THE BROKEN GOD

GARETH HANRAHAN

orbit

orbitbooks.net

ORBIT

First published in Great Britain in 2021 by Orbit

1 3 5 7 9 10 8 6 4 2

Copyright © 2021 by Gareth Hanrahan

Excerpt from *The Bone Shard Daughter* by Andrea Stewart
Copyright © 2020 by Andrea Stewart

Map by Paul Bourne, Handiwork Games

The moral right of the author has been asserted.

A CIP catalogue record for this book is available from the British Library.

ISBN 978-0-356-51436-9

Typeset in Garamond by M Rules
Printed and bound in Great Britain by Clays Ltd, Elcograf S.p.A.

Papers used by Orbit are from well-managed forests and other responsible sources.

Orbit
An imprint of
Little, Brown Book Group
Carmelite House
50 Victoria Embankment
London EC4Y 0DZ

An Hachette UK Company
www.hachette.co.uk

www.orbitbooks.net

This one's for Cat.

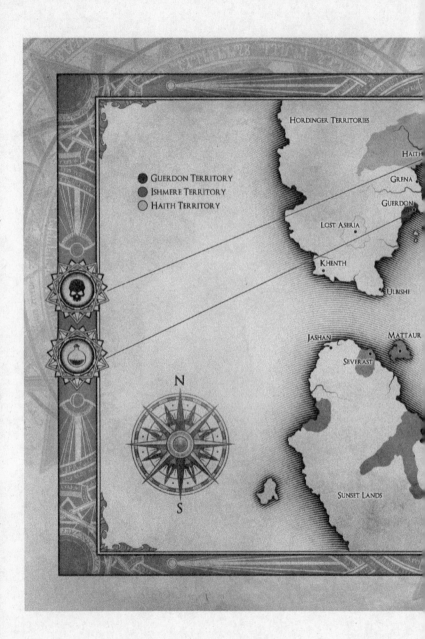

GUERDON TERRITORY
ISHMERE TERRITORY
HAITH TERRITORY

HORDINGER TERRITORIES

HAITH

GRENA

GUERDON

LOST ASERIA

KHENTH

ULBISHE

JASHAN

MATTAUR

SEVERAST

N

S

SUNSET LANDS

PROLOGUE

The same dream, again.

That same day, again. More than a year ago, now.

In the dream, Artolo of the Ghierdana swaggers down a street in the New City of Guerdon. Spring is in the air, and there's a spring in his step, too. He looks across the unlikely vista of the New City, this realm of fanciful spires and bridges, as if the froth of a breaking wave froze and turned to marble. He looks up at the towers, all conjured in an instant by a creation of the alchemists gone awry – or so rumour claims. Across the world, Guerdon's chiefly known for the wonders wrought by the alchemists' guild. Weapons from their foundries and cauldrons flow out across the sea to the Godswar and streams of gold and silver come flowing back.

In Artolo's eyes, this New City is a sieve, straining the city, skimming off gold and silver for him and his family. It was born of chaos and crisis, and chaos always brings opportunity for those with the nerve to seize the moment. That is why Great-Uncle chose Artolo, out of all the family, to oversee operations in Guerdon. He's got the strong hands needed.

In the few months he's been here, he's proved it. He broke the local criminal syndicate, the Brotherhood, operating out of the pisspot district of the Wash – he owns them now.

And he's dealt with anyone else who crossed him.

Because when you cross Artolo, you cross the Ghierdana, and no one crosses the Ghierdana.

No one crosses the dragons.

This is only the beginning. The New City doesn't belong to anyone, not really. Half these enchanted spires are empty, or claimed by squatters and refugees who have no one to protect them, who can easily be driven out. Guerdon's still knitting itself back together after the Crisis. The city watch's wax golem-things, the Tallowmen, banished off the streets. The alchemists are rebuilding their broken factories, the Brotherhood's gone, parliament's staggering around stunned, run by some cobbled-together emergency committee. Even the local gods are moribund.

All wide open. All ripe to be plucked. Artolo runs his big hand along the smooth marble railing of the balcony, delighting in the sensation. He taps the Ring of Samara off the railing, and he can almost feel the whole city tremble, feel it quiver beneath his touch like it fears him. A horse to be broken, a woman to be taken.

It feels good. It feels right. It feels like the first time Great-Uncle took him flying. The New City around him might be a cloud in a shimmering sky, and he's soaring towards his glorious destiny.

In the dream, he walks down a stairwell. His men bow their heads as he passes, murmur words of respect. Soon, the whole city will bow to him, too. Boss Artolo, Great-Uncle's favourite. Great-Uncle's Chosen.

He enters the cellar room. Two of his men wait, his cousin Vollio and Tiske. Loyal men, even if Tiske's only Eshdana. Ash-marked, not one of the dragon's kin. They're holding a prisoner between them. A woman, young, dark-haired, struggling like an alley cat. Yowling like one, too.

"Quiet," he snaps. He grabs her by the chin, twists her head so he can see her face. Her skin is marked by a dusting of little dark marks, like scars or burns. An ugly amulet of some black metal hangs around her neck. "I'm told that you've been spying on me. That you stole from me. That you stabbed three of my men."

"Three that you've found," she whispers.

"Do you know who I am?" He squeezes her mouth.

"Tolo," she mumbles.

"Wrong!" he shouts.

He releases her. Takes out his knife. The hilt is gold and studded with jewels. The blade is a dragon's tooth, given by Great-Uncle. It's more than a weapon – it's a symbol of Great-Uncle's trust, of his authority as a Ghierdana prince. He lifts the knife, enjoying the weight of it, the way it fits in his hand. It was made for him.

Artolo slams it into the woman's face, hilt first. He holds the weapon up so she can see it.

"See this? Know what it is? I'm a boss of the Ghierdana. I'm Chosen of the Dragon."

He puts the knife to her throat, pressing the blade against her skin.

A little more pressure, and the skin will open in a red spring.

A little more work, to saw through the cartilage, and then there'll be that parting, that hot rush as the windpipe gives way.

"Cross me, and you cross the Ghierdana!" There aren't any witnesses, down here in this cellar. Just Vollio and Tiske. Just the glimmering stone of the impossible New City. Still, Artolo likes to say his piece. He's said it before, many times. It's for his own good as much as anything else. Reminds him to be tough. Reminds him not to fail.

He looks the girl right in the eyes. There's no fear there. She doesn't think he's going to do it. That makes him even angrier.

"Take from me," he snarls, "and you take from the dragon!"

He draws the knife across her throat.

There's a screeching, scraping noise, like he's drawing the blade across solid stone. Sparks fly where the knife grinds across the soft skin of the girl's throat. The knife – *his* knife, the dragon-tooth knife – can't injure her.

Somehow, though, it injures the room around them. A dozen wounds open in the glimmering white walls, deep wet gouges tearing the stone, mimicking the path of the knife across her unblemished, still-uncut throat.

A miracle. It's a fucking miracle.

But Great-Uncle told him there were no saints left in Guerdon.

The stone floor convulses, flinging Vollio and Tiske away from the girl. They land in opposite corners of the cellar room. The ceiling melts, long fingers of glistening stone cascading from it like stalactites, intertwining and blooming flowers of solid rock, walling off the corners from the rest of the room. In an instant, Vollio and Tiske are immured, locked away behind stone. Artolo can hear their muffled shouts of alarm.

The girl stands up slowly, a wicked grin on her face. Flushed with excitement, drunk on power.

Behind her, the cellar door quivers, and then the stone lintel above it melts, too. The only way out of the room clenches shut. He can't call for help.

The knife can't cut her. He slams the hilt of the blade into her nose.

The walls of the room — no, gods below, it's the whole New City that takes the force of the blow. She's untouched. He punches her in the face, and it's like punching a wall. His knuckles come away bleeding, and it's a game to her.

He can't hurt her. He can't kill her. He doesn't have a gun, or anything more destructive. He needs a gun. Why didn't he bring a fucking gun? He's killed saints before, across the sea, but not without weapons. Not without Great-Uncle.

He can't fail Great-Uncle. He can't fail the dragon.

There's no air down here; he can't breathe. He can't stand, and, in his panic, he can't tell if it's the floor or his knees that have turned to liquid. She looms over him, suddenly terrible and monstrous. He crawls backwards away from her, or tries to, but the ground is mirror-smooth and slick.

She picks up his dragon-tooth knife, admires the jewelled hilt. Flips it around expertly, examines the blade.

"You've blunted it," she says. "It's shit now." She throws his knife to the floor. "But I've got my own," she says, laughing, and produces her own blade from some hidden fold of her cloak.

Vollio was supposed to check the bitch for weapons.

"Call me the Saint of Knives," says the girl, advancing on him. Then she stops, glances at the ceiling. "What? It's a good name!" She pauses, as if she's listening to some voice Artolo can't hear. "Fine, I'll get a magic knife then. A fucking flame sword, maybe. But first—"

She turns her attention back to Artolo. Her eyes glitter like the stone of the New City in the sun.

"This is my city. I know what you're doing here. I know what you're looking for."

She can't know that, Artolo thinks. Great-Uncle entrusted him with a mission so secret that it could only be given to one of the family. She can't know about the Black Iron weapons. Who is this girl?

"I'll kill you," threatens Artolo, summoning the tattered remains of his bravado. There has to be some way to hurt her. Poison gas. Acid. Sorcery. Dragon-fire. She's human. "I'll fucking kill your family."

She laughs. "Bit late for that. But if we're swapping threats—" She closes her fist, and the wall holding Vollio mirrors her movement. There's a muffled scream, and red rivulets squirt from the cracks in the stone.

"I'll find a way."

The woman ignores him. "The Ghierdana aren't welcome here. Go back and tell the dragon that. You won't get a second warning." She gestures, and the wall opens behind him, ripping and reflowing to form a new doorway. The graveyard stench of ghoul tunnels wafts from this second portal.

She steps over him like he's nothing.

Ignores him like he's nothing.

No one treats him like that. He is Artolo of the Ghierdana. Great-Uncle's favourite. Chosen of the dragon!

The dragon-tooth knife is in his hand. He finds his footing, leaps at her. The bitch is half his size, small and weak, and, for all her miracles, she's just a girl. Take her by surprise and—

—The dream ends like it always does. She turns around, like she saw him coming. Her knife goes in just under his ribcage, and his momentum carries him on as she twists, and now the white walls are all red, red, red. And he's falling, like he's slipped from Great-Uncle's back.

The dragon flies on and does not look back.

CHAPTER ONE

S ome days, Cari has to remind herself that it wasn't all a dream. The rolling of the ship is so familiar to her. The smell of sea air, the stink of the bilges. The creaks of rope and timber, the slap of water on wood, the shouts of sailors, all this was her life before, is now her life again. The wide world, sea under sky. She leans on the railing by the prow of the ship, watching the horizon. The empty expanse makes her feel deliciously anonymous. The open ocean accepts no name that mortals or gods might try to put on it. It admits no history, existing in one present and eternal moment. On the ocean, it feels like she could be born anew with each swelling wave.

On the ocean, her life ashore feels like a dream.

But it wasn't a dream, was it, she thinks to herself, her fingers closing around the black amulet that once more adorns her neck. She's not expecting an answer here – Spar is half the world away. And even if Cari was back in the New City, standing in the heart of the great metropolis that she inadvertently conjured from his corpse nearly two years ago, she doesn't know if he'd be able to answer her.

Still, she prays for an answer. Strains whatever the psychic equivalent of an ear is.

Nothing.

Just the jagged whirling of her own thoughts.

She can't help but be amused by the irony. She ran away from home long ago because she was haunted by the fear of unseen powers that called to her, and she found solace in the anonymity of the ocean. Distance muted the voices. Every mile she sailed away from Guerdon was a balm to her scarred soul.

Now, she's terrified by the absence of one particular voice, and every day she sails is time she can't afford to spend. If she could have teleported across the world, instead of spending months travelling around the Godswar, she'd have done that, and damn the cost.

Nothing's ever simple with you, is it, she thinks to herself. Again, there's no answer. Just a memory of her cousin Eladora, lying bleeding in an alleyway off Desiderata Street, whispering to her: *You ruin everything.*

Not this time.

"Ilbarin!" comes the shout from the crow's nest. "Mark, the Rock of Ilbarin."

Cari stares at the horizon, looking for the distant hump of the mountain, but she can't see it from down here yet. She suppresses the urge to climb up into the rigging and get a proper view. She spent half her old life aloft, and the swaying of the mast holds no fear for her. But she can't abandon her prize. She pats the heavy oilskin bundle that hasn't left her sight in six months, feels the comforting weight of the book inside.

Comforting weight? More like fucking inconvenient weight. The book's absurdly huge, and the cover is shod in metal, with a hefty lock built into it. Probably magic wards, too. The thing could stop a bullet, and not a small one either. If Cari's ever caught in an artillery bombardment (*again*, she adds), she's hiding under that fucking book.

The Grimoire of Doctor Ramegos, to give the book something like its proper title. From what Eladora explained, it's some sort of magical diary. Cari wishes she knew which pages were actually important. If she knew what was valuable, she could just steal that, cut the pages out and wrap them up in a nice neat bundle. But no – it's all incomprehensible arcane runes in there. She can't distinguish between the world-shattering secrets and the magic equivalent of "day eight of gastric distress. Today's bowel movements were mostly greenish and inoffensive" so she has to carry it all. She's dragged this fucking book from Guerdon to Haith, across the sea to Varinth, down south to Paravos, across to the Caliphates into the Firesea, and now nearly to Khebesh.

Thinking about it, six months with this book can be counted among her longest relationships, and she can't even read the thing.

She listens again. Spar was always amused when she got ranty. She's still curating her own thoughts, storing away things that he might enjoy. But he's an absence in her soul, an unseen wound. A phantom limb that other people don't have. She's left only with her own thoughts, and Cari's always been poor company for herself.

Some of the crew of this ship might understand. Some of them, too, have walked in the shadow of divinity. It's not a Guerdon ship; she boarded this ship in . . . one of the occupied Caliphate ports? Taervosa, maybe, or some other stop on her long, meandering journey. Not a Guerdon ship means not a Guerdon crew – there are god-touched on board. They've got a weatherworker, Eld, a minor saint of Cloud Mother. Waddling around, complaining about his swollen ankles and swollen belly, occasionally called on to birth sylph-spirits to fill the sails and speed the ship along. Another sailor has a Tomb Child from Ul-Taen riding on his shoulders, the shade of a child sacrifice. Cari can see the Child, sometimes, if the sun catches it at the right angle. And there's one mercenary who has the Lion Queen's sigil tattooed on his chest.

She's stayed away from him, this whole journey.

She's made enough enemies for one lifetime.

The Rock of Ilbarin grows as the ship struggles to make headway through a sea of debris. Floating wreckage bumps against the hull.

The crew rush to the rail to take soundings, check the depth beneath the keel. They have charts, of course, but charts are useless these days. The gods can tear up the foundations of the ocean to throw at each other.

It's been five years since she last saw the Rock, but she still remembers Ilbarin City. Other travellers might speak of Ilbarin's glittering fountains amid the lush green gardens, or the golden-roofed temples, but Cari chiefly remembers the crowded quays and the alleyways between the warehouses, the dockside inns and chandleries. She spent her formative years there, and on the *Rose*. She'll be able to find her way on from there.

The ship's course shifts. The distant Rock of Ilbarin vanishes behind the bowsprit, reappears a moment later on the other side. They're no longer heading for Ilbarin City, but instead making for the north end of the island.

Cari stuffs Ramegos' grimoire into her pack and swings it on to her back. The weight of the loaded satchel makes her feel lopsided, and the waters are choppy here. She finds Captain Dosca nearby, standing at the rail, spyglass raised. Something's coming.

"Hey," she calls. He ignores her, so she puts her palm across the end of his telescope, blocking his view. That gets his attention.

"I paid for passage all the way to Ilbarin City. I paid you extra to go straight there." In fact, it was the first time in her life she'd ever had the money to *pay* passage instead of working it, and she's damned if she's not getting her money's worth.

Dosca sucks his stained teeth. "We must change course," he says slowly. "Ilbarin City is no longer safe. There has been, ah, flooding."

"You said you'd take me to Ilbarin City."

"We cannot land there."

"I've got friends in the port." Using the present tense is a risky assumption on her part; she had friends there, long ago. Family, sort of. She spent five years aboard the *Rose*. Hawse or Adro will help her. She'll even go to Dol Martaine in a pinch – she's got money to pay her way, now. Captain Hawse came from Ilbarin, and always said he'd retire there. She'll take any ship that'll bring her to the forbidden land of Khebesh, but secretly she's harboured the fanciful notion that it'll be the *Rose* that carries her there. "I need to go to Ilbarin City."

Dosca pauses for a long moment, then says, "We're going to Ushket instead."

"Ushket ... Ushket's halfway up the fucking mountain!" How bad was the flooding? Shit, how out of date is her information? Sailing from Guerdon to Ilbarin usually takes four or five weeks, but Cari did it all arseways, took the long way around. She had to – there was no way she dared get anywhere close to the gods of Ishmere, not after what she did to their war goddess. She's been travelling for months, with little news of the south until she reached the Caliphates. And she was so eager to find passage onwards to Ilbarin that she didn't take any precautions.

"We will put you ashore at Ushket. There is nothing else to be done." He raises the spyglass again.

"What is it?" Cari asks. She can see some other vessel approaching, a smudge of dark smoke above it. Alchemy-powered, probably a gunboat from the size. Ilbarin military, maybe? She reaches for Dosca's spyglass, but he folds it up and tucks it away before she can take it.

"An escort." He glances down at Cari. "It would be best for you to stay hidden. I will tell them I have no passengers."

"Are they Ilbariners?"

Dosca shakes his head. "No. They are Ghierdana."

Ghierdana. Fucking dragon pirates.

Run. Hide. Cari sprints below deck, leaping down the narrow ladder, ignoring the curses of Eld as she shoves past him. His big, wind-pregnant belly nearly takes up the entire gangway. She races to the corner she's been sleeping in and gathers her other few possessions. The hold stinks of rotten eggs, and the smell is bearable only if they leave the hatches half open most of the time. From down here, she can look up and see a bright blue sliver of sky, hear movement on the deck above.

Acrid smoke crosses the sliver of blue, and she catches the whiff of engine fumes. The gunboat's alongside. She hears shouts, thumping against the hull as people climb on board. Cari discovers a hiding place under a bunk, pressing herself into the shadowy corner, a child hiding from monsters. Knife clutched in her hand, ready to strike. Her heart pounding so hard it feels like it's going to break her ribs.

All her instincts are off. Back in Guerdon, she was fucking unstoppable. She was the Saint of Knives. With Spar's miracles backing her up, she was invincible. Spar shielded her, took on any wounds that might hurt her. With his help she'd single-handedly stabbed the fuck out of the Ghierdana crime syndicate. Kicked them out of Guerdon without taking a scratch. Only a few months ago, she wouldn't have had to hide. She'd have known where every Ghierdana bastard was, felt their footsteps on the stone floor. The walls would open for her, the New City reshaping itself according to her desires. She'd have shrugged off gunfire with marble-hard skin, defeated a dozen men with a saint's cruel grace.

Made them beg her for mercy.

Pray to her for mercy.

Sometimes, she'd given it. Sometimes, she hadn't.

Do you think they know who I am, she thinks to Spar, wildly. Hell, maybe they won't. Maybe she's overreacting. The Ghierdana are a big outfit, a syndicate of criminal families, each headed by a fucking no-shit fire-breathing dragon – there's no guarantee that any of the ones here in Ilbarin know anything about what happened back home. Three times so far – twice in Varinth, and once on Paravos – she thought she'd spotted someone was following her, but she lost her pursuers each time. She doesn't even know if they were Ghierdana or not – she's made a lot of enemies.

Maybe she can bluff her way out. Stick the knife in a pocket and stroll up on deck all casual. *Who, me? I'm just another deckhand.*

But they might find the fucking book.

So she stays hidden and waits. Her shoulder muscles and her legs ache from being crammed into the tight space under the bunk. The metal edge of the book digs into the small of her back. Roaches crawl over her hands, her collarbone. She doesn't move. She cowers like a frightened child.

Two men open the hatch and climb down into the hold. Both are wearing military garb, but it's a mismatch of bits and pieces from different uniforms, all stripped of markings. They're both armed. All she has is her little knife clutched in her hand. Two's more than she can handle – two, when once she'd have laughed at a dozen of the bastards. They sweep through the hold, kick open the door to the bosun's locker, give the place a cursory search, and leave. The creaking of the stairs under their boots signals they've gone above.

She exhales. *Amateurs, right? Not even worth my time.* Spar might chuckle at that.

Cari relaxes a little, but she can still hear the grumbling of the gunboat's engines nearby.

The sliver of blue light turns golden as the sun begins to set. From above, she can hear Dosca shouting orders. Sounds of sails being furled, the rattling of chains and the distinctive jerk as something starts tugging the ship forward. They're being towed into port, presumably by the Ghierdana gunboat. Presumably into Ushket. The gunboat's engine downshifts and strains, and the ship rocks.

Plan: wait till they're tied up at the quay. Wait till it's dark out. Slip ashore; head south around the rock to Ilbarin City and the last leg of the journey to Khebesh. Even without Spar's miraculous guidance, even with the weight of the fucking book, she's still sneaky enough to get ashore without being seen. And if she is spotted, well, she's had a lot of practice knifing the Ghierdana. *But you're not invulnerable any more, so don't get hit*, she tells herself in Spar's voice.

The golden sliver of light turns orange, then grey. Sunset's quicker this far south.

Outside, the noise of engines ceases, gives way to the creak of ropes, the muffled thump of the ship coming to rest against some jetty. Shouts of dockworkers. The journey's end. Captain Hawse taught Cari always to thank the local sea-gods after a safe voyage, but she dares not even whisper.

Not long to wait now.

Then the stairs creak again, groaning under a heavy weight. There's a hiss of a breathing apparatus. The daylight's mostly gone, so Cari can only see a silhouette. A metal helmet. A rubbery suit, covered with tubes and metal plates that glimmer with arcane sigils. The armoured figure clomps into the middle of the hold and stops, scanning the room. Cari presses herself back into her hiding place again, heart pounding again, mouth dry.

She's seen things like the armoured figure before. Suits like that were originally intended to protect wearers against alchemical fall-out, plagues and toxins and knife-smoke and shit, but she's also seen them adapted as containment suits for the incurably contaminated. Back in Guerdon, there's a dealer in second-hand alchemical stuff called Dredger who uses one. Then there was the Fever Knight, the enforcer who worked for Guerdon's old criminal boss, Heinreil.

Spar killed the Fever Knight, but he nearly died in the process, and he had the strength of a Stone Man then. Cari broke Heinreil with a thought, but that was when she could work miracles. Here, she's got nothing but this knife, no miracles or unnatural strength to back it up.

The Fever Knight's armour was a boiler with legs, the ironclad of the alleyways, all rivets and armour plating. This suit is delicate, ornate — more fragile, maybe? The helm is made to resemble a boar, and the mouth of the beast gapes wide to reveal a dispassionate metal face. A woman's face, cold and cruel. Green lenses for eye sockets.

Go for the breathing tube, go for the joints, she thinks, *you won't pierce the armour.* The knife handle's slippery in her grasp. She wipes her palm on her shirt, grips the weapon again. *Go for the tube.*

The armoured figure raises a hand, gurgles something – and the hold's suddenly flooded with light. A dozen little floating globules of liquid illumination dance through the air. Sorcerous werelights – the armoured bastard's a sorcerer. Shit. Cari's fear is now titrated with a cold flood of uncertainty, which she really hates. Sorcerers are hard to judge, hard to fight. You can't tell how good they are until they start throwing spells. Can't tell how strong they are, because that really depends on how desperate they are. Magic burns them up from the inside.

A memory, the same memory she always sees when she closes her eyes: Spar falling, tumbling over and over as he plummets from the ceiling of the great Seamarket to break on the floor far below. His terrified face, eyes pleading with her as he falls, while she's held paralysed and frozen by a spell.

Hell, what can she do against a sorcerer? If she was still a saint, she'd have a measure of divine protection. Saints and sorcery both exist in the aether. Saints can brute-force their way through spells, smashing enchantments and breaking wards like they were physical barriers. If Cari were still in Spar's grace, still the Saint of Knives, maybe she could charge through the sorcerer's spells like a brick thrown through a spider's web.

Now, she's powerless. Harmless as a fucking fly.

The lenses whir and click as the helm slowly rotates, scanning the room. Cari tenses, ready to scramble out of her hiding place and attack if she's spotted.

Sorcery takes time. If she's quick enough, maybe she can get out from under the bunk and get to the sorcerer before her foe gets a spell off. Maybe.

The werelights follow the sorcerer's gaze, sweeping towards her.

Go for the breathing tube, she thinks, *and get lucky.*

"Witch?" calls one of the Ghierdana from above. "Need you up here."

The armoured sorcerer snaps a hand shut. The werelights go out. Again, the mercifully, blessed, best sound in the world – footsteps creaking on the ladder.

Cari slithers out of her hiding place, dragging the heavy pack behind her. From above, the sounds of an argument – the Ghierdana want Eld, the saint of Cloud Mother to go with them, and he's not budging. From what Cari can tell from the noises, Eld's trying to squeeze out a sylph-spirit on the spot to fight the Ghierdana.

Terrible combat tactic for him. Brilliant distraction for her, especially when Eld starts bellowing in pain.

She creeps through the hold to the aft hatch. She scales a stack of crates, hooks her pack on a convenient nail, then pulls herself up through the half-open hatch on to the deck. She glances towards the prow. Eld's writhing around on the deck. She can see the phantasmal shape of a wind-spirit halfway out of a fresh cut on Eld's stomach, but the armoured sorcerer's standing over him. One armoured gauntlet extended, glimmering with power. The sorcerer's pinning the spirit in place with magical force, half in and half out. Gusts of wind hiss from Eld's distended belly, from the edges of his caesarian cut. Most of the Ghierdana have gathered around the contortions, other than a pair of gunmen who are watching Captain Dosca and the rest of the crew.

No one's looking her way.

Cari reaches back into the hatch and unhooks her pack. The weight of it nearly pulls her back into the hold, but she drags it out, secures it on her back. There's a boarding plank, but Eld's thrashing about next to that, so she sneaks to one of the ship's toilets – a precarious little platform that hangs out over the side, near the stern.

From there, she climbs down on to the quayside.

The quay's newly built, the concrete smooth and unweathered. There's something deeply strange about her surroundings – it's like they've docked in the middle of a market square. She finds a hiding place amid stacked boxes near a chain fence. It's deathly quiet, and the streets beyond the fence are deserted. It's hard to be sure in the dim light, but it looks like they've carved this harbour out of a flooded part of Ushket. She can see a narrow channel that must have once been a street – the gunboat must have towed Dosca's ship along that route. It's the only path that leads back to sea. The ruins on either side of that channel are scorched and blasted. Dragon-fire maybe. Or a miracle.

There are four other ships tied up at the dock, like prisoners in a chain gang. That's what this is, Cari realises – a prison for ships. Only way in or out is by tug, and with a pilot who knows the waters. She can imagine all sorts of obstacles and dangers in those waters, ruined buildings like reefs that'd tear a hull open. A prison for ships – and she can guess who the fucking gaolers are. The Ghierdana.

She scurries, shoulders bowed under the weight of her back, running along the edge of the quay, staying in the shadows. As the last rays of the sun vanish, Carillon vanishes into the night.

The streets are unfamiliar, the buildings strange: the ones nearby are closely packed along steep lanes, but she can hear birdsong, smell greenery not too far away, so there must be gardens here, too. It's a moonless night, and the twilight's going fast. She splashes through puddles, skirts around the silt and debris that's everywhere. It reminds her of parts of Guerdon after the Kraken-fleet of Ishmere attacked. That must be what happened here, too – the gods seized the sea and wielded it as a weapon, dropped an ocean on this place.

She needs to get off the streets before she's spotted. The lower floors of the buildings look flooded out and abandoned. She spots an open door – broken, one half off its hinges, leaning against its mate like a drunk looking for support. Cari slips through the gap into a once-grand hallway. Paint peeling from rotten timbers stains her hands. Stairs in front of her lead up, but she hears the sound of distant snoring and guesses the upper floors must still be inhabited.

This ground floor is caked in drifts of mud and flotsam, but there are no fresh prints past the stairwell. She forces a door into a derelict apartment, long since looted of anything valuable.

That's fine. All she needs is a place to hide for the night. In the morning, she'll get her bearings, get out of town, walk around the mountain to Ilbarin City and find a ship going south. She sits down in a dry corner, aching and exhausted.

Cari opens her pack and checks, for the thousandth time, that the grimoire is still there. It's the only thing she has to trade to the sorcerers of Khebesh.

Eladora's words replay in her mind: "Bring them this. Trade it for what you need. I don't know if they can help Mr Idgeson, but I hope it's possible."

Not long now, Spar, she tells herself. Maybe, somehow, she tells him, too.

The lapping of the water in the street outside lulls Carillon to sleep.

CHAPTER TWO

The dragon Taras circles over Guerdon.

Great-Uncle's massive frame soars through the sky, gliding on leathery wings so wide they cast a shadow over the world. Titanic muscles move beneath his ancient hide, marked with thousands of scars. Some are centuries old, made by arrows and crossbow bolts, by the javelins and lances of saints. Others are fresh: bullet wounds, acid burns, the bloody patina of knife-smoke or the marks left by the tendrils and claws of divine monsters. The Godswar has wounded everyone, thinks Rasce, even Great-Uncle Taras.

But the dragon is invincible.

He circles lower. Rasce's mask was damaged by a stray shot during the bombing raid, leaving a spiderweb of cracks across his field of vision. He has to tilt his head this way and that to see different parts of Guerdon as it spreads out below him. From here, Great-Uncle seems to fill the world – no matter where Rasce looks, there's always some part of the dragon, a wingtip or claw or tail.

"Is it not a pretty thing?" rumbles Great-Uncle. Rasce feels the words rather than hears them, the vibrations running through his thighs, his spine, echoing around inside his helmet.

He would never disagree with Great-Uncle, but the city below strikes him as singularly ugly. From this altitude, it feels as though he could reach out and pick up the whole city with one hand. The factories of the alchemists resemble intricate machines, stained with oily clouds of smoke, embedded in a fruiting mass of streets and tenements that sprawls inwards along the track of a mostly buried river. As Great-Uncle circles down, the light of the waning sun reflects off some canal or an exposed stretch of water, making the city flash like a signal-glass. In other places, the city's scarred by recent wars. The fortress of Queen's Point lies in ruins; out in the bay, nothing remains of the old prison at Hark except blasted, fire-blackened stone.

There are jewels here, too. Cathedrals and palaces up on Holyhill. The sullen lump of the Parliament atop Castle Hill – ugly to look at, but valuable. And directly below, their destination – the great shining pearl of the New City. An unlikely beauty, a district of marble domes and spires, of boulevards that shimmer in the sun and alleyways like frost on the veins of a leaf.

Conjured, the Dentist told him, through some alchemical accident, a whole city springing up overnight.

Nearby, is another district, equally unnatural these days. The roofs of Ishmerian temples rise like shark's fins through the purple gloom that hangs over what some call the Temple district, but in the staccato language of the Armistice is officially the Ishmeric Occupation Zone. Just like the New City is termed the Lyrixian Occupation Zone, and a swathe of the city from the edge of Holyhill to the north-eastern suburbs is the Haithi Occupation Zone. IOZ, LOZ, HOZ.

Abbreviations serve to sweep away the strangeness and the shame, neat boxes to categorise the unthinkable. The city escaped destruction and conquest only by inviting all its prospective conquerors in to share the prize. Like a woman, offering herself to the victors – take my body, do what you wish with me, only spare my children.

Or, in Guerdon's case, spare my vital alchemical factories, spare my mansions and palaces. Spare my markets and my unfettered access to the arms trade, spare my wealth. The city's found safety by balancing itself on a knife edge.

Is the city a pretty thing? Rasce considers the question. He's seen many cities from the air, and many of them were glorious. He's seen temples like blossoming flowers of crystal, stepped ziggurats of obsidian, golden-roofed longhouses where heroes feasted. He's seen prettier places – but when the dragon was done with them, they were all ash. Guerdon's an ugly place from the air. A great misshapen stone beast, rent by many wounds, that has crawled down to the shore to die – but even from this height he can see the thronged streets, the busy docks.

He can smell the money. Sense the power.

It is not a pretty thing, but that is not why the dragon desires it.

A rumble of disquiet runs through Great-Uncle's titanic form as they pass the Temple district, and the clouds writhe in response. Cloud Mother's monstrous offspring hide there. Rasce feels the dragon's displeasure in his bones.

"We should fly over the HOZ," says Rasce, "and dismay them." A tube carries the sound of his voice to Great-Uncle's earpiece. Otherwise, he'd have to shout at the top of his lungs to be heard from the dragon's back.

"Not today," rumbles Great-Uncle. "No provocations. We've had enough war. Now for business."

Enough war. Rasce tugs at the unfamiliar badge on his flying armour – the sigil of the Lyrixian Army. Twenty years ago, they'd have been the ones shooting at Great-Uncle.

They descend towards one of the domed structures in the New City. Another dragon – Thyrus – patrols the air over the New City, banks towards Great-Uncle as they circle lower. The face of the Ghierdana rider on Thyrus' back is hidden by her mask, but Rasce can imagine her scowl. He grins back at her.

A Lyrixian banner flutters in the breeze from the sea, then gets blown the other way, buffeted by the wind from Great-Uncle's massive wings as the dragon lands on a plaza. Lyrixian soldiers guard the perimeter of this military enclave. Great-Uncle stalks through a hole blasted in the side of the dome, his movements suddenly clumsy and heavy now that he's on the ground. Dragons are meant to soar.

Rasce dismounts. His own limbs are stiff and sore after the long flight. He, too, has become a creature of air and fire, not lumpen earth. He stretches, feeling the ache in his limbs. He's young and strong, but only mortal. Many generations of his ancestors have ridden on Great-Uncle's back, and they're all gone now, while Great-Uncle remains.

Inside the dome, both dragon and rider shuck their military trappings. Lyrixian soldiers help Rasce out of his heavy breathing mask, strip off his flight armour. They remove, section by section, the armoured barding that protects Great-Uncle's belly from anti-aircraft fire. They unhook the empty webbing that recently held alchemical bombs. The soldiers are nervous in the presence of the dragon; Great-Uncle puts up with their hesitant fumbling for as long as he can, but the dragon's impatience wins out. He rips the last of the barding off, then stomps off towards the exit.

An officer – Major Estavo, Rasce recalls – hurries up, stammering something about a report on the bombing raid. A folder of documents clutched in his hand – damage reports, maybe, or proposed targets for the next sortie. He starts to salute, then catches himself. Rasce and the dragon are still criminals in the eyes of the Lyrixian state – it's just that one of them is a criminal who can tear a warship in half or incinerate an army from above, which makes the dragons vital to the war effort. For the duration of the war, there's a truce between the authorities and the Ghierdana families.

"Great Taras—" begins Estavo, addressing Great-Uncle by name.

"My nephew will deal with that," rumbles Great-Uncle without stopping, and Estavo's not stupid enough to stand in the path of the dragon. He turns helplessly to Rasce.

"I'll report to you later, sir," says Rasce, smirking at the "sir".

Both the major and Rasce know that this is all an absurdity, a wolf pretending to solemnly consult with a sheep. "Maybe tomorrow. Or the next day." He dumps his damaged helmet in Estavo's arms and follows Great-Uncle out.

There's business to attend to first.

Long ago, the priests say, the people of Lyrix were wicked and sinful. They were greedy and gluttonous, lustful and wrathful. They lied and cheated, blasphemed and murdered. The gods grew angry, and they took the sins of the people, and from those sins were born the dragons – creatures made to be divine scourges, to turn sin into redemptive suffering. But instead, the dragons went to the worst of the worst, the criminals and pirates of the Ghierdana islands, and said, "Are we not alike? We are both hateful in the eyes of others. Let us be one, and show those bastards."

And in their way, the dragons did scourge the people of Lyrix, and reminded them of their sins, and drove them into the loving arms of the gods. But they made a profit while doing so.

The street outside is too narrow for Great-Uncle to pass easily. His wingtips cut grooves in the walls on either side. Children run after the dragon, picking up pebbles dislodged by his wings for good luck. Great-Uncle grunts in amusement, and deliberately leans into one wall, sending a cascade of plaster tumbling down for them to collect.

Rasce ducks under Great-Uncle's foreleg and jogs along by the dragon's head so the two can converse.

"Estavo will want us to fly south again within the week. How long will this business take?"

"That, nephew, depends on you. There is work that needs doing, here in the city. But wait until we are in private." Great-Uncle has claimed part of the New City as his temporary residence while in Guerdon; everyone in that compound is Ghierdana or Eshdana, sworn to the service of Great-Uncle or one of the other dragon families. There are three other dragons in Guerdon – no, two, now that

Viridasa has gone south – but none of them are half so glorious or mighty as Great-Uncle.

"We should press the advantage, while the Ishmerians are in disarray." Ever since the death of the Ishmerian goddess of war, the once-mighty Sacred Empire of Ishmere has faltered. Lyrixian forces have pushed back on many fronts. Rasce doesn't give much of a damn about the fortunes of those Lyrixian forces – if pressed, he'd admit to a mild preference that Lyrix triumph over its rivals, that the gods of his homeland cast down the temples of Ishmere and all the rest, but that's more a preference for familiar food, familiar devils. Lyrix can go to hell with the rest; it's the fortunes of the Ghierdana that matters. Victory opens up new ways to grow the dragons' hoard.

And it's glorious to be up there, on dragon-back, to have the strength and the fire at his command. To point at a temple, or a fortified guard tower, or a formation of infantry on the ground, and to know that he could destroy them all with a snap of his fingers. Who cares who the enemy is when you wield that much power?

It's glorious to be Chosen of the Dragon.

"In my way, nephew," says Great-Uncle. "And in a time of my choosing. But now, I must speak with Doctor Vorz."

Vorz. The Dentist, some call him. As Great-Uncle's physician, he's responsible for removing a tooth from the dragon's maw whenever a new member of the family comes of age and wins their knife. More than that, though, he's Great-Uncle's counsellor – the one member of the inner circle who's not a member of the family. He's only Eshdana, bound by oath instead of blood. He can never be Chosen of the Dragon. Maybe that allows him to speak more honestly to Great-Uncle; maybe it's the knowledge that he's reached the zenith of his possible ambition and can never rise higher.

There's always a counsellor, whispering in Great-Uncle's ear. When Rasce was a young boy, it was a former pirate queen from the Hordinger coast, tattooed and savage. She ate seal blubber, and grease dripped from her lips as she talked to the dragon. The family hated her, and she slipped from a clifftop and died when Rasce was five. After the Hordinger came Marko – no, after the Hordinger was that old priestess, the one who knitted burial shawls, and after *her* was Marko, everyone's friend with his easy grin, making deals and slapping backs, mopping his flushed forehead in the summer heat of the island. Always someone useful to Great-Uncle, some skill or connection that the family could not provide.

And then one day Marko was gone, and in his place was Vorz. The Dentist, with his leather bag of physician's instruments, his collection of potions and philtres. A renegade alchemist, it's said, exiled from Guerdon's alchemists' guild for unspeakable experiments. Grub-pale skin, face like an undertaker. Never raises his voice above a whisper or a hiss. He dresses all in black like a priest and walks as if moving too quickly he would tear his ill-made body apart. Rasce's seen that sort of play-acting before, beggars and con men affecting divine stigmata or the ravages of sorcery, hinting they've paid some terrible physical price for ultimate power. Most of the time, it's just an act, a way to suggest they've got access to supernatural abilities while also getting out of actually having to do anything.

Most of the time. The way Great-Uncle uses Vorz suggests the man has some genuine power.

And even if Vorz is just a man, Great-Uncle demands privacy. Rasce slaps Great-Uncle's scaly shoulder and peels off. Conversations with Vorz are tiresome, anyway – like talking to an accounts ledger. The man's got no fire in his soul.

The crowds do not part for Rasce.

Back home, no one would dare stand in his path. Everyone would make way for the Chosen of the Dragon. Back home, men would come up and greet him, shake his hand, seek his blessing. Women would watch him, whisper about him, the young prince of the Ghierdana. Back home, all know he has the dragon's favour.

Here, as soon as he steps out of Great-Uncle's shadow, he's lost. Oh, a few know him, but only as one of the Ghierdana. They don't know how high his station; they do not see the significance of the dragon-tooth on his hip. He's anonymous in this crowd. Earthbound, no longer soaring.

He pushes through the crowd, and instead walks the twisted streets of the Ghierdana enclave in the New City. He wants to feel the wind on his face again. There are many spires and towers in the city, rising like frozen waterspouts or icicles towards the clashing clouds. Yellow fumes from the alchemists' factories, the natural slate-grey of Guerdon's skies, and, over the IOZ, weirder clouds — living spawn of the sky goddess, trailing tentacles like jellyfish over the rooftops, plumes of incense from the temples, ephemeral stair-cases and citadels that fade into empty air. There must be a way up somewhere, but the New City's absurdly confusing, a labyrinth of bridges and walkways, stairs and arcades.

Rasce finds a stairway that seems to lead up to the level above, but it peters out before it reaches it. The whole New City is unfinished; the miracle that made it ran out before it was done. Cursing, he hurries back down the steps.

"Cousin. Are you lost?"

Vyr calls to him from the foot of the stairs. Looking at Vyr is like looking at a phantom conjured by a fortune teller as a warning about some horrible fate. Vyr and Rasce are first cousins. They're about the same age, the same height and build. The same olive skin, the same dark hair. Even their faces are similar, though Vyr's spent too long here under these bleak skies, and there's something sickly about him now, the perpetual impression that he's about to throw up and is moving cautiously to avoid upsetting a delicate stomach. And, of course, Vyr doesn't have a dragon-tooth dagger, nor the enchanted Ring of Samara that adorns Rasce's finger.

Vyr glances at the ring, and he can't quite hide his envy.

And my father never brought shame on the family, like Uncle Artolo did.

"Clearly, I've become accustomed to flying. It all looks different from on high."

"How goes the war?" asks Vyr.

"Like the gods are cats and the world's a sack," replies Rasce. "How have you been? Do you still have all your teeth, or has the Dentist been plying his trade on you?"

"Truth be told, I've seen little of him. I've been tending to our business here. I know not what he's doing, save counting coin and brewing his elixirs," grumbles Vyr. "The New City's ours, every whorehouse and gambling den – but only in the New City. We're penned up here, by the peace lines. We got the worst of the deal when they carved the city up, and there's little enough gold to be found here. We should have demanded Serran and Bryn Avane, not here." Vyr rambles on about problems – disputes about passes and permits, legal entanglements, a litany of names and factions that Rasce doesn't bother following.

He yawns. Business is so dull. It's for dull people like Vyr and the Dentist to take care of. A dragon sleeps on a bed of gold, resting and dreaming for months at a time until it's time for action. Time to fly. "I need a bath, a cup of wine and a bed, cousin. Quickly, now."

Vyr hurries off in the direction of the Ghierdana compound. Night's falling, and the walls of the New City glimmer slightly, a glow rising from within. It looks like fire buried deep within the white stone, and Rasce finds it pleasing.

Rasce follows the path Vyr took, but the city's confusing. He takes a wrong turn at some point, and finds himself back at the foot of the staircase. No – it's one almost identical to it, as similar to the first as he is to Vyr. This staircase, though, is complete, running up to the tower entrance he desired. What a mad folly this New City is! It's almost as though the staircase grew new steps to accommodate him.

He climbs, up and up, until he can feel the wind on his face. From this perspective, looking inland from the shore instead of down from dragon-back, the various districts of the city blend into each other, and he can't clearly distinguish the various occupied zones from each other, can't tell where the IOZ ends and Venture Square begins. It's all one great urban wilderness, a jungle bristling with chimneys and church spires. A labyrinth in its own way – the rest of Guerdon may not be as bizarre and mutable as the New City, but it's still strange to him, and he has no desire to know it better.

It's much better to be up here, unentangled and aloof from the city below. To soar free.

Tomorrow, though. Right now, he wants a glass of arax and a warm bed, so he descends.

At times, it seems like he hears another set of footsteps on the stairs behind him, but when he turns there's no one there.

The next morning, Great-Uncle summons Rasce.

Back home, on Great-Uncle's island, there is a cavern beneath the family villa. Rasce remembers playing on the cavern steps as a child, his cousins daring him to take a few more steps down into the dark, until he could see the red-golden glow from the slumbering dragon. None of them would ever dare trespass into Great-Uncle's chamber without permission; even the head of the family would wait on the threshold until the dragon acknowledged them.

There are rumours of equally large vaults and caves below the New City, but none are accessible to the massive dragon. Today, Great-Uncle suns himself on a wide plaza. One edge of the plaza ends abruptly at a sheer drop down to the sea; armed Eshdana guards patrol the other entrances. The dragon sprawls out across a row of ruined houses, occasionally scraping his back against the rubble. Vorz the Dentist has applied some alchemical salve to the wounds Great-Uncle took in the recent raid; ugly black scabs on the golden-red magnificence of the dragon. Nearby, marring the pristine stone of the plaza, is the scorched carcass of a goat. Great-Uncle's breakfast.

People file up to Great-Uncle, one by one, to whisper into the dragon's ear. Reporting to him, begging for favours. Or offering tribute – there's a growing pile of coins and bank notes on a black cloth in front of the dragon, a microscopic fraction of the dragon's hoard back home.

Rasce walks across the plaza, head held high. Swaggering, the dragon-tooth knife at his belt gleaming bone-white in the sun. The onlookers watch him as he crosses the open ground, but few dare meet his gaze. They bow their heads, offering respect. He spots his cousin Vyr. Unlike most of the Ghierdana, Vyr doesn't look away, but the expression of naked jealousy on his face is tribute enough for Rasce.

He reaches the head of the dragon and kneels smoothly, drawing his knife in the same motion and holding it out so that Great-Uncle can see his own carved tooth, symbol of the bond between the two.

"Beloved Uncle."

"Rasce. Come, sit." The dragon nudges a block of masonry forward with his chin, a seat so close to the dragon's maw that Rasce can feel the fiery heat of Great-Uncle's breath.

"Vorz," rumbles the dragon. Doctor Vorz glides out of the shadows, holding his black bag. He hands Rasce a folded sheet of paper, then reaches into his bag and draws out a glass vial. The Dentist closes Rasce's fingers over it as if it's something precious. Vorz's own fingers are soft and very, very cold.

"There is other business," says the dragon. Great-Uncle extends one bat-like wing over Rasce, angling it to create a leathery tent overhead. The dragon's long neck slithers out, twists around and tucks under the edge of the wing. Stones crack and tumble as Great-Uncle coils his tail round them, making a perimeter wall. Suddenly, Rasce's entirely surrounded by the dragon, cocooned in a hot little box of wing membrane and scaly flesh. Alone, facing the dragon's head.

Great-Uncle snorts, and the sulphurous smell fills the space. Rasce swallows hard, trying not to gasp for air. Beads of sweat run down his back; it's furnace-hot in the dragon's embrace. A private conference is an honour.

"I have a task for you," says Great-Uncle. "Look at what Vorz gave you."

Rasce opens his hand. The glass vial glimmers softly with silvery light. It's full of liquid and some whitish-grey crystals, like salt. "Yliaster," says the dragon, "spirit brine. Used in great quantities by the alchemists. The substance is vital to their industry." Great-Uncle licks his lips, and the scraping of tongue over scale is deafening in the enclosed space, like a sword being dragged across stone. "And we have secured control of a vast deposit of yliaster. Soon, we will begin importing it. The alchemists' guild of Guerdon relies on a handful of merchants here in Guerdon for their needs. Deny them yliaster, and the factories grind to a stop. They must have a constant supply."

"Where's our supply?" asks Rasce.

"Ilbarin," says Great-Uncle.

The Firesea region is a long flight. The direct route is perilous, but going via Lyrix and on through safer territory adds days to the journey. "I'll get my flight gear," says Rasce.

"No. Doctor Vorz will ride in your place," says Great-Uncle.

"Alone?" Rasce can't believe the dragon's words. A dragon might – rarely – carry a passenger, bundled up like cargo, but for someone who isn't family, who isn't Ghierdana to ride in the saddle is unthinkable. "He's not one of us!"

"Your place," says the dragon, "is here. There is work to be done, and it may be that you are best suited to it. The yliaster importers . . . they must buy from us." Great-Uncle's massive tongue scrapes again over his scaly lips. "Give them the dragon's choice."

Take the ash, serve the Ghierdana. Or perish.

Great-Uncle withdraws his head. The wing's edge comes down, closing the gap, leaving Rasce alone in the hot darkness of the dragon's embrace. Outside, the sound of bone crunching, meat tearing as Great-Uncle takes another mouthful.

Rasce is momentarily blind-sided by this. Why him? It must be a test, he tells himself. Artolo was high in Great-Uncle's favour, but failed, fell when he was given a mission here in Guerdon. Rasce tries to breathe, but there's no air in here. The merchants who currently supply this alchemical stuff, this yliaster – he needs to persuade them to serve the Ghierdana. To take the ash, even. All of them are outside the Lyrixian Occupation Zone, so he cannot draw on the strength of the Ghierdana directly. A hundred ways this could go awry.

He must not lose Great-Uncle's favour. He will not.

He squares his shoulders, lifts his head proudly, as a Ghierdana should. He is Chosen of the Dragon. He never fails.

Great-Uncle's head returns, his chops now covered in blood and goat entrails. Rasce wraps the paper around the yliaster vial, stuffs both inside his jerkin. "It shall be done, Great-Uncle."

"Good boy," says the dragon. He lifts his wing, and abruptly Rasce is back in the bright courtyard.

Vorz is now wrapped in an expensive fur coat, with a breathing mask strapped to his head. The Dentist doesn't look any more or less human with his eyes hidden behind bulbous glass goggles, with a breathing tube snaking from his mouth to a tank on his back. He clutches his black bag tightly.

Vorz lays a gloved hand on Rasce's arm. "You are far from home, here, and there are powers in Guerdon you do not know. Your Uncle Artolo moved without caution, and it cost him dearly." Vorz's fingers spider down Rasce's bare forearm, linger a moment too long on Rasce's knuckles. "But it is written: there are moments when the forces balance, and one man in the right place can change the world. Be brave, Rasce."

"Thank you for your counsel," says Rasce, scornfully. He has little time for Vorz's mystic mummery.

"I have prepared the way for you. Speak to Vyr."

Great-Uncle growls, eager to be off. Vorz climbs into the saddle on the dragon's neck. Instead of the long rifle, the spear, the scale-brushes and hooks and other supplies that would normally be kept within easy reach, there are bags, chests of alchemical supplies, an ornamented metal case that Race doesn't recognise.

"Be ready, Rasce," says the dragon, "for my return." The dragon spreads his wings, and steps forward over the edge of the sea wall. He catches the rising air and soars up, circling higher and higher over the New City.

Ascending, without looking back, into the heavens.

The city feels different in the absence of the dragon – fragile, weightless, like it's made of spun sugar and the rain's about to fall. Rasce tries to cling to his bravado, discovers he's clutching his dragon-tooth dagger like a talisman. He shoves it back in his belt, takes a breath. By the grey god's balls, he's fought in the Godswar. He's been a pirate, a soldier, a dragon-rider. He's Chosen of the Dragon, and he's never encountered a foe he couldn't best. In all his life, he's never lost. Convincing some withered old merchants to take the ash should be easy.

He beckons his cousin over.

"Vyr. I'll need somewhere secure as a headquarters."

To his credit, Vyr takes to his new role with great efficiency. Before the first day's out, he's found Rasce a large house on Lanthorn Street, on the lower north side of the New City, close to the edge of the district. It was occupied, but Vyr had the families squatting there moved up to the towers.

Like the rest of the New City, the house sprouted from the same miraculous stone. No one built it. Still, as Rasce wanders the freshly scrubbed rooms, stinking of some alchemical cleaning agent, the shape of the house is strangely familiar to him, like a childhood memory.

Vyr stations guards at the door. A sniper's nest in the attic. Promises to hire a street sorcerer to draw spell-wards at the entrances. "And I've put poison down in the basement." Vyr taps the floor of the cellar with the point of his sword, and there's a faint echo. "The whole city is riddled with tunnels. The cursed ghouls aren't supposed to cross into the LOZ, but they do anyway. They're informants for the city watch so don't say anything down there you don't want repeated."

The list of merchants. None are based here in the New City, but a few are close by, in the neutral zone along the docks. Others are on the far side of Guerdon, past the other occupation zones, in the region called Fog Yards. It's almost funny. In the air, that distance from the New City to the Fog Yards is a heartbeat, a single sweep of Great-Uncle's mighty wings. Here on the ground, it's a considerable obstacle.

"Vyr, we shall need to hire some local ruffians. Blades, smugglers, footpads." Rasce forces himself to smile at his sickly shadow. "I shall be boss, yes, and you shall be my counsellor."

"As the Chosen commands."

CHAPTER THREE

Something taps on the window.

Cari's awake in an instant, blade in hand. *Spar, show me*, she thinks, before she remembers that she's far, far away from the New City, far from her friend. She's alone here, far from home, and there's something at the window *so get it together, Carillon*.

Again, the tapping. Wet thumping, really, like someone's slapping the outside of the building with a dead fish. The window's shuttered; bluish light seeps through the slats.

Run, her instincts tell her. Running used to work for her.

Instead, she crosses the muddy floor of the abandoned room, stepping so softly she makes no sound. She readies her blade, positions herself to one side of the window, keeping the solid wall between her and – whatever's out there. It's big, she can tell that from the sound of its laboured breathing, from the weight of it as it thumps at the shutters. But probably not hostile – the shutter's not that sturdy. If it wanted in, it could get in.

She peers through a slat and finds herself looking into a fish's eye the size of a dinner plate. Unblinking, an awareness both terrified and placid, as if all it has ever known is suffering. The eye stares back at her without recognition, then the thing thumps on the shutter again, hard enough this time to pop the latch. The shutter bounces back, swinging open to give her a better look at the thing.

It's either a huge fish that's eaten the head of a drowned man, or a drowned man wearing a giant fish like a cloak or headdress, the two fused where the headless neck of the human portion meets the underbelly of the fish. She wonders if she'd see a face if the creature opened its mouth. The human body bends under the weight of the huge fish on its back, its knees and hands caked in mud. The body's bloated, its flesh pockmarked with bites from smaller fish, water oozing from old wounds. Naked, but the fish have eaten away the genitals. The hands are caked with salt or something similar, little crystals clinging to the skin. More of the crystals smeared on the window.

The fish-part is still alive as far as she can tell, its brownish-green flanks beaded with moisture, gills pulsing in the pre-dawn air. The fins twitch, brushing against the window frame.

It stands there for a moment, then a ghastly sound bubbles from the drowned man, like he's trying to talk even though his head's got a fish clamped to it – or maybe fused to it, because she can't tell if the man's head is in the fish's mouth, or if it's more like a monk's cowled hood instead of a mouth. The groaning gurgle goes on, a terrible keening, and she can nearly make out words in the sound.

Glass smashes – a bottle, thrown from a window across the street. Bluish blood runs from the fish's back. Then a hail of stones rains down on the creature. As far as Cari can judge, the attackers aren't scared, just irritated to be woken by the creature. Like it's the town drunk, singing at the top of its gills in the middle of the night. The thing's just standing there, taking the punishment.

It slaps on the window again as if it's waiting for her.

Fuck it. She's got no reason to stay. Cari grabs her pack and slings it on to her back. The weight of the fucking book makes her slip in the mud. She climbs out into the street. Someone above shouts a curse, and flings a bottle at her, too. It shatters on the wall nearby, showering her in broken glass. Cari grabs a stone and throws it up at the window. She's a better shot; there's a second, and considerably louder curse, and the window above slams shut.

The fish-headed thing – Monkfish, she decides to call it – begins to walk. There's something absurdly solemn, even dignified about the way it staggers through the muddy streets, dragging the train of its massive fish-body behind it. The absurd entity makes its way downhill, and she follows, staying in the shadows cast by the creature's radiance. As far as she can tell, she's the only person on the streets of Ushket at this hour. The sun's only just crested the shoulder of the Rock, sending long shadows striding west. The light shows her the town. Houses with large arched windows, flat red-tiled roofs, whitewashed walls. Shady green courtyards, to provide relief from the summer's heat.

She was right about the transformed terrain. Ushket sits on a hillside, once high above the sea. Now the sea laps at the heart of the town. Through gaps in the buildings, dawn light flashes off the water, blindingly bright. The sea level has risen hundreds of feet; either that or the whole island's sunk, buried by the divine wrath of the Kraken of Ishmere. When the gods go to war, the way the world works is the first casualty.

The Monkfish leads her through the streets. A different route to the hill she climbed last night. The streets are still eerily empty, but she can hear the town waking up on the upper levels. Glancing up, she sees rope bridges and walkways crossing overhead, linking the various buildings. The people of Ushket have moved up, ceding the streets to the tides. She spots early risers on some of the walkways, and some of them might be armed. She tries to stay hidden, but Monkfish doesn't stop moving and the muddy ground is treacherous; at least one of them spots her. She hunches her shoulders and keeps moving. Moves her pack around, so it's less obvious she's got anything worth stealing.

More Monkfish come shambling down different lanes. It's a congregation, a whole pack of animated-corpses-hauling-giant-fish-things.

The fish all goggle at one another; their zombie host-bodies just keep trudging through the mud. Cari sticks close to her Monkfish, although she's having second thoughts about this whole idea. Maybe she misinterpreted the creature's intent entirely. Fuck, maybe it has no intent at all, and it's as dumb as it seems.

The parade of Monkfish passes through an archway, and suddenly they're at the edge of town, on the open hillside. There are sentries on the walls of Ushket, but they don't spot Cari as she slips out and follows the parade down to the new shore, where waves break on the remains of drowned vineyards. It's a graveyard of ships – there are a dozen hulks here, carcasses drawn up and left to rot. Their prows face the road, and the ebbing tide washes around their sterns. Mastless, some partially broken up. Dragged out of the water judging by the gouged tracks they left behind them, by the heaped and broken earth like frozen red-brown waves around their keels. Something big – a dragon, she guesses, if the fucking Ghierdana are in town – dragged those ships out of the sea and left them broken on the shore. It puts her in mind of beached whales.

One by one, the Monkfish wade into the water. As they enter the sea, the creatures become suddenly graceful, their human bodies going limp and trailing behind the dancing, leaping fish. They surge through the surf, joyfully, vanishing into this new sea.

All except her Monkfish. That one wades into the surf and stands there. The fish-eye stares are her, and then it haltingly raises a human arm and points to one of the more intact ships.

She recognises it. Gods below, she knows it. It's the *Rose*.

Cari runs across the muddy hillside towards the wreck. When she glances back, the Monkfish is gone.

It's the stillness that disturbs her. She still knows every inch of the *Rose*, could find her way through the compartments by memory alone. This was her ship, her home, her salvation. The *Rose* carried her away from Guerdon, away from the legacy of her family, away from her aunt's curses and torments, away from the black iron dreams. This ship gave Cari her life.

But it's all too still. *Rose* used to roll with the waves. Cari could feel every breath of wind or pulse of ocean through the decks. Now, the ship's like another dead body washed up on shore, cold and still.

She climbs in through a hole in the hull and makes her way through the forward hold. The aft hold looks to be mostly flooded. She sloshes through stagnant water on her way to the ladder that brings her up on to the deck. *Rose* is listing over to the side; the deck slopes, like the ship's caught in a never-ending wave. The door to the forecastle, the crew cabin, is open, and Cari stares at it for a long while. For five years, that was her home, her first real home. Her aunt's house in Wheldacre was never as welcoming or as loved as that little nook under the bowsprit. Unconsciously, as if enchanted by her own past, she re-enters the room, finding memories with her fingertips.

That bunk on the right, that used to be where the first mate, Adro, would sleep. Dol Martaine on the other side. She still instinctively steps to the right to avoid the empty bunk – Martaine would beat anyone who woke him. Gods, she hated him, still hates him, but somehow it's a fond memory, too.

She ducks to dodge the lamp that used to hang there, steps over the memory of Cook's boxes. There are rusted hooks in the walls, for the hammocks were once slung there, a labyrinth of canvas, the crew of the *Rose* crammed in tighter than sleepers in a flophouse. Storage lockers and boxes, all broken open and empty. The floor's dirty, too, and that's so wrong it hurts her bones. Cari's stolen from temples, faced down saints, even killed a goddess, but this is blasphemy.

Finally, she sits down on her bunk. For a moment, she imagines what she would do if she could step out of time and reach across the years, speak to the girl she was when she first came aboard, curled up and seasick on this little bunk. Dressed in boy's clothes, frantically trying to work out how to go to the toilet without giving away her secret. Thinking that was the only secret she had. *If you ever go back to Guerdon, Cari thinks to her twelve-year-old self, things will get fucking weird. You'll make friends, and one of them will turn into the king of the ghouls. And you'll get the other one killed. And then you'll be an avenging saint for a while, and that'll be fun – only it's killing him again, and you've got to cross the world to save him. And don't get me started about gods and alchemists.*

Oh, and you'll have to put up with know-it-all Eladora again.

Look, don't go back to fucking Guerdon, all right.

But if she never went back to Guerdon, she'd never have known Spar.

And Spar would still be alive, she reminds herself. Her presence in Guerdon brought ruin to the city. So much of the suffering is her fault.

Her eyes fall on another wonder. There, kicked into a corner, is her own little box that used to stand by her bunk. She filled it with treasures collected across the world. Coins from Lyrix, stolen – she was told – from a dragon's hoard, blessed with the monster's luck.

A playbill from a theatre in Jashan. Captain Hawse brought her there for her eighteenth birthday. They both dressed up for the occasion; Hawse had insisted. Cari wore a ballgown, and it was like a glimpse into another life, one in which she'd been born into a regular, wealthy family, instead of crazed demon-worshippers who bred her to be a herald to nightmare gods.

A petrified dragon's scale. Scrimshawed whalebone. Blue jade from Mattaur.

But the box is empty now. There's nothing there.

She only has one of those treasures left, and it wasn't what she thought it was. Cari once thought the amulet she wears at her neck was a gift from her unknown mother. It was only years later, in Guerdon, that she learned the truth – that it was made by her grandfather, a ritual talisman for communing with the Black Iron Gods. She treasures it still, for her own reasons. It's a reminder that she can take whatever the world throws at her and refashion it into a weapon. Everything's a weapon if you're willing to use it. And she has a second treasure, now – the fucking book. The weight of it reminds her she can't linger here.

Wiping her eyes – it's very dusty in there – she emerges back on deck. The masts have been cut down. The stumps that used to be the *Rose*'s graceful masts offend her to her core, and she adds whoever wrecked the ship to her shit list.

Across the deck, there's the door to Captain Hawse's cabin.

And in the doorway, Captain Hawse. Older, greyer, smaller somehow, but still himself.

A sword in his hand.

"Are you a dream?" demands Hawse. "A spirit, sent to torment me?"

Part of her wants to rush across the deck and hug the old man. Another part, the part that fought on the streets of Guerdon, watches that sword. *He's got reach, you've got speed*, thinks that part of herself, and she hates it.

"It's me. It's Cari."

"Cari," echoes Hawse. He blinks, raises one hand to shade his eyes from the rising sun. "It is you. You came back."

"Sort of." Cari shrugs awkwardly.

"You left!" says Hawse, with apparent surprise, as if he just remembered the circumstances of their parting. "You just jumped ship. It was in Severast. We were in Severast, and you left without a word." He shakes the sword at her. "After all I did for you."

"There were fucking words beforehand," Cari replies before she can stop herself. This isn't what she wants, to go over decade-old arguments. "You didn't listen to me."

"Oh, I remember. Full of ideas, you were. Stealing from the Eyeless priests! Saying we should smuggle wine-of-poets out of Jashan. Making a run to the Silver Coast! A slip of a girl, telling me how to run my ship!"

Cari glances around at the wreck of the *Rose*, at the empty hulk lying in the sun. "Yes, well, you've clearly made a great success of it without me."

He laughs at that, a chuckle that's half a snarl. He waves the sword at her. "Cari. Where have you been? Why are you here?"

"All over. Guerdon. And . . . " She shrugs. "A dead guy with a fish for a head led me here."

"That was a holy Bythos. Emissary of the Lord of Waters," says Hawse reverently. Cari vaguely recalls the Lord of Waters as the Ilbariner sea-god.

"There was a shoal of them out there before dawn."

"I know. The war broke the Lord of Waters, child, and his servants are lost. They wander the streets every night." Hawse yawns, and Cari notices how old he's become, how his jaw trembles. How much it costs him to lift that sword. She takes a step towards him, hesitantly, then another and another.

The sword comes back up. "What do you want? Nothing here for you to take."

"I was looking for a ship. I need to get to Khebesh." She nearly adds "sir".

"The *Rose* is wrecked. You can see that."

"But you used to know people in Ilbarin City. You've got to know someone with a ship, Hawse, you've got to. I've got to get to Khebesh. *Please.*"

Hawse lowers the sword. Cari takes another step forward, but he turns away from her. He digs around in his pockets, finds his pipe. Fills it, his hands shaking.

"I took you in. I remember you trying to sneak on board, making enough noise to wake the dead. With your hair cut short, wearing trousers pinched from some farmer. And that voice!" Hawse mimics an absurdly deep, gravelly voice. "Begging your pardon, captain, but I'm a boy who ran away to sea. I'll work my passage. I'll scrub the decks, do whatever."

"I fucking did work, though," says Cari, cheeks flushing. It's ancient history now, of course, but she thought she'd kept her secret for years. She remembers nervously admitting to Hawse that she was a girl, the look of surprise on his face giving away to laughter. She'd always believed he was laughing at his own foolishness in not seeing the truth.

"You did. I can't fault you on that. Best topman I ever had. You proved Adro wrong – he said I should have sent you home."

"Adro said that?" She and the first mate were friends for years; he was like a brother to her. A big ox of a man. They'd planned to conquer the world together, go crawling the dockside taverns together. She smiles at the memory.

"I stopped Dol Martaine from hurting you," says Hawse, harshly. "He'd have cut your throat and dumped you over the side. But, no, I gave you a place on my ship. And then you left."

"Look, I was pissed. I'm sorry, I should have—"

"Do you still have that amulet?" asks Hawse, turning back to her.

Cari unclasps it and hands it to him. Hawse holds it up to the light of the rising sun. "Remember that time in Ilbarin, you ran off and pawned this ugly thing. Threw the ticket into the bloody sea. Then came crying to me that night, begged me to help you get it back."

"I remember," says Cari. "I . . . look, I didn't know back then, but I . . . my family, back in Guerdon, they . . . " She struggles for words. How can she convey the strangeness of her origins, the terrible destiny that was made for her? The dreams that haunted her when she was a child, the nameless terror that drove her to flee across the world. She knows now that it was the Black Iron Gods calling for their herald from their prison, but, back then, she only knew that she was always, always in the wrong place. Always feeling dangerous, like some great doom was following her, and if she stayed in one place too long it would fall upon her. "I can't talk about it."

Hawse snorts in anger. "You always had one eye on the door.

Always looking to the horizon, to the next port. Six years on board my ship, and you just walked away." He throws the amulet back to her. "So walk away. Go on. Go to Khebesh, if they'll take you. Or go back to Guerdon for all I care. There's nothing for you here."

The door of his cabin slams shut, leaving her alone on the deck.

CHAPTER FOUR

B aston Hedanson debates the best way to kill the man standing at his doorstep.

"Can I come in?"

Tiske stands there, hands twisting nervously, beefy face half hidden by a hood. Laughing no longer. He looks like he's been through the wars – he has that hunched, furtive look of a man who fears the wrath of the gods.

The proper thing to do, of course, is hang him from a drain-pipe. That was what the Brotherhood used to do to traitors. String them up, where everyone could see them, as a reminder that the Brotherhood owned the streets of Guerdon. It was a warning, too, to the politicians and priests that they weren't the only powers in the city. The authorities hung Idge, the great leader of the Brotherhood, from the gallows on Mercy Street, after Idge refused to recant, refused to betray the movement he'd led. A gutter death in some alley in the Wash wasn't a mockery of that martyrdom; it honoured it.

"I just want to talk," says Tiske.

Drowning? The murky waters of the harbour are only a few streets away. Many a better man than Tiske has met an end there. You have to weigh the body down with stones, so it's eaten by fish and not by ghouls. These days, even the corpse-eaters are informants.

"I don't mean you any harm. The dragons didn't send me, I swear."

Burning? Now there's a strong candidate.

It could be argued that Tiske deserves to burn.

Tiske makes the sign with his hand, the old distress signal of the Brotherhood. By tradition, no member of the Brotherhood of Thieves can refuse aid to one who makes that sign.

That sign shouldn't hold any power over Baston now.

It does, though. A little. Enough to buy Tiske another few minutes' life.

"Come in." Tiske pushes past him, down the narrow hallway, into the kitchen. He peers out into the cramped yard behind the house

"Who is it?" calls Baston's sister Karla from the floor above.

"Tiske."

"Don't murder him until I'm dressed."

Baston advances into the kitchen. There was a time when Tiske would have been a regular visitor to this isolated house, Tiske and the rest of the Brotherhood's inner circle. Heinreil, Tammur, Pulchar. Baston's father, Hedan, too. His father grew up in this little house, and kept it even after his fortunes rose and he bought the big place up in Hog Close. Fortunes made and lives lost over this little kitchen table.

Baston recalls the Fever Knight standing guard outside that back door, the sound of rainwater dancing on the bodyguard's armour.

Every one of them is dead, or gone – just like the Brotherhood.

"Your father," says Tiske, "always had a bottle of wine to hand, for guests."

"No. For friends."

Tiske's face falls. "I'd never wish harm on you and yours. I stood with you at the funeral, remember?" *Funerals*, thinks Baston, *plural*. Two in the last two years. His wife, Fae, was never part of the Brotherhood. She was nothing to do with this life at all. Fae was his second chance, his clean slate, and she'd died, too.

"I'd have carried your father's body to the sisters with you," continues Tiske, unaware he's stepped on a mine, "if they'd ever found his remains."

"And then you took the ash. You broke faith with the Brotherhood, and joined up with the Ghierdana."

Tiske bristles. "I never broke faith. But I wasn't going to shackle myself to a body that was already halfway down the corpse-shaft. The Brotherhood was as good as gone before I left." He holds up his hands, like a priest giving a blessing. "I know you don't see things the same way, Baston, but truth's truth."

We could have rebuilt, thinks Baston, *if you and the others stayed true*. It would have been hard, he knows that, with so many of their number dead in the chaos. But there'd been opportunity, too. The New City sprouting from the ruins – a literal rebirth of hope. If the Brotherhood had been united, they could have seized that divine blessing, taken the New City for their own. Instead, it fell into the claws of dragons, and the Brotherhood stayed broken.

"Tiske," says Baston, "what do you want?"

"I want you to come up to the New City with me."

"I won't take the ash."

Tiske rubs his forehead. "I'm not saying that. But—"

From outside, an uncanny sound, a chittering whisper.

"Quiet," snaps Baston. Both men freeze.

Through the window, they see a spider's leg the size of a tree trunk in the yard outside, stepping over the adjoining derelicts. Fine hairs bristle on the leg of the god-thing, twitching like antennae. Baston peers out – the spider-spirit straddles the house. The creature is only half real, its substance skittering in and out of the mortal world, moonlight reflecting off a shifting fog-bank. Eight eyes stare down at Baston as it probes his mind. He feels it, or imagines he feels it, picking its way over the folds in his brain.

He pushes his thoughts down deep. Weighs them down and drowns them in the dark recesses of his mind. Lets his conscious mind fill with quotidian thoughts – he wonders if there'll be work down at the docks tomorrow morning, tries to recall if there's bread in the cupboard, reminds himself to fix a broken window upstairs.

Finding nothing, the spider moves on, picking its way with unnatural lightness over the terraced rows of houses. From the street outside, Baston hears the chanting of the Ishmeric priests as they follow the emanation of their god on its nightly inquisition.

Tiske exhales. "By all the hells, Baston, how do you still live here with those things crawling around?"

It's a fair question. And not one for which Baston has a good answer.

"Have you killed him yet?" Karla enters the room, pulling a shawl around her shoulders. "Hello, Tiske. Baston, if you're going to murder someone here, put down a towel first."

"There was a sentinel," warns Tiske hastily. "It just passed."

"I felt it. Oh, the gods of Ishmere don't care much what we faithless do to each other. They only look for threats to the Sacred Realm." Karla bustles around the kitchen. "Do you want a drink, Tiske?"

"Listen. This is for you, too, Karla," says Tiske. "There's a new Ghierdana boss. A young fellow, Chosen of the Dragon. He needs locals who know the streets. He'll pay. Come on, lad, come up to the New City and meet him."

"No," says Baston.

Karla laughs. "Baston won't take the ash, Tiske. He's Brotherhood till the day he dies."

Tiske reddens with frustration. "And when will that be? When some giant fucking spider decides you're a sinner? When the clouds eat you? When High Um—"

"Don't say a name," snaps Karla. Mentioning a god by name is perilous.

Tiske catches himself. He spreads his hands across the table, takes a slow breath, smiles a sad, weary smile. "Do you remember what it was like before the Tallowmen?"

"How young do you think we are, Tiske?" says Karla from the window. Tiske knew their father, knew them when they were children. He still thinks of them that way. It's how he can get away with calling Baston Hedanson "lad". Baston's north of thirty.

They'd have been nine or ten, still living up on Hog Close, when the alchemists' creations were first loosed on Guerdon. The wax monsters were made out of condemned thieves, remade to hunt down their former brothers. Baston used to have nightmares about looking out of his bedroom window and seeing the face of his father lit from within by candle-flame.

"Ah, back then, things made sense to a simple man like myself. No gods except the Kept up on Holyhill, and the watch were flesh and blood. You could bribe 'em to look the other way, and they all knocked off at sundown. Then they sent the Tallows, and we were fucked."

"The Brotherhood," says Baston, "was fucked when Heinreil took over."

Tiske sounds bashful, like he's speaking beyond his remit. "The Dentist was running things in Guerdon, but he's left now. The new boss, Rasce – he's just a boy, green as canal-weed. He doesn't know the city at all. I came to you first, Baston, I came to you because it's an opportunity. They have money, power – and they can't be touched, up in the New City." Tiske peers out of the window at the distant shape of the sentinel, and shudders. "Get in with him now, and you'll have the dragons on your side when you need 'em."

Baston stays seated until the front door shuts behind Tiske. He doesn't trust himself not to do something violent to the older man, so better to stay put until he's gone.

Karla studies her brother from across the room, letting the rain and the distant chanting from the temples fill the silence. It's a comfortable silence. Karla's silver-tongued and can talk for hours with people she despises, charm them and enchant them, and they'll never know it's an act. Words are a costume for her; it's in silence that she's her true self.

Baston's house has been very, very quiet since his sister moved in to take care of her widowed brother. A long, slow silence, where he could heal.

Karla watches, and waits, and thinks. Finally, she speaks.

"You should do it. Meet with this Rasce at least."

"Why should I go to the Ghierdana to sell my soul, when I could spit on a dozen temples from here?"

"So long as spitting is all you're doing to them," says Karla. She pulls the shawl up over her head. "I've got to go out. There's dinner in the pot – or are you going out to Pulchar's?" Pulchar's restaurant used to be a Brotherhood haunt, back when there was a Brotherhood. Now, it's just a few tired old men reminiscing.

"Not tonight."

A quick kiss on the cheek, a reassuring squeeze of his shoulder. "Think about what Tiske said. We don't have many friends left. It might be good to make some new ones."

And she's gone. Baston doesn't know where his sister goes, which temple she worships at, or if she has some other business. He wonders if she'll come back tonight, to sleep in that little attic room intended for a child's bed.

He hopes she does. This house feels like it should be haunted, but it's empty of ghosts.

Too full of gods.

The next morning, he goes down to the docks. That means leaving the Ishmeric Occupation Zone, means waiting in line at the checkpoint for an hour, shuffling along until it's his turn before the sentry-clerics.

"Name?"

"Baston Hedanson."

"What business?"

"Docker."

The mad-eyed cleric studies him for a moment, as if he can see into Baston's soul, then reaches up and anoints him with foul-smelling oil.

"Blessing expires at sunset," snaps the cleric, "and then thy soul is forfeit to Cruel Urid, watcher of the night hours."

Baston trudges down the hill, joining the crowd of dockworkers who jostle for labour every morning along Guerdon's wharves. The others back away from Baston, give him space. They remember who he used to be.

These docks are neutral territory, but they're sandwiched between the Lyrixian and Haithi Occupation Zones, between the dragons and the mad gods, so there are fewer ships berthed here than there might once have been. No captain wants to leave his ship in between two warring powers, and trust to the fragile Armistice to preserve the peace. The big freighters go to the new docks in Shriveport, on the far side of Holyhill, long piers running out into deep water. Fewer ships mean less work.

He waits in the chilly spring drizzle for his name to be called. Distantly, he knows that he's better off than most of the poor bastards huddled along the dockside. He won't starve if he misses a day's work. For others, there's the span of a single coin between a good day and a bitter one.

Gunnar Tarson sidles up to him in the crowd. Another Brotherhood boy cast adrift. Tarson's young and eager, starts talking about some job he has in mind, breaking into a merchant's house. It's not the time. Not with the spider-sentinels crawling over the district. It hasn't been the time for months. Maybe it won't ever be the time again.

He imagines himself as part of a broken mechanism. A coil or spring, wound ever more tightly, but disconnected now from whatever apparatus might once have given him release or function. He bows his head, waits to be called, and feels the tension in his belly ratchet forward, an inch of bile at a time.

The foreman starts calling names.

"Baston Hedanson?"

He steps forward.

"Sheds on Acre Lane. Boss wants 'em cleared."

The sheds are a maze of rotting timbers. Raindrops swelling through narrow cracks in the roof, like a man bleeding from a dozen cuts. Floor slick with foamy run-off. This place hasn't been used in months. Abandoned when an alchemist's freighter went aground off the Bell Rock, and the evening tide ran yellow with poison. Another bit of the city gone rotten, ceded to something toxic and inimical to mortal life. Baston sniffs the air – as a creature of Guerdon, the smells from the alchemists' smokestacks are as familiar to him as church bells. The burned sourness of phlogiston, the effervescent, tickling saltiness of yliaster, the cloying stench of melting wax.

There's something else as well. A faint, floral scent. Perfume, maybe?

He's not alone here. He tenses, his broad shoulders hunching. Hands bunching into fists. This isn't the occupied zone, he tells himself. There's no reason to assume trouble.

He prowls through the sheds, moving deeper into the maze. There's a large space in the centre. Once, it was a trade hall, ornate iron pillars supporting a high ceiling, glass skylights green with moss and scum. The green light shifting like the whole place is underwater.

Two figures wait for him there. One's an old man, bald, a face like a gargoyle. He's wearing a priest's cassock, but there's a gun in his hand. The other's a younger woman, a black velvet dress like a guildmaster, but no guild sigil or badge of office. Hair pinned back, one hand pressing a scented handkerchief to her nose. The light catches her face, and for a moment Baston thinks he recognises her.

"Cari?"

"You're not the first to make that mistake," says the woman. "But no."

She raises her other hand and invisible chains lock into place around Baston's arms, legs, throat. Even his eyes are held by the spell. He can't blink, can barely breathe.

The woman's a sorcerer. Even as he's held there frozen, Baston's mind is racing. Sorcery's rarely seen on the streets, and she's clearly no thief or hired assassin – although he's not so sure about her companion.

The old man searches Baston's paralysed body expertly, finding the knife tucked into his boot, the garrotte in his pocket. He checks Baston's hands, probes the wedding ring for a concealed needle. One horned finger pokes at the spot on Baston's forehead where the cleric anointed him. The old man sniffs the oil, grimaces. "He's clean."

"Thank you," says the woman. "Mr Hedanson, forgive me. I shall release you momentarily, but please don't do anything, ah, provocative."

The old man tucks Baston's knife into a fold of his cassock, then backs away out of arm's reach. The gun appears again, pointed at Baston's belly. The man is old, but his aim is unwavering.

The woman closes her hand, and the spell vanishes. Baston watches the woman closely – he's heard sorcery puts a terrible strain on its practitioners – but she seems unwearied.

"My name," says the woman, "is Eladora Duttin. I understand you knew my cousin Carillon, once." She produces a slim black notebook from a pocket, makes a note.

"I haven't seen Cari in a long time. Is this about her?"

"Not quite."

"Then who are you people?"

"Our remit," says Duttin, "is safeguarding the Armistice. It would be disastrous for the city if the war were to resume. The terms of the peace accord provide some restraint on the occupying powers, but it's our role to, ah, deal with potential problems before that restraint is tested."

Baston stays silent. His father drummed into him never to talk to the city watch. These people aren't watch, but they're something like it.

"The Armistice works by balancing the ambitions of each occupying power against the other two – if the Ishmerians attack, they risk creating an alliance between Lyrix and Haith. The Ghierdana are, ah, challenging. The dragons are an essential part of the Lyrixian military. Without the dragons, the Lyrixians would struggle to fulfil their part of the accord."

Baston shrugs. "I just shift cargo down the docks. I don't—"

"Oh, spare us the mummery," snaps the priest. "We know every fucking thing about you. We know every one of your little secrets. We know your crew, that shit Tarson and the rest. All the scum that you scraped out of the gutters after the invasion. And, honestly, we don't care. This is much bigger."

Duttin continues with her lecture. "The Ghierdana operate independently from the Lyrixian armed forces—"

"Wild as bloody devils," mutters the priest, rolling his eyes. "Anathema upon 'em."

"Sinter, enough! We don't have time for this." Duttin silences him. Sinter – it's a name Baston's heard before. A Keeper priest, a fixer. Reputation as dirty as the hem of his cassock that trails through the slime.

Baston folds his arms.

"We are aware," continues Duttin, "that you were offered a job. We require you to accept this offer of employment. The Ghierdana are tightly knit, and we require a w-window into their plans."

"You want me to spy on the Ghierdana for you?"

"Precisely." Duttin's face lights up. "You will be recompensed, of course."

"Why me?"

"Never you mind," growls the priest, but Duttin overrules him again.

"You were well connected in the Brotherhood, well respected. An able lieutenant, able to recruit and motivate, by all accounts."

"One of Heinreil's legbreakers," interjects Sinter.

"You are precisely the sort of man the Ghierdana need. Your former associate Tiske certainly thinks so. We know he visited you last night." She smiles, and it's unexpectedly genuine, a moment of satisfaction at her own cleverness.

"Looks like you do know everything." Baston spits on the floor, a big gobbet of saliva and mucus, halfway between him and Duttin. Anger rises up in him. "So, you know that you bastards have shit on the Wash time and time again. The alchemists poisoned us. When the Ravellers rose, you let them eat us, so the fighting wouldn't spill into the *quality* districts, right? Same thing happened in the invasion – you drew the fucking line of no retreat at Holyhill and the Viaduct, not in the Wash. You say you want to protect Guerdon – you mean, *your* Guerdon, up on the heights. The churches and the palaces and the guildhalls. Not my Guerdon. My Guerdon's possessed by mad gods. So, you all-wise cunts, you know where you can stick your plan, right?"

"The Armistice saved thousands of lives," says Eladora, quietly.

"How fucking nice for them that lived."

"Show some respect, you little shit!" croaks Sinter, spittle flying from his lips. He steps forward, waving the gun—

—and Baston strikes, grabbing at the priest's wrist, twisting his body as he moves to dodge the bark of the gun. His coat tugs as the bullet passes through the folds of cloth, but he's not wounded. He grabs Sinter with one hand, hammers the priest in the face with the other, swings the old man's body around as a shield, then charges Duttin, hoping that any spell will catch the priest and not him.

But he's a fraction too slow. Duttin's paralysis spell locks around Baston again and he goes down in a tangle of limbs, landing heavily atop the priest, face down on the muddy floor. Fucking magic. Sinter wriggles out, twitching like a half-crushed insect, cursing and spitting. Bony limbs kicking and hitting Baston's frozen body as he pulls himself free. There's a knife in the priest's hand now, wicked and bright, and he scrabbles at Baston's collar, searching for his throat. "Little Brotherhood shit," he mutters, "fucking guttersnipe."

"Sinter. *Enough.*" Baston's face down in the mud; he can't see Duttin's face, but he can hear the strain in her voice. Holding him like this costs her. He struggles against the spell, trying to force his limbs to move against the unseen hands that grip every muscle. "The poor man's wife perished in the invasion," she adds. "We must be understanding."

Understanding. How can they be understanding, when he can't understand? How can anyone give meaning to the terrible suddenness of Fae's death? One moment there, and the next, gone, washed away by the Kraken-waves that crashed down on the city. As though she were no more real than a figure drawn in the sand of the shore – to be erased by a passing whim. How do you understand, when nothing stands, nothing lasts, and the world changes in a heartbeat?

"Roll him over," orders Duttin. Groaning, the priest hauls Baston's paralysed body over. He's lying on his back now, staring up at the green light.

Duttin stands over him. Her hand still glows with arcane energy, blood welling up from the edge of her fingernails to drip down and mingle with the mud.

She sighs. "Three points. First, please understand that we are trying to preserve a very delicate balance. I brought the Ghierdana back to Guerdon – at a not inconsiderable personal cost – to ensure that balance between the occupying powers. We need the dragons to remain in Guerdon. We are prepared to overlook a certain degree of, ah, illicit activity, as long as it doesn't threaten the Armistice.

Second, we only require information from you, nothing more. If action is warranted, we have our own resources. We do not require you to do anything more than report on the Ghierdana's plans. And, thirdly . . . " She purses her lips, like she's tasting something unpleasant. "I know your wife perished last year, but, ah . . . "

Sinter steps in. "We've been watching you. We know your sweet little sister. Your sinful mother. Your friends in Pulchar's bar. Any of yours that hasn't gone up to the New, we know. You think you're the only one with gutter-water in their blood? I was running saint hunters in the Wash when your shit of a dad was an altar boy in St Storm's. If you don't do as we tell you, we can ruin any of them." Sinter jerks a thumb at Duttin. "You work for her now, understand?"

Baston really wants to punch that old priest. To bring down Eladora, too, this woman who looks like Cari and talks like a lawyer. Move fast enough, the Fever Knight once showed him, get your hands around a sorcerer's throat before they can breathe a word, and you've got a chance.

But it's not worth it. The Ghierdana and their dragons, the Ishmerians and their gods, and this woman and her murderous priest – and behind her, other forces he can only faintly perceive, money and influence and parliament, as real and dangerous as any other power. Fuck them all – they're all uncaring giants, trampling the wreckage of his home underfoot.

They step back. The priest ostentatiously takes another cartridge from his pocket, reloads the pistol. Once the weapon's ready, Duttin releases the spell.

Baston sits back up, draws himself back to a standing position.

"One job. And I'm not taking the ash. One job, and you leave me and mine alone after that."

Duttin glances at Sinter, who scowls.

"Assuming you're able to ascertain the nature of this Rasce's plans," says Duttin carefully, "that would be acceptable."

"All right. I'll do it." Baston extends his hand.

Neither of the other two moves. Neither shakes his hand to seal the deal. Neither risks coming within arm's reach. Oh, they think they know him.

"There's a tailor's on Greyhame Street, up Holyhill," says Sinter. "Go there after, and we'll take your measurements, understand?"

Baston nods. "What happened to Cari?" he asks. "Is she dead?"

"Oh." Eladora's flustered for the first time. "S-she's alive, but she had to leave Guerdon. I sent her away. She's safe."

The first to arrive at the house on Lanthorn Street is Tiske. Rasce could guess Tiske was ash-marked even if Vyr hadn't already told him – there's something in the demeanour of the Eshdana, an instinctive deference in the presence of Ghierdana. Middle-aged, heavy-set, balding. A barrel of a man, in that he's been filled with salted pork and you could use him to barricade a door, but he doesn't strike Rasce as a great wit. One of Artolo's lieutenants, hoping to worm his way back into the dragon's favour.

He kneels, kisses the dragon-tooth when Rasce presents it. His hands shake, slightly.

"They're on their way up, sir," he says.

"I'm looking for soldiers, Tiske, not the sweepings of an alehouse. This friend of yours had better be worth my time."

"I'd wager my life on him."

Rasce toys with the dagger. "Oh, you have."

The door opens, and Vyr shows two people into the room.

One, Rasce assumes, is the fellow Tiske spoke of, Baston Hedanson. Broad shoulders straining the fabric of his grey suit. His face puts one in mind of an animal, but which beast? The build of a bull, but no – he's a wolfhound. Strong, fierce, but used to being part of a pack. He moves unhurriedly across the office, taking in everything. His gaze flickers to the exits, marks the guards at the door, the dagger on the desk.

The other is Baston's sister. Hair dyed an unnaturally pale blonde.

Her dress is of cheap fabric, but she wears it well. Back home on the isles, the fisherfolk would parade their pretty sons and daughters on market day, hoping to be noticed by a Ghierdana. He wonders if that's why Baston brought her along – but then she meets Rasce's gaze, and doesn't look away. None of the fisher-folk would ever show such a lack of respect to the children of the Dragon.

To his surprise, he finds it enhances her allure in his eyes.

She smirks as if they're sharing a private joke. "So, Tiske tells my brother there's business to be done, and you need a few good hands. What sort of business?"

"I intend to burn Dredger's yard."

"Thought you had dragons for that sort of thing."

"My Great-Uncle is away, and this is family business," explains Rasce.

Baston frowns in confusion, and Tiske leans down, whispering. "There's a dragon at the head of each family. The families work together on some business, but not all."

Rasce continues. "You will be well paid for your work. And if you prove worthy, you may be rewarded further, with the favour of the dragon." Back home, just the chance of the dragon's favour could induce one man to kill another. To be Eshdana, ash-marked, is to share in the dragon's fortune, to have the syndicates behind you. Rasce's mildly surprised when neither Baston nor Karla react. "The ash," he adds.

Baston's unimpressed. "Why Dredger?"

"Does it matter?" snaps Vyr. "That is the target the Ghierdana have chosen."

"Dredger's got friends in the Wash," says Karla, "he's been running his yards for years. Paid his dues to the Brotherhood regular as clockwork."

"That was when the Brotherhood had the docks," says Tiske. "Nowadays, they go unclaimed." His tone is that of some old aunt running her finger over the mantlepiece and finding it dusty.

"He gave work to the plagued when no one else would touch 'em," says Baston.

"But he was an informant to the thief-takers. And the watch, when it suited him," argues Karla.

Vyr scowls at her. "He is who I have chosen. Are you in?"

Tiske reaches forward and squeezes Baston's shoulder, but the younger man still has reservations. "What's our payment?"

"Chaos is all we want. We'll break the yards. You may rob what you wish in the process." He's handing the Guerdon thieves a small fortune in stolen alchemical weapons, but the sum is of little concern to the Ghierdana. Great-Uncle sleeps on a bed of treasure worth a thousand times as much.

"Not coin?" grumbles Baston.

"I'm sure we can move whatever ye steal through the New City," says Tiske. "Baston, lad, the Ghierdana operate all across the world. They can sell those weapons off in Khenth or Ul-Taen, get you a good price. Assuming you're not going to ..." He trails off, glances at the Ghierdana. Use them here, Rasce assumes. On the Ishmerian occupiers.

"What's the plan for containment? And protection? Dredger handles poisons and worse in the yards."

"A small explosion, at the far end of the yards, to draw guards away. A second team at the front, to strike the main office as you counsel. The risk of wildfire should be minimal. We know how things burn, of that have no doubt." Baston's caution is justified – alchemical weapons are immensely potent, and indiscriminate in their killing. A leak from Dredger's yard could be disastrous.

Karla leans over to her brother. "It's worth a shot, to my mind. Bring some of the canal crew. See if Yon Bleak will still talk to us."

"Listen to her, lad," pleads Tiske.

Baston's face is unreadable. "That's a fine dagger, there," he says, nodding at the dragon-tooth blade.

"Taken from the dragon's maw, and it marks me as the dragon's favourite. Do not touch it, or I would be honour bound to kill you."

"So I've heard. Can you use it, or is it an ornamental piece?"

"I can use it."

"Aye, aye." Baston watches the light glimmer on the blade for a moment. "I'm in – on one condition. You're coming, too."

"The point of hiring you," says Vyr, "is to ensure the attack cannot be blamed on the Ghierdana."

"Or maybe the point of hiring us is so you can set us up."

"You come to our house and you dare accuse us of treachery?" Vyr goes for his own dagger, but Baston's quicker. He springs to his feet, grabs Vyr's wrist and pins it. "It was your father who tried to move in on the old Brotherhood territory last year, wasn't it? Artolo, right?

"Baston, I wouldn't lie to you!" shouts Tiske, leaping up, too.

"You did take the ash, Ben," remarks Karla lightly. Like Rasce, she too has remained seated.

"If the dragon wanted you dead—" begins Vyr, but Rasce interrupts him.

"The dragon does not want you dead." Rasce picks up the dagger, flips it in the air, and thrusts it into his belt. "And battle holds no fear for me. I shall be with you at Dredger's yard. And to put your fears at ease, we'll bring Vyr, too. Isn't that right, Vyr?"

CHAPTER FIVE

Waking is always bad. The long scar on Artolo's belly hurts, a dull ache. Groaning, he throws back the silken sheets, reaches for the glass jar that holds his pills.

The idiot servants have put the lid back on. How many times must he tell these Ilbariners to leave the lid off in the morning? Artolo snarls and bats at the lid with his maimed hands. No fingers, no thumbs, just stumps. The horror still hits him every time he looks at his ruined body.

He sweeps the heavy jar off the nightstand. It shatters on the tiles. Shards of glass and brownish lozenges scatter across the floor, some becoming lost under the ornate furniture. An oil-painting portrait of some long-dead Ilbarin minister or priestess stares down at him from her golden frame, as if disapproving of the criminal that now rules in her palace.

The door opens a crack. One of the servants looks in. "My lord? I heard something break."

"Where is my witch?

"I don't know, my lord. I'll go and look—" the servant pleads.

"No. Come in here. Help me." The servant enters the room like a mouse, his hands twitching, shoulders flinching as broken glass cracks underfoot.

"Get me a pill," orders Artolo. The servant rushes over, finds one of the pills, holds it out. "In my mouth." He sticks out his tongue, and the servant places the pill there with outstretched arm, outstretched fingers like he's reaching into a dragon's maw. Artolo sucks the sticky lozenge, feeling it numb the inside of his cheek, his throat.

The servant's *wholeness* irritates him. The servant comes from Ilbarin. His homeland is drowned and ruined, his gods broken, his leaders fled. He's lost – so how dare he stand so proud? How dare he remain unblemished? It's an insult. A deliberate insult.

"Now my boots." The servant glances at Artolo in confusion – Artolo slept naked. "There is glass everywhere – would you have me go barefoot?"

The servant fetches Artolo's heavy boots from the wardrobe. They're his old dragon-riding boots, armoured, steel-toed. Steel hooks at the ankles, designed to lock into the saddle-straps. He hasn't flown since he lost Great-Uncle's favour, but they're still his boots. The servant helps him pull them on, one at a time. Artolo gives the servant a reassuring smile as the Ilbariner works the buckles. Artolo's useless hands sit in his lap.

"Now, clean. Be sure not to lose a single pill. Each one's worth more than your life."

The servant nods. Crawls over on his knees, starts picking up the pills and piling them on the nightstand.

Artolo stands. The pain of the old knife wound in his belly's gone. He stretches, feels the warmth of the morning sun on his back as it shines through the window. "Did Dosca's ship come in last night?"

"Yes, my lord."

"Good. Good." Artolo looks out of the window at the rooftops of Ushket, at the cluster of masts in the port. Contemplates the light dancing on the water, the reflections on the walls of the buildings around the half-flooded streets.

Then he slams his boot into the servant's face. Stamps on the servant's hand, grinding his boot to press the servant's fingers into the broken glass. Kicks the man in the stomach, twisting his heel so the boot-hooks tear the flesh. The servant's other hand, too, deserves attention. Artolo wrenches the portrait off the wall. The thing's fucking heavy, and he can't get a proper grip with his maimed hands, but he manages to sort of twist it as it falls, so the sharp-edged corner of the heavy frame lands squarely on the servant's palm. The painting falls with a crash. The servant starts to scream, but Artolo fumbles a silk pillow off the bed and shoves it at the man's face. The servant buries his mouth in the pillow, muffling his whimpers and groans.

"Gods below." The witch stands at the doorway. Her voice drips with revulsion, but the metal face on the helmet is expressionless.

"You're late," snaps Artolo. He kicks the servant again for emphasis. "This is your fault."

"There was a problem with Dosca," says the witch. Her suit whirs and clicks; some clever magical clockwork hisses as it injects her with her own painkillers. They're both damaged goods, debris from the wars. Discarded on this ruin of an island.

"Gloves first," he orders. The witch opens the wardrobe, takes out Artolo's heavy riding gloves. She removes her own gauntlets, studded with little shards of ruby like spots of blood, exposing her hands. Her flesh is marbled, scarred with forking, coiling burn marks. The lines of nerves set alight by sorcery, Artolo guesses – humans aren't made for working magic. She needs to be free of the unwieldy gauntlets, though, to strap on his gloves properly.

"Any word from my son?" asks Artolo. His son Vyr has hired doctors and artificers in Guerdon to make him a set of mechanical fingers, like the witch's suit.

"I told you, that sort of precision work takes time."

"And much money," says Artolo sourly. "For the price they charge, they should be done by now. If I was there—"

"Would you beat them, too?" mutters the witch. "Ready?"

Artolo grunts in acknowledgement. The witch takes his gloved hands in hers, and concentrates. Artolo can feel the invisible filaments of sorcery pushing against the stumps, worming their way into his own nerves. The gloves flex, inflate, stiffen. A thrill runs through his hands as the witch's spell takes hold. He feels the ghosts of finger-bones form within the gloves, feels spectral muscles and sinews sprout and knit themselves into his living flesh. He flexes his new hands, feeling the strength in them again, better than any drug.

The witch lets out a groan, and her suit fusses over her. It clacks as it injects more drugs, leeches poisons from her. Aetheric energy discharges from the suit in crackling arcs of blue light. She leans heavily against the wardrobe as she laboriously pulls her gauntlets back on. Tendrils of smoke rise from her blistered fingers.

Artolo whistles as he pulls on a shirt and watches the servant laboriously pick up every spilled pill with broken fingers. Fastening each button is a joy. It's the little things. The witch's spell will only last a day or so before it will have to be cast again, but until then he's whole.

He wonders how long she'll last at this rate. If she dies, he'll have to hire the fucking Crawlers again, and he has no desire to sit across a negotiating table from those wormy horrors. They demanded a fortune the last time he dealt with them.

"What happened with Dosca?" he asks.

"The gunboat caught him trying to go to Ilbarin City first."

"What was he planning on doing? Stealing raw brine?"

"He had a passenger on board who paid for passage to Ilbarin," says the witch. "That's all. He'll know better in future."

"Who was this passenger?"

"No sign of them. Must have jumped ship as soon as they got here." The witch starts to reattach her own gauntlets, laboriously plugging little wires and veins back into place.

"But you have a description, yes? Dosca told you who this passenger was, yes?" Something's amiss. Artolo takes the witch's blistered fingers, squeezes them – gently, but with enough pressure to hurt, enough to remind her who's in charge.

"A woman. From Guerdon. No name, but the crew said she was

dark-haired. A thief, some of them said." Artolo squeezes a little more. "Scars on her face. Little scars!" admits the witch, wincing in pain.

"It was HER. The Saint of Knives. She has followed me here." Artolo rushes to the wardrobe, pulls out a gun, as if Carillon Thay might be hiding under the bed or behind a curtain.

"I'll deal with her," says the witch hastily. "You should go to the refinery, make sure the yliaster is ready."

"No," says Artolo. "No. I will find her. I will find her, and I will do to her what she did to me ten thousand times over." He rushes over to the nightstand, pulls out his dragon-tooth dagger. The edge is blunt, but the blade is still strong.

His fingers are gone, but his grip is still strong.

Artolo drives the blunt blade into the servant's stomach, putting his full weight on the knife's hilt to push it deep. The servant shrieks in pain, bellows, hammers his bleeding hands against Artolo's face, but Artolo is much, much too strong. The blade sinks in. Hot blood gushes across Artolo's bare legs, stains his half-closed shirt.

Then he tears, ripping the stomach like a wet sack, spilling the man's entrails out across the tiles.

Better than any drug.

"Witch!" calls Artolo from the puddle of gore. "Read this fortune!" He lifts up a handful of guts, feeling them drip through his fingers. "Read it and tell me where I will find Carillon Thay!"

By mid-afternoon, Cari thinks she might die here on the fucking Rock of Ilbarin. She pulls at her sweat-soaked clothes. She'd forgotten how hot the sun could get down south. Firesea's well named.

The mountain's steep-sided and treacherous, and she's had to go higher and higher on the rocky slopes to avoid being spotted, picking her way past scraggly bushes and little thorny trees. There's salt in the air from the unnaturally swollen seas, and white patches of dried salt on rocks around her. Below, she can see the white scar of the road from Ushket as it snakes around the mountain. The road shimmers and dances in the haze until it vanishes around the side of the Rock on its way down to Ilbarin. Beyond the road, the new shore, a treacherous silty slope, red mud dissolving into the sea like the mountain's bleeding.

She couldn't take the road. It's guarded by armed men – she's guessing Eshdana, The Ghierdana's ash-bought mercenaries. There's a lot of traffic on the road, too, mules hauling carts full of metal casks. She has no idea what they're transporting, but she doesn't want to get too close. There are plenty of hiding places amid the rocks, but Cari's a creature of the alleyways and the docks, and feels horribly exposed without walls around her.

So, she went higher up the slopes, picking her way past unstable patches and the scars of recent landslides, only to discover there are farms up here. Fields of freshly cleared brownish-grey earth. The soil's thin and full of stones. Cari doubts they can grow much of anything, but what choice do they have? Most of Ilbarin's farmland got drowned by the Kraken – it's spread out there before her, under the glittering waves. So, the survivors scrape what they can out of the rocky hillside. She watches them for a while from a hiding place beyond the barbed-wire fences: a host of people labouring in the parched field, working the ground with their bare hands. Thin and grey, faces aged by hunger and exposure, the commonality beneath the skin overcoming distinctions of age or sex. A field of almost-skeletons.

Watching over them are armed guards. Well-fed Eshdana, with clubs or guns. They're running the farms now, running everything, it looks like. She saw the same thing back in Guerdon, in the early days of the New City. The crooks and the criminal syndicates were quickest to adapt to the catastrophe, and grabbed power. *You'd hate that*, she thinks to Spar. *You'd go on about your father, about the Brotherhood, about making a fairer world out of the ruins. And where did all those good intentions and self-sacrifice get us?*

You dead, and me here on this bloody Rock. It's a thought she'd never allow herself back in Guerdon, but Spar's half a world away and can't hear her anyway.

Her only route around the farms is to go higher, scaling the uppermost slopes where the air grows cooler and the terrain more broken. Up here, the mountain is a fantastic labyrinth of shattered stone, the only living things a few thorn bushes. She guesses that gods fought here. Those scars on the hillside were probably left by the acid-tripping tendrils that trail behind the creatures of Cloud Mother. These three parallel chasms must have been torn by the claws of Lion Queen. The damage is fresh, the rocks underfoot jagged. Broken goat paths end prematurely.

Not that she's seen a goat all day. Her empty stomach rumbles. She's getting weak with hunger. It's getting harder to carry the weight of the fucking book, not to mention the rest of her gear.

She forces herself to keep going. She imagines that she's back in the New City, Spar miraculously transforming the uneven terrain into a smooth path for her. Once she gets around the Rock, it's downhill. Down to Ilbarin City. Even if most of the city's gone, there'll be places to hide there. She'll find someone with a ship, someone who'll take her coin.

Further up the slope there's an area that's less smashed up than the rest. Tired of slipping on jagged rocks, Cari climbs, pulling herself up on tufts of tough grass and the exposed roots of thorn bushes, until she reaches the unbroken section. Up ahead, she can see a small stone building. A goatherd's shed, maybe, or a little shrine for pilgrims.

She can walk for a bit here, instead of having to climb through shattered terrain. She drinks the last of her fresh water, kicks herself for not collecting more before setting off. She blames Hawse for pissing her off, tries to keep that anger alive in her belly. Anger's better than hunger. Anger keeps you sharp.

She sets off again, trudging across the hillside. She'll be around the Rock by dusk. She can make it to Ilbarin City by noon tomorrow. She may not have any food left, but she still has money. She doesn't need the captain to find her a ship to Khebesh. She hasn't needed Hawse in years. *The Ishmerians want to kill me, the Ghierdana want to kill me, and my best friends are a city and a ghoul. I've clearly made a fucking great success of it without you.*

The wind picks up, flinging dust in her face. She pushes on, head down, one step after another after another. She'll get to Khebesh, she tells herself. Get rid of the fucking book, trade it for the sage counsel from the master sorcerers of the forbidden city. She doesn't even know what she's going to say to them when she gets there. *My grandfather made me to be the centrepiece of a ritual to bring back the Black Iron Gods, and I sort of accidentally dumped all their power into the corpse of my dead friend. And then he turned into a city. And I could hear him in my head, and together we beat the shit out of the Ghierdana, and fought off an invasion, but now he's fading. Is there a lotion you'd prescribe?*

What happens if it doesn't work?

What happens if it works?

For a moment she feels a strange friction in the air, like there's an invisible wall blocking her path that she has to push through. It scrapes against her skin, then becomes a weight inside her skull, a building pressure.

She suddenly has the terrifying sensation of motion, like the whole hillside is trying to push her off. She falls to her knees, clutches at the ground, and the dirt stings her bare skin.

Then, as quickly as it came, the sensation passes. The mountain's just a mountain again.

"Okaaay," she mutters to herself.

Then she's flung bodily into the air.

Sun and sky and sea and Rock whirl around her, and then she lands heavily in the dirt, the impact knocking the breath from her lungs. Stones digging painfully into her face, her chest. The weight of the book sends her pack sliding forward, slamming into the back of her skull. Fuck. She tries to scramble back up, pain shooting through her wrist as she puts weight on it. The ground shifts and slides underneath her, and she falls again.

She glimpses a blur of movement. Not human, a whirling blur of dust and stones, but as it rushes towards her Cari suddenly sees it as an old woman, hunched and grey, her face scarred by claw marks. Stones for teeth, thorns for nails.

It's the spirit of the mountain, Cari thinks a second before it hits her again, square in the chest. Ribs crack, and she's sent tumbling back, rolling down the mountainside.

The earth around her screams and roars. Rocks fall with her, pelting her with debris. Clouds of dust block out the light. The old woman's everywhere around her, everything around her, hammering and clawing at her. The wind spits curses loud enough to deafen. All Cari can do is curl up, a mortal in the face of divine wrath.

In Ilbarin they worship Usharet, goddess of the mountain.

And the mountain lands on Cari.

Cari wouldn't put much money on it, but she thinks she's still alive. She feels like a sack of bone shards and pulp. Her thoughts drip slowly through the mush of her brain. It takes her a while to work out that she's moving, not lying on the hillside. She's in the back of a wagon. Creaking of wheels, whispered voices, the clank of heavy metal kegs next to her. Hands bound with rope, but she can tell from the way it's digging into her back that she's still got the fucking book. They haven't even searched her satchel. She tries to whisper a cheer, but the effort sends a spear of pain through her side.

One of her eyes has swollen shut. Four men she can see, all armed, but they're not watching her. They're all looking up the slope of the mountain, watching the slopes. Fuck, that thing that attacked her, that goddess or whatever it was, it nearly killed her. It must have kicked her all the way down to the road.

The setting sun's on her left, falling behind the Rock – she's heading the wrong way. They're going back towards Ushket. Shit, she thinks, but that's the least of her problems. She fights down the feeling of panic, and the effort makes everything go dark again for a minute.

Spar? I'm hurt. Spar was able to take her injuries back in Guerdon, protect her from harm, but she's far away from him now. Her wounds are her own, and they're bad. Everything around her seems so much harder now, a world of sharp stones and cruel foes, and she's small and broken.

Think. She's too hurt to move quickly, but she can still move. Her hands and feet are bound, but it looks like a rushed job. The same coarse rope used to secure the kegs in the wagon, and it's not drawn tight. She can wriggle free, if she gets a chance. The four guards around her sound like they're local boys, Eshdana conscripts, and they're as scared as she is. Carrying sticks and knives, no real armour. Not soldiers. Just hired muscle. *And they don't know you're awake. Wait for your moment.* She imagines Spar giving her the advice. She'd never tell herself to stay still. *Wait for the opportunity. Until then, play unconscious.*

That part's really easy. She blacks out again for a moment as the wagon rolls over a bump in the road. Liquid sloshes around in the kegs beneath her. Pain sloshes around within her, like it can't decide which of her many bruises and cuts deserves primacy. Settles in her wrist, her knee, the ribs down her left side. She tastes blood in her mouth.

"The old woman's after her," mutters one of the guards. "We should leave her."

"Word came down from Ushket this morning," replies another. "The boss wants this one. She came off a ship yesterday."

The first guard glances over at Cari. She forces herself to stay limp and feign unconsciousness. "For what? Who is she?" She watches him through a red haze of blood-matted hair and flying dust. He sounds young and scared. He keeps shooting nervous glances up the mountain, flinching at every breath of wind. Only the mule is calm, untroubled as it hauls the cart around the Rock of Ilbarin.

"Keep watch for the old woman," hisses the other voice. "I have the gun. I'll shoot her when she comes for us."

Whoever this boss is, the one who wants Cari, they're more scared of him than they are of a demigoddess.

Cari waits until the wagon hits another bump in the road, lets her head loll about until she happens to be looking in the right direction. Through her mostly closed good eye, she can see a man clutching a heavy rifle. Phlogiston charge, big bore – the sort of gun you'd use for fighting saints and godspawn. Not an equaliser, but enough to piss off a divine monster.

The Ghierdana tried using guns like that on her, back when she was the Saint of Knives.

Back when she had power.

"Lord of Waters, protect us," mutters the nervous boy. A brief echo of the strange feeling she had on the mountain passes over Cari again. It feels like pressing on a scab. The hot, dusty wind blows.

"Idiot!" curses the rifleman, his ire directed at his young companion. "Don't rile her up more! Don't say a name."

I trespassed, Cari realises. That must be holy ground up there. The mountain goddess, Usharet – she could tell that I was a saint of another power, and fought back. Cari shivers, can't stop shivering. She's freezing despite the heat of the day.

Cari's avoided temples and churches for a long time. The last time she set foot in one was back in Guerdon, years ago, and that was a church of the Kept Gods of Guerdon when they were piss-weak. (*They came back*, she thinks bitterly. *Why can't Spar?*) On her journey south, she kept mostly to godless territory, to Haithi outposts and empty lands, or she was at sea. Still, at times, she felt something similar – a tension, a burning. Like she was standing exposed to the desert sun at noon. Or the feeling in a crowd before a riot kicks off, this sick anticipation of violence.

The Ishmerians want to kill me. The Ghierdana want to kill me. And the gods want to kill me if I trespass on their turf.

Fine. She can use that. Everything's a weapon. She learned that long ago.

"Holy Beggar," she mutters under her breath. "Mother of Flowers. Holy Smith. Saint Storm." The weak Kept Gods of Guerdon.

The hot wind blows. The mule whinnies.

"Fate Spider. Smoke Painter." The gods of the Sacred Empire. "High Umur. Cloud Mother."

Pain, like her head's in a vice. The guards hear her prayers. They grab at her, wrenching her legs as they pull her from the wagon, but she keeps chanting, forcing the names out even as she's coughing up blood. She spits them like insults.

"Fucking Kraken." Hot dirt rains on her face. "Fucking Pesh, the Lion Queen!" She remembers the sight of the goddess Pesh marching on Guerdon, taller than a mountain, waves breaking against her golden thighs. Pesh in her glory, her words an artillery bombardment, her gaze fire and destruction. Pesh, so beautiful and terrible that Cari had to stifle a prayer even as she pulled the trigger on the god-bomb that murdered her . . .

The mountain's roaring again, earth thunder, the whole hillside writhing and groaning. Cari's eyes are tightly closed, but she still gets the impression of the old woman rushing towards them.

Cari cries out, shouting the names of the Black Iron Gods — names she didn't know she knew, never heard before, but they're in her somewhere, and now she calls them aloud. Screams them, and they echo off the mountain.

The gun goes off, a flash of phlogiston and a barking report that half deafens Cari. Again, and again, and the third time there's a hiss — not pain, but uncomprehending anger and amazement at the insolence of mortals.

Then the landslide hits them, sweeps guards and wagon and mule off the road. Cari's already moving, already rolling off the wagon before it topples. Everything's a confusion of dust and smoke, noise and flying stones. The screaming of the Ghierdana drowned out by the rumble of the falling mountain, of the goddess Usharet in her wrath.

The mule's to her left, legs broken, squealing in agony. The wagon's fallen over, the kegs spilling down the mountainside. One smashes open, spilling a glowing liquid out in a brilliant spray, mixed with a sludge of crystals like sea salt.

Guards to her right, one trying to dig himself out of the stones that half buried him. Another, buried and unmoving, one outstretched hand a marker for his grave. Somewhere off in the swirling dust, flashes of red as the gun goes off again, firing blind.

Cari twists around, finds her knife – pain shoots through her wrist. She's half buried herself in moving stones as the landslide ebbs. She kicks free of the stones, brings her legs up to her bound hands so she can cut at the rope, once, twice, until it gives way.

One of the guards grabs at her, but Usharet grabs him first, thorn-fingers tearing his throat open, hands of dust seizing him with terrible force and flinging him away.

Down, she thinks. *Got to get off this fucking mountain.*

The guard with the rifle emerges from the dust. He fires at point-blank range, so close that Cari can hear the glass ampoule inside the phlogiston charge crack as the hammer comes down. Usharet whirls around, leaps on to the guard's shoulders, rakes his face with her thorns. Howling all the time, a mindless keening.

Cari runs. Crawls. Falls, bouncing off boulders, slipping on loose pebbles – and then on mud. She falls to her knees again, sinks her hands into the deliciously salty mud of the shoreline. Pain bursts through her, broken ribs and twisted muscles. Bruises exploding like artillery beneath her skin. She fears that she might burst or break, but still she crawls.

Behind her, up the slope, the distant roaring of the goddess. The ground quakes beneath her, the earth cracking and sloughing away from the hillside, great gobbets of soil sliding into the sea, brown stains like blood spreading across the waves. The air is full of dust, full of pressure, like a great iron bell is tolling right next to her ears. Blind, she wades forward through the catastrophe until her feet find the road.

Stumbling, limping, falling, crawling, but always moving, always running away from the wrath of the mad goddess she offended. She wipes away the dust that's caked on her face and hands, but it's futile. She must look like the goddess, she thinks distantly, a thin and broken thing covered in dust and mud and thorns.

She hears shouts from up ahead, and acts on instinct, a thief's reflexes. She hurls herself into a ditch, muffles her own yelps of pain as armed men rush past to vanish into the roiling chaos of the dust cloud, and then there are more gunshots, the howl of a flash ghost detonation.

She staggers on. The act of walking becomes mechanical, a mantra spoken by her twisted ankles, by her tortured shoulders. Her own momentum carries her forward. She feels as though she has to keep moving, or the road around the mountain will rise up and strike her. Above her, the sun wheels through the sky; clouds white and dust-grey circle above her. Vultures, too, she thinks.

At one point, she reaches around to adjust her satchel, move it around so the fucking book isn't digging into her spine quite so sharply, and her hand comes back wet with blood. She draws her knife, confused, unsure what she's thinking.

It's not like death is something she can cut. Her fingers are powerless, and the knife slips from her grasp. Lands in the middle of the road, the metal gleaming bright, unsullied by the dust that coats everything else. She stares at that knife for a long, long time, scared that if she bends over to pick it up, she'll fall over, fall apart. Break the delicate balance between the weight of the book and her own forward momentum, disrupt the arrangement of wounded limbs that lets her keep going.

She can't think straight. She's inhaled so much dust, it feels like it's coated her brain with a thick crust of earth. Her skull's fit to burst. She wonders if it's her fear, or if it's Spar's. He was always nervous about falling.

But that was when he was alive.

No, she tells herself. *He's still alive. I'm still alive*, she thinks. *And I'm going to fix this. I'll go to Khebesh and fix this.*

She steps over the knife. Keeps going. Keeps going. Keeps going.

Until she's crawling through the hole in the hull of the *Rose*. Finding her way blindly up the ladder.

Falling down in her own bunk.

Home.

CHAPTER SIX

Three thieves running down a street. A heist gone wrong. An explosion.

That was how it began, wasn't it? Is this a memory, or something that's happening now? The footfalls of the thieves agitate his thoughts, the vibration in the living stone shaking his mind free. For a moment, part of Spar's attention is drawn to that particular street in the New City, to these thieves. Enough of his consciousness gathers for him to be aware that he's conscious.

This city he's become is too big for his mortal mind — he can feel himself slipping away, parts of him following raindrops down windowpanes, ghouls down gutters, the delicate constellation of thought and memory that used to be a man named Spar Idgeson dissipating into the labyrinthine streets of the New City. Dissolving into the stone, like a drowning man.

Focus. Fight for focus. Pay attention. Stay awake. Hold on until she finds you again.

Three thieves run down a street. The street winds steeply down towards the edge of the New City, towards the docks where black water laps against white stone. They cross a narrow bridge that spans a gap in the streets. The bridge is made in the semblance of an angel, and they run across its outstretched wings. The angel's face is that of Spar's mother. Water cascades past her memorial, falling into the lower parts of the New City. A canal below.

(His mind slips, chasing the memory: fighting the Fever Knight. Charging the armoured warrior, sending both of them plunging into the stagnant water of a different canal. He couldn't beat Heinreil's bodyguard in a fight, so he tried self-sacrifice. That's the thing about living with a fatal disease – death stops being unthinkable. You contemplate long enough, and it becomes just another thought.)

It's no good. He's falling again. He still senses the three thieves – he can feel their footsteps on the cobblestones that are his skin. He can watch them through every window. All three wear dark rain-coats against the downpour. The rain's washing away his mind, he thinks. How can he think when he also has to feel the impact of every raindrop, all clamouring for his attention? What's the differ-ence between a raindrop and a human, anyway? Both mostly water. Both burst on impact with the stone.

He burst on impact, too. Beneath the wide boulevards and twist-ing alleyways of his thoughts is an underworld of memory, a sucking sewer that traps him and drags him down. In memory, he falls from the dome of the Seamarket, his calcified joints and heavy limbs betraying him; all that strength and he can't beat gravity. Failing at the last challenge. Cari's eyes full of horror. Knowing as he dies that she's doomed, that Guerdon's doomed and the Black Iron Gods will reign in tyranny forever . . .

That's a memory. Focus on the now. Focus on the thieves. They're important, somehow. Two are foreigners, new to the city. They're wearing raincoats, but he can see beneath those, too. He can taste their weapons. The one in the lead carries a dragon-tooth knife that burns in Spar's vision. A Ghierdana boy, from the dragon families. (Spar remembers another knife, just like that one, cutting into Carillon's throat. Cutting, miraculously, into his own stony flesh – but that's another door into memory, another stairway leading down to the underworld. Close it, quick. Focus.)

The Ghierdana boy swaggers along. Hair cut short to fit under a flying helmet, a thin moustache to show he's a man. Olive skin marked by dozens of old scars, knife cuts, on his hands and forearms, but no bigger wound. A boy who's fought many, many times, but never lost. He's got a well-used breathing mask hanging from his neck; he wears the distinctive leathers of a dragon-rider under the cloak, heavy gloves and fur-lined collar. Is he a fool to wear such an outfit on a heist, or is he declaring his rank to those who recognise it? Arrogance or pride? The difference between them is one of balance – take pride just a little too far, and you'll slip and fall. (Fall from the dome of the Seamarket, to burst on the rocks below.)

The boy is important. Spar doesn't know how or why he knows this; an instinct he cannot name, a way of sensing that mortals do not possess.

Rasce. That's his name. It's a name that Spar's heard many times, whispered in his streets.

The other Ghierdana, also male, about the same age, but wearing street clothes. Hands sweaty on the grip of his pistol. No dragon-tooth knife for him, no mark of the dragon's favour. Strapped to his side is a cloth bundle, carefully wrapped to keep the contents in place. Thieves' tools, lockpicks and cutters. And explosive charges, little glass balls of phlogiston. This second Ghierdana man scowls at the dragon-rider when Rasce's back is turned, malice mixing with fear. Bile rising the man's throat, like rainwater rising in a blocked drainpipe.

The third man, Spar knows. Familiar people are a trap for him; watching them, it's too easy for him to lose track of time, to slip into his memories of them instead of tracking their present existence. Carillon anchored him in the present, focused him – but thinking of her is like falling.

(From the dome of the Seamarket, tumbling end over end, bursting on the stone. The memory reaches for him hungrily, like a Raveller's tendrils, flensing away another portion of his consciousness.)

Focus! Pay attention! The third man ... the third man is ...
Baston Hedanson. A Brotherhood man. The Fever Knight's appren-
tice. Spar used to be friends with Baston: they ran together when
they were younger, before the Stone Plague took Spar's youth and
friends and standing in the guild away from him. Two versions of
Baston war in what remains of Spar's mind. In the present, Baston's
glancing at the shadows, scanning for trouble. The years haven't been
kind to him – he looks worn, face gaunt. In memory, Baston's fifteen
years younger. A few years older than Spar, half a man when Spar
was but a boy. Sitting on a wall in Hog Close, watching Spar run
with Karla and the other kids. Baston acting aloof, but twitching
to join the game.

Hog Close. The memory of Spar's own youth rears up, hoary and
potent. He tries to fight it, tries to pay attention to the present city,
to these three thieves, but he can't hold on. He can feel his consciousness breaking apart again, pulled apart by the sheer size of the New
City. He's grown too large to encompass himself. His mind is like a
little spider trying to weave a web around the whole city.

Spar wonders, as he breaks apart for the millionth time, if
there are other fragments of his consciousness out there, other
parts of his mind that have found each other, hung together long
enough to think the same thoughts. Is he Spar, or just one of Spar's
many ghosts?

He falls. His awareness like droplets of rainwater running down
the walls, dividing and recombining and breaking apart again, a
silver tracery of thought that pools in the deepest parts of the New
City, in the deepest parts of his soul. He can no longer tell past from
present, distinguish his own memories from the shadows that play
on the walls of the New City.

He falls.

In Hog Close, Spar plays watch and thieves with Karla and a gang
of other kids, dodging in and out of the alleyways. He's the tallest in

the group, the fastest. No one can catch him. Karla shouts after him, threatening to invoke the wrath of her big brother the way a saint calls on a god. Spar vaults over the garden hedge that represents the edge of the Alchemists' Quarter, pretends to gather up handfuls of gold coins and flings them over the wall, then runs before the watch can get him. He runs down the street, racing ahead of his pursuers.

A group of older men enter the close. Brotherhood all.

"Gods below, it's the son," says one of them. "Get his mother, she should be the one to tell."

"No," says another, softly. The old man kneels down, puts his hand on Spar's shoulder, looks him right in the eye. His breath smells of tobacco. "The city watch arrested your father. He's done for. Listen, the Brotherhood will take care of you, but there's nothing that can be done for him. We can't help him."

"Will they hang him?"

They will hang him. They hang Idge.

It's twenty years ago, and it's always now.

Spar watches in the garden of the Hall of Law. The bell tolls the noon hour, and the gallows drops beneath his father. Idge falls, and in Spar's memory the fall seems to go on forever, far longer than any rope could possibly allow. He clutches his mother's hand, imagining somehow that his father will fall through the earth, fall into some subterranean wonderland of the ghouls, escape through the endless tunnels below the city. Survive, transformed into some strange new form. Survive through his writing if nothing else.

The fall an escape, a miraculous victory in the face of death.

But the rope snaps taut, and the fall ends.

In a tunnel under the New City, a ghoul crouches by a stone wall. It's dark, but darkness means nothing down here – both Spar and the ghoul have transcended the need for anything so mundane as eyes to see in the dark.

He knows the ghoul. It's Rat. When he contracted the Stone

Plague, that mysterious disease that slowly ate away at his flesh, transmuting it to rock, his Hog Close friends abandoned him, one by one. Their father hustling Karla out of Spar's room, Baston hovering at the threshold, unwilling to leave, too scared to come closer.

Some saw that he would never take his father's place at the head of the Brotherhood. Others, he drove away. But Rat stayed. Ghouls can't get the Plague. Ghouls don't care about bitterness, or self-loathing, or despair. Everyone else, Spar could find some leverage, some weak spot to push, but Rat had decided Spar was his friend, and that was that.

Rat, but not Rat. Rat has suffered a change almost as complete as Spar's. His friend was a street-ghoul, a young ghoul, lurking in the alleyways and stealing carcasses from slaughterhouses to slake his hunger for dead meat. But Rat was – possessed? Chosen? Consumed? – by one of the Elder Ghouls of Guerdon, the necrotic demigods who dwelled in the depths below. All the other elders are gone now, killed in their war with the Crawling Ones, all save the thing called Lord Rat.

Rat scratches at the tunnel wall with his massive paws, tapping on it. His huge jaws part, his long purple tongue licking at his teeth. Sharp fangs for ripping corpse-flesh from bone, wide flat molars for cracking bones to get the marrow, the residual soul-stuff. Haltingly, Rat speaks. He's trying to tell Spar something important. The ghoul gestures, says something about Black Iron. Something about alchemy.

The vibrations echo through Spar's mind. He fights to pay attention again, to pull fragments of his mind together so he can listen, but it's so hard to focus. To . . . coagulate.

Rat's voice becomes an echo, robbed of meaning. His words join the chorus of other words spoken in the New City, lost in the tumult of noise. He strains to pick meaning out of the seething chaos of life. Spar's aware that he's only been a city for a short time, but his grasp of the mortal world is slipping. To distinguish individual words, individual days, individual lives from the masses that swarm through him, their passage clear to him only in aggregate, in the way their feet wear away well-travelled steps, in how their hands rub certain lucky carvings smooth.

Frustrated, Rat scratches on the stone again.

Spar's eyes are the tunnel wall, the ceiling, the stones all around. His eardrums are every surface. He sees Rat from a hundred different angles, and every one of those viewpoints is a portion of Spar's attention that threatens to slip away. His thoughts are a host of children in a crowded city – it's all too easy for him to lose them down the twisting alleyways of memory.

He follows the scratching sound, back three years.

Scratching at his door. It's Rat. Spar puts down his papers and levers himself up from his chair. If he grabs on to the edge of the shelf nearby, he can pull himself up, avoid putting added pressure on the left side of his back. There are jagged plates of stone on his skin there that dig into the underlying muscle if he puts weight on them, and every time he does he feels the chill numbness of petrification take hold.

The shelf creaks under his weight. Dents in the wood match his stony fingertips. He stands, but his left leg seizes up, goes numb. Like he's balancing atop a precarious pillar of stone.

He's in danger of falling. The room spins around him. Terror seizes him; he can't breathe.

Falling's always a danger for him – if he smashes to the floor, the impact might cause internal damage he can't see, damage he won't catch until it's too late. He imagines smashing heavily on to the dirt floor. Maybe hitting his head, or getting dirt in his eyes that scratches the delicate tissue, blinding him with stony cataracts.

He tells himself that he's not that fragile. He's seen Stone Men like him shrug off bullets, smash through brick walls, endure terrible beatings. As long as he takes the hit on a part of his body that's already gone to stone, it doesn't matter. He's just got to protect his dwindling stock of flesh. Measure out his life in square inches of flesh, in nail breadths of unpetrified skin.

"Give me a minute."

"Hurry up," mutters Rat. "It's pouring out here."

There's a vial of alkahest on the shelf, just within reach. Spar leans over, pressing his other hand against the wall for balance. He scoops it up, finds the gap between stone scabs on his leg, and drives the needle home. Fiery sensations, exhilarating and agonising in equal measure, rush through his leg. The paralysis in his knee melts away, and the limb moves freely again. He can feel his toes for the first time in days. The alkahest seethes through his bloodstream in a blazing flood. It feels as though the stone has melted away to become supple flesh again. He knows it's only a temporary relief, but, still, it's enough for now.

He strides across the little room, unbolts the door. Rat's outside, with some human girl leaning on him for support. She's deathly pale, shivering, her lips and sleeve caked in fragments of vomit. Spar's first instinct is to pick her up and carry her to the bed, but the Stone Plague is transmitted by touch. "Put her on my bed," he tells Rat. There are old bandages hanging on the back of the door; Spar begins wrapping his hands.

"Found her down by the docks," mutters Rat, "tryin' to pick a pocket. She threw up all over the mark. I figured keep her here. If she gets better, she owes us. If she dies, I'll take the carcass below." The ghoul licks his chops.

"Fuck you," says the girl, weakly. She paws at her throat. "Did you . . . ?" Rat brushes her hand aside, pulls a necklace out from under her shirt. He holds it up to the lamplight – dangling from the chain is a black stone, set in an enamelled amulet.

The girl reaches for it. "No," she moans, "that's mine."

Spar closes his hand around it. "I'll keep it safe for you. Just rest."

He draws a blanket across her thin form. The girl closes her eyes, seems to fall asleep.

Rat sniffs her. "She's off a ship. Not local." He sniffs again, wrinkles his muzzle as if trying to identify some subtle scent.

"Here." Spar hands the ghoul a few coins. "Run down to Lambs Square, get some food in. Stuff that's easy on the stomach – Ranson's Chemical Food, maybe." Alchemical paste, sweet and sticky. Stone Men with calcified stomachs swear by it; Spar isn't there yet. "And some clean clothes. Maybe ask Silkpurse."

Rat hurries off. Spar returns to his chair, carefully lowering himself like a crane righting a derailed train engine.

He waits there, reading his father's old papers. Turning her necklace over and over in his hand, testing to see if there's any sensation left in the skin of his palm. Not much – he'd have to dig the metal edges of the little amulet into his flesh to feel anything, and that might damage the girl's treasure.

After a few minutes, he becomes aware that she's woken up, but is still pretending to sleep, watching him through half-closed eyes. Waiting for him to move, so she can escape out of the door and die in a gutter somewhere. He reaches over, drops her amulet on the bed next to her.

"You're safe here," he says again, "I'm Spar Idgeson." Putting the emphasis on his last name, his father's name. Everyone in Guerdon's underworld remembers Idge – the great leader, the philosopher-thief, the man who was going to right all the injustices of the guilds and make the city fair. Invoking Idge's name is a declaration of responsibility and trustworthiness. Everyone in Guerdon would understand that Idge's son is a man of honour.

But Idge's name clearly means nothing to her. She stares blankly, then repeats "Spar," in a scratchy voice. "Is there water?"

"Would you like me to fetch some?"

"It's okay." She sits up – how easily she does that, without any hesitation, without any cracking of stone scabs or shooting nerve pains – and swings her legs out of the bed. She takes two barefoot steps, then her knees buckle and she nearly falls, catching herself on Spar's chair.

"Little help?" she asks, reaching out.

Spar takes her hand, careful to ensure the bandages are between her skin and his stone. With his other hand, he lifts himself out of the chair. The room's cramped, and he's much bigger than she is, so he has to carefully manoeuvre himself to avoid brushing against her, like he's dancing with her.

They walk the few steps to the little sink, hand in hand. The girl finds a cup of water, sips it slowly. "Gods, that's better. Thanks."

"I still don't know your name," says Spar.

"Cari. It's Cari."

Cari looks down at him as he falls.

Tumbling, head over heels, from the roof of the Seamarket to the stone floor of the market far below. Three hundred feet straight down.

As he tumbles, he sees it all.

Below him, the terrified crowds. People of the city, corralled into this ancient temple as sacrifices to the Black Iron Gods. The people his father tried to inspire, tried to lead, to protect.

Above him, the black iron bell. A monstrous god, reforged and trapped in the shape of a bell.

Below him, the city. Through the great arched windows of the Seamarket, he glimpses for an instant the spires of Guerdon, but an instant is all he needs to recognise his city. The Victory Cathedrals up on Holyhill, the church spires of the Holy Beggar, St Storm's by the sea. Castle Hill, like a sleeping dragon, its back saw-toothed with towers and roofs. Across the harbour, the mighty bastions of Queen's Point. The new spires of the alchemists, the smokestacks and cooling towers. His city, his Guerdon.

The city is eternal, says an old rhyme; the city must finally end.

Above him, Cari. Caught by a spell, paralysed, unable to reach him. For an instant, he dares to imagine a last-minute reprieve, a miracle. He imagines her taking the terrible bargain offered by the Black Iron Gods, becoming their high priestess. Sharing in their divinity. She could pluck him out of the air and carry him to safety. Cure the Stone Plague with a thought. Bring down the alchemists and the arms dealers, the politicians and the priests. Shatter the world and remake it.

But no. Below him, he sees the dark writhing tide of the Ravellers, the other agents of the Black Iron Gods. Monstrous things, living knives of shadow, nothing but hate and hunger made manifest. Nothing good could ever spring from such things.

Above him, the vast dome. A magnificent tomb for a street thief.

Below him—

The fall is eternal. The fall must finally end.

Spar falls into darkness.

Darkness.

And then a distant flare of light.

CHAPTER SEVEN

A distant flare of light. There, for a moment, across the dark waters of the harbour.

Time to move.

"Lead on," hisses Rasce. Baston leads them down the silent docks, using stacks of crates and mooring posts as cover. Their target's just ahead. A wide pier, sectioned off from the rest of the docks by a wire fence. Rasce can make out a long, low building, and beyond it, tents and temporary storehouses – Dredger's yard. The arms dealer used to run part of his operations from an island out in the harbour, but Shrike Island was washed clean in the invasion last year, so now everything's crammed into the yards.

They come to the fence. A row of red flags flutter limply in the breeze. Red's a warning: it means the yard's handling highly volatile phlogiston. Vyr shudders at the sight.

Poor, nervous Vyr. He needs to learn how to fight, how to act. Vyr should learn from his father's bad example – Uncle Artolo came to Guerdon and lost everything through weakness. Rasce's not going to make the same mistake. He'll show Vyr to be bold, as befits a son of the Ghierdana.

He glances from Vyr to Baston. The local man's face is dour, downcast. Does he doubt their chances of success? Or is it something else – Tiske mentioned a tragic backstory, but everyone has sorrowful tales to tell. Cling too tight to your sorrows and they'll drag you down. These bastards need to feel alive again, to feel the dragon's fire in their souls.

There's an explosion at the far end of the pier. A flash of blue flame so bright it briefly lights up the low clouds over Guerdon, outshining the lights of the alchemists. Tiske's work – Vyr gave him the most dangerous job, and he's carried it out bravely.

Shouts and sirens ring out. The business of the yards is recycling and reselling alchemical weapons. A fire here could drown Guerdon in toxic smoke, or detonate some other weapon, like a phlogiston charge. Everyone stops working, drops everything to lend a hand when fire breaks out. Workers run out of the warehouses, out of the workshops, to grab buckets of water and canisters of fire-quenching foam. Rasce sees the blocky shapes of Stone Men, hauling wagon-loads of salvage away from the hot zone.

"Wait for it," mutters Baston.

A side door of the main building bursts open. Flames reflect off a burnished helmet.

"There goes Dredger," whispers Baston. The salvage dealer, pro-tected by his armoured suit, stomps off into the maelstrom leaving his offices unguarded.

More importantly, he's also left the shed where Dredger's stock of yliaster is stored. That's Karla's job – to smash open the casks and spill the yliaster into the water, as a warning to other dealers in the stuff.

Then the black harbour blazes red. A second, much larger explo-sion erupts near the first, showering burning debris down across the pier. The whole area's aflame, now, red flames lighting the night sky, flaring blue and green and lurid violet shades as alchemy burns. Tiske's misjudged where he set his fire, it seems, and paid for the error with his life. Neither ghoul nor god will ever find the man's remains – the blast is big enough to scatter his ashes across the harbour.

Vyr quails at the sight of the devastation, looking nervously into the sky as if expecting to see an attacking dragon circling over the New City. Baston doesn't flinch, but he looks to the Ghierdana for a decision. Lead on or fall back? Abandon the mission – or plunge into the flame?

"Onward!" cries Rasce. He darts forward, shoves open the door. Baston and Cousin Vyr follow. The air's thick with smoke; this building isn't supposed to be on fire, but, well, you don't blow up a pier full of dangerously volatile alchemical salvage and expect everything to go as planned. They just need to be faster. Baston leads them into Dredger's office.

"Vyr, to the shelves. Baston, you find the safe," orders Rasce. He searches the desk himself. The worktop's littered with machine parts – alchemical scrap or parts of Dredger's armour, Rasce can't tell, but none of it's useful. He forces open the drawers, finds a bottle of nectar-wine, more junk, more junk, and . . .

"Behold! This bastard," he mutters, holding up the weapon he has found mounted beneath the desk. The blunderbore looks like its maker harboured a subconscious death wish and tried to make a weapon that was guaranteed to explode when test-fired. Given its placement under the desk, muzzle pointing at the chair opposite, he suddenly has more respect for this Dredger as a negotiator. He's glad he picked Dredger as the example, instead of burning down some other merchant and then trying to cut a deal from that chair of death there.

Baston tears a painting of a burning ship off the wall, revealing a heavy safe. He peers at the mechanism, coughing as the room begins to fill with acrid smoke. "This is going to take a few minutes, boss."

Vyr's looking out of the window. "Longer than we have, I fear." Outside, flames leap and roar.

Rasce hefts the blunderbore. "Stand back."

"Are you crazy?" Vyr flinches away from the weapon. Rasce tosses the heavy blunderbore to his cousin, who catches it with a squeak.

Rasce draws his dragon-tooth knife, advances on the safe. The blade cuts through steel like straw, and there's a little puff of sulphurous smoke as whatever magic wards guarding the safe pop. The tooth still retains a trace of Great-Uncle's magic. Little mortal spells can't stand against the dragon's might.

The door gives way under its own weight and falls to the floor. Rasce grabs the heavy ledger books, folders full of contracts and secrets. He grabs the petty cash for good measure.

"Come on, let's . . ."

The strangest feeling overwhelms him. His vision doubles – he's looking down at the yard from a great height, able to see Karla and her crew staving in the casks of yliaster, the flames raging along the pier. She moves like she's dancing with the flames, eyes bright behind her breathing mask. He sees the foaming slime beneath the pier, thick with alchemical run-off. He feels like there are hollows in his skull, and furtive, feral shapes move through them, within him. Ghouls. Ghouls are coming.

Rasce knows all this like he might know he has a stone in his shoe, like he might feel the sun on the back of his neck. But how? Where did this knowledge come from? He reels, steadying himself against the wall. He can feel the heat of the fires on the far side, outside the window. It's getting hard to breathe in here, with all the smoke. That's all it is – a lack of good air, making his mind play tricks on him. Like his ancestors who went flying on Great-Uncle's back before the invention of breathing masks, tormented by phantoms of the thin upper airs.

That's all it is.

"Are you all right?" asks Vyr, studying his face closely. Rasce grins, tries to speak, but another wave of dizziness washes over him – another building, a great stone hallway, the smell of burning paper, the desperate tolling of a distant bell. He's seeing double. Baston's face is cast in shadow, but the light from the fires outside makes Vyr look sickly, his face all rotten ghoul-flesh. Ghouls. Those are ghouls in the tunnels. How does he know that?

Rasce grabs his breathing mask, presses it over his nose and mouth. It has to be the fumes. He opens the window and drops the ledgers and documents into the fires burning outside.

"Let's go!" he orders. "Now! Make haste!"

Outside, Rasce glances back at the burning yards. In the distance, he can still make out the figure of Dredger, outlined against the inferno. The weapons dealer is no longer directing the effort to save his yards. Instead, he stands there, staring into the flames as a lifetime burns around him. The salvage dealer is no fool; Rasce wonders if he recognises the hand of the Ghierdana in his downfall.

Rasce gives his defeated foe a nod of respect. Rasce always wins.

Whistles in the distance. The city watch are on their way.

The three thieves run along the dockside. Ahead of them, looming over the harbour, is the alien citadel of the New City. It looks different tonight in Rasce's eyes, brighter somehow. But there's a long, dark stretch of old Guerdon between him and the New City, a waterfront district of alleyways and tenement. Once they're back in the New City, they'll be back in the Lyrixian Occupation Zone. The watch won't be able to touch them in there.

Shapes rise out of the darkness and the drifting haze of ash. Not ghouls – it's Karla's crew. Most of them are local Guerdonese, but a few are Lyrixian, sent by Rasce to make up the numbers. Every one of them groaning under the weight of stolen alchemical weapons – boxes of ammunition, canisters of knife-smoke, blisterlight lenses. Karla pulls off her breathing mask to talk, gags at the smoky air. Her green eyes rimmed in red, face shiny from the heat.

"Come on," she shouts, "this way!"

No. Ghouls have come out of the sewers. That way is blocked. They can't get out that way. He knows that with an impossible certainty.

Rasce turns to Baston. "How close are we to the Ishmeric Zone?"

"Three streets over, top end of Heavengut Wynd," replies Baston, "but why—"

"There are ghouls there. We cannot return to the New City by the route you planned."

Vyr mutters an oath under his breath. "How—" Baston begins to ask a question, then shakes his head and changes tack. "We can stash this stuff at Tarson's."

"Then, I pray you, lead on," orders Rasce. "The rest of you dogs – be ready to become fine upstanding citizens as soon as we cross the border. Vyr, we may have to sacrifice you to some Ishmeric god, just to be sure of salvation."

They rush up the steep steps of Heavengut Wynd. The tenements along the wynd are waking up, the inhabitants' fitful slumber disturbed by the commotion in Dredger's yard. People peer out of their windows, wondering what fresh hell has come to Guerdon.

At the end of the stairs, the Ishmeric Occupation Zone begins. Two statues with the heads of beasts stand watch at the top of Heavengut Wynd – Sammeth and Cruel Urid. Even at a distance, Rasce can sense a divine presence in both statues. Beyond the icons, the narrow streets of Guerdon twist into an enchanted realm. Purple fog that smells of incense coils around the temple precincts. The sanctum of the Smoke Painter hovers in the sky, held aloft by illusory pillars. Tentacles stir the waters down by what was once some Keeper church, now a temple to the Kraken. Even at this late hour, devotees of Cloud Mother gather in a market square, reading portents in the clouds illuminated by the burning dockyard.

As a son of the Ghierdana, Rasce is not permitted to enter the Ishmerian Occupation Zone. The inverse is true for the Lyrixian Occupation Zone up in the New City. If one of those mad Ishmerian priests showed up in Ghierdana territory without permission, his life would be forfeit. His soul, too – no ritual burial, no final offering to the gods. Dragon-fire burns away all evidence.

The ghouls aren't supposed to cross the border, either.

"In here," hisses Karla. She leads them into a building off Heavengut, three doors shy of the border. Through a hallway crammed with old furniture and debris and up another staircase, until they're nearly to the roof. Then down a narrow corridor, its walls covered with old graffiti and thief's marks, into an adjoining building. From there, they cross through an attic, down another set of stairs, across a little rope walk strung across an alleyway, through a dozen secret paths. The border's porous to a Guerdon thief.

Karla brings them down yet another staircase and stops at a door. She makes an intricate series of hand signals. A chain's drawn back, the door opens and they're in, a dozen heavily burdened thieves crammed into the hallway of a little flat. Karla and Baston are like conjurers, making everything incriminating vanish into hiding places. A cupboard with a false back swallows the alchemical gear and the ledgers stolen from the yard. Their soot-stained cloaks and gas masks are stuffed into sacks for disposal. Guns get bundled up and hidden up the chimney. Rasce hands over the blunderbore with reluctance. He really wants a chance to fire the thing. He keeps his dragon-tooth knife, of course, and no one dares ask for it.

Karla passes around a damp cloth to wipe the ash from their faces. Her brother Baston hands around a flask of brandy. A hulking sailor with a scarred face hustles them back out through the door, and they leave by a different route, emerging on to the streets of the Wash well inside the boundary of the IOZ.

Cousin Vyr stares up at the temples of the Ishmerian gods.

"We should get back to our zone. Get out of here." The presence of the gods in those temples – in all but one of those temples – is as palpable as the heat from a furnace.

"The ghouls will still be on the streets," says Baston.

"Or under them," adds Karla, looking warily at a sewer inlet at the side of the street.

Rasce takes a deep breath. The air of the IOZ smells of incense and the ozone tang of magic, but his head's stopped spinning. That strange fit he experienced at Dredger's has passed. No more bizarre convictions. Whatever touched him on the docks can't reach him here.

"We'll wait a few hours." Rasce claps Baston on the back. "The gods send dragons to scourge the sinner and honest man alike." An old saying in Lyrix, meaning *this is our fate, we just have to live with it.* "Find us somewhere profane, eh?"

The restaurant, Baston mutters, was part of a theatre once. They enter by a back door. An old man with a long moustache greets Baston like a long-lost nephew, then smuggles them up some stairs to a back room. Rasce peeks through a door into the main bar. The walls are a deep crimson, smoke-stained; the ceiling overhead is an ornate plasterwork, the details lost in the gloom. The clientele there are Ishmerians. Soldiers in dishevelled uniforms, priests in flowing robes, huddled around hookahs. The priests smoke to find the gods; the soldiers, Rasce guesses, to hide from their memories. The war's turned against Ishmere in the last half-year.

Rasce follows the others up the stairs. The back room is equally opulent, although there's a musty smell in the air that tells him this room hasn't been used in months. Rasce sinks into the welcome embrace of an overstuffed leather chair, and his gang gathers around him. Baston and Karla on either side of a sofa, their men perched on the armrest or pulling up armchairs. The old man returns with a tray of drinks. Brandies and alchemical gins for locals, a bottle of arax for the Lyrixians. The thieves laugh, joke with one another, tell tales of narrow escapes and alchemical monsters. The two groups beginning to mingle. *They'll take the ash soon*, thinks Rasce.

Only Cousin Vyr remains standing, shifting awkwardly from one foot to the other.

"Sit down," orders Rasce.

"We should get back to the New City."

"Vyr, trust me. We'll lie low here, have a few drinks, wait until it's quieter."

"We're in the Ishmeric Occupation Zone. This is madness. You'll provoke—"

Rasce draws his knife, points it at his cousin.

The laughter stops.

"Sit," he orders again.

The knife's a sign of Rasce's rank in the Ghierdana, of his favour with Great-Uncle. Vyr has to back down. He sits.

To break the tension, Rasce slams the knife down on the table, spins it with his fingers. The dragon-tooth blade whirls around and comes to point at Baston.

"Give us a toast, my new friend," says Rasce.

Baston hesitates, and Karla steps in.

"To Tiske," she says. She tips out the last of her brandy, then refills her glass with arax. She produces a cigarette lighter and ignites the liquor. She lifts the blazing glass, the flames reflected in her green eyes.

Rasce takes the lighter.

Tiske, he realises, was the first man to die under his command.

The man who carries the knife cannot carry any burdens, any dead weight. He cauterises any regrets.

Rasce sets fire to his own drink. A more fitting toast to doomed Tiske.

"To Tiske."

More bottles of arax. The Guerdon thieves are drinking it now, faces grimacing at the gritty, ash-flecked taste. Like licking an ash-tray, says Karla. Vyr tells them how it used to be made from the seared grapes from vineyards on the Lyrixian mainland that got burned by dragon-fire. These days, the farmers themselves set fire to the fields every season and smuggle it out to the Ghierdana islands. Good arax is expensive.

"You should call it the Wash," mutters Baston to Vyr, "not the Ishmeric Zone."

"Call it what you will," replies Vyr. "It doesn't change the fact that we're surrounded by foes."

"We're surrounded by friends, Vyr," says Rasce. "Admittedly, those friends are then surrounded by foes."

"Why—" Baston coughs, to clear his throat of the smoke. "Why take down Dredger? He was always willing to pay his money to the Brotherhood."

"Ah, the famous thieves' guild of Guerdon!"

"Not a guild," snaps Baston. "We fought the guilds, and stole from 'em, same as you."

"A revolutionary Brotherhood, yes? Sworn to overthrow corrupt politicians and crooked guildmasters."

"That's how it was," says Baston.

Rasce grins. "Mortal men are easy for the dragon to kill. But the dragon sees further."

"Everyone knows Dredger," adds Vyr. "Everyone will pay attention to this message."

He sips his own arax, throws one leg over the arm of his chair. "Yliaster! Next on the list is Craddock & Sons. Mr Craddock will see sense, or he'll have fewer sons, and I do not anticipate any difficulty there."

"I know Craddock's'," says Baston, leaning forward. "I used to go there with the old master." Talking business draws him out. "When?"

"A few days, for Craddock. But my aim is higher still. Bend your thoughts, please, on the problem of the other yliaster importers."

"About a third of 'em import by sea," says Baston. "They're all along the docks. The rest go by rail, or caravan. They're based mostly in the Fog Yards. Far side of the city." He sits back. "Close to impossible, now that the city's chopped up into occupation zones."

"Ah, the invaluable insight of a local," laughs Rasce. "See, Vyr, this is why we need our new friends!"

Vyr looks queasy, and he's hardly touched his arax. "We shouldn't be discussing business here."

"And yet, we are. Baston – if I wished to strike at a foe in the Fog Yards as we burned Dredger, how would I do it?"

Baston considers the problem. "Without knowing the specifics . . . you'd need a hell of a lot more men than we had tonight. And you'd have to get them all the way across Guerdon without the watch crying foul. Tunnels, maybe. Go through the undercut."

"Is that not under the control of the ghouls?"

"It is. You'd need to cut a deal."

"With the Rat?" asks Rasce, or tries to, but as soon as he says that name, the world seems to lurch around him. For an instant, the entire room is transformed from the back room of a bar to some little bedsit down in the Wash. Everyone vanishes, or almost everyone – only Baston and Karla remain, and they're transformed, too. Baston has become ghoulish and hunched, his face lengthening into a wolfish muzzle. Karla's replaced by another woman, smaller and slighter with gamine features, her hair darkening, her fingers toying with a chain around her throat. Rasce tries to speak, but his throat is blocked as if he's swallowed a stone.

The vision lasts only a moment, but when reality snaps back the conversation's moved on and Rasce has lost the thread of it. An argument about some gang from Five Knives. Karla looks to Rasce, obviously waiting for him to respond to a question.

He coughs, covers for himself. "Actually, my good cousin has the right of it. We shouldn't talk business any more tonight."

Awkward silence falls over the table. Baston and Karla glance at each other, some unspoken signal between siblings. Vyr reaches over and sniffs the empty arax bottle.

"I'll say this for old Dredger," says one of the thieves, breaking the silence, "he was good to the Stone Men. My cousin got the pebble-pox, and he worked in the yards for ten years before he went to the isle."

"I've heard that Dredger has the plague," says another, "and that's why he always hides in that armour."

"He doesn't have it," says Rasce without thinking. How the hell does he know that? The adrenaline's wearing off now. The arax sits heavily in his gut — and it's gone right to his head, too, skipping past merry and straight to a pounding pain in his temples. He slips away from the table, leaves the clamour of the back room for the quiet of the stairwell.

Outside, there's a landing. A few yellowing playbills from old performances in the vanished theatre. *The Sewer Children. The Tragedy of Gethis. The Badger and the Nightingale.* The last one's got a notice stamped across it — CLOSED BY ORDER OF PARLIAMENT. PUBLIC GATHERINGS FORBIDDEN. DANGER OF CONTAGION. He examines them in what he first thought was moonlight spilling in through the high window, but now he realises it's not the moon — it's the nocturnal glimmering of the New City, its magical radiance lighting up the night.

Without quite knowing why, he feels compelled to raise his glass in salute.

"My mother." Karla's voice.

He turns around. She's followed him out, and now stands by one of the playbills. She taps the poster with a fingernail. There's a sketch of a woman's face, and he can see the resemblance now. "She played the nightingale."

"Ah." At the mention of Karla's mother, he feels unwell again, and sways at the top of the stairs. The image of glass shattering pops into his head, the sounds of a loud argument, a man and a woman screaming at each other. It feels like a memory, but it's not. He has no idea where it came from.

"Are you all right?"

"I just need some air," he says. "This city chokes me, yes? All the chimneys and the factories spread a miasma through the sky."

"You get used to it."

He sits down on the top step, to avoid showing any more weakness. Great-Uncle would be displeased.

"Does she still act, your mother?"

Karla sits down next to him. Back home in the isles, it would be unthinkably presumptuous for someone like her to sit next to a scion of the Ghierdana. Her unwitting insolence amuses him. "Not professionally, any more. Not since she met my father. She taught me. In another life, maybe I'd be up on the wall, too. But I was always my father's daughter."

"He was a thief, yes?"

"He was one of Heinreil's crew from the start. Rose with him." She raises her glass in a silent toast and takes a sip.

"Tiske said your brother worked for Heinreil, too."

"Bodyguard. No one's better in a fight than Baston."

Rasce laughs. These Guerdonese thieves are so *provincial*. "Indeed? A mere mortal man, and yet he can wrestle a wereboar or stand against a Nightshade! What a prodigy!"

"I'd take those odds," says Karla quietly.

Rasce was trained from a young age to excel and catch Great-Uncle's eye. Baston's bigger than him, doubtless stronger – but Rasce's sure he could defeat the Brotherhood enforcer in a duel. He always wins.

"And you? What was your place in the Brotherhood?"

She smiles. "I kept my hands clean."

"Tiske told me your father has passed. The war?"

"Before that. The Crisis. He went down a crypt on Gravehill, and we never saw him again. Ghouls got him." She sips her arax, tries and fails to hide the scowl. "What about your parents?"

"My mother is still alive, of course—"

"Of course?"

"On the isles of the Ghierdana, the daughters of the dragon are princesses, and treated accordingly. They rarely leave the family compounds."

Karla snorts. "Sounds boring. And your father?"

"They hanged him." The words come out of Rasce's mouth, but they're not his words. He grabs Karla's glass of arax from her, washes his mouth out, swallows, gagging on the ash. "Ach! No. Why did I say that? No, my father is alive, but – weak. Too many scars, and he can no longer fly. A broken knife, we say. No matter. No matter."

"Are you sure you're all right?"

"The fumes, I think."

She rises. "Come back inside."

"In a moment."

She slips away, returning to the upstairs room. He should follow, but for a moment he feels rooted to the stone steps. The solitude is welcome, too – he's used to spending long days strapped to Great-Uncle's back, with no company expect the dragon and his own thoughts. A little silence is balm, and he sips the last of the arax.

From the bar downstairs he can hear the Ishmerians singing a familiar hymn of mourning, a song that's sung many times a day in Guerdon. It tells of the death of their war goddess, brought down by treachery. The death of Pesh was more than a defeat for the Sacred Realm. It tore a wound in their souls and destroyed their ability to conceive of war. The empire's collapsing – and in that chaos, the Ghierdana thrive.

A door at the bottom of the stairs opens. The sound of the hymn mixes with the sound of an argument.

"Who's drinking that filthy arax? Who've you got up there?" An Ishmeric soldier shoves the waiter against the wall, heavy bottles clanking together as the waiter's tray wobbles.

"No one," insists the waiter. "Just a storeroom."

"Kraken take your lying tongue," slurs the soldier. He grabs one of the bottles, raises it like a club. He's a big man, shoulders corded with muscle. A killer, forged in the Godswar. He won't hesitate to smash the waiter's brains out with the bottle.

The waiter, Rasce suddenly remembers, is named Pulchar.

Another former member of the Brotherhood. He's lived in the Wash all his life, watched the city change around him. Memories flash through his brain. Pulchar serving him a drink, shouting at other customers who refused to share a bar with a Stone Man. Pulchar, during the invasion, cowering on these stairs as water flooded the bar downstairs, as monstrous Krakens swam through the streets outside.

It's not Rasce's memory. It can't be. He's never met Pulchar before. These memories are coming from the same place as the visions that warned him of the ghouls, of the fires. But none of that matters right now. Pulchar doesn't deserve what's about to happen to him.

The soldier, Rasce decides, does.

Rasce jumps over the banister.

The split second in midair is liberating, like flying again. He feels thoroughly himself in that instant.

He lands squarely on the Ishmerian. The soldier crumples under the impact, ribs cracking. For good measure, Rasce grabs the wretch by the hair, drives his skull into the nearest step, and the Ishmerian goes limp.

The waiter stares in horror. Rasce barely notices. His mind is elsewhere. The memory of Pulchar hiding on the stair, the vision of Dredger's yard – in both, it was as though he was looking down from some vantage point in the heights of the New City. He's looked down from Great-Uncle's back often enough to visualise the city spread out below, to imagine the angles and perspectives. Something has touched his mind. Something unnatural.

Something connected to the New City.

"Baston! Vyr!" calls Rasce. Faces appear at the top of the stairs. "We're leaving."

He kneels down by the terrified waiter. "Listen! We were never here, yes?" Rasce presses a purse of gold into Pulchar's hand. "Take this, for the drinks. And the shelter. And the fire damage."

"What fire damage?" mutters Pulchar weakly.

Unlike the soldier, the bottle of arax is still intact.

Rasce plucks a rag from Pulchar's apron, stuffs it into the neck of the bottle. The Guerdon thieves did well tonight, he reflects, and it's only fair to honour their efforts with a little extra payback. "We shall leave by the front door," Rasce announces.

"The bar is full of Ishmeric soldiers," says Vyr.

"The dragon walks where he pleases."

A burning bottle of arax isn't half as impressive a weapon as that blunderbore, but it still makes for a marvellous beginning to a quick and bloody brawl as the thieves charge through the front bar, scattering the soldiers of the Sacred Realm.

To Rasce's delight, Baston comes alive in the fight. The man fights with brutal efficiency, moving across the bar like some remorseless engine. He wields a table leg as a weapon, bringing it down again and again on the skulls of Ishmeric soldiers. Never a blow wasted.

"We have to go," shouts Karla. Blood runs down her face from a cut on her cheek, but she's grinning broadly. Rasce claps her on the back. "Lead us out!"

She grabs him by the hand, fingers intertwined with his. The thieves spill out on to the streets, Ghierdana and Guerdonese alike, and vanish down back alleys and passageways, out of the sight of the city and its many gods.

CHAPTER EIGHT

Carillon wakes at dawn, hears the waves washing against the hull through a haze of dull pain. Hears Captain Hawse's gruff voice in the distance. She thinks, maybe, that she saw a Monkfish – a Bythos – standing in the doorway of the cabin, but it might have been a dream. She's dreaming again—

Waking in a cold panic, unsure where she is. She lunges for her dagger – unexpected, unfamiliar pain, how can she be wounded? – and reaches out for Spar with her mind. She's the Saint of Knives, she's got a thousand enemies in Guerdon. She can't let her guard down. *Spar? Who's out there? Show me*, she thinks, even as she falls out of the bunk to land heavily on the floor of the little cabin. Falls through the floor, into blackness. Into another waking dream.

Hours later, in the dead of night, she's awake again. The bitter taste of medicine in her mouth; her lips numbed. Someone – Hawse? – has put a blanket over her, and it's drenched in sweat. She kicks it off, awkwardly, her limbs heavy and disobedient. She looks out of the door, sees a sky full of strange stars, and none of the smog that usually covers the skies of Guerdon. *I'm in Ilbarin. I've got to get to Khebesh.* Her satchel's on the floor by her bed; she fumbles for it, tries to pick it up, but she doesn't have the strength. The weight of the fucking book is too much for her. She falls back into the bed. Sleep. Heal.

She wakes to the reassuring bulk of Hawse as he wipes her brow with a cool cloth. "Rest," he tells her. "The Lord of Waters will bear you up." Somehow, coming from him, it's comforting. He leaves a plate of fried fish by the bunk, and a flask of water. She sips the water, eats as much of the fish as she can. It twists in her stomach, so she twists herself face down on the bunk, as if she can keep the food trapped inside her by her posture. She falls back asleep.

Half awake, she wanders through confused recollections. She hasn't been this sick in years, not since her return to Guerdon, when Rat found her, shivering and feverish, in an alleyway, and brought her to Spar. *How close to death must I be*, she thinks, *before I can ask for help?* She sits up, has a little water, then lies back and rests, listening to the sound of the birds on the shore. A curious cacophony – gulls and other seabirds, but also inland birds, screeching threats at the unfamiliar expanse of the encroaching sea. The harsh sounds are not restful, but, still, she sleeps.

She wakes again to a man sitting on her bed.

"Hello, Cari."

Dol Martaine.

She tries to back away, recoiling from Martaine like he's a scorpion. Pressing herself up against the wall again, reaching for a knife that isn't there. A figure out of a nightmare, a shadow from her past. She can't run. Her legs still feel boneless.

"Never thought I'd see you again," says Dol Martaine. He's a lanky man, all limbs and long hands. Head shaved; a thin black beard. A high-collared shirt that probably hides the armoured vest he used to favour, leather treated with alchemical curatives until it's tough enough to stop a bullet. "Young Cari, all grown up." His gaze runs over her hungrily. "What are you doing back here, Cari?"

She tries to speak, but her throat is clogged with fear. She's faced down far worse things than Dol Martaine, fought Ravellers and Crawling Ones and mad saints, killed a fucking goddess, but that was when she had power. And Martaine's another order of terror. The bastard tormented her on the *Rose* for years, played with her like a cat toying with a mouse. Adro – and Hawse, usually – gave her some protection, but the *Rose* wasn't a big ship, and she couldn't avoid Martaine. He taught her to hide, to move unseen. To hate.

"Let's see." He grabs her satchel. Instinctively, she tries to snatch it away, but he's faster and stronger. He paws through the contents. "Oh, she has money," he crows, letting a handful of coins from her bag slip through his fingers. "But I always guessed that, from how she joined us. Spoiled little runaway. And what's this?"

He rips open the inner lining of the satchel, pulls out a little derringer pistol, a handful of Haithi letters of credit. All given to her by her cousin Eladora, back in Guerdon. Emergency supplies for the journey, in case she encountered trouble she couldn't run away from. He pockets the pistol. Spreads the Haithi papers out on the bed. "What are you?" he asks, a note of surprise, even respect in his voice. "A spy? For Haith, maybe?"

"I stole them, you moron," she lies. He hasn't taken the book out yet. How can he miss it? It's gigantic, heavy, obviously valuable. Why isn't he asking her questions about Ramegos' grimoire?

Because, Cari realises with mounting horror, the book isn't there. It's already gone.

The room darkens as Hawse appears in the doorway. Martaine hastily folds the letters of credit and shoves them inside his jacket. The captain carries two steaming cups of tea; he hands one to Martaine.

"Well?" he rumbles.

Cari tries not to panic. Hawse took care of her. He's always protected her from Dol Martaine. He's always been her friend – *until you ran away*, she reminds herself. But he's always been Martaine's friend, too. He needed Martaine a lot more than he ever needed Cari; Martaine was the captain's right hand back in the day, his counsellor, his scourge. Adro was the muscle, but Martaine was the one the captain trusted to get things done, at sea or on shore. She remembers seeing Martaine come back on board with bloodied hands, being told to help throw cloth-wrapped bodies overboard. The *Rose* survived by smuggling on the fringes of the Godswar; a dirty, dangerous business, and Martaine handled the roughest parts.

Cari swallows the bile rising in her throat and stays perfectly still as the two men talk over her.

"Here's the thing, captain," says Martaine. "The Ghierdana are looking for a young woman, just come to Ilbarin. Dark-haired, like our Cari. Secretive, like our Cari. Little scars on her face." Martaine reaches out, runs his thumb over Cari's cheek. "And our Cari's got some scars since she left us. They didn't say anything about her being insolent or treacherous, but we'll take that as read."

"Is there a reward?" asks Hawse, sipping his tea.

"Passage off the Rock. That's all they need to say to get every poor bastard on Ilbarin looking for her."

Hawse groans as he sits down on the bunk opposite. "Cari, why are the Ghierdana looking for you?"

Cari shuffles away from Martaine as much as she can. "Stuff happened back in Guerdon." Both men frown in confusion. "Look, have either of you heard news out of Guerdon in the last few years?"

Martaine sounds gratifyingly unsure of himself. "Ishmere invaded. Guerdon used some alchemical weapon on the Lion Queen. Killed Her, I've heard."

"Impossible," says Hawse harshly. "Gods cannot die."

Martaine rolls his eyes, "Ishmere signed a peace treaty, guaranteed by Haith and Lyrix. Guerdon's partially occupied by all three, now, and they've all agreed not to fight in the city."

"And there's a king in Guerdon again," adds Hawse. "Chosen by some god or other."

"Now what," says Martaine slowly, "does any of that have to do with you?"

Cari's tempted to boast about killing the Lion Queen, to show them that she's risen far beyond them, but, instead, she picks her words carefully. She doesn't want to give away too much. "I was running with the Brotherhood – the Guerdon thieves' guild, right? We kicked the Ghierdana out of Guerdon. Killed a bunch of them. That's why they want me, I guess."

Martaine leans back. "But the Ghierdana are back in Guerdon now. The peace treaty let them back in."

"Yeah. That's why I'm here and not there."

"Why here?"

"I need to get to Khebesh."

"Khebesh has sealed its gates. No one can pass the Ghost Walls." Martaine leans back. "You're lying."

"Believe me or don't, I don't care. Look, I just need passage off Ilbarin. I'm not looking to make trouble here, not looking for payback or anything. Don't tell the Ghierdana you saw me, Dol, and you can keep the money."

"Oh, I'm keeping the money." Dol Martaine laughs. "As for telling the Ghierdana . . . the captain already told me you were here."

Shit.

Martaine's Eshdana. She should have guessed he would take the ash.

Carillon throws herself at Martaine, hands scrabbling for that little pistol, but her limbs are like wet seaweed against the solid rock of his arm. Pain explodes in her wrist again. His hot tea spills down his leg, making him flinch, but she's too hurt to take advantage of the opening. He pins her in the bed, puts the gun to her head. "I know the boss, Cari! This much hate – it's more than business! It's a vendetta!" He hisses into her ear. "Why does Artolo want you so badly?"

"Dol." The captain doesn't look up, doesn't move, but there's still a weight to his words, an iron bar dropping. Martaine twists around to look Hawse in the eye.

"We need to know! We need to know what she's worth to him!"

"Dol. Not like this. Get off her."

Martaine snarls, but he obeys the captain's order, releasing his grip on Cari. He stands up, slips her pistol into a pocket, tugs his shirt down. He backs away, keeping his eyes fixed on Cari, all of him in motion somehow, hands flexing, body twisting as he withdraws from the cramped cabin.

"Keep her here," he tells Hawse from the doorway, "until I get back. Don't tell anyone – and if Artolo's men come calling, drown her like I told you."

"Dol," says the captain, in that same leaden tone, "*He* has not forgotten."

"Your god is dead, captain," spits Dol Martaine, and then he's gone. Cari hears him slithering down the side of the *Rose*, the distant wet squelch as he lands in the mud.

"You're still weak," says Hawse. He throws back the last of his tea, then rises, groaning as his old bones creak. "I'll get you more to eat."

"You fucking turned me over to the Ghierdana?"

Hawse grunts in irritation. "I found you on the shore, and there were other Ghierdana out there this morning, looking for your trail. If they'd caught you, you'd be in their citadel in Ushket, and I'd have my throat cut for sheltering you. So, aye, I went to Martaine. He took the ash after they beached the *Rose*. He can make sure they won't search here."

"You mean, he won't let anyone else turn me over. He'll do it himself."

"If it comes to it. But a promise to me is not one he'll lightly break."

Cari scowls. Her head's spinning. "You sound very sure."

"I have faith. I shall show you, when you're stronger."

"Hawse, my book. Where is it? Did he take it?"

Hawse sits heavily back down on the bunk opposite. "I spoke with the Bythos this morning." It takes her a second to recall he means the Monkfish-things that came out of the ocean. "There's much I don't understand about you, Cari. But your book is safe. I hid it from Martaine. And you're safe, for now. I swear this by the Lord of Waters."

By the evening of the next day, Cari is able to walk a little. Her whole left side is blue with bruises, courtesy of the goddess of the mountain. She creeps out on deck, moving like an old woman herself, like Spar on a bad day. Her ribs feel like they're made of glass – fragile, cracked, fragments grinding into her flesh – but she's getting stronger.

She crouches down by the railing, and looks out at the shore, squinting through the bandages over her battered face. In the fading light, the Rock is visible only as a black void looming above her, blotting out the stars to the south, although she can see an eerie radiance from the far side, streamers of light of no colour she can name rising from what must be the ruins of Ilbarin. It puts her in mind of the new Temple Quarter back in Guerdon, the Ishmeric Occupation Zone.

Off to the right, she can see the lights of the town of Ushket. More lights – campfires and farms – on the upper slopes beyond the town. Floodlights now illuminate the harbour where she landed, and she can make out parts of a fortress on the far side of the town, through gaps in the skyline – a tower there, a bastion there. It's like some great beast hiding in the undergrowth, hunting her, waiting for her to break cover. And on the shore between the wreck of the *Rose* and Ushket, she can see a few thin figures stalking up and down the muddy fields, poking at weeds or searching through the other wrecks.

They're looking for her.

For them, passage off Ilbarin. Hawse told her that the first thing the Ghierdana did when they arrived, after Ilbarin City drowned, was make sure they controlled all the ways off the island. Their dragons destroyed the ships that weren't Ghierdana. Burned most of them, dragged others – like the *Rose* – out of the water to rot. Tens of thousands of people died in Ilbarin City, but tens of thousands survived, too. For now – this island is dying, she can taste it in the air like a ghoul. Not enough food, not enough drinkable water. The farms up the slopes look like they don't produce much, and she's got no idea where Hawse got the fish he fed her, because the only others she's seen are the piles of rotting fish-kill along the water's edge. The seas are fucked, too, ruined by the battle between Kraken and the Lord of Waters. She wants passage off this rock, but so does everyone else.

What about Dol Martaine? Hawse claims she can trust their former crewmate, that Martaine won't break his word to the captain – but Cari needs to know the source of that certainty.

She leaves the rail, makes her way slowly downstairs into the dark bowels of the ship.

The forward hold is pitch-black apart from the wan light that spills in through the breach in the hull. She has to navigate by touch, by memory, until she finds the doorway that leads into the aft hold. The tide's coming in, water gushing through the wounds in the aft hull. She climbs down the ladder, wincing at every rung, cold and slimy tongues lapping against her ankles, her calves. The salt stings the cuts on her knees.

There's another sensation, too, like she's passing through invisible veils. She has to push at the empty air; something unseen and unnamable passes through her. It tickles her skin, her bones, her mind – it's like the feeling she experienced on the mountain, just before the goddess of the mountain nearly beat her to death, but she doesn't get the same feeling of hostility here. Just a feeling of presence. One time, back in Severast, Cari robbed the house of a dead man. He was a wealthy merchant who died suddenly, and all his family and servants were away at the funeral rite in the temple of the Dancer. Cari had slipped away from the rites, swapped her acolyte's robes for the more practical garb of a sneak-thief, and made her way through the cobbled lanes of Severast until she found the empty house.

She remembers making her way through the rooms, knowing the owner was gone, but still sensing him everywhere. Papers left on a desk, a half-finished bottle of wine, a caged parrot demanding attention – as though the merchant had just stepped out for a moment. A house that was unoccupied but not empty.

The aft hold is like that.

Captain Hawse is there, waist-deep by a makeshift floating altar, on which he's laid the sacred icons of the Lord of Waters. Blue light wells from the water when he touches it. As Cari enters, there's a sudden splash and ripple from the far side of the room. One of the Bythos, maybe, vanishing into the water.

The expression on Hawse's face is one she's never seen before. His eyes are closed – in prayer? In pain? – but he senses her approach.

"I said I would tell you, did I not?"

"What is this, captain?" asks Cari. It's obvious what it is – a little temple to the Lord of Waters, with Hawse as priest. But in all the time she knew him, Hawse's approach to religion was pragmatic. He made offerings to the Lord of Waters, but also to all the other sea-gods, to Kraken and St Storm and Vas and the Whale-God. Sailors are syncretists; you never know which god, if any, is going to have influence over the shifting currents and storms of the open ocean, so you hedge your prayers. "Have you gone hallowed on me?"

"The man you knew is dead, Cari," says Hawse.

"How metaphorical are you being, here?"

Hawse ignores her, and speaks without opening his eyes. He recites rather than replies, as if he's quoting some ancient prayer from thousands of years ago. "When the Sacred Realm of Ishmere made war upon the land of Ilbarin, there was much suffering. From Ishmere came the Kraken, bearing the temple-fleets, the armies of the mad gods. The sky darkened with the demon offspring of Cloud Mother. The hearts of brave men were dismayed by the horrors conjured by Smoke Painter, and the minds of women were poisoned by the whispers of Fate Spider. Woe and suffering came from Ishmere. Anathema upon the gods of Ishmere!

"The kindly gods sent forth a host of saints to defend the shores of Ilbarin. Their battle cries shook the mountain. Their blades were fire and thunder. To look upon them was to go mad with joy."

She's never heard him talk like this. Never heard him talk for so long. Hawse was always a man of few words.

"The *Rose* was caught between them. We were on our way back from Paravos, and I sailed us right into . . . into . . . " He opens his eyes, fixes his gaze on Carillon. Moistens his lips. "The Krakens stole the seas, and we couldn't move. I saw the clouds eat my crew. I saw everything breaking. And they were in me, too. I was their battlefield. We all were. They'd command us, and we obeyed. Gods sending us this way and that. Jumping into the water. Or the sky. It was all one. Everything was broken. Pesh told me to kill, and I killed. But death was no release from their commands. Even the men I killed kept fighting. It was madness."

She remembers the attack on Guerdon, the Kraken-waves that carried temples full of saints and monsters, the things in the clouds reaching down with their tentacles. The feeling that everything was breaking, everything was slipping away. She saw hundreds of people go mad as the gods approached. She had Spar to anchor her, but the things she saw that day still wait in her dreams.

She had power then. She could do something. How much worse to be utterly powerless before the wrath of the mad gods? To know that no matter how hard you tried, all your efforts could be brushed aside in an instant. To know that you were nothing compared to them, a mote of dust, a drop of water in a torrent.

Like the whole world is theirs, to be remade as they wish, and you count for nothing.

Captain Hawse plunges his hands into the water, and the blue glow intensifies. He closes his eyes again. "All was lost. My ship was lost. My crew . . . I had to save them. And the Lord of Waters heard my prayer. I swore that I would serve him with all my soul, and with His great hand, he lifted the *Rose* out of the storm and carried us to safety."

Captain Hawse cups his hands, lifts them out of the water. He splashes the glowing blue water over the icon of the Lord of Waters on the altar. "I saw, too, the hateful gods of Ishmere attack my Lord. I saw the Kraken wrap tentacles around Him to drag him into the blackest depths of the ocean, where the damned dwell. Smoke Painter poisoned him. The Lion Queen tore open his stomach, and the waters poured out. I saw my god sacrifice himself to save me and my crew." Tears run down Hawse's cheeks, and they too glow blue, leaving luminescent tracks on his face.

"That's what will bind Dol Martaine, Cari. His life and mine belong to the Lord of Waters."

Cari leaves Hawse at prayer, or communing with the Bythos, or whatever he's doing down there, and climbs back on deck. She's glad to be back in the open. A cool night breeze blows in from the sea, and she shivers.

She wants to climb. She's always liked to be up high, up in the rigging, or on rooftops and spires. She likes getting to places where no one can follow her, where no one can see her but she can still watch the world below. Back in Guerdon, when she could choose where to live, she made herself an eyrie atop one of the tallest spires in the New City. It's a stupid thought, she tells herself – even if she wasn't limping and sore, even if the *Rose* still had her graceful masts, she's supposed to stay hidden.

So, she walks around the deck, prowls through the empty cabins.

The sound of Hawse's prayers from below mixes with the endless washing of the waves, but it's not a restful sound. She's not sure if she likes this new side of Hawse. Faith in the gods is not something she trusts – it's a form of madness, surely, to put your trust in such things. Or anything, for that matter. She trusts Spar. Trusted Rat, sort of. And once, she'd have said she trusted Hawse.

She trusted the captain he was. Not the priest he's become.

The urge to run wells up in her. Well, limp, but she can still move. There's food in Hawse's cabin, maybe money. A sword, at least, perhaps some other weapons. She could try to get around the mountain again. Dol Martaine said that the Ghierdana control all the ships leaving Ilbarin, but that means that people do leave. She could sneak aboard. All she needs to do is reach the mainland, and then she can find her way south to Khebesh, right. *Maybe that's why Hawse took the fucking book – to keep me from leaving. What if he's in league with Dol Martaine, and Martaine's gone to get the Ghierdana?*

The stairs creak. She tenses, ducking into a hiding place, hand reaching for the knife that isn't there, but it's just Hawse coming back up, wringing out his shirt and pulling his coat around him against the chill of his wet clothes. He digs through his pockets, searching the wrong hip pockets first, just like he always does. A gesture made so very familiar over the years.

That's the Hawse she wants to be here.

"Dol Martaine said your god is dead," she says.

He lights the pipe, ambles over to her. "Gods cannot die. They always return in some form. They are outside death."

"I killed Pesh."

His face is unreadable.

"In Guerdon. They made an alchemical bomb, a god-bomb. It annihilates gods. No coming back. That's why the Ishmerians left Ilbarin. I killed their goddess, captain."

He's silent for a long time before he speaks again. "The Bythos already told me. They would not have guided you here otherwise.

And Martaine's half right – the Lord of Waters fell in the invasion. But nothing is ever wholly lost. He shall come back, not as he was, perhaps. Nothing will ever be as it was. But he'll come back." He sighs. "I'm a poor priest, Cari. I've never studied the scriptures, and I don't know much about interpreting omens. But I believe that the Lord of Waters has a special purpose for you. If you must get to Khebesh, then I'll help you. But you must be patient: you need time to heal."

CHAPTER NINE

Artolo runs his ghost-fingers over the barrel of the gun. Flexes them, to make sure they've got the strength and speed to pull the stiff trigger when the moment comes. He looks up at the barren hillside and imagines Carillon Thay popping up from behind one of those rocks. Would shooting her be enough? The rifle's chambered with oversized phlogistonic rounds, and the witch has woven spells around each bullet to make them even more potent.

No. Shooting would be too quick, too painless. Something slower.

Anyway, Thay isn't his quarry today.

The witch points up the slope. "There's the shrine," she says, pointing with her armoured hand. She sounds breathless from the effort of weaving protective spells around Artolo, but this is dangerous work – the hunting of a god.

The shrine on the shoulder of the Rock of Ilbarin is an ugly thing, squat and rough-made, cut from the same stone as the mountain. There were other shrines and temples dedicated to the goddess of the mountain, but they're all gone now. The rising seas drowned most of them, and the Ishmerians defiled the rest. This little shrine, high on the upper slopes, is perhaps the last.

He hesitates. "You said tearing down this shrine would provoke her."

The witch shrugs. "She's already provoked. She's already active.

Demolishing the shrine will make it harder for her to reform coherently. She'll come back even more disorganised."

Artolo raises the rifle, presses his eye to the scope. He trains it on the shrine. There's a statue there, depicting the goddess Usharet. The statue is beautiful, a work of ecstatic devotion, every careful chip with the chisel a prayer. It depicts a young woman, tall and athletic, defiant as the mountain. Usharet, before the war.

"We'd better be quick, before she finds someone to saint," mutters the witch. No doubt there are many souls among the survivors of Ilbarin who know the rites and prayers to please Usharet, to attract the attention of the goddess; if the whirling pattern of Usharet alighted on some compatible soul, that'd be trouble he doesn't need.

Especially with Great-Uncle on the way back to inspect the yliaster refinery.

He sweeps the scope left and right, up and down the slope. Other than a few lazy whirls of dust, there's no sign of movement in the blasted landscape.

"Nothing," he mutters. "The bitch must be over on the west side of the Rock."

"You're thinking like a mortal," replies the witch. Her armoured suit whirs as she surveys the landscape. "She's everywhere on the mountain. She is the mountain. We need to get Her to concentrate Her being. Make Herself manifest. And then you shoot Her."

The other two riflemen on either side of Artolo signal their acknowledgements. When the goddess Usharet was at the height of her power, she'd have shrugged off attacks from little weapons like these. But like the other gods of Ilbarin, she was broken by the Sacred Realm. She's nothing but a mindless godhusk now. Greatly diminished, and soon, she'll be diminished again.

Artolo grunts in acknowledgement. He checks his gun again, checks his fingers. There was a time when he'd have laughed in the face of a broken little goddess like Usharet. Laughed, then shot her in the face. But he's not laughing now.

"Martaine!" he calls. Dol Martaine turns and hurries over to Artolo.

"Aye, sir?"

"Take four men. Blow up that shrine. Be on your guard – this will call Her, my witch says."

"I've set up trigger-wards," adds the witch. "They'll go off before She manifests. That'll give you a little warning."

"How much warning?"

"Better than none. But not by much."

"My life's in your hands, boss," says Martaine, shooting a sidelong glance at Artolo's gloved fingers. That borders on insolence, and Martaine's only Eshdana. He doesn't get to speak out of line.

"Go," snarls Artolo.

Martaine picks four men from the gaggle of beaters and sentries they've brought to this not quite godforsaken hillside, and they begin their slow ascent, carrying a bundle of alchemical explosives. They walk gingerly over the unstable rocks. Avoid the tangles of dead thorn bushes. Flinch at every shift in the wind.

Some of them look back, as if worried they're being abandoned on this cursed hillside as sacrifices to Usharet. Martaine, to his credit, never looks back.

Artolo's still not completely sure about Martaine, but it's obvious the man has ambitions beyond this ruined island. Most of the other survivors just stumble around, hollow and confused, unable to reconcile their memories of what Ilbarin was with what it's become. They cling to what can be salvaged from the past, as if they can wait out the destruction. Artolo's seen survivors out of Ilbarin City dragging furniture with them, as if the floodwaters might soon recede and they can return to their homes. Trying to find some government official to complain to, when there hasn't been a functioning government in Ilbarin in months. Wasting food on children, though there's no hope of them seeing the next year. Idiots, all of them.

Martaine's not like that, reflects Artolo. Maybe it's a mark of a well-travelled man – seeing the world gives a breadth of vision that's necessary to survive. You learn there are possibilities elsewhere, and there's no sense tethering yourself to a dead cause, a dead past. There are always new lands to conquer.

"You travelled before I found you, yes?" he mutters to the witch.

"I did. All over the south, then up through the trading cities. Nearly went to the Archipelago. Ended up in Guerdon instead."

She's distracted, working her magic. He should pay attention himself. The goddess could manifest at any moment.

The glow of the warding runes laid down by the witch is unchanged. Martaine and his men have nearly reached the shrine.

His mind returns to Carillon. She deserves a slow death at his hands. Yes, it'll have to be with his hands. She wasn't the one who cut off his fingers – it was a punishment decreed by Great-Uncle – but it was her fault. Curse the gods, and all their fucking mad blessings. Handing out power on a whim, or according to some twisted philosophy that meant nothing in the real world – it disgusted him. Power should go to those strong enough to claim it, brave enough to use it. When Great-Uncle punished him, hard as it was it made sense. He'd failed the dragon, and so he suffered. Not because of some nonsensical sin, not because the gods were randomly cruel, and not because of some heavenly war. No, the dragons knew how the world really worked, once you stripped away all pretence, all the holy scriptures and divine commandments.

You were strong, or you suffered.

Ilbarin was his proof of that. This land of crushed and broken gods, without the wit or strength left to them to spawn a saint. Lawless and godless, too many people and not enough food. There's only one way off Ilbarin, and he controls it. He can reward the worthy, the ones with the courage and sense and strength to become Eshdana, and the others suffer.

He'll make Carillon suffer. He'll . . . he'll bury her on this mountain. There must be hidden caves in the depths of the Rock, cracks and crevasses where he can entomb her alive, down in the darkness, surrounded by stone, the roots of the thorn bushes pushing into the fecund stickiness of her eye sockets, drinking her soul . . .

That's not my thought, he realises.

The warding runes flare. The ground shakes.

She's right below them.

The witch senses it, too, but she's clumsy in her articulated armour, too slow to react. Artolo grabs her and sprints forward as the hillside explodes behind him. He shouts a warning, but it's lost in the thunder of the eruption. Boulders crash around him. Dust billows up, and through the choking clouds he sees the goddess. He tries to bring the long rifle to bear, but she's too close.

Witless, broken, but cunning like a fox. The goddess recognised the long guns, knew they were a danger to her.

The goddess is a leafless tree, barren and bare, twisting in the force of some unseen gale – but every time she bends, every time her long tangled arms reach down, they come up dripping with the entrails of one of Artolo's men. She shakes her arms, scattering the gore like dew, and green shoots begin to sprout across the mountainside. Bits of rifle and rifleman land in front of Artolo, both horribly mangled.

Ghost-fingers close on the trigger. The recoil hammers through his body and tears at every old wound. He feels it in his finger-stumps, in the belly-wound, in his spine. The flash blinds him; his nose fills with the caustic stink of sulphur and phlogiston.

Usharet roars in pain. The blast catches her in the chest, nearly severing one arm. She comes running towards him, sliding – he's standing in the path of a landslide. Thorn-fingers reach for him—

—And stop. Usharet's frozen, held paralysed by the witch's sorcery. A cage of ebony lightning flickers around the goddess, tendrils flickering and snatching at the human-shaped assembly of rock and dirt that makes up Usharet's form.

"Can't. Hold. Her," groans the witch. Unearthly light blazes from every joint of the armour; black liquid drips from the witch's wrists, sizzles on the ground. Every syringe in the armour clicks into position, pumping drugs into the witch's sorcery-riddled body. If it were not for the rigidity of the locked armour, she'd be writhing in agony from the arcane backlash.

Artolo draws his dragon-tooth knife. The blade is blunt, but it's still got power. He leaps on to the back of the frozen goddess, drives the blade like a chisel into the wound, cleaving the arm from the body. The arm falls apart, dissolving into its components in a rain of stones and roots and rot.

The knife breaks the spell, too, freeing Usharet. She crumbles, hunching over, keening like a wounded beast. Turning, she scrambles away from Artolo, loping up the hillside towards the shrine. Her monstrously long strides carry her away across the mountain. If the goddess escapes, she can draw power from the shrine to heal herself. Maybe come back and hunt them down for profaning her mountain, or go and find a potential saint.

"Hold her again," he orders the witch.

"I might not be able to," the witch whispers, but she tries anyway. She extends her hand, chants the spell again, and again the goddess is caught mid-stride, paralysed by the spell. Bolts of arcane energy leap from the witch's body to the soil. The smell of burning flesh.

Artolo ignores it. He cups his hands, shouts an order. "Martaine! Bring the explosives back here! Quick!"

He can't see Martaine in the dust and confusion, but a few moments later there's a flash, a roll of thunder, a rain of stone. The witch collapses at his feet, gasping in relief. As the smoke clears, the ruin of the goddess becomes apparent. A blackened thing that somehow recalls a woman, lying at the bottom of a fresh scar in the mountainside.

Artolo marches across the hillside, stepping over the remains of his soldiers. Ignoring the witch's whimpering behind him. There's a job to do first. He climbs down into the hot pit, holding his breath to ward off the acrid fumes. The withered god husk raises the stump that used to be her head, and for a moment he sees the statue, the girl from the shrine, superimposed over the ruined form of Usharet. Her expression hasn't changed – there's no pleading for mercy, no fear. Just defiance.

The dagger's blunt, so it takes him several long, lung-searing minutes to saw through the thorn-root sinews of her neck, to cut through the mud-flesh and part the stone vertebrae.

Fuck saints and fuck gods.

It takes them nearly an hour to rally the scattered Eshdana, and to gather any dropped weapons or unused explosives. By then, a living veil has grown over the slopes like a spreading bloodstain. Artolo tugs at one of the new plants, pulling it out of the dusty soil. The miracle-spawned growth is the only patch of green on the whole mountainside. The plant is misshapen, a weird amalgamation of different species that once grew on the Rock, on the foothills now lost beneath the new sea. It's probably poisonous or tainted – eating the flesh of miracles is foolish in the extreme. Letting a god into your body . . . madness.

"Clear the corpses from the mountain," orders Artolo. If they don't, worshippers of Ilbarin's broken gods could use the remains as offerings, extract the residuum with funeral rites. "And when you're done with that, search the upper slopes. The Guerdonese woman might be hiding up there."

Martaine hesitates. "What should we expect if we find her? Anything I should know?"

"She's not to be killed."

"Anything else? Is she armed? Alchemy?"

"She's alone. Maybe armed. Bring plenty of men."

Martaine looks across the corpse-strewn hillside. The skirmish with Usharet killed half a dozen Eshdana. "We're going to run thin on ash-marks."

"Take what you need from the work camp. Get it done, Martaine." Artolo spits into the pit, listens to his saliva sizzle on the smouldering corpse of the goddess. He turns on his heel and walks away.

The witch waits for him by the roadside. "'Take what you need from the work camp'," she echoes. "What about the production quotas? What will you cut off to atone this time?"

"Watch your tongue," snaps Artolo. "Let me handle my Great-Uncle."

"I'm not taking the blame for any delay," says the witch.

"Great-Uncle will understand."

A carriage arrives to bring them back to Ushket. Artolo would prefer to ride – sometimes, when riding fast, it's almost like flying on Great-Uncle's back again. But the witch is exhausted, and she's too useful to neglect.

It's dusk by the time the carriage reaches Ushket. After curfew, and they speed through empty streets to the citadel.

The citadel in Ushket was once a provincial fort, home to a small garrison of troops. The prefect of Ushket province dwelled here. For a few chaotic weeks after the fall of Ilbarin City, the citadel was the seat of the government, when senators and prefects came scrambling up the Rock in search of higher ground and shelter from the Godswar. There's still a government in exile, off in Paravos, but the only law in Ushket now is his word.

"It's not the dragon I'm worried about. He's bringing the Dentist." The witch removes one of her gauntlets and scratches at the flaking skin beneath. Her fingers come away bloody. "I don't like him. And I've never heard of anyone *leaving* the alchemists' guild in Guerdon, other than in a gilded coffin. They seal their secrets with *wax*, aye?"

"Vorz is ash-marked, as are you. Vorz serves the Ghierdana loyally. As should you."

"You think an oath and a pinch of ash means anything to him?"

"It means something to you, does it not?"

She falls silent. Sits back, her armour creaking, and stares out at the discoloured sea. Soil from the mountain has stained it a ruddy shade. The witch holds her hand up, examines it in the light. Most of the skin has long since withered or burned away, exposing the muscle and sinew beneath. Bizarrely, the ornate tattoos on her wrists and the back of her hands are unaffected. She reminds Artolo of the ruined goddess he killed earlier. If he struck the witch hard enough, would she too crumble into dust leaving behind only a tracery of tattooed flesh?

Sorcery is a quick route to power, if you've got the talent for it. If you're willing to light your soul on fire. Artolo flexes his ghost-fingers. He could kill the witch with one blow in the right spot. Drive those ghostly fingers into her throat, for instance. Even if her sorcery-ravaged windpipe didn't collapse, she'd be unable to speak, unable to cast a spell. She's physically weak for all her power. What's the point of power without endurance? She needs to be sheltered. Like the long gun – very powerful, very precise. A wonderful piece of engineering and alchemy, but easily broken.

He clears his throat. "Why do you fear Vorz?"

"I don't fear. But either he's not as clever as he thinks he is . . ." She scuffs a bit of dead goddess with her shoe. "Or he is, and that's even scarier. He's dangerous, boss. I want to stay clear of him."

"Find Thay for me, and I shall protect you."

"I'm working on it. Divinations take time. I can't just read a pile of guts." She sounds irritated. "It'd be easier if you *didn't* have the whole island looking for her. It stirs up the aether, creates all sorts of echoes. You should leave it with me. Martaine and the rest are needed in the camp."

"Don't bother with your spells, then. Conserve your strength. The dogs in the street will find her."

"No. I can do it. I'll do it."

CHAPTER TEN

I t's double shifts down at the docks all week, working night and day clearing warehouses contaminated by the fire at Dredger's yard. Baston brings down the breathing masks from the raid and hands them out to the dockers working on the worst afflicted areas. It's a risk, but he'd prefer to field awkward questions about the masks than watch some poor bastard vomit the dissolved remnants of their lungs up. Baston knows all about necessary evils, about justifying violence to himself. He tried to scrub his conscience clean many times over the years, working for the Brotherhood in the bad times. He told himself that the Brotherhood could still be a force for justice, a way to kick back against the oppressive rulers of the city. He told himself that those he hurt deserved it; they'd broken some rule of the streets, and so brought their suffering on themselves. He could tell himself, maybe, that the burning of Dredger's yard was an accident, and that he shares no blame for what happened.

All excuses fall hollow in the end, though, and so all week he takes the hardest work on himself, wading into tainted floodwaters to scoop up deposits of alchemical gunk with gloved hands. He works through the night until they send him home.

At the blackened ruins of the yard, the guild alchemists have erected a containment screen of some silvery cloth that glows in the dawn light, as if the New City has spawned a new district. Wearily, he makes his way back through the streets of the Wash, in the shadow of the temples. In Cloud Mother's floating sanctum, they greet the dawn with torches, setting fire to the horizon. Baston's perspective warps when he gets too close to the temple – for a moment, that symbolic act of worship becomes real and true, and the priests really are igniting the morning sun. He's too close to the goddess's influence. He crosses the street hastily, and reality snaps back.

He tries to cut up Crascuttle Walk, up the worn steps with the rusted black handrail running down the centre, but his path is blocked by a monstrous bull-scorpion creature. An umurshix, they're called. Sacred animals of the father-god, High Umur. Baston can't tell if the monster is sleeping, or meditating, or just unmoving. It's not a natural beast, anyway – it's godspawned. Maybe it only moves when the god wills it.

A bomb under it could kill it, he thinks, remembering the weapons they stole from Dredger's yard. Then he hides that thought as quickly as it came to him. There could be sentinel-spiders nearby, scanning for blasphemous or seditious thoughts. Tiske was right – things were simpler in the old days. Back then, it was enough for a thief to hide from sight. Now, he has to patrol his thoughts, too.

He wonders how many of his neighbours in the Wash have given in and bowed to the Sacred Realm. The occupying forces of Ishmere favour those who convert. More potent, though, is the favour of the gods. Worship Blessed Bol, god of trade, and your business will thrive. Worship Smoke Painter, the divine muse, and your dreams will seep into the waking world. All you have to do is submit, and be exalted.

He breaks his fast in a food hall across the street from Pulchar's restaurant. He hasn't been back there since the raid on Dredger's, since Rasce got them involved in that absurd bar brawl with the Ishmerians. The stupid arrogance of the Ghierdana, drawing attention like that. Baston spends his days hiding from psychic spiders, always holding back, always waiting for his moment, and Rasce just comes in and starts punching.

But damn, it felt good to hit the bastards.

In recent weeks, it's become Baston's habit to go to the church of the Holy Beggar and watch as the congregation spills out through the doors. The crowds grow smaller every week. The Keepers have already abandoned one of the Wash's great churches, the church of St Storm down by the water. How long before some alien god squats in the vestry of the Beggar's sanctum?

This morning, Baston scans the crowd, marking the faces. Some are defiant, but most are furtive, or worse, empty, walking downcast like automatons. They deny the strangeness of the city around them by clinging to old customs and habits.

One face is missing from the crowd – his mother.

Reluctantly, Baston trudges up the hill to Hog Close. The lower Wash is stinking and grimy in a way that defies even miracles. The temple of Blessed Bol had two idols of solid gold outside the doors, two saints so holy they transmuted into precious metal when they perished. Within a day of the statues being installed in the Wash, they were covered in a thick scum of soot and grease and alchemical run-off. (And within a night, one statue was missing its ears, nose and three fingers, and the other had vanished entirely.) Hog Close, though, borders on respectable – literally. It's right up next to a high, sheer wall that divides the Wash from other, better parts of the city. That wall has become the border of the IOZ; another umurshix patrols atop it, an unsleeping guardian monster out of myth prowling at the bottom of the garden of Baston's childhood home.

He lets himself in, unlocking the heavy door. Notes the unwelcome smell of incense.

"If you're here to rob me," calls his mother from upstairs, "my jewellery case is on the table in the front room. First door on the right. If you come upstairs, I shall throw shoes at you."

"It's me," shouts Baston.

"Oh, then ignore the case. All that's left is costume jewellery and contact poison."

"What about the shoes?"

"I haven't decided yet."

He risks it and climbs the stairs. The wallpaper's peeling in places, and there's a damp spot on the plaster that wasn't there last month. There's a portrait on one wall of Karla, standing next to her former betrothed. Karla never speaks of him any more. It wasn't a love match. The boy was the scion of an alchemist family, immensely rich. The match arranged when there was a secret alliance between Heinreil and the guild. All gone now, of course, all the money and connections. No house in Bryn Avane for Karla.

He finds his mother kneeling before a small shrine to the Ishmeric god Smoke Painter. Incense fumes from two braziers coil around her. Multicoloured streamers of smoke twine and dance. Baston coughs.

"Nearly done," says his mother, her eyes closed – in concentration or prayer or just making him wait, he can't tell. The smoke slithers in and out of her nostrils, flows across her face like a veil.

"You weren't at the Holy Beggar this morning."

"You were at Dredger's last week."

Baston considers his response carefully. Elshara Teris spent thirty years married to Hedan, thirty years married to the Brotherhood. Hedan may be two years in the ground, but those connections don't just fade away. She still has connections, still hears whispers in the underworld. At the same time, she was never really part of the Brotherhood, not like Hedan. Not like her children. And she's kneeling in front of an Ishmeric shrine. It would be folly indeed for Baston to hide from the spiders and the spies, only to be turned in by his own mother. If she's gone too far, and fallen under the divine influences of the god . . .

"All right," he concedes, "I'll stop checking up on you, if that's what you want."

"I don't mind what you do, as long as it's you doing it, and not your father." She turns. "What do you think?"

She looks thirty years younger, and radiant. She looks like Karla.

He blows gently in her face, and the illusion dissipates like dust in the wind. Elshara scowls. "Damn, I can't hold it."

"An illusion."

"A miracle of the Smoke Painter, Veiled Master, God of Revelation and Inspiration, Lord of Poets, Dweller in the Room Without Walls, Maker of . . ." She goes a little glassy-eyed as she recites the names, and he gently pokes her in the arm. She recovers and continues talking as if she'd never slipped into that near-trance. "I spent years shivering in the Beggar's church, and never once did the Kept Gods answer any of my prayers. I thought I'd try another."

"You hardly went without," says Baston. This house on Hog Close is one of the largest in the Wash. Not the sort of wealth the Ghierdana have, but rich enough, thanks to the Brotherhood. Every time he visits, though, he spies some empty spot on wall or shelf that once held a treasure, now gone to the pawnshop. How much is she spending on necessities, and how much is on offerings to the gods? "And speaking of – do you need money?"

"Have the dockers started paying more than five coppers a day?" Elshara sniffs. "No, your sister came by earlier, so I don't need anything. Fewer children hovering over me, maybe. I thought Karla had enough to do looking after you. She left a message for you, by the by, in case you called. Said to meet her at the Seamarket Arch at seven."

"You've been talking about me."

"Of course we have. We worry, Bas. It's been a hard few years, but we'll always take care of you."

"I have to go." Baston pauses at the top of the stairs. "You don't need the smoke, you know."

"You think I went to Smoke Painter's temple out of vanity?" Elshara sounds hurt, but as always, Baston can't tell if his mother is genuinely offended or putting on a dramatic performance of her woes. "There's truth in the smoke. The priests have shown me visions."

"A mad god's ravings."

"I can't make you see, Bas. Only you can look into the smoke. Come down to the temple with me."

"I can't."

She snorts. "What, are the boxes getting impatient?"

"I've other things to do."

Elshara turns back to her shrine, throws more incense on the braziers. The smoke begins to braid around her face, again, and Baston wonders how long it will be before he no longer recognises her. She's becoming as strange to him as the Wash, the gods of Ishmere taking yet more from him. Elshara waves her hand through the smoke, studying the shapes that form.

"Be careful, please," she says, without looking at him.

He grunts. He's not the one in danger.

"I mean it. I always told your father, you've got to be a ruthless bastard to hold on to power. Not everyone can do it. Your father, Mercies take his soul, he couldn't. So I told him to stay close to the cleverest, cruelest bastard he could find. If you go up to the New City, Bas, make sure you do the same."

"I can take care of myself."

Elshara clucks her tongue. "You give me crow's feet, you and Karla."

A memory trails across Baston's mind as he leaves Hog Close. It was back before the Armistice, before the Crisis. No New City rising across the skyline of Guerdon, no alien gods planting their nightmare twisted temples amid the ruins. He hadn't recognised the Stone Man waiting for him outside in the dusk. No Stone Man would dare come up to Hog Close.

"Baston, we need to talk." The words were ground out, like he'd got millstones in his throat.

"Gods below – Idgeson?" The face he'd known lost beneath scales, pebble-like scabs, sprouting plates of stone. Only the eyes were recognisable, staring out of that stony mask. "Heinreil's looking for you."

"Heinreil's trying to kill me. He poisoned me. I'm not going to let him get away with it."

"He's not here, if you're looking to kill him." A part of Baston's mind wondered if he'd be willing to kill his friend, and prayed Spar wouldn't push it.

"I'm going to challenge him. For the title of Master." Spar had to gasp out the words, the stone plates pressing on his lungs. He stamped on the ground, sending a shock running through his whole body, shaking the windows of Hog Close. The vibration shook some blockage loose, and he spoke more easily. "I'll see him in Thieves' Court. I know your father's supported Heinreil in the past, and has done well out of it – but I'm asking you, Baston. It's our Brotherhood now. We can make things better. It's time for a change."

"You'll never get the votes. Heinreil's too secure." He tried to convince himself of that, tried to tamp down any embers of hope. The idea that Heinreil could go, that the Brotherhood could be redeemed . . .

"By tomorrow, I'll have Tammur's support," said Spar. "I'll have Tiske's. I'll have the Cafstans. And I've got something Heinreil doesn't have – I've got a saint."

"What saint?"

"Cari. She gets visions – of real things. She can see everyone's secrets. Even Heinreil's, soon. He won't be able to hide anything from me. I can bring him down. It's the right moment to turn the wheel." Quoting his father's writings. "Are you with me? Both of you?"

Baston glanced over his shoulder. Karla had followed him out, and stood there like a shadow, listening to Spar's plea. "Hedan's upstairs," she whispered. "He'll call Heinreil if he sees you, put the Fever Knight on your trail. You've got to go."

"I'll see you at Thieves' Court." Spar drew his hood back over his scaled head, stepped back into the shadows. Moving quietly despite the stone.

"Spar," Baston called after him, "I'm with you." He never knew if Spar heard him.

Two nights later, Spar challenged Heinreil at Thieves' Court, and won. But Heinreil had an insurance policy – a bargain with the Crawling Ones. The best of the Brotherhood died that night in a barrage of death spells.

Baston wasn't there. Karla had convinced him not to go.

The subway in the Wash has not run since the invasion, after Kraken flooded the tunnels. So Baston walks, his long legs carrying him steadily across the district. It starts to rain, a fierce downpour that sends muddy streams cascading down the alleyways. Rats scurry from the drainpipes – the rainwater's picked up some caustic gunk from the clouds, and it makes his eyes sting.

Greyhame Street's up near Holyhill, outside the Ishmeric zone and near the Haithi border. Under the terms of the Armistice, papers must be produced when entering or leaving any of the three occupied zones. Occupying forces from one zone are supposed to stay out of the other two, and require permission to enter the neutral portion of the city. In theory, citizens of Guerdon are supposed to be permitted to enter any of the zones, but unusual movement risks scrutiny. One of the guards at the checkpoint sports a broken nose – from the bar fight, maybe. Baston keeps his head down, tries to avoid showing his face until he's at the head of the queue. There's no watch-priest at this gate – it's Cruel Urid himself, a manifest demigod. Nine feet tall, bird-headed, a beak that can pluck out the hearts of the unworthy.

Urid crows something in a language Baston doesn't know.

"What business among the faithless?" translates one of the priests.

Baston holds out the tail of his coat. "I'm going to see about getting this mended."

Urid croaks, then anoints Baston with oil and lets him pass. The oil smells different – maybe they use different oil down at the other checkpoint, or it's some ritual he doesn't understand, or Urid's presence changes it. Or they know what he intends, and they're marking him. He imagines Urid stalking him through the streets, that curved beak smashing through his breastbone to pluck out his heart.

Somehow, he can't envisage his heart as a beating thing. In his imagination, it's a hollow grey shell, an engine part.

He passes through one of the scarred areas of the city. Buildings so damaged they cannot be repaired, awaiting demolition – and, for those blasted by miracles, exorcism. If he turned left instead of right here, Mercy Street would bring him up past the HOZ, to the place called the Peace Grave. The spot where Pesh, Ishmerian goddess of war, perished. The spot's sealed off, buried in a containment vessel, an empty tomb. Alchemists are still studying it, and it's said that those who were too close to the goddess's death will never be whole again.

The city was too close, says a despairing voice in the back of his mind.

Despite the effects of the war, the city's commercial district still hums. Traders and speculators scrambling over the rubble, ignoring the damage around them. Shares in weapons shipments, in alchemical components, in companies and ventures overseas. More money changes hands here in a day than a thief could hope to steal in a lifetime – a thief from the Wash, anyway.

He climbs up Holyhill, finds the tailor's shop. The place mostly deals in robes for priests and students, a wasteland of grey and black cloth. It reminds him of an old railway tunnel near the Viaduct he knows, a haunt for thousands of bats, all hanging there, wings neatly folded. Sinister, lurking presences.

The young woman behind the counter appears to recognise him. She takes his coat, folding it over her arm like it's an expensive garment and not a filthy rag, and ushers him into a fitting room. There she fishes out a key, opens a cupboard. A magical sigil glows drawn on the wood for an instant, then fades back into invisibility. A mass-produced concealment ward, one of the more recent innovations of the alchemists. Sorcerous sigils drawn by machine.

Inside is another creation of the alchemists. A strange machine, a typewriter awkwardly mated to a glass tank of some glowing fluid. A thick silver cord runs from the base of the machine to a hole drilled in the back of the cupboard.

"Have you used an aethergraph before?"

Baston hasn't. The woman shows him how to position his hands over the keys of the communications device, then presses a switch, and the machine comes to life. He thought it might speak, or show him his interlocutor, but it's stranger than that. While the aethergraph's live, it feels like Sinter is in the room with him, looking over his shoulder, breathing down his neck. He can smell the priest's odour, feel the scratchy robe rubbing against his wrists as he reaches for the keyboard. Baston's fingers move of their own accord, tapping out a message.

REPORT.

He waits for a moment.

Baston's never touched a typewriter before, but the machine compensates, and the words fly from his fingers as fast as he can shape them in his mind. Such a device is dangerous; a stray thought could escape and be transmitted. He guards his thoughts as carefully as he would back in the Wash when the spiders are near.

THE GHIERDANA BURNED DREDGER'S YARD.

GOING AFTER YLIASTER SUPPLIERS.

LIKELY CRADDOCK & SONS NEXT. NEAR TARGETS FIRST.

THEN FOG YARDS.

He can almost hear Sinter lick his dry lips. Baston's knuckles twinge with phantom stiffness as the echo of the priest's hands moves his own fingers over the keyboard.

RETURN HERE IN ONE WEEK, replies Sinter.

Baston types again, his fingers stabbing the keys. ONE JOB.

The reply comes quickly, and carries the echo of a sadistic smile. DO YOU KNOW WHAT THE GHIERDANA DO TO INFORMANTS?

And then the light from the machine fades, and the sense of the priest's presence is gone. The girl returns instantly. She bustles about, handing Baston his mended coat, closing up the cupboard with its secret machine. Baston just sits there, admiring the neatness of the trap. Once, no one would have dared treat him like this. The Brotherhood looked after its own. The city watch had tried to find someone to inform on Heinreil for years, and never succeeded. Everyone knew that the protection of the Brotherhood meant more in the Wash than anything the city watch could offer, knew that the Brotherhood's threats had more bite. But all that's changed now. The Brotherhood's gone, leaving Baston as a man without a roof, without a shield against the powers that stalk the city.

All very neat. But Sinter doesn't see everything. The priest may have his spies and watchers, but he doesn't know everything. He doesn't know Baston's soul. That's the last redoubt, the one place they can't reach.

"See you next week," he mutters to the girl as he leaves the tailor's, and he can't help but wonder if that's a lie.

Karla's waiting for him around the corner from the Seamarket.

"Rasce wants to see us," whispers Karla, "another job."

"Craddock's."

"Yeah. They want to see us up on Lanthorn Street. Tiske was right – this is the chance we've been waiting for. We'll stick close to the Ghierdana boy and grow strong again. Better days are coming." Karla's excited by the prospect, her eyes bright as she looks up at the shining citadel of the New City. Baston, though, feels the familiar grime of the Wash cling to him, call to him. These are his streets, the old lanes and wynds and alleys between Castle Hill and the docks. He was made for these streets, not that eerie labyrinth. His feet drag as he approaches the border, but Karla pulls him onwards.

They cross into the New City. The Eshdana at the checkpoint recognises them, waves them through, and from there it's only a short walk to Rasce's headquarters. A short walk in the New City, of course, is always a confusing and tangled thing, but that's to their advantage – any pursuers would be shaken by the twisted route they take through the shimmering arcades.

Baston pauses outside the house. It's uncannily similar to his mother's, to all the houses along Hog Close. It looks like a ghost of a house, a pale apparition in stone.

Karla doesn't hesitate, and walks straight in.

INTERLUDE I

The aethergraph on Eladora Duttin's desk spits out a brief message, wreathed in Sinter's distinctive combination of musty odours and spite. HEDANSON IN.

Eladora sits back in her chair and allows her eyes to close for a blessed moment of rest. The situation with the Ghierdana is an unwelcome distraction from other, more important duties, and it's a relief to know that their stratagem is working. There's something satisfying, too, about using one brutish criminal to counter another.

The work continues. Officially, Eladora is the city's special thaumaturgist, in charge of regulating sorcery. She picks up a stack of applications for licences to practise magic and leafs through them. A few renewals. A greater number of cancellations – sorcery takes its toll. She skims them all, then scribbles her approval on each.

The new applications are of more interest. All from newcomers to the city, refugees from the Godswar or agents of occupying powers. They'll go to the minister of security for investigation. There are less than a dozen, all told. Kelkin wants to put a law through parliament rescinding the right of the alchemists' guild to internally regulate its own sorcerers, instead putting them back under the thumb of the special thaumaturgist.

Eladora wonders if she'll still be in this seat when that happens.

She wraps the stack of new applications in a length of purple ribbon and walks out to her assistant in the outer office.

"Rhiado? I'm going to walk over to Minister Nemon's office."

"Excuse me, miss, but you've a visitor."

Waiting for her is a round-faced little man, red-cheeked, his black robes mottled with spilled droplets of bleach or acid. A golden eye-and-flask chain of office around his neck, studded with gems.

Of course, they had to make a new chain. The old one was lost with Rosha in the Crisis.

"Guildmaster Helmont," says Eladora, curtseying. "Forgive me, I didn't know you'd made an an appointment."

"Oh, I haven't, I haven't. This is just a brief social call. May we?" He gestures back towards Eladora's office.

"Of course."

She stuffs the applications into a warded drawer and checks to ensure the aethergraph is locked down before settling back into her chair. Helmont – the master of the alchemists' guild – waits patiently until she's done.

"You never considered a career in alchemy?" he asks.

"No."

"A pity. I'm sure you'd have done very well in the Crucible."

The alchemists' guild holds tests for schoolchildren at the age of fourteen; those who meet the grade have their further education paid for. For the worthy, an apprenticeship and a lifelong career in the guild. "My m-mother never let me attend the Crucible."

"Well, you've risen very high, nonetheless. Still, what might have been, eh?

Eladora considers the man as she clears her desk. From what she understands, Helmont was a compromise candidate – elevated as a caretaker guildmaster. A cautious, plodding lab worker, not a brilliant mind or respected captain of industry like his predecessors. The weakest master, her informants tell her, since the founding of the guild.

"What can I do for you, Guildmaster?"

"Nothing. I'd like you to do exactly nothing. Simplest thing in the world."

"In connection to . . . "

"The guild intends to recover certain treasures that were buried under the New City when the Alchemists' Quarter was destroyed. Valuable experiments, relics of the guild, and whatnot." He waves his hand, as if he's talking about mere trifles – not the remaining god-bombs, or Guildmistress Rosha's phylactery, or all the other horrors entombed there. "I'll put a proposal before the security committee. I just want you to refrain from objecting to it."

Eladora gives him a pinched smile. "Guildmaster, you know that previous attempts to open that vault met with disaster. In any event, the vault's beneath the Lyrixian Occupation Zone and any intrusion would endanger the peace."

His face falls theatrically. "Oh, I see. I see. Endangering the peace, yes, that would be a grave concern." He rubs his jaw. "You know, I've heard the strangest rumour. Damnedest thing. I've heard that *you've* already done exactly what *I* propose to do. Broke into the vault under the New City and looted the place."

"I- I," begins Eladora, but Helmont rolls on.

"Nonsense, I'm sure. I mean, you'd have to have the help of the ghouls, wouldn't you, to pass through their domain and open the vault?" He sniffs the air. "By the by, have you seen Lord Rat lately? Or does he not show up in person any more? Maybe you've recently met one of his proxy mouthpieces. I understand you and he worked together closely during the invasion."

"Lord Rat," says Eladora, "serves the city. As do I. Now, if you'll excuse me, Guildmaster." She rises.

"Now, if you had taken those relics from the vault," says Helmont, almost to himself, "you'd need somewhere to store them and repair them. And it's not like you've got an alchemical factory under this desk." He raps the desk with his knuckles. "Or down in your little prison in the Wash."

Eladora probes with her mind, invoking a little sorcery. Unsurprisingly, Helmont's chain of office is woven with potent countermeasures. Her spells have no chance of piercing his defences. She sits back down, her fingers resting on the handle of a desk drawer.

"Where indeed could you keep such dangerous alchemical relics? Oh!" Helmont feigns a gasp of revelation. "You also know Johan Mandel, don't you?"

"Mr Mandel is a family friend."

"Of course, of course. Nothing untoward there. A friend of your father's, no doubt. I'm sure Mandel had lots in common with ... what was it? Ah, a dairy farmer in Wheldacre."

Eladora loses what patience she had with Helmont's feints and insinuations. "Mr Mandel is a member of your own guild, is he not? If you have questions, speak to him. I have work to do."

"You're so *clever*, Miss Thay!" Helmont claps his hands. "That's exactly what I'll do. I'll speak to Mandel. It's an internal *guild* matter, after all. Nothing you need to *concern* yourself with. You just do *nothing*, like I said."

"If I did nothing," snaps Eladora, "the Godswar would consume you. Good day, Guildmaster. You can see yourself out."

Helmont grins. "Before I go, I have a present for you. I understand you're a historian." He claps his hands, and Rhiado enters carrying a wooden box. "We found this when clearing out some old stores. It's at least a hundred years old."

He opens the box. Inside is a glass jar, two feet high, sealed with a wooden lid. Brimming with murky liquid. A figure floats in the jar – a figurine of a naked youth, blue-tinged, a waxy sheen to its flesh. "It's a homunculus," says Helmont. "One of the first attempts by the guild to produce artificial life." He taps the jar, and the creature's eyes flicker open. It swims to the glass, peering out.

Its features remind Eladora of Miren.

"You know," muses Helmont, "back then, they used horseshit. To get the right temperature, you see. They buried the jar in warm horseshit so the homunculus would grow. Nowadays, we have athanors and furnaces and spawning vats. I think it's good to remember our roots. To remember the guild was founded in horseshit, but moved on to greater things. We can always move on." He bows. "I'll have words with Mandel. Good day, Special Thaumaturgist Duttin."

After Helmont goes, escorted out briskly by loyal Rhaido, Eladora contemplates the homunculus in its jar. The thing stares back at her, its beautiful features impassive. Homunculi are mindless and soulless, but they can be animated with magic, used as an extension of a sorcerer's will. Is the thing listening to her? She imagines it crawling out of its jaw in the dead of night, unscrewing the jar from within, creeping naked and dripping through the corridors to relay its stolen secrets to Helmont. Imagines it finding her in her bed by night, and cutting her throat.

She opens the drawer and takes out her gun. A twin to the one she lent to Carillon. Sturdy, reliable, unassuming. Easily overlooked, just like Eladora.

She opens the jar, removes the twitching homunculus.

Eladora smashes the wax effigy with the butt of the gun, beating it into a waxy pulp.

History no longer concerns her. The future is coming too fast for her to look back, even for an instant.

CHAPTER ELEVEN

Early evening in occupied Guerdon.

Across the city, in the Fog Yards and the New Alchemists District, the whistles sound a shift change. Workers spill out of the factories, a human tide pouring through the streets, breaking into tributaries that fill the taverns and the playhouses, waterwheels of commerce. They pour down spiral stairs into underground rivers where the subway trains thunder. They pool in Venture Square. Different districts of the city flow with their own colours – the grey cassocks of the university students, the tawdry sequinned glamour of Glimmerside, black suits and starched collars of parliament clerks. It's hard to distinguish one droplet of life from another, when they all mix in the churning rivers that race down the streets.

But the rivers are dammed, and cannot flow free. At the borders of each of the occupation zones are checkpoints and guard posts, each according to their own methodologies. In the Haithi zone, it's all regimented, with undead soldiers, bureaucratic ledgers, an arrangement of chits and passes, while Ishmere's borders are watched by gods and monsters. The routes into the Lyrixian Occupation Zone are guarded, too – some by Lyrixian soldiers, nervously holding on to this little foothold on the edge of the city. Others by Ghierdana thugs, hungry for bribes.

The flow of those rivers of life is strangled. The city's arteries cut.

Spar sees all this, and now he can know all this, too. For months, his mind was broken and scattered, unable to form a coherent thought. Now, suddenly, he has focus. A fixed point of reference, one that is here and now.

Rasce. Rasce of the Ghierdana.

It's the second time Spar has gone through this strange experience of reintegration, and it's very different this time. The first time it happened, after he died, after the Gutter Miracle, it was Cari who saved him, and she did it deliberately. She reached out and found him in the darkness, and pulled him back into awareness. She went looking for him, took him by the hand and led him back to life, or whatever bizarre quasi-life he has now – the embodied spirit of the New City.

Cari, he calls, *can you hear me?*

Nothing. He didn't think she would be able to hear him. She's half the world away, and Spar's reach is limited to the New City.

Rasce, though, isn't even fully aware of Spar. It's more like the two have become entangled, like Rasce blundered through a dark alleyway and emerged with Spar's mind clinging to him like a cobweb on his sleeve.

He feels as fragile as a cobweb. Spar strained himself with miracles during the invasion, spent his power profligately. He's not a god – all he had was the stolen divine potency of the Black Iron Gods, and he's used up all he could carry. For now, he can only observe through a hundred thousand windows, a hundred thousand eyes.

Spar watches Baston visit the house on Lanthorn Street. Rasce now keeps a little snuffbox of ash taken from the ruins of Dredger's yard on his desk. Spar wonders how much of Tiske is mixed into that black dust.

Baston doesn't take the ash, but some of the other thieves from the Wash do.

Spar finds that he's able to watch Baston without falling into the traps of memory – Rasce keeps him anchored in the present.

Rasce, can you hear me? he calls. Rasce shivers, like Spar's thought is a breath on the back of his neck, but he still cannot hear.

Cari couldn't hear Spar either, at first. It took time to build that connection. He can afford patience, even as Rasce paces the halls of the house on Lanthorn Street (his footsteps echoing through Spar like a new heartbeat), eager to press on with his campaign. Spar can share Rasce's excitement – and his fears. Anticipation of the dragon's return is a constant presence in the back of Rasce's mind, the shadow of great wings. Fragments of emotion bleed through.

Why Rasce? Spar can only guess. He's not a god, but the terminology of sainthood is all he has to use. From what he knows, gods don't exactly choose their saints – it's a question of potential, like lightning striking the tallest point in the landscape. It can be the work of a moment, too. Cari's Aunt Silva was a Safidist, an adherent of the branch of the Keeper's church who sought sainthood. She diligently performed the rites, offered sacrifices, mortified her flesh, but the gods ignored her for years until that lighting flash finally came. And then, once the connection was established, it endured even after Silva's mind was broken. Compare that to Saint Aleena, who had no time for rituals or worship, who was endlessly profane in every sense of the word – but for one moment she'd attracted the attention of the gods, and that was enough to bond her to the gods for the rest of her life.

So, why Rasce? Spar and the Ghierdana are both of similar age – well, Spar's been dead for two years, but set that aside for now. They're both heirs to criminal dynasties. Spar's father Idge was master of the Brotherhood; Rasce's Chosen of the Dragon. Was that enough for a moment of congruency?

If Spar could choose, he would not pick Rasce. The Ghierdana boy may have had a similar upbringing, but they're very different men. Rasce has no love for the people of Guerdon, no thought of a higher calling. He'd pick another connection instead. Baston, maybe. They were friends, before Spar's illness, before Baston became the

Fever Knight's lieutenant. There were others Spar would have chosen before Baston, but most of them are dead. Can he give Baston that saint's grace, instead?

He reaches out with his soul. Exerts his will as best he can.

Baston, can you hear me?

Nothing. He pushes harder, slips – and now it's a day later. Maybe two. Mid-morning, and Rasce's walking out of the New City, passing the checkpoints along the border. Spar's disorientated, his consciousness as slippery as wet soap. He clings to Rasce with what strength he can muster, desperate to avoid those chasms of oblivion.

He can't let himself fall again.

Rasce shivers as icy raindrops trickle past his collar and run down his back. Another advantage of soaring above the clouds denied to him. No wonder everyone in Guerdon seems to wear hooded cloaks or drab, heavy coats. Streams gush from the drainpipes, making the pavement a series of rivers that must be forded. This afternoon's downpour has emptied the streets of Glimmerside. Only a few hardy souls can be seen on the street, and half of them are his Brotherhood recruits. Baston strides along just ahead of Rasce and Vyr, and Rasce can almost imagine him growling faintly. Karla's already gone ahead, to keep watch on Craddock's.

Vyr sniffles into a handkerchief. "I need to stop along here for a moment," he says. "An errand for my father."

"As you wish." They're in the free city, but he and Vyr are the only Ghierdana members of this little expedition, and he's not expecting trouble. Burning Dredger's yard was the artillery barrage; today, they're bonepicker priests, collecting the souls of the fallen.

The streets here are lined with bookshops, stationers, cafés. Tailors with academic robes and tasselled hats in their windows, makers of alchemical paraphernalia, dealers in reagents and relics. Rasce notes the shimmer of yliaster amid jars of other alchemical substances – dilute phlogiston, aetherated salt, tincture of divinity, mother's milk, sweetened vitriol. Vials and syringes of alkahest, the drug that the Stone Men use to slow the progress of their horrible disease.

Vyr enters a curious little establishment. At first, Rasce mistakes it for a jewellers', but when he wipes away the rain that beads the heavy slate-glass window, he discovers it's a dealer in prosthetics. A display of mechanical arms, peg legs carved from wood or bone, alchemist-grown organs floating in life-support jars. A partially disassembled suit of armour, like Dredger's. A peeling sign pasted to the door gives notice that priority will be given to accredited members of the alchemists' guild, and no charity will be extended to victims of war or industrial accident.

In the dim shop beyond, he can see Vyr arguing with the maker of mechanical limbs.

Rasce crosses the street to a little newspaper kiosk, nods at the haggard crone behind the counter, and takes a copy of the *Guerdon Observer* off the table. He starts to walk away.

"Thief! Thief," she croaks, "two coppers!"

Of course – he has to pay. Back on the isles of the Ghierdana, no one would dare charge the Chosen of the Dragon for anything. Even in the New City, most now know better than to ask him for coin.

Rasce gives the woman a gold coin, worth enough to buy the kiosk and all its contents. Gives her a smile, too, a dragon's smile, with the promise of teeth.

The headlines, pleasingly, are still dominated by the fire at Dredger's yard. Fears of contamination from the toxic smoke. It's not the first such incident in recent years, and Rasce's lost count of the number of infants he's seen with twisted limbs or other malformations. Among the wealthy, gilded gas masks have become a fashionable accessory.

The newspaper does not mention the Ghierdana in connection with the attack on Dredger, which does not surprise Rasce. The truce between Guerdon and the three occupying powers is a delicate one, and everyone knows that Lyrix's main contribution to the balance of power comes from the dragons. Openly accusing the Ghierdana of the crime would risk the peace, even if everyone knows the Ghierdana are responsible. A gap in the armour, and the knife goes in. He imagines parliament sending out its agents, bribing and threatening and whispering, trying to right the ship of state.

Speed is of the essence. He needs to get this done before Great-Uncle returns, but also before the authorities push back at him. If he seizes the yliaster trade quickly enough, then parliament will have no choice but to bless this new status quo.

Empty eye sockets watch him from across the street. Skull-faced undead sentries from Haith. Glimmerside's on the edge of the Haithi Occupation Zone. If he climbs up Holyhill, he'll be in their territory – and Haith doesn't have the same compunctions about maintaining the truce. The rules of the Armistice are clear – if one of the three powers breaks the truce, the other two are compelled to ally against the offender. Walking into Haithi territory could be enough of a provocation to start the war.

Rasce gives them a cheery wave and crosses back to meet Vyr.

"Still not finished," grumbles Vyr. "It needs a specialist sorcerer to enchant it. Five thousand just for the consultation."

"And they call us criminals."

They walk side by side through the rain, shadowed by the body-guards. High atop the hill to their right, emerging from the rain like snow-capped mountains, are three great cathedrals of the Kept Gods. The singing of a great choir, slightly ragged, drifts down from the churches like incense.

"I'm told they never used to do that," murmurs Vyr, "until the Ishmerians came. Now the singing never stops."

Craddock & Sons is situated off a steep lane that runs down to Venture Square. Lawyers, speculators, brokers – and dealers in alchemical reagents. Unlike Dredger, the warehouses of Craddock & Sons are far across the city, in the Fog Yards. Their offices, though, are within reach of the Ghierdana.

At a nod from Rasce, the Eshdana go in first. Rough men in grey cloaks swarm the office in a practised flurry, a swarm of pugnacious fish, each man with a task assigned. Sweep for guards. Secure the back exit. Keep the staff quiet. Close the door once the boss is in.

The heavy door shuts behind Rasce. He scans the office, desks of dark wood laden with papers and ledgers, alchemical weapons and supplies reduced to notes and sigils. A dozen clerks of varying ages, ink-spots on their shirts, eyes wide. One fellow attempted to make a break for it, and is now hunched over in his chair, clutching a broken nose. Otherwise, no damage or injuries, and every ash-marked is in their assigned place. Good. Executed with military discipline.

Judging by their chins and thinning hair, three of the clerks are Craddock's sons. "Those three."

Three ash-marked move to mark the three sons. One of whom actually shakes his fist at Rasce.

"You won't get away with this!" he blusters from behind his desk.

"Yes, they will," calls a voice from the inner office. "I'm in here. And don't break anything else, please."

Craddock's hair has gone entirely, and his chin is lost behind his white beard, but there's a keen intelligence in his eyes. Rasce sits down – then, on second thoughts, shifts the heavy chair a few inches to the right, just in case Craddock picked up some negotiation tips from Dredger.

Vyr drifts to the window behind Craddock, checks the alleyway outside, then closes the blinds.

"Well, then," says Craddock, "do you have terms, or should I dig up my old agreements? I've been in business long enough to know the score."

"We have terms," says Rasce, "but you shall find them reasonable. A small fee to ensure that your yards are safe from the same fate as Dredger's – and two conditions. First, you'll henceforth buy your yliaster from us, and only from us."

Craddock narrows his eyes. "Yliaster? At what rate?"

Rasce waves his hand dismissively. "A reasonable one, I'm sure. Cheaper than the blood of your sons."

"There's no need for such threats. As I said, I've done this before. The Brotherhood. And later I paid the tallow-tax to the alchemists. Hah! The protection money was cheaper. What's your other demand?"

Rasce produces the snuffbox, offers the ash. "You know what this means?"

Craddock's hand shakes. "I did business in Severast, too, before the war. I dealt with the Ghierdana there. Aye, I know what it means to take the ash, and what will happen if I break my word to you."

"Terrible," says Vyr softly, "is the vengeance of the dragon."

In a quick spasm of motion, Craddock takes a smear of ash and rubs it across his forehead. "Done, then."

"Two down," says Rasce.

Vyr glances back down the street. Craddock and his belligerent son stand in the doorway. The rain has already washed away much of the ash from the old man's forehead. "He didn't seem as cowed as I'd have liked."

"He's taken the ash. That gives him a measure of indulgence. Let him keep face, so long as he does as he is told." Rasce glances to his left, looking north across the side of Holyhill. He can dimly make out the shape of the Duchess Viaduct that runs between Holyhill and Castle Hill, although the fog makes the structure look like some primordial serpent-monster, a dragon about to assail the Parliament. Somewhere beyond that, lost in the smoke clouds and serried rooftops, are the Fog Yards. "I have it in my mind to go for Mandel & Company soon. Vorz listed them as the largest supplier of yliaster to the guild. Great-Uncle may return more swiftly than we expect, and we must be ready."

"Our new recruits haven't taken the ash yet," grumbles Vyr, loud enough for Baston to hear. "We cannot rely on them until they do.

There are many smaller dealers, closer to the LOZ. We should consolidate our holdings first before risking the Fog Yards."

"Have faith, Vyr," says Rasce.

Baston stands at Rasce's shoulder like a dour shadow. "You should get back to the New City."

"Indeed. You know, I think I am growing to like the place."

They head back along Philosopher's Street, the New City rising before then. The rain slackens off, rays of sunlight breaking through the clouds and turning the towers to blazing pillars. Once they secure Mandel's supply of yliaster, the job will be mostly done. Great-Uncle will return, and he'll lift Rasce from these streets, return him to his proper place as Chosen of the Dragon. Vorz can oversee the dull details of the yliaster trade, and whatever intrigues and schemes he intends.

Or, perhaps someone other than Vorz. The Dentist has grown arrogant and must be shown his place. The ash buys a measure of indulgence, but only a measure. Once Great-Uncle returns, Rasce will suggest that Vorz be placed in charge of the yliaster trade, and someone more suitable be given his role as adviser. Someone who knows Guerdon, if the Ghierdana are to have a permanent presence here in the New City.

Baston, maybe, once he takes the ash. Or Karla. The idea of an alliance with her certainly has its appeal. It's strange how comfortable Rasce feels with the two of them, as though he's known them both for a long time.

Someone calls his name.

He stops, looks around. The whole procession of thieves stops, fanning out across the pavements.

"What is it?" asks Baston.

"You spoke."

Baston shakes his head, confused. Vyr flinches and looks up at the clouds.

Rasce. There. Danger.

Rasce's vision fractures, like he's looking at the world through broken glass. Simultaneously, he's standing on Philosopher's Street, surrounded by his guards, but he's also looking down on himself from the heights, his attention focused on one rooftop – *there*.

A brief glimpse – a humanoid figure, long, spindly limbs, clad in rags – and then the thing's leaping, flinging itself from the roof of a nearby hostel to land right next to Rasce. Face burning with its own inner flame, the wax of its skull burned paper-thin in places. The horror's got a dagger in its pale hand, and it stabs at him, moving inhumanly quickly.

The first shallow cut opens up his forearm, spraying blood across the Tallowman's thin ribs. The monster raises its knife, then freezes for a split second, the flame in its wax skull flickering as if in thought, an instant of hesitation that gives Baston time to tackle it. He's bigger than it, heavier. The pair go down in a tangle of legs, but the Tallowman's quicker. It slithers free, stabs at Baston's back once, twice, but its thrusts aren't able to penetrate the armour he wears beneath his shirt.

Rasce tries to go for his own knife, the dragon-tooth blade, but his wounded arm betrays him. His fingers are slick with his own blood, and he drops the knife. Falls backwards as the Tallowman slashes at him. The Tallowman's burning bright now, head flaring with murder-lust. The guards in disarray, trying to grapple with the nimble assassin that prances madly around them, dagger flashing in the fresh sun. A scream as one of the thieves loses his fingers to the wicked blade. Some of them strike at the Tallowman, but they can't injure it. Wounds in the wax close instantly.

Baston's up again, attacking the Tallowman from behind. He gets his forearm across the creature's throat in a chokehold, and pulls with all his might. The Tallowman doesn't need to get air to its lungs – if it even has lungs – but Baston tugs with such force that the waxy neck stretches, pulling apart, gooey strands of wax snapping and parting. Rasce ducks forward, scoops up the dragon-tooth blade – and the Tallowman kicks him in the face, sending him sprawling once more. Again, it twists free of Baston's grasp, scrabbles across the pavement on all fours like some nightmare insect, melting face scuttling ever closer.

It's on top of Rasce now, pinning him, hot wax dripping on him. The dagger's in its wax hand, and then it slashes him across the throat, quick and neat.

No pain. No blood.

He feels the blade skitter off the skin of his throat, but he's uncut.

The Tallowman frowns, opens its mouth, and a bubble of hot wax bursts on its lips. It drops the dagger, tries another murderous approach. Fingers – horribly soft and malleable, boneless, but terribly strong – close around Rasce's throat. The other hand probing at his nose, his mouth, fingers slipping past his lips, closing his nostrils.

Rasce fights for air. He slams his fist into the monster's side, tries to push it off him, but it's locked on tight. The other thieves are there, too, but somehow they're very, very far away even as they tug at the Tallowman's limbs, to no avail.

Vyr's shouting. Baston's shouting. Where's Karla? He'd like to see Karla.

The heat of the Tallowman's blazing wick on his face is like Great-Uncle's fire.

The dagger is by your left hand, says a voice in his head. Blindly, he reaches out, finds the dragon-tooth. He stabs it into the Tallow, and there's a hot gush of molten wax, an inhuman bubbling shriek, but the monster doesn't let go.

Then Baston takes the dagger from him, and drives it into the Tallowman's spine, severing the wick. The wax horror spasms, limbs flailing until the flame in its skull goes out. Wax mingles with blood and rainwater on the pavement of Philosopher's Street.

Voices, all around him, but Rasce can't move. A tremendous exhaustion suddenly lands on him. He feels drained, his energy utterly sapped. His limbs as distant as the towers of the New City, as heavy as stone. It's like he's falling away down some deep shaft into darkness, leaving everyone far behind. The voices of his companions echoing down from far, far above.

Vyr, angry and accusing. Snatching the dragon-tooth blade away from Baston.

Karla, running up. Cursing herself for arriving late. Cradling Rasce's wounded arm, his blood welling up between her fingers.

More shouting. Baston, intercepting a carriage in the middle of Philosopher's Street, throwing the driver down into the gutter. Hands, lifting him. But all so far away as the stone drags him down.

That night, Rasce's dreams are confused. Usually, he dreams of flight, but not now. The dreams are vivid and insistent, pressing on his brain, less like passing fancies and more like a cavalcade of unwelcome spirits that sit on his chest and show him visions, some of which he would rather not see. Over and over, he dreams of the people who live along the dockside wards of the New City. Acrid smoke from the burning yards blowing in their windows, leaving streaks of black soot on the white walls of the New City. They cough and wheeze, breathe through dampened clothes or flee their tainted homes. Children in their beds, retching. Childen, found stiff and cold in the morning.

Another vision. Black smoke from the burning yards mixes with the rain to coat the world in ash.

Black smoke from cities scorched by dragon-fire coats the world in ash.

Through the haze, he sees Baston and Karla on the streets of the Wash, far below. She's gesturing up at the New City, at the Ishmerian temples that dominate the skyline of the Wash. They fall silent as a stalking spider moves down the street, then resume their argument. Baston's sullen and impassive, but Karla's face is animated, passionate; Rasce feels a great swelling of lust for her, suddenly, and the dream fragments and shifts. Now she's in bed with him, limbs intertwined with his, coiling around him, the heat of her body like a naked flame, and he's not sure if this is part of the dream or the waking world. He pushes into her, eagerly. Her face changes – it's a different woman, dark-haired instead, a knife in her hand. There's a knife in his hand, too, his Great-Uncle's dragon-tooth dagger.

The dream shatters. Rasce wakes for an instant – he's in his room in the house on Lanthorn Street, his sheets soaked with sweat. The stone walls of the room are ablaze with light. They flow and crack, like melting ice. There's liquid beading on their surface, caustic and foul-smelling. Alkahest, some distant part of his brain identifies it.

He tries to struggle out of bed, but his limbs become immeasurably heavy, like he's turned to stone. He falls back, and as soon as he hits the pillow he's asleep again.

Rasce falls. He's in a tunnel now, alone. He snarls, furious to have been snatched away from pleasure. Greenish walls, marked with carvings scratched into the stone over thousands of years. Pitch-dark, but he can still see. He can see gradations of darkness – the fragile cobweb darkness that fills the void when the light leaves, darkness so small that it can be banished with starlight. The settled darkness that accretes over time, leaving a patina of grime, a deep chill that never quite goes away. The thick, hoary darkness of the old tunnels, where no one has dared bring a light for generations. The darkness of the deeps that has learned to slither. Ghoul tunnels.

Out of that darkness comes a huge figure. Hunched, but still its horned head scrapes the ceiling. Massive cloven-hoofed feet, the stench of its rank fur filling the tunnel, claws scratching against the tunnel wall – and Rasce can feel the sensation of the claws against stone, like they're skittering across his ribcage.

The elder ghoul, Lord Rat of Guerdon.

Rat stops, sniffs the air of the tunnel. Its yellow eyes pass over Rasce without seeing him, like he's not really there.

The ghoul opens its massive maw, but it doesn't speak. Instead,

Rasce feels pressure at his own throat, invisible fingers forcing his mouth open, seizing his tongue.

SPAR? HOW IS THIS POSSIBLE? HAS CARILLON RETURNED?

There's no response – no spoken one, anyway. But the earth creaks, and dust falls from the ceiling of the tunnel.

THEY HAVE OPENED THE VAULT. TAKEN THE BLACK IRON BELLS, AND THE RUINS OF THE ALCHEMISTS' QUARTER. THERE WAS NO CHOICE.

The weapons Artolo sought! Great-Uncle commanded Artolo to find the weapons of black iron – and that failure doomed Artolo. But who is the Rat talking about?

The horned ghoul sniffs the air. Yellow eyes peer into the darkness.

A low growl.

YOU ARE NOT CARILLON THAY.

CHAPTER TWELVE

V yr snarls in Baston's face. "My cousin's blood is the blood of the dragon, and it has been spilled on the streets. This is an unforgivable insult – and an unforgivable failure."

Vyr sounds a lot tougher when he's got half a dozen Eshdana backing him up. All Lyrixian by the look of them. Two of them wear black jewels on their foreheads, symbolic reminders that they're ash-bought.

"I snuffed the bloody Jack," snaps Baston.

"After it maimed four other men. After it nearly killed my cousin. It's a miracle he survived. You failed to protect us."

"It was a fucking Tallowman, Vyr," argues Karla. "No one's seen a candlejack in more than a year. They're all supposed to be gone. How could we have known?"

Vyr's gaze is reptilian in its coldness as he turns his attention to Karla. "Your absence was noted, too. You should have seen the danger. You also failed the Ghierdana."

"I'm going to talk to Rasce," says Karla, stepping towards the door.

"No. The doctors are attending to him." Vyr folds his hands tightly in front of him. "Your services are no longer required by my family, and neither of you have taken the ash. If you are found on this size of the LOZ border by nightfall, your lives are forfeit. The same applies to any associates of yours."

"I see what this is!" shouts Karla. "You're trying to take over!" She addresses the Eshdana standing behind Vyr. "You all see it, right? You see what this shit is doing?"

"If you speak again," says Vyr, "I shall have your tongue torn out."

"And how are you going to get to the Fog Yards without us? None of those louts can cross the border!"

"That's none of your concern."

"You fucking need us, you idiot!" shouts Karla, loud enough to be heard upstairs.

"Her tongue," orders Vyr.

One of the Eshdana lunges at Karla. Baston grabs the man's wrist, pulls him off balance, punches him in the throat, leaves him gasping on the floor. The other Eshdana draw blades, but they hesitate to attack. Baston shakes his head. "We'll go."

"No!" Karla protests, but the Ghierdana close ranks. Baston takes his sister by the arm, pulls her out of the room. No one stops them walking out of the ghost-house, although the sniper on the top floor tracks them as they walk down Lanthorn Street in the pouring rain. It's dusk already, the New City beginning to glow faintly beneath their feet.

"Little Ghierdana shit," complains Karla. "He'll have the fucking leeches bleed Rasce dead. What a disaster!" She keeps ranting all the way down the street, but Baston's hardly listening.

"Where," he asks, "do you think that Tallowman came from?"

"I don't know. What, you think Vyr sent it? Where would Vyr get a Tallowman?"

The idea is nonsense. The things were made by the alchemists' guild, hired out to Guerdon's city watch. Each Tallowman was human once, a condemned thief. Heinreil's bargain with the alchemists meant the old Brotherhood paid a secret tithe to the guild – as long as Heinreil handed over a few bodies every month for the vats, the Brotherhood was permitted to continue its criminal ways. But Heinreil's in prison, and the vats were shut down years ago, the monsters banished from the city. The alchemists are banned from making new ones, too. There are still a few left, Baston's heard, guarding the new factories, but there shouldn't be any on the streets.

It was an old Tallowman, its wax thin and flaky. The things had to be remade every few weeks to replenish their waxy bodies. Could this one have somehow survived all those months, rotting in some attic? But why attack Rasce? No, far more plausible is that someone must have activated an old Tallowman, relit its wick and sent it on a new mission. But who else knew that Rasce would be visiting Craddock & Sons? *We only require information from you, nothing more. If action is warranted, we have our own resources.*

The thought weighs heavily on Baston's shoulders. He tries to tell himself that it's not his fight – if Duttin and her cabal want to plot against the Ghierdana, it's none of his concern. He hasn't taken the ash, neither has Karla. And any prospect of an alliance between the Brotherhood and the invaders is dead now, washed away into the gutters up on Philosopher's Street.

The coil inside him snaps. The machine's finally broken.

To hell with them all.

"Tell our lot," says Baston, "that they need to get back to the Wash before nightfall. I'm going home to rest up."

"Are you all right?" asks Karla, face full of concern.

"Just a few cuts."

"I won't be back tonight," she says, "but I'll see you tomorrow. We'll figure out what to do next."

Baston descends, trading the strange, shimmering heights of the New City for what should be the familiar streets of the Wash. The streets of his boyhood, the streets he knew, now turned monstrous. He steps over rubble, passes buildings scarred by claws or bullets or explosion. Skirts around pools of rainwater – the razor-edged water of the Kraken has mostly retreated, but he's seen unwary travellers cut their feet to ribbons by splashing through the wrong puddle. The Ishmerian temples are crowded this evening – he can hear the chanting of the priests, the ecstatic responses of the crowds. He wonders if there's some reason behind this intensity. Have the Ishmerians won some victory in some other part of the Godswar or is it one of their seemingly unending parade of holy days? Flames leap from the great sacrificial brazier atop Smoke Painter's pyramid, hissing and crackling far above, lighting up the rooftops. He passes the former cathedral of St Storm, now a temple to the Kraken. Dark shapes swim on the far side of the stained-glass windows. Kraken-cultists shamble past him along the alleyways that run down to the sea. They look bloated, the touch of the god slowly turning them into something inhuman.

The dockside taverns are busy, too, crowded with people sheltering from the downpour. He walks past the lighted doorways, keeps walking in the rain. The clouds are so dark it's hard to tell when the day finally slips into evening.

The few people who recognise Baston know better than to get in his way. In moods like this, he walks. He walks like he can outpace the darkness that follows him, as if it's a black cloak that might be torn from his shoulders if he moves fast enough. He walks until his legs ache, but the city's still wrapped around him, clutching at him.

Karla, he tells himself, will be fine no matter what happens. His sister always lands on her feet, and she'll take care of their mother. He comes to Sumpwater Square, an unexpected opening in the narrow streets of the Wash. Tenement blocks rise from all four sides of the square like sheer cliffs pockmarked with narrow windows. Water pours down the storm drains, gurgling into the entombed rivers under Guerdon.

He moves faster now, heading for the heart of the old Wash. The worst of the rookeries, streets the city watch never dared go. Not even the Tallowmen went down here. A place that no Kept God ever held sway over, where neither act of parliament or royal decree ever mattered a damn. These are the Brotherhood's streets, and the clubhouse is at the centre of the maze.

Baston turns a corner, and there it is. The headquarters of the Brotherhood for as long as anyone can remember. An anonymous house, a tavern without a sign or a name, a door like any other, except for the wear on the step outside, the shine on the brass handle from generations of eager hands. But now, sprouting from the roof of the clubhouse, is a structure that calls to mind a nest as much as it does a temple, bulbous and papery. Phantasmal spiders scuttle around its crenellations, vanishing into hiding places or crawling along cables that run from the temple's upper levels to some unseen realm, fading from view above Baston's head. Endless whispering, chittering, the susurrus of billions of spiders crawling over one another in the darkness within. The buildings around the clubhouse are covered in thick webbing, and Baston can make out cocooned shapes – offerings? Informants? Hanging there. The hanged man, a sigil that's haunted the Brotherhood since Idge's death. The same pattern repeated in a corrupted form.

The headquarters of the Brotherhood, now the temple of Fate Spider in Guerdon.

He finds himself walking down to the lock-up on Hook Street. The lock-up on Hook Street isn't that far away, and the weapons stolen from Dredger's yard are there. He retraces his steps, winding his way back. These streets, he realises, are replicated in the New City, too. Not quite the same – it's the same configuration, but exaggerated, grown larger. Alleyways become boulevards, the rookeries exalted into miraculous spires and castles. A strange thought, and he puts it aside. He's become very good at hiding his thoughts, but he's tired of that burden.

His fingers shake as he fumbles with the cold metal of the padlock. His thieves do good work – at first glance, the lock-up looks like it hasn't been used in years. Dusty tarpaulins covering battered tea chests and old crates, junk crammed into every corner. Baston shoves crates aside, searching through the prizes stolen from Dredger's yard until he finds what he seeks. A phlogiston siege charge. The thing is a brass sphere, about a foot in diameter. Beautifully baroque, covered in inlet valves and detonator rods and spikes of obscure purpose. Liquids slosh within it as he lifts the weapon. Elemental phlogiston, the essence of fire. At the heart of the weapon is a reaction chamber where fire burns itself, exploding and imploding all at once until there's nothing left. Brighter than the sun. He imagines himself standing there, holding that blazing sphere, thrusting it into the face of the gods even as he's blasted away. A thief emerging from the shadows for the last time, stepping into the brightest light of all.

He won't hold back this time.

He puts everything else back, just as it was. Closes the door and locks it – his father drilled into him that a small error can ruin the best-planned heist. It'd be the worst luck of all for his grand gesture to be foiled because some well-meaning citizen spotted he'd left the padlock off and called the watch. Someone in the Wash calling the watch would be a miracle, of course, but miracles are two a penny since the invasion.

Baston wraps his cloak around the precious bundle, cradles it like a baby.

"Baston, we need to talk." Baston's head snaps around, startled. He nearly bolts, then he recognises the voice.

Rasce steps out of the fog. His face is flushed, and he sways on his feet. He's wearing a cloak, but little else, like he wandered down here from his sick bed. His feet are bare and there are bruises on his chest and throat smeared in some alchemical cure-all. A stained bandage trails from his arm. "Something strange is happening to me. It – it knows you." He stumbles forwards, steadies himself by grabbing on to Baston's shoulder. "Such dreams. He's shown me such sights. I must put it right."

Godshit. Rasce is Ghierdana. If he's found wandering in the Wash, within the Ishmeric Occupation Zone, he's dead. The man clinging to Baston's left arm is as explosive as the bomb cradled in the crook of his right.

"Come on." Acting on reflex, like he'd protect any member of the Brotherhood, Baston hustles Rasce off Crane Street, into the alleyway behind the lock-up. The nearest hiding place is ... hell, it's Baston's own house. Fine. Downhill, then, towards the docks.

"How did you find me?" mutters Baston.

"I saw you. From up there." Rasce waves up in the direction of the New City.

The few streets from the lock-up to Baston's home have never seemed longer. The distance stretches, and the bomb grows heavier with every step. Fortunately, Rasce sways like a drunk, so they don't draw as much attention as they might. To mortal eyes, Rasce is just another dockworker who's already spent the day's wages. To divine eyes – well, who the fuck knows?

Rasce is muttering to himself: "Argh, it's like bees buzzing inside my head. A needle, quick. Steel, to pierce the skull. That way, isn't it? Down there?" He tries to lurch off down a side street, but Baston restrains him.

"No. Just follow me."

"Listen. He showed me ... we hurt people, Baston, when we burned the yards. It's not right. Here, I brought this to put it right. Take it." Rasce pulls a purse from inside his jacket, spills the contents on the cobblestones. A fortune in gold falls around Baston's feet. Rasce reaches down awkwardly, like his joints are stiff, his limbs heavy. Moving like a Stone Man.

Baston hauls him upright. "Come on! Leave it!"

"He keeps showing me their faces! Misery piled on misery – how can I stand it? He won't let me look away." Rasce lunges for the coins again. Baston kicks the money away – let the streets find a use for the dragon's gold – and drags Rasce forward.

"We have to go," he insists. The Spiders will come soon.

The front door's locked. Karla must not be home yet. Baston juggles the bomb from one arm to the other as he fishes out his keys. There's a spider two streets over, picking its way with silent grace over the terraces, eight glowing eyes like moons. What will it see if it looks at Rasce?

Baston shoves the Ghierdana inside, drops the bomb in the umbrella stand, shuts the door and bolts it. Presses his forehead against it, as if he can hold the world out by sheer willpower.

"Why," asks Rasce, "do you have such a thing? Even in Guerdon, I did not think it customary to carry bombs of such size." He talks like he's half asleep, or drugged.

"Never you mind." Baston grabs Rasce, shoves him down the little hallway into the cramped kitchen. "What are you doing here?"

"I don't know. I think ... I think I am going mad. My head is crushed by heavy stones. I see – I see too much." Rasce presses the heels of his hands into his eyes. "What is this?"

"You're seeing visions?"

"Would that it were only seeing!" moans Rasce. "It's feeling them, knowing them. I saw the Tallowman on the rooftop. I should have died! But I live, while others die. There's a woman dying of the flux in the New City, Baston! Too far gone for medicine, she gasps for breath. I am the rattle in her lungs! I smell the rank stench of her pissy sheets! And I know her husband's fled. I see him in a tavern off the Street of Saints!" Rasce staggers across the kitchen to the window, looks out through the grimy glass. "And it's easier down here, damn it! Up in the New City – it's flying through a thunderstorm. I'm going mad. Help me!"

"What do you want me to do?"

"He knows you! Tell him to stop!" Rasce brandishes his dragontooth dagger, but he's clumsy, his limbs as stiff as stone, and the blade goes flying out of his grip. It flies through the kitchen window, shattering the glass, and lands in the yard outside. Baston flinches; Rasce doesn't react. His mouth moves, but the only sound he makes is the grinding of stone.

He knows you. What god knows Baston? He's never knelt to any, not even in the churches of the Keepers.

The clouds overhead shift and roll, like the sky's boiling over. Lightning flashes, illuminating for an instant the suggestion of titanic figures in the heavens. Across the Wash, ecstatic shouts. Whatever's happening to Rasce echoes in the divine realm – they're drawing attention.

In the months since the Armistice, Baston's witnessed the gods of Ishmere claiming more than one saint. The Spider took a six-year-old girl on Slaughter Lane. Her mother put her to bed with a fever, and the child awoke eight-eyed and whispering prophecies, and the priests took her away. High Umur's chosen was a beggar, legless and blind, who pushed himself around the alleys on a wheeled hand-cart – until he rose up, lifted by unseen hands, and looked down upon the rabble with a sneer, his eyes flashing with lightning, and spoke in a voice of thunder. Umurshixes drew his cart then, transfigured into a golden chariot.

Baston watched both transformations, and he's learned a trick, too, from the priests who follow the saints like gulls after a fishing boat. Speak a saint's name – their mortal name, their true name – and it grounds them, like an aetheric current returning to earth. It isn't a sure thing. If a saint's so far gone to identify more with the god than their mortal self, it won't work. But here . . .

"Rasce," declares Baston loudly, proclaiming the name. Putting as much weight on the name as he can.

"Rasce of the Ghierdana." Nothing. Not even a twitch. The man's name holds no sway over him. Baston thinks for a moment, and then tries again, one last time.

"Chosen of the Dragon."

The title strikes Rasce like a blow.

"Ah," says Rasce, "that's better."

And he falls to the floor of Baston's kitchen, unconscious.

Spar's closer to the mortal realm than he's been in months, closer even than he came with Cari. Closer than he's been since he died. He'd never have dared push like this with her, for fear of injuring her – but with Rasce, he's willing to risk it. To press the psychic weight of the whole New City against the Ghierdana's mortal brain. Rasce is on the very edge of Spar's influence, outside the confines of the New City itself, but it makes it easier in a way. All of Spar's mind, all his attention, his divided strands of thought all strain in a single direction, like a city's streets all gathering at a crossroads, at a single bridge—

But the bridge breaks. The anchor-rope to consciousness shatters. He's falling again, plunging into oblivion. Spar's mind tries to seize on to Rasce, seize on to anything, but it's no good. He's cut off again from the mortal realm.

There are miracles in the New City as Spar falls, spasms of wild magic. In the tunnels below, passageways open or close spontaneously, like a dying man losing control of his bowels. Towers shake and convulse. Old memories, given shape in stone, lurch out of walls – spontaneous cryptic statuary depicting moments from Spar's thoughts, old and new. Along Sevenshell Street, the sea wall collapses, sending chunks of stone splashing into the waters below. A child in the Armistice Gardens collapses, frothing at the mouth and reciting extracts from the writings of Idge.

They sound the alarm in the Lyrixian barracks. Soldiers scramble out to their guard posts, hastily donning what protective gear they can against divine assault – warding talismans, holy relics of the Lyrixian deities, armour shot through with aetheric dampening rods. Guns and swords in hand, they look out into the night, unsure if they're under attack. The dragons of the Ghierdana bellow in alarm and take flight, flapping around the spires of the New City like startled crows.

Spar falls out of time. Above him, Cari's frozen on a ledge, caught in Professor Ongent's spell, and he's falling. He's out in the harbour, salvaging the last god-bomb from the wreck of the *Grand Retort*, and he's falling into dark waters. Cari's drowning, too, lungs filling with searing water.

And then – a connection again.

Penetrating his consciousness like the steel tip of an alka-hest needle.

Hot, honey-sweet pain.

He's himself again, coherent again. From the heights of the towers, Spar looks down on Guerdon. All his attention focused on a single point. He looks across the familiar streets of the Wash, their pattern more familiar to him than the back of his own dead and shattered hand, more constant than the plague-scales and scabs that ate his flesh. He sees a small yard at the back of a house near the docks. Baston's house.

He's lost hours. The night's rolled on.

Rasce emerges into the yard from the kitchen door. He lifts his head to look at the New City on the horizon, and he's looking right at Spar, recognition in his gaze.

"Spar Idgeson, I presume," he whispers, but the words echo down every street and alleyway in the New City.

Rasce walks across the little yard, glass cracking under his borrowed boots. He searches around in the debris, and finds his dragon-tooth dagger. He holds it up, blade levelled at the distant city, and somehow it's not an entirely absurd threat. The thought of being cut off again terrifies Spar. He's unsure if he can survive another dissolution without going mad.

Yes.

Rasce glances back at the kitchen window and nods. Baston emerges from the house, almost shyly, not daring to believe.

"I know you, now. Baston has told me a great deal about you, about you and Carillon Thay. My uncle, too – he told me a lot about

Guerdon, back home. Other things, you showed me. And you aided me in Glimmerside, yes? Tell me, what are you? A ghost? A god?"

Honestly, I don't know.

"In truth, it matters little. We may be friends, but you will not *use* me. I am not some empty vessel for you to fill. Understand this – I am a prince of the Ghierdana, Chosen of the Dragon. Cities burn at my command, yes?"

I'll help you, says Spar, *if you help me. A partnership.*

Rasce considers. "Among my cousins, only one can be Chosen of the Dragon. Each of us strives alone to win Great-Uncle's favour. I am Chosen, and so I have no peers. How can I have a partner?"

A friend, then.

"Friends may prove false. I know what Carillon Thay did to my Uncle Artolo – with your help, yes?" Rasce's grin is visible across the city to Spar. "But the dragons are here now. Soon, my Great-Uncle will return. It is better for us all – for you, for me, for this city – if he is satisfied with my progress when he arrives."

The Ishmerians are coming. You're surrounded. Spar can see some of the Ishmerian forces closing on the house – phantasmal spiders skittering over the rooftops, cloud-spawn swimming towards Rasce, saints and soldiers on the streets. Other forces he perceives with senses he has no mortal words for – High Umur's judgement coalescing, Fate Spider weaving an unseen web to catch the thieves in misfortune. *You've got to run.*

"Well then," says Rasce, "let us put you to the test. Do for me what you did for Carillon Thay. Shape the stone."

I had more power then. Spar still feels as weak as gossamer. Merely talking to Rasce at this distance is taxing him. Having Rasce as a focus helps, but it's still an effort. His mind is scattered across the whole New City, so his thoughts arrive like footsore pilgrims, stumbling as they march. *I'll try.*

"Do more than try, spirit, or we are both lost." Rasce ducks back into the house, calling for Baston. The saints are nearly at the door.

The borders of the New City are not clearly drawn. At the edges, the two cities – New and Old – intertwine. Buildings half made from wood and brick, fused with miracle-spawned stone. Bridges and walkways like marble filigree, leaping above the old streets.

And as above, so below. Under the New City are many miles of tunnels and passageways, and some of those too connect to older ghoul-runs and smugglers' tunnels under the Wash.

Now, Spar puts what remains of his strength into one of those. The stone softens, like a Stone Man's sinews under alkahest. It melts, flows, re-forms, remaking itself according to Spar's will. The tunnel becomes a serpent, burrowing through the earth, questing for the surface. Inside, the floor reshapes itself into a stairwell. The tunnel mouth breaks through, emerging out of the ground in Baston's yard.

The two thieves rush down the stairs, nearly falling down the tunnel in their haste. Baston's carrying two large bags, everything he could take from his house with a moment's notice. Rasce carries only the dagger.

The effort of conjuring the tunnel exhausts Spar. He summons up an image of the route through the deeper tunnels, and gives the knowledge to Rasce. He also sends a warning – he's too weak to reseal the tunnel mouth. The way into the tunnel remains open in Baston's yard, the clearest possible sign of the thieves' escape route. *They'll follow you.*

"That," laughs Rasce as he descends the stairs, "shall not be a problem."

Back on the surface, an agent of the Fate Spider is the first to arrive. An assassin, dispatched by the cult to deal with saboteurs and traitors. Her thin blade drips with the Poison Undeniable. Behind her cluster umurshixes, spiders, cultists of one god or another, all eager to punish whatever intruding saint breached the sanctity of the Temple Quarter. The assassin reaches out and slowly turns the handle of the front door, anticipating an attack. Anticipating martyrdom.

She does not, however, anticipate the detonation trigger for the siege charge just inside the door.

For an instant, a new sun blooms in the street.

CHAPTER THIRTEEN

The days go by, falling one by one behind the flank of the Rock of Ilbarin.

Hawse insists they must be careful to avoid any sudden changes that might draw attention. He's even more insistent that Cari not leave the *Rose* at all. So, for a few days, Hawse spends his time in the temple to the Lord of Waters, chanting his rough prayers, and Cari lies in her bunk in the forward cabin, stewing. She tells herself that she needs time to heal, that a few days' delay isn't much compared to the months she's already squandered, and it's true, but still every part of her soul cries out for action.

She finds the ship's carpentry tools, busies herself with them. Fixes the holes torn in the roof of the cabin by dragon claws. Repairs the broken steps leading up from the darkness of the hold. Wanders the little country that she dwells in now, the portion of the deck that cannot be seen by unfriendly eyes on the shore, and looks for things to do.

She's lost her knife, so she borrows Hawse's old sword, and practises with that instead, though the weapon's unwieldy for a fighter of her size. Cari's never had any formal training in fighting, except what she learned on the alleyways and docksides. Her instincts are still off, she discovers. When she was the Saint of Knives, Spar could miraculously take her injuries from her and on to himself, on to the New City, thus shielding her from harm. That let her be as reckless as she wished, quick and savage, her approach focused solely on slashing and stabbing with the sharp blade, on wounding her foe. Now, she has to think about self-preservation, too. Every movement makes her ache, reminding her of what she's lost. She imagines making Spar laugh with her clumsiness with the sword, and that thought aches, too.

She reads, which was previously something she only did in dire need. Not the fucking book, of course – it's hidden wherever the captain put it to conceal it from Dol Martaine. Instead, she reads sodden, half-destroyed religious texts from a temple of the Lord of Waters. Chunks are missing, pages stick together, words become a mush of paper and ink, so reading them is listening to the ravings of a mad god. Still, she reads, because it's better than sitting there in the dark, listening to the Bythos bump against the hull.

The Bythos rise every night, ambling out of the surf and marching off into the darkness. Usually, they parade through the streets of Ushket, or try to stumble up the slope of the Rock – they're absurdly ungainly climbers and don't get far – but sometimes they gather around the *Rose*, keening and burbling in a strange echo of the captain's prayers. Cari learns to distinguish one from another by their markings. The fish-portion of the creatures always remains the same, but the rotting human corpses that carry them on land change, although they're all so bloated and half eaten that it's hard to be sure. The discarded remnants wash up along the shore from the *Rose*, and a few mountain vultures pick at them, shrieking angrily at the unfamiliar sea.

The Bythos wander around, aimlessly, then slip back into the waters. She's certain that they're psychopomps, like the ghouls of Guerdon or the sacred birds of Cloud Mother. They're supposed to collect the freshly deceased and bring that potent residuum, the corpse-dregs of the soul, to the gods. Now, what's the point of them?

Captain Hawse makes tentative expeditions to Ushket. Carefully scouting out the town, planning his route, making contacts, waiting for moonless nights. Like she's a hot cargo that he's trying to smuggle past customs patrols.

She pleads to be allowed go to town with Hawse, but he shakes his head. Everyone knows that the mad old hermit of the wreck lives alone, so he goes alone. He brings a basket of fish to trade. Without the gifts of the Bythos, he and Cari would soon starve to death, as there's little food for sale in Ushket – unless you have connections with the Ghierdana, of course.

Each time the captain goes, Cari spends hours crouched at the rail, watching the empty shore for his return. Carts go by under armed guard, carrying food and supplies from the mountain farm, or casks of that glowing silt. From what Hawse tells her, she guesses those casks come from the work camp on the far side of the island. They're doing some sort of alchemical work there near the ruins of the drowned city. The only way to leave the island is through the Ghierdana. Want out? Then pay. Can't pay? Then work for the Ghierdana until you've earned your passage. Ilbarin's a corpse-land. No one wants to stay here, except maybe Captain Hawse with his weird vigil for the Lord of Waters.

She confronts him about it one morning, after a sleepless night spent wondering.

"Captain . . . you said there was a storm when Ishmere attacked, and the Lord of Waters pulled the *Rose* out of it. That's why you think you owe him, right?"

"I asked the Lord of Waters to save me and my crew, and we were saved."

"Right. But . . . the ship was safe, then, wasn't it? There was a time between Ilbarin getting fucked by Krakens, and the Ghierdana bastards showing up with their dragons and beaching the *Rose*, when you could have just sailed away, yeah?"

"I could have. I chose not to. Or it was chosen for me. It is folly, I say, to deny the gods."

"Deny them – what? Deny them what you owe, is it?"

Hawse shakes his head. When he speaks next, it's with slow deliberation, like every word must laboriously be twisted around the capstan of his mind. "I think that we do not ... admit, as we should, that we are ... flotsam on the waves. Everything we are, all we think, is shaped by the gods. By all the gods, blowing us this way and that."

He looks across the table at Cari, frowning. "You told me that when the war goddess Pesh was destroyed—"

"When I fucking killed her."

"Foul language is unbecoming of you," he mutters, then continues. "When you slew Pesh, the people of Ishmere forgot how to make war."

"Sort of." A wave breaks loudly at the stern of the ship, and the sudden noise startles her. She can't hear the cries of the birds on the shore, either, any more, although she can hear scraping and scratching on the cabin roof. She can't shake the feeling that something's eavesdropping, a prickling feeling in her soul. "After I hit Pesh with the god-bomb, the Ishmerians were confused. They could still fight, but it was like they'd taken a blow to the head."

"It was like that everywhere. Pesh was war. She was on every battlefield, in the heart of every soldier."

"Every Ishmeric soldier." Cari pushes her own bowl away, feeling unwell.

"Every soldier," repeats Hawse. He dips his spoon into the dregs of his stew, lets chunks of fish fall back into the gruel. Watching them splash, little droplets of grease landing on the table, like an augury. "Some more than others. A ... way of war, of thinking about war, died by your hand." He takes a deep breath. "When I sailed, I was more ... no, there is no 'I'. This ... mortal shell ..." He gestures down at his own body, "was inhabited more by an aspect of the Lord of Waters than any other god. When I bargained in the ports of the trader cities, was I not more Blessed Bol then? When I smuggled and stole, was I not Fate Spider? This thing I call my mind, what is it but, a – a weathervane for gods?" Hawse's voice quavers with the effort of articulation, like he has to use his whole body to force out the word. Shoulders, hands, belly, all labouring. Something about his movements makes her think of a man wading through rough water, trying to make his way back to shore to tell her what he saw in the deeps.

"Godshit," snaps Carillon. She hasn't heard that exact philosophy before, but she's heard variants. Safidists back in Guerdon, trying to hammer their souls into perfect alignment with the gods. Mystics who mutter that the physical world is an illusion, and that all that matters is the invisible, aetheric realm of the gods.

"No. The Lord of Waters filled me that day. I saw Him. I was Him. I am Him, I pray. What is time to the gods?"

"Godshit," says Cari again. She's about to say more – to decry Hawse's fatalism, to say that it all means nothing anyway, that blaming the gods is just a coward's excuse – but suddenly her stomach empties itself, everything rising up in a burning torrent and gushing out of her mouth. Unreasoning terror catches up with her, a wave crashing over all the walls she's built around herself. *It's not true. People are more than puppets for gods.*

She falls to her knees, shivering.

In the hollowness that follows the bout of vomiting, she finds a horrible thought. If Hawse is right, if mortals are nothing more than walking vessels for the stray thoughts of disembodied gods, then what is Carillon? She was made to channel the thoughts of the Black Iron Gods, to be their saint, their herald. Monstrous, murderous gods, full of hate and hunger. Machines for torture, great iron weights squeezing the breath out of the world.

But Cari ran away from home, ran away to the *Rose*, because the Black Iron Gods called to her. They called to her – they weren't her. She's not an embodied echo of a monster, a puppet without free will. She refuses to believe that. There has to be something inside her that doesn't spring from the Black Iron Gods or any other deities, and wasn't made by her grandfather's sorcery, some inner core that's uniquely hers.

Can you be sure? a cruel voice within her asks, and in that moment she doesn't know if it's a part of her mind or if it's coming from outside her, or if there's even any of her at all, and not just the Godswar in miniature inside a mortal skull. *Rat was possessed by a ghoul demigod, and tried to kill you. Your friend tried to murder you. You've seen saints channel the gods, talk for the gods. Silva channeled the Kept Gods, and they tried to kill you, too. You've seen gods intervene in big ways. Why not in small ones? What if you don't exist, and it's all just the gods pulling this way and that? What if you'll never be free of the Black Iron Gods because they're you?*

She refuses to believe it, rejects the poisonous thought. Spar, she thinks, is the counterargument. Spar disproves everything. Her friend isn't a god. She watched him live as a mortal, watched him struggle with the twin burdens of his disease and his legacy. Spar Idgeson, forever the son of the great Idge, the man who was supposed to remake the city. When Spar talks to her in her mind, it's not like he's controlling her.

What if this very thought you're having now is just some fucking god of mischief fucking with you, she thinks.

Hawse's rough old hands on her elbows, helping her sit down. "Ach," he mutters, stepping around the pool of vomit.

"Sorry." She forces a grin. "If you want to have that sort of deep philosophical conversation with me, I should get drunk first."

"It is of no importance, and I am no philosopher. I only say what I think – ach, I say what seems true." He wipes her chin with a cloth. "When you first came on board, you were seasick everywhere. This is nothing in comparison." He bends over to clean the mess on the floor.

"I'll clean it." She takes the cloth from him, and he sits down heavily, letting out a groan. Cari scrubs and wipes, cleaning the worn planks, digging into the gaps between them to erase any trace of the thought.

"I should go," she says after a few minutes. "I'm putting you in danger here. Martaine or some other Ghierdana could show up here."

"Stay. Give me more time." There's a plaintive note in his voice that she hasn't heard before, but when Cari looks up Hawse's face is unchanged, as impassive and weathered as a figurehead. "I told you, the Lord of Waters guided you here, and He has a plan for you."

"But if ... if you're right, and we're all just receptacles for the stray thoughts of gods, and you're especially attuned to the Lord of Waters—"

"His last priest," says Hawse quietly.

"—then you're channelling a broken god! You're like the Bythos, just flopping around at random." She wants to be angry, discovers she's scared and full of worry, and not just for herself or for Spar. She slumps down at Hawse's feet.

Hawse takes her hands. "I know. This thought, too, is in me. But I believe that I am ... like a lighthouse. I shall guide the Lord of Waters back home."

The Ishmeric priestess sits like a beggar on the doorstep of the prefect's palace in Ushket. Her sea-green robes are stained by the reddish mud of the Rock, and soaked in briny water. Her long fingers are so bloated that the gold rings and jewels she wears on them are almost lost in the pale bluish flesh. Her face, though, is ageless and proud, a temple statue come to life.

"Blessings of the gods upon you," she says as Artolo emerges from the main gate.

"Fuck your gods. What do you want?" Ishmere may be in disarray, but the Sacred Realm is still an enemy. Artolo remembers sitting in the villa back in Lyrix. Outside, Rasce, Vyr and the other youngsters preparing to defend the isle against invaders, swords flashing in the sun. Lorenza and her sisters laying in supplies for a siege. Artolo in the middle of it all, sitting by the fire like an old man, useless and broken.

The invasion never came. Ishmere struck at Guerdon instead, and foundered there.

The priestess rises, leaning on her staff for support. Amulets hang from it, depicting the gods of the Sacred Realm. High Umur, Smoke Painter, Kraken, Fate Spider. And the Lion Queen, although that amulet is scorched and cracked. "May I enter?"

Artolo addresses one of the guards. "When did she show up?"

"At dawn, lord. She said she would speak only to you."

"She came alone?"

"Yes, lord. But not by ship. I . . . I think she walked here, over the ocean."

"My name is Damala. May I enter?" she says again.

Artolo grunts, and they pass through the tall green gates of the palace into an inner courtyard. His steel boots scrape the mud away from the elaborate mosaic inlaid in the floor, revealing glimpses of lost beauty. Two Eshdana follow close behind, ready to strike down the priestess if she invokes any divine powers. There's no Armistice here, no truce between Lyrix and Ishmere. Not that such a truce would bind the Ghierdana – sons of the dragon walk where they wish, take what they wish.

"I dreamed of this place," Damala murmurs, "when my gods conquered Ilbarin."

"You lost," snaps Artolo. "You failed to hold the island. It's mine now."

"The mortal portion of it. The gods of this land are broken, and no longer challenge the Sacred Realm. Without offerings, they shall fade, driven before us as hollow phantoms. Your little gods in Lyrix, too, shall fall to us, in time." She has to force the last words out, as if they stick in her craw. It's true, then – the Ishmerians can barely conceive of war since the death of the Lion Queen.

"If you came here to threaten me, you wasted a journey."

"I come to bargain, not to threaten. You shall have the murderer. The one who loosed the god-killing weapon. Carillon Thay."

Artolo's jaw clenches. "Who says this?"

"Fate Spider. He has foreseen this. He has seen you strangle the life from her with your own hands. I have followed signs set before me, read omens given to me. The gods have decreed your fate, and I have heard them speak it."

"The prophecies of your gods are worth shit." Artolo tears off his right glove, holds up his maimed hand to the priestess so she can see the stumps of his fingers. The witch's ghost-fingers glimmer, but they're not his. "How would I strangle anyone with these hands?"

The priestess grabs his hands. "Our purposes are aligned. We both thirst for revenge! Your mortal body is wounded – and so is the soul of my pantheon! Her death shall be offering and memorial to blessed Pesh! Lion Queen, goddess of war, goddess of the hunt, sacred killer—"

Artolo snatches his hand back and punches the old hag in the face. Sends her sprawling into the dirt, blood spraying from her broken cheek. How dare she touch him! How dare she remind him of his wounds!

"That's what I think of your gods and their prophecies. Fuck your gods."

"You have blasphemed against the Sacred Realm," says the priestess, clutching her cheek. "And there shall be a price. But it changes nothing. Your fate is ours."

He could kill her. Fuck her prophecy – it's *her* life that's in his hands.

"Strip her," he orders. One of the Eshdana hesitates, unwilling to lay hands on a priestess, but the others fall on the old woman eagerly. They tear off Damala's rich robes, grab her staff, rip the rings from her fingers. Her treasures are piled at his feet.

"All this," says Artolo, "belongs to the dragon."

Damala drags herself back up. "The gods sent me."

"Throw her out."

Somehow – stripped of her finery, bloodied, mud-soiled – Damala retains that infuriating serenity even as the guards fling her back on to the muddy streets. A confidence born of the knowledge that greater forces watch over her.

He had that once, when he was Chosen.

He'll have it again, he swears.

The captain goes off again, trudging across the mud, towards the town. The Bythos crowd around him, pulling at his coat, and he waits patiently until their curiosity is exhausted before continuing on. Cari spends the day assembling her gear, repacking her bag. That fucker Martaine took her money and the gun, and the fucking book is still in the captain's hiding place. It only takes her a few minutes to put the rest together.

So, she does it again.

And again.

She's well enough to travel. She can't wait any longer, can't stay patient with Hawse's slow and careful approach. As soon as the captain's back to fetch the book for her, she'll go. Sneak into Ushket by dark, stow away on one of the Ghierdana ships. Screw it, maybe she'll have to backtrack a bit, but she'll soon be on her way to Khebesh again. Hawse will be safer when she's gone.

She picks up her mother's amulet. Holds it in her hands. She remembers an afternoon, long long ago, back in Guerdon. She'd have been five years old, six maybe. A few months after the Thay family were murdered, their mansion attacked by unknown assailants. She knows now that it was the Church of the Keepers who executed her hateful family, but, back then, she wasn't even really aware anything had gone wrong. It was just a visit to the countryside, to her aunt's house that went on forever.

Aunt Silva brought Cari and her cousin Eladora back to Guerdon. She had business in the city, meetings with lawyers and the watch, talk of wills and inheritances, so she left Eladora and Cari playing in the Meredyke Park, under the supervision of Silva's husband, Wern. It was easy to slip away from Wern, and Cari went running off into the tangled trees on the north side of the park, with Eladora following her, slow-footed and indecisive, looking back to her heedless father but still trying to keep Cari in sight.

There was a tree, a gnarled oak, perfect for climbing. In her memory, it's tall as a church spire. She'd scaled it, laughing, intoxicated by the immediacy of the challenge, risk transmuting to certainty as her fingers closed around the next branch, her bare feet finding purchase. She remembers pushing her head through a gap in the leaves, seeing the city – and then sudden, unreasoning, directionless terror, and the confused impression that the tree was trying to eat her. She'd fallen, screaming, tearing at herself, as great invisible forces reached out of the sky, reached out of the darkness, reached out from inside her to seize her and carry her away.

And even after Aunt Silva was done with her business, even when they were in the carriage and the city dwindled behind them, Cari could still feel invisible hands at her throat, at the base of her skull. Claiming her.

She opens the clasp of the amulet and puts it around her neck without fastening it.

Spar, are you—

Drops it like it's poisoned.

She's being foolish. Spar's half the world away, and he can't help her. He can't reach her.

She's got to get to Khebesh. He's the one who needs saving.

The captain's late. He misses the slack-tide prayers. The stars come out above the Rock, and he's still not back.

Cari goes down to the lightless shrine, just in case she somehow didn't spot him returning across the muddy slope, but the hold's empty. There's that feeling again, a faint, distant feeling of pressure, which reminds her of a dog growling when another animal trespasses in its territory. A god growling – but nothing happens when she brushes her hand across the blue stone of the altar.

The stairs in the forward hold creak.

It's not the captain.

She moves through the waters as silently as she can and climbs through from the aft hold to the forward. She can barely see the intruder, a darker shape in the shadows. He's big, but he moves quietly. A heavy sack slung over his back as he crosses to the ladder.

Shit, she doesn't have her knife, but there's an old crowbar to hand. She sneaks up and—

—the intruder bangs his head on a low beam, just like he always did.

"Adro!" she squeals, and hugs him.

They sit down in the forward cabin, and Cari lights the lamp so she can get a better look at her old friend. Adro was the heart of the crew when she sailed with them, her closest friend. They'd been a pair of laughing rogues, treating smuggling and thievery as a great game, running off and exploring every port. The gods watch over fools, the captain always said of them.

"The captain'll be here soon," says Adro. "It's better we arrived separately, in case anyone's watching, so I came ahead. And look, look, I brought wine."

The wine's awful, but that doesn't matter.

"Look at you!" laughs Adro. He pokes her in the bicep. "You look like a Guerdonese sell-sword! I was counting on you running home to your rich aunt, then taking us all in."

"I wish I'd done that." The thought of a crew of smugglers marauding around Aunt Silva's kitchen in Wheldacre is delicious. "She would have hated you. It would have been glorious."

"Oh, aunts love me," says Adro. "But, Cari, if you didn't go back home, where did you go? What happened to you?"

"Gods below," says Cari. How to summarise her experiences since leaving the *Rose*? How to talk about the revelations about her family, the Black Iron Gods, Spar and Rat, everything that happened? The Gutter Miracle. The war. "Magic shit."

"Say no more." Adro raises his glass. "We've had plenty of that down here, too. We're better off out of it. I miss the days when we could look across at some city like Ul-Taen," – he puts on the portentous voice of some epic-taleteller – "lo! with its stepped ziggurats, the fabled underworld of the spectral tomb children, the sorcerers in their jars, and gribbly things in the city, and say 'fuck it' and sail off somewhere else."

He scowls at the taste of the wine. "Remember that time in Jashan, when we got drunk on wine-of-poets?"

"We wrote a play."

"We thought we wrote a play!" laughs Adro. "We had three scribbled pages of nonsense, and then we broke into a playhouse and held those poor actors hostage! What was it you said?"

"'Either you spill your heart on the stage, or I will.'" Cari quotes her younger self. "We were idiots back then, Adro. And the captain was so angry."

"Ah, he should have listened to us and taken the cargo for smuggling. Then we wouldn't have had to drink the evidence."

Her memory of Adro and the reality of him swim in and out of focus. He looks pretty much the same, so it's easy to ignore the intervening years, to slip back into their old camaraderie. But it's not quite real – they'd both be playing a part, acting the role of their younger selves, pretending nothing's changed. It's so tempting, to fall back to that simpler time.

She fights against it. "So why did you stay here? I asked the captain this morning, and he talked about gods without giving a clear answer."

Adro drains his glass. "It's not like we made the decision to stay in this shithole. It wasn't one thing, it was a lot of little things. The captain had a flea in his ear about the Lord of Waters, and you've heard him preach. The *Rose* came through the storm all right, but she still needed a lot of work before you'd trust her in the Middle Sea. And everything else was a mess, too – Ilbarin drowned, and folk crawling all over the Rock, looking for a place to hide. Mad priests telling everyone to throw themselves off cliffs. We all thought the Sacred Realm would come back at any moment." He's moving now, unable to sit still. "Prefect's men came down and seized all the ships, but they didn't know what to do with them. One day, the plan was to evacuate everyone to the Caliphates. Then the rumour was they need all the ships to bring in food and stuff, or they're going to invade Serpent's Mouth. It was bad, Cari. People were cheering in the streets when the Ghierdana showed up and took over."

He sits down, breathing heavily. Then looks over at her and grins. "And . . . did the captain tell you about Ren?"

"What's this?"

"I'm married now, Cari. We've a little girl, too. And, gods, I've never been so scared. Ren was in Ilbarin, see, when the gods came. We got separated in the invasion, and it took me months to find him, and Ama, but they made it out. They're both all right. I found them again. Captain calls it a miracle. But by the time I'd found them, the Ghierdana had taken control of the port. You can only leave if you pay their toll, and we couldn't afford it. Not for Ren and myself and Ama."

Fuck you, Dol Martaine. If she still had that money, she'd give it to Adro without hesitation.

Adro fills his glass again, fills hers. "I wish you could come see them. You'd like Ren. He's a good man."

It's very tempting.

"I need to get to Khebesh, though. I have to."

"So the captain said. But more importantly, you should see what the captain has." He grins. "The last pork in Ilbarin, I'll wager. Who gives a damn about long-lost friends? I'm here to eat!"

Captain Hawse arrives, puffing up the ladder, laden with packages. "Lazy dogs," he jokes, "no cooking fire in the galley? No table set? I should whip the pair of you! But the Lord of Waters is merciful. Instead, I shall feed you, and then speed Cari on her journey. I have found a ship to carry her forth."

There isn't much food, and it's not much good, but by the standards of the benighted isle of Ilbarin it's a feast. It feels like one, too – there's merriment and song, the warm glow of friendship in her heart and the wine in her belly. A long-delayed reunion, and the farewell she missed when she left the *Rose*.

They're in the ship's common room, seated around the long table. The captain, in his hermitage here, has taken over the space; they had to shove piles of rotten books off into the corner, fold and store the ceremonial vestments salvaged from a temple of the Lord of Waters. Having Adro back makes the space feel more like it used to.

The captain speaks little, save to call for a song or to interject, full of mock gravitas. Still, satisfaction radiates from him like heat from a hearth. He's put aside the role of the priest, and is more like his old self again, like a father at the head of the dining table. He even skips the night prayers.

Adro's full of excitement, humming with manic energy, like they're drinking wine-of-poets and not cheap Paravosi red. Cari can't tell if it's just sheer excitement, or if he feels compelled to put on a show for her, to cram all the jokes and conversation they missed out on over the last five years into a single evening.

Cari curls her legs under her, listening to Adro tell for the hundredth time the story of how they stole from the Eyeless. All three of them were there, but Adro's told the story so many times it's transmuted into something unfamiliar and new. She barely recognises herself in the swashbuckling, devil-may-care rogue he describes – although it reminds her of tales of the Saint of Knives. She envies those past selves, who weren't so laden down with fears and worries, or who had miraculous powers to strike back against the world.

She lets herself imagine what her friends in Guerdon would make of this. Imagines Rat – Rat as he used to be, the hunched little ghoul, not the hulking, horned Elder Ghoul he became. Rat would be skulking in the corner, grumbling as he picked stringy vegetables out of his bowl. He'd only eat the pork. But when Adro sang, Rat would sway back and forth, his hooves tapping along to the melody.

And Spar – Spar as he was when he was alive, before the fall. Spar would sit over there, at the far end of the table from the captain, so he wouldn't risk touching anyone and spreading the Stone Plague. Spar would be a cooling presence, a counterweight to Adro's levity. She can imagine him getting into an argument with Captain Hawse. Or coming up with some plan to save the survivors of Ilbarin. Leaning forward, earnest. His voice grave. *You have a ship, sir. And, for what it's worth, the favour of a god. And you, Adro – you have a child. Do you really want your daughter to grow up in chains? My father Idge wrote there are moments in time when things can change, when forces balance and it's possible for individual people to remake the world.*

And she'd shout for everyone to take a drink whenever he mentioned Idge. Their old drinking game.

She becomes gradually aware that Adro stopped talking several minutes ago; she's the one talking now, the words flowing out of her like her heart's been opened. She tells them everything, all her burdens slipping from her as she explains about the Black Iron Gods, about the Thay family and her grandfather's experiments. About coming back to Guerdon, finding Spar and Rat. About the Tower of Law, Professor Ongent, the Ravellers. The Gutter Miracle. Spar's strange survival after death, and becoming the Saint of Knives. How she drove the Ghierdana from the streets of her city, about how Ishmere invaded and Spar exhausted himself fighting to defend the New City and those who'd taken refuge there.

How she killed a goddess.

It all comes out, a wild confession, disorganised and tangled. She has no idea if she's making any sense, or if she comes across as a madwoman raving about gods and monsters.

The captain just listens, drinking it all in. He nods in recognition when Cari tries to describe the awful feeling of direct communion, and it's reassuring.

Adro looks like a man caught in a tidal wave, buffeted and battered by the rushing words. He grabs on to what he recognises – when Cari talks about kicking Artolo out of the New City, Adro grips her arm tightly and hisses, "He'll fucking kill you", like she doesn't know that already. Mostly, though, he's slack-jawed, his energy draining away until he's gnawing on his knuckles, staring at Cari in mounting confusion.

"Your friend, Spar – is he dead?" asks Adro.

"Death," intones the captain, "is a shedding of long burdens. It is in death we know who we truly were in life. We are scraped clean of distractions and doubts, washed and refined, until that singular quality is known."

Adro throws a frightened glance at the captain, but his attention is on Cari.

She shrugs. "He died. He changed. He's dying again. Or he's still dying, I don't know. But it's not ... it's not right. It's not fair. It's why I've got to get to Khebesh."

"What if you don't?" asks Adro. "What if they can't help you?"

She searches for a response, but can't find one. The thought's like a black abyss, a fall without end. Her old life ended when the Tower of Law fell on her back in Guerdon, when the Black Iron Gods started communing with her. Spar's been the one constant in that new life. Hell, worrying about Spar has been a constant thread. Taking care of him is the thread she's been holding on to. It tied her to the New City.

If that thread breaks, what does she have left?

Once, she might have toyed with the idea of returning to her old life. Coming back here to the *Rose*, to Hawse and Adro and the rest, to go adventuring again, buccaneering across the seas. But the *Rose* is beached and broken, and the captain's become a crazy hermit, Adro's married, and the rest are dead or scattered.

She could go wandering, go see the world – but the world's breaking, too. Everyone said Guerdon was the last safe city, the last place untouched by the Godswar, but that's not true any more. Gods can't die, not without a god-bomb, and how do you end a war where the combatants can't die? They'll just keep fighting, keep stumbling back into the fray. There's no sea wide enough to hide from the gods. Running's always been her first and last resort, but there's nowhere to run to.

"We do not know ourselves," says the captain, "until we fall. We mistake our everyday circumstances, whatever equilibrium we have found, for what we truly are. You cannot know yourself until you stand alone against the storm." His voice is sonorous, deep as the sea that rushes against the flanks of the ship.

Cari sees the waters rise, surging forward. The sea floods the room, water gushing through the open door, through the portholes, rising through every gap in the floor. The sea claims the ship, drowning them all. The shapes of Bythos in the murky gloom, the holy fish claiming the drowned bodies of Hawse and Adro. Cari tries to scream, but she's underwater, she can't breathe—

Adro catches her as she stumbles, knocking her plate to the floor.

The hallucination vanishes. The pressure lifts.

"I'm all right," she insists, "I'm all right." *What the fuck was that*, she thinks? Adro didn't even notice it, whatever it was. The captain, though – he called something up with his words, or something spoke through him. It stinks of a divine vision, but not from the Black Iron Gods.

"You've gone pale as death," Adro says. He helps her sit down again, then turns to Hawse. "Captain, the Ghierdana will gut her if they find her here."

Cari clings to the arm of the chair. The deck heaves and lurches beneath her even though they're on solid land. She grabs her glass of wine and throws it back. "You said you'd found me a way off this fucking island. Let's hear it."

"On the Street of Blue Glass—" begins the captain.

Adro interrupts him. "No! Begging your pardon, sir, but fuck no. You can't send her there."

"They have a ship, Adro, and the Ghierdana won't dare hinder them. I have spoken to them."

"Gods below," swears Cari, "let him talk, Ad. It can't be that bad. Who are they?"

Adro opens his mouth to speak – and then they all freeze. There's noise outside on the deck, the sound of people climbing up the sides of the *Rose*, clambering over the rail.

The captain moves to the door, opens it a crack. There's light outside.

It's not moonlight.

Werelight.

Shit. The armoured sorceress must be out there.

Hawse gestures, pointing towards the other door. It leads to his cabin.

"Go," he hisses.

"Come with us," insists Cari.

"The Lord of Waters watches over me. I have nothing to fear."

Adro tugs her arm. "We've got to go!"

"Wait!" she whispers. "The fucking book."

"It's safe," Hawse replies. "They won't find it. Hide! I'll see them off."

Cari grabs the carving knife off the table without thinking. Weirdly, the imminent danger of being captured and killed by the Ghierdana makes her feel so much better. She's either going to live or die in the next few minutes, she's going to bury this knife in someone's guts or she's not, and there's no time to think about anything beyond that.

The captain's cabin is dark, except for the little moonlight spilling through a round window. In all her years on the *Rose*, Cari rarely trespassed in this room, and it still feels more like a sanctum to her than the rough temple below. Adro grabs the captain's sword from where it hangs on the wall, but he doesn't look like he's spoiling for a fight. He's scared, too.

Cari presses her ear to the door.

"Your table," says the sorceress, "is set for three." Her voice is distorted by her helmet, but it's still faintly familiar to Cari.

"For the gods!" shouts the captain, playing the holy fool. "I set a place for the Lord of Waters! And another for Usharet – behold, she comes to dine!" It's not going to fly – if nothing else, the fact that there are heaps of gnawed bones on the plates gives the game away. Hallucinatory guests don't have Adro's appetite.

"Search the ship," orders the witch.

"Down here!" whispers Adro. There's a trapdoor in the floor of the captain's cabin, a square of blackness. Adro climbs down, his limbs folding like a spider's, squeezing his lanky body into the little gap. He hangs and lets himself drop as softly as he can, landing in the half-flooded hold below with the quietest of splashes.

"Catch me," whispers Cari, and slithers through the trapdoor. Adro's strong hands catch her by the hips, hold her aloft so she can grab the hatch and close it soundlessly behind her, a heartbeat before the Ghierdana goons blunder into the captain's cabin.

They're not safe. The room above is dark, but the trapdoor's not that hard to find. Cari creeps through the dark waters, brushing past the altar to the Lord of Waters. It's nearly time for the Bythos to rise. Every other night, the captain came down here to pray as the tide rolled in. The water's already rising, seeping into this temple. They can't hide here for long. If they can get to the hole on the starboard side of the forward hold, maybe they can crawl out without being seen by the sorceress.

Cari takes the lead, sneaking forward until she can peek out of the hole in the hull. She spies more Ghierdana, out on the shore. Signals to Adro to stay back. Their lamps flood the shore with unwanted light, but they're not moving. They're standing guard, making a perimeter around the *Rose*.

"How many?" whispers Adro.

"Too many."

She ducks down behind some debris, a pile of empty crates and wooden carving of some god, riddled with rot. She crouches in the darkness, trying to work out how to play this bad hand. Make a break for it, and hope she can slip away in the darkness? Stay here, hidden in the hold, and hope that the captain's bullshit is enough to convince the sorceress? Sneak out and try to swim for it, turn right rather than left and plunge into the waves as they break on the shore?

Adro's got the captain's sword, but the Ghierdana will have guns. Charging out is almost certainly suicide. But maybe, maybe, one of them could break through the line. Is Adro willing to take that risk? Once, she'd have known exactly what he was thinking, moved when he moved, but those days are gone.

So, too, are the days when she could just swagger out there, the Saint of Knives, girded in miraculous armour. Hard as stone, glorious as the soaring spires of the New City. Power isn't a card she can play any more, and she misses it. Once, she could have saved everyone. Once, she wouldn't have had anything to fear.

Movement, outside! The lamps bob around, their beams shining back towards Ushket, lighting up the slope. More men have arrived. More Ghierdana – but they're arguing with the others. Shouting, shoving, the two groups lining up and posturing. Cari knows a gang dispute when she sees one. No one's drawing weapons yet, but they're paying more attention to threatening each other than to watching the shore.

This could be the moment.

The leader of the newcomers pushes through the line,

strides across the stony strand to the *Rose*. It's dark, but he's outlined against the torchlight, and Cari still knows his walk. Dol Martaine.

"The fucker sold us out," she whispers, her grip tightening on the carving knife. If she still had her powers, she'd walk out there and kill Martaine for betraying them. She wouldn't even hesitate.

Adro sounds like he's about to say something, but she shushes him. She watches Martaine clamber up the side of the ship. The deck creaks overhead as he crosses to the sorceress. Cari can only make out a few words, but it sounds like a turf dispute.

Adro swallows. "You should run!" he whispers in her ear. "They'll kill you if they catch you!"

She tenses, about to make a break for it, when the watchers outside the ship turn to face the rising sea. Shining their lamps out into the dark waves, drawing swords as if they've seen some danger.

If she runs out of the gap in the hull now, she'll be running right into that light. They'd see her instantly.

The scrape of the trapdoor opening, the splash of someone dropping into the aft hold. Martaine's voice, calling down from above. "Be respectful, you dolts! It's a holy place. Do you want to bring a curse down on your heads?" Another splash, and another. Light flaring in the aft hold behind them.

They're trapped. Three ways out – the stairs up to the deck, the door aft, the breach in the hull – and Ghierdana watching all three.

Then comes a wet slap against the hull, the sound of squelching mud, the hooting of the Bythos. The light from the sentries' lamps outside becomes a flickering shadow-play as the Bythos march up the shore, hooting and belching. There are dozens of them out there, parading out of the sea, more than she's ever seen before. A stream of glistening black scaly things, carried on shambling, stumbling host bodies, marching out of the surf and proceeding along the shore towards Ushket. The line of Ghierdana sentries parts to let the creatures through.

For a moment, a Bythos lingers at the entrance to the hold, the unblinking saucer of its fish-eye staring right at Cari, beckoning her. It's the Monkfish, the one she saw on her first night on Ilbarin. She can still see the scars left by the broken glass.

"Now," she hisses at Adro, grabbing him by the arm. They run out, staying low, and plunge into the midst of the procession.

The Bythos on either side of her extend their fins over her, soaking her with dripping seawater and slime.

The fishy stench is all-consuming; she can taste it in her throat, in the back of her sinuses. Slime coats the ground, making it slippery, and if she falls the Bythos might trample her to death. She can't see anything except confused fragments of Bythos – a rotting buttock or forearm here, a wriggling fish-tail or gaping mouth there. She has to trust that the creatures will keep to their usual parade route, that they'll march along the road to the town of Ushket.

Cari desperately wants to look back at the *Rose*, to see what's happening on deck. Where's Dol Martaine? The sorceress? Is Hawse all right? She can't see anything except zombie fish-men, can't hear anything except the hooting and yawping of the Bythos. She can't tell how long they've been marching for.

Her lungs feel choked with their slime, her skin slick with goo. She feels them pressing on her. Their fishy gurgles and hoots become a hymn to the Lord of Waters, a plaintive cry for a missing parent. She's not sure if their voices have changed, or if they've worked some change on her ears so she can suddenly understand. Is this how Hawse hears them?

Her fingers dig into Adro's sleeve, holding his wrist tight. She can hear him cursing and complaining through gaps in the Bythos chorus.

Slimy rocks and mud give way to the packed surface of the road.

The parade picks up speed, the Bythos wriggling with excitement as they rush towards Ushket. They've made it.

As they enter the town the parade breaks apart and the Bythos go their separate ways. Some turn down alleyways and streets; others just stop and amble aimlessly around. Cari tugs Adro into a sheltered doorway.

They've fucking made it.

"What the hell are we going to do?" Adro whispers, fearful of attracting attention. "We've got to get off the streets."

"What about your place?"

Adro's face is a mask of anguish. "No, no. I can't bring you to Ren, Cari, it's too risky. What were you thinking, going up against the Ghierdana like that?"

"We're clear," she says. "No one followed us."

"Not that. In Guerdon. You stabbed Artolo! You crossed the dragon! Godshit." He paces back and forth, rubbing his forehead. "I thought you'd just stolen from them."

"Things were different back there." She doesn't know what to say. She's already told Adro everything about her sainthood, but she can't make him understand. He's never known the strangeness of being close to the gods, the intoxicating and terrifying power to remake the world. And what terrifies her, almost more than anything else, is the thought that Artolo was *nothing* to her, back in Guerdon. He wasn't the only crime boss or foreign spy she destroyed when she was the Saint of Knives. How many others are out there? How many enemies has she made in her heedless course? "It doesn't matter anyway. Hawse said to go to the Street of Blue Glass – where's that? Show me where to go, and I'll go. You'll never see me again."

She knows she should leave him behind. She's the source of the danger. He'll be safe if she goes, right?

Until Dol Martaine finds out he was there. Until the witch finds him. Until her friend ends up as one of those poor starving slaves she saw working the hillside farms. There's no "safe" on Ilbarin. Only degrees of suffering.

Cari grabs his hand. "Or come with me. We'll get out. We'll get Ren and your kid. We'll come back for the captain, and we'll all get out."

CHAPTER FOURTEEN

Guerdon was like the open ocean. Cari could easily lose herself in the sea of people, the flow of life in the streets. The choppy waters of the Wash, the fast-flowing river of Mercy Street emptying into the whirlpool of Venture Square.

By comparison, Ushket's a small pond, and full of sharks. It's not the first time Cari and Adro have run through the streets of a city, evading the Ghierdana, but back then they risked nothing but their own lives, and weighed the risk lightly. Tonight, they're both conscious of their burdens, of how much they have to lose.

Cari's got a better feel for Ushket, now. She almost feels like she knows the town, thanks to Hawse telling her about his excursions. Half the town's been abandoned to the rising seas; the new harbour near the prefect's fortress marks the dividing line. Downslope of that harbour, it's all tidal ruins, inhabited only by the most desperate. The only way out of there is through the Ghierdana. Work in the labour camps, or the yliaster refinery. Or, if you want to get out faster, try jumping the fence that divides the town and take a Ghierdana bullet. Cari was very lucky, that first night. If the Monkfish hadn't found her, she'd likely have ended up on the wrong side of the line.

Upslope of the harbour, life in Ushket is almost normal. People still have jobs there, still go to the market to shop, meet their friends for a drink. Oh, the lower levels flood when the tide's high, and the temples are all ashes, but you could close your eyes and imagine that the Godswar never came.

But you're still the dragon's property, there. Cross the Ghierdana, and you lose everything. You go downslope, beyond the chain link fences and the barricades. Ushket isn't a place where humans live, not any more. It's a machine for enforcing compliance, for grinding every scrap of service out of a captive population.

The Street of Blue Glass, Adro tells her, is as far downslope as you can go without drowning. So, they go down, through alleyways choked with mud and driftwood, along walkways over flooded streets. She'd be lost without Adro as a guide, but when it comes to sneaking and slipping through the fences, she takes the lead, drawing on skills she learned in Guerdon. She and Adro make a good team, even after all these years.

It gets easier once they're past the rotten heart of town – the prefect's fortress. Cari glances up at the towers, wondering if Artolo's behind one of those lighted windows. She tries again to recall her first clash with the Ghierdana boss, back in the New City – there were so many bastards to destroy in those glorious months of power. Slavers, rapists, murderers, arms dealers, god-touched – anyone who threatened the people under Spar's protection, she broke. She looks up at those windows and tightens her fist, imagining the stone obeying her, blotting out the light.

The Street of Blue Glass looks to be entirely abandoned. Floodwaters surge in and out of the ruined buildings, like the street's breathing.

"I can't figure out the seas here at all," mutters Cari. "Did the whole island sink? The sea level around the rest of the Firesea hasn't changed, far as I could tell."

"It's all fucked." Adro sounds shaken. "Kraken piled the seas up on Ilbarin – they're not level any more. The Ghierdana have to use motor-tugs to pull ships up the slope. And it's worse on the far side."

The buildings that line the street were once physicians, artists' studios, solariums. Most have shattered panes of blue glass in their upper storeys. There was a belief in Ilbarin that light filtered through such windows had healthful properties, and rich folk from the city used to travel to Ushket in the winter to bask in the blue-tinged sunlight. Now it's all filtered through a murky soup of silt and broken glass.

"Do you know who we're meeting?"

Adro shakes his head. "I've heard there are evil sorcerers living down this way — I've seen a black ship sailing through the ruins. Moving against the wind." He probes the water with the captain's sword. "The rumour is that they've got an arrangement with the Ghierdana, so no one dares come here."

Something slithers past Carillon's ankle, something sinuous and slimy. The waters around her churn with sudden animation. It's dark, and the faint moonlight dances on the leaping water without revealing what's beneath. Adro ineffectively slashes at the water with his sword. It's not one creature down there, it's hundreds of them. It's thousands.

It's worms.

The worms boil out of the water, piling on one another, a pillar of writhing slimy bodies rising above Cari like a putrid wave. Two long fronds emerge obscenely from that central mass, growing in length and thickness. They shrug on a cloak of darkness, pulling the night sky around them as a garment. A worm-fingered hand passes over what approximates the entity's face, and suddenly it's got a white porcelain mask for a face. The mask smiles in an expression of bland reassurance.

The Crawling One extends a hand to Cari, offering to help her out of the water.

Adro runs forward, hacking at the Crawling One with his sword. It's as ineffective as slashing the floodwater. His sword slips right through the monster, comes out covered in worm-goo, but the Crawling One isn't wounded.

"We mean you no harm," says the Crawling One. Its voice is rich and deep, soothing in its confident warmth, but there's a disconcerting accompaniment – barely audible, at the edge of hearing – of other voices saying the same words. "We have been expecting you. Please, come with us."

The long night has made Artolo's eyes feel raw. He shuffles through the papers, and the columns of numbers dance in his vision. To the abyss with it – he's no clerk to fuss over accounts. The shape of the problem is clear enough – the yliaster produced by the work camp is barely enough to meet the quotas demanded by Great-Uncle, and the supply of workers is limited and dwindling. Either fewer of the bastards get to leave, or they stop dying – or Artolo sends more bodies to the camp.

He tries to shove the papers away across the desk, but his gloves bend under the pressure. The damn ghost-finger spell has worn off again. He slams his palm down on the papers and paws them across the table. He storms across the room and fumbles with the doorknob but he can't get a grip on the slick brass. Infuriated, he steps back and kicks the door down, splintering the lock. A passing servant in the corridor yelps in alarm and scuttles backwards.

"Where's the witch?" demands Artolo.

"Shore! The shore! She's down there!" The words come spilling out of the servant in a jumble, a frantic defence against Artolo's anger. "Someone reported seeing the Guerdonese woman there!"

Artolo snorts, like a bull about to charge. The witch should have told him there'd been a tip-off. Has her sorcery rotted her brain? Damn Eshdana should know their place! The ash-mark can be wiped away as easily as he put it there, he thinks, but his limp fingers mock him. He remembers the first time she woke his ghost-fingers, and how pleasurable it was to dip his thumb in the ash and smear the grey dust across the brow of her helmet. She won her life with that spell.

But she must learn her place.

"Find Dol Martaine. Tell him to fetch my horse—"

"Begging your pardon, lord, but Dol Martaine's gone down to the shore, too. Soon as he heard the witch was gone, he took his men and followed."

"Get my carriage ready. Now."

Cari doesn't know if the Crawling One found this loft room intact, or if it salvaged furniture from all over Ushket. The shattered blue windows look out on the troubled stars over Ilbarin.

Adro sits down next to her on the rotted sofa, his eyes fixed on the Crawling One. His face has a sickly greenish cast, and his hands grip his knees tightly to keep from shaking.

"You may call us Twelve Suns Bleeding," said the creature. "Forgive us – we were not expecting you until tomorrow. We intended to provide more pleasant environs for any negotiation."

"But you have a ship, right?" asks Cari.

"One that suffices for our purposes," says the Crawling One. "You will not find it a pleasant voyage, I fear."

"And you've got an understanding with Artolo? With the Ghierdana?"

"We do," says Twelve Suns Bleeding. "We do not interfere with their harvest of yliaster, and they do not interrupt our consumption of the remains." There's a sickening relish in the way it says the last word, a sort of leering. The Crawling Ones devour the dead, capturing what remains, reading the lingering patterns in the brain. The colony in front of her has the knowledge of hundreds of people, all their minds trapped within the grubs. There must still be corpses down there in the ruins of Ilbarin City. Most of the human remains would have rotted by now, but there could be the relics of saints and divine monsters. A banquet for the worms.

"Do they search your ship when it leaves?"

"We have, as you say, an understanding."

"All right, let's talk business." Cari's eager to get out of here. If things turn sour, they've got nothing that can hurt the Crawling One.

Twelve Suns Bleeding doesn't so much sit as engulf the chair. "Do you desire refreshment? Dry clothing, perhaps?" The creature's black robes are bone-dry.

Adro looks to Cari for guidance, and she shakes her head. Accepting anything from the Crawling Ones is perilous. Cari rarely dealt with them directly, back in Guerdon, but she knows they're not to be trusted.

"You need not fear us, Carillon Thay." It must notice her involuntary frown, as it continues. "Your friend Hawse did not tell us your true name. We knew it through other sources. We are exceedingly well informed on many matters."

"Does my name make a difference? I just want passage to Khebesh."

"We knew your grandfather." The porcelain mask remains impassive, the voice measured. "He too sought the city of Khebesh."

"He did?"

"When he was a young man, as humans reckon age. He came to Ilbarin as a merchant, trading with the prefects and the spicers by day, but by night he visited the crypts and the temple of Rammas, Recorder of All Deeds, seeking wisdom. He tried to enter Khebesh, but the gates of the sorcerer's city open for few." The mask tilts slightly, asking the unspoken question: why would they open for you?

"What was Jermas looking for in Khebesh?" Cari can't resist wanting to know more. Her grandfather was a lunatic – he squandered the family fortune on a deranged attempt to remake the Black Iron Gods, to turn them from monstrous deities of carrion and suffering into something more *tractable*. Civic gods, protectors of Guerdon. Guardian spirits for the whole city.

"He sought the most skilled mortal sorcerers." Twelve Suns Bleeding turns their pseudo-palms up, as if to say, *what are we, invisible?* Crawling Ones are far more able than fragile mortal flesh at surviving the devastating side effects of sorcery. "He found a renegade from Khebesh who was able to assist him in his efforts. We greatly admired your grandfather's ambition. He foresaw what the Godswar entails for your civilisation. In time, he turned to us. We were *honoured* to be able to preserve part of his indomitable will."

"The fucker's ash now. And the ghouls kicked you worms out of Guerdon." She knows she shouldn't antagonise the Crawling Ones, but the way they're talking about Jermas like he's a visionary to be admired sickens her. The old man was a monster in human form even before he came back as a pile of worms.

The mask doesn't slip. "A regrettable situation," replies Twelve Suns Bleeding, "Guerdon holds much knowledge that should be preserved. The pioneers of alchemy were the greatest minds of their generation, and their souls were tossed down the corpse-shafts to be food for the savage ghouls, or burned as offerings to the Kept Gods. We offer a new path. A form of survival."

Cari shudders as an unwelcome mental image appears in her brain – the towers of the New City, but they're made out of a gigantic seething pile of maggots instead of heavenly stone. She perceives Spar's soul locked within that worm-city. Another form of survival – and can she say it's any worse than Spar's current state? She imagines the worm-towers collapsing in on themselves, unwinding, taking on a new shape. A cloak of black, and then a white porcelain mask with familiar features. Spar's face, no longer disfigured by the scales and carbuncles of the Stone Plague, but preserved for ever in perfection—

"Get out," says Cari through clenched teeth, "of my fucking head!"

The Crawling One doesn't react, but the thought vanishes, snuffed out like a candle-flame.

"We seek only understanding," says Twelve Suns Bleeding mildly. "We are akin, are we not? All psychopomps, custodians of the souls of the dead."

"Passage to Khebesh. For me." Cari wonders how far she can

push it. Ask for the moon, and get a silver coin. "And Adro, and his family. And Captain Hawse. After we're done in Khebesh, you bring us back to a safe port. Not here – Paravos or the eastern Caliphate."

Adro reaches over and squeezes Cari's hand in gratitude. Of course, it complicates things. They'll have to pick up Adro's family. And circle back for Hawse and convince him to come. Hell, maybe it'll be like old times. A pile of malign sentient grave-worms can't be that much worse than sharing a cabin with Dol Martaine.

Twelve Suns Bleeding considers. "The city of Khebesh is closed to outsiders. None may pass the gate. How do you intend to gain entry?"

Cari tries a bluff. She shrugs. "I'm a thief. I'll find a way in."

The worms withdraw, the Crawling One seeming to recoil. It reminds Cari of a sea anemone pulling back its tendrils. "Khebesh is not as other cities. It is locked away behind the Ghost Walls. Even we are not able to force entry. Your skills will not avail you."

"All right. If that doesn't work, I've got something they want. A book."

The mask slips a little. When Twelve Suns Bleeding speaks, the grave worm chorus is louder, more discordant. "What book?"

Adro shoots her a curious glance, too. Cari takes a deep breath before answering. The book's her only leverage. It's Spar's only hope.

"A journal belonging to Guerdon's chief thaumaturgist, Doctor Ramegos. She came from Khebesh. They'll want her spell diary back, right? Much knowledge that must be preserved."

"Doctor Ramegos was known to us." Twelve Suns Bleeding studies its gloved hands like it's examining the fingernails it doesn't have. "Might we examine this tome?"

"No. The book's somewhere safe." It's only half a lie – Hawse has hidden the fucking book somewhere safe. She's just not entirely sure where.

The important thing, though, is keeping the Crawling One's wormy fingers away from the fucking book.

"You intend to trade Doctor Ramegos' grimoire for entry into the city. A plausible exchange," continues Twelve Suns Bleeding.

"So, what do you want?" asks Cari.

Twelve Suns Bleeding raises an empty hand. The fingers – more than five, and no discernible thumb – fold inwards, squeeze, and unfold again. Now there's a jewelled box in its hand, about the size of Carillon's thumb. It looks like a tiny coffin. The Crawling One opens the clasp, and a worm wriggles out of its glove and into the casket. The lid shuts again, and Twelve Suns Bleeding lays the casket down on the table between Cari and Adro.

Neither of them move to take the box, even though it's made of gold and studded with rubies.

"What do we do with that?" asks Adro.

"The sorcerers of Khebesh worship no gods. When a sorcerer dies, the body is placed in a lead sarcophagus and locked away in the Vault of Aeons. You will bring the casket within the walls of Khebesh, and find a dark, moist place. A patch of earth, perhaps, or a drain, or a midden. Let the worm do the rest. We shall multiply, and grow strong, and we shall find a way into the vault. Stone cracks, lead corrodes, and flesh decays. The worm always conquers, in the end."

"That's it?" Adro's surprised. "And for that, you'll get us all out of Ilbarin?"

"Passage to Khebesh, and from Khebesh to another port of your choosing within the Firesea. There are no safe ports any more, but we shall ensure your protection as much as is reasonable." The mask tilts. "We gave your grandfather a similar arrangement, Carillon Thay. You shall see the wisdom of an alliance with us."

Cari hesitates as she considers the gleaming casket. She never met the wormy resurrection of Jermas Thay – it was Eladora, instead, who fell into their grandfather's slimy clutches. Eladora who got used in his attempt to bind and remake the Black Iron Gods. But she saw the other Crawling Ones that infested the city. Their malignity is something other than the crazed fervour of the gods – it's a slow rot, a cancer. There's a horrible inevitability about it. Everyone knows that the sorcerers of Khebesh are the best at sorcery, just like Guerdon's alchemists are the best in the world, far beyond their competitors in Ulbishe or Paravos. What will happen when the worms get into the Vault of whatever-it-was and eat the knowledge of the dead archmages? How much stronger will the Crawling Ones become?

But if she doesn't take the deal, what then? Spar dies, she probably dies here on Ilbarin when the Ghierdana find her, and the worms find some other way in. The next pilgrim seeking Khebesh might not hesitate. *What should I do?* she thinks. She wishes she could ask Spar, even though she knows what he'd say. Spar would tell her that it's too dangerous to give the Crawlers such power, that he should do the honourable, self-sacrificing thing instead. He'd martyr himself, and say something inspiring about his father Idge.

You martyring yourself is how we got here, she snaps. *I'm saving you no matter what.* What's the value in thinking through the consequences, in considering the morality of your action, if your conclusion is that it's wrong, but you have to do it anyway?

Her hand hovers over the casket, her fingers flexing, unable to decide.

It's Adro who jumps up, Adro who grabs the casket, stuffs it roughly into his pocket. "It's a deal? Right, Cari?"

"Fuck it. Deal."

The carriage can't cross the mud of the shore. Artolo climbs down and strides across the muddy slope towards the wreck of the *Rose*. Werelights glow on the deck – the witch must still be there. Ropes trail over the side of the hull, and it's clear from the footprints that most people took that route up on to the deck, but with his maimed hands it's denied him, because of Carillon Thay. He searches until he finds a breach in the hull and squeezes his broad shoulders through, makes his way through the stinking bowels of the wreck. It's pitch-black and he has to shove his way through the debris, kicking and pushing junk out of the way until he finds the cramped stairs up to the deck.

Dol Martaine rushes over to him like a hound greeting its master, licking the bleeding stumps of Artolo's fingers. Too eager. Too eager by half.

"We got a tip-off, boss, but it didn't pay off." He jerks a thumb towards an old man sitting on the deck. "Just some crazy hermit. God-touched, I'll wager. Seeing things that aren't real."

Artolo ignores him. "Hands," he says to the witch, "now."

The witch recites the spell, and the ghost-fingers awake. Strength runs through his hands.

"She was here," whispers the witch.

"You've searched the ship."

"She's gone. I'll find her. You need to focus on the yliaster supply. The dragon will be—"

Artolo turns away. He picks up the old man, ghost-fingers gripping the collar of his priestly robes. The old man's mumbling to himself, snatches of a prayer to the broken gods of Ilbarin.

"Hawse, yes?"

"Blessed be the Lord of Waters. My soul shall sail over calm seas until the Bythos carry me down to the fathomless palace."

Artolo strikes the old man in the face, but he keeps mumbling through broken lips. A fanatic. It'll take time to break him. He drops Hawse at the feet of another Eshdana – Rauf, he recalls.

"Hold him. Make sure he doesn't run off. Or die."

Rauf's a little slower than he should be, wary of laying hands on a holy man. Infuriating – he should fear Artolo, not the broken gods. All these bastards need reminding who rules Ilbarin. It's because of his fingers. They don't respect a maimed man. They don't respect him because of Carillon Thay.

"Martaine," snaps Artolo, "search the shore. She was here. Find out where she went."

"First light, we'll sweep the shore."

"Now."

"It's too dark, boss."

Artolo takes a breath. More and more, it feels like he's wrestling with the whole of Ilbarin, like the whole island is conspiring against him. Godhusks, foot-dragging workers, cursed weather. Crops that won't grow, ships that won't sail, alchemical machines that break down. Every time he pins one problem down, another sprouts, and the only tool left to him is fear.

Very well. He'll make them scared.

"Oh? It's light you need, is it?" He grabs Martaine, spins him around, ghost-fingers seizing the smaller man by the wrist, arm locking across Martaine's neck. He bends Martaine's sword arm back painfully. "Witch! Burn this fucking ship."

The witch raises her hand, makes an arcane gesture. Blue flames flicker in the captain's cabin, then catch on the piles of salvaged books. Artolo force-marches Martaine over to the burning pile and shoves his face towards the flames. "You belong to the Dragon! You don't question my orders! You belong to me!"

Martaine struggles, but Artolo's too strong for him. "I'll find her! I'll find her!" whimpers Martiane. Artolo drops him to the floor, kicks him in the side, lets him crawl away. Martaine's men, the witch's men, all Eshdana, all gathered in a gaggle around the deck, faces lit by the dancing firelight, all watching Martaine's humiliation. Artolo roars at them. "You think the ash-mark means you're safe? You're mine, too! I can put you back in the camps! Make you dive until your lungs burst! If any of you want to get off this stinking rock, you'll do as I say. Find her! Go!"

Led by a limping Dol Martaine, they scramble down the side of the ship.

Artolo's left alone with the witch. The fire's blazing now; the whole cabin's aflame. Soon, it'll consume all the rotten timbers of the *Rose*. It bathes his left side in uncomfortable heat. He can only imagine how hot it must be inside the witch's metal suit. All that exposed brass and steel, next to the open flames.

Servants, he can break. Martaine, he can hurt. The witch requires special handling.

He stands there for a long minute, watching the fires dance. Great-Uncle is coming. Hasn't Artolo done enough to atone? Hasn't he done enough to be forgiven? It wasn't his fault; it was Carillon Thay who ruined everything. His fingers weren't enough to satisfy the dragon. Carillon Thay – he'll stake her out like a goat. Roast her. Gut her. Burn her.

There's a hiss of steam from below as little burning fragments of the deck fall into the waters in the flooded hold underneath. Little ticks and creaks from the heating metal.

"Someone told you she was here."

"You told us she might know a sailor. And there were stories on the street about the hermit behaving oddly."

"Why come yourself, on so thin a tale?"

"I was doing what you told me. You want her caught."

Finding Thay is an irrelevant distraction. His head knows this. His blood, though, roars in his ears. It knows another truth, deeper and more vital.

"I want her dead."

CHAPTER FIFTEEN

Spar watches Rasce's triumphant return to the house on Lanthorn Street. Vyr blusters, argues that Rasce should rest, but he cannot deny his cousin's rapid recovery. Like Cari, Rasce's vitality is renewed when he enters the New City.

"Baston," orders Rasce, "tell your allies that they may return, that Vyr misspoke. Tell them the New City was made for them, and they have a place here." Spar's lifted by those words – in his dying moments, he dreamed the New City into being as a place of refuge, out of reach of the oppressive guilds and grasping priests that rule Guerdon. His father's writings made real in stone.

"Vyr," continues Rasce. "There are those here who require our charity. Open the coffers! We shall not be miserly!"

"That's not what Great-Uncle sent us to do," objects Vyr.

"I am Chosen. Do as I say."

"I'll handle it," volunteers Karla. "Just give me the money."

Spar can follow every coin. He can feel every scratch of Vyr's pen on the ledger, hear every grumble and complaint. Rumour quickly spreads to the other Ghierdana families – and the other dragons – of Rasce's odd behaviour, his swift recovery – and Spar hears every whisper. He relays them all to Rasce, who leans his head back in his chair and listens to the song of the city. Spar can sense the man's soul expanding, intertwining with his own. Even as the city flows into Rasce, so too does he inhabit part of the city.

On a warm evening, three days later, Rasce leaves the house on Lanthorn Street, and walks the ways of the New City again. Baston follows, a wary shadow, still unsure of what to make of this strange hybrid, now that he's been reborn in the grubby heaven of the New City.

They come to the base of one of the City's great towers, and Rasce ascends, hurrying up the endless flights of stairs. This tower is among those that burned during the invasion, but Rasce keeps climbing when he comes to the ashen region. Like much of the city, the tower is unfinished – the miracle of its creation ran dry before it was done, and the topmost levels of the building trail off into stalagmites and unformed fingers of stone, like melted white candles.

It's easier for Spar to think up here. Easier to focus. Rasce is the only living soul at this height.

"So," says Rasce. "Show me the city."

He closes his eyes, looks within. Taps into Spar's own perception from within. When Cari tried this, it overwhelmed her, and she had already experienced similar visions from the Black Iron Gods. It took weeks for her and Spar to find the point of balance, to drip-feed revelation into her mind. Rasce, though, eats the visions hungrily and demands more.

"It's not so different," he says, "from seeing the world as my Great-Uncle does." Rasce points north, down Mercy Street towards Castle Hill and the city beyond. Towards the Fog Yards. "Show me the yliaster dealers yonder."

I can't see clearly beyond the New City. Images flicker between their two minds – glimpses of high walls, fortresses mated to factories, great holding tanks – but it's all fleeting, all strained.

"That's of little use," says Rasce. "Mandel & Company must fall – my Great-Uncle has commanded it. But there are lesser prizes closer at hand that can be swept up, while I learn how you can best aid me." He plucks idly at a piece of scorched stone, marvelling at the experience – he can feel the stone with his fingers, but also experiences the sensation of the fingers brushing the stone, through his communion with Spar. "You burned."

It was miraculous fire. A saint burned Carillon with a sword of fire, and the injury was transferred to me. It set the stone alight.

"On Glimmerside, you saved my life. Am I now invulnerable to knife and gun?"

It's not easy. I couldn't always do it for Cari – and I had to draw on your life force to save you from the Tallowman.

"If I stepped off the edge, would you catch me?"

I'd try. I might be able to take the force of the impact, or give you something to grab on to.

"You can reshape the city."

A little. It's an effort.

"I did as you asked me," says Rasce. "I gave money to the wretches you showed me. They will be helped, you have my word. Tell me, O spirit, what did my coin buy me?"

What do you want?

"An army of stone golems, each one twelve feet tall and armed with poleaxes. I desire a fortress suitable for a prince of the Ghierdana, with a dracodrome for Great-Uncle. Walls thick enough to endure a siege by all the gods of Ishmere. A great juggernaut that rolls across Guerdon to the Fog Yards and crushes my rivals in the yliaster trade. Conjure those for me from the stone of the city."

I can't tell if you're joking or not.

"In Lyrix, the priests of Culdan can put a death-curse on a blade, and every wound from that sword is henceforth mortal. The priests of Velthe can command demons. A saint blessed by the Moon Goddess can walk among the clouds and hurl spears of moonlight. Can you do any of those things?"

No.

"But you conjured this city."

We stole the power of the Black Iron Gods. They had a vast reserve of miraculous energy, accumulated over years of worship and sacrifice. We used all that to make the New City.

"Had I the power of those dread gods at my command, friend, I would have spent it more wisely."

I was mostly dead at the time. The memory of Spar's fall from the apex of the Seamarket wells up, overlaps with the thought of Rasce falling from this ruined spire. The tower shifts, sending dust and pebbles cascading over the edge to plummet down to the streets far below. Portions of Spar's consciousness fall with the pebbles. Rasce grabs the wall for support.

"Of course. Forgive me, friend. As with any new Eshdana, I must know your particular talents."

I'm not one of your recruits!

"You've already taken the ash," laughs Rasce. He holds up soot-stained fingers. "Very well. Our partnership shall be one of equals, for I bow to neither god nor man, only to my Great-Uncle."

The thunder of great leathery wings scatters Spar's mind like leaves in a hurricane. Has he lost track of *time* again, slipped forward a few weeks to the return of the dragon? No – it's a smaller dragon, one of the other Ghierdana family heads. Spar reconstitutes himself (a flurry of minor miracles across the streets near the tower: a pot falls from a stove, shattering; a pistol in an Eshdana armoury goes off spontaneously; birds take flight, cawing out the name of Idge) and refocuses on Rasce.

The dragon circles the tower twice, the winds from its wings nearly knocking Rasce from his perch. A young woman in riding gear clings to the dragon's back; through her goggles, she watches Rasce with suspicion. The dragon lands, clinging to the side of the burned tower like a gigantic bat, claws sinking deep into the masonry for purchase. The long neck cranes so the head can look in at Rasce.

"Young Rasce," says the dragon Thyrus, "why are you all alone atop this spire?" The rumble of its voice sends ash and debris tumbling from the tower.

"I seek the pure night air, great Thyrus, for this city is full of miasmas and foul smoke. And I seek to remember what it is like to fly."

The woman on Thyrus' back whispers to her mount. The dragon's head twists around. "Be kind, Lucia," she admonishes. "Or perhaps I shall make you walk, too."

"How goes the war, great one? Does Major Estavo work you hard?"

The dragon extends one wing, displaying an ugly suppurating wound on the inside of the forewing. "Not Estavo. This I got from some Ulbishan trade ship, crossing the sea. The Ulbishans trade in alchemy now, too, in imitation of Guerdon. I thought to take one of their ships, and they drove me off with death-glass."

"The dragon is invincible."

"The dragon needs more than aphorisms," says Thyrus, ruefully. "Next time, the dragon shall fly low, and Lucia here shall slay their gunners from afar before they can wound me. A week, and I shall hunt again – unless Estavo comes knocking. With my brother's long absence, we must all work harder to fulfil our bargain with the mainlanders." The dragon's lip curls, exposing three rows of fangs each as long as a man's hand, but Rasce can't be sure if the dragon's distaste is aimed at the mainland of Lyrix or at Great-Uncle. "My brother has still not returned from Firesea. What is he doing there, I wonder, that keeps him so long away?"

"Family business, great one."

"Does he know you have dipped into his hoard, Rasce? I would not be so quick to forgive such a thing, were one of my kin to steal from me."

"My Great-Uncle trusts me, great one. He has given me a task, and I shall spend the dragon's gold as needed."

The dragon snorts. "We watch you, Rasce. Remember that we are all bound by the Armistice. Be careful, child, that you do not break what you cannot mend and do not own."

"All things," says Rasce, "belong to the dragons."

"Flattery." Still, the dragon preens. "There is something different about you, boy. I smell it."

"I have been across the border. Even into the zones held by our enemies. Unlike you, great one, I can move unseen. Your presence is too glorious to go unnoticed by our foes."

The dragon stretches its wide wings. "Your Uncle Taras had better hurry back. This peace, I think, will not last for long. Haith is too withered. Ishmere is a caged beast. And Guerdon is too rich a prize to be left unplucked. The gold of the alchemists may be made in their factories, but it is gold nonetheless."

Silver, mutters Spar. *Ishmeric miracles devalued silver, years ago.*

Rasce ignores him. "All things belong to the dragons."

"Yet you employ thieves who are not ash-bought. I hear you overruled your Cousin Vyr, and brought the unmarked back into your house. Why?"

"Family business, great one." Rasce bows, affects a mocking smile, but Spar can feel the man's heart pounding in his chest.

"It stays family business," says Thyrus, "only so long as it does not trouble the other families. We must share this miserable city, boy. Do not overstep."

With that, the dragon's gone. It opens its claws, falling from the tower, then spreads its wings and catches the air, swooping low over the New City and flapping away. Rasce waits until the dragon has vanished into the clouds before speaking again.

"You will listen, won't you, to what is spoken in the compounds? To know what Thyrus whispers to her Chosen, or to her counsellor, that would be a precious boon indeed."

I'll try. It's not always easy for me to focus.

"I'm told that you struck down Ishmeric godspawn in the war, when they dared enter the New City," says Rasce. "Could you strike down, say, a dragon in flight, if you had to?"

Just making that tunnel cost me almost everything I had left.

"I see." Rasce pulls off one of his riding gloves, touches the stone with his bare hand. Toys, for a moment, with the jewelled ring he wears.

Then steps forward, off the edge of the building.

What are you doing!?

"Catch me if you can!" shouts Rasce as he falls. His words are lost in the wind, but Spar hears them nonetheless.

Spar gathers himself, a whirlwind of power. There are fragments of his soul all over the New City, tangled in objects. Now, with a desperate effort of will, he pulls them to the locus of his concentration, rupturing and straining his very soul as he draws all his remaining power into a point.

Rasce tumbles down and down—

—The past threatens to swallow Spar, to pull him back to that fall from the Seamarket, to the moment of his death, but he pushes it away, focuses on *here* and *now*, on the living man who falls, not the dead man who fell—

At the moment of impact, Spar catches him, redirects the energy of the fall. The New City quakes, walls cracking, towers swaying. Like a sorcerer swallowing a spell, the worst damage is unseen, internal. Far below, tunnels collapse, foundations crumble.

But it works. Rasce falls more than a dozen storeys to land as lightly as a cat. He looks up at the tower, at the ash falling around around him, and laughs. "See! You are stronger than you think, my friend! You need only a little encouragement!"

Spar's too broken even to form words. The stone around Rasce fluoresces dimly, as portions of Spar's soul combust from the effort of the desperate miracle. Flurries of indignant fury and confusion burst from him, but his mind is too shattered to hold even those gusts of emotion. His feelings blow away from him, his anger like wild dogs running through the streets of the city, howling in the distance until they vanish.

Rasce pulls the Ring of Samara from his finger. "An heirloom of my family. Enchanted to save a falling man. A useful thing for a dragon-rider – but you are more useful still!" He tosses it in the air, catches it again. "Forgive my deception! My Great-Uncle has commanded me to accomplish a perilous quest, and I had to know if you were ready for the battle to come!"

The New City changes.

Spar can feel the shift in mood. He feels the quick, subtle footsteps of thieves gathering in the house on Lanthorn Street; they come, sneaking out of the Wash and Five Knives, out of the Fog Yards and Glimmerside, from under the skirts of the Duchess Viaduct. Drawn by tales of dragon's gold, by rumours of a new prince in the underworld, a new master. Some smugglers have thrived in this divided Guerdon, sneaking across the lines between occupation zones, but more have suffered. Neither Haith nor Ishmere have any love for thieves, and the free city's new minister for security is eight times more vigilant and cunning than his predecessors.

The LOZ border is porous to them, secret ways opening as needed.

In the evenings, Lanthorn Street is the Brotherhood clubhouse reborn. They toast the fallen, naming their kin who were taken by the gallows, or the Tallows, or the war. Idge, Ven the Goat, the Cafstan boys. Silken Tammur. Even Heinreil gets a round. Karla leads the toast to her father Hedan, gone underground two years ago tonight, and never came back.

Another toast, to Spar Idgeson.

Karla whispers into her brother's ear, unheard by any in the room save Baston – and Spar.

"What the fuck happened between you and Rasce?"

"Trust me."

"Of course *I* trust you," she whispers. "Make sure Rasce does. We should take the ash."

"There's no need for that," says Baston. "It's Spar. Idge's son came back."

Trust. Spar has to trust Rasce, trust this slender connection to the mortal world. This narrow crack in the walls of his living tomb.

His trust is rewarded. Those poisoned by the fumes from the burning of Dredger's yard are given money by Karla. She hires back-alley alchemists and whisky saints to tend to them, rough healers of the streets, but at least it's some help. Rasce's campaign against the city's yliaster dealers continues – one by one, other merchants of raw alchemical materials along Guerdon's docks take the ash and swear allegiance to the Ghierdana.

Take the ash, or are given it. There are no more accidental conflagrations like the debacle at Dredger's yard, but there are incidents of arson. Sabotage. The occasional beating. Spar learns much of this second-hand – the other alchemical supplies have their operations outside the New City, in the old docklands to the south or the new docks beyond Holyhill. From his spires, he sees columns of smoke, shadows moving on rooftops, but most of his knowledge comes from whispers heard by his walls. Thieves boasting about coin stolen from rich alchemical merchants (like they did in Idge's day, thinks Spar, when his father led the Brotherhood against the crushing power of the alchemists' guild). Grumblings from the other Ghierdana families, the subsonic rumbles of disquiet from the other dragons. The clatter of typewriter keys as Lyrixian soldiers write up worried reports about their unreliable allies.

Spar relays all this information to Rasce, and Rasce puts it to work. Secrets are weapons if you know how to use them. Rasce sets dragon against dragon, buys off Major Estavo with the promise of intelligence gleaned from the other occupation zones, rallies the thieves. His swagger is infectious; the younger thieves feel like these streets are theirs. They no longer need to be furtive and god-fearing – Rasce offers them a chance to be respected, to take what they wish from the city.

Spar watches Baston follow loyally behind Rasce, eclipsing Vyr as his right-hand man. It's Baston who knows how to evade the city watch in Guerdon, Baston who knows who to bribe and who to intimidate, Baston who knows when to fall back to the inviolate fortress of the New City. No streets were ever so friendly to thieves and rebels as those changing alleyways of Spar's mind.

Listening to Rasce's quick heartbeat, Spar no longer finds himself losing track of time. He's anchored to the present now, no longer falling into regretful labyrinths of the past or fragmenting into confusion. Time proceeds in an orderly fashion for him. Days passing into weeks. He still feels fragile, still dares not work any miracles, but he's himself again.

In the dark of the night, while the New City sleeps, Spar's mind scans the southern horizon, listening for a whisper.

Hearing nothing except the mutterings and yowling of ghouls, deep underground.

"What do you have for me?" asks Rasce. He flings himself down on a couch, closes his eyes, and Spar relays the day's stolen secrets.

The last shipment of Craddock's yliaster has arrived; henceforth, he's to buy only from the Ghierdana. Rasce orders Baston to pay a visit to Craddock, remind him of the oath he swore, of the ash he wears.

More thieves out of the Wash; three are trustworthy, but the fourth is sworn to Fate Spider, a spy for the Sacred Realm. Rasce marks the woman's face.

Gossip from the Lyrixian quarter, rumours about places and people Spar's never heard of. Rasce drinks it all in, his mind bloating on the flow of secrets. His appetite for this hidden knowledge is insatiable, and he consumes it very differently from how Cari did.

A creature of instinct, she would seize on one image, one fragment, and go haring off after that secret. Spar might show her, say, a single act of injustice in the New City, some rape or murder or cruelty, and she'd spend the next week hunting the perpetrator. Rasce, by contrast, treats Spar's revelations like a glimpse of some wide terrain. He looks at the city spread out beneath him like a great map and spots connections Spar does not.

Always, in the back of Rasce's mind, Spar can dimly perceive the remembered presence of the dragon. Even this ragged sort of saint-hood with all its attendant miracles is nothing compared to the joy and glory of being Chosen of the Dragon.

"Show me the Fog Yards," says Rasce. He sips arax, and Spar finds he can taste the burning alcohol.

They're far away. Spar does his best to comply, drawing up an image from his tallest towers. The industrial district is on the far side of Guerdon, blocked by the cathedral-spangled shoulder of Holyhill and the eponymous smog. It's hard to focus at that distance, hard for him even to think about a place so far from the New City. City-dredged visions jostle with memory-fragments of the few times he visited the Fog Yards in life. As supernatural visions go, it's blurred and confused.

Sorry.

"Ach! It's like having a broken spyglass shoved into your eye socket. Enough!" Rasce waves his hand, and the vision vanishes. "I couldn't see a single thing about Mandel & Company. They control the bulk of the remaining trade in yliaster. Great-Uncle demands I bring them to heel." Outside the room, Karla approaches. Spar sees her through the stone, and thus so does Rasce. The Ghierdana prince drains the arax. "Come in," he shouts.

Karla slips in, shuts the door behind her. She peers curiously around the room. "I heard you talking to someone. Is . . . is he here?" she whispers in awe.

Tell her I'm here.

"He's here. He says hello." Rasce moves over on the couch to make space for her, pours her a glass of arax. "And he will leave, now, I think".

I'm omnipresent. I exist throughout the New City.

"Exist elsewhere, please."

"It's all right," says Karla. "This is business."

Rasce pouts. "Just business?"

"What did you expect?"

"Back home, the peasant families would happily send their comeliest daughters into my bed, in the hopes of winning the dragon's favour."

Karla rolls her eyes. "Well, I'm not some cow-eyed doxy, here only to warm your bed." She dances away from him, leaving him alone on the couch. She crosses the room, and toys with the box of ash. "It's about Mandel & Company, actually. I asked around a bit. Talked to some of Dad's old cronies. Turns out you're not the first to contemplate making a move against old Mandel."

"And?"

"There's a secret way in."

"Where is this secret way?"

"It wouldn't be very secret if I told you, would it? I don't know it, but I know who knows it." She grins, then dips her finger in the ash. "There's a price."

"The dragon," says Rasce, "does not bargain."

Karla brushes the ash across his lips. "But the dragon," she says, "could favour some of his servants above others. The dragon could lift up those who have been cast down."

He kisses her forehead, leaving the trace of ash on her brow. Claiming her.

"Who knows this secret way?" he asks again.

She speaks a name, and a shudder runs through the New City.

CHAPTER SIXTEEN

Twelve Suns Bleeding offers to go across town and collect Adro's family, but they decide the best thing to do is for them all to go. The Crawling Ones are exempt from the Ghierdana curfew – or so Twelve Suns Bleeding says, anyway. Cari pities the poor Eshdana guard who tries to tell a Crawling One to stay off the streets.

Cari and Adro fall into their old habits, keeping to the shadows. The Bythos have departed with the falling tide, although Cari hears the occasional distant bellow. The streets are mostly empty.

Mostly. Ahead, a trio of Eshdana. She ducks into a doorway, clutching her little knife, but Twelve Suns Bleeding just glides up the street towards them, its worm-voices chanting. The three men freeze, caught in a spell.

"You may pass freely," says the Crawling One. "They cannot see or hear you. I have their attention." Like it's something you can seize in your hand. The three men stare unseeing into the night. Cari wonders what Twelve Suns Bleeding has made them see instead of their quarry. Are they wandering the empty streets of Ushket in their minds? Or somewhere darker? The lips of one of the trio quivers, like he's about to say something.

She'll need to be careful. The Crawling One could do the same to her, just as easily. It could kill her, or Adro, with a word.

Adro's place. The tall, narrow houses remind her of Guerdon's

Gethis Row. Here, though, the stairwells are open at the top, an internal ventilation shaft to cool the buildings in the Ilbarinese heat – but that was when Ushket was far from the cooling sea. Now, water drips down in unlikely cascades from the tiled roof above. They climb the stairs without incident.

Adro knocks on the door twice, a heartbeat pause, another double knock. A code. Instantly, the door's opened from the inside revealing a smaller man, his features fine as china, marred by an odd mottling of the skin on his neck and left cheek. "Thank the gods! How did—"

He sees Carillon. Sees the looming shape of Twelve Suns Bleeding behind her.

"Adro. What's going on?"

"A thousand pardons for the disturbance," says the Crawling One, gliding in past Ren.

Inside, Adro moves quickly, stuffing clothes and other belongings into bags. "Change of plan, love," he says to Ren. "We're getting out, tonight."

Ren pulls Adro away into a side room, where they talk in quick, angry whispers. Cari glimpses a child's bed in there before Ren shuts the door firmly in her face.

Cari glances around the little apartment. Clothes drying on a rack. The embers of a fire in the stove. An unwashed pot with a crusted residue. A piece of blue jade on the shelf, twin to her own lost souvenir from that botched heist in Mattaur. She tries to imagine Adro's life here; all she can visualise is an idealised scene, like an oil painting. Adro and Ren talking by the fire, some rosy-cheeked cherub of a child playing on the floor.

That sort of cosy domestic normality would have her crawling up the walls in days.

Ren and Adro's argument gets louder.

"We must go," says Twelve Suns Bleeding, "before we are discovered."

Cari joins the Crawling One at the window. Down on the street — the armoured witch, and four Ghierdana soldiers.

"Godshit. Can you magic them?"

The Crawling One stares down at the witch, and there's a moment of pressure in the air, a roll of thunder as unseen wills contend. Humans aren't usually a match for Crawling One sorcery, but the porcelain mask snaps back as though struck with a hammer. "They are protected by a powerful sorcerer. A talented brain." The worms squelch, like he's licking his lips only it's his whole body, and Cari really wants to set him on fire at that moment. "I shall delay them." It glides over to the door of the apartment and draws a blazing sigil on the wood.

Adro emerges from the bedroom, a light-haired child clinging to him. Ren follows, carrying a bundle wrapped in cloth.

"Come on, we'll go up," she urges, making for the door.

Adro and Ren don't move. They look at each other, a moment of silent debate. They could turn Cari over now, save themselves.

Ren moves. He reaches inside the room, fetches the captain's sword. "Adro will have to carry Ama," he says. "You take this." He hands the blade to Cari.

Out over the rooftops.

Cari's the fastest of the four, the most at home in the uneven landscape. Adro's burdened by the precious weight of the child, which seems exaggerated, multiplied by the four-storey drop to the street below. Ren moves cautiously, too, and he's got a cough that speaks of some long illness. He has to stop, twice, to catch his breath, as Cari leads them back across town. Twelve Suns is gone — the Crawling One crawled into a drainpipe and is now back on ground level. She's spotted him twice, keeping pace with them on the streets below, illuminated by flashes of sorcery.

It's easy to navigate from up here with the Rock behind her and the moon-dappled sea ahead, the bulbous towers of the citadel to her right. She just has to find a route they can all traverse. She darts ahead, looking for walkways over the flooded streets, for gaps between buildings they can jump.

Encumbered by her armour, the sorceress can't follow.

Her guards can.

One of them catches up. Cari gets a glimpse of his face – young, his features reminding her horribly of Adro's kid. His armour's mismatched, and he holds his weapon as awkwardly as she holds the captain's sword. When he sees her, he snarls and charges her, swinging his blade wildly. She brings up her own sword, but the thing's heavier than she likes, and it's an awkward parry that knocks her off balance. He comes at her again, and she dodges away, dancing over the roof tiles. Even without Spar to guide her and anchor her, this is her element. Heights and unsure footing hold no terrors for her. The boy tries to follow her, but he's clumsy, and he slips.

She brings the sword down on him, putting her whole weight behind it, and, fuck, it's awful. The blade bites, sinks in, and he lets out a ghastly gurgle, blood and spittle bursting from him with the sound. He whimpers, one leg kicking against the tiles, hands grabbing at her shoulders, clawing at her face.

Cari's not a stranger to bloodshed, but not like this. When she was just a thief, she cut and ran. A quick slash with a sharp blade to slow down a guard, to slice her way free when someone tried to grab her. For all she knows, maybe someone she cut like that bled out, maybe the wound festered and they died from it, but she never hung around to find out. Cut and run.

And when she was the Saint of Knives, it was different. For one thing, she knew who she was killing. Spar could see everything that happened in the New City, so she could watch them. She could judge them with the perfect knowledge of a god. And when she did confront them, it was like a game. She had all the power, she was sainted and invulnerable, and they were – for the most part – only human.

It's not like this. She has to work to kill the boy, to kneel on top of him and push the blade in. She doesn't know how to do it clean, or quick. She has to look into his eyes as she does it, and they're full of confusion and fear. What does the boy see when he looks at the woman who murdered him?

He's still moaning and dying when Adro finds her, pulls her away. "Come on! Come *on*!"

She lets Adro lead her to a rotting roof garden when Ren and the boy wait. Ren's shaking with the effort of stifling his cough, to avoid giving them away to the other guards searching for them. A swaying rope ladder gets them down to street level. No sign of Twelve Suns. Adro lifts the child like a sack, and Cari and Ren run after him. There's a pinkish glow in the distance, beyond the Rock. Sunrise is coming soon. Right now, curfew's working in their favour, but once dawn comes there'll be more eyes, more desperate people looking for their own ticket out. Speed's their only hope now. Sprinting through the mud, Ren spluttering and spitting, Cari's own legs aching. It's hard to catch her breath, and every step sends sharp pain stabbing into her right lung. The bloody sword a dead weight in her hand.

Every moment, she expects a gunshot to ring out, a Ghierdana soldier to block her path.

Or, worst of all, the unnatural grip of a paralysis spell, locking her in place, freezing her like a statue, forced to watch, unable to act.

There! There, rising above the rooftops, the masts of a small sailing ship. No sails, bare as a tree in winter, but it's a ship, just like the Crawling Ones promised. They race down the Street of Blue Glass, wading through the waters now. Knee-deep, waist-deep, shoulder-deep – and then Twelve Suns Bleeding's sickeningly soft fingers clasp around her wrist, and lift her on to the deck of the derelict ship.

The mask smiles blankly. "To Khebesh, then."

Cari falls to her knees as the ship begins to move. No sails, no oars, no engine, just sorcery. The boards of the deck beneath her fingers are rotten and waterlogged – this isn't a ship, it's an animated wreck, drawn up from the seabed by magic. Pale shapes squirm in the swollen planks, and she realises the wood is riddled with grave-worms. The whole ship's a Crawling One.

With unlikely grace, the dead ship pulls away from Ushket, navigating the narrow channels of the flooded streets. Cari follows Adro and his family into a cabin and sinks down against the slimy wall.

"Hey, Cari."

She can't remember how to speak.

"That was almost like old times. We made it. We're out."

Twelve Suns Bleeding slithers out of the cabin walls, forming itself in front of them. The writhing worms fascinate the little girl. She reaches out to dip her fingers in the slime, but Ren pulls her back, gathers her close.

"Where is the grimoire?" asks the Crawling One.

Cari hesitates for a split second. The fucking book is her only leverage here – but she's under no illusions about the honour of Crawling Ones. She'll have to play this very carefully – but right now, she's got to co-operate. "Captain Hawse has it. It's on the *Rose*."

"A brief diversion, then." The worm-ship shudders and changes course. Twelve Suns sees the child, and bends down. The porcelain mask changes, becoming more clownish. "We shall play later, child," it says, then dissolves again.

"Those fuckers are never not creepy," mutters Cari.

Ren lifts up Ama, hugs her and hands her to Adro before extending a hand to Cari. "Adro spoke of you often, but I didn't think I'd ever meet you."

"Yeah, well, here I am."

"Adro trusts you, and he's got a good heart – we're all in your hands now." Ren glances around the rotten cabin. "I brought a little food, but we've a long journey ahead of us. Let's hope the worm-men eat something other than bodies."

"I don't think they do, but we can make it to the coast before we starve."

"Before we starve," echoes Ren, looking at the child in Adro's arms. "All right."

"Come on, Ren. We're off the Rock." Adro grins. "This is one of those adventures I told you about. Cari, come over here, meet Ama properly."

Ama's younger than Cari was when they sent her away to Aunt Silva's. She barely remembers that time, just the confusion of everything changing around her. People talking above her, transforming her world for reasons she couldn't understand. Being sent to live on a farm in the countryside outside Guerdon isn't quite the same as being kidnapped on to a worm-ship and sent on a mad quest to a city of sorcerers, but maybe it's not any weirder to a child.

Ama looks up at Cari with dark eyes. She seems less enchanted by Cari than she was by the Crawling One, and Cari tries not to take it personally.

"Where'd you get her?"

"Ren found her," says Adro, dandling the girl on his knee, "but we don't talk about those times, do we?" Ama laughs, and Cari wonders how much of the Godswar and the fall of Ilbarin the child recalls – and how much she should know. The child seems immensely fragile in Cari's eyes all of a sudden, ignorant of how much peril she's in. They're sailing from one land blasted by the gods to another ruined region, and who knows what they'll run into along the way. Cari imagines Ama running up the hillside near that shrine, the goddess manifesting. Thorn-fingers ripping Ama's soft flesh apart.

The child laughs, and Cari forces herself to smile.

Ren whispers something to Adro, who stands and carries Ama out on deck. She can hear him poking around the other cabins on this rotten ship of worms.

"When the Ghierdana come after us," Ren asks, "will that Crawling One protect us?"

When, not if. She tries to be reassuring. "Sure. Maybe. Look, we're out – we'll put as much distance between us and the Rock as we can. I need to get to Khebesh—"

"Paravos is closer, and much safer."

"That's the deal. Khebesh first."

"Once, long ago," Ren says softly, "I was a servant in the house of the prefect of the ninth district of Ilbarin. When especially complex or arcane matters came before her court, she would dictate a letter to the sorcerers of Khebesh. The greatest scholars in the world, she said, wiser than the gods in these troubled times." He makes a sign with his hands, to ward off evil. "She'd write to the temple of the All-Seeing One, too, of course, but everyone knew the god was mad, and we discarded the replies from His priests without reading them."

"Did the sorcerers of Khebesh reply?"

"Sometimes they'd send letters back, giving sage counsel. And a few times, they'd send a sorcerer with a white staff and a great book. The sorcerer would never do anything except stare and mutter, and make notes in their grimoire. I was always disappointed – the conjurers in the market could call up demons, and make the fires dance around the square, which seemed far more impressive. But one day, the sorcerers stopped coming, and the gates of Khebesh were shut. That's when I realised they truly were wise – they saw the war coming and hid from it."

"I've got a key to those gates."

"So Adro said." Ren runs a finger over his close-cropped greying hair. Cari notices that his earlobes are both torn; he'd worn earrings there, and someone tore them out. "I know some people who fled Ilbarin tried to take refuge in Khebesh, but the gates stayed shut, and they had to turn back. I wonder about the sort of people who wouldn't open their doors to people fleeing the mad gods."

He looks like he might be about to say more, but they're interrupted by a child's cry. Cari leaps up, grabbing the captain's sword, but Ren seems unruffled, unhurried.

Adro comes back in, the sobbing child in his arms. "Moon came out, and she saw where we were."

"I'll take her." Ama's transferred from one parent to the other, still shrieking and keening. A breathless whole-body shriek, over and over. "She's scared of the waters," explains Ren as he cradles Ama.

"There's another cabin," says Adro, speaking over his daughter's screaming. "Full of salvage and crap. I'll clear it out. No other supplies. The captain will never let this stand. He'll be barking orders at the worms until the whole deck is spotless." He strokes Ama's head, and she starts to quieten down.

"Go and clear the cabin," says Ren. "And keep looking for something she can eat."

Cari sits there a moment, listening to Ama's sobbing diminish. The makeshift ship creaks, and the creaking's answered by a whispering of worms, weaving more spells to keep them afloat. Everything around Cari suddenly seems immensely fragile, and Ama most of all. Gods below — she doesn't know if Adro's immensely stupid or immensely brave to love such a thing. If there was anywhere safe on the way to Khebesh, she'd happily leave Adro and his family there. Slip away, like she'd done before, taking no more than she could carry while keeping her knife-hand free.

She remembers an argument with Spar, years ago now. Back when he was alive, back when she was offered the power of the Black Iron Gods. *I don't want it to be up to me*, she'd told him. *I want out. The open sea, and a place where no one knows where I am.* To leave her family name behind, and all the gods and horrors and responsibility that comes with it. He argued she should stay.

There's so much out there beyond Guerdon, she told him. *The Godswar isn't everywhere yet.*

That's not true any more. There are fewer places now that the mad gods haven't reached, and fewer still untouched.

You should have come with me, Spar, she thinks, but he won that argument, hands down. They'd taken the power and used it, remade the city. And after that, he'd won again. She'd stayed, and it had all been up to her. As the Saint of Knives, she'd protected the people of the New City – but that had been easy. Nothing could harm her, and she'd made no promises. If she saw something that offended her – some act of cruelty, some injustice – hell, some score she wanted to settle from her old life in the Wash – she'd been able to drop out of the heavens and smite. She'd driven herself hard, gone without sleep, taken immense risks, thrown herself into battle against all sorts of weird foes, but it was all her choice. She'd had the power to carry it all.

Get to Khebesh, she tells herself. Find a way to help Spar. Then go back. Kick the Ghierdana out, and this time do it all better. That vision of Adro and Ren in their little apartment crosses her mind again, but this time she imagines them in the New City, happy and secure. Ama running in the streets, heedlessly climbing the towers, laughing and playing – all watched over by the Saint of the New City, all protected from the war and sorrow.

She files that thought away. It's an image Spar would like. An image she'll share with him when she makes it home.

The ship creaks again. Twelve Suns Bleeding appears at the entrance to the cabin.

"There is a problem."

She follows the Crawling One outside. Looking on Ushket in the dawn light, Cari can see the whole sorry place laid out before her – the bulk of the citadel, white stone painted a delicate pink by the dawn. The new harbour, ugly as a freshly sutured wound. The thick mud staining everything. And off to the left, the long shore of wrecked ships.

Black smoke. From near the *Rose*. Maybe, maybe, from the *Rose*. Too far away to be sure.

"Oh." Cari's voice sounds small and childlike in her ears. The *Rose* was her home. And she's brought disaster to it. *You ruin everything.* She looks for some sign the captain's still alive. Surely they'd have brought him to the work camp in Ilbarin City. They can rescue him – she'll demand the Crawling One help her break the captain out. Hawse has to still be alive.

"Has the grimoire been destroyed?" Twelve Suns Bleeding's cultivated voice expresses sympathy and deep concern, but she's quite sure the Crawling One is about to cut its losses. Without the grimoire, the gates of Khebesh stay shut. Without access to Khebesh, the Crawling Ones have no use for her, or anyone else on board.

"It's safe. The captain hid it." She puts as much fervour into her words as she can. "But we've got to go back."

The ship turns smoothly, the useless rudder bumping against the hull, the masts quivering under the shock of the sudden change of course. They're not so much sailing as being carried in a wooden box. A floating coffin.

Adro notices the smoke and comes running up. "Is that the *Rose* burning?"

"I don't know." Ilbarin swells before them once again, as if the Rock exudes some malign gravity, pulling them back.

"This won't take long," Cari insists, to herself as much as Adro or Twelve Suns. "I'll just grab the captain, and the book, and we'll be gone again. Straight to Khebesh."

Adro digs the box out of his pocket, holds it up to show Twelve Suns that he still has it. "We'll plant your little wriggler for you, soon as you get us there."

Twelve Suns doesn't answer. The Crawling One shudders, the whole ship, too. From all around them there's a sudden cacophony of chirping and hissing, like fat in a frying pan.

The ship slows, almost stops. Abruptly, they're drifting on the waves instead of being propelled by the Crawling One's sorcery.

"Twelve Suns?"

The waters around them whiten with worm-flesh. The ship's leaking, worms wriggling out from every timber and hole, pouring out in pale torrents. She can see shoals of the worms swimming away from the ship, knotting together into new shapes like eels or dolphins.

"What's going on? I'll get you the book, I swear! Don't—"

"A thousand pardons." The human form of Twelve Suns collapses. The Crawling One topples forward, vomiting itself over the railing into the muddy sea.

"Cari, what are they doing?"

Cari tries to grab at Twelve Suns Bleeding, but the worms wriggle between her fingers, or burst in gobbets of slime. There's no way to stop the Crawling One from abandoning them again. The whole ship sags, creaking as the sorcery ceases to support it. They're riding lower in the water now, the lower decks flooding.

Ren, coughing, struggles out on to the deck, clutching Ama, pressing her face into his shoulder so she doesn't have to see the ocean. They're close enough to the shore that they should be able to make it if they swim, but the waters here are treacherous. Cari imagines their bodies washing up by the *Rose*, to be picked through by the Bythos.

The last of the worms leaves the ship. They're alone on a sinking wreck. But why have the Crawling Ones suddenly fled? She looks around, scanning for the Ghierdana gunboat approaching, or . . .

There.

There, in the sky.

Circling down towards them. Lazily, unhurried, its great wide wings outstretched like storm clouds. It comes lower and lower, and Cari can feel heat radiating off the dragon's underbelly, a promise of the terrible fires within.

Closer and closer. She can see the monster's armoured flanks now, the gigantic claws, the sinuous serpent tail. She can see the jaws, a crocodile smile. The eyes fix on her – not on the ship, on her – and she can't move. Terror roots her to the deck, even as water begins to well up between the boards.

Closer and closer. The sword drops from her nerveless hands. Far away, Adro's running back and forth, looking for a weapon, looking for a way out. Looking for anything, but they're powerless in the face of the dragon. Ren crouches down, holds Ama, waits for the fire.

Closer, but the fire never comes. The sky is full of dragon, pressing down on her. A hemisphere of scale and muscle, fire and bone, awful in its undeniable existence. This is no god, nor it is a conjured monster like a Kraken, dependent on unseen forces, bound by arcane rules. No, the dragon's as solid as she is, as free as she is, but infinitely stronger, infinitely more powerful. As solid as the bells of Guerdon.

Closer, and the stench of the dragon rolls over her, sweat and soot and rotten meat. It circles around once more, beating its wings as it turns, hurricane winds whipping up waves that crash over the wreck, cracking the timbers. The ship lurches, sinking faster now.

The dragon hovers above them, filling the world. Cari won't kneel, won't look away. There's nowhere to run and there's no way to fight back. No god will grace her here, she's got no clever tricks to hand. All she has left is defiance – to look into the dragon's eye and say, at the last and for all time, fuck you.

Claws dig into the ship's side, grabbing the wreck's ribs, and the dragon lifts the whole ship out of the water. The worm-ship doesn't have the strength to hold together for long, but it's only a short flight to land. The dragon drops them in the mud, another in the line of wrecked ships along the shore.

Then it slithers forward, touching down just inland of them. Its tail bats Cari, knocking the wind from her lungs, sending her sprawling on the deck. The wings fold back along the monster's flanks.

A cavalcade of figures from Cari's nightmares climb on board.

First, the armoured witch, sorcery crackling around her hands. She moves to the side to allow the others to follow her up the ladder, staying in the back of the crowd.

Dol Martaine, hustling Adro and Ren away from her at sword point, telling them to yield. Snatching Ama away from them. There's a brawl, Adro throwing punches, but there are too many foes, and he goes down. Ama shrieking at the sight of her father's blood soaking the deck.

And then Artolo of the Ghierdana. Powerful gloved hands gripping the top of the ladder. He's bigger than she remembers. He strides across the deck to her, steel boots ripping out chunks of the rotten wood.

"Bring him up," he calls.

They've got Hawse. Two more Ghierdana come up the ladder, the captain between them. Hawse's face is bloodied, his nose broken. Soot and blood cake his features. Every one of his finger bones has been snapped, his hands dangling like the fronds of some sea creature. His bloodied lips move – a message or a prayer, Cari can't tell.

Artolo takes out his dragon-tooth knife.

"When last we met, Carillon Thay, I told you I'd kill your friends."

He rips her amulet from her neck.

"I told you I'd kill your family."

He takes the blunt knife, hefts it, smashes the pommel into Hawse's forehead. The old man staggers and falls. No one else moves.

Artolo kneels on Hawse's chest, brings the knife down again.

And again.

Dol Martaine holds Adro back. Cari crawls forward, head spinning. She feels like she's drowning in a nightmare.

And again.

No sounds except the wet thud of bone and flesh against the wood. The waves crashing on the shore. The low rumbling laughter of the dragon.

The world doesn't move, but it breaks.

Artolo stands up, letting the gore drip from his fingers.

"I said," he says thickly, "that I would kill you."

Something breaks inside her, flooding her with furious energy. Her anger unravelling like a fraying cable, snapping around inside her. Cari snatches up the sword, swings it like a club. Everything

Hawse showed her about technique is forgotten – all she wants to do is smash Artolo's skull. To open him up again, like she did back in the New City. To break him like he broke Hawse.

The ferocity of her attack takes him by surprise. He leaps back, flipping his dragon-tooth knife in the air, catching it in his other hand. Urging her on. She stumbles across the blood-slick deck, feeling the worm-eaten timbers give under her weight. She slashes at him, and he dodges again. His face flushed red, taunting her, toying with her. Cari's aware, distantly, of the massive dragon watching them from the beach, of Adro and Ren huddled behind her, of the Eshdana forming a circle around the pair, cheering on their boss as he takes Carillon apart, of the Rock on the horizon, rising up to dash all her dreams of escape.

All of them, even the dragon, are remote. A painted backdrop.

There's nothing but Artolo, and the fight.

She steps over a pool of the captain's blood. Hawse's dead eyes stare up at her. *Sorry, captain.*

Cari knows she's going to die here. She has no alchemical trickery that could deal with those guards, nothing that could stop the sorceress, and, well, there's a bloody dragon right there, too, just to tip the whole situation over from merely doomed to thoroughly, absolutely no-question fucked.

Sorry, Adro. You should have stayed away from me. I can't save you.

But Artolo's only human. A vile shit of a human. If killing him is her last act, then she can live with that. So to speak.

Sorry, Spar. I tried. I did.

She has to keep Artolo at arm's length. Up close, he's too strong for her. She keeps moving, the sword between her and Artolo, feinting with the point to keep him at bay. On another ship, she knows exactly what she'd do – climb. On the *Rose*, she'd be up in the rigging by now, or up on the rail, walking on it like a New City alley cat. But the fucking worm-ship is too rotten for acrobatics. Even the deck is a gamble.

Artolo makes a grab for her wrist, trying to wrestle the sword away. She twists, tries to slash him with the blade, but it's too heavy, too slow; he dodges, backs away.

Artolo switches his knife from hand to hand. It's a streetfighter's trick she knows – forcing her to second-guess how he'll hold the knife, where the attack will come from. This sword is as heavy as the fucking book, more than she can manage. She'd give anything, right now, for the gifts of the Kept Gods. Strength and speed and a flaming sword – Saint Aleena would have slaughtered Artolo in five seconds flat. Hell, Cari would give Aleena good odds against the dragon.

Maybe the thought of Aleena shows on Cari's face, somehow, because Artolo hesitates, just for an instant. She takes the opening, thrusts with the sword, puts everything into the attack—

—and Artolo steps aside, casually. Drives his knife into her side. The dragon-tooth is blunt and it doesn't cut deep, but it's still harder than a steel bar. Cari goes sprawling, the sword flying out of reach across the deck, a mouthful of wooden deck and worm-husks.

She rolls over, but Artolo's already standing astride her.

He raises the dagger.

"Great-Uncle," he cries, "this is the one who stopped me from finding the weapons of Black Iron! This is the one who drove us from Guerdon! I offer you her heart!"

The dagger falls to the deck. Artolo's gloved hands suddenly lose their strength, deflating and drooping. He roars, a furious animal noise. "Witch!"

Sorcery crackles around the armoured sorceress. The guards back away. "Don't kill her! That's Carillon Thay," shouts the witch. "She's more valuable alive! I know all about her – her family, her gifts. She's the Herald of the Black Iron Gods – the alchemists were willing to pay a fortune for her!"

Cari wonders how the sorceress knows all that, but her confusion is eclipsed by the spike of hope. She's not dead yet.

The dragon snakes forward. "Carillon Thay? Truly?" The monster laughs, and it's like deafening thunder. "Oh, oh, here is a jest for the ages." The dragon chuckles and shakes its massive head.

"She's mine to kill!" roars Artolo.

"No, nephew," says the dragon, suddenly cold and humourless, "she belongs to me. How was she able to command this ship, I wonder?" The dragon lowers his massive head to the deck and takes a sniff. The rush of air nearly knocks Cari off her feet. "Aaah. Worms." He draws the word out, making it a low rumble. Flames edge his smile.

"What . . . what should I do with her, Great-Uncle?" Artolo asks.

"Store her until I decide what to do with her. Put her to work in your camp. Everything is in order there, Artolo, isn't it?"

"Of course, Great-Uncle."

"Good." The dragon's head turns to address the witch. "That was a worthy suggestion. I commend you. But . . . you are only Eshdana, and you contradicted the command of a member of my family. Must I remind you of your place?"

The sorceress' face is hidden by her mask, but she bows her head, kneels before the dragon. Great-Uncle grunts with satisfaction. "Now," says the dragon. "I have flown long, and I hunger. I must hunt. I shall see you at the refinery, and we shall examine the fruits of your labour."

The dragon takes off, the beating of its wings cracking the rotten timbers of the worm-ship. He rises above the smouldering wreck of the *Rose*. He soars over the town of Ushket, his wings darkening the sky, the walkways and rope bridges tearing in the hurricane of his passage. For an instant, he dips out of view – and there's a flash of fire over the Street of Blue Glass.

Cari, Ren and Adro are marched up the wet muddy hillside towards the hard-packed dirt road, where the carriages wait. A procession of the damned: Adro cursing, shouting at the Eshdana, calling for Ama. Ren grimly silent. Dol Martaine, dragging the child through the mud, one hand clasped over her mouth to keep her from crying out.

On the shore behind them, the few stragglers of the morning-tide Bythos watch them with bemusement, until the Eshdana throw Hawse's body into the sea.

They're loaded into the carriages, into the carts, and set off down the road to Ilbarin, the road around the Rock.

And then they're gone, and the shore is empty again.

Gulls settle on the newest wreck, and burrow in the rotten boards looking for fresh worms.

CHAPTER SEVENTEEN

For all its many great civic buildings, those grand monsters of slate and glass that squat sullenly on the city's hills, Guerdon is singularly lacking in prisons. There was little need for them in several periods of the city's history. During the terrible years when Guerdon was under the sway of the Black Iron cult, prisoners were sacrificed to the Ravellers, their souls flensed and consumed by monstrous gods. For more than two centuries, the city was ruled by the Church of the Keepers, who were more concerned with building marble cages up on Holyhill for their own Kept Gods. Criminals were scourged with divine wrath, cursed by the Mother of Mercies. Few prisons were built in that era – but when the Stone Plague struck, those prisons were converted into lithosariums, where the infected were contained until they petrified. Most of those prisons were demolished afterwards, out of fears the plague still lingered in the walls. The rubble of prison and prisoners dumped in the harbour to make sea walls and artificial islands.

The last forty or fifty years, the free city period – again, there was little need for prisons. Effro Kelkin and his Industrial Liberals built a new prison out on Hark Island, a symbol of their war on crime, but that prison rotted once the alchemists' party took parliament, and the Tallow Vats took over. More efficient to recycle condemned prisoners into enforcers.

All gone now. The Tallow Vats are shut down. The various occupation zones have their own ways of dealing with criminals – Umur's law-giving sphinxes in the IOZ, something called Supplication in the Haithi district, and the Lyrixians use a prison hulk docked off the New City.

But there's still one prison left in Guerdon.

The grey walls of the Last House rise up above Baston and Karla.

"I'm going in alone," says Baston. "You didn't need to come."

Karla draws her cloak tightly around herself. "I'm going to wait out here for you, all right? Just remember to keep your head, Bas. You're there to get what we need to know, that's it."

Baston flexes his knuckles. He knows how to get information, all right. The Fever Knight taught him that.

"Stop it," says Karla. "Just ask him about Mandel's, and then come back to me."

"I'll just talk," growls Baston. He glances up at the walls of the prison, sees armed guards patrolling. Sinter's threats run through his mind. *We know your sweet little sister. Your sinful mother. Your friends in Pulchar's bar. We can ruin any of them.* He imagines Karla being dragged by the city watch through those prison gates. "You get back to the New City. It's safer there."

"Here." Karla presses a small golden object into his palm. A box, half the length of his thumb, like a little casket or a snuffbox.

"I've got the dragon's gold for bribes." The bag's heavy on his belt. Even with the value of gold debased by miracles, there's still a fortune in there, more money than Baston's ever carried.

"That's from Mum. It's for *him*, all right. Do it for her."

Baston scowls. His mother's admiration for the old guildmaster is a point of contention between them. He puts the little golden box into his pocket.

"Be quick."

Baston advances into the shadow of the Last House. Guards at the gate usher him through a side door into an office. A brief moment of haggling. Beneath a portrait of Guerdon's new minister of security, a guard captain takes the money, then ostentatiously closes a ledger of visitors without entering Baston's name. They don't search him. They bring him like a condemned prisoner through a maze of dank tunnels. He's heard tales that the prison is haunted, that the first Tallow Vats were made in secret in the cellars, that even the Holy Beggar turns his face from those sent here, but the Last House doesn't need horror stories to chill the soul. The despair of the place sinks into his bones. The weight of the dead stone is enough to crush the spirits of those condemned to the dungeon cells on the lower levels.

But they bring up him up out of the mire, up to the tower cells once reserved for the nobility. Just as that bag of dragon's gold bought Baston access to the prison, money works its own miracles. Here, the air is fresher, the floor warmer.

The guard captain knocks respectfully on one door, then unlocks it. Inside is a cosy room, the walls lined with bookshelves. A fire burns in the hearth, and a side table bears the remains of an evening meal. Seated in a wheeled bathchair by the window, head bent as if in prayer, is a little man in a dressing gown. A blanket on his lap cannot conceal his extensive injuries – his left leg is missing, and his right foot is twisted inwards, and painfully swollen. His abdomen, too, is bloated, pockmarked with needle scars, and there's an undeniable stench that the smoke from the fire cannot hide.

"Ten minutes," whispers the guard, and the door shuts behind Baston.

He spends thirty seconds of his precious ten minutes just waiting, breathing, letting the anger that wells up in him at the sight of the prisoner slowly drain from his blood.

"Boss."

"Ach, Baston. There's no ash on your brow, so it should still be master to you." Heinreil's voice is only just above a whisper. The master – former master of the Brotherhood – gestures at an empty chair. "Sit. Let us talk. Tell me of my city."

Baston scowls. "The Ghierdana sent me. I'm here on business."

"Are you, now? You never had a head for business, in the old days, but I still found a use for you. There was a whole crop of you youngsters – Idgeson, obviously, but you, too. Lem, Rynn the Red, poor Hosker Venson – all raised on tales of how the great Idge defied the interrogators and preserved some dream of a better tomorrow. Thank the gods that Idgeson got the plague, or you'd all be dead in some ill-thought revolution. I tried to take you in hand, make something of you."

"They are all dead." Spar and Hosker died in the Crisis. Lem in the invasion. Rynn, eaten from the inside out by spider-spirits two months ago. "And you made me do the things you didn't have the stomach for."

"At least you're not dead, lad."

"I always thought you were clever," says Baston. "But you're a bloody coward. You were so fucking good at undermining anyone who opposed you, anyone who questioned you, but you never did anything that could have made things better. You squandered the promise of the Brotherhood. Skimming off your take, while the city got worse, the guilds went unchecked—"

"You said you were here to talk business," interrupts Heinreil, "and you don't have much time left. Old men like me will ramble on about the old days if you let us."

"The old days, then. Mandel & Company. Karla said you had a way in."

"Your sister is cleverer than you. You should listen to her more. She knows the proper way of things." Heinreil's stomach gurgles; he leans over in his chair and farts loudly, wincing in pain as he does so. There's a metallic edge to the stench, like blood. "Ach. I *was* clever, Baston, but what did all my cleverness avail me when my carriage ran off the road? At least Myri made it out. Now there was a girl who understood business. Like your sister, aye? I should have put more trust in women, I think. They're better at handling the slow days, the between days, and that counts for more than you think at first. Men tend to rush about shouting, and that's what you need in a fight. But if it gets to a fight, something's gone wrong, eh? There's a woman who comes in to wash me. To talk to her, you'd think her empty-headed – but she listens, and watches, and I've no doubt reports everything. Not to the guards here, mind you, but—"

Baston reaches over, puts one finger on Heinreil's belly, and presses hard. The old man doubles over in agony, retching. "You sold us out. You think you're broken now? The Fever Knight teach me how to hurt people."

"Gods below, boy!" Heinreil dribbles blood. "There are guards outside!"

"They're well bribed. You taught me that, too."

"Aye, well, I bribed the whole watch so well that they made the Tallowmen, so what do I know?"

"Mandel & Company."

"Why them?"

Baston reaches forward again. Heinreil raises a hand like a shield. "I'll tell you, but I need to know the shape of the thing. Are you trying to rob Mandel? Kill him? What does the Ghierdana boy want?"

"Control of some trade that Mandel's involved in. The yliaster supply."

"Yliaster," Heinreil echoes. "Where's the profit in that? They dig it up for two coppers a sack."

"Talk."

"You have something for me, first."

"What is it?"

"The last of my gold. Your mother kept it for me."

Baston digs out the little snuffbox. "This belongs to the Brotherhood, then. You stole from us."

"I earned that payment," croaks Heinreil, "after Idgeson kicked me out. It's mine by right."

Baston flips the snuffbox open. Inside is a fat white grub, its ridged body pulsing gently. The sudden light makes it curl up, wriggling into a corner.

"It's what you think it is," said Heinreil. "If you're going to go after Mandel on some fool's errand, you'll need sorcery or something like it. Alchemy, miracles – this is no city for mortals any more. Can't do anything without power. I had Myri and the Fever Knight – and brave boys like you. I had the Crawling Ones. I had the support of Rosha herself, and the backing of the alchemists' guild – yet Idgeson and his sainted bitch still took me down. Your Ghierdana boy can't use their dragons, and I hear the Dentist isn't around either. Muscle won't be enough – what's his edge?"

Spar, thinks Baston. He wants to gloat, to torture Heinreil with the revelation that Spar Idgeson not only survived, but is now guiding Rasce.

"You've got something," says Heinreil. "What is it?"

Baston plucks the worm out of the box and holds it aloft.

"Careful with that. It's one of the last in the city. Ghouls killed the rest."

"And when you die, you live on in this, is that it?"

Urine dribbles down from beneath the blanket. "Ach, boy, does it matter? You don't have much time. You want to know about Mandel? I'll tell you."

Baston sits back down, still holding the worm between thumb and forefinger. The grub writhes around as if trying to bite him. It has two teeth that look horribly human. He squeezes it, enough to hurt it. "Talk."

"Mandel used to work for the Thay family, years ago. Long before my time. He went off with Erasmus' boy, Jermas, on trading expeditions. Now, Jermas comes back from one of these trips to Firesea with a head full of madness. He squanders the Thay fortune on who-knows-what, and we all know how that ended. But Mandel saw which way the wind is blowing, and started up his own trading house. He took over a lot of the Thay business – as they declined, he rose. He started importing alchemical components on the side—"

"From Ilbarin?"

"Nah. Overland, mostly. Jashan. Ulbishe, too, I think."

"He's an alchemist himself?"

Heinreil shrugs. "High in the guild, aye. Mandel was in thick with them in the early days. I do know he got into trouble with the Keepers – they sent a saint round, to put the fear of the gods on him, and after that he stuck to business. Made his fortune when the alchemists' guild was founded. Sensible man. More people should do that."

"Stick to the topic. What was your way in?"

"Mandel took over part of the old city walls to house his refineries and holding tanks. There was a temple there, dating back to the bad old days. I dug around in the archives, found some old drawings, mapped the tunnels. There's a way in there. That's one thing I love about this city – so many hidden ways."

"They'll have sealed it, surely."

"Oh, no doubt. They sealed all the deep ways. But this tunnel was different. You'll see if you go there. It'll be watched, but I don't think they could close it. It wouldn't stay closed."

"Where is it?"

"You know St Styrus' Shaft? There's a branch off that. The ghouls know." Heinreil coughs, his body wracked with pain. "Mortality is such shit. The gods and their spawn go on, undying, and what do we do? Rot when we're alive and rot when we're dead. Nothing lasts. You have children, and they're ungrateful little scrotes who think you're all that's wrong with the world. You build something, and fools come in and break it."

"Why didn't you use the shaft? If Mandel was that rich, why did you never go after him?" For a moment, Baston has an inkling of another Guerdon, another strand of some web of fate – a world in which Idge survived and used this tunnel to sabotage Mandel. No Mandel, no alchemical components. No alchemical components, no guild. This blight on the city, excised before it could fester.

Heinreil grins, revealing a mouth of rotten teeth. "Because I was sensible. We were only mortals, Baston. Even back then, I knew that we weren't enough."

Business is over. Baston holds up the grub.

"You corrupted the Brotherhood. You could have done what Idge promised, fought the guilds instead of taking their scraps—"

"Oh, for fuck's sake," groans Heinreil, "how many times does Idge get to throw that argument in my face? The man's twenty years down the shaft, and still he vexes me."

"Ideals can't die," says Baston.

He squeezes the worm.

Or, at least, he tries to.

His fingers don't move. He's paralysed, caught in place by a spell.

"Ideals are like gods. Fucking troublesome. And when you kill 'em, they come back warped." Heinreil reaches forward, groaning with the effort, and plucks the grub from between Baston's frozen fingers. As he does so, he whispers, "Be like Idge, boy. Say naught. All's in hand."

Then he raises his voice. "Come and take him, if you want him."

The bookcase opens silently. A secret door. Rough hands grab Baston, lift him from his chair, drag him into the darkness.

They drag him down a secret passageway. Too dark to see, he can only smell the dust that tickles his nose, feel the bump of each stone slab as his frozen feet pass over them. From the curve of the corridor, he guesses it runs behind several cells on this level.

A door opens, and he's flung to the floor. A lamp on a rough wooden table illuminates a room that Baston guesses doesn't appear on any plans of the Last House. Old rusty manacles on the wall. Old rust-coloured stains on the floor.

Duttin staggers past him to sit in a chair. She cradles her right hand, and there's a lambent glow to the blood that stains her fingers. She's breathing heavily, and waves at the other two men to begin while she catches her breath.

One of the two men Baston recognises. Sinter. The priest is armed, as before, and this time is careful to stay out of Baston's reach, pressing himself against the wall as he circles around. The second man would be forgettable, if Baston had not seen his portrait downstairs. It's Alic Nemon, minister for state security. Nemon gives Baston an encouraging little smile, then Sinter flings a chair in Baston's direction.

"A week, you little shit! You were supposed to report in after a week!"

Baston stands, considers throwing the chair back at the priest with a lot more force. Instead, he rights the chair and sits. "I couldn't get away, could I? The Ghierdana are watching me closely."

"It's unwise to lie to me," advises Nemon, like he's remarking on the weather. "We know you returned to the Wash on the evening after you visited Craddock & Sons."

"The clue," adds Sinter, "was when you set off a fucking siege charge in the middle of the Wash."

Baston stays quiet. What is there to say?

"Talk, you little shit. Explain yourself."

"Who sent that candlejack? The one that tried to kill Rasce?"

"The Ghierdana have many enemies," says Nemon, blandly.

"That's not an answer."

Duttin dabs her bleeding fingertips with ointment. "As I explained when we first met, Mr Hedanson, my sole interest in this matter is keeping the Armistice intact. Your own actions severely imperilled it."

"I nearly got killed, too," Baston mutters.

"Martyrdom is no excuse for poor planning," says Duttin, wincing as she applies her medicine.

"Idiot. If you want to die, that can be arranged with a lot less collateral-bloody-damage."

"Out of curiosity, how did you escape the blast?" asks Nemon.

Do they know about Rasce? About Spar conjuring up a tunnel? Heinreil warned him to stay quiet, give nothing away. Is this what he was referring to? But how could Heinreil know, when he's locked away in his prison cell?

"Ghoul-run. Out through the sewers." Only half a lie.

"Rasce's criminal acts so far, while distasteful, can be tolerated for the sake of peace," says Duttin. "I was aware of the nature of the dragon families when I invited them in. However, a move into the Fog Yards is impermissible. Guerdon's alchemical industry requires a secure supply of yliaster, and it cannot be monopolised by a foreign power. The ambition of the Ghierdana must be curtailed."

The sight of the three bastards in front of Baston makes his anger swell, blood pulsing through his frame. They're the worst of Guerdon made flesh, injustice and cruelty given form. Duttin stinks of money and alchemy; Nemon's part of the corrupt parliament, and Sinter's a Keeper priest. He can imagine the three of them agreeing to carve up the city, to hand the Wash over to the mad gods.

Nemon continues. "Tell him that you saw Heinreil. Tell him that it was a fruitless meeting, that Heinreil said there's no viable way into Mandel & Company. Slow him down. Give him nothing." He stares intently at Baston, his piercing eyes incongruous in his doughy, unremarkable face. Some insect picks its way down Baston's spine. "Do you understand?"

He nods. Plays dumb, plays the whipped dog.

"I'll tell him there's no way in." He swallows his anger, even though it's spiky and bitter going down his throat.

Nemon stands. "I must leave. I'll talk to the alchemists' guild and bring the new guildmaster to heel."

"Very well. Sinter and I shall finish up here."

Nemon looks back at Baston for a moment. "My blessing upon you," he says, and then he's gone, slipping out through a side door.

"Let the fuckers run to Ulbishe," mutters Sinter. "The city would be the better for it."

Duttin rubs her eyes. "We need the alchemists, just as we need the dragons – and the Kept Gods. We must work with the tools we have, no matter how unreliable. Mr Hedanson, I trust you will leave peaceably, and I shall not have to exert myself again."

"Who sent that jack?" he asks again. "Was it you?"

Sinter grins, a mouthful of broken teeth like a graveyard. "There was a time," he says wistfully, "when I'd have sent Aleena Humber or Holger Carlson to do a job like that, 'stead of some ratty candle. Make sure your boss stays on his side of the border, boy, or there'll be worse coming."

"Our previous arrangements stand. Report back in via the aethergraph in the tailor's shop. Once the danger from the Ghierdana is contained, we shall reward you commensurate with your service," says Duttin. "Oh, one final question. I've had reports of . . . " She shakes her head, rephrases the question. "Have you seen or heard anything that might suggest Carillon Thay has returned?"

"No," replies Baston, and it's the only wholly honest word any of them have spoken in the entire conversation.

Baston finds Rasce in the house on Lanthorn Street, lying back on his couch, clad in a silken dressing gown. His eyes are closed, but he's awake. Dreaming awake, guesses Baston, wandering the New City in his mind.

"You just missed your sister," says Rasce dreamily, without looking up. He smirks in response to some comment only he can hear. "Spar wishes to know what tidings you bring from the old master. Did Heinreil speak of him?"

"Not really." The casual nature of the question makes it uncomfortable. Baston can get his head around the concept of some spirit or ghost of his friend haunting the New City, and he's lived in the occupied zone long enough to be familiar with the supernatural intruding into the mortal world. But spirits are supposed to be distant and inhuman, to talk in riddles and prophecies, not talk like this. His gaze flickers nervously around the room, unsure where to look.

Stick to business. It should be safer footing, but it's all tangled up with Eladora Duttin and that priest and their secret threats. The urge to confess wells up in him. He owes Duttin and her coterie no loyalty, but he doesn't know how Rasce would take the admission.

He could take the ash. If he swore an oath to the Ghierdana, then he'd have some protection from Rasce's wrath. He'd be fully on the inside then – and it's not like he'd be alone. He's brought half the old Brotherhood up to the New City, and they're all ash-marked now. It's only his own stubborn pride that keeps him from swearing the oath. Rasce's eyes are still closed, but Baston can somehow tell that he's watching very, very closely. All the walls here are eyes.

"Boss, there's something. Something you should know." His tongue feels like it's turned to stone in his mouth. He stumbles over the words, uncertain of the path forward.

He's interrupted by Karla's return. She enters, towelling her wet hair. Baston looks from her to Rasce, all thoughts of confessions and conspiracies falling out of his mind for a moment. "I thought I heard you. How did it go?"

"Heinreil's still alive, at any rate."

Karla gives him a furtive smile. It's clear that she used him to smuggle that grub past the prison guards – the Ghierdana's money ensured he wasn't searched. Using him like that is the sort of trick Heinreil used to play, and it rankles.

"What about the alchemists, my friend? What did your old master say?" asks Rasce.

Give him nothing, they told Baston. Fuck that. "Heinreil said there used to be a tunnel or something under Mandel's place. An old one. The Brotherhood thought it was too dicey to risk."

"And what do you think?" asks Rasce, quietly.

"I don't know. I'd need to take a look at the place, and I don't know how we'd manage that. And I don't trust Heinreil. But . . . I think we go for it," says Baston.

Rasce's eyes flick open. "Karla, my sweet," he says, "hand me my knife."

CHAPTER EIGHTEEN

I t's waiting that hurts the most. It's lying here, hollow in belly and soul, knowing there's nothing to be done. No escape route that hasn't been tried by a hundred others, no appeal to be made, no hope of rescue, no clever plan. No divine revelation. Just the sound of the gulls, the clink of the metal fences shifting in the wind, the breaking of the waves on the shore. The sucking noise of garbage-clogged alleyways draining as the tide retreats.

Everything tastes of salt, but no one weeps here any more. An ocean of tears has already been shed in this camp, to no avail.

So – wait. Wait and rot.

A small part of Ilbarin City that escaped the flooding has been turned into a work camp. The Ghierdana have cordoned off the streets, turned the ruins into an open-air cage. Fences, guard towers, heavy locked gates. Walkways overhead like in Ushket, gantries for the guards to move between rooftops. The stairs up to walkway level blocked or collapsed. People staring blankly, watchful but too exhausted and hungry to do anything except stay on guard, a hollow place on the far side of fear. It all barely registers on Carillon – these places are the same the world over. She was locked away in one back in Guerdon, on Hark Island. Anywhere humans draw a line and declare that everyone on the other side has to be contained, it's the same. They start out as prisoners, as refugees, as victims of illness, and the fence works its alchemy, turns them into problems to be overcome or caged animals to be tamed instead of people.

Cari's a special case. An especially dangerous animal. She still gets thrown in the camp with everyone else, but the guards all know who she is. They give them a room to sleep in, but the roof's missing, so the guards can watch Cari. There's nothing between her and the pitiless stars. Twice now, she's seen the armoured sorceress watching her from the gantry, werelight flooding the cell, but both times the woman left without speaking.

Each day, the prisoners are sent out to gather yliaster. They gather at the main gate, and the Eshdana split them into work teams. Each team gets a raft and a bunch of sacks, and then wade out into the flooded city. If they come back with sacks full of yliaster, they get a chit, stamped in some bureaucratic joke with a seal from the provisional government of Ilbarin. Trade chits for food. Trade enough chits for passage out, or so the sign in the commissary claims. In the camp you can trade chits for food, for medicine, for sex. Trade chits so the gangs leave you alone.

But, fucking hooray, she's a special case. She knows the guards won't let the gangs murder her. But she's also damn sure they won't step in for anything short of murder, so she stays on her guard. They've taken everything from her, not that she had much left. They took the captain's sword, her amulet. They even took her clothes and gave her a grey shift to wear.

Yliaster, Ren tells her, is a precipitate of clashing miracles. Two gods hammer the shit out of each other, and you get yliaster. Here, it mixes with seawater to form this phosphorescent gunk, like a wet scab. They process it in the refinery near the camp, to get the glowing brine that they're shipping out from Ushket. There are still a few patches in the shallows where yliaster can be found. The prisoners gather it with their bare hands, scraping it off the rubble and smearing it into the sacks. It stings, and Cari quickly learns to recognise the prisoners who've been here the longest. The god-brine's in their bloodstream, dissolving them from the inside. Mottled patches on their skin, like Ren.

They have to dive for the yliaster deposits, swimming down to the drowned city below. Ren tells her that it clusters around the temples, around the sunken battlefields where saints and monsters clashed. Sometimes, it looks to her like the yliaster collected around the bodies of the slain. The remains are mostly gone, eaten by scavengers or washed away, so only the outline remains – humanoid figures sketched in glimmering slime, bodies huddled in doorways or fallen in the streets.

The biggest deposits are in the lightless chasm where the Lord of Waters perished, but Ren cautioned her against diving down there.

"You've been here before."

"Yes."

"How did you get out? Did you earn enough chits or—"

"Adro found me. He was one of the guards. He'd taken the ash, and that bought him a favour. Me."

But now Adro's down with them, another prisoner. On good days, Cari manages to get assigned to the same raft as Adro or Ren, but usually the guards partner her with strangers. Strangers to Cari – but they all know her. All daring her to make a move, to try to escape. Some prisoners do try – they float their rafts to the fringes of the harvesting zone, then make a break for it. But there's nowhere to go. South and east and west, there's the ruin of Ilbarin City and the drowned lowlands, a handful of small islands that used to be the southern hills, and then the open ocean. North, there's the Rock, and Ushket.

To ensure Cari doesn't escape, the guards shackle her every morning. A collar around her throat, and a long rope tying her to the raft. The rope is long enough that it doesn't restrict how far she can dive, but it's a heavy drag, especially when wet, and she has to constantly worry about it getting fouled on some protrusion in the ruins.

They dive almost naked. The hot Ilbarin sun scorches her bare shoulders, and the saltwater and god-brine aggravate any scratches or wounds. Her fingernails are soon raw from scraping at the glimmering slime.

Down, down, into the chill depths. Ilbarin City is almost unrecognisable, a corpse city, but sometimes the rippling blue light catches the outline of some monument or street corner, and it all snaps back in her memory. The strange impression that if she swims deep enough into the darkness she'll reach the old docks of ten years ago, before the war, with the *Rose* waiting for her. Captain Hawse on the deck, looking up at her swimming down out of the sky. But she can never go deep enough.

Swim up. Claw back the light. She breaks the water, drags herself over to the raft, and slings another sack of yliaster on to the pile. Then down again. They can only work for two or three hours a day before exhaustion and cold defeat them, and if they don't have enough yliaster by then they won't eat.

Adro's the best of them, his lanky frame and big hands and feet thrashing through the water. Cari's a powerful swimmer, too, but her injuries and the rope slow her down. Ren has the most experience of the trio when it comes to diving for yliaster, but the drowned city holds many horrors for him. There are more dangers than the cold down there. Ilbarin City was a battlefield for warring gods, a graveyard for broken gods, and miracles still crackle and blaze beneath the waves.

The Kraken of Ishmere touched this land, and spawned horrors. There are places where the Kraken-shape was imposed on everything, a fractal pattern of tentacles and teeth repeated over and over. Tentacled fish warped into tiny Krakens, dust clouds swirling in the water that form into ghost-kraken of mud and slime, rubble that's sprouted razor-edged tendrils of stone. Swim through those cursed regions, and the Kraken-pattern replicates in your flesh. A doctor in the camp trades her services for chits, and excises Kraken-tumours with a stolen knife. In other places, other gods have left their mark. Ren warns them of traps left over by Smoke Painter: divers have found themselves in lush pleasure gardens under the summer moon, where veiled maidens teased them and fed them wine – only to discover it was all an illusion, and the wine drowned them. Where High Umur smote his lightning, the sea still rages and boils, fierce currents that drag unwary swimmers to their doom.

Cari dives again, looking for the telltale glimmer of the yliaster amid the broken stones. Swim down, scrape, scrape, claw at the rocks until there's blood, smear the glimmering slime inside the sack. Then the moment of indecision – swim back up, or risk gathering a little more? Each return to the surface takes time, and even though her body craves the relief of fresh air, her soul is a leaden weight, dragging her down.

On the surface, everyone knows her. Her anonymity is gone. The guards know her. The other prisoners know her. The dragon and the Ghierdana know her. Worst of all, Adro and Ren know her, as the woman who ripped them from their safe lives in Ushket. As the woman who took their child away. They don't say anything, but they don't need to.

It's all there in their hollow eyes.

Every time she swims down, she stays a little longer.

Cari reaches the surface again, gulping in great lungfuls of air. She throws a full sack on to the raft, grabs an empty bag and takes another, calmer breath. Adro grabs her by the arm before she can dive again. "You're blue. We're going back in."

She drags the rope around so she can join the other two at the rear of the raft, and they start kicking, pushing the raft in towards the shore. Bits of flotsam bump against their makeshift vessel, and twice it gets caught on unseen obstacles, but soon they reach the shallows. They change to dragging the raft, wading through thigh-deep water. Ghierdana guards stand sentry on rocks like predatory seabirds, watching the rafts come in. Counting them, to make sure there have been no escape attempts.

Cari has tried escaping, of course. The fourth day, when she was partnered with three strangers, she waited until they were all diving down, and then swam for it – but she'd been spotted and dragged back. A gang of ten or twelve men, all grabbing her, pulling her back to the camp. They'd dumped her in front of one of the Eshdana guards. The guard threw a handful of chits into the middle of the mob, and laughed as they'd scrabbled for them, fought for them. After that, they started putting a rope on her, tethering her to her raft.

The ninth day, when she and Adro were together, he'd tried cutting her rope with a sharpened stone. The rope was tough, but gave way in the end – and then the Ghierdana showed up instantly in one of their little motorboats, nosing their way through the drowned streets. Cari suspects the rope was magically warded, and cutting it alerted the sorceress. That, or her luck is absolutely cursed, which she'd also believe.

The twelfth day, she'd suggested they ambush one of the guards. Maybe steal a weapon. Maybe fight their way out. But Ren refused.

"Then what? Even if we escaped, where is there to go?" His voice matter of fact, something of the bureaucrat he once was, like he's reporting to some prefect, discussing a trivial case instead of pronouncing his own death sentence.

Cari pleaded with Adro, begged him to help. One last madcap heist, just like old times. They'll dress up as guards and set fire to something. Setting fire to things always works, right? But Adro shook his head, went off to trade chits for food for them.

So on this, the seventeeth day, she just waits.

Cari's special. They want something from her.

Maybe, maybe, it'll give her something she can use. Everything's a weapon, right?

They drag the raft on to the makeshift dock, adding it to the pile of other rafts. The guards take the yliaster sacks, weigh them, give them a measly handful of chits. Unlock Cari's collar.

Cari's too tired to eat, so she staggers to their room and collapses.

Time passes. She thinks she might have got up, worked another shift on the raft, come back here again, but she can't be sure. It might have been a dream. She's losing track.

She's lost.

A shadow passes over the camp, waking her from fitful sleep. A few ragged cheers from the guards.

"Dragon's back," says Adro. "Here, I've got you breakfast." He passes her a bowl of some unidentifiable slop and gives another to Ren. "Eat up before they send us out again." Adro's own bowl is less than a third full. "I already ate," he says.

Both Cari and Ren protest at the same time at the obvious lie.

"We're out of chits." Adro shrugs. But he lets them divide the slop evenly, and they all eat. From the sea, the spluttering roar of the motorboat, following in the dragon's wake, heading towards the refinery along the shore.

"Maybe," says Ren, "they'd move us up there."

"What's up there?"

"They process the raw yliaster. Wash it, filter it. Do things to it. Some alchemical procedure. It might be easier work."

"Up there, breathing those fumes? You've already been exposed enough, love." Adro gestures at the striations on Ren's skin. Since they started gathering yliaster, the marks have become angrily inflamed, and sometimes even glow softly in the dark.

Cari watches the dragon settle on the roof of the refinery. She wonders how swiftly that dragon could fly her home. *I need three days*, Eladora said during the invasion, three days to somehow teleport to Lyrix and bring a fucking army of dragons to the city. Cari only needs one dragon, to fly her to Khebesh and then back home.

Those three days cost Spar everything he had left.

"Let's steal the fucking dragon," she suggests, as a gallows joke. When all else fails, try the impossible.

Adro gets it, and chuckles. Ren just stares at her. "How?"

"Let's go and earn some chits," she says in resignation.

Artolo watches from the roof of the refinery as the great ship approaches. The titanic freighter is too large to sail safely through the ruins of Ilbarin City. She'll dock at the new harbour in Ushket, by the yliaster stores.

"Is she not magnificent?" breathes Great-Uncle, admiring the freighter. "*Moonchild*, she is called. Doctor Vorz has overseen her refitting, to carry the yliaster you have gathered for me."

Artolo grunts. "She's big enough to be a warship. We could have made her a corsair. Does the dragon not take what is desired?"

"This is business, nephew. There are greater prizes to be claimed." Great-Uncle scratches a loose scale. "I asked if she was magnificent."

"Not half so magnificent as you, great one."

A boat's lowered from the iron deck of *Moonchild*. Artolo's eyes are still keen, and he can make out a hunched figure at the back of the little boat. Doctor Vorz has returned to Ilbarin.

"Vorz also brought glad tidings from afar," whispers the dragon, half mantling a wing around Artolo. "Now, my boy, fetch Carillon Thay."

"Ten sacks," says Cari, "let's go for ten sacks."

She slips from the raft, limbs numb in the cold water. The rubble directly below has already been scraped bare, so she emerges from the first dive with nothing. They agree to sail the raft further, closer to the heart of the ruined city, closer to where the Godswar hit. The waves break on broken spires and shattered temples, and Cari spots the carcass of some gargantuan sea monster washed up on one bank of rubble. She can't tell what killed it, but it looks burned.

Adro sees it, too.

"You stay up," he says to Ren. "Help us with the sacks. Keep watch. I'll dive with Cari. If you see anything Kraken-shaped, you tug on the rope, right? And we'll come up."

"Keep watch," Ren echoes. The waters are so silty, it's impossible to see any distance. He finds a length of mostly rotten wood amid the floating debris, holds it up as a crude club.

They dive. Cari kicks ahead, using the weight of her iron collar to pull her down swiftly. The slime-bearing ruins are deeper here, so it takes them longer to descend to where they can gather yliaster. The pickings are richer, though – Cari's filled most of her sack before Adro even touches bottom. Lungs burning, she shoves another handful of glowing muck into her bag, starts helping Adro fill his. Their hands tangle, and one glimmering lump gets knocked from Adro's palm and floats off. Adro curses, angry bubbles bursting from his lips.

Cari swims after the glowing lump, snatching at it as it bobs out of reach. The ruined city drops away beneath her – they're on the edge of the great rift, where the Lord of Waters fell. Looking down, the silt clears, and Cari glimpses strange fish swimming through the waters below.

Not fish – Bythos. She can see their dead human-halves trailing behind the living godfish. The way they swim makes their limbs wave, like they're signalling to her. Fuck, maybe that's a way out! The Bythos have helped her before! Hawse said the Lord of Waters had a plan for her, and she'll take a crazy mostly dead god's plan over rotting in the camps. If the Bythos can animate a dead body, then maybe they can keep a living one alive!

It'll be a good thought to share with Spar. *How did you save me, Cari? Well, it all started when I stuck my face up the bum of a divine fish and swam all the fucking way to Khebesh with a flounder on my head.*

She and Adro swim back up. Dump their sacks. Fill their lungs.

"Eight more!" gasps Adro. "We can do eight."

They dive again.

This time, Cari heads straight for the rift where the Bythos cluster.

Pressure as she descends – a pressure in her soul, just like she felt on the mountainside. She's entering into the presence of a god.

She swims down. Leaves Adro far behind.

There's something else down here, too, moving in the dark. Not a Bythos – somelike else, a congregation of dark shapes. A glimpse of many teeth. It vanishes into the mud as Bythos circle around her protectively.

Think. All godshit is the same shit, right? Self-perpetuating structures in the aetheric field, to quote someone who was at the top of the to-stab list for a while. Cari was made to be a saint of the Black Iron Gods, but ended up channelling Spar. Her cousin Eladora – for all her prissiness, El's a spiritual slut, touched by the Black Iron Gods and the Kept Gods, too. Once the channel's opened by one god, it's sometimes easier for another one to make contact.

Cari opens her mind, tries calling. Recites in her head the prayers she overheard from Hawse. *Come on! If you've got some divine plan, fucking show yourself.* She can't see the Bythos overhead any more. Can't see anything apart from the glimmer of yliaster in the dark waters, and she can't tell if those dim lights are five feet or five hundred feet down.

Then – building in the back of her mind, washing over her like a familiar drug – a vision.

Not like Spar's crystalline regularity, his architectural mind, his voice guiding her through the images discarded on the streets of the New City.

Not like the screaming, desperate hunger and hatred of the Black Iron Gods, every thought stained dark and cruel, her soul blood-soiled and tattered afterwards, a thing sewn together from carrion birds.

No, this time the knowledge flows into her, fills her, then recedes. A tidal vision, a wave of revelation. It floods her mind completely, then retreats, leaving prophecy behind on her lips, little tide pools of memory left behind by the drowning god.

She sees—

Two men walking through the streets of Ilbarin long, long ago. Both young. One's dark-skinned, keen-eyed. Dressed in bright robes adorned with the images of colourful birds, a heavy book in his hand. A heavy book, almost identical to the fucking book she haunted all the way from Guerdon. The other's pale like Cari, black-haired like Cari. Memories of the father she barely knew, a dim shape from her childhood, colour the vision. It's not him, though. It's got to be Jermas Thay, like the Crawling Ones said. Jermas, hauled all the way from Guerdon. Hauled all the way from her nightmares.

Jermas looks up at her in the vision. In the memory. Like he knows she's watching.

The scene ripples. Only the book remains constant, and now it's being carried into the deeps by a shoal of Bythos. Cari struggles in confusion, unsure if this is another vision or if she's opened her eyes and spotted the actual book, Ramegos' grimoire, being carried away into the deeps.

Even as she thinks that, the image breaks, and she's storm-tossed, hurled from the heavens to the fundament of the world and back again into a different vision. Powers thunder and spit around her, reality cracking. The Lord of Waters rises, and she's caught in his net. She's the point of his spear, too, at the same moment. It's the invasion of Ilbarin, simultaneously years in the past and happening to her, to the Lord of Waters, right now. Cloud Mother breeds monsters in the sky. Kraken steals the seas, and the saints of the Lord of Waters cry out in agony, for the sea is their blood, and they're transformed into desiccated husks in an instant, a legion of bone-dry corpses standing in a line on the shore. The stolen water draws back, and a host of horrors marches across the suddenly dry seabed, crosses the dry Firesea to lay siege to Ilbarin. At the head of the host is Pesh, Lion Queen, war goddess of Ishmere.

Her eyes are the golden fire of burning cities. Her voice is every battle cry, her roar every explosion, every cataclysm. She is bloody-clawed war, tawny-flanked victory, glory and power.

The churning waters draw back, and Cari spots a tiny speck tossed in the waves. The *Rose*! *Save them*, she thinks. She prays. The Lord of Waters reaches down and picks up the *Rose*.

She's back in Guerdon. She's in the ship made from Spar, in the ship that is Spar. They've got the last god-bomb, but the Ishmerian invasion is all around them. Pesh stands in the flood-waters of the Wash, her legions advancing into Guerdon. Artillery thunders from the heights, and somewhere in there the city's last defenders rally along Mercy Street. Cari aims the ship, Rat lights the fuse and the bomb launches, arcing over the city to explode into nothingness.

Hands grab her, pulling her. Darkness all around. She struggles. Adro, the fucking idiot, her brave moron of a friend, pulls her out of the rift, drags her back towards the surface.

He doesn't understand. She's made contact, but she hasn't got through. The Lord of Waters is an idiot, too, a broken god, spitting out whatever random thoughts and memories he thinks might connect to Cari. He doesn't understand. She's got to make him understand, got to find a way to use his power. The Bythos can carry them home. The Bythos can get them to Khebesh.

Her lungs are full of water. Her head's full of gods.

Adro shoves her roughly out of the water, throwing her on to the raft like a sack of yliaster. He drags himself out, groaning, rolls her over so that she throws up over the edge. He's bleeding from a fresh wound on his chest. A small bite mark.

"I've got. Go back," she moans between gushes of seawater and vomit. Her puke glimmers with yliaster, and she doesn't know if that's some mystical side effect of the vision or just too much exposure to the raw stuff.

"I tugged on the rope," says Ren, "when I saw them."

Cari raises her head, and sees the approaching shape of the Ghierdana motorboat, and the armoured sorceress is standing at the prow like a figurehead made from the same gunmetal.

CHAPTER NINETEEN

B aston sits in silence as the train rushes under Guerdon. Vyr squirms, nervous at being so far from the safety of the New City. The air down here is hot, full of soot and steam. Flashes of light give unconnected glimpses of the tunnel outside – here a brick wall, water from some buried river beading on its surface, there a graffiti-marked arch. Now darkness, darkness, ghoul eyes, darkness again.

"My cousin . . . he is not wholly himself," Vyr begins, keeping his voice low. "You were there when it began. Tell me what you know about the thing that speaks to him."

"We shouldn't talk about it," grunts Baston. "Not here, not now." They've got a job to do.

"Here is exactly where we should talk about it. He cannot eavesdrop on us here." Vyr shakes his head. "Back home in Lyrix, they lock saints away in madhouses and call them monasteries. It's for their own protection. Saints have their eyes fixed on heaven and cannot see the mortal world. Cannot see the harm they do. We never use saints." He mutters to himself in Lyrixian, a quick litany of curses or prayers, then glances back up at Baston. "We walk a dangerous path. He goes too fast, without supervision. He shall bring ruin on us."

"Not here." Baston leans forward. "And you're going to be speaking for your cousin, right? So you'd better fucking swallow that doubt. Just tell Mandel that if he doesn't take the deal, he'll end up like Dredger. That's all you've got to say, but you have to show steel. If you're weak, they'll never take the ash."

Vyr scowls. "You're not even Eshdana. You don't speak to me like that."

"And what," says Baston quietly, "will you do about it?"

The answer, it seems, is nothing. Vyr sits back, pressing himself against the seat to get as far away from Baston as he can. He looks strangled, his body twisting with nervousness and bile. He mutters to himself again, and it's definitely a curse this time.

The funny thing is, Baston's instincts agree with Vyr. Baston's cautious by nature; a good right-hand man has to be. You're supposed to keep the boss from walking into danger, from getting overextended. To attend to practicalities instead of chasing bold visions. But he did all that, and where did it get him? Lost, left behind in a changed city. Play things too cautiously, and the world leaves you behind.

There's a certain quality in a great leader. The ability to see the gap between what everyone agrees can be done, and what's actually possible, to push you into going beyond yourself. A catalyst, they'd call it, enabling things that would otherwise be unthinkable. Of course, go too far and that quality becomes dangerous, becomes explosive.

Baston runs through his own litany – the masters of the Brotherhood. Idge, of course, was a perfect example of a leader who saw what was possible, but went too far. He gave the Brotherhood a dream and a purpose, warned them about the power of the alchemists, about how they would be more callous than any priest or god. But Idge pushed too hard, and the city pushed back. He died on the gallows when Baston was a boy.

After Idge came a quick succession of forgettable men, bosses who just tried to hold the Brotherhood together. Even their names blur together in Baston's mind – Tomas Whoreson, Starris, Gaern the

Shipwright. All cautious by nature. Baston knows that if he'd ever risen to the rank of master, he'd be counted with them.

Then, Heinreil. Even after all these years, Baston still doesn't quite know what to think of Heinreil. He'd done things that no one else had thought could be done, but they were the wrong things – bringing in sorcerers and other monsters like the Fever Knight, cutting deals with Crawling Ones. Selling out to the alchemists. A twisted vision of the possible. He took the Brotherhood and twisted it. Twisted Baston, too, by apprenticing him to the Fever Knight. No one could deny Heinreil's cunning – he led the Brotherhood through the candlelight, bargained with the alchemists, made more money than any of his predecessors – but the price was too high.

Spar – Spar, the lost hope. All of Idge's moral clarity, but tempered with grief, with an understanding of the costs of failure. If Spar had been master, then the Brotherhood might have become more than a band of thieves – a movement, a counterforce, something to grab the wheels of the terrible machinery behind the city and force them to turn the other way.

On his own, Rasce's just an interloper, a spoiled dragon-prince with no understanding of Guerdon's history, of the Brotherhood's purpose. But Rasce is not on his own. He's got Idgeson's blessing; he's got Baston by his side. He may be an outsider, but he could be the leader they need. That's the Guerdon way, isn't it? Everyone's from somewhere else. Even the first people to settle in this city found it abandoned and empty.

There's the dragon, though. There's the dragon. Baston sticks his hand in his pocket, grinds the white pebbles he carries against each other as a nervous gesture, like a priest toying with prayer beads.

The train grinds to a halt. Baston opens the door on to a platform crowded with grey-faced factory workers, coughing as the fumes fill the underground station. The Fog Yards.

The dragon is a problem for another day.

*

Mandel & Company is a big enough problem for today.

Mandel & Company is a big enough problem for a lifetime.

Mandel & Company is, literally, a fortress. Before Guerdon swelled in size and influence, the old city was guarded by walls and towers, and Mandel's yards straddle that border. Most of the walls have long since been scavenged by stone-hungry masons, but not here. Mandel's fort incorporates part of the old city wall, new fortifications piled on old stone. The wall's scarred in places, which Baston realises must be damage from the siege of Guerdon three hundred years before, when the saints of the Kept Gods overthrew the cult of Black Iron. If the old wall's intact, then that lends some credence to Heinreil's claim of a secret tunnel in the depths, but he has to know for sure.

The Fog Yards sprawl out from the line of that former wall – an industrial landscape, trail tracks spilling out like steaming steel entrails, sheds and factories and sullen red-litten mills. The streets here are wide. They have to be, to make room for the heavily laden wagons that crawl between the factories, drawn by teams of raptequines. Off in the distance, rising like skeletal giants, are the new towers of the alchemists. All steel and corrugated iron and vat-grown bone, not the dark stone of the city proper.

The Mandel fortress may be older than the rest of the Fog Yards, but the defences are brand new. The guards walking the walls wear helmets with thaumic lenses and breather masks, the same as the city watch. Ensorcelled to spot hostile magic and miracles. A man could scale those old stone walls, but Baston doesn't like the look of those gaps between the blocks. You could hide anything in those dark fissures. Biters. Green slime. Knife-smokers, spitting mist that cuts your fingers off. The four walls form a rough square around the Mansel compound; tanks and aetheric vanes rise above the parapet, suggesting the yard inside is filled with industrial machinery.

It reminds Baston of the old Alchemists' Quarter, with its impenetrable sheer stone walls rising like cliffs, looming over the lesser structures in the Fog Yards. It took the Gutter Miracle, Spar's martyrdom and miraculous rebirth, to destroy the old Alchemists' Quarter; it'll take something equally divine to breach the wall of Mandel & Company.

Vyr looks equally daunted. He shakes his head as he spots gun emplacements and aetheric vanes on the upper levels. "Even Great-Uncle would balk at this."

"It has to be doable." From the shadow of the subway entrance, Baston gives the fortress a quick once over, casing it as best he can. There's a statue at the subway entrance, depicting some dead guild-master, cradling the cup of the alchemists. Baston reaches up, drops a marble pebble into the mouth of the cup. "Let's go," he says.

Vyr squares his shoulders. His face adopts a cold sneer that makes him look like Rasce. He marches across the street, head held high, dodging the wagons. Pounds his fist on the door. The walls seem even taller up close, looming like a Kraken-wave of black stone. Above the door is a recess, and nestled there is a glass tank filled with greenish liquid – and a giant eyeball, as big as Baston's fist. The thing's alive – it stares down at Baston, and it seems to him that it's pleading with him.

"Mandel & Company export all over the world." Vyr looks up at the eyeball, presenting his face to it. "They know the Ghierdana's reach."

The door opens. A footman welcomes them in. "Mr Mandel will see you now."

They're let through the outer walls of the fortress, but instead of passing into the central courtyard the footman leads them through another door into a long carpeted corridor. Portraits on the walls tell of the glorious works of the alchemists' guild, and long series of studious men and women, pale faces lit by glowing flasks or blazing crucibles. Baston recognises some of the faces – a red-haired woman holding a candle must be Rosha, the former guildmistress who vanished in the Crisis. A few politicians he vaguely recalls, mainly because they took bribes from the Brotherhood of old. A group portrait, showing the founding of the guild, watched over by a frowning Keeper priest.

Other pictures show other fruits of their labour – the burning ruins of cities, armies vanquished by alchemical weapons, new forms of life sprouting in vats. A Tallowman, and no amount of talent on the part of the artist could make that waxy horror appear noble. In the image, the Tallowman in city livery stands before a gallows, displaying Idge's body like a prize catch.

At the end of the corridor, a gigantic canvas shows the last moments of the invasion. The war goddess Pesh stands astride a shattered city, her claws tearing down churches and towers. There's no sign of the hasty alliance of city watch, Keeper saints, and Haithi soldiers who fought against the invasion, nor is there any sign of the dragons, the threat of whom sealed the final Armistice. The only resistance to the invaders is the god-bomb in the sky, depicted as a pure, searing light. The giant form of Pesh seems ephemeral in comparison to the alchemists' bomb.

He also notes that the frame of that huge painting is decorated with silver leaf and sapphires. A fortune squandered on extravagant folly that only a handful will ever see, while people starve in the shadow of those dark walls. In the painting, Pesh's gigantic feet trample the familiar streets of the Wash.

Baston's hand brushes against the painting. He hides a second pebble of stone in the frame.

The footman brings them to another double door and shows them into Mandel's chamber. The room is long – you could fit Craddock's whole building in here twice over – and lit by glowing panels of gold that cast patterns of light shimmering over the polished tiles of the floor. Marble walls rise in flowing shapes to meet in the arched ceiling overhead, giving the unsettling feeling of movement, as though the stone might without warning transmute to fluttering fabric. A dark-skinned scribe sits on a stool near the altar, scratching notes in a great ledger, but the shifting light makes it hard to see his face. Baston wonders if the creature is really a man at all, or something grown in a vat. Certainly, the scribe doesn't react to their presence at all. Only his withered hands are clearly visible, moving ceaselessly across the page, recording everything.

Nothing is solid here, nothing certain except the great black altar of Mandel's desk at the far end.

Mandel himself looks like a judge, white hair worn long enough to touch the collar of his dark suit. A golden amulet on his chest, the eye-and-cup of the alchemists his only adornment. Gloved hands steepled in front of him.

It's all theatre, Baston guesses. All to make people feel small. He holds his head up, refuses to let the weight of Mandel's gaze intimidate him. *The Brotherhood will get you in the end*, Baston promises silently, *and we won't need a picture to remember*. Still, he finds his pace slowing, and has to fight the urge to bow his head. Instead, he sits in one of the two low chairs in front of the massive desk.

He slips a third pebble out of his pocket, tucks it into the lining of the chair.

Vyr draws his knife again, holds it up. "I am here as a representative of my cousin – and my Great-Uncle, Taras the Red. I speak for the Ghierdana."

"Speak, then," booms Mandel, his voice brassy and deep.

"We offer a simple arrangement. My family has secured a large supply of yliaster. We ask that you purchase all your yliaster through us, instead of your existing sources.

"My present arrangements are satisfactory to me. I have no interest in bargaining with you. Good day."

"Ah," says Vyr, "but our rates are cheaper. You shall profit greatly by agreeing."

"Your supply comes from Ilbarin." The scribe makes a note. "Much farther away than my existing sources of yliaster. Your rates cannot be cheaper – unless the dragon is subsidising the cost for his own ends. I have no intention of surrendering control of the guild's yliaster to the Ghierdana."

"Your—" Vyr's voice cracks. He swallows, tries again. "Many of your competitors have already taken the dragon's bargain, and you would be wise to do the same. It is better to be the dragon's friend than his enemy!"

"The whelp threatens us, Tym," laughs Mandel, and the scribe makes another note. "The whelp mistakes us for grubby dealers in scrap. Out of respect for the dragon – not you, and certainly not your cousin, who lacks the courage to come himself – I shall say this: the alchemists' guild sees no profit in a pointless quarrel with the Ghierdana, but we shall not tolerate thuggery or insolence. Walk away now, whelp, and I shall forget you ever spoke so unwisely."

Vyr opens his mouth like a gaffed fish, unsure of how to respond. Baston steps in. Time to growl, to be the savage brute that makes Vyr look reasonable and statesmanlike in contrast. He launches into a snarl, a rant, hunching his body forward like he's about to fling himself across the deck and go for Mandel's throat.

"In case you haven't noticed, you fat prick, this isn't the guild's city any more. You're not in charge. You're fucked and you know it!" Baston's intimidating enough for the scribe to lay down his pen, to raise his hand in a curious contorted gesture. He keeps going, droplets of spittle mottling the pristine surface of the desk, waiting for Vyr to say *something*, to lay a restraining hand on him or to interrupt him, but Vyr's just sitting there gawping. Baston's words keep coming, exploding like the siege charge. He rises from his seat, slams his hand on the desk. "You haven't got parliament in your pocket. Your Hawkers lost last year, and you can't buy enough votes to cover your shame. There's a king up in Holyhill now, and every dog in the street knows he's on our side, not yours. The Keepers are back, and they hate you, too. There are fucking mad gods squatting in the Wash. You don't even have your candlejacks no more. This city hates you! The streets will rise and we will finish you!"

"Enough." Guards in Mandel & Company livery flood from concealed side doors, faces masked by black helms.

Hands grab at Baston. He breaks them, twisting free, grabbing fingers, twisting them too, then driving his knee in hard enough to snap ribs. Elbows one man in the face, punches another.

He knows that this is stupid, but his blood's up.

A fourth guard moves in – Baston grabs the chair he was sitting on, flings it towards the man, but the guard's not there any more. The fucker moves far faster than any human could, ducking under the flying chair with easy grace, and now his too-soft, too-strong hands are at Baston's throat, pushing him to the floor with horrible ease. He can feel the heat of the candle-flame inside the guard's skull – a Tallowman.

Not like the one that attacked Rasce in Glimmerside. This candlejack's fresh, its waxy form recently recast. He doesn't have a fucking chance against this one.

He tries anyway. Slams his fist into the monster's flank, its neck, anywhere the wax might be exposed. The Tallowman doesn't react, it just pins him to the floor. Little drools of melted wax from its mouth drip through the faceplate of the helmet.

Vyr pulls himself free. "I'm Ghierdana! I'm Ghierdana! Blood of the dragon!" he shrieks.

The guards – the human ones – hesitate and glance towards Mandel. They know the reputation of the Ghierdana, and how laying hands on a member of the dragon's own family is an unforgivable offence. Mandel makes a dismissive gesture. "Let him go. As I said, I want no quarrel with the dragon. Your blood will not be on my hands."

Vyr darts to the doorway, then looks back at Baston, still pinned by the Tallowman. Baston still hasn't taken the ash. He's not Eshdana. Just a stray dog. By the customs of the Ghierdana there's nothing stopping Vyr from walking out the door and leaving Baston behind.

Vyr knows it. He wavers at the threshold, looks down at Baston for a long moment, his breathing fast and shallow, weighing the risk to himself against Rasce's anger if he returns alone.

"Wretches like him," remarks Mandel, "are fit only for rendering in the Tallow Vats. I have it in mind to remake him into something useful to society."

The scribe coughs. Mandel nods, and the Tallowman releases Baston.

He crawls clear, staggers to his feet, leaning against the wall for support as he and Vyr stumble out of the fortress. A fifth chip is tucked behind one of the glowing panels as he passes.

"A disaster. A disaster," repeats Vyr to himself. "Rasce should have gone himself. I was doomed from the start, yes? The fault is his, not mine. I must tell them that."

"There was every chance it was going to play out like that." Baston rubs his neck. "Rasce knew there was little chance of Mandel taking the deal straight off. It was always going to get rough."

"You made certain of that, dolt, by shouting in Mandel's face! Useless bluster!"

Baston rolls the last of the pebbles between his fingers. "Wasn't useless."

Vyr stares at him, uncomprehending, then says: "Go and tell my cousin of our failure here. Tell him that Mandel is secure in his fortress, and will not bargain. Perhaps we can bring another of the families in, pay Carancio or one of the other great ones for aid. Nothing short of a dragon could break those walls, yes?"

"Looked like." Unscalable, invulnerable walls, patrolled by Tallowmen and gods know what else. A challenge. Definitely a challenge.

Vyr narrows his eyes. "This is a ploy. Some scheme of *his*? We're far outside the New City. The thing that Rasce communes with – it can't do anything here . . . can it? What have you done?"

Baston scowls. "Stay quiet. Wait till we're safe."

"Safe? *Safe?*" echoes Vyr. His whole body quivers with nervous excitement or fear. He shakes his head. "Meddling with divine powers is never safe. This has gone far enough."

It's not some mad god, Baston thinks, *it's Spar Idgeson. The son of the man who made the Brotherhood.*

The train slows, stops at Venture Square station. Vyr rises.

"This isn't our stop."

"I need a drink. And not in the New City. That cursed place hurts my eyes. I can't sleep properly up there. Too many eyes." He vanishes into the throng on the platform. A few other passengers consider getting into Baston's carriage, but take one look at him and pick another seat. He closes the door, lets the jolting of the train lull his tired bones.

Alone, he opens his hand and stares at the pebble. It glimmers with a faint light that seems to grow brighter as the train crosses the border and into the New City.

So what if the alchemists have their candles? The thieves have their own light, now.

CHAPTER TWENTY

The Eshdana unshackle Cari and take her on board the gunboat. At the sight of the armed guards, Ren lets his stick fall into the water. There's nothing they can do against armed guards – and that's not even considering the sorceress.

One of the guards on the gunboat is Dol Martaine. He pulls Cari down to sit next to him as the boat turns around, engine alternately growling and idling as they try to find the best course through the hazardous ruins.

"Help them," she whispers.

"Got their brat at home, don't I? That's all I can do for Adro."

"You sold me out to the Ghierdana," she spits at Martaine.

"If I'd sold you out," Martaine whispers, "you think I'd still be here? Instead, I'm wiping up after the wretch." He shakes his head. "I should have done it. I wish I had done it. I'd off this cursed island and halfway to Paravos. But no use crying over it now, yes?"

"Are you taking me to Artolo?"

"No. The Dentist." He hands her a grey shift to wear. The coarse cloth is spotted with someone else's blood. As Cari pulls the garment over her head, she turns around, looking for something she can steal. A knife or some other weapon. Anything to give her an edge – but Martaine knows her too well. He grabs her, drags her back down to the bench next to him, and keeps a close eye on her. The sorceress, too, watches her like a silent idol.

There's a ship in the distance, beyond the ruins of the city. An alchemy-powered freighter, her funnels trailing pale blue smoke as she steams north around the coast. Cari stares at her, trying to judge her size. The horizon's as fucked up as the sea, but Cari guesses it must be huge.

"What's that?" she asks.

"*Moonchild*," answers Martaine. "The Dentist brought it. Big beast of a ship, eh? Armed, too. She's to bring the yliaster to Guerdon." He shakes his head. "Maybe I'd be on her if it weren't for you."

Cari half rises for a better view of the distant vessel, but Martaine hauls her down. "Sit still and shut up for once in your bloody life," he hisses, and there's terror in his eyes. "I won't end up like Hawse."

She sits still. She shuts up. She pulls the grey shift around herself, like her touch is tainted.

The refinery reminds Cari of the Alchemists' Quarter in Guerdon, but only a little. In the district, the pipes were polished mirror-bright and ornamented with astrological sigils. The factories were palaces of industry, temples to transmutation. The Ghierdana refinery, though, looks like a distillery for making rot-gut booze. All ramshackle, dripping with grease and oil, barely holding together, and built from whatever salvage they could find in the ruined city.

There are a few sections, though, that look new-made. The innermost components – reaction vessels, industrial athanors – are clearly imported from beyond Ilbarin, incongruous as a hat on a Bythos. Guerdon-made, she guesses, although they look somehow off to her. Fanciful, brass and steel decorated with serpents and flowers. Admittedly, her expertise on alchemical factories is limited to one burglary and two near-apocalypses.

Below, she can see the loading docks where they bring in the sacks of yliaster; on the right, a queue of carts, laden with casks bound for Ushket's docks, then *Moonchild*. And then far-off Guerdon.

And above it all, perched on the roof of the refinery, is the dragon.

Martaine and other guards drag her, kicking and biting, through the refinery. She knows it's a waste of energy, but she gets a really satisfying elbow into the ribs of one of the guards. If she managed a bite, too, it would have been a better meal than she's had in days, but they don't give her the opportunity.

They wrestle her across the main floor, past rows of troughs filled with yliaster, being washed by miserable workers who don't dare look up. Past the huge main athanor, an alchemical furnace. They bring her to a narrow metal staircase that leads to a gantry. There's a room up here overlooking the main factory floor, and they shove her through the door.

It's a laboratory – there's a mask and robe of woven silver hanging from a hook, rows of bottles and jars, aetheric instruments, things in tanks. Windows so he can monitor the athanors. Another window, looking out over the ruins and the sea and the muddy shore. The room's all cold and clinical, all scrubbed clean. A room for dissections.

The alchemist's there. The Dentist. Vorz. Cari's seen him before, sort of – through Spar, in the last days before she fled Guerdon. A black crow of a man, stalking through *her* streets in the New City. Another alchemist, grubbing in the dirt for poison.

The guards troop out, but the armoured sorceress remains. "I'll paralyse her," she says, raising a gloved hand limned in purple light.

Vorz clicks his tongue in irritation. "An active incantation would affect my instruments. Restrain her only if necessary."

Cari nods meekly. Lets her shoulders drop, her hands go limp. No point in fighting a sorcerer.

From a shelf, he takes down an object she recognises – it's a gilded skull. Once Professor Ongent used a skull like that one to determine her connection to the Black Iron Gods. She recalls the horror of that early contact with the deities, how it drove her into a frenzy of terror. She'd ended up breaking Ongent's nose with a headbutt.

"First, I shall ascertain what thaumic anchors remain," murmurs Vorz. He's talking to the sorceress, not Cari. He hasn't even looked at her – she's a specimen to him, an experiment. His voice is a solemn whisper. "At this distance, I doubt there's active congruency to any Guerdonese powers, but there may be spiritual pollution from the local aether. I may require you to conduct an exorcism."

He bends over to put the skull in Cari's hands, just like Ongent did.

Cari skips the frenzy of terror, and just head-butts the Dentist straight off. His nose breaks with a very satisfying crunch. She flings the skull at the sorceress – purple light flares, but it catches the skull, not her. More bone shatters. Cari springs across the room, grabbing jars of alchemical shit and smashing them down, throwing them at the sorceress – *fuck, please, would SOMETHING just explode!* – then running. There's a door across the room. She darts to it, grabbing a scalpel as she flees, broken glass bloodying her feet.

Out of the door on to the gantry. Refinery floor below her. Above her, the whole building shakes with a furious animal roar. Oh yeah, there's a dragon on the roof.

Suddenly, there's no ceiling above her, as a massive claw rips a hunk of it away. A furious dragon's eye peers through the hole, boggling at her insolence, so she adds injury to insult by flinging the scalpel straight into it. She runs down the metal gantry, charging headlong. No fucking idea where she's going, but at least it's not waiting around to die.

She hears shouts from the factory below. Eshdana guards below spot her, start stomping up the metal stairs towards her, so she jumps from the gantry, grabbing on to the metal bars that support the tin roof. She swings across, bar to bar, until she reaches the outer housing of the main athanor, the big bell-shaped tank in the middle of the room. It's hot to the touch, like climbing on a stove, but after a morning diving in the chilly depths it's almost pleasant. Easily the best part of a doomed attempt to escape from a gang of crazed dragon-pirates and their alchemical freak show. She sways, deliriously, from the top of the machine. She doesn't have a plan, but maybe something will happen. And, if not, then at least, for a brief moment, she's free. She laughs wildly.

Roars from outside. Surely the dragon won't smash up his own refinery. The workers and guards mill around beneath her, but none of them can climb up here. None of them dare shoot at her, either, for fear of damaging their precious machinery. Cari laughs again as they come to the same realisation and lower their weapons.

A door below bursts open, and Artolo rushes in, red-faced and furious, carrying a long-barrelled rifle. He raises the weapon, and she can tell that the risk to the yliaster isn't going to dissuade him. Shit. She climbs higher, trying to keep the athanor between her and that gun.

Artolo roars in frustration and races to the side, trying to get a clean shot. She dodges back the other way, trying to guess his intention. She wishes that she had Spar's sight to back her up, instead of having to peer through the tangle of struts and pipes that sprout from the upper section of the furnace.

He fires. The section of pipe she was clinging to explodes in a burst of fire and shrapnel. Cari leaps awkwardly at the last second and manages to catch on to a dangling loop of chain, but there's nowhere else to go, and she's left hanging thirty feet above the ground, ears ringing from the blast. The world sways and spins around her.

Artolo takes aim.

"ENOUGH!" roars the dragon. "Artolo, put the rifle down. *Now!*"

Artolo's face contorts in fury, but he drops the gun.

"You, Thay, enough of this folly. There is no escape. There are only degrees of suffering. Yield."

All Cari can do is hang there. The only defiance she can muster is spitting in the dragon's face, and he's too far away for the little gobbet of phlegm to get anywhere near him. It splashes in a yliaster trough, far below.

"Your courage is noted," continues the dragon, squeezing in through the loading dock. Its folded wings scrape against the sides of the massive door. Workers scurry out of the way, and the liquid in the yliaster troughs jumps and ripples with every thunderous footfall. Gods, the thing is gigantic. It fixes its fiery eyes on Cari, and she's frozen − not by magic, but by sheer animal terror, a little mouse facing off against a lion. She tries to clamber around the athanor again, get the furnace between her and that thing, but, fast as a striking serpent, the dragon's head darts forward. The jaws close around Cari, and she lets go of the chain in shock. She shrieks as it whips her around. The dragon holds her in his mouth without biting down − he could devour her in an instant, the slightest pressure from those mighty jaws would crush her, drive those huge teeth through her, she can feel them digging into her, and for a terrifying instant she thinks that he's going to *eat* her − and then spits her out, dropping her on to the hard ground.

He leans down, his hot drool dripping on her skin. Flames lick the air when he speaks. "Your cousin Eladora Duttin came to my lair. She offered me tribute. A share of Guerdon's wealth. A territory on the mainland. The fate of two empires, at my command. She bargained with gods to reach me. Praised my magnificence. She bowed before me and *begged* for my aid. She understood her *place*." The dragon stares down at her, eyes blazing.

"You will, too."

They dress Cari's wounds before returning her to the prison camp. The dragon's teeth have torn a dozen ugly cuts in her thighs, her side, her shoulders. None too deep, but they all have to be washed out with stinging antiseptic. While the Eshdana healer treats her, she glances up, spots Vorz sitting on a walkway above the factory floor, another doctor fussing over the alchemist's bandaged nose.

"Worth it," she mutters.

She expected them to punish her. To beat her. Feed her to the dragon. Instead, they feed her. It's better than camp food – she guesses it's Eshdana rations. There's even something pinkish that might conceivably have once been introduced to meat, and she wolfs it down. It doesn't even cost her any chits. Somehow, it's more sinister to have her special status underlined. They want something from her.

Back in the camp, the guards thrust Cari through the gate and close it behind her. Other guards watch her from the gantries as she makes her way through the ruins to the house she shares with Ren and Adro. The other prisoners watch her, too, but she can feel a barrier between her and them. She's tainted, made toxic by her mysterious association with the Ghierdana. It's like having the Stone Plague back in Guerdon.

Adro's lying on the floor. They're always exhausted after diving, falling asleep where they drop, so she thinks nothing of it until she sees Ren's face.

"Oh fuck. What happened?"

"He got sick after they took you. Something in the water struck him. Maybe poisoned him." Ren presses a rag to Adro's brow. His big body shakes with the effort of breathing. His skin's clammy, his hands limp, sprawled across his heaving chest like jellyfish. The wound's small, but the flesh around it is swollen and raw. Little droplets of liquid pus ooze from it and run down Adro's flanks.

"You're hurt, too," says Ren, seeing Cari's bandages.

"It's nothing." She kneels down on the other side of Adro, takes his other hand in hers. "We've got to find him a healer."

"I tried," says Ren quietly, in his matter-of-fact way. "They won't come. We need to be here for him."

Cari sits. Waits. Holds her friend's hand, as shudders run through him. She doesn't know what to do. Her instincts tell her to run. She hates to stay and watch, to sit and wait for the inevitable.

Don't stay in Aunt Silva's house, waiting for the nightmares to come. Leave. Run away in the night.

Don't sit and quarrel with Captain Hawse day after day. Leave. Run away in the night.

And Spar – Spar was dying from the moment she met him. And she nearly did flee, when he needed her most. When he was in a prison – a prison like this one – and Heinreil poisoned him, Cari fled down to Guerdon's harbour, went looking for a ship to carry her away. It was the fucking Black Iron Gods that convinced her to turn around, to stay.

How shit a person is she, to need moral guidance from tyrannical carrion gods?

Is Khebesh another way to avoid hanging around, waiting for a friend to die? She told herself that Khebesh was a destination, not an excuse, but it got her out of Guerdon. Should she have stayed, born witness as Spar slowly faded into nothingness? Maybe it's all her fault – she used so much of him during the invasion . . .

Adro groans, and it floods her stomach with sick guilt. She's supposed to be here for Adro, and instead she's thinking about Spar. *Focus on one sick friend at a time.*

She searches for something to say. "Your little girl – Dol Martaine has her. She's safe. I mean, Martaine's a fucker and I'll kill him if he touches her – no, *we'll* kill him – but she's staying with him."

"Hear that? Ama is safe. You don't need to worry," echoes Ren, talking to Adro. He even manages a thin smile. "We'll find her again, like before. You brought us out of this camp, remember? You saved us."

Adro groans, but doesn't say anything that might be intelligible speech. He coughs, blood-flecked spittle bursting from his lips. His eyes open, but they don't focus on anything. Ren dribbles a little water into his mouth.

"He's not going to make it," whispers Cari, and Ren's eyes flash with anger.

"He's strong. You know how strong he is. He'll bury us all – won't you, Adro?"

The sun vanishes behind the Rock of Ilbarin. The stars come out. They've changed again, Cari notes distantly. The Godswar fucks up the heavens, rewrites the celestial sphere. The tide comes up the slope, waves breaking against the ruins of the city. It's beautiful in the darkness – the yliaster deposits make the whole sea shimmer like liquid moonlight. She describes it to Adro. Talks about old times, telling the same old stories Adro recounted at that last dinner on the *Rose*. She doesn't tell the tales as well as Adro, but she tries. She even adds a new one to the rotation – *remember that time we nearly escaped Ilbarin on a boat made of worms? Wasn't that crazy? Wasn't that a lark?*

When she can no longer talk, Ren takes over. He reminds Adro of their shared history, how Adro got him out of the camp. Talks about the fragile little life they built in Ushket. He speaks with a courtier's eloquence, and a diplomat's evasion: he never mentions that Adro was ash-marked, a prison guard for the Ghierdana. Ren never mentions his own job in Ushket directly either, but Cari guesses it was something to do with the Ghierdana, too. Either you serve the dragon, or you die. *There is no escape. Only degrees of suffering.* Ren describes a little island of tranquillity, a fiercely defended bubble of normality in a dying land. He talks about teaching Ama to read, about friends they can stay with in Paravos when they finally leave Ilbarin, about his idea to keep roaming Bythos out of a little vegetable garden at the back of their home.

Her own dragon-inflicted wounds begin to ache. Her shoulders, especially, as she hunches over Adro's body. At some point in the night he begins to shiver, his whole body shaking convulsively. They pile their thin blankets on top of him after the heat leeches from the air.

Sometime close to dawn, Ren comes around to sit next to Cari.

"I want to tell you something," he says, not looking at her. "Adro asked me to remain silent, but I owe you honesty. That night, when Adro visited Captain Hawse and dined with you – he told me where he was going, and who he was going to see. I told the Ghierdana that you were at the wreck of the *Rose*. That's how they found you."

"I- I thought it was Martaine—"

"No. It was I. They were offering passage off Ilbarin." Ren adjusts Adro's blanket. "Adro didn't know. He was furious when I told him. And I don't suppose it's worth anything, but I am sorry. I don't bear any malice towards you. There's no space for such things, now." A thin smile. "It's always easier to deal with abstracts, isn't it? In the prefect's court, one of my duties was overseeing the paperwork regarding executions. We always had to excise all the names – it was always Prisoner Number such-and-such."

"It's all right," mutters Cari. Once, she'd have been filled with wonderful righteous anger at this confession. She'd have leaped up, shouted *fuck you* at Ren, stormed off. Knifed him, maybe. Plotted revenge, or just run. Another city marked off the list. Sailing off, never to return.

Strangely, though, she feels it is all right. Self-sacrifice has never been in Cari's nature – all her life, maybe from the moment she was conceived in Jermas Thay's fucking laboratory-slash-Black Iron Cult sanctum, she's had to fight to have a self, to be something more than a tool of the gods. Somehow, the fact that it all went wrong for Ren, too, makes it easier to forgive. Ilbarin's run of cursed luck extends to him, too.

Also, later that night, when she burst into his carefully built little fortress of normality with a Crawling One and a mad plan, he hadn't said no. That willingness to take a chance counts for a lot with Cari.

She peels back the blanket, takes a look at Adro's injury. It's bad. It's very bad.

Spar, what should I do? she thinks, but there's no answer. Two dying friends to save, but one's right here.

"Back in a while," she lies.

Cari walks the streets of the camp, stepping over bodies – sleeping or dead, it's hard to tell – until she finds a guard post.

"Hey!"

It's too dark for her to make out his features. He's just a dark outline against the pinkish sky, looking down at her.

"Go and find the Dentist. Tell him I'm ready to co-operate."

CHAPTER TWENTY-ONE

There's a glass of arax waiting for Baston at Lanthorn Street. He wishes it was something else – the smoky liquor echoes the smoggy air of the Fog Yards instead of washing away the taste – but he still raises his glass when Rasce toasts his success. There's a third glass on the table. For Karla, maybe. Or for Spar.

And next to the glass is Rasce's snuffbox of ash, for anointing new Eshdana. Its presence unsettles Baston. It reminds him of the grave-worm in Heinreil's little gold casket.

"A daring raid," says Rasce, "into the heart of the enemy!"

"All for naught, unless you can find the tunnel. Have you looked, yet?"

Rasce shakes his head. "I'll wait until nightfall. It's easier for Spar, then. I don't know why."

"What's it like? The visions, I mean?"

"Perilous, in its way. Like walking along a parapet." Rasce sits down, swirls his arax. "No, better. Sit down and I'll tell you what it's like. Sometimes, in the summer, Great-Uncle would play with the children on the island."

"The dragon . . . would play with the children."

Rasce nods enthusiastically. "It was wonderful. We'd climb all over his back, slide down his tail. Go hunting and seeking in the folds of his wings. He'd throw us up in the air and catch us, or blow smoke rings the size of wagon wheels to jump through. He'd whisper secrets to us, too – things we weren't supposed to know. Who had gained his favour, or lost it. Who was strong, who was weak. Marvellous it was to be a child and know that a dragon watched over you. That's what the visions are like, my friend. I am watched over by something great and glorious, and it whispers secrets to me."

"It's strange to hear you talk of Spar Idgeson like that," says Baston. It sounds wonderful, in truth. The Brotherhood, blessed and cleansed, watched over by Idge's son. "In my head, he's still living off Crane Street in the Wash."

"What was he like, in life?"

Baston shrugs. "His father's son. A good man. A great one, I think, had he lived." He throws back the arax. "We moved apart, and I regret it."

"And Carillon Thay?"

"I hardly knew her. Spar and I . . . once he got the Stone Plague, we had to stay away from him, right? It's catching. So I only met her a few times. Once or twice in the clubhouse, and on the streets. Sour-faced. Skittish." Baston rakes through his memories, searching for some early sign he missed. That flighty little cutpurse became the dread Saint of Knives, powerful enough to hold back the Ghierdana.

"You said the visions could be perilous."

"Ah, yes. Once, Great-Uncle was playing with my cousin . . . cousin . . . ah, what was her name? Tero's girl? He'd fling her into the air with his teeth and catch her again. How we laughed – and then Great-Uncle flung her up, and gobbled her up instead of catching her. Like that!" Rasce's hand mimes a snapping jaw closing.

"Gods below!" Baston's stomach turns. He didn't think he was still capable of feeling revulsion, after all the things he's done.

"Oh, she deserved it," laughs Rasce, finishing his drink. "Tero had failed Great-Uncle, and so he had to atone. We all belong to the dragon, my friend, and he shall reward or punish as he sees fit. But you have nothing to worry about – you've done well, Baston."

He pushes the snuffbox across the table. "I need a strong right hand. Take the ash, and I can send Vyr back home. You can have his place."

Baston shakes his head. "I've already given you my word. That'll have to do you."

Rasce frowns, and the room seems to darken for a moment, the light in the stone walls guttering out. "For now."

"Show me."

Rasce hardly needs to say the words, now. Every day, he becomes more adept at calling on Spar's miracles. The visions grow more tactile, too, Rasce sharing more of Spar's strange perceptions of the city. Rasce can feel his mind moving through the streets, feel the people of the New City as soft, hot, fragile things amid the stone. His own body, lying on the couch in the upstairs room on Lanthorn Street — he sees it from the outside, sees it from every angle, an eye in every wall of the house, and he beholds the whole house, too, the whole street, his mind's eye shattering and re-forming to encompass the new way of seeing. He sends his thoughts dancing over the streets, leaping invisibly from spire to spire, then leaping into the sky like a dragon to spy on the other Ghierdana families. He glimpses Major Estavo bent over a desk full of maps. Glimpses the Street of Saints up near Ghostmarket — and the slumbering gods in those temples sense him, too, a profane presence searching their altars for hidden gold.

He sees the dragons Thyrus and Carancio in private conference, their wings a black leathery tent, blocking out all eavesdroppers — but he's there, too, listening from the stone. He hears the dragons grumble about the war. Ishmere's collapse has thrown the southern portion of the continent into chaos. Lyrix vies with Ulbishe and Khenth, and with wild gods from the interior beyond the forest. Without the foothold in Guerdon bought by the Armistice, Lyrix's forces could never hope to compete against mainland deities. Lyrix needs the New City as a supply depot, a secure port and a nest for dragons, who are much more vulnerable on the ground than in the air. Thanks to the Armistice in Guerdon, there's a chance for Lyrix to greatly expand its influence inland. There's war in the south, with Lyrixian forces ranging upriver as far as Asegata. Rasce fought in those battles with Great-Uncle, but he never paid much heed as to *why*. Now, he finds himself listening intently.

No. *Rasce* is not listening intently. It's Spar. The distinction between the two blurs; Rasce has to examine his own thoughts and impulses closely to see which are solely his, and which spring from the stone of the city around him. Sometimes, the visions are things Spar wants him to see, showing him people in need, people he can help. The Brotherhood took care of their streets, and all these streets are Spar's.

"Enough!" Rasce cries. "We have work to do, friend. Baston has done his part, now you must do yours. Show me the secrets within Mandel's fortress."

I'm not some demon conjured to grant wishes. I want something in exchange.

"What do you desire? More coin for beggars?"

I want to talk to Rat. I'll need you to speak for me. He can't hear my thoughts like you and Cari can.

"The Lord Rat of Guerdon. He was your friend, yes. Karla told me. He was a common ghoul, and you a common thief. Now you are both very much changed." Rasce finds he can't lie on the couch any more; too much nervous energy to stay still. He paces the room, feels the sensation of his footsteps on the stone floor through Spar. "Will the Rat come if you call him?"

He's still my friend.

"And he is chieftain of the ghouls, in league with the city watch. I must tread carefully, friend. Show me Mandel's secrets, and I shall do as you ask. Now, no more hesitation," he tells Spar. "Reach out."

I'll try. Spar's soul is gargantuan, swollen beyond mortal recognition by the miracle of his rebirth. His mind encompasses and inhabits the New City. Now, Rasce demands that his conscious mind – perhaps the greatest portion of what remains of Spar's consciousness – balance itself on five little pebbles, five shards cut from the living stone. It's a psychic high-wire act, crossing an abyss where you can only cling on to a narrow ledge by the fingernails of one hand.

Spar tries. The first attempt is a dismal failure; his soul pratfalls, sending him tumbling down alleyways of memory, his consciousness shattering like a fallen vase. He remembers toddling into Idge's paper-strewn study at four years old, interrupting his father's work. Idge gently but firmly putting him out, closing the door, choosing the work over the child. Not knowing they'd only have a few more years.

He remembers lumbering across that side street near the House of Law, knowing there were Tallowmen around the corner, trusting in Rat and Cari to unlock the door and let him in before the candles got him.

Rasce draws him back together, sends him out again.

The second attempt is better. Birds take flight, frantically racing north along Mercy Street, and for a moment the flocks resemble a humanoid figure, a giant rising from the rooftops. The suspension bridge at the Viaduct sways and creaks, even though the day is windless. On Holyhill and the University District alike, the keen eyes of saints and the subtle instruments of alchemists alike discern an invisible wave crashing across the city. The ghouls smell it, too, in the dark pits beneath Gravehill, where the Rat of Guerdon sits on a hexagonal pedestal and dreams of elder days. They yelp and hiss, all but one unsure of the meaning of this omen.

But he falls again. The wave of his mind breaks far short of the distant Fog Yards, squandering the strength of his will amid the alleyways and tenements of the Five Knives.

It's too far.

"Gather your strength! Try again!"

Every time I try, I diminish, says Spar, his thought edged with exhaustion, and, beneath it, despair. An inverted horror – once, he feared his body turning to stone, his mind remaining healthy and whole as it became trapped in a living tomb. Now, his worry is that he shall erode his soul to nothingness, expend all that he is on failed miracles, and be reduced to nothing but a hollow structure, a corpse grotesquely fossilised and bloated. A horrible image flickers through his mind – Carillon returning to Guerdon too late, after he's gone. He envisages her walking through the streets of the New City, and finding them empty. He would let that thought go if he could, but it haunts him, clinging to his mind. In his mind's eye, he watches Cari wander lost through dark passageways, lonely and despairing.

"You say you are weak," whispers Rasce to the wall. "How can we make you strong again?"

My – no, this *strength,* Spar replies, *was stolen. It's the accumulated power of the Black Iron Gods, accrued through their reign of terror. Three hundred years ago, they ruled this city. They forced everyone to worship them, and conducted mass sacrifices through their Ravellers.* Cari's perverse inheritance, and she gave it all to him.

"Do you want me to praise you?" sneers Rasce. "To sing hymns glorifying your name?"

I'm not a god, says Spar wearily. *I don't want worship.*

"I speak of need. If it would strengthen you—"

I don't think it would. Spar gives the psychic equivalent of a shudder, which manifests in the New City as a moment of quiet. For an instant, every conversation comes to a natural pause, the wind off the harbour drops, silencing the flapping of the flags and banners. Even the seabirds cease their cries. *During the invasion, the people of the city prayed to me – to Cari – for help. I protected them, but I'd have done that even without their prayers. I could hear them, but they were just words.*

And then footsteps. *Karla's coming. Something's wrong.*

Rasce runs downstairs and is waiting at the door before Karla even reaches Lanthorn Street.

"It's Vyr," gasps Karla. "He's been attacked. The Green Inn."

"Show me," he demands of Spar.

Rasce's vision blurs, doubles, and it's as though he's standing atop one of the tall towers of the New City, looking down at the inn from a distance. It's near Venture Square, off Mercy Street – not that far, as the dragon flies, from the border. He can't see inside the inn, but he can peer in the windows from every angle. There, on the floor of an upper room, he can make out what must be Vyr, lying on the floor. The room's in disarray, papers scattered across the floor – and then a dark shape moves across the window.

Someone's still inside.

"Let's go," says Rasce.

Baston appears at his shoulder like a loyal shadow. "I'll go. This stinks of a trap. Like that candlejack."

"This is an attack on the Ghierdana! On the blood of the dragon! I must go." Rasce hurries out of the door.

Baston protests. "The place could be crawling with city watch! Or—"

"It's not. I can see it." Rasce strides down Lanthorn Street, steel boots sounding out a call to arms. Eshdana gather in his wake. "Baston, go and tell the other dragons. An attack on one is an attack on all."

Baston hesitates. He grabs Karla by the shoulders, whirls her around so he can look in her eyes. For a moment, he seems to be about to speak, but then he just snarls and pushes her away. Karla reassures him. "I'll stay with Rasce. Go, go."

Baston vanishes down a side street. Absently, Spar watches him sprint up the winding stairs and alleyways of the New City, heading for the dracodrome on the southern face of the city.

Karla takes her brother's place at his side. "Who raised the alarm?" he asks.

"It's not the first time Vyr's gone to that inn. I had a friend of mine watching, just in case anything happened. She came running to me, said she heard fighting inside Vyr's room."

Something is very wrong. Spar feels it in the streets, feels it in the invisible divine currents that eddy around Holyhill, around the IOZ. Gods are abroad tonight.

CHAPTER TWENTY-TWO

Artolo seethes at the sight of Carillon Thay. Clenches his ghost-fingers, imagining they're closing around her throat. The bitch sits there shivering, clad only in a grey shift, but she's still dangerous. Don't they see how dangerous she is? Yesterday, she nearly wrecked the refinery. What if she'd sabotaged the athanor and destroyed their ability to process yliaster? That's what Thay does – she ruins things. A bomb on legs.

Vorz's laboratory is much too cramped for Great-Uncle to enter. The roof creaks under the dragon's weight as he cranes his head down to peer in through the little windows. Carillon on a metal chair in the middle of the room. The witch standing sentinel at the door. And Vorz gliding around like he's Chosen of the Dragon, even though his nose is a mess of bandages.

"Now, let us begin. A physical examination first."

"I want Adro healed before we continue," demands Thay, folding her arms and staring up at the dragon. Insolent, arrogant. How dare she make demands of Great-Uncle!

The dragon snorts, clouding the glass window with its breath. "If it spares us more embarrassment, very well." Great-Uncle smiles. "You have the word of the dragon that he shall be spared. Artolo, see to it."

Vorz looks over at the witch, who follows her cue and seizes Cari in a paralysis spell. She freezes, every muscle locked in place by arcane bonds. It would be so easy to cross the room and kill her. Would it be more or less satisfying if she couldn't struggle or scream?

The Dentist lives up to his name. His first action is to open Cari's mouth and examine her teeth. With gloved hands, he probes beneath her fingernails. Examines the scars on her face, an old scar on her shoulder. Studies the skin between her breasts with his eyeglass.

Great-Uncle stirs. "Well? Can we make use of her, or not?"

"Patience," replies Vorz.

"When our business is concluded, you can play all you want."

"This," says the Dentist, "is not play." He bends over to shine a light into Cari's eyes. Held open by the witch's spell, she can't even blink, and they're reddened around the edges. Tears run down her cheeks, tinged purple by the arcane light coruscating around the witch as she holds the spell.

One of Vorz's instruments chimes. The metal box he arrived with.

"Release her," he orders. Both Cari and the witch sag. Cari eyes a tray of scalpels. *Go for it*, Artolo urges her. He'd have to kill her then. Smash her. Cut off her fingers, one by one.

Vorz glances over in irritation. "Please, breathe more quietly."

A hurricane-gust of amusement from the roof. "Get on with it, Vorz."

The Dentist opens the metal box. Inside, Artolo catches a glimpse of a keyboard attached to a glowing tube wrapped in silver wire. The machine chimes again, and the Dentist spreads his long-fingered hands over the keys like a musician. He presses a stud, and the machine hums, a discordant noise like a key being dragged over piano wire.

"Is it Ulbishe?" asks Great-Uncle. Is the machine communicating with someone in Ulbishe, all the way across the ocean? In Guerdon, they have aethergraphs, but those machines are connected by silver cables. This is something new. Artolo's coming to despise new things. Give him a ship, give him a flight on dragon-back and a fat merchant to rob. One with sails, too, sails that burn and masts that break. Not a stinking alchemy-driven iron hulk of a ship. Give him his youth back, give him his hands back.

Make him Chosen again.

She took all that away. She's less than ten feet away. Kill her. Kill her. Kill her.

"No," says Vorz. "Guerdon."

"Ah. What does my nephew report?" asks the dragon.

Does he mean that arrogant brat Rasce, or Artolo's son Vyr? Artolo hasn't spoken to Vyr since he was exiled to Ilbarin. His only communication with the boy is through Lorenza. Artolo can hardly blame his son – pleasing Great-Uncle is more important than any other relationship. Artolo displeased Great-Uncle, so it's right and proper that Vyr abandon him. But the betrayal still rankles. Artolo sacrificed his fingers to ensure that Vyr retained standing in Great-Uncle's eyes – the boy should be grateful!

"A moment, please." Vorz taps out a message on the keyboard. He flicks a switch, and the machine changes to a slightly different, but equally unpleasant noise. Vorz types again, fingers flying over the keys. Steam rises from the metal coil, and the liquid in the tube bubbles. His work done, he switches the machine off and closes the box.

He takes down the gilded skull from its shelf. Carillon threw down everything from that cabinet in her escape attempt yesterday, smashed all the jars, but this morning there's not an item out of place, not even a stray shard of broken glass glinting on the floor.

Vorz places the skull in Carillon's hands, then steps back to a safe distance. Aetheric energy crackles for an instant, leaving after-images when Artolo blinks, making his ghost-fingers tingle. Cari stares into the skull's eye sockets, and shudders.

And that's it.

There are no demons conjured, no magical blast. No mad god appears in the lab, the skull doesn't come to life and start disgorging prophecy. Everyone else in the room – Vorz, the witch, the dragon, even Cari – seems to perceive that something meaningful has happened, but it's all opaque to Artolo. It adds to his frustrations – he has no desire to know anything more about their mystical nonsense, and it's always been his philosophy that sorcery is all either portentous mummery or self-destructive madness, but he's at a disadvantage here, in front of Great-Uncle.

"Are you done with her?" Artolo demands.

The Dentist ignores him. "There's minimal spiritual contamination", whatever the hell that means. "She remains primarily congruent with the Guerdon entity. And we are fortunate in the circumstance of her conception, too. If she were not the offspring of a formless one, the tincture would require much more denaturalisation. As it is, I can proceed to the next stage immediately."

From his black bag, he produces a metal syringe. Again and again, he takes blood from Cari. Wrists, ankles, chest, even from between her eyes. Each sample squirted into a neatly labelled glass jar, then tucked away inside his black bag. Cari shudders each time the needle pierces her skin, but she doesn't struggle. She just bites her lip and endures. Artolo watches her throat move, imagines her swallowing all her clever retorts and insults. Imagines his ghost-fingers strangling her instead.

"What do you have for me, Vorz?" demands the dragon.

"Not yet," replies Vorz, distracted. Cari chokes and shudders as he pulls two teeth from her mouth and collects the bloodied spittle from her lips in a vial.

Vorz holds the last vial up to the light. He taps it with a gloved finger, and for an instant Artolo seems to see darker shapes congealing and then unravelling within. "A catalyst, I think. An accelerant." His hands shake.

"Come up. You, too, Artolo," orders the dragon. Vorz closes his black bag and carries it with him as he crosses the gantry and climbs the rickety metal stairs to the roof.

"Watch her," snarls Artolo. The witch nods and turns to face Thay, catching her in the act of reaching for the tray of scalpels.

"What?" says Cari, snatching back her hand. Artolo growls and follows Vorz up to the roof.

Great-Uncle waits there, sitting on his haunches. The whole roof of the refinery flexes when he shifts his weight. Below, the athanor's at full heat, and thick clouds of white mist whip across the rooftop, stinging Artolo's eyes.

"Vorz." The dragon extends one wing, folds it to enclose the Dentist, then tucks his head beneath. A private conference. Artolo waits, enduring yet another snub. Great-Uncle may consult with his counsellor, of course, but the Dentist is only Eshdana. Artolo is Ghierdana. Has he not done enough to earn redemption? How much more must he sacrifice before Great-Uncle favours him again?

He roams the tin roof, the metal creaking under his boots. What was Vorz talking about, with his black box and his secret messages? Again, Artolo is left on the outside, exiled to this cursed Rock, banished from the councils of the family. His heart pounds; his blood thunders furiously through his veins, thick and hot with anger. He can feel it curdling in his brain, the fringes of his vision reddening.

He needs to kill again.

He can *smell* Thay downstairs. A few steps, and he'd be on top of her. Those blades are just *there*, in his mind's eye. His own wounds ache with remembered pain. Gods, does he not deserve revenge?

"Artolo!" roars the dragon.

Slowly, he turns away from the stairs. Turns to face Great-Uncle. There's an expression on the dragon's face he has not seen before – a combination of bemusement and anger.

"I am not accustomed," says Great-Uncle slowly, "to repeating myself."

Artolo hastily kneels. "Forgive me." Had he been so lost in his own thoughts that he failed to hear the dragon's command? Thay's fault, of course. It's all Thay's fault.

"There was some benefit in your obsession. We can use the Thay girl to hasten our plans in Guerdon."

Artolo flinches. "Are you taking her away?"

The dragon chuckles. "Quite the opposite. Hold her here. She must not return to Guerdon."

"Great-Uncle, there is no surer way to keep a prisoner than in a grave."

The dragon laughs. "You have the right of it, nephew. Take your revenge, and know this – you failed me in Guerdon, but you have atoned here. You shall not be my Chosen again – but your offspring shall be favoured."

A fierce joy blazes through his soul, hotter than dragon-fire. "I shall remind Thay that no one crosses the Ghierdana," vows Artolo. He rises, bows and runs back towards the stairs. His ghost-fingers flex. He won't use the knife. The dragon-tooth knife is the dragon's symbol. No, no, he'll strangle her. He'll break her. He'll—

The explosion from below nearly knocks him off the roof.

Artolo stumbles down the stairs, ears ringing. Vorz's lab is afire, flames leaping purple and green and blue from the shelves of burning alchemical materials. There's a gaping hole in one wall where the shoreside window used to be – and no signs of Carillon Thay.

The witch lies slumped in a corner, her armour scorched by the explosion. Artolo darts over to her, but she holds up a hand. She doesn't speak – jerkily, she points to her helmet, indicating that some mechanism has been damaged.

"Where is she?" roars Artolo.

The witch rises, unsteady on her feet, and points down at the shore below, a stone's throw from the refinery. There's a covered motorboat down there, one of the smaller skiffs used to patrol the ruins – and as Artolo watches, it takes off. Moving jerkily, as if the pilot is unfamiliar with the controls.

"Contain the fires!" Vorz shouts from the top of the stairs, unwilling to leave the comparative safety of the roof and enter the growing blaze that used to be his laboratory.

To hell with that. Thay will not escape him again! Artolo climbs out of the ruined window, clambers and slides down the outer wall of the refinery, clinging to pipes and vents until he lands heavily on the muddy ground at the foot of the wall. The boat's already moving, its engine suddenly roaring as it rushes away. He charges down towards the water. She's *taunting* him, waiting until he's almost in reach and then dancing away. The boat's pilot finds the throttle and opens up, the little motorboat shooting like a reckless rocket over the waves, racing south over the drowned streets of Ilbarin City.

Massive wings cover the sky as Great-Uncle swoops down from the refinery roof to land in the surf. He lowers his neck for Artolo to climb on board, and Artolo does so joyously, his face breaking into a wild, incredulous grin. He's Chosen again, exalted again, flying again! Oh, the thunder of the wings! The rush of air! The thrilling leap as the dragon takes to the air, the lurching glory of the downsweep, the steel-cord strength of Great-Uncle's muscles between his thighs. Artolo's ghost-fingers cannot grab the ridged scales of the dragon's neck – the magic of the witch's spells pales in comparison to the divine vitality of the dragon – but he doesn't need to. His hooked boots find the catch-scales instantly, leaving his hands free to wield a gun or spyglass.

Each stroke of Great-Uncle's wings lifts his heart. One wing beat, and he forgets his failure at Guerdon. He couldn't find the words to win forgiveness from the dragon, but what are words compared to the headlong rush of flight, the sensation of it, the defiance – dragon and rider, defying sky above and earth below, hunting, devouring, burning as they choose.

Another, and he forgets his maimed hands, his whole mind afire with the joy of flying.

The dragon twists in the air above the boat, and Artolo leaps down, landing cat-like on the aft deck. He should have a sword in his hand, should have the Ring of Samara on his finger, but it's still the most alive he's felt in years. Oh, to be raiding Haithi trader vessels again!

He stomps forward, eager to find Thay. It's just her and him on this little boat. His revenge is finally at hand! Artolo tears back the awning, an overture to the violence he will do to Carillon Thay when he finds her.

But she's not here.

The boat's empty.

The controls move of their own accord. They're limned by faint traceries of purple light, the lingering after-energies of a spell.

Hollowly, feeling like he's operating his own body at a distance, Artolo takes the helm. He throttles back on the spluttering engine, turns the boat around in a wide arc. The dragon circles overhead once, then flies off towards the shore. Artolo follows.

The fire in the refinery is still burning, but is still contained to the upper room. Workers hastily drag the troughs of unrefined yliaster out, so the smoke doesn't contaminate the brine. Other workers drive cartloads of casks down the road to Ushket, in case the fire spreads. Black smoke mingles with white vapour from the athanor. He imagines Vorz gliding around on the refinery floor, the Dentist's well-ordered realm of calibrated gauges and titrations thrown into disarray. A little taste of the chaos and ruin that Thay brings.

Refinery crew call for his aid. Artolo ignores the commotion.

He abandons the boat close to the shore and steps into the surf. His steel boots sink deep into the mud as he climbs up the last slope. Waiting for him in the shadow of the refinery is the witch. Unmoving, as if frozen in fear.

"You did this," Artolo growls – and then he sees it. The stillness of the armour. The syringes do not hiss, the tubes don't gurgle or throb.

He shoves the armour in the chest, and it falls over, collapsing and breaking apart as it lands in the mud. A dissipating haze of purple light as the animating-spell breaks. Sections of the suit go rolling down the slope to be swallowed by the sea.

Other parts land at his feet, metal tapping against metal like a distant bell.

Artolo falls to his knees, pawing through the empty armour with his fading ghost-fingers. Trying to read his future in entrails of rubber, casting syringes like runes upon the sand.

CHAPTER TWENTY-THREE

T he city takes on Rasce's fury as he marches downhill. His passage becomes a hurricane, pebbles and dust flying up around
him, as though an invisible dragon flies overhead. Crowds part to
let his host pass, and church bells jangle in alarm. A mob forms
around him – ash-marked Eshdana, Ghierdana kinfolk, Brotherhood
thieves, and even ordinary folk of the New City, who take up sword
and club and follow him without knowing why.

When he comes to the border, the Guerdon city watch soldiers
stationed there try to bar his path, but there's an unseen contortion
of the ground, and they topple as he strides past. Guerdon shivers,
struck by an earthquake. Broken glass from a hundred shattered
windows crunches under Rasce's steel boots. He marches down
Seamarket Way, Mercy Street, the thoroughfare emptying as the
crowds flee from his mob of thieves.

"Secure the inn," he orders. In his mind's eye, he sees the building,
sees every way out. Watches his mob of thieves and pirates swarm
in, smashing through the door of viridian glass that gives the place
its name, forcing their way through the side doors, the back. Even
scaling the walls to climb in the upper windows.

Rasce enters through the wreckage of the front door. The inn's
customers – rich merchants, speculators, lawyers, alchemists – are
all frozen in their seats, staring in confusion as the place is suddenly

overrun with thieves. Rasce ignores them, ignores the whistles of the city watch sounding in the streets. He climbs the stairs, enters Vyr's room.

He shuts the door behind him, plunging the room into a stilled silence, as if the chaos of the world outside is suddenly paused. He watches himself through the window. It seems safer, somehow, to think of himself as something remote. To imagine his body as a tool.

Rasce watches himself cross to Vyr's side. His cousin is quite, quite dead. Vyr's face is purple, his tongue bitten and bloodied. His fingers are scraped raw, too. A strange apparatus is clamped around his neck, and it's clear that this machine strangled him. Carefully, Rasce prises the machine away with his knife, and it's only when it falls away that he recognises what is it. The prosthetic hands that Vyr commissioned for his father Artolo, like a jewelled crab cunningly wrought of brass and steel. Patches of skin from Vyr's neck caught in the gears.

I'm sorry. Spar's presence in Rasce's mind is awkward, uncertain. Shuffling around the edges of perception, trying not to intrude. Still, it's impossible for some of Spar's thoughts to avoid leaking into Rasce; when he looks down at Vyr, he sees, from certain angles, the face of Spar's father Idge. The faces of strangled men have a grisly commonality. They hanged Idge slowly, as a warning to the Brotherhood, and his face had the same cast to it. The same desperate air-hunger, the panic reducing the features to something animalistic and primitive and scared.

"I didn't even like the boy," says Rasce quietly. Gently, he lifts Vyr's body from the floor, lays it on the bed. Draws a sheet over the contorted face. "But he was family. He belonged to Great-Uncle. This insult cannot go unavenged."

What was Vyr doing in this room when he was attacked? Not sleeping. No sign of a woman. Rasce finds a heavy case of dark wood, lined in velvet, that must have contained the mechanical hand. Inside, a letter from the shop on Glimmerside, a certificate of authenticity, heavy with the wax seals of various craftsmen who worked on the prosthetic. The eye-and-flask design of the alchemists repeated on each seal.

Including the last – a stern and stately capital M, a fortress flanked by two towers. The "&co" almost an afterthought. Aetheric enchantment services. Rasce imagines his cousin opening the box, and the hands coming to life, scuttling towards him, strangling him. An alchemist's assassin. He imagines it as clearly as any of Spar's visions, sees the hands throttling the life from Vyr.

This insult cannot go unavenged.

Trouble, warns Spar, and, moments later, Karla hammers on the door. "Boss! City watch! Lots of them!"

Rasce ignores them both. He lets himself drift from his body again, shares Spar's perspective. Sees the little specks moving in the streets, a stain of blue-cloaked city watch surrounding the inn. A little spurt of red, a puff of smoke as some thief panics and lets off a pistol, but the line of the watch holds. Rasce can see the house on Lanthorn Street in the New City; he can see the Inn of the Green Door only a short distance away. He's aware of the underground line below, like he's aware of the bones beneath his skin. Why did Vyr come here to open the box, instead of continuing on a short distance into the safety of the New City? Such a treasure as these hands would doubtless be sent by Ghierdana messenger, maybe even by dragon, to the distant land of Ilbarin where Uncle Artolo serves.

There must be something else here. Rasce prowls around the room, ignoring the shouts from outside. The nightstand on the far side of the bed has toppled to lie against the wardrobe – and the wardrobe has been ransacked by the attacker, all except one compartment. Rasce tries the drawer, but it does not budge. He pulls on it with all his might, and it still doesn't move, even though the whole heavy wardrobe rocks slightly. He kneels down and examines the drawer.

"Rasce! Are you all right? Let me in!" Karla shouts from outside, a note of mounting panic in her voice.

A carriage is coming, intones Spar, *many guards, and parliament livery on the doors.*

"Shut up, both of you," snaps Rasce. The drawer's not locked. It's got to be magic. A spell-ward is one of the easier sorcerous enchantments, but Vyr's no sorcerer – someone else sealed the drawer. Another trap? Or did Vyr want to keep something safe? Wards can only be opened with the right token. Blood's the most common key, but it might be something else – and, for all he knows, Vyr's murderer has already stolen the token. Rasce draws his dragon-tooth blade, presses the tip into the wood like he's picking a lock. The magic in the blade reacts against the magic of the ward, giving the illusion of physicality, and he gingerly cuts the threads of the spell until they give way.

Inside – papers, handwritten notes in Lyrixian. Vyr's handwriting. By the Scourge! Notes about the yliaster trade, about all their crimes outside the occupation zone. Names, dates – the burning of Dredger's yard, the brawl in the Haithi zone, Craddock's, all the yliaster merchants. Even the explosion in the Wash, at Baston's. What is this – Vyr's archive of blackmail material? Did he think to present all this to Great-Uncle when the dragon returned, to replace Rasce as Chosen? Or, far worse, has Vyr *betrayed* the Ghierdana?

Mixed in with these accounts, other notes. Words Rasce doesn't understand, like *congruency*. Names he knows – *Idgeson. Carillon Thay. Eladora Duttin.* A description of the visit to Mandel & Company.

"What's taking so long? Let me in!" cries Karla, slamming her fists against the door.

These notes cannot be allowed to fall into the hands of the city watch, or any of the Ghierdana's enemies. There's a fireplace in one corner of the room, the grate full of cold ash. Rasce stuffs handfuls of the papers in there, sets them alight, stirs them as they burn so nothing legible remains.

At the back of the drawer is a metal box, decorated with curlicues in some silvery metal. He opens the clasp – inside is another machine of some sort, with a set of lettered keys and a tube of some alchemical goop. Rasce has a pirate's eye for design – he grew up in Great-Uncle's palace back on the isles of the Ghierdana, and that was decorated with treasures stolen from all over the world. He can tell that this box was not made in Guerdon. The smiths and alchemists of Guerdon drew on the aesthetics of the Keeper's church for inspiration – their works are stern and imposing, with little unnecessary adornment. Images of cages, lanterns, the solemn faces of saints and martyrs. The machine in the box, by contrast, has fanciful touches. The connectors where orichalcum wires enter are made to resemble blossoming flowers, and silver fish dance along the circuits.

Rasce catches a glimpse of his own face in an inset mirror, and for an instant he can't remember if he's the living man in the mirror or the dead man watching from the New City. He slams the box shut. It's some sort of communications machine, he guesses. The alchemical equivalent, maybe, of his clever pebbles.

It, too, must be destroyed.

"Boss!" calls Karla. "We have to go!"

The little fire in the grate isn't hot enough to damage the machine. He takes his own dragon-tooth blade and cuts the box, slashing it over and over. The thin metal tears. Components break like small bones, and the glass tube shatters and spills its vital fluid over the floor in a visceral rush. He drops the corpse of the machine to the ground, wipes his hands on the bedsheet. Kicks the burning papers in the grate, to ensure everything's erased.

"Vyr," he whispers to the corpse. "Your blood is my blood, and you shall be avenged. I don't know what you were doing in this place, but I know who murdered you."

He unlocks the door, and Karla practically tumbles in. "Gods below!" she curses as she sees the body on the bed. "We'll find whoever did this, Rasce, I swear. But I think they got away – we had all the exits secure. Maybe they got away before we arrived."

"Or they had some arcane means of escape," says Rasce. "Some trick of the alchemists." Who knows what devilry Mandel has brewed in that fortress? Oh, for him there will be no chance of atonement, no offer of ash in exchange for fealty. He will burn. No one crosses the dragon.

"Either way, we'll track them down, I promise."

No one left the inn by any path I can see, adds Spar. *Maybe the attackers are in the taproom below – but you can't hold them. The inn's surrounded by city watch. Either you fight your way out, or you talk your way out. Alic Nemon is here.*

Karla picks up the wax-seal letter from the desk, scans it. Her face pales. "Godshit. See this?"

"I did." Rasce stands, brushes little shards of metal off his trousers. "Gather up my cousin's remains," he orders, "no ghoul or god shall have his soul." He takes the letter from the alchemist from her and tucks it into his pocket, careful to avoid cracking any of the wax seals.

Through Spar's eyes, he watches Karla lead his body down the stairs.

Outside, a stalemate.

The inn's become a besieged fort. Rasce's men are at the windows, hiding in alleyways, crouched behind crates and barrels, or holding fat merchants as human shields. Lined up along Mercy Street, the city watch. Mostly street guards, armed with no more than truncheons or swords, but a detachment of armoured watch, too, with firearms. And this isn't the New City, or even the Wash – these streets are unfriendly. Pale faces look down from the surrounding trading houses and offices, waiting for the iron fist of the city watch to crush the invading thieves, to drive them back where they belong. No doubt there are packs of ghouls in the sewers below, waiting to intercept anyone who tries to escape that way.

Beyond the watch's line is the carriage that Spar spoke of. A quartet of raptequines, sweat steaming from their flanks. Beyond them, a crowd of onlookers, held back by more city watch. In the distance, a growing traffic jam of carts and carriages. Venture Square's clogged with crowds.

And beyond them, all the way down Mercy Street, past the ghost of the Duchess Viaduct, past Parliament and Gravehill, past Five Knives and Scuttle, is Mandel. Rasce's anger wants to take flight, to spread its wings and soar over the city. To burn Mandel's fortress from the sky.

The Fog Yards are a heartbeat away as the dragon flies, but he's rooted to the ground. His path barred by the city watch, by the ghouls, by all of Guerdon's impediments.

Alic Nemon, the minister for security, stands by the carriage, speaking with a pair of city watch captains. Nemon's a forgettable bureaucrat — but when Rasce draws on Spar's sight, and views the scene from above, Nemon seems weightier, more significant. All the people in the crowds are ephemeral to Spar, wispy shades of water and flesh moving through the stone and brick of the city, but Nemon has a solidity to him the others lack. The mantle of his office, maybe, the embodiment of Guerdon's tattered establishment, even though Nemon's no more a native to this city than Rasce.

Eladora Duttin watches from Nemon's carriage. Rasce has met Duttin before, under strange circumstances. Six months ago, during the invasion, she appeared out of thin air in Great-Uncle's palace. Somehow, through some secret sorcery, she teleported across the ocean from Guerdon to Lyrix. Rasce recalls the tolling of unseen bells that heralded her arrival, and when she appeared she was covered in a thin film of reddish dust, like rust or dried blood. Still, despite the trauma of her unnatural mode of travel, she had the presence of mind to demand to speak to Great-Uncle. She carried with her a message from the rulers of Guerdon, and she pleaded her case before the dragon while barely able to stand. As much as anything else, the sheer bravado of her act impressed Great-Uncle and sealed the bargain that led to the Armistice.

Like Nemon, Duttin is more dangerous than she appears.

She's Cari's cousin, adds Spar. *She's a friend.*

"My cousin," murmurs Rasce, "is dead." To the abyss with the Armistice and all the laws of this city – the blood of the dragon has been shed. No one crosses the dragon and lives.

Spar's vision shows Rasce one more thing – there's a gap in the line of the city watch. Nemon's deliberately refrained from stationing any guards along the street back to the New City, obviously leaving a line of retreat open to the thieves.

Spar also shows him snipers on the rooftops, the long guns used in the war against saints and monsters.

You're too far away from me to protect you if they shoot.

"They don't have the stomach for it. They don't want a fight."

They might not. A fight might happen anyway. A flicker-vision – the clouds twisting and boiling in the sky over the Ishmeric Occupation Zone, as the gods there sense destinies colliding. There are spies in the crowd, Rasce guesses, who'll report events back to their masters in the Haithi Bureau, too. The rules of the Armistice are clear – whoever breaks the truce is the enemy of the other three signatories. Lyrix and the Ghierdana would be set against the unlikely temporary alliance of Haith, Ishmere and Guerdon.

Be careful, urges Spar. His voice is fainter, weaker than before. Failing, just when Rasce needs him.

Again, Rasce sends his mind aloft, climbing Spar's soul like a ladder to the sky. Again, he looks down at Mercy Street from the heights of the New City. He can see the heaving crowds behind the watch lines, see Baston shoving his way towards the inn (an unfortunate watchman tries to stop him at the border; there's a moment of violence, and then the watchman's unconscious in an alley and Baston hasn't broken stride). He sees a knot of dignitaries, debating and blustering like they mean something. There's the

Lyrixian ambassador and Major Estavo, both red-faced and angry, arguing with some Guerdon official, Eladora Duttin lurking in the background. Gods and politicians alike, all trying to seize the thrashing serpent of events. Everything could change, here on Mercy Street.

But it's all in the decisions of two people. In this moment, only two men command the city's destiny.

Rasce walks forward, leaving the cover of the inn. From the New City, he can see snipers on rooftops aiming at him.

Alic Nemon pushes forward through the ranks, to meet him in the middle of Mercy Street.

"Prince Rasce."

"Minister Nemon."

"You're well beyond the truce line here, my lord. Can we resolve this without bloodshed?"

"Blood has been shed. My cousin, Vyr, was murdered in that tavern."

Nemon bows his head. "You have my condolences, for what they're worth. But the Inn of the Green Door's in free city territory, not the LOZ. March your Eshdana back across the border into the New City and I'll see that the case is investigated promptly and thoroughly by the city watch."

"I'll save you the bother. I know who was responsible. The alchemist Mandel."

"Do you have proof?"

Rasce flings the sealed letter at Nemon's feet. Wearily, the minister bends down in the dust of the street to pick it up. "This is a receipt for a set of prosthetic hands."

"Mandel enchanted them to murder my cousin. It is proof enough for me."

"And why would Mandel do such a thing?"

"That is between Mandel and the Ghierdana, but know this – he will pay."

"The Ghierdana," says Nemon, "have no business beyond the truce line. Take your Eshdana back to the New City, now."

"You dare—"

Do as he says, urges Spar. *This isn't your moment. Fall back, regroup, come up with a plan first. Don't rush off blindly.*

Some of Rasce's anger bleeds off into Spar; it's like pressing his forehead against a cool wall, soothing and calming.

"We shall bear my cousin's body home. But this is not over. Do not come between the dragon and his foe."

"Should I ever meet an actual dragon, I'll remember that," needles Nemon.

Rasce raises his voice, calls out to his followers. "We are leaving! We gather again at Lanthorn Street."

The way they leave the inn speaks much about each man. Many of the Eshdana in Rasce's entourage are veterans of the Godswar, veterans of fighting in other cities. They move in ones and twos, scurrying from cover to cover. They move as though the buildings around them were burning and about to collapse, as if the massed lines of the city watch were about to open fire. The few full-blooded Ghierdana, distant cousins from minor branches of the family, march out proudly, an honour guard for the sheet-wrapped corpse they carry with them. The Ghierdana do not give their dead to any god or psychopomp; Vyr's body will be interred in the haunted crypts back on the isles.

The new recruits, the Brotherhood thieves, they slink out of the inn, hiding their faces from the eyes of the watch. They'd melt into the shadows if they could, vanish down the alleyways and side streets off Mercy that run down towards the Wash. Karla's there, close behind the corpse. Baston at the corner of Seamarket Way, as close as he can get without breaking the watch line, urging them onwards with his eyes. A motley host, marching back up towards the New City on the hill.

"Your kin can go. Your Eshdana can go," says Nemon. "But I mark some in that crowd who are Guerdonese. Criminals known to the watch. They're under arrest." At a nod from Nemon, the watch level guns at the Brotherhood thieves. Baston's suddenly seized by plainclothes watchmen in the crowd and slammed up against the wall. Karla breaks from the line and runs towards her brother; the watch closes on her, too.

The Lyrixian ambassador huffs up, followed by Major Estavo. "Don't—" he gasps for air, "don't argue. Otherwise – breach of Armistice. They'll—" Out of breath, he waves an arm towards the New City, gesturing in the direction of the Lyrixian Occupation Zone and their military toehold here and the Godswar and everything. "All fucked," he explains, undiplomatically.

Rasce's hot anger has been quenched, congealed and cast like metal into something hard and cold. He turns to Nemon.

"No. All of them are mine. All under my protection. They all get to leave."

"That's not going to happen," says Nemon.

Rasce closes his eyes for a moment, sees a shadow cross the New City.

"Yes, it is."

For months now there have been dragons in the skies over Guerdon. Ever since the Armistice, ever since Eladora Duttin crossed the ocean and invited the Ghierdana to occupy part of the city, there have been dragons in the skies. But all that time they've been a distant threat, easily forgotten by a city eager to return to its grubby ways of commerce and corruption. They've nested in the heights of the New City, where there is all manner of strangeness anyway, not part of the real city, the old city. They've soared beyond the clouds, vanishing into the smog above Guerdon on their way to war in the south or west, problems for some other unlucky city, just like the crates of alchemical weapons piled on the docks. For months now, the people of Guerdon have had the luxury of forgetting they share their city with living dragons.

Not today.

Thyrus lands atop the Inn of the Green Door, her massive claws sending roof tiles cascading to shatter on the street below. Screams of alarm and terror break from the crowd, triggering a panicked stampede. The watch take a step back – for all their weapons, for all their authority, they're only mortals, prey flinching in the presence of a predator. She spreads her wings, plunging the whole street into darkness. She extends her long sinuous neck; her massive head, her terrifying maw so close to Nemon and the others that the heat of her breath is like standing before a furnace.

Thyrus twitches her tail, smashing another part of the inn. "One of my brother's children," she hisses, "was murdered here. The Ghierdana must grieve. Do not try my patience today."

For a long, long moment, everyone stops. The city swirls around them – the crowds further up Mercy Street flee in terror, the gods in the Ishmeric zone and on Holyhill rumble in their temples. Smoke curls from the gaps in Thyrus' teeth. The Armistice balances on a knife edge.

It's Eladora Duttin who moves, who breaks from the crowd. She hurries up and whispers in Nemon's ear, and it's Duttin who curtsies to the dragon.

"They may all go."

I told you she's a friend, says Spar.

"If she stands between me and Mandel, then she is an enemy of the dragon."

CHAPTER TWENTY-FOUR

When the armoured witch begins to remove her helmet, Cari braces herself for a shock of recognition. The witch, whoever she is, knows her from back in Guerdon. Knows all about her, too – her mysterious Thay heritage, her connection to the Black Iron Gods, her involvement in the thieves' guild. Cari stares as the helmet comes away – a slight sucking noise as damaged flesh adheres to the inside of the faceplate.

No recognition; it's a shock of a different kind. The sorcerer's face is scorched, half melted. Every vein is like a lightning bolt crackling beneath the skin, burning the flesh to grey ash. Hairless, the curve of the skull visible. Runic tattoos crowning the scalp, tracing the vanished hairline, and somehow the tattoos protect those patches of skin, remaining grotesquely pink and healthy, islands in the ruin. Cari's met Haithi undead who look healthier.

"If you want to live, help me with this," demands the witch. Her voice is still damnably familiar.

More of the armour comes away, syringes tearing through dead skin like wet paper. Cari's heard that practising sorcery is ruinous, she's even seen the toll incantations took on Professor Ongent or Eladora, but this is much, much worse. It's why most sorcery is performed by godspawn and inhuman monsters like Crawling Ones . . .

And then it comes back to her. Guerdon, Thieves' Court – the night she and Spar thought they'd taken Heinreil down. Heinreil had allied with Crawling Ones – but he had his own sorceress there that night, too. Myri, her name was. Cari saw her only briefly, but she'd glimpsed her in Black Iron visions, too. Tall and proud, bare arms rippling with arcane tattoos. Beautiful, like a coral snake.

"I saw you. I know you."

A scowl crosses the parts of Myri's face that can still move. "No time for that now. Get in the barrel." Myri points at a yliaster cask outside the door of the lab. Cari hesitates for an instant, but what's she going to do, *not* get into the barrel? Hang around and wait for the psychotic Ghierdana and the creepy alchemist to come back for her?

She climbs in, squeezing into the metal cask. The mouth of the cask is narrower than her shoulders, but Cari's lithe enough to wriggle down. Inside, she folds up as best she can, a foetal position inside the jar. Like one of the alchemical creatures on the shelves of Vorz's lab, only a few feet away. Myri hastily closes the lid of the cask, plunging Cari into darkness.

Outside, the sounds of uproar. An explosion, breaking glass, shouting. There's a clank of metal as someone attaches a metal hook on to the outside of the cask, and she's lifted, painfully rolled as the cask is hoisted off the platform and lowered to the refinery floor below. Cari manages to keep herself from crying out in pain as the cask slams into the ground. It's lifted again, roughly, and thrown to the side so Cari's now lying horizontally, her spine crushed against the metal.

Movement. She's on a cart from the sounds, from the rattle of the wheels on the stony road. The sounds of the chaos at the refinery die away.

Now all she can hear is the creak of the cart's axle. The laboured breathing of the mules. Her own breathing inside this fucking coffin.

Her skin stings from where Vorz stole her blood. Her back aches from her contorted position inside the cask. How long should she wait? Is this the sort of escape attempt she might have devised herself — *badly thought through and desperate, right Spar?* — or is there a plan? Is Myri out there, or has she been handed off to some accomplice? Should she call out? She's literally in the dark about what to do next.

Hell, for all she knows there's no one out there — maybe the mule ran off while still hitched, and she's technically its prisoner. From Dol Martaine to Twelve Suns Bleeding to the fucking Ghierdana to Myri, and now a mule — her captors are getting worse. She giggles, and realises that there isn't much air in the oven-hot casket, so waiting for the right moment might not be an option.

Still, she waits. After all, every minute spent in the cask gets her further away from the camp.

Cari's had too much experience with gods to pray to them, but still she hopes that Adro's still alive. The dragon promised to send a healer, and while she knows that the promise of a dragon means nothing, it's all she can offer.

She rubs the needle wounds, wondering what Vorz was doing to her. Something to do with her sainthood — Professor Ongent did the same experiment with a skull, back when she had no idea what she was. Sometimes, Cari wishes she could find some alchemist or sorcerer she could really trust, get some answers.

The confinement and darkness of the cask are familiar to her on some deep, atavistic level, familiar to some part of her she prefers to flee from. Fuck. The damn thing is like a bell, isn't it? She's inside a bell-shaped steel vessel. Or maybe it's the resemblance to an alchemical jar. Jermas Thay *made* her, bred her from his son's seed and a Raveller — a shapeshifting horror from the underworld, a living sacrificial knife for the Black Iron Gods. Ravellers can steal human forms, human faces, but they're not human. Malign emanations, the hunger of the gods oozing into the material world.

Cari doesn't know if she was even *born*. Did the Raveller keep its shape long enough to give birth to her, dissolving back into its amorphous slimy form even as she came into the world? Or did Jermas grow her in a jar like this one? When she broke into the Alchemists' Quarter back in Guerdon, she saw other embryos growing in tanks. Was she *cultivated* the same way?

Is she even really human? Is her soul her own, or is she an emanation, too, a little tendril of god-stuff in the physical plane? At least she's replaced the Black Iron God with something better. Human or not, mortal or not, at least she's got Spar.

From outside, there's a thump, and the cart slows. Swerves slightly in the manner of a mule halting at the roadside verge for a snack, then stops.

It's as right a moment as she's going to get – and Cari feels that there's nothing out there that can be as bad as spending any more time with her own thoughts in the dark. Cari presses her fingers to the lid and turns it as best she can. It moves a finger's breadth, but it moves. She twists it over and over, pain shooting through her wrists, until finally it pops off and she can crawl out into the glare of the sun.

The mule is munching contentedly on some thorny plant that sprouts in unlikely profusion along the side of the road. Two more casks of yliaster on the wagon. And behind her, lying face down in the dust, a crumpled human figure wearing a hooded cloak.

It's Myri.

Cari considers leaving the sorceress to die in the dirt. Even considers speeding her along. The woman served Heinreil back in Guerdon, serves the Ghierdana here. She's an enemy – but she got Cari out of that lab, and clearly has some plan in mind. So, fuck it, Myri gets to live a little longer.

The woman is disturbingly light, like she's burned herself hollow. Unconscious, from some combination of the scorching heat and whatever sorcery she's performed. Something big, from the state of her. Soot cakes Myri's mouth and nose, and bloodless wounds have opened on her wrists. Cari looks around for some shelter, spots signs of a landslide, a patch of green on the mountain, and then realises she's been here before. Up the slope is that little shrine to the god-dess of the mountain. Also the Goddess of Kicking the Shit out of Cari – but she's heard the Ghierdana attacked the goddess, disrupted her. They can't permanently kill her, but it takes time for a deity to re-form. Maybe the shrine is safe – and it's probably not the sort of place anyone else would willingly go.

She huffs up the mountain, Myri thrown over her shoulder like an evil carpet. Approaching the small shrine does bring on the same prickly tension feeling as before, but it's much weaker this time. She passes the marble statue of Usharet that adorns the front of the shrine, dumps the unconscious sorceress in the shade and goes around the back. There's a small room there, entered through a doorless archway. She freezes for an instant, thinking she glimpses someone sprawled in front of the altar, but when her eyes adjust to the shadowed room, it's just a thorn bush sprouting from a crack between the tiles that just happens to resemble a hunched woman, thorn branches growing across the altar like a drowning swimmer clinging to driftwood.

The walls are decorated with mosaic tiles soiled with dust that's blown in, and there are little alcoves on either side where attendant priests must once have stayed. And – miraculously – there's a basin of fresh water, filled by a spring that trickles from one wall. No food, but Cari ate yesterday, so she's doing well by the standards of this dying rock.

Cari drags Myri into one of the alcoves and sits down on the floor opposite.

That thorn bush really looks like a person, the more she stares at it. She can make out the curve of a spine, the suggestion of legs in that tangle of roots, even a hint of a face.

"She's coming back." Myri speaks through cracked lips, a throaty whisper.

"Figured that."

"Don't say her name."

"I know!" snaps Cari.

Myri gestures weakly towards the basin. Cari scoops up some water in her palm and trickles it into the sorceress's mouth.

"Where's . . . the food?"

"There isn't any."

"Idiot. In other casks! I brought supplies. Food, medication, money."

"Oh. Shit. They're down the hill. I thought they were just full of yliaster."

"There are waterproof sacks floating in the brine."

Cari hurries out of the shrine, looks down the slope at the distant ribbon of the empty road. There's no sign of the mule, or the cart. She doesn't know if the animal wandered off, or if pursuers from the refinery got it. Or, hell, if the dragon swooped out of the blue sky and grabbed it.

"The cart's gone."

Myri taps her head gently against the tiled wall. "Idiot." Her fingers twitch spasmodically over the hollow of her elbow. An injection site for her suit's vitalising fluids. "Don't go outside again. Until nightfall. The dragon will be searching."

"So," says Cari, "are you fucked without that stuff? You gonna die?"

"No. But it'll hurt."

"I'm sort of fine with that." Cari grabbed a scalpel as she fled the lab, and she produces it now. "Why'd you pull me out of there?" she demands.

"Don't." Purple light crackles around Myri's fingers, she says, looking at the scalpel. The whites of her eyes aren't white; they're mottled brown, a mass of scars. "Khebesh, of course. They wouldn't let me back in."

"Back?" echoes Cari. "You've been there before."

"Trained there." The lightning snakes around her hand again.

"They won't let you in, either. Not unless you've got some key, something to trade. What is it?"

"A book. There was this sorceress in Guerdon, Doctor Ramegos. She died in the invasion."

Myri nods. "She was working on the god-bombs. Her grimoire would be enough to open the gates. So, where's the book? It wasn't on the *Rose*."

"Captain Hawse hid it. I think I know where."

"Show me," orders Myri.

"Fuck off."

"I—"

"And don't bother fucking threatening me." Cari puts on a mocking imitation of Myri's voice echoing within her helmet. "'I shall blast you with dread sorcery.' You want to kill me, the Ghierdana want to kill me, the Ishmerians want to kill me. Heinreil wanted to kill me, back in Guerdon, and you saw this thorn bitch wanted to kill me," she adds, kicking at the Usharet-tree.

Myri rolls her scarred eyes. "Maybe you should stop provoking . . . well, everyone. And I was about to say, I have a *ship*. Well, a sailing boat, but it'll reach the mainland."

"You've got a sailing boat. They've got a fucking dragon."

"He'll leave for Ulbishe soon. We just need to stay hidden until he does." Myri coughs. "Vorz got what he wanted from you."

Cari rubs her own wounds. "They took my blood. Why?"

"You're an interesting specimen. A synthetic saint. Breeding saints is commonplace – drooling sacred idiots, inbred to be pleasing to Culden or whoever. But you were made for a singular purpose." Myri licks her lips, and bits of dead skin flake off. "A freak."

"You're one to fucking talk."

"This?" Myri holds up her scorched hand, as if seeing it for the first time. "I brought this on myself. I chose this, and I live with my choice." She coughs again. "And, yes, if I don't get to Khebesh, I'll die with my choice. But it will be my choice."

"They can cure you in Khebesh?"

"They can help me."

"That's why I'm going there. To find help for Spar."

Myri laughs, coughs, laughs again. "Who told you the Khebeshi could help with that?"

Cari's cheeks redden. "Eladora Duttin. My cousin. Was she wrong?"

"Wrong? Not necessarily. The Khebeshi are the greatest sorcerers in the world. But what you did, your Gutter Miracle – that wasn't sorcery. Facilitated by sorcery, maybe, but it was a botched miracle." Myri shrugs. "Maybe if you had a few dozen archaeotheologists studying it for months, they could begin to reconstruct the aetheric currents. But from what I understand, the New City wasn't exactly a conducive environment for research while you were ... what was it, the Saint of Knives?"

Cari sits back. Certainly, she drove away anyone that stank of sorcery when she was the Saint of Knives – she and Spar feared they might discover the secret vault under the New City that contained the remaining Black Iron bells, the unfinished god-bombs. And Eladora told her, once: *there are theological engineers trying to calculate how much divine power you disposed of.*"

Was Eladora lying to her, when she told Cari to go to Khebesh? Once, Cari would have found the idea absurd – her cousin was dully honest when they were children. But Eladora's involved in politics now, in international affairs and intrigues. Even if she wasn't lying, it's certainly possible that Eladora had some ulterior motive for getting Cari out of Guerdon for a long time.

But there has to be some truth in Eladora's words, too. The fucking book is too valuable for her to just give it away.

"I'll get the book," mutters Cari, "you get your boat."

"Like hell. We'll go together. I'm not letting you out of my sight." Myri groans as she reaches for the water. "And I'll need to lean on you to walk, anyway."

*

Myri does let Cari out of her sight, though, to sleep. The sorceress draws a warding rune on her side of the shrine first, barring Cari from entering her little alcove.

Myri's woken by the sound of Cari slicing open waterproof sacks with a scalpel and spilling the contents across the yliaster-slick floor. Cari sorts through the junk, scooping up most of the vials of Myri's drugs and stuffing them back into one of the sacks. Leverage.

"How?"

"Found the mule. Some kids found it. I took it back." Cari holds up one large black box. "I found this, too. This is the thing Vorz was using, back in the lab. Some sort of aethergraph?"

"An advanced model. I hadn't seen anything like it before. It might be useful."

Cari grunts. The aethergraphs she saw back in Guerdon communicated through fat wires that the alchemists planted across the city like choking vines. This one works without wires, presumably transmitting messages through the invisible aether, the realm of the gods.

Another synthetic saint, sort of.

"Can they track us through this?"

"I don't think so. Certainly not when it's switched off."

"Can I talk to Guerdon with this?"

"Perhaps. Vorz was able to talk to someone in Guerdon."

Into the sack it goes. Myri paws through the other bags.

"Hey, most of the food is missing. And my money. And—"

Cari shrugs. "Had to leave the kids something."

Bolstered by the contents of one of the vials, Myri's able to walk the next morning. The sorceress knows the routes the Eshdana take, and they're able to cross much of the island without being seen. Cari feels a sharp pang of guilt as they pass into the shadow of the peak – she wonders if Adro lived through the night, if Ren's still waiting for her to return with help. To bring hope in a handful of chits.

She could have kept going, last night. Returned to the camp under cover of darkness. Maybe, maybe she could break in. Cut a few throats. Find Adro and Ren – and then what? Their chances of escaping would be minimal, and even if they made it out of the camp, they'd still be stuck on Ilbarin, hunted by the Ghierdana. It comes down to power, doesn't it? She doesn't have the strength to drive the Ghierdana off this island, to bring them down or to carry her friends to safety. Better to run, to hide, to conserve what she has, instead of dying beside them in a futile gesture.

By the time they reach the little cove west of Ushket, Cari's almost convinced herself she's doing the right thing. *Can't afford guilt*, she tells herself. *Have to move fast now.*

"Cove" isn't the right word – before the war, this would have been a stony cleft high up on the north-western face of the Rock. Now, the floodwaters break against cliffs that in a rational world should be hundreds of feet above sea level. Cari wonders if Myri can see the churning of the miracle that piles the waters up on Ilbarin.

Myri's boat is a small one, drawn up on a low shelf of rock. The tide's rising towards it – at high tide, Cari estimates she'll be able to refloat the boat on her own, with only a little sorcerous help.

"Does she have a name?" asks Cari.

"*Tymneas.*"

"Who's that?"

"A sorcerer of Khebesh. A renegade, they called him. An inspiration of mine." Myri struggles to lift the remainder of their scanty supplies on board. "Khebeshi masters don't usually leave the city except on matters of great importance. The outside world is considered perilous – and corrupting. They hide behind the Ghost Walls."

Cari hurries over, grabs the sacks off Myri, hoists them on board. "I've heard that name before. What are the Ghost Walls?"

"A mystery only for the initiated," mutters Myri, with a sarcastic edge. "That's what they told me." She lowers herself painfully on to a flattish rock, takes a sip of water, another vial of her painkilling drug. "What do you know about sorcery?"

Cari shrugs. "Chant words, wiggle fingers, shit explodes. Oh, and it fucks you up. Sorcerers I've known include bloody Jermas Thay himself, the treacherous bastard who killed Spar, a bunch of fuckers I knifed back home. Oh, and you. On the whole, I'll pass."

"So, you know nothing." Myri snorts. "I suppose that's to be expected."

"Fuck you."

"You understand what you are, don't you?" Myri's gaze is uncomfortably intense.

"What?"

"Back in Guerdon, I studied you. It was Heinreil who spotted you, but I helped him put the pieces together." She smiles. "Vorz had the right idea. I would love to dissect you. Unravel you, and find out how you were created. You were made as a tool, Carillon Thay. You never needed to understand the supernatural any more than my boat needs to understand how to navigate, how winds and currents work. You were made to be used. You need guidance, not comprehension. A hand on the tiller. To act, not to know. You'll note that all those who sought to make use of you were sorcerers."

Eladora too, thinks Cari, a spike of doubt stabbing her in the stomach. She hides it with anger. "I honestly don't fucking know if you're trying to teach me or insult me."

"I'll try teaching. Everything exists on two planes. The physical, and the spiritual – or, as sorcerers prefer to call it, the aetheric. The gods exist primarily on the aetheric plane; mortals, primarily, on the physical. But the two worlds are interconnected."

"Oh, really? I hadn't noticed."

"It goes both ways. Mortal thoughts shape and agitate the aether, pushing it in different directions. Over a long, long time, those eddy currents become self-perpetuating and—"

"That's all a god is, right?" Cari does know something about this. "A self-perpetuating structure."

"From one perspective – yes. Gods are structures in the aether, given motion by the action of human souls. And freshly dead souls are most potent of all, for they are free of mortal entanglements. Hence the divine hunger for sacrifices and funeral rites, and the preponderance of psychopomps."

"Preponderance of psychopomps," echoes Cari. "Gods below, if you don't die on the way, this is going to be a hellish journey. Go on, what does all this have to do with the Ghost Walls?"

"The aetheric plane is perilous. It's elemental chaos, churning with gods and demons. Worse, it's timeless – effects ripple and echo there back and forth in time, from a mortal perspective. Now, when a sorcerer casts a spell—" Myri conjures a werelight, snuffs it out, "I'm reaching into the aether with my mind, and agitating it just so as to create a physical effect. To do so, I must expose myself to the currents and storms of the aetheric plane – and, often, endure cross-currents and backwash. And, because I am human and thus a creature of the material realm, such backwash takes on material form. Material consequences." With a hideous grin, Myri wipes away a little blood from her lips and flicks it into the surf. It glimmers for a moment before a wave washes it away.

"And the Ghost Walls? It takes you longer to get to the point than it does to get to Khebesh."

"They cut the aether of Khebesh off from outside influences, creating a placid zone. And the sorcerers record every act of magic, so they can compensate for it. Maintain the balance of the world." Myri's grown breathless. And irritated, as if the discussion of the Ghost Walls angered her. "But speaking of Khebesh – where is the grimoire of Doctor Ramegos? Where did Hawse hide it?"

Cari takes a deep breath. She's been anticipating this moment for some time, and hopes she's right.

"I think – right here."

She shucks off her rags and steps off the rock shelf.

Diving down, to reach the muck of the drowned land.

Falling into the hands of the Lord of Waters.

Cari thinks of that thorn-bush goddess on the mountain, renewing herself after being destroyed. Tethered to that shrine, to the Rock of Ilbarin. Thinks of Hawse's altar on the *Rose*, his devotion to a vanished god. His promise that the Lord of Waters had a plan for her.

And her vision in the rift — the Bythos swimming over the grave of the god. Something must have survived. Gods cannot die. There has to be something left, some meaning to Hawse's long vigil, his martyrdom.

Her thoughts become a prayer.

She reaches the seabed and holds on, sinking her fingers into the mud. Holding on as her lungs burn, her vision darkens. Hoping she's right.

Movement, in the deeps.

Cari kicks back up, breaching the surface, gasping for air. She swims back to the rock and pulls herself out of the sea, turns in time to see the first of the Bythos emerging from the water behind her. Half a dozen of the fish-creatures swim towards her, lowing softly, their iridescent scales gleaming wetly like jewels.

Only one follows her out of the water. It stumbles as it climbs up the rocks, the sudden weight of its fishy upper body nearly too much for the withered human frame beneath to bear. The human portion of the Bythos is naked, headless, bloated from weeks underwater, but Cari still recognises it by its gait, by its broken hands.

It's Captain Hawse.

How much of Hawse survives in this hybrid being? Is there still something of the captain in there, or it is just using him, a divine parasite animating that stumbling human form? Did the captain want this, in the end? Is it reward or punishment – or is she applying human words, human intent, to something beyond human comprehension?

As the Bythos approaches, her eyes are drawn not to the holy fish-body that trails behind the creature, nor to the remains of Hawse that carry it, but to the point of union, the spot where Hawse's neck fuses with the underbelly of the fish. She doesn't know why it fascinates her so, nor can she draw any meaning from it, but that point of balance draws her eye, as if she can discern whether the Bythos is more god than man.

It stops, and extends its ruined hands – Hawse's hands, familiar and loved – offering her a bundle wrapped in oilskins. The fucking book, at last.

She takes it, reverently, and lays it on the rock beside her.

Without a word or gesture, the Bythos turns and slips into the ocean, vanishing instantly from sight.

Cari chooses to take it as one last jest from the captain, that he walks away without a word, just like she did six years ago. He doesn't speak, but the return of the book is proof enough of his friendship.

"To Khebesh," she says through the tears.

CHAPTER TWENTY-FIVE

I n the house on Lanthorn Street, Rasce holds a wake for Vyr. He was not well liked by any of the thieves: not by his Ghierdana kinfolk, nor the Eshdana, nor the Guerdon thieves, but he was one of them, and they honour that bond if nothing else. Bottles of wine and casks of arax, then the common ground of whisky.

Vyr's body, still wrapped in the sheet, lies on the table in the room downstairs. In time, they'll bring it back to the isles of the Ghierdana and bury him in the crypts. Once, it was the tradition of the Ghierdana to murder a priest as part of the funeral ceremony, to show that the sons of the dragon bow to no god, but in these days of alliance between the isles and the Lyrixian mainland it wouldn't be politic. At least, it wouldn't be wise to kill a Lyrixian priest; no doubt Baston would happily murder some cleric from the Sacred Realm of Ishmere and drag the corpse back across the border, but that wouldn't be wise either. They've already strained the bounds of the Armistice this day.

Rasce feels restless no matter how much arax he drinks, and the singing irritates him. There's too much he doesn't know about Vyr's death – and how he feels about Vyr's death. He had no love for his cousin, but he's honour-bound to avenge the murder of a Ghierdana. Those papers suggest Vyr was plotting against him, or at least reporting on his efforts in Guerdon – and if Vyr was reporting to

Great-Uncle, then Vyr might have lied to the dragon, poured deception in Great-Uncle's ear.

Worse, it's a sign that Great-Uncle doesn't trust Rasce. That Great-Uncle fears Rasce might *fail*.

He wants to act. To strike. Instead, he feels weighed down, surrounded by obligations and duties. Surrounded by people. It was so much easier to soar heedless, to take and move on, to let the dragon-fire scorch the cities and move on – this connection to Spar is a curse as well as a blessing. He's aware of Vyr's body in the house, aware of those who were wounded on Mercy Street. One woman was shot – an accident, her gun went off when the watch grabbed her. She's dying a few streets away, despite the efforts of the surgeon. The sensation of her blood running down on to the floor mixes with the taste of the arax.

Outside, another obligation. Rasce emerges on to Lanthorn Street and bows before Thyrus.

"My thanks, Great-Aunt, for your assistance earlier."

"My assistance," she echoes. "Nearly breaking the truce, and for what? A band of stray dogs from the Wash?"

"Allies. Trustworthy allies, so we can extend our reach beyond the occupation zone."

The dragon enfolds him in a tent of wing-leather. Thyrus' green-tinged scales eclipse the world.

"Dragons have servants, not allies," hisses Thyrus. "Have they all taken the ash?"

"I – almost all, but—"

"Almost all. Ah, you clasp only a handful of disloyal vipers to your bosom! My estimation of your competence only decreases. So tell me, nephew, who shall pay me for my assistance? Who is to blame?" Her eyes burn in the hot darkness of her embrace. "Do I blame the dead boy, for whatever foolishness got him killed? Do I blame you, for breaking the truce line and marching a host down into the free city?" She snarls, acidic spittle steaming on the cobblestones of Lanthorn Street (and distantly, Rasce feels the acid eating into the stones). "Or do I blame my brother? He has still not returned! What did he command you to do?"

"To take control of Guerdon's trade in yliaster," replies Rasce. Great-Uncle commanded him to remain silent, but he owes Thyrus a debt.

"Are we pedlars now? Do we grub in the dirt for the leavings of gods to sell on for a few coppers? The margins on yliaster are miserly." Thyrus hisses again. "End this. Do not cross the border again, for any reason."

"My Great-Uncle set me a task, and I would sooner die than fail."

"My child," says Thyrus, "you are mortal. Death and failure are inevitable for you. You only get to choose which comes first." Her tone suggests she's done with the conversation, but Rasce isn't finished.

"A Ghierdana has been murdered. All of us are honour-bound to avenge him."

Thyrus yawns, showing him three rows of razor-sharp teeth. A few small gaps, where knives were harvested for her adopted children. Tooth-buds are already sprouting in the gaps. "Bring me those responsible, and I shall devour them."

"The alchemist Mandel—"

"You have no proof of that."

"This letter," says Rasce, producing the sealed letter. "Mandel's company enchanted the hands that strangled the life from Vyr."

The dragon breathes softly. Wax melts. Paper scorches and burns. "I am not unsympathetic, child, but young Vyr is dead, and the dead can wait. Sometimes, vengeance must be slow, and it may be all the sweeter for it." Thyrus spreads her wings, releasing him from the confessional. "Know your place, Chosen, and be the better for it."

Spar watches the dragon depart, part of his mind following Thyrus as she climbs, circles once over the New City, then strikes out for the designated hunting grounds north of Guerdon. He can feel her, too, with senses he doesn't have a name for.

I think she may be right. If the Armistice fails, then everybody loses. Secure what you've won.

"You owe me," says Rasce, rising to face the house on Lanthorn Street. "I saved you. We made a bargain, you and I." He shouts, his voice echoing off the New City. "Show me my enemies!"

Spar tries. Again and again, he reaches out. He can see the pebbles planted by Baston, across the city, gleaming in his mind like a constellation of stars, but it's too far. He strains until his mind dissolves, until his soul burns, all to no avail. He can no more reach those stars than he can fly.

"Damn you!" Rasce roars. "I shall not fail Great-Uncle!"

Inside Lanthorn Street, Baston rises to investigate the commotion outside. Karla looks down from an upstairs window.

"On Glimmerside," says Rasce, "you took my strength to fuel the miracle. Do so again, then."

Spar hesitates. A Stone Man must be cautious. If he takes too much from Rasce, the spiritual loss could kill him – and then Spar himself would be lost, falling back into the abyss. He tries to think – and then Rasce's knife plunges into the wall of the house, or into Rasce's own flesh, Spar can't tell. The overlap is too complete, and his mind's already scraped over the city from the seawall to Gethis Station. Pain rushes through him, although he cannot be sure what "he" refers to at this juncture.

Is he the Ghierdana boy on Lanthorn Street, sawing madly at the glowing stone walls like he's trying to cut the house free from its foundations? Is he the New City, defiant labyrinth, a thing sprung from neither victory nor defeat, but something else entirely, an act of faith in no known god? A thing the scholars have yet to name, a magical accident as misshapen as the alchemical waste-poppets that crawl from their birthing vats in agony?

Is he the spiderweb of consciousness drawn across Guerdon, the ghost of a Stone Man who died two years ago, animated by miracles stolen from the Black Iron Gods, his brief afterlife bought with the coin of a thousand thousand sacrificial victims?

He falls.

He flies.

His consciousness leaping across the city, focusing on another point. His stepping stone across the abyss is a single pebble, lodged in the wax of a Tallowman.

This Tallowman is new-made and knows it. Life flows through it, artificial but no less sweet. The flame burns clean and bright, a tongue of fire dancing across the finely drawn glyphs and runes engraved on the inner surface of its skull, illuminating them in order to form ersatz Tallow-thoughts, an approximation of mind. Artificial but no less cherished.

For now, it's content to follow orders. It was told to stand guard, and stand guard it will! It's so young that the simple act of standing and watching is fascinating and novel. Why, it could stare at a blank wall for hours, and find joy in watching the light moving across the bricks. Some part of it knows that, as the wax hardens, so too will it become jaded, and it'll be harder to think. It'll have to do cruel things, hurtful things, to feel anything. It'll have to be blood spraying across the bricks. But for now – bricks! So intricate, the lines and patterns like veins and arteries.

And this Tallowman has something much more interesting to look at. This room is circular, the ceiling a glass dome, ornate ironwork made to resemble astronomical glyphs – although only a tiny patch of sky can be seen through the forest of pipes and storage tanks above the dome, and that sky is choked with fog. This place was made as an observatory, but instead of a telescope, an aethergraph has pride of place. A Guerdon-made model, its thick connecting cable of rubber-sheathed orichalcum running into a socket in the floor.

Mandel – the Tallowman's maker – sits at the aethergraph, his lined face bathed in the glow from the machine. His lips move in silent communion with the other minds in the circuit. His scribe waits patiently, heavy ledger balanced on his knees.

There's something in the Tallowman's side, between where its ribs used to be, before rib and lung and everything else got rendered down in the vats. It doesn't hurt but having something lodged in its flank is *interesting*. A chip of stone. Oh, yes, when it fought that human. Humans, so slow and stodgy and messy on the inside. The Tallowman's glad to have left that behind. It thanks the alchemists, thanks Mandel, for making it *better*. Nearly perfect.

The glow from the aethergraph fades.

"Cowards," says Mandel, "Rosha left us with a guild of jellyfish pretending to be human."

"What was the consensus?" asks the scribe.

"There wasn't one. Most of them are just piddling around in their breeding vats or sniffing around the edges of the Great Work. Demanding praise for creating condensed aether or grinding mummy to ninety-nine-parts pure. The rest ... either they talk only of rebuilding the factories, or they see the peril posed by the Ghierdana, but think fleeing is the better option. That the Armistice is unsustainable, and the threat to the yliaster supply is the final straw. The new guildmaster ... gah, what's the fool's name again?"

"Helmont," supplies the scribe.

"He leans towards decamping to Ulbishe. But he doesn't command the guild the way Rosha did. He can't bring them with him, so it's war between the jellyfish and the accountants." Mandel shoves the aethergraph in irritation, sending the fluid inside sloshing against the glass.

"You should let me talk to them."

"Ha. Wouldn't that be a thing? 'Twould be almost worth the risk of revealing you to see their mouths drop open like gaffed fish." Mandel groans. "Maybe we *should* consider evacuating. Third time's the charm and all. Khebesh was too isolated, Guerdon too welcoming. Maybe Ulbishe will be right. Ready supplies of the base *materia*, and while their athanors may not be as advanced as Guerdon's, at least we would be away from the front lines."

"And end up as Kept as the gods. You know you cannot trust the mirror princes of Ulbishe." The scribe lays down his pen, rubs his weary eyes. The Tallowman watches in fascination, enchanted by the idea of having little flaps of skin that cover the eyeball! Tallowmen do not blink.

"And anyway," adds the scribe, "young Duttin has us in a vice."

"Ach, I know. What a debacle it was to let Aloysius Ongent of all people get hold of *both* Thay heirs. Now Duttin's got her stable of monsters and rogues to meddle with us. Not to mention Ongent's homunculus skulking around the city. I swear, I'll wake some morning to find the creature sharpening his knife on my ribcage."

The scribe passes Mandel a letter. "This arrived while you were in conference. Parliament has voted in emergency session. In response to, ah, the growing threat to the peace and stability of Guerdon, they've agreed to reopen the Tallow Vats. They'll be under the auspices of the Ministry of Security, not the alchemists' guild."

The Tallowman doesn't have a heart. Or blood. Or, really, anything but wax and wick and fire. But wax and wick and fire all thrill at the thought of *more* of its kind. There have been so few since the making of new Tallowmen was banned.

"Under Nemon, then. Bah. Another of our works taken from us, and all in pursuit of Duttin's lunacy."

"Like old times," laughs the scribe. "A Thay ruining us."

"I fail to see the humour," says Mandel.

"The Great Work endures, my friend. We are close. A little longer, and we can set all the world to rights."

Mandel replies, his mouth moving and making sounds, but the Tallowman's lost interest. Now, it's fascinated by the motion of Mandel's jaw, the way his beard hairs move when his mouth opens, the moistness of his tongue, the pulsing of the arteries in his neck. Wouldn't it be enlightening to bludgeon his skull open with a brick? Or a knife, a sweet sharp knife?

The flame in the Tallowman's skull dances through random fantasies of cruelty. Unseen, the stone in its side begins to slip as the wax around it softens.

Spar's mind retreats from the Tallowman, the backwash of a psychic wave.

"What are you doing?" hisses Rasce. He's distantly aware that his body is soaked with sweat, the dragon-tooth knife slipping from his slick grip, but that body is many streets away and mostly irrelevant.

I can't hold on.

"We must divine if there's a way in. Heinreil's tunnel – does it still exist? Look deeper! I care not for the mystic jabbering of alchemists!"

The Great Work. In his death throes, Spar swallowed the old Alchemists' Quarter of Guerdon. Portions of their library are still lodged in his bowels, in the tunnels below the New City, and knowledge leeched into the stone. The Great Work is the long-held mystic obsession of the alchemists' guild, the goal of spiritual transformation and perfection. For some, it was metaphor – lead in gold and flesh into transcendent matter just another way of talking about coaxing fire from phlogiston. A secular philosophy in a godless city to lift the alchemists' work above grubby commerce, just like the Brotherhood clung to Idge's writings.

A memory opens up beneath Spar, triggered by words he heard while eavesdropping. Professor Ongent's querulous voice, asking him, *Are you familiar – I would assume not, not to cast aspersions on your education – with the Theory of Forms?*

He once was. He's not any more. That knowledge is scattered across the city, tucked away in odd corners and alleyways, memories left stranded on rooftops and attics, buried in cellars, and he doesn't have the strength to collect it all. Something to do with the movement of souls, with the physical plane of mortals and the aetheric plane of gods and spells. It's important, he knows that. *Help me*, he pleads to Rasce. Rasce is the fixed point of his consciousness now – he can use Rasce as an anchor as he collects his scattered thoughts.

It's important, thinks Spar.

"NO!" Rasce drives the dragon-tooth blade into his own thigh.

And then he's flung forward, as though a volcano of pure willpower has erupted beneath the New City—

The flame in the Tallowman's skull flickers and bends as some unseen wind breathes on it. A new impulse fills the Tallowman. It wants to go down. Down and down.

So it goes, leaving the maker and the scribe behind. The cellars under Mandel & Company are a labyrinth of pipes and valves, holding vats and deep-storage vaults girded with dampening rods and containment wards. The Tallowman slips by them all, sniffing its way to the oldest, deepest part of the fortress.

Down.

It leaves the hiss and hum of industry behind, the rumble of the trains and the complaints of the roaring furnaces in the high-pressure athanors. A stray moment of sympathy crosses the Tallowman's mind, a thought of kinship between itself and the caged infernos in those furnaces. They're both things of flame, and would delight in running rampant across the city, consuming all those lovely breakable flammable things – oh, imagine the screaming! – but they're both chained in houses built by the alchemists. Both yoked to useful tasks. It moves on. Stainless steel and orichalcum wiring give way to grey stone blocks mortared with blood.

Down. Down.

And oh – what is this? The Tallowman enters into a large underground chamber. The only light here is from the candle-flame inside, and the fiery light dances over flagstones carved with runnels, over walls with depictions of mass sacrifice at the knife-tentacles of hideous formless horrors, over an altar of onyx.

Over two great lumps of iron that rest here in this tomb. Both deformed, half-melted and half-congealed, neither bell nor icon. The Tallowman's flickering gaze passes over the pair of junked effigies without pausing. The flame flickers again, compelling it onwards.

Silently it moves through this unholy place, through this temple to forgotten gods, until at last it comes to the brink of a dark well. A tunnel of black stone, dug long, long ago.

The Tallowman leans over the edge, staring down into the darkness.

And it is not only the flickering of the candle that makes those shadows move.

"The tunnel exists!" crows Rasce. He imagines Baston and the rest climbing up that tunnel, bearing guns and bombs. Revenge for Vyr! Great-Uncle's commands achieved!

Spar doesn't respond, but Rasce senses their shared awareness unspool, their prolapsed soul unravelling as it retreats across the city. For an instant, he feels Guerdon as Spar must, streets like veins, his mind slithering down Heinreil's tunnel to brush against something dark and deep.

And then he falls back into his body, and is met with pain.

CHAPTER TWENTY-SIX

They fall into a simple routine on board Myri's little boat. Cari does all the work, and Myri concentrates on staying alive.

To be fair to the sorceress, she does one other thing, and it's key to their chances of making the voyage to Khebesh. Each morning, Myri binds wind and wave, commanding them to carry *Tymneas* swiftly over the ocean. It's the easiest sailing Cari's ever done.

Myri claims that the spells are easy, too. The gods have already fucked up the aether here with discordant miracles, Kraken and the Lord of Waters clashing over command of the seas, so it's trivial for her to take the tatters of reality and weave them into a new spell. But Cari can see the strain on her face, the way she braces herself against forces that Cari cannot feel. She watches Myri measure out her remaining drug vials like Spar used to space out his alkahest shots. They split the boat between them, an unspoken border zone running amidships. Cari spends most of her time aft, Myri forward.

Sometimes, a strong gust whipping off the Firesea tears through Myri's spells, and Cari has to scramble to trim the sails to match, but for much of the journey there's time to kill.

Or not kill. The sorceress may be quite far down Cari's list of enemies, but she's on there – and a lot of the names above her have been scratched off. But it's not the time. Get within sight of Khebesh, then their little private Armistice ends.

Cari's not much for conversation, but maybe talking will take her mind off the gnawing hunger in her belly. Her attempts to figure out the aethergraph have yielded nothing but frustration. She'd hoped, somehow, that the machine would work like her amulet and let her thoughts reach Spar all the way across the world, but so far the contraption's proved unresponsive. She has to fight the urge to throw the damn thing overboard.

And maybe talking will stop Myri from staring at her like she's something dangerous, something venomous. The sorceress is the dangerous one here, right? Far from Guerdon, far from Spar, Cari's got nothing.

"What's Khebesh like?" Cari asks.

"When I first went there, I thought it was the most marvellous city in the world. It was only later that I realised it's a hermitage. Tranquil, deliberate, all things carefully balanced." She glances at Cari. "You'll hate it."

Cari shrugs. "As long as they help Spar, doesn't matter. Where'd you come from? Before Khebesh, I mean."

Myri rubs her tattooed wrist. Little crackling bolts of aetheric energy dance around her hand. She flings them out over the railing like snot, the magic dissipating over the wide ocean. Then she begins to speak, her voice a painful whisper that's often lost in the wind and the creaking of the sails . . .

She was born in the forests of Varinth, and it was whispered she burned her way out of her mother's womb with words of fire, nursed by a boar-spirit from the dark of the wood. A wild talent – a twist of mind and soul that gives a natural ability for sorcery. They called her a witch, too, and apprenticed her to the priestesses who wove effigies of green branches for the boar god.

In those days, the tribes warred with the Empire of Haith, and Myri made her first kill at the age of six. Men of Haith marched on the forest villages in orderly columns, living and dead soldiers advancing in lockstep, indistinguishable until the blasts of sorcery struck them. The flesh withered and the living bones collapsed, but the dead kept on walking.

The boar god died a hundred times, brought down by massed artillery fire. Each time a new saint or avatar emerged from the thorn forest, the men of Haith would kill it again. They burned the temples, toppled the effigies and spilled the offerings in the mud.

The tribe surrendered. The warriors exchanged swords for saws and axes; Haith's shipyards were hungry for timber. The surviving priestesses fled into the dark, where no man could follow. But they left Myri behind, and the dead men captured her.

Cari drops a fishing line into the water. They're nearly out of food, and while Myri hardly eats, Cari's belly is pressing against her spine, and it's making her irritable.

"If you want to play who had the shittiest childhood, I'm game."

"Oh, please. I know all about your past, remember? I was with Heinreil when he found out who you were, Carillon *Thay*. You were sent to live with your aunt. Your childhood was scraped knees and picnics and farmyard animals."

"My aunt tried to murder me."

"Because you were bred to be the Herald of the Black Iron Gods and bring doom upon the world? Because you were spawned from a Raveller summoned up by your mad grandfather? Or because she had to spend time with you?" Myri rolls her eyes. "And I don't want to play, as you put it. The circumstances of my childhood were harsh, but there's no point complaining to anyone. My past doesn't define me. I choose my own future."

Her story's interrupted by a fit of coughing so intense that Cari crosses the demarcation line to help Myri breathe. After a few moment's retching over the side, the sorceress continues.

All things have a place in the orderly Empire of Haith, even wild girls from the wood. They sent her to a Bureau school for sorcerers in the mountains north of Paravos, where they shaped her talent, taught her rote incantations from musty grimoires. Her classmates an unlikely mix: children like herself, the others from poor families hoping for advancement, criminals judged to have enough wit to attempt thaumaturgy, the desperate or god-touched, who had nowhere else to go. There were other schools, she learned, where sorcery was treated as an academic discipline, a prerequisite to the high science of necromancy, but the Empire of Haith also needed disposable war-sorcerers. Spellcasters to let off a few big blasts before the aetheric feedback ruined them. Even in Myri's youth, such practices were seen as crude and old-fashioned – alchemical weapons promised more destructive power, and did not require any souls to be torn asunder in the process. But the Empire of Haith changes very, very slowly; if military protocol called for each cohort to have a combat sorcerer attached, then combat sorcerers they shall have.

But they would not have Myri. She learned all they had to teach her, honed her natural talents for sorcery – then escaped.

Cari's attention is distracted when she hooks a big snapper on her fishing line. Myri keeps talking while Cari wrestles with the fish. Something about wandering the lands around Paravos, sometimes alone, sometimes with criminals or godbands or mercenaries. Something about angst and fireballs. The other woman's casual power irritates Cari – if she could throw spells like that, she wouldn't have ended up in a tin can playing sidekick to fingerless Artolo Dragonshit. She imagines what she could do with a sorcerous talent like Myri's. Imagines zapping Aunt Silva with a blasting spell. Imagines stealing blue jade from the Eyeless with Adro, using the same invisibility spell Twelve Suns used.

Imagines countering Ongent's paralysis spell, and saving Spar from falling.

That's what she wants, that sort of controlled power. Call it Saint Aleena's paradox. The sweet spot is enough to stop other people fucking with her, enough to hurt those that deserve hurting, but not so much that people look to her for salvation.

The fish thrashes on the hook, pulling hard against the line. Cari's forearms strain to hold on.

Once, back in Guerdon, they thought there might be a way for Cari to command the Ravellers and control the power of the Black Iron Gods, and the thought had filled her with a cold horror unlike anything she'd felt before. The thought of being *responsible* for everything terrified her. Her immediate reactions: run away. Failing that, give it all to Spar. Let the clever people like Spar, like Eladora, figure it all out.

The line goes slack, suddenly. The bastard got away.

"I asked about Khebesh," says Cari, sullenly.

"I'm telling you about Khebesh."

"No, you're not. You're rambling about fucking mercenaries in the Pultish Waste. Get on with it."

"Khebesh won't make sense unless you understand."

Every act of sorcery is a risk. No matter how talented the sorcerer, no matter how prepared, there's always a risk. Eventually, the dice turn against them, and the spell turns on the sorcerer. Sorcerers are thieves and gamblers, stealing little fragments of the power of the gods and betting they can ride out the storm that follows in the wake of blasphemy.

The Khebeshi sorcerer who found Myri, though, claimed to have a foolproof system. A way to use sorcery that was a sure thing. He didn't try to force her. Didn't abduct her. Didn't threaten her. He just walked into the mercenary camp in the middle of the Pultish, strolling past sentries and wards like they weren't there, and offered her knowledge.

She sailed with him for Khebesh the next day.

All the maps place Khebesh along the southern coast of the Firesea, but that's like trying to mix cartography with poetry. The city is where it needs to be; where magic rhymes with reality. They saw the spires from afar, flashing like silver spearheads in the summer sun. They passed through the Nine Perilous Gates that are the only way through the fabled Ghost Walls, and at each gate Myri overcame some challenge, solved some riddle, proved her worth, until at last she came to the spiritual oasis of Khebesh, where the chaos of the outer worlds, both mortal and divine, cannot trouble the tranquillity of the school.

In Khebesh, there were no gods, and there were no nations. Myri was not a Varinthian barbarian nor a prisoner of Haith; neither an initiate of the priesthood of the boar god nor a war-sorcerer of the Empire. There are only students in Khebesh—

"So who cleans the toilets?"

"What?"

"Who cleans the toilets?" repeats Cari. "Look, I was the Saint of the New City, right? I know fucking plumbing from the *inside*. Blame Spar. I don't know what it says about the man that he had the presence of mind to imagine a remarkably intricate and functional sewage system while *dying*, but yeah, I've had more toilet-centred divine visions than I ever wanted. Even in the New City, miraculously conjured and all, someone has to clean the shitter. You're telling me about some equally magical fortress of academia – gods, it sounds like Eladora's wet dream – but I'm asking you, who cleans the toilets there?" Cari shrugs. "I'm trying to get a handle on who I'll be dealing with."

"There were servants." Myri frowns. "I didn't pay much attention. I was busy learning."

For there was much to learn there, in the city of sorcerers, and Myri drank knowledge like pure water. For uncounted centuries, the sages of Khebesh have gathered arcane lore from across the world. They depart the city cloaked as pilgrims, as beggars, as adventurers, as hedge-sorcerers, hiding their true nature as masters. They wander the world, observing and learning, never interceding – for the sorcerers of Khebesh understand that the outside world is broken, like a clay pot that has been shattered. Every act of sorcery risks widening the cracks, so every spell must be carefully considered. Every word of power weighed out, coins from a miser's purse. No magic may be used unnecessarily; anything that can be done by mundane means should be done by mundane means, no matter how arduous. Myri studied the works of past sorcerers who summoned demons and challenged gods, but she was not permitted to conjure the feeblest werelight when there was a candle to be used instead.

The method to glue the broken pot of reality back together has yet to be found, so it is the custom in Khebesh to record every spell cast, every miracle observed in a great tome that each sorcerer bears with them at all times. When a pilgrim returns to Khebesh after long, lonely years away, their book is added to the great archive.

One day, the masters of Khebesh predict, a Mind shall arise of such profound complexity, an intellect beyond the comprehension of anything save itself. That Mind shall encompass all the knowledge in the archive, and all the wounds of the world, and all shall be renewed. The Mind shall—

"Was that you?" asks Cari.

"What?" Myri chokes, coughs so hard she spits out something black and shrivelled. "What do you mean?"

"The Mind they talked about. I mean, you're a shit-hot sorcerer, and they went looking for you."

"Am I the prophesied one who'll restore the world to balance? No, Carillon Thay, we're not all chosen by destiny. I'm good, but I'm not some fabled arch-mage. It's just a philosophic theory, not a mystic prophecy." Myri wipes her lips. "My tale was not unusual.

The pilgrims look for talent. Khebesh gathers the best minds to itself. They look for keen intellects, and souls that have not been corrupted by divinity." Myri nods at the book, wrapped in its oilskin. "They'd never let something like you through the Gates, normally. You'd endanger their precious equilibrium."

Cari scowls and throws the fishing line out again.

"Anyway," says Myri, "it's all bullshit. Their theories are bullshit. Take the two of us, for example. All the spells I've worked in my whole life, all of it — they're *nothing* compared to the chaos you unleashed as a Saint. I lit a few candles, but you set the world on fire."

Cari doesn't answer, but her shoulders hunch. *I didn't*, she wants to argue, *it was the gods.* Shapes are visible in the water. More big fish. *Come on, one of you, bite.* For all her divine connections and mystical experiences, she can't even command a fucking fish to bite. Her wrists ache where Vorz bled her.

"I told them as much," says Myri. "I told them that the world outside the walls had gone beyond salvaging, and that choosing to restrain our own power was folly. I wasn't alone in this. Others agreed with me, and I wasn't the first to make the argument."

"Tymneas, right?"

Myri's eyes widen in surprise. "How do you know that name?"

"You told me." Cari slaps the side of the boat. "You named this boat after him, and said he was an inspiration of yours."

"He'd left Khebesh long before I arrived, but I found some of his grimoires in the library. He was a pilgrim sorcerer, a wanderer. He often travelled to Ilbarin. Further, sometimes. I took Tymneas' grimoire with me when I confronted the masters, but they wouldn't listen."

"So you told the guys we're going to beg a favour from to shove their whole philosophy up their arse. What happened then?"

Myri left without winning her staff. Instead, she inscribed sigils on her living flesh, a map of her own soul. A declaration that the rest of the world could shatter and burn, but she would remain true to herself. She would not hide behind the Ghost Walls, nor give up her talent for sorcery. Five years after she entered Khebesh by the Perilous Gate, she left by the same route. She fled in the night, wrapped in a warding-cloak. The masters are not vengeful or cruel, but neither do they tolerate the theft of their secrets. If they caught her, they would take her back to Khebesh and never permit her to leave again. She travelled, never lingering anywhere for long for fear of meeting a disguised pilgrim-sorcerer.

She returned to her old ways. The mercenaries of the Pultish were all dead now, so she went west, to the Trading Cities, where a sorcerer might easily find employment. She would prove to those cloistered masters that it was foolish to remain in obscurity, to leave the gift of sorcery to moulder out of some misplaced sense of obligation to a future that will never come. The Godswar shatters the world more thoroughly than she ever could, and she intended to make a better life for herself amid the ruins, before the end.

Better than she ever was before, thanks to her training in Khebesh. Better than any graduate of Haith's dusty institutes, or Smoke Painter's academies. The alchemist-scholars of Guerdon might be her equals in finesse or technique, but not in strength. She worked her sorcery, and the dice never turned on her. Her luck wasn't faultless, and the power that runs through her burned her, but she did not relent. The power was worth the price.

Severast to Jashan, to Khenth, to a dozen other places, and in the end to Guerdon. Some of those cities are familiar to Cari, but Myri's descriptions of them make them sound alien to her. Weird shit attracts weird shit, she guesses – no one's going to hire a sorcerer like Myri just to steal a cargo of blue jade or rob a warehouse full of wine-of-poets. No, you hire a sorcerer when you need to fight a demon, or spy on the dreams of some politician, or . . .

"When did Heinreil hire you? When he stole my amulet?" Cari's hand involuntarily grabs at her neck, remembering that her treasure has been taken from her again. This time, the loss of the amulet doesn't hurt so much. It's tainted now she knows the truth of its origin. Back then, though, the amulet was all she had of the mother she never knew, all she had to give her a home.

"No. I'd worked with him before, several times. He kept me a secret from the rest of the thieves' guild."

"Brotherhood," Cari corrects automatically. She spits over the side. "That slippery bastard."

"He treated me well, and he wasn't crazy like Artolo. As employers go, I rate him highly."

"He poisoned Spar!"

Myri shrugs. "That's between Spar and Heinreil." She gestures at the grimoire. "That's an account of all the spells Ramegos cast. All her sins, all her worries about how her actions distort the world. Fuck that. My actions are mine. Let the world attend to itself." She takes a moment to catch her breath, then continues. "Heinreil brought the amulet to me. I could tell it was a potent talisman, but I couldn't divine much about it. I figured you'd stolen it somewhere, but Heinreil found out that you got it from your grandfather."

"They told me it belonged to my mother."

Myri smiles, and it's an ugly sight – her lips have been scorched by the words of power that rested upon them, so it looks like a wound opening. "More accurate to say that it *conjured* your mother. The amulet was a relic of the Black Iron Cult, repurposed by Jermas Thay's sorcerers to be a link to the sleeping gods. But it also housed a fragment of the god's hunger, a manifest emanation."

"A Raveller," says Cari. The thought sickens her and fascinates her in equal measure, and Myri's the first person she's met who might be able to answer some of her questions. Well, the first person she's met that wasn't trying to use her in some arcane ritual, throw her in a prison for saints, or that she wasn't actively trying to murder. "But I'm human, right?"

Myri wrinkles what remains of her nose scornfully. "What a stupid question. Humanity is an accident of birth, not something to cling to or take pride in."

"Well, I'm not a fucking Raveller, am I?"

The sorceress rolls over, draws a blanket around herself. "Clearly not. I'm tired. Wake me when the wind fails."

"Hang on. I want the rest of the story."

The rest of the story is short, painful, and Carillon's fault.

Cari doesn't mention that part. She stays quiet as Myri describes her attempt to flee Guerdon at the height of the Crisis. Myri and Heinreil sold Eladora and the amulet to the Crawling Ones in exchange for a fortune in gold, and tried to drive out of the city in a carriage. But Cari had power that night, and from across the city she saw her enemy and struck at him. With a thought, she could have crushed Heinreil's soul, smashed through all Myri's wards and destroyed her. Instead, she snuffed out the life of one of the raptequines drawing the carriage, sent them careening into a wall.

Heinreil, his legs shattered, was arrested.

Myri escaped. She fled south, to Ulbishe. To survive, though, she had to use sorcery despite her wounds. Like a gambler on a losing streak, taking double-or-nothing bets to turn it all around. The cost paid in stigmata on her body and scars on her soul. In Ulbishe, she traded what coin she carried out of Guerdon for the containment suit. The first time she'd passed through Ulbishe, the quality of the alchemy work there was far behind that of Guerdon, but the alchemists of Ulbishe had improved greatly in the intervening years, and anyway, she had little choice. Augmented by the iron prison, she continued south. Skirted the Godswar—

"Is that when you signed on with Artolo?"

"No. Ilbarin was under siege by the gods of Ishmere. I took *Tymneas* east, beyond the Isle of Fire, and reached Khebesh by that route. Only the Gates were closed to me, and they would not open." Myri shivers beneath the blanket. "I tried every opening spell I knew. I hammered on the Gates. I argued, demanded, pleaded, begged. But the city remained closed." Her gaze lights on the book. "But I shall return there, and the Gates will open."

"Say you get back to Khebesh—"

"I will."

"Say you abandon me to get eaten by wild gods or something."

"I may."

"And you show up with Ramegos' journal, and they let you in, and they heal you. What then?"

Myri's words are a whisper. "Then I spit in their faces and depart again. My present circumstances have no bearing on the fact that I am right and they are wrong."

Cari sullenly checks the fishing line. There's little chance of them catching anything at this speed, but they've nothing else to eat. The dark coast of the mainland slips by to starboard. Dark shapes in the water, too – she wonders if they're not fish at all, but Bythos. An escort sent by the Lord of Waters? Some ghost of Captain Hawse, still watching over her? More likely they're just carrion hunters, waiting to collect two fresh corpses, brimming with residuum for their broken god.

She shakes the line, taking her frustration out on it. She wonders why the end of Myri's tale angers her so much. The sheer selfishness of it, maybe – Myri threatening to take Spar's one chance for survival. It's her only chance, too, of course, but Spar's a better person than Myri, damn it. If Cari gets to choose, she chooses Spar.

Oh, now *you want it to be up to you. Now you want to be the one who sorts the living and the dead.* It was easy, back in the camp, to choose between her freedom and Adro's health.

Tymneas rolls and shivers. Cari leaps up and scans the seas behind them, a lifetime of instinct warning her of danger. There's a long band of oddly still, glassy water stretching out from the north, from the smudge on the horizon that's the Rock of Ilbarin. The band rolls west, reaching and rotating, like the spoke of a tremendous wheel – and there's another band moving in from the east, visible in the distance as waves break along it.

Cari's seen it before. At Guerdon, before the invasion. She knows that if that glassy, stolen sea touches *Tymneas*, they'll be caught like a fly in amber. It's the Kraken's miracle.

"Kraken!" she cries, slicing the line free with her knife. She leaps to the tiller, hauls it around. She kicks the wood next to Myri's head to wake the sorceress. "Kraken! We've got to get out of the water!"

Myri wakes, and with a word she wakes a hurricane.

Tymneas races west, the sails straining to contain the conjured wind. So fast they leave the Bythos far behind.

The Kraken-miracle reaches for them, like the fingers of some gargantuan hand, searching and probing, but they outrun it, too. The mainland coast swells ahead of them. As they draw closer, Cari sees the distant flash of miracles reflecting off the low clouds.

"We have to get off the water," she repeats.

"That's the Godswar," warns Myri. "We'll have to pass through the Godswar."

"Let the fuckers try to stop us."

Artolo watches the *Moonchild* approach from the tower of the prefect's villa in Ushket. The freighter is too large to make its way through the flooded streets of the city to reach the new docks. Instead, swarms of smaller boats ferry cargo out to her, emptying the warehouses of their yliaster stocks. Iron-hulled *Moonchild* looms above them, taking all they can bring her yet remaining unsated.

Great-Uncle is gone, and Vorz with him. All of Artolo's pleas ignored. They have left him here on this cursed island to oversee the loading of *Moonchild*. The witch is gone, too, and she's taken his *hands* with him.

"How can I serve, Great-Uncle, when I have no hands?" he'd asked.

"You have a tongue," the dragon replied. "Command in my name." And then he vanished into the bright sky.

The new dragon-tooth dagger hangs at Artolo's belt, like a cruel joke. The witch's spells have faded, and he cannot wield the blade.

So Artolo uses his tongue. He commands. He sends his remaining Eshdana to search the island once more – Carillon may be able to hide, but how can the fucking witch escape him? She can barely walk! Dol Martaine returns empty-handed and says there's no trace of the treacherous pair.

Hollow, lost, Artolo walks the streets of Ushket, aimless as a Bythos. His bodyguards shadow him, confused and nervous. Sometimes, beggars approach him, pleading for passage off Ilbarin. They offer to work in the yliaster camp, offer to crew the *Moonchild*, offer him treasures salvaged from the drowned city, offer their daughters to warm his bed. He ignores them all.

Unable to touch, he just walks and stares. He returns to the ruins of the *Rose*, as if there's some answer hidden there. Returns to the Street of Blue Glass and wades through the ash-flecked waters, through the tide of dead worms. He walks the decks of the *Moonchild*. She's Maredon-built, a prize taken by Ghierdana pirates. In another life, Artolo imagines himself as captain of this great ship. Fit her out with stolen cannons, gird her in warding runes and sail her into the maelstrom of the Godswar. Loot and pillage, like a proper Ghierdana, and never go to Guerdon. Never go to Ilbarin.

Never lay eyes on Carillon Thay.

Tides rise and fall. Boats go in and out. Figures melt away as he passes, scurrying in terror. He doesn't eat – he cannot endure the shame of having some servant spoon-feed him. He doesn't sleep.

How can he use his tongue? He needs it for screaming silently.

Another beggar emerges from an alleyway, blocks his path. A bodyguard steps forward to shove the old woman aside, but she moves with surprising grace, filthy rags whirling as she ducks past to stand in front of Artolo.

"Your fate has not changed," she says.

He searches for his tongue. "You. You're the Ishmeric priestess. Damala."

"Carillon Thay is still within your grasp. Fate Spider has foreseen you strangle her."

He holds up his ruined hands, his finger-stumps. "With these hands?"

Damala takes his hands, raises her voice in a prayer to the Kraken. Waves crash against the hull of *Moonchild*, the spray glittering like shards of glass in the sunlight. Artolo suddenly feels *doubled*, simultaneously standing in this muddy street in Ushket but also out in the sea, observing the town from afar with cold, inhuman eyes.

"With these," she says, and she releases him. Tentacles sprout from his hand, writhing and slimy, the Kraken in miniature. His own skin giving way to the mottled squid-flesh. He flexes his transformed hands, feels the god-given strength flow through him. For a moment, he has the sensation of brushing his fingers against the wooden hull of a little boat, and through taste-receptors in his knuckles he smells the sweat of Carillon Thay, the ozone stink of the witch.

And then it's gone.

"Make an offering," whispers the priestess. "Seal the bargain."

What does he have left to give? His tentacle-fingers close around the hilt of the new dragon-tooth dagger, and the priestess nods. "Most fitting. You shall please the gods." She points down towards the harbour. "Cast it into the Kraken's seas, and He shall claim you as His instrument."

"No," he says thickly, his tongue too big for his mouth. "Not from this fucking town. Not from Ilbarin. To the abyss with this place." He turns to the bodyguards. "Find fucking Dol Martaine! Tell him to get the *Moonchild* ready to depart immediately!"

"My lord, only half the yliaster has yet been load—"

Kraken-fingers close around the Eshdana man's throat. Kraken-fingers squeeze, and the bulging of the man's eyes, the choked gasps that escape his purpling lips are a prayer to the Kraken.

Moonchild departs with the evening tide, pushed clear of the Rock's shallow waters by tugs. In the open ocean, her mighty engines growl, her screws spin, taking her south.

He casts the blade from *Moonchild*'s stern deck, and the Kraken's glass seas accept the offering of the dragon-tooth dagger, swallowing it like they swallowed Ilbarin.

CHAPTER TWENTY-SEVEN

Days pass, and Rasce is still abed.

Baston sat around the house on Lanthorn Street for most of the first day, waiting for the boss to recover. He called a doctor to treat the wound in Rasce's leg, but the injury itself wasn't the problem. They needed a sorcerer. Or a priest.

Or an exorcist, some of the Ghierdana whisper.

Fuck them. The Ghierdana doesn't understand the transformation Spar has wrought through Rasce. It's a thief's city now, a lucky city. Every day, there's another story from the borders of the New City, about how some thief escaped through a gap in a wall that wasn't there before, or a watch patrol managed to get lost in a single blind alleyway for half a day, or how some old woman dreamed of where to dig to find hidden alchemists' treasure. How an alleyway was smooth when a pickpocket fled down it, but the stones turned uneven and treacherous when the watch pursued.

They used to tell tales of the Saint of Knives, the vengeful guardian of the New City. Now, they speak of a more subtle angel.

With Vyr dead, and Rasce drifting in and out of consciousness, the responsibility to run the business falls on Baston and Karla. There are yliaster merchants to bully into line, goods to be smuggled across the zone borders – in the last few weeks, Baston's arranged alliances between Ghierdana smugglers and local sailors and dockers, and the wharfs of the New City are busy day and night. He visits friends he hasn't talked to in years, reactivates old networks, puts coin into the hands of those that can use it. Puts knives and guns into other hands, too.

It's good work, balancing the scales. He can feel the old mechanisms coming back to life, the customs and connections of the Brotherhood returning in a new form.

Baston returns to Lanthorn Street each night and checks on Rasce, who sleeps, and mumbles in his sleep. Karla sits by his bed with medicines, but also a notebook for their ad-hoc oracle. Baston's nightly visits take on the aspect of ritual obeisances, a ceremonial blessing. He takes on a portion of Rasce's authority, speaks for the boss, and no one questions his orders. The other Ghierdana whisper and grumble about an outsider – not even an ash-mark! – having such influence, but Baston's too busy with the business to pay them much heed. The gold of the dragon flows through his fingers – and Karla's. When she's not with Rasce, she's out in the New City, distributing coin and kindness, like the Brotherhood used to share a portion of their thievery with the poor folk of the Wash.

Each night, he looks at Vyr's map of yliaster suppliers. Two clusters, on either side of the city. The dock cluster, a long arc from the ruins of Queen's Point to the new docks under construction up at the Shad Rocks, they've all taken the ash. Everyone from established merchants of good standing with the alchemists like Craddock, to the smallest mudlark with a few casks of old yliaster salvaged from the war, they're under Rasce's control.

Under his control.

He can't deny it feels good, but it's all built on sand. If Rasce wakes, if the dragon returns . . . what then?

Karla comes down and hands him a steaming cup of tea.

They sit in silence for a few minutes, but it's different from the companionable silence they enjoyed in Baston's old house down in the Wash. It's like they're intruders, sneaking into somewhere they don't belong. Or is it only he that feels unworthy of this place? He hasn't reported to Sinter in days – not that he wants to do so. Karla's safe here, but Sinter threatened other people.

"We should check on Mum."

"She's safe. She's with friends." Karla sips her tea. "I'm staying here, in case I'm needed. You should, too."

Baston stares at his hands. He wants someone to tell him what to do, who to hit. That's what he's trained to do, what he's good for. He can organise, he can build the Brotherhood, but it needs a leader with vision. He wants Spar to speak to him, to tell him what needs to be done to make a better city. Who needs to be taken out? Is it Mandel, as Rasce wants? Duttin and her cryptic allies? Gods below, he'd enjoy that. Is it the invaders from Ishmere, and fuck the Armistice?

Tell me what to do. Tell me before this opportunity slips away. Tell me how to atone.

"We need some lads to look after the Ghostmarket. And the old docks. I'm thinking Gunnar and maybe Sten Cantcount," says Karla, breaking the silence.

Both Brotherhood. Both ours. "I'll sort it out."

"There's a ship going to Lyrix next week. We should send Vyr's body home."

"He'll need an escort, I take it."

Karla smiles. "His kin should take him. Full-blood Ghierdana family, not ash-bought. I'm thinking we send some of them home to Lyrix. If you tell them the order came from Rasce, they'll go."

"And what do we do when the dragon comes back, and finds his kin gone, one grand-nephew dead and his Chosen bedridden?"

Karla's about to answer when a messenger hammers at the door. "Boss! Boss! Trouble up the Shad Rocks!"

At the Shad Rocks, Baston finds worse than trouble.

There's a long jetty there, shit-encrusted pylons sunk into the scummy water of Shriveport Bay. Beyond, ramshackle warehouses, thrown up in the aftermath of the Crisis. All owned by an alchemical trader named Barrow. A month ago, Baston waded into that scummy water, held Barrow's face under until he yielded and took the ash, swore eternal loyalty to the Ghierdana.

Now, there's a squad of city watch there, blue cloaks flapping in the sea breeze. On the roof of the warehouse, the fiery lights of a trio of Tallowmen.

Baston studies them through a spyglass. They're freshly cast, like the ones he ran into at Mandel's, unlike the one that attacked Rasce. City watch cloaks nailed on to wax shoulders, hunched like gargoyles. Tallowmen, back on the streets. The bad old days on top of all the new strangeness.

"We came down to collect off Barrow, like you told us. The jacks came at us without warning," says one of the thieves, clutching his wounded arm. "We tried to fight, but they're too fast. Watchmen came after. They're questioning Barrow, yonder." The spyglass shifts to a small office adjoining the warehouse. Baston can make out Barrow's lean features. He's talking to a watch captain.

"How many of ours did they get?" asks Baston.

"They arrested Sten Cantcount and young Leo. Jahn tried to fight, and they cut his throat. Rest of us made it out."

"Back to the New City," orders Baston. "Watch can't follow us back there."

"What about the jacks?"

The Tallowmen are in the livery of the city watch. The last time the candlejacks were allowed out on the streets of Guerdon, just before the Crisis, they were bound by the same rules as the watch. So, by law, the Tallowmen shouldn't be able to pursue them freely across the border into the LOZ. They'd need a pass from Lyrix to cross.

And all of that and two coppers will buy you a two-copper meal. Tallowmen go where they please.

"Run fast," orders Baston. He digs in his pocket, finds a key. "There's a lockup down on Crane Street, in the Wash. Send some lads down there, tell them to bring the contents back up to Lanthorn, all right? Every bit of it."

The thief nods.

"And give me your rifle."

Baston lifts the weapon, tests its weight, its balance as the other thieves flee. They'll need a distraction to get back to the New City safely, but more, there are rules to be observed. Those who take the ash must be loyal to the Ghierdana. To take the ash and then break the oath is unforgivable. A man's oath has to mean something. Baston's own refusal to take the ash is testament to that – if he can't swear allegiance to the Ghierdana and mean it, then he cannot swear, no matter how useful it might be. There's a special hell for oathbreakers.

He cracks open the breech, checks the phlogiston cartridge, slots it back into the receiver.

It's not the first time Baston's killed, far from it. His first kill came when he was fourteen, a thieves' war against the Five Knives gang. They went after Heinreil and his lieutenants, went after Hedan. Went after the families, too. A gullhead broke into Karla's room, he can still see its little black eyes, still hear it screeching. There were Brotherhood men there, guards sent by his father, and they'd wounded the thing, given their lives to save Hedan's kids, but it was Baston who killed it. Hacked its seagull head from its human shoulders. He remembers the tangle of viscera in the neck bursting, high-pressure sprays of blood and gore, staining the world red.

Heinreil apprenticed him to the Fever Knight after that. "The boy's got a talent for it, Hedan." The Fever Knight was Heinreil's enforcer, his leg-breaker. More than legs. Name the limb, name the bone. Name the pain, and the Fever Knight knew how to cause it. In the Knight's service, Baston killed several times, and hurt many, many more, some so badly they'd wished they'd died. Gods below, one boy they broke so badly he sold his body to the alchemists while still alive, volunteered to be sent to the vats to end the pain. It was Heinreil who made him do it, Heinreil who ordered the beating.

Every time he'd killed, it's been on the orders of someone else. At Heinreil's command. At the Knight's. Every kill had soiled him, until he was armoured in filth. He wants to wash it all away, but instead he's wading deeper into the muck. His faith in the tenets of the old Brotherhood a thin cord that he hopes leads to a better place.

Barrow's still talking. Still spilling his guts to the watch. It doesn't matter what he's telling them. It matters that Barrow took the ash once.

He aims the rifle, adjusts the sights. Barrow's face in the crosshairs.

Another step through the muck. A squeeze, and the window turns red.

Baston drops the rifle, turns and runs even as the city strobes with fierce candlelight around him. This part of Guerdon is new, and he doesn't know it well, so he has to guess which alleyways lead uphill over the headland and which come to dead ends. The pursuing Tallowmen are strong and light enough to spring from rooftop to rooftop, their heads flaring searchlights as they hunt for him. Shrieking, one to the other, in high-pitched squeals, like he's being stalked by a pack of boiling tea kettles.

Which way now? If he turns right, he might make it to an outcrop of the New City, a curious little cove on Shriveport Bay. Ghierdana ships dock there now. There's a mess of buildings between him and the cove, though, a warren of sheds and lean-tos, built by rough folk out of Mattaur. If he gets lost, or if anyone slows him down, the jacks will have him.

The other option's a ghoul tunnel, straight ahead. It runs through the headland like a worm through an apple. Once, he wouldn't have hesitated at taking the tunnel – this close to the surface, there's little chance of running into feral ghouls. But now, the ghouls are working with the watch—

—A flicker of light on the rooftop to his right, and the decision's made for him. Baston lowers his head and sprints towards the tunnel, legs pounding, huffing like a freight train. Behind him, the Tallowmen closing, wax limbs tireless, the fires of hell behind their faces.

He's swallowed by the darkness of the tunnel, but that darkness is all too brief. It's driven away by leaping light as one of the Tallowmen follows him in. Candle flickers on carved green walls, damp, beaded with water that shines like jewels, but the floor's slick with slime.

He's not going to make it. The border's at the end of the tunnel. Hell, for all he knows the Lyrixians have barricaded the far end anyway; it'd be just his luck. He runs ahead blindly, slipping on the wet rocks, splashing in the slime, picking himself up again. Somewhere in the distance, the sound of water gushing through some pipe. Maybe they'll flood the tunnel, wash him and the Tallowman back down into Shriveport Bay. He'll drown like Fae did: wouldn't be a bad end.

The Tallowman catches him, trips him up and he's down in the mud again. A fist slams into his stomach, winding him. It catches him by the hair and slams his face into the wall, then throws him to the ground again. Giggling to itself, knife in hand, candlelight turning the bright blade to fire.

"THIS ONE IS NOT FOR YOU."

The words come out of Baston's mouth, but they're not his words, not his voice. They taste of earth and rot and meat.

The Tallowman freezes for a long moment, its flicking flame the only movement. The creature contemplates the voice without fear. Wax fingers probe Baston's throat with surprising gentleness, as if amazed he could produce such a noise.

"LEAVE."

The Tallowman flips its knife around, pushes Baston's chin up, as if determined to dissect his larynx. Then it convulses, dropping the knife, scrambling backwards across the floor of the tunnel like a startled insect. The flame in its head flares, then turns a lurid blue, Its mouth opens, and it splutters gobbets of hot wax. It screeches something that might be a few words, then turns and runs.

Baston lies there in the mud for a moment, his whole body aching. The voice vomits out of him again.

"BASTON. TELL YOUR MASTER THAT I MUST MEET WITH HIM. TELL HIM I KNOW THINGS HE DOES NOT. TELL HIM I WANT TO SPEAK WITH SPAR."

Rasce wakes, jarred from his sleep by dreams of ghouls. He opens his eyes, but the room's too dark to see, and for a moment he's confused – is he in the tunnel near Shriveport? Or is the tunnel part of him?

He opens his inner eye, taps into Spar's perception, and sees everything. Sees the body in the bed, the stained sheets. He has to swim down towards it, reclaim the flesh – and then he's in his bedroom on Lanthorn Street. It's night outside, and the streets are slick with rain. It was daylight and dry a moment ago – he's lost time again.

No. It's Spar who fears being adrift in time, Rasce reminds himself. The lines between the two are blurring.

"Was I—" his throat is dry and painful, his voice a croak.

"Sssh. Don't move." Karla kneels at his bedside, pulling the coverlet back. Unwrapping a bandage on his leg. Pain shoots through him again.

"My leg! What's wrong with it?"

Karla doesn't look at him. Instead, she begins to change the dressing. "You stabbed yourself. You'd stabbed the walls a few times, then you started on yourself. Baston had to wrestle the knife off you."

Rasce grapples with the memory. "I had to do it. The pain helped. It was like a sacrifice."

"I know, I know. Stay still. Rest."

The wound, when revealed, is deep and ugly, a gash in the muscle of his thigh almost to the bone. Karla gently cleans out the wound, slathers it with a healing ointment, then opens another jar and starts to rub a gritty slime into the skin around the injury. The ointment is numbing, making him feel detached from the experience of the pain.

"What's that?" asks Rasce drowsily. There's something odd about the injury. The skin around it is stiff, encrusted with greyish pus, and seems to glisten in the dim light.

"Alkahest," says Karla. "For the stone skin. It's just a little pebbling."

"I have the plague?" Horror rushes through him, a cold bile-flood carrying memories that are not his – memories of Spar's slow corruption by the Stone Plague.

Karla shakes her head, puts a reassuring hand on his chest. "I got to it in time, but I need to keep treating it. You've got to stay still and rest. It's all right. Baston will handle things."

He wants to protest. He tries to get up, but she pushes him back down. She puts a cup to his lips; a bitter draught, thick and medicinal, and it washes him back down into oblivion.

CHAPTER TWENTY-EIGHT

This stretch of coast is a seawall of mountains, an absurd profusion of peaks. Cari can't recall any mountain-gods of Ul-Taen, but one must have walked here. Or perhaps some expeditionary force from the north brought the miracles of Uriah Mountainmaker with them. Certainly, these mountains weren't there the last time Cari passed this way, but Myri's unperturbed. "Godswar," she says, and shrugs.

They find a place to land *Tymneas*, a little cove where two mountains have toppled against each other, creating a gap in the seawall. As they sail through the titanic arch of stone, Cari glimpses white-furred apes clinging to the rockface far overhead. The creatures scream and hiss at the boat as they pass, and their faces are skulls.

Beyond the mountain wall, the lands are half familiar. The salt marshes and dunes of the Ul-Taen coast, the remnants of old roads and settlements dotting the broken landscape like scattered pebbles.

The other half is nightmare. Chunks of broken heavens, fallen from the sky and made material in the moment of their destruction. Malformed miracles leaking into reality, scabs of divine works. God-touched creatures crawl across the land, screaming hymns of gratitude. Strange plants grow, fiery-red bushes that ignite when touched, mountain-flowers disgorging virulent blue poison on to unseen winds. They travel through the meadowlands of some hunting god, through the burned-out stacks of a seemingly infinite library, through a desert of broken glass.

They are not alone here. Ghosts dwell in this land, the shades of divinities broken over and over until there is nothing left but mindless fragments. They move with the wind, trying to impose their pattern on to whatever they happen upon. Pebbles spontaneously pile themselves into little mountains, dust clouds take on the aspect of wolves and serpents. Tufts of grass become strings of angelic lyres. At one point, the stolen aethergraph tunes into some divine frequency and goes mad, keys hammering out incomprehensible prophecies until Myri finds the off switch.

Carillon and Myri, too, risk being remade by these vanished gods. Both women are fortified against the touch of the divine – one through her sorcery, the other through the remnants of her sainthood, through her eldritch heritage, and both have enough willpower to resist direct assault by these diminished spirits. These gods are still perilous in an oblique manner; at times, Cari's attention strays from the dusty path, and alien thoughts infiltrate her mind. Once, she imagines what it would be like to tear Myri's throat out with her teeth, to howl and call her vanished pack (Rat would howl back at her, she knows, and Adro if he was drunk enough). Another time, she finds herself reciting poetry, her words so sweet that honey comes dripping from her mouth. She has the presence of mind to keep reciting for a few minutes after the fit fades, and Myri collects the honey so they have something to eat at least.

"We can't make it all the way by land," mutters Myri. "Maybe we make for the coast again once we're south of Ram's Head. Find another ship for the last leg to Khebesh."

She sounds like Cari. Just get south of Ram's Head. Just get to Ilbarin City.

Khebesh is always just out of reach, a retreating mirage.

Other thoughts that cross Cari's mind are equally disturbing, but they're all her own. She thinks about Adro, and hopes he's recovering from his wounds. Thinks about Ren and Ama, and how glad she is that they never came here. The child, especially, would be vulnerable. Children are impressionable, easy clay for the gods to work. *Jermas meant to use you when you were nine*, she remembers, and thinking of her grandfather puts her in mind of the Crawling Ones. Would Twelve Suns Bleeding have been able to find a better path to Khebesh?

Most of all, she thinks of Spar, and how far from home she's strayed.

Cari suggests they head south for the market town of Erephis. It's years since she was last there, and all she remembers of it is watching soldiers from Ul-Taen marching through the square on their way to war with Ishmere. The crowds cheering, and robed priests scattering holy sand in their path. Back then, the Godswar was far away. Now, it's all around them, in their lungs, on their skin, seeping into their souls. Writ on the ruined world around them. And this still isn't the front lines – the real fighting's moved back north-east, she guesses, towards the heart of Ul-Taen. Ever since the Sacred Realm of Ishmere lost their war goddess and had to fall back, the resurgent deities of these conquered lands have reasserted themselves, broken gods shambling to war once more.

Cari shivers; she killed the war goddess, she launched the last god-bomb. How much of the devastation around her is her fault? It's not like she has any love for Ishmere and its mad gods, but there's still that sickening doubt in the back of her mind that she's only made things worse. How do you trust your actions when you can't predict the consequences? Fuck it, look at Artolo – if she'd killed the fucker stone dead back in Guerdon, then everything would be different.

"Carillon. Watch yourself," warns Myri. Carillon glances down, realises she's nearly walked straight into a patch of poisonous flowers. "Stick to the path. And let me lean on you." Myri's hand, trembling and scabby, threads through the crook of Cari's elbow, but the sorceress is hardly any burden at all. She's burned hollow.

They cross the broken land. The spirits of this place seem especially offended by Cari's presence. The same feeling of friction and pressure that she felt before encountering Usharet, but it's a constant here, like the air's made of sandpaper that only affects her soul. Several times, godhusks manifest to strike at her. Most of these manifestations are more pathetic than dangerous, the god appearing as nothing more than a cloud of dust, a single serpent that speaks with a human voice, or a shambling mound of rubble that crawls slowly across the landscape towards them. Other manifestations, they flee or fight, Myri's spells flashing in the twilight. Mostly, though, it's just mud and dust and shattered stone. A no-gods-land where nothing lives.

The fighting seems worse to the west. That way lies the Sacred Realm of Ishmere. It's over the horizon, too distant to affect them directly. The sky over there looks like it's on fire, and Cari discovers she can't sleep when facing that way without being troubled by nightmares of a hammer falling on her. She wakes screaming about the judgement of High Umur.

They do not go west. They go south, stumbling for days through the ever-shifting lands.

Erephis is gone. "I think a really, really big snail ran over it," says Myri, and Carillon wished she didn't agree. By the edge of the glistening canyon, Myri bargains with some ghosts, trading a handful of coins for the location of a cache of food and news of the wider war.

"What the fuck do ghosts want with cash?" mutters Cari as she digs a handful of tin cans out of a mudbank. There are more bodies buried here, too, the flesh seared by slime, and the bones turn to mush in her hands as she pulls them out of the way. A military expedition, she guesses. She salvages a miraculously intact jacket from one of them.

"The Empire of Haith broke the local death-god, years ago,"

explains Myri. "It was the custom of these people to put coins on the eyes of the dead, to pay for their passage into the afterlife. The Haithi forced the goddess to only accept Imperial currency, but now Haith is in retreat and it's hard to get Haithi coins this far south. So, the dead souls go unclaimed and the dead walk the earth." She counts out her remaining coins, hides them away. "Just in case we need to pay for passage elsewhere. Anyway, they said there are living folk a day's travel south. We'll head that way."

Cari brushes mud, ichor and soldier-bits off a can and tries to read the label. "Don't we want to stay the fuck away from people? Anyone we meet here is probably going to try to kill us, right?"

Myri injects another vial of her medication before answering. "The presence of the living to the south implies that conditions there currently permit life to exist in that region. That's not true everywhere in the Godswar."

On the fifth day in hell, they come to the ghost of the city of Gissa. Even Cari knows that Gissa was destroyed, ten years ago or more, Gissa of the red roofs and the counting-houses, Gissa of the temples and the red walls, Gissa of the deep wells.

Gissa should be a lot further south.

They hide in a ditch and watch the city march past them. People, thousands of them, dragging sacks of rubble and brick, shoulders bowed under cloaks of red slate. Skins red with brick dust. They march in columns that mimic the layout of vanished streets – and a presence moves with them, invisible forces flattening the ground ahead of them, stamping the map of the crawling city into the mud. Some hold street signs like battle standards, others stumble through the mud with absurd pomposity, clad in the ornate robes of civic officials, of judges and councillors. There's a carnival touch to the whole procession, wild abandon mixed with civic pride. All of their faces, from the starveling children to the oldest greybeard, touched with divine ecstasy. They live in Gissa, and Gissa is the heavenly city.

Cari feels that sandpaper sensation again, and presses her face into the mud as a great temple-barge passes. It's a huge pyramidal temple, the house of the civic god, mounted on gigantic runners of teak wood and dragged by a crowd of ecstatic worshippers. Atop the temple stands a young man, beautiful and shining, chosen of the god of the city of Gissa.

"Tell me when they've gone," whispers Cari, but before Myri can answer the saint raises his left hand. Trumpets sound, the earth shakes and the city settles around them. Their ditch is now surrounded on all sides by the memory of a ruined city, by the shambling crowds of the displaced and the divine.

After a whispered conversation in the ditch, they agree that Cari should sneak out at twilight and try to find how close they are to the edge of this mobile city. Myri's too weak to move quickly, so she'll stay in their hiding place, drawing protective wards to ensure she stays undetected.

"If you can't find a quick way out, come back here," says Myri.

"Maybe we can wait 'em out," suggests Cari. "Hide here until the city moves on."

"For all we know, they might be here for months. I don't know why they're digging in here."

"All right then. I'll go. Just give me the money."

"You want to go *shopping*?"

Cari shrugs. "It's a city. There'll be a market. At the very fucking least, we need a can opener."

"It's not a city. It's the ghost of a city, preserved by the husk of the city's god."

"People still need to buy shit. Give me the coins."

"No."

"All right, I'll steal."

Myri curses and hands over the pouch of coin, which Cari takes as a damning indictment of her talents as a pickpocket.

"You'll move faster if you leave your pack." The fucking book is still slung on Cari's back, along with the aethergraph, tied across her shoulders with a length of line salvaged from *Tymneas*. The rough rope digs into her skin, and the weight of the damn thing does slow her down. At the same time, she instantly imagines Myri staggering off with the book, sneaking out of this hallucinatory city the way she crept out of Guerdon years ago.

"You're right." Cari unties the knot, lets the bundle fall. Then she darts forward, grabs a handful of Myri's vials of medicine, stuffs them into her pocket as insurance. Myri scowls at her, but is too exhausted to object. "See you in a few hours."

The twilight makes the city even weirder. There are pillars of piled stones everywhere that seem to mark street corners, a few low walls, too. Cari can't tell if these stones were carried all the way by the people of the city, or if the stones themselves walked along as part of the procession. Or maybe the stones were always here, only now they've been incorporated into the city, structure imposed on chaos. Many of them are topped with bone fragments, which put her in mind of sacrificial altars, and that's always guaranteed to put her in a great fucking mood. This place makes her skin crawl.

In the dim light, the suggestion of structures loom out at her. Ghosts of vanished temples and houses, giving her fleeting impressions of mighty buildings all around her. Godshit, why did they have to run into a city-god? It's an uncomfortable reminder of her grandfather's plan for Guerdon, to transmute the Black Iron Gods into something tame and civilised, civic spirits to guard the city. A reminder, too, of Spar. That boy atop the rolling temple is like she used to be, an avatar of the city, their version of the Saint of Knives. Only this place is a dead city tethered to a mad and broken god.

No. Nothing like me. Nothing like Spar, she tells herself.

Also, fuck you, Myri. Told you there'd be a market. Cari passes under an archway decorated with great bronze horses – no, under the *memory* of an archway – and wanders through the market. There aren't any stalls, just merchants and hawkers standing around in the places stalls should be, like they're play-acting. It's all mummery – Cari watches a line of people pretend to eat at the counter of a nonexistent food stall, shoving imaginary food into their mouths, chewing and swallowing with gusto. One of them lets out a belch, and his breath smells of meat and spices. A low-grade miracle – for them, the illusion of food is enough to sustain them. She wonders what would happen to these poor people if they left the city and the realm of their city-god. Nothing pleasant.

One passer-by grabs her arm, gestures at an empty spot on the far side of the market. "Look! Are the fountains not beautiful tonight? And tomorrow may never come! Join me for a cup of wine, and we shall celebrate Rhan-Gis!" He's dressed in tattered rags, a long beard tangled with twigs and thorns, but he talks like he's some handsome courtier. The remnants of the cloak around his shoulders look like it was once an expensive garment.

"Very beautiful," agrees Cari, in the same tone of voice she'd say *nice horsey* to a slavering raptequine, "but I have to, uh, go and pray at the temple."

"All these streets are His temple," says the man, "and so all acts are acts of worship!" His tone leaving no doubt what sort of act he has in mind. Cari twists away from him, stepping into the press of traffic, vanishing into the crowd. The flow of people in the marketplace skirts around the empty spot, and Cari spots some young women sitting as if bathing their feet in the dust. The fountain exists for these people. Divine madness.

Thunder rolls, somewhere in the distance. Cari tenses – such omens often accompany divine intervention, miracle bombardments. But the people of Gissa ignore it, secure in the knowledge that their city is inviolable, that Gissa will never fall. No foe will ever breach their walls.

She does find one woman who's selling actual food – a rack of dried fish and eels.

"Do you take these?" The Haithi coins. The fishmonger says something in Taenish. Cari nods, uncomprehending, suddenly alarmed – if everyone in the city is a worshipper of the god of Gissa, then maybe they can instantly spot strangers. But the woman smiles and speaks in broken Haithi. "Yes, yes, praise Rhan Gis."

"Where'd you get the fish?"

"Little village just east of here. Yhandin." Uncertainty creases the woman's face – Cari's question exposes an inconsistency in the miracle of the city. If Gissa is as it once was, before the Godswar, then it's located far from the village of Yhandin. The question forces the woman to complete actual reality. Cari grabs the fish and hurries away before she raises any more existential doubts.

Finding the edge of Gissa is harder than she expected. The city can't be that big – it's not even a fucking city, it's one minor god and his band of deluded worshippers, all dragging the corpse of the city with them – but space and time twist on the imagined streets. Cari can see the city walls in the distance outlined against the horizon, which is a whole other level of fucked she's not going to contemplate right now, but she can't find her way there. Straight streets don't run straight here.

The stars that come out in the night sky above Gissa are not the same ones she saw over Ilbarin.

Defeated, she turns back towards Myri's hiding place, and things instantly get worse. Her first clue is the fact that she can now see *buildings* around her, full-on towers and citadels, not the ruins of five minutes ago. At first, she guesses that she's spent so long in Gissa that she's fallen under the sway of the shared delusion, but then she hears a beautiful voice like a trumpet call, and her stomach sinks even as her heart sings.

"Bring the unclean one to me," commands Rhan-Gis, His voice echoing from the stones around her, resonating with her very soul. "She is nearby. I see her." It's the saint from the temple, and it would seem the fucker can do her trick, Spar's trick, the seeing-through-stone miracle. She doesn't know what "nearby" means—

As if conjured by the saint's commands, a group of soldiers appears at the top of the street. She'd almost mistake them for Stone Men, their bodies marked with stony growths, but in a flash she sees the distinction. These guys were all mortally wounded in the past – that one's got a wide gash in his belly, that one was stabbed through the heart, another doesn't have a fucking head – and the wounds were filled with pieces of the city. They've got chunks of brickwork and mortar shoved into their bodies, working as muscles and organs and, apparently, a head. One of them points at her with a hand salvaged from some marble statue, and Blockhead swivels to look at Cari like the thing's got eyes.

Fuuuuuuuuuuuuck this.

She runs.

Sprinting forward, flagstones giving way to mud beneath her feet. The resurrected city fades as she gets further away from Rhan-Gis, returning to the mummery of ruins and lunatics. The guards keep chasing her with equal zeal, though, regardless of her perception of their surroundings. "Halt, in the name of the city!" cries one, and she guesses they're still seeing the dream of Gissa. The guard's words have power here, too – her limbs become leaden weights, almost too heavy to move, the streets grabbing at her feet. She can barely move, and the guards are gaining.

She staggers around a "corner", around one of the piles of stone, and then throws herself to her right. According to the rules of the imaginary city, she's now inside a building, even though the streets are just lines drawn in the mud here. The guards run past her, even though she's lying right there. The guards don't share their saint's power of perception. To them, the ghost of a wall is a wall. There are downsides to seeing heaven, she thinks, lips too numb to laugh.

Cari lies there in the mud waiting for the paralysis to fade. She listens to distant drumming, interspersed with horns and trumpets.

It reminds her of the Ishmeric temples back in occupied Guerdon; there must be some sort of ceremony or celebration happening at that big temple, which probably isn't a good thing. She hides as dusk gives way to darkness. The night sky's riven by fractures, and the stars shudder as gods fight far far above.

A smaller procession halts outside her hiding place. A dozen or so citizens of Gissa, thin and ragged. Four of them pallbearers, carrying the body of a young woman; another walking behind, carrying a little bundle pressed to her chest. Two of them mime lifting tools, swinging them against the nonexistent wall like pickaxes. If there really was a wall there, Cari would be covered in debris and dust. The other mourners kneel by the wall, pretending to clear fragments of brick. They're lifting nothing but memories, but still they huff and strain. Still their fingers bleed.

They lay the body down in the imaginary hole they cut in the wall, then brick it up again. Every god has their particular rites and methods for consuming the souls of the dead. Some use particular funerary rituals, like this. The city-god has its worshippers interred in the walls, blood mixed with mortar.

The dead woman's eyes stare blankly at Cari. The woman's belly is swollen, and there's a lingering smell of old blood. She died in childbirth. That bundle must be the newborn. Gods below, what sort of life is that? At best, a lifetime spent wandering this god-torn world, blindly worshipping Rhan-Gis, force-fed tales of the glories of Gissa and the ghost of harvests pasts, until the walls close. Ilbarin's better than this, and Ilbarin's a prison camp in a dying land.

If Eladora were here, lying in the mud instead of Cari, she'd stammer about confluences of geography and history, wealth and culture. Guerdon was spared because it was sheltered by Haith, able to stay neutral through economic independence. She'd talk about how a series of quirks of fate led to Guerdon being the epicentre of the alchemical revolution. But it's all just fancy words for luck.

Cari thought she was unlucky to be born – fuck it, admit it, *made*, not born. She fled, left everything behind and called herself unlucky for having to start from nothing. But she looks into the eyes of the dead woman and sees that starting from nothing is a blessing.

The New City was supposed to be a place where people could be safe. Spar made it for the people of Guerdon's poor districts. He tried in his dying moments to fulfil the promise of the Brotherhood, but that's still thinking small. She's guilty of the same sin, Cari thinks. When she first discovered her gift for visions, she used it to get revenge on Heinreil and bring down the old master of the Brotherhood. And after, when she was the Saint of Knives, the vigilante guardian of the New City . . . what did that achieve, really? She hurt some bad people, stopped anyone getting their hands on the remaining Black Iron Gods, but was that enough? She and Spar, together against the world, but everything she did drained him. Every miracle ate his soul away.

The world's too big to handle, too broken to fix. Even when she had power, she didn't know where to start.

Her face is wet with tears. Angrily, she wipes them away.

Get up, she urges herself. *Get to Khebesh. Then go back and do better.*

Hawse thought she was worth helping. Hawse saved her.

And in the camp, she was able to save Adro, right? She sacrificed herself to get him a healer. That has to count for something.

A city starts with one brick laid on another. Get to Khebesh. Save Spar.

She pulls herself upright, leaning on the dead woman's tomb until she's able to stand.

Take all you can. Use it to better ends.

This time, she ignores the streets. She steps over the imaginary walls, refusing to let the delusions of mad gods shape her world. She walks in a line straight as a gunshot, heading for Myri's hiding place.

Make your own luck.

But when she gets there, the sorceress is gone.

CHAPTER TWENTY-NINE

S hriveport wasn't the only place they got hit.

In the house on Lanthorn Street, another half-dozen reports of attacks. All outside the borders of the Lyrixian Occupation Zone. Craddock's is gone – there are Tallowmen on the streets of Glimmerside, along the border of the HOZ. Craddock was arrested and taken to the Last House; one of his sons is now in charge. The other yliaster merchants in Glimmerside and along Mercy Street, gone, too. The thieves bring the bodies of the fallen back to Lanthorn Street, so the ghouls don't get them. Baston orders them brought down to the cool cellar, to be laid alongside Vyr's wrapped corpse.

Along the waterfront, Tallowmen have raided the warehouses, hitting anyone connected with the Ghierdana or the Brotherhood in a concerted effort to push the Ghierdana and their allies back beyond the Armistice Line. They came in from the sea, on city watch gunboats. Bloody hard there; the lads got the cache of weapons from the Crane Street lockup in time, and were able to fight back against the Tallows. The candles are stronger and faster than any human, and bullets don't do much to wax that doesn't bleed or break, but there are alchemical weapons that do the trick. Knife-smoke to trim a wick, and transmutation clouds can melt wax as well as flesh. Phlogiston-shells work, too. Fight fire with fire that's on fire.

The Tallowmen fell back to their boats. First time Baston's ever heard of the jacks retreating, but, then, the thieves never had this sort of firepower before. But one victory among a half-dozen defeats is scant comfort.

"How's Rasce?" he asks Karla for the hundredth time.

She shakes her head. "No better." She glances at the walls, the ceiling. "We need to talk about what we're going to do now."

"The jacks aren't crossing the border into the LOZ."

"Not yet," echoes Karla, "but they're everywhere else in the free city. Kicking us out of everywhere we've taken."

"We still have the old docks."

Karla makes a derisive noise. "You've got them tonight. Who knows about tomorrow? Or next week? And when Rasce's Great-Uncle comes back and finds everything's fallen apart, we're fucked. Either we staunch the bleeding, get back all we've lost *and* take down Mandel, or . . . " She lowers her voice to a whisper.

"Or?"

"Baston, you've got the loyalty of the thieves. We've got the Ghierdana's money. We could go."

"You shouldn't talk like this." He killed Barrow only a few hours ago for betraying his oath. Karla took the ash, too. If she runs, the Ghierdana will be after her forever. They'll want to make an example of her. The image of his sister dead, her throat cut by a dragon-tooth knife . . . He shakes his head. "Go and see if you can wake Rasce. I ran into Lord Rat earlier, I think. He wants to talk."

Karla wrinkles her nose at the mention of ghouls. "What's going on?"

"I don't know. Magic shit." Baston rubs his head. His hair is rank with sewer-water. "I'm going to go and talk to the other dragons. Convince 'em they're in danger, too, maybe."

"Is that going to achieve anything?" She kneads the back of his neck. He reaches up, takes her hand, holds it.

"Come with me. You've taken the ash. What did Rasce say – it buys a measure of indulgence? Let's see what they'll do for you."

*

The New City juts out into the harbour of Guerdon, skirted by a towering seawall. There are few places to moor a ship in the original design (if the word design can be applied to the dream of stone that is the New City), but Guerdon is always quick to adapt. Ugly concrete platforms, stained with alchemical run-off, now abut the seawall. Most of the ships docked here are Lyrixian military vessels, taking advantage of the only secure port friendly to them in the west. They'll refuel here, then steam south, laden with supplies for the Lyrixian war effort against Ulbishe and Khenth. The strange sight of convoys escorted by Ghierdana dragons, instead of being preyed on by them.

There are two dragons on the docks, Thyrus and Carancio, lazing in the afternoon sun. There are few places in the New City where a dragon can stretch out to its full length, and Thyrus sprawls along the dock. Carancio has slithered into the water, his tail snaking off into the mud. His wings are extended to dry in the sun; he has propped himself up by his elbows, like a fat man in a steam bath. Beside him, a cargo ship newly arrived from Lyrix unloads crates of supplies – most of which are destined for the markets of Guerdon, not the war. Lyrixian silk and jewels pass through Ghierdana hands to be smuggled across the border into the city proper, to come washing back as coin and armaments. The dockworkers have to shuffle awkwardly to avoid treading on Carancio's wingtip; Baston fights the urge to hurry over and give them a hand shifting the boxes.

Each dragon is accompanied by a host of Ghierdana attendants and other bodyguards. The dragons are more dangerous than any assassin, but there are other forms of assault. A brigade of mercenary priests chant and ring bells, in the hopes of disrupting any divination miracles targeting the pair. Hired sorcerers, too, ready with defensive wards and dampening rods. A cowled figure in a porcelain mask stands near Carancio – a Crawling One. Baston hasn't seen one in months.

A few passengers disembark from the Lyrixian ship and gingerly pass between the dragons. One – stooped and thin, with a broken nose – casts a curious glance at Baston and Karla, and seems almost to recognise them, but he hurries on without a word.

The dragon Carancio, too, notices the pair. He beckons them with a lazy wave of a claw that could rip through steel armour like tissue paper.

"Look, Thyrus – Taras' Chosen sends his servants to treat with us."

"It is the way of this city. These people have no understanding of civility or respect. Is that not right, little ones?" Thyrus rolls her neck to fix Baston with the full glare of her reptilian eyes.

"We need to talk," says Baston, awkwardly. "Sharpish. It's business."

Karla steps in. She sweeps back her hair to show her forehead, marked with fresh ash. She raises her voice, projects like she's treading the boards of the Great Metropolitan Theatre in Bryn Avane. "Great ones, I have heard many accounts of your magnificence from your kinfolk. Carancio, Bane of Cities. Thyrus, Queen of Calamity. I beg leave to address you in the name of Rasce, Chosen of Taras. The matter is urgent."

Thyrus smirks, then furls her long body. She extends one wing, mantles it into a tent. Baston hesitates for a moment, then Karla gives him a sharp shove, pushing him forward. The dragon curls around him, enfolding him. All he can see is Thyrus' eyes, glowing with inner fire, inches away from him.

"Speak." Her voice is a subsonic vibration, shaking his bones.

"City watch Tallowmen are attacking us. So far, they haven't crossed the border into the occupation zone, but—"

"'Us?' I smell no ash upon your brow, mortal. You are not Ghierdana. You are not Eshdana. You are nothing to me. I could swallow you whole, here and now, and no one would gainsay me."

"I'd taste foul." Baston opens his jacket, revealing a metal cylinder tucked inside. "Withering dust." He has no idea if the alchemical poison would work on a dragon, but at this range, it certainly wouldn't be pleasant. "Rasce is my employer, and my friend. He's saved my life, and I've saved his."

Thyrus snorts, and the wing-tent fills with sulphur. It's hard to breathe. "And yet you have not sworn fealty to him. He must be a fool to trust one such as you." The dragon yawns. "Rasce has brought this misfortune on himself. You mortals are hasty and lack wisdom. It was careless of my brother to leave the child without adequate supervision."

"That's as maybe. But now they're attacking the Ghierdana."

"The things of wax have not crossed the border. They are attacking you and your cutpurses, not my kin."

"They attacked Rasce, too, on Glimmerside. A jack nearly cut his throat. And Vyr got killed down on Mercy. And let me tell you something – the last time they let the Tallowmen loose on the streets, it wasn't long before there was martial law. Curfews, mass arrests, raids. All sorts of trouble."

"That was before the Godswar came here. They would not dare do so now."

"Maybe. Maybe not. Jacks are hard to keep under control. And even if they don't cross the border, you're not just a *soldier*, are you? Not just here for the war effort. You've got business, same as me. How hard do you think it'll be to smuggle goods across when there are Tallowmen watching?"

The dragon growls in irritation, which Baston takes as an acknowledgement of his point.

"My lads know the city. That's why Rasce recruited us. We can help your family, too."

"And in exchange? What will this cost?"

"Your presence down on Mercy Street stopped the city watch from arresting us when Vyr was killed. So, we need you and Carancio to watch over the old docks. There are still a few places in Glimmerside they haven't gone after yet. And—"

"You ask too much," says Thyrus. Her wing begins to open, letting in the world again.

"You don't have to fucking do anything!" shouts Baston in her face. "Just be there! They won't dare act while there's a dragon present!"

"Unlike my feckless brother," hisses Thyrus, suddenly rearing her head above him, flames flickering in her nostrils, "I still play my part in this bargain. I have responsibilities to my children back on the isles, and so I fly to war for Lyrix. I keep the peace of the Armistice. I owe little to my brother's chattels—" she snarls at Karla, "and I owe *nothing* to you."

That night, they lose the old docks.

The Tallowmen attack again, but this time they come via the ghoul tunnels, cutting the thieves off from the New City. It's like the burning of Dredger's yard all over again, recapitulated in a nightmare. The scorched ruins of the yard are alive with dancing flames again, only this time the flames pursue Baston and his crew, chasing them through the alleyways and warehouses, a whirl of knives and fixed, distended grins.

Some of the thieves try to retreat up Heavengut Wynd, just like before, but some bastard's informed the Ishmerians they're coming. The demigod Cruel Urid stands at the top of the stairs, spear in hand, judging the unworthy wretches who flee up the stairs. None are deemed worthy to enter heaven. Caught between the candles and the demigod, they perish. Baston hears their screams across the night. Their souls forfeit to the Ishmeric gods.

Baston leads another group west, towards the spires of St Storm. It's not St Storm's any longer, not since Kraken took it, but he knows those spires – and knows the little streets around them, the ones that slope down to the shore. There, on the edge of the IOZ, there are still a few fishing boats, near the houses of the harbour-priests who bless the ships and pray for fair winds.

They steal these boats and cut back east, trying to thread a course between the Tallowmen on the docks and the city watch patrol boats in the deeper harbour. Oars dip into black water; thieves hunch against spotlights. One boy, his stomach cut by a Tallowman, coughs wetly and dies at Baston's feet, the warmth of his blood soaking through the leather of Baston's boots. They heave him overboard. Let him go with Fae, the poor lad, and they can't afford the extra weight.

One of the Tallowmen hears the splash. The crazed monster takes a running jump, leaping impossibly far out into the harbour, a grasshopper arc, head-flame like a signal flare. It falls short. Splashes loudly in the water, thrashing around and shrieking, until a wave quenches the fire in its wax skull and it freezes, bobbing up and down. Its fellow Tallowmen cluster along the edge of the docks, straining to get closer to their quarries.

Searchlights find Baston's boats. The city watch bellow some command, an order to surrender. The whole city's against them, watch and jacks, gods and governments. *Rasce went too far*, part of him says, *pushed them too hard*, but the truth is this was always going to happen. There's no place for Baston's kin in this new Guerdon, this city ruled by gods and alchemists who think they're gods. Rasce just made it happen faster.

The city watch boats close in, their alchemical engines driving them, faster and stronger than the arms of the rowers. Acrid smoke drifts across the water. A searchlight falls on them like a blazing eye.

A loudhailer crackles, calls out.

"SURRENDER."

Baston stands, casts off his coat. Braces himself.

Opens fire.

The gun's a heavy repeater, fresh from the foundries. A beautiful piece of engineering, really. Something the Fever Knight would have appreciated, a weapon for laying waste to one's foes. You could never get a gun like this for love nor money on the streets of Guerdon in Heinreil's day, but the city's changed, and Ghierdana coffers run deep.

The thunder of the repeater deafens him. The recoil nearly sends him backwards over the side. The nearest city watch cutter lights up in a dazzling shower of sparks, bullets ricocheting off the hull, smashing through the cabin. The searchlight explodes, and he turns his fire on the other boats. "Row!" he roars. "Row for fucking home!"

And stroke by stroke they draw closer to the New City, last refuge of scoundrels.

Spar can feel himself fracturing again. His mind falling apart, his thoughts wandering off and never coming back. *I'm dying.* Rasce still acts as an anchor, but he's drifting, like an anchor skipping over the seabed instead of holding fast. He's a maelstrom in Spar's mind, pulling Spar into darkness instead of giving him a beacon to rally around.

He's coming apart. His consciousness is already overstretched, spread all around the New City, and now it's cracking under the strain. Even *thinking* has a cost now, he can tell. He's a clockwork engine running down.

He's been here before, when it was his body and not his mind that was dying – but that doesn't have to change anything. When he lived, he resolved once to spend his remaining days helping the Brotherhood, fighting the Black Iron Gods that threatened the city. He fought to save Cari, and she ended up saving him instead. So, if he's got only a little of this strange second life left, he'll use it like he used his first life.

It's tricky. Observing is less costly than thinking, and thinking is less costly than acting. He has to build instincts, autonomic responses, cut his conscious mind out of the loop as much as possible. Simple rules first – *help running thieves escape. Block the Tallowmen. Give shelter. Help those who want to be found, and those who seek to be lost.* The Tallowmen come like falling stars, like a siege, each burning wick an incoming shell, and he deflects them as best he can. No stairs for you, candle-man! This alleyway has a doorway at the end when a thief passes through, but not when you follow! And those roof slates are treacherous, and prone to falling on wax heads.

In truth, he's unsure how successful he is. Without Rasce as a focus, time and space become distorted. He reacts to block one Tallowman, and a day later the streets change. Or a day before. Or he moves the wrong stone, warps the city the wrong way. He observes far more than he acts, for few of the attackers cross into the part of the New City where he has the most power.

It's easy for him to observe. Easy for a Stone Man to cut himself off. Loneliness and isolation are old companions of his.

His thoughts spin out, escaping him. Vanishing like runaway children down twisted alleyways of memory or might-have-been. Phantom conversations haunt him. He imagines long conversations with Rat. His old friend is the one other soul in Guerdon who might understand his situation. Both he and Rat underwent strange transformations during the Crisis. Spar became the New City, and Rat became an Elder Ghoul, something closer to dragon or godspawn than mortal.

Rat wouldn't see it that way, of course. Like most ghouls, Rat is a survivor at heart. Relentlessly practical, unsentimental, even amoral. Rat would speak in his old voice, the voice he has in Spar's memory, not the borrowed heralds the Elder Ghoul uses. *You should have died when you fell from the Seamarket. Anything that keeps you going after that is life. I haven't eaten you. That's how you know you're alive.* And Rat would grin, showing his corpse-tearing teeth, and his eyes would burn with this fierce faith in Spar, this belief that his friend could endure anything.

Spar observes Rat moving through the New City. *Now. This is happening now.* Sees him speaking with Baston. Watches them descend to that empty vault in the depths to where Cari waits for them *but that hasn't happened yet.*

Conversations with Cari, too. Most are memories from her time as the Saint of Knives, those madcap days after the Crisis, after she'd come into her power. Her happiness when he answered her from the stone, the zeal with which she threw herself into her self-appointed

rôle as guardian of the New City (the eagerness to forget the trage-
dies and mistakes of the past). The two of them against the world,
souls intertwined, unable to hide anything from the other. The city
was hers, and she embraced it with violent joy.

Rasce was like that, too, he reflects. Both Rasce and Cari are wild,
quick to act, fiercely loyal to their friends. But Rasce's alliance with
Spar is a temporary thing; he's a shooting star flashing over the New
City, crossing Guerdon in an eye blink.

Another memory – the god-bomb arcing over the New City,
striking Pesh, the goddess of war, and annihilating her. And his own
voice, saying *we can remake the world*, and Cari replying *who wants to
do that? You get it wrong, and the whole world is your fault. How do you
live with that?*

But later, she said, *if you ask me, I'll do it.*

Spar can feel himself fracturing again. *I'm dying*, he thinks.

Cari, he thinks. *Goodbye. I wish we had time.*

The flames of the Tallowmen look like stars, he observes, and then
everything vanishes behind grey clouds.

In his dream, Rasce has slipped from Great-Uncle's back. He's falling
from the sky, falling through endless roaring storm clouds. Falling
for hours, buffeted by winds, scorched by lightning. Plummeting
through cloud-cities, falling through sheets of rain, and no end to
this fall in sight.

He hears Spar's voice like thunder, but he cannot make out
the words.

He senses his body, lying in bed, but cannot find it.

He breaks through the clouds, falls towards a black ocean. It
writhes, glistening like a sea of tentacles. A living darkness. He
would scream if he had the breath for it, if he had the body for it.
In the distance, beyond the rim of the world, the sound of chanting.

And then – miraculously, he's rescued. For a moment, Rasce
fumbles with the thought that he has the Ring of Samara, that its

magic has saved him from this fate, but no – it's something else. There are hooks in his elbows, his thighs, his chest, even between his eyes, burning bright as fire, wrenching him into the sky. Heat floods through his veins, like alkahest – *no, that's Spar, he's the Stone Man, he's got the plague, not I* – as he flies in the dream.

Soars like a dragon.

CHAPTER THIRTY

Cari's initial assumption can be summarised as *I'm so stupid*. Myri seemed too exhausted to move. Righteous fury wells up in her as she imagines Myri sneaking off into the wastes with the grimoire, cackling evilly. Immediately, Cari imagines what will happen next – she'll track the sorceress down.

Maybe it'll be a desperate chase all the way to the gates of Khebesh. She'll hunt Myri through the Godswar, always one step behind her, stalk her just as she stalked her foes in the New City. The very moment Myri tries to use the book to get inside the walls, Cari will appear out of nowhere and cut the witch's throat from behind. Serve her right for stealing from a thief. Or maybe it'll be the lack of pills that does her in, and Cari will find Myri's corpse in some ditch, all curled up and stiff like a dead insect.

As she searches, though, she finds clear signs of a struggle, of a magical blast of some sort. Myri was surrounded, attacked on all sides. Scorched areas, with drag marks nearby – Myri used sorcery to kill some of her attackers, and their bodies were later removed. No doubt they'll be interred in the walls, too, the dregs of their souls fed to the god of Gissa. And that deformed building wasn't there earlier. Cari's one of the few people in the world who can give constructive criticism on weaponised architecture-miracles; she guesses that Rhan-Gis himself was here, the saint of the city, using the power of Gissa to counter Myri's spells. No wonder Myri fled.

Cari climbs down into the ditch where Myri was hiding. The epicentre of the battle seems to have moved away from their original hiding place. She guesses that Myri was already sneaking out with the book when she was spotted, had to fight her way clear.

Cari's foot brushes against a stone, and there's a pop as a concealment ward fizzles out.

Oh.

Oh fuck.

There, hidden beneath the stone, warded against discovery – there's the fucking book. The remainder of their supplies. The aethergraph in its case.

The sorceress *left* the book. She drew her attackers *away* from the book. She left it for Carillon. She saved it for Cari, sacrificed herself so Rhan-Gis and his minions wouldn't find it.

Cari sinks down in the mud, unsure what do with all her anger. She shoves the rock in frustration – betrayal she can cope with. Bastard sorcerers with their schemes and treacheries, she knows how to deal with. Someone *helping* her? What do you do with that? She can imagine Myri's thought process. The sorceress is cold enough to weigh the odds, to decide that Cari's got a better chance of reaching Khebesh on her own than the sorceress has of escaping Gissa without her. To decide that the optimum outcome is for her to hide the book and draw the foes away.

Hawse did the same, but that's something Cari can understand. You take risks for your friends, for your crew. Myri hates her, and it's fucking mutual. She was looking forward to stabbing the witch, and now that joy's been taken away from her.

With shaking hands, she picks up the grimoire. She hesitates, then grabs the aethergraph and the rest of the bundle, too. There has to be some configuration of the controls that'll let her contact Spar. Or, failing that, someone in Guerdon. Some military channel, maybe. *Carillon Thay calling Queen's Point, calling Parliament, fuck it – calling Eladora Duttin, are you annoying, over?* She's maybe got enough supplies to make it to that fishing village, Yhan-something. It can't be that far. And she's got some coin to buy passage to Khebesh. That, or she steals a fishing boat. Dodge the Kraken somehow.

Walk away, she tells herself. *Get to Khebesh. Get moving, while you've still got cover of night.*

Her feet seem rooted to the ground, like they've turned to stone.

Myri's probably dead. If she isn't, she's the prisoner of a mad god, and she'll be dead soon anyway. That Rhan-Gis is as powerful a saint as you used to be, back in the New City, she tells herself. *You broke the Ghierdana, remember? Remember all the shit you did to people who came after you with guns and magic? Walk away.*

She takes a step in what is utterly, unambiguously, the wrong direction.

Myri told you to run. She might as well have painted a big sign on the ground saying "leave me and go".

A second, stupid, step.

Spar would tell you to leave.

But she knows, sure as anything, that that's a lie, and it only makes her take another step, and another, and fuck it, now it's a rescue mission.

A few hours sneaking around Gissa, and Cari's learned three things.

First, it's really easy to work out where Rhan-Gis himself is. There was a trail through the city that led from his big mobile temple to Myri's ditch and back again, a trail of reassertion. Places where the dream of old Gissa condensed into mortal reality, where muddy ground transmuted into paved streets, where scattered stones rose up as towers and walls. Divine urban renewal. Cari saw flowers blossom where saints of the Mother passed, back in Guerdon. Same thing, only with the city. Unlike the miraculous flowers, though, the renewed buildings *wilt* pretty quickly, rotting and crumbling away. She hopes that means that Rhan-Gis is low on divine strength, that he's depleted himself. Keeping the city intact, keeping his worshippers fed, his motley-guards alive, and fending off rival gods – all that has to sap his strength, and there aren't that many people in the city.

Another clue – she can feel that same friction that she experienced on the mountain at Ilbarin, and in the water. Thinking about it, she felt it in Guerdon, too, but back then she either had the Black Iron Gods screaming in her head or had far more powerful divinatory senses through Spar, so she hadn't paid much attention to the feeling. (*Also, you were drunk a lot*, says a whisper in the back of her mind.) Other saints can do it, too, she guesses – she remembers Saint Aleena talking about sensing Ravellers and the Black Iron Gods, but no one ever trained Cari in sainthood.

The presence of Rhan-Gis scrapes her mind, but not that much. She guesses – and this is very much in the realm of things that Eladora or Myri or someone should be dealing with, not her – that it's to do with divine congruency. Spar's not a god, but he's similar enough to the god of Gissa if you squint your inner eye. Maybe the sandpaper effect comes from the friction between Cari's lingering sainthood and the sort of holy ground she treads on. The more different the god, or the more hostile, the more friction.

She wishes she had Spar to help her make sense of these thoughts. Part of sainthood is not knowing which thoughts and impressions are really *yours* and which stem from the gods. Still, she tentatively adds "risk of spontaneous combustion" to her long list of reasons sainthood is shit.

Thing Number Two: it's really easy for her to move around the city, because the citizens of Gissa are mostly out of their skulls, stumbling around like sleepwalkers, mouthing litanies at each other. She gets the impression that Rhan-Gis doesn't tolerate dissent, and anyone who argues with the divine tyrant got walled up years ago.

Between the general inattention of the populace, and their inability to distinguish reality from their memories of what Gissa was, she can sneak around without being seen. There are parts of the "city", too, that are empty, scars that move with the wandering metropolis. She guesses these are districts that got hammered in the Godswar. They're empty of anything living, so she can cut through them when she needs to hide. Best not to linger there, though – in one, the shadows were ice-cold, and drew blood.

Her working assumption is that Rhan-Gis can track her if he tries, but as long as she doesn't provoke him, she's as safe as anyone can be in a phantom city of religious lunatics situated in a blasted hellscape in the middle of the Godswar.

Part of her wonders who Rhan-Gis was – not the god, the human who's become His saint. She doubts there's much left of the mortal; the body's just a tool now, a channel between the god and the mortal world. Hollowed out. Did he welcome it, she wonders, a faithful follower of the god of Gissa, thinking he was being exalted instead of being eaten alive? Was it forced on him? Was he horribly aware the whole time? Or did he know the cost, know the truth, and do it anyway? Towards the end, when Spar was getting really weak, his miracles took a toll on her soul. If she'd stayed in Guerdon, would Spar have consumed her? Cari always thought that self-sacrifice was a fancy word for surrender, but if it was the only option – would she have let him do it, if it kept him alive? If it was the only way to protect people she cared about?

Another horrible thought wells up from the seemingly inexhaustible reserve of horrible thoughts the Godswar engenders in her – what if it all works, and this is how Spar turns out? She gets to Khebesh, finds a way to help him stay alive – and in a few years she's a drooling husk like the saint of Rhan-Gis, and everyone in the New City is running around with stones for heads or something? At this point in her life, Cari's grasp of what counts as sane and normal is shaky, but she knows that's not right.

The third thing she discovers on the afternoon of the second day. Artolo's here.

Moonchild's a huge ship, but she moves swiftly through the ocean when lightly loaded. The thunder of the alchemical engines and the wild rolling of the deck exhilarate Artolo. If he closes his eyes, he could imagine himself on dragon-back.

He doesn't sleep. Not after the first night on board. The dreams of the Kraken came on too strong, flooding his brain with images of the Ishmeric god. He doesn't want to fall under the spell of the Kraken. He shall not kneel again, not be chosen again. Kraken is his tool. The priestess, Damala, is his tool.

His destiny is clear. First, he'll find Carillon Thay, the woman who ruined him, and he will destroy her. Kill her slowly. Strangle her. Break her, finally and completely. He'll mount her as a figurehead on *Moonchild*, as a warning – this is what happens to those who cross Artolo of them . . .

No. Just Artolo. Artolo alone. Artolo, the Pirate King. He'll take *Moonchild* into the war. Outfit her with weapons, show those cowards in Lyrix how a true pirate marauds. Maybe he'll go back to Guerdon and put the city to the torch. He'll burn the world.

Damala tells him – or maybe he dreams it – that they're on the trail of the witch's boat. The witch will suffer, too. He's brought along the witch's armour. He's going to use his new hands – his new, dextrous, boneless inhuman fingers – to weld her into the suit. Fill it with hot lead, then sink her. He'll shoot down Great-Uncle and mount the dragon's skull on the prow, too. He'll piss on the world, strangle every living thing until the scales balance and they've all suffered like he's suffered!

In his more lucid moments, he thinks of his son Vyr. Thinks of his wife Loranna. He cannot remember either of their faces. No matter – they are better out of hell. They are safe across the world, in Guerdon and Lyrix respectively. No harm will come to either of them. All the harm has come to him, instead.

Damala tells him they are close, very close. And on that night, he walks the many decks of the *Moonchild* instead of sleeping. Walks through the cavernous cargo bays that should be loaded with casks of Great-Uncle's yliaster. He finds one of the deckhands and strangles him until the boy is unconscious, then ties a leaden weight to him and throws him overboard, while chanting a prayer in Ishmeric that he does not know.

The next day, there is no sign of Carillon on the sea. *Moonchild* cruises the coast until the lookouts spy the witch's boat. The cove is too narrow for the great ship to enter, so Artolo orders his crew to sail south, a course parallel to the mountains. They are to anchor at the first harbour they find, and await instructions.

Await omens.

Artolo goes ashore, taking with him Damala and a host of Eshdana. The soldiers quail at entering the Godswar, but once Artolo offers one to the Kraken, the rest find their courage. On the shore, they find a curious trail, as though something has slithered out of the ocean. They follow it to Erephis, finding the footprints of two women in the dirt as they go. Artolo lies down, laps rainwater from Carillon's footprint like a dog, and tastes her scent.

But in the chaos of the ruins there they lose the path. Some foe has torn up the land, drawn arcane sigils that baffle Damala's divinations. Artolo's hunters scout the surrounding lands, come back empty-handed. The last one to return, Artolo strangles without noticing. Two do not return at all.

Carillon has escaped him again. For a day and a night, he screams, and his screaming is like a storm at sea. His anger as jagged and sharp as broken glass.

He drowns another offering in a pool of mud, and the gods reward him. Aerial saints, devotees of Cloud Mother, spot them from the heavens. Cloud Mother whispers that there is a city to the south, the city of Gissa.

Damala speaks with her fellow priests and soldiers of the Sacred

Realm and explains their quest. At the mention of the name of Carillon Thay, the heavens quake. The gods of Ishmere share his hate. His quest for vengeance is more than sanctified, it is fundamental, as true and certain as day follows night. He could no more turn from this quest than water could flow uphill.

The world is like *Moonchild*, huge and ponderous to turn, but driven by great engines on a course he dictates, and he directs it at Carillon Thay.

The world is like his rifle, heavy and hard to aim, but it shall wreak such terrible suffering, and he directs it at Carillon Thay.

Not just Artolo.

Cari hides amid the wandering ruins, behind a low pile of stones that's only a wall if you worship Rhan-Gis, and watches her enemies approach Gissa under a banner of truce. A bunch of Eshdana, and some old hag that seems to be in charge. No sign of a dragon, which is a small mercy. Weirdly, they're all damp and shivering despite the heat, and there's a small boat stranded in the mud outside town, even though they're miles from the sea.

They're met by Rhan-Gis and his courtiers, who emerge from the temple into the great square to meet the newcomers. Rhan-Gis strides out, fragments of a beautiful mosaic appearing under his feet. His courtiers follow, pomp diminished by the need to struggle through the mud, their gold hats made to resemble the towers and palaces of the vanished city, their procession forming a cityscape in miniature. At Rhan-Gis' right hand slithers a Crawling One, clad in the standard-issue dark cloak and porcelain mask that all the worm-colonies favour. *Do you know that Artolo's dragon torched the Crawling One colony on Ilbarin?* she wonders. Maybe she can turn the Crawler to her advantage.

She can't eavesdrop on the conversation between Rhan-Gis and Artolo. All she can do at this distance is read body language. *Spar, I really wish you were here*, she thinks. *You could drop chunks of masonry on them all. Help me spy on Artolo. Find sodding Myri. And I miss you.* Cari's never been homesick before. You need a home for that.

Rhan-Gis is preening and disdainful, which clearly pisses off Artolo. The big bastard's face turns so purple it's visible even from far away, and he clenches his fists. There's something weird about his hands, Cari can tell, and he's not wearing his gloves. The old woman seems to be playing mediator. Several times, she gestures off to the north-west, towards the front lines with Ishmere. When she does, the Crawling One stretches up and whispers in Rhan-Gis' ear.

From the size of the crowd in the square, Cari guesses that half the temple clerics and servants have followed Rhan-Gis out. Plenty of those motley brick-and-mortar guards, too. *So, the temple's only lightly guarded, right?* She slips away, circling the fringes of the great square, sneaking along in the shadow of the massive oiled runners that allow the temple to be dragged across the land, bringing the ghost of the city with it. She scans the temple's crumbling walls, looking at the little barred windows, the doors that once led out on to the street, and now step out into empty air ten feet above the muddy ground. Ancient weathered statues of the god Rhan-Gis, depicted as a sphinx, but the god's face is identical to that of the saint who's negotiating out in the market square right now. The temple's scarred in places – targeting temples and shrines is a standard tactic in the Godswar. Maybe she can climb in through one of those breaches, then sneak around until she finds Myri. And then . . . then she'll come up with something.

Rescue missions aren't like stealing. If she was just going to rob the temple, she'd shove a handful of jewels into her bag and run. Myri's going to be harder to rescue, assuming she's even still alive. *This is a stupid idea, Cari,* she tells herself. But her voice in her head doesn't sound like Spar's voice, so she doesn't give it much credence.

"Ho there!" calls a voice from a balcony above her. She glances up, and it's Beard Priest from the market, the sleazy courtier who tried to show her the fountains.

Con artistry of this sort isn't Cari's strong suit, but she knows when to grab a lucky break.

She looks up, waves, puts on her biggest smile. "Isn't it wonderful to be in Gissa in its glory!" she calls. "Why, the only thing that could make this perfect city even more perfect would be that cup of wine you spoke of!"

Another thing Cari's learned: one of Myri's painkilling drug vials, mixed with a cup of wine, makes for a quick-acting sedative. Within twenty minutes of Beard Priest admitting Cari into the temple through a side door, he's snoring on the couch in his little chamber. He told Cari his name at some point, but she wasn't listening.

From the look of the chamber, being a temple acolyte of Rhan-Gis means a much better life than the average citizen, but that's starting from a very low mark. Still, Cari loots the room, grabbing spare clothes, coin, a few other treasures and relics. A sacrificial dagger, too, which always puts her in a good mood. At least, she hopes that's what she's grabbing – at one point, she glances out of the balcony window and sees a glorious city of marble and gold, which means she's falling under the spell of Rhan-Gis. For all she knows, the temple treasures and holy robes she's stealing will turn out to be handfuls of pebbles and ash when she leaves the city, like fairy treasure in some kid's story. She slips one of Beard Priest's robes over her head in a gesture towards a disguise, makes sure Beard Priest is still breathing, finishes the undrugged goblet of wine, and then it's off on her rescue mission.

She walks swiftly but not hurriedly, head bowed so no one sees her face. That won't matter when Rhan-Gis comes back, of course, so she doesn't tarry. Not even when she passes one chapel that's dripping with jewelled treasures, including a golden sphinx with ruby-eyes the size of pigeon eggs. *Spar, you had really better be worth it*, she thinks. *Myri certainly isn't.*

Up one level, and she finds a door with one of the motley

part-masonry part-living guards in front of it. Cari's getting that sandpaper-itch at the back of her mind, so she has to go for the direct approach. *Please be really, really stupid.*

"Uh, I'm here for the prisoner. In the name of Rhan-Gis the, uh, glorious."

The guard frowns, brow furrowing where it meets the half-mask of stone. "Who commanded this? Who are—"

Cari puts the sacrificial knife to his throat, but it doesn't intimidate him, and she flinches when he moves. He grabs for her, slamming her against the wall. Cari twists away, tries to run, but he tackles her, sending them both to the floor. There's a brief moment of struggle, and then – shit – the knife ends up in his side. He stares at it in confusion, blood bubbling out of the wound with every gasping breath, and he makes a hideous wheezing noise that stops only when Cari swings her satchel and catches him in the flesh-face with the edge of The Fucking Book. He goes down, and she feels sick to her stomach at what she's done. The sentry didn't have it coming, not really. Maybe Rhan-Gis can patch him up. Maybe as he bleeds out, he'll see the perfect city of his dreams, and be at peace. *Please, let him have been an utter bastard.* Another virtue of her lost sainthood – she could see, through Spar, who deserved mercy, and who didn't.

Keys. Door. The floor's a mess of blood, so all pretence at stealth is gone. Speed's her only friend now.

Inside is, as she'd hoped, a small row of cells. A rescue mission's equivalent of a treasury full of gold. Most of the cells are empty, but in one she finds Myri. Unconscious, bound hand and foot, and surrounded by a weird arcane binding circle drawn on to the stone floor. The air above it shimmers. Crossing it wouldn't be a good idea.

She bends down and starts scraping at the runes with her sacrificial knife, frantically trying to scratch away enough of the inscription to break the spell. The little cell fills with the ozone tang of aetheric discharge. Faster and faster she scrapes, the knife handle slick with sweat or blood.

Come on, before Rhan-Gis comes back. Break.

"Cari," says a familiar voice behind her. "Look at you. You look like an altar-server who dropped the sacred wine."

Her heart leaps. Adro's voice. Impossibly, it's Adro. She turns around.

Looks into a mask of porcelain.

CHAPTER THIRTY-ONE

"**Y**ou're awake. This is promising."

Not Karla's voice. Remote and cold, barely above a whisper. Rasce opens his eyes. The light is almost blinding, but he makes out a black-clad figure and a pale face that naturally falls into a scowl.

Doctor Vorz.

The bed's covered with alchemical paraphernalia, knives and scalpels, too, and the white sheets are spotted with red. A complex thaumaturgical pentagram scrawled on the floor. Rasce's head, though, is clearer now than it has been in weeks. He feels no pain, no fear; it's like his spine and his skull have been flooded with icy water.

He looks down. Radiating out from where he stabbed himself in the thigh is a ghastly wound, like a grey scab that covers him from his lower ribs to his right ankle. He stares at it, revulsion crawling beneath the icy calm of whatever drugs Vorz used on him. "The plague," he says, weakly.

"Yes. I cannot tell if the wound became infected due to poor care, or if this is some divine stigmata. The condition can be managed, though, as I'm sure you're aware." Vorz pulls the corners of his mouth into an ugly smile, meant to be reassuring. "I am aware of your *other* condition, too. You have served the dragon well."

Hope like a spike, breaking the thickness of the ice. He's done well! The dragon is pleased. "Great-Uncle – you flew back with him? Where is he? I must go to him." Rasce struggles to stand. The living skin on his right side tugs painfully as it's held back by the weight of the stone.

Vorz shakes his head. "He has not yet returned to Guerdon. He flew me as far as Lyrix, and there we parted company. He had business to attend to, overseas. He shall return soon. But you have done well, my prince."

"I dreamed Tallowmen were attacking our yliaster merchants," says Rasce. He tries to sort dream from vision. *Spar, show me*, he thinks, but there's no response.

"That is true, but irrelevant. There are far greater opportunities here. Tell me, what can you *see*?"

"Nothing." No visions. He's earthbound, limited to the perceptions of this body. He can't even tell who else is in the house, other than Vorz perched at the end of the bed.

"Good. I conducted an exorcism while you slept. I have banished the entity that troubled you, while augmenting your congruency with the underlying divinity."

"You killed Idgeson?"

"Dissipated, to be accurate. The entity may reform, in time. But it need no longer distract you."

"How did you know?" snaps Rasce, infuriated at the insolence of the man. Vorz may be Great-Uncle's adviser, but he's only Eshdana. He's a servant.

"Know?" echoes Vorz, fitting a strange device to his eye. He peers at Rasce, adjusts the lens, peers again.

"Vyr was reporting to you. You knew sainthood this would happen."

"*We* knew it was a possibility." Vorz closes the lens with a snap. "No more than that. After the defeat of your Uncle Artolo, the dragon sought ways to counter the threat of Guerdon's new saints. I advised him on methods that could be used. I have made a long study of similar techniques."

"You did this to me?"

"Your Great-Uncle commanded you to take control of the yliaster trade." Vorz digs around in his bag. "Is there any weapon you would dare not use? Any challenge you would not dare attempt, if commanded by the dragon?"

"No. Never!" responds Rasce without thinking.

Vorz takes a vial from the bag, holds it up to the light. Blood-red, and something darker. "Then give me your arm," he says to Rasce. "This, too, is a weapon."

Baston smells the change as soon as he enters the house on Lantern Street. The familiar smell of the Brotherhood clubhouse – leather, sweat, tobacco, the lingering scent of phlogiston – has been replaced by the harsh tang of chemical cleaners, like an alchemist's lab. A rotting stink, too, coming from the basement, the stench of decay. Everyone here seems to be Eshdana, faces he hasn't seen before. The Brotherhood thieves must have scattered to adjoining buildings, or be out on the streets holding the line against the Tallowmen.

"What's going on? Where's my sister?" he demands. Shrugs, blank faces. She left in the night, he's told. Business down in the Wash.

He hurries up the stairs. Rasce's bed is empty, the stained sheets littered with empty alkahest syringes and soiled bandages.

He eventually finds Rasce in the cellar, in the temporary mortuary they set up here for Vyr and the others who fell to the Tallowmen. Twelve neatly wrapped bodies on twelve trestle tables – but now the bodies are spread out across the broken floor. Some dismembered, gutted, their entrails spilled out across the white marble of the New City. Some buried in graves dug right into the floor of the cellar, or bricked up in holes smashed in the walls. One hanging from the ceiling, a noose around its neck. Another in a fucking *bathtub*, dissolving in a vat of alkahest, a thick scum of melted flesh and fat bubbling on top of the liquid. A trio of Eshdana stand by, pickaxes and shovels and bone saws at the ready.

Standing over it all, a man in black, gloved hands dripping with gore, moving like a conductor in front of some mordant orchestra. He seems quietly satisfied with this scene of horrors, a craftsman at work. It makes Baston want to punch him.

"Who the fuck are you? Where's Rasce?"

"I'm here, my friend." Rasce steps out of a shadowed corner. Up and awake. His face is pale, glimmering with sweat, and the colour of it almost matches the glowing stone of the New City. "There's no need to shout. I hear everything." He gestures at the alchemist. "This is Doctor Vorz. My Great-Uncle's counsellor, newly returned from overseas."

"What is this? What are they doing?"

"Necessary things."

Vorz interrupts. "Try again," he says to Rasce. With a wave of his hand, Rasce causes a fresh grave to open up in the floor. The stone flows sluggishly, a reluctant miracle.

"Should you be up? Karla said you were still sick."

Rasce grips Baston's forearm, leans on him. His grip is very strong now, but he's breathing quickly, like he's got a fever. "I have lain abed too long. Now is the time to act." His grip tightens until it's painful. "I owe you, my friend, for all you did while I was godstruck. I saw the secret path into the fortress of our foes. I saw the path we must walk." He leans close, whispers in Baston's ear.

"Tell the Rat it's time to meet."

They descend.

It's Rasce who leads the way, and he seems to grow stronger as they go, striding so quickly that Baston has to hurry to keep the other man in sight as they descend down endless stairs and tunnels. They wind through the bowels of the New City. They leave the streets behind, entering into a labyrinth of stone. Baston carries an aetheric lamp to light their way, but there's little need for it, for the stone glows where Rasce touches it. The glow fades after he passes, though, so the light is like a bubble, a fragile vessel sinking into a vast darkness.

Sometimes, Baston glimpses strange things down a tunnel branch – the glowing eyes of a ghoul, crushed pieces of machinery embedded in the walls, slithering creatures that flee the light. Rasce doesn't pause, and Baston can't linger. The air's bad, a miasma of fumes and subterranean exhalations.

Once, he thinks he sees a youngish man, rake-thin, with lank black hair. Well-dressed, like he's on his way to dinner in Bryn Avane. A silver blade in his hand. His gaze meets Baston's – and he vanishes into thin air, face contorting in pain for a moment, then gone, leaving Baston to wonder if he dreamed the whole thing.

Abruptly, the tunnel enters into a huge vault, so vast that Rasce's stone-light is lost in the yawning reaches. Baston turns the aetheric lamp up to full so they can see their surroundings. Well, so *he* can see them, as it's obvious that Rasce's miraculous perceptions have returned. The light leaps, and Baston gasps as he beholds the full scale of the chamber.

This hollow beneath the New City could swallow any of the cathedrals atop Holyhill and have room to spare. Littered around him is the wreckage of huge machinery, athanors and containment vessels, industrial crucibles and spawning vats. Littered around him, too, are the remains of products of those vats – corpses of splattered wax, corpses with organs from disparate creatures fused together, things he cannot name.

The light from his lamp falls on a cleared area, a wide road cut through the debris. It's obvious that someone – a great many someones – has dragged material out of the cavern. It might be a salvage operation, but some instinct tells Baston it was more of a heist. There's something in the air, along with dust and the stink of incipient lung cancer.

The trail leads across the cavern to a partially demolished curtain wall, a barrier breached by an ugly gash. There's another vault through there, equally huge. Rasce hurries off that way, limping slightly now, sloshing through puddles of spilled alchemical run-off without care. Baston follows, unslinging his gun just in case something in here isn't quite dead.

"What is this place?" he breathes. He can't bring himself to speak loudly. It seems oddly disrespectful, like this place is a church. Or a tomb.

"The ruins of the Alchemists' Quarter," says Rasce. "Spar buried their works here. Ghouls guard the tomb. Behold!"

He flings his arms wide, and the curtain wall flares with light, like there's fire buried deep within the stone. The light outlines a figure sitting cross-legged in the breach. Gigantic, hunched, its horns like antlers, long clawed fingers caked with grave dirt. Hooves crusted with a mash of wax and ordure.

"Gods below," mutters Baston, and then invisible fingers grab his tongue, his throat, and words exhume themselves through his mouth. "SO, AT LAST, THE DRAGON'S BOY SHOWS HIMSELF. I AM TOLD YOU CAN DO WHAT CARI DOES." The ghoul's long tongue, like a black snake, slithers out and tastes the air. "I WOULD SPEAK WITH MY FRIEND."

"He is here," says Rasce. "He is all around us. But first, Lord Rat, I would bargain with you."

The ghoul laughs, a sound like an earth slip, like an open grave caving in. Then he speaks through Baston again. "I KNOW ALL ABOUT YOUR PLANS AND DESIRES, DRAGON'S BOY. I KNOW WHERE YOU SEEK TO TRESPASS. KNOW THIS – IF YOU SET FOOT OUTSIDE THE NEW CITY, I WILL EAT YOUR BONES AND SEEK MY FRIEND IN YOUR MARROW." Rasce takes a step back. Baston's grip on the gun tightens.

"SPAR – THERE IS MUCH WE MUST DISCUSS." Rat waves a paw towards the inner vault. "HOW MUCH DID YOU SEE?"

"He – he says he was confused," says Rasce. "Weak and scattered, after the invasion. What happened here?"

"HURRH." The massive elder ghoul scratches the ground with one paw, hunches his shoulders. Its claws stir up piles of slag, intermixed with blackened bones, scraps of metal and leather. A shattered Haithi helmet. Rat's *nervous*. The thing seated before them is a necrotic demigod, one of the most powerful entities in Guerdon, but Baston can tell that Rat is ... embarrassed. "I FAILED IN MY VIGIL. SINCE THE ARMISTICE, ELADORA DUTTIN'S INFLUENCE HAS GROWN. SHE HAS SOME HOLD ON THE NEW MINISTER OF SECURITY, NEMON. AND THROUGH HIM, THE CITY WATCH. SHE HAS GATHERED OTHERS TO HERSELF, TOO. SAINTS. WILD TALENTS. MERCENARIES, INCLUDING A DEAD MAN OF HAITH. NOW, THANKS TO THIS FOOL'S ACTIONS" – he waves a claw at Rasce – "SHE HAS CONVINCED THE ALCHEMISTS TO GIVE HER THE TALLOWMEN."

Baston has to gasp for breath, interrupting Rat. The ghoul frowns in irritation. "WITH CARI GONE ... WITH YOU GONE ... SHE CONVINCED ME THAT THE NEW CITY WAS NO LONGER A SAFE RESTING PLACE FOR THE THINGS YOU BURIED HERE. SHE TOOK THEM AWAY."

"What did she take?"

Baston's stomach turns. It feels like his guts are overflowing with dirt, like he's swallowed handfuls of earth and stone. Still, the words come, the ghoul using him as its herald, like Rasce speaks for Spar Idgeson. "THE BLACK IRON BELLS. GUILDMISTRESS ROSHA'S CASKET. OTHER TREASURES OF THE ALCHEMISTS' GUILD."

"And where does she keep these treasures?" asks Rasce.

Like Rasce's *supposed* to speak for Spar Idgeson.

"I WISH TO SPEAK WITH MY FRIEND," Rat growls.

"Oh, he is here," replies Rasce. He speaks quickly, like he's rehearsed this speech. "But my services as mediator are not without cost, and here is my price. Your ghouls control the underworld. You will help me get to St Styrus' Shaft."

"YOU DO NOT DICTATE TO ME!"

Rat rises to loom above them – and there's an earthquake, right there, a spasm of the New City. Baston falls to his knees, and the Rat's flung backwards as the hexagonal hunk of stone he was seated on suddenly rebels, knocking him over. He lands heavily on the far side of the curtain wall, a grunt of pain escaping both his lips and Baston's simultaneously. Then he's up like a panther, leaping back towards the breach.

But before he can reach it, Rasce gestures, and the stone of the curtain wall melts, flows, knits together. It's sluggish, and seems to fight against him, pseudopods of stone rolling backwards against the flow. Fires blaze within the wall; bloodstains appear on Rasce's leg, his side.

Across the great cavern echoes the hooting and yelping of ghouls. A great many ghouls.

The hole's become too small for Lord Rat to squeeze through, but one of his long ropy arms snakes through the gap. The claw grabs Rasce's foot and yanks him over. Baston glimpses Rat's drooling maw on the other side of the wall, eyes blazing with fury.

He reacts on instinct, the way the Fever Knight taught him. Reacts the way any right-hand man should.

The gun in his hand barks as he shoots Lord Rat in the face.

The ghoul flinches – the gun's too small to do real damage to such a monster – but it only takes a moment. Rasce pulls himself free and deliberately slams his hand into a shard of jagged metal. Blood sprays across the white marble of the wall as the breach suddenly seals, leaving Rat trapped on the other side.

They lie there for an instant, amid the rubble, in the brief silence.

Scratch.

Scratch.

Scratch.

Baston opens his mouth, finds the words are his own. "What the fuck have you done?"

"What's necessary." Rasce hauls himself upright, leaving bloody handprints on the wall. "Reload." Dozens of ghouls lope and skulk across the cavern towards them. Feral ghouls, savage and unthinking. This little handgun is useless against such a horde. Fuck, even if he'd brought that lovely repeater, Baston wouldn't have a hope in hell against so many.

"I WILL EAT YOU." Rat's voice comes from a chorus of ghouls as the circle closes.

"The gun," says Rasce, holding out his hand. Baston passes the loaded weapon to him, and Rasce aims it at his own temple. "Listen! Carillon Thay's gone. I'm the only connection left to Spar Idgeson. If I die, so does he! So, O Rat of Guerdon, what is it to be? Your friend's life – or shall you be a thief again, instead of Duttin's bootlick?"

"YOU DO NOT KNOW WHAT YOU ASK," say the ghouls in unison.

Rasce grins, showing bloodied teeth. "The dragon does not ask. The dragon takes."

Baston feels Rat's mind settle on him again, feels the ghoul's thoughts worming their way into his jaws. He tastes Rat's mordant humour, tastes some cynical joy. Despite being imprisoned, Rat still somehow thinks he has the upper hand.

The ghoul pack snarls, but they do not advance. "Threaten us!" shouts Rasce, "and I shall bring the ceiling down upon your Lord!"

The assembled ghouls howl and gibber. Shit, most of them are ferals, middle-ghouls. Baston prays there are a few young surface ghouls in the mix, ghouls like Rat used to be, ones who understand human speech and can relay the threat to their feral kin. Rat is now the only Elder left – without him, the ghouls are kingless.

"Behold," shouts Rasce. "I lay a curse upon this place. Should anyone, ghoul or human, living or dead, touch yonder prison wall, then the chamber beyond shall collapse, and all within shall perish. The power is in me to do this."

Baston's got no idea if Rasce's bluffing, but it's clear that the ghouls buy it. The ferals closest to the wall shuffle away. Rasce advances, and the pack parts to let him through. The gun still pressing on his forehead. "Come on, Baston," he says.

"WAIT. SPAR. SPAR, ARE YOU THERE?"

Rasce's face contorts. He takes on the same expression Baston had, as words try to fight their way out of his mouth. He breaks stride, the hand holding the gun shaking for a moment. Then, he regains control. Swallows hard, spits.

"He's here. But you shall not speak to him. Not until I have done what my Great-Uncle commands."

Rat does not respond, but the thought of his unspoken words flickers through Baston's mind.

THEY KNOW ALL YOUR PLANS. YOU WILL FAIL.

"My lord, I never fail."

The words come out of Baston's mouth reluctantly. DO AS HE COMMANDS.

They leave the vault, and behind them the only sound is Rat's claws scraping on the stone.

Scratch.

Scratch.

Scratch.

Scratch.

The sound, the sensation of Rat's claws on the stone.

Like a beacon. A point of reference. The claws scrape on the stone. The stone of the New City was born from stone that was once flesh. That flesh was the flesh of a man, and the man was Spar Idgeson.

Spar hangs in the abyss, the sound a thin cord drawing him back from oblivion.

Scratch.

*

A memory.

Spar's standing guard outside a house off Sumpwater. Baston's there, too, staring nervously at passers-by on the street. Keeping the width of the door between the two, not looking at Spar. Saying nothing, because what is there to say to a terminal diagnosis? The notion that he is *unclean* settles around Spar like a heavy mantle, a wall coming down between him and the rest of humanity. Never again shall he know touch. Never again shall he know hope.

Inside the house, a muffled scream. A thump. A moment's silence.

Heinreil emerges, jingling a bag of coin. "Well, that was unnecessarily messy. Spar, boy, you wait here. There'll be a cleaner along presently, for ... for ... "

The Fever Knight follows his master out, bending and twisting to get his massive armoured form through the narrow door. "Varot, wasn't it?" He adds, "cloth", as he passes, and Baston fishes out a scrap of fabric so the Fever Knight can wipe the blood from his gauntlets.

"We've more work to do," says the Fever Knight. "Bloody work, up in Five Knives district. Come along, Baston."

The armoured knight beckons Baston to follow. Baston glances back, but doesn't speak; he follows doggedly along behind his tutor, leaving Spar alone on the street with Heinreil.

"We'll take care of you, boy," says Heinreil. "The Brotherhood way. Make sure you have enough alkahest. Keep you useful. There'll always be a place for Idge's son in the Wash, aye? But not up in Hog Close – somewhere more, ah, private."

"More isolated."

"A bit of peace and quiet, aye – gods below, I'd give anything for time to just sit and think!" says Heinreil. "I'll take care of you, and you'll stay true to the Brotherhood."

Spar nods. The movement hurts his neck. He swallows, nervously, imagining his throat seizing up. The terror of the Stone Plague grabs him and freezes his bones, giving him a momentary presentiment of what the future holds.

Scratch.

Staring into the glimmering lens of Vorz's loupe. The sharp pain of a syringe piercing skin, and Vorz has to try three spots before he finds soft tissue.

"I'm still too weak!" says Rasce. "That brute nearly got me."

Vorz frowns. "Residuum is being absorbed much more slowly than I would have expected," he admits. "I did not expect this resistance."

"My uncle will be displeased if you fail."

"There are other options." He turns to examine one of the dead thieves in the mortuary at Lanthorn Street. "In any event, Taras' displeasure will fall on you, not me. The dragon gave you this task."

"Then I shall not fail." When he flew with the dragon, Great-Uncle would breathe his glorious fire and move on, and Rasce would never have to see the remains of the fallen. Now, the cellar is littered with all manner of corpses, but Rasce will not turn his eyes from them. He climbs down into one of the graves and begins to dismember the corpse with his knife. Digging for the soul within the carcass, the precious offering of residuum.

Scratch.

The ghoul slinks up Sumpwater Row. Pauses outside the door.

"Boss sent me," he says, licking his lips. Taps himself on the chest. "Rat."

"Spar."

"Idgeson, right?" The ghoul sucks his teeth. "I heard. Hard. Hard."

"Varot's in here," says Spar, opening the door.

"Can smell him." Rat slips into the house. Some morbid impulse makes Spar follow the ghoul in, and watch as Rat begins to expertly dismember the corpse. Limbs are cut off, wrapped, stowed away in a sack. A cross between a mortician and a butcher.

Some bits, the ghoul pops in his mouth immediately.

"That's disgusting," says Spar.

Rat looks up at him. "Survive first. Can't do shit if you're dead. No dead man ever got a lucky break."

It's good advice.

Advice Spar remembers when they give him his first shot of alkahest. The sharp pain of a syringe piercing skin, and the doctor has to try three spots before he finds soft tissue.

Scratch.

Survive first. You can't do the right thing if you can't do anything.

Spar can sense the bodies interred within the house on Lanthorn Street. Interred within him. He can feel their soft flesh, like moon-shadows, ephemeral and fleeting. He can feel their bones, a little denser, a little more like stone. He can sense Rasce digging there, too.

And he can feel, too, something else. He can feel their souls like they're a physical thing. A dark, heavy liquid, pooling in the corpses. Condensing out of the aether.

It's different in each corpse. Vyr's soul-residue, for example, con-geals in the man's hands, in his throat, in his brain. Gingerly, Spar tastes it – and immediately recoils. The stuff is a soup of memories and stagnant thoughts, and he's so fragile that he nearly drowns in it. Part of Spar's consciousness carves off, sinking into the Vyr-ness of the residuum.

Scratch.

A lingering memory. Spar, lying on his reinforced bed, his body wracked by the Stone Plague. Rat squats by the fire, munching on something unmentionable, but he's there. He's the only one who didn't leave Spar's side. He's loyal.

Scratch.

A memory. Rat at the door, in the rain. Bringing Cari home for the first time.

Scratch.

"Better," says Vorz. The alchemist kneels by one of the graves in the basement of Lanthorn Street. The corpse is covered by a cairn, but beneath the pile the stones become knives, probing and slicing. Rasce's will moves like the stone plague, consuming the flesh, consuming the bits of soul-stuff that remain in the nerve endings, in the deep pools of the brain. He gestures, and a dozen more grave-pits open up in the ground like hungry mouths.

"Will that be enough, do you think?" he asks Vorz.

Scratch.

They bring in more dead thieves, each one stabbed or shot or poisoned or starved, and they're laid to rest in Lanthorn Street in Spar's name.

And while Rasce takes the dragon's share of each soul, Spar steals a little – just a little – from each, and hides it away.

Can't do shit if you're dead, Rat taught him. So survive first. Wait for a lucky break.

Scratch.
　　Scratch.
　　Scratch.

CHAPTER THIRTY-TWO

"**M**iss Thay," says the Crawling One, in Adro's voice, though Adro never called her that in his ... in his ...

Fuck. He's dead. He's dead and a worm has eaten his brain and stolen his voice and she wants to scream.

"Call me Twelve Coins Bleeding. Forgive me for the circumstances in which we parted."

She doesn't know if he means the way the Crawling One abandoned her on her first attempt to escape Ilbarin, or if it's Adro, regretting what happened in the camp.

"How ...?"

She can barely speak; words aren't equal to the maelstrom of horror and anger and self-loathing and confusion that churns in her brain. The Crawling One only picks up on the confusion. "Ah, I should explain. My kind are not as singular as yours. The names we apply reflect our constituent parts. Some parts of the entity you met in Ilbarin that you called Twelve Suns Bleeding exist in me. I hoped to liberate you from the prison camp, but the risk was too great, so I followed you after I learned of your escape. Other parts of me are derived from a Crawling One that advises Lord Rhan-Gis, the Cornerstone of the World." He leans closer. "All cities are our home, in the end, so rest assured that our previous bargain endures! I shall assist you in getting to Khebesh."

"What happened to Adro?"

The Crawling One pretends to kneel down next to her. She knows, distantly, that the thing is boneless, formless, only pretending to be humanoid. Only pretending to have legs that bend, feigning a hand that rests reassuringly on her shoulder. "I was badly injured, Cari. I succumbed to my wounds, and the Ghierdana threw my remains into the sea. But the Crawling Ones found me, and saved me."

"You're dead."

"Everything I am, everything the individual you knew as Adro," says Adro's voice, "endures. I have the same memories, the same thoughts, the talents preserved. But we cannot linger here, talking philosophy as though we were sharing a bottle of wine-of-poets, can we? Come on. I must present you to your cousin."

She's so shaken that for a moment she imagines him bringing her to Eladora. Two images of Eladora war in Cari's mind – her cousin as she usually thinks of her, nervous and prissy, a well-read churchmouse, and Eladora as Cari glimpsed her in the days around the Armistice. Somehow, it wouldn't surprise her to hear of her cousin's presence here.

Then she realises that it means cousin in the *royal* sense. If Rhan-Gis is the embodiment of Gissa, then Cari's the embodiment of Guerdon.

"Wait. What about Myri? I can't just leave her here."

"Artolo's sorcerer?" Twelve Coins Bleeding sounds surprised. "I assumed she came with Artolo." His hand – pseudo-hand, whatever – passes over Myri's unconscious face.

"No, with me."

"As your prisoner?" There's a note of respect in Adro's voice. In the simulacrum of Adro's voice. She's talking to a pile of worms, she has to remember that.

"No. She wants to get to Khebesh, too. We've been helping each other."

"Ah." It's Adro's voice, but she can't read the emotion behind it.

Surprise? Amused acknowledgement of yet another absurd situation involving wild Cari? A piece of a puzzle slotting into place? "I must present you. Emissaries of Ishmere are here in Gissa, and it is necessary to convince Rhan-Gis to protect us from them so we may travel in safety. Come with me."

The Crawling One glides out of the cell, and she follows. She doesn't have much choice – it's as powerful a sorcerer as Myri, if not more so, and it doesn't suffer the same ill effects as she does when it uses magic. And the little sacrificial knife she stole isn't going to cut it, so to speak. They pass back the way she came – the corpse of the man she killed is now covered with little white dots that must be worm eggs. Soon, they'll hatch and bore into his brain, and eat whatever remains of his soul, his memories. Gods below, he'll come back and know she murdered him. She wants to tell him to get in line behind Artolo and the whole bloody Sacred Realm and everyone else, but she can't summon up the bravado right now.

Instead, she whispers, "I'm sorry" as she passes.

"That reminds me," says Twelve Coins Bleeding, "I presume the Ghierdana took the worm I gave you. No matter – I have a prodigious supply." Putting just enough of one of Adro's leers in to sound right. "You recall what you are to do with it?"

"Put it in the sorcerer's tomb in Khebesh."

"Exactly. I shall ensure your passage to Khebesh is untroubled. Trust me, Cari."

She really, really doesn't.

Apparently, getting presented to Rhan-Gis first means getting bathed and anointed by handmaidens, then putting on the most absurd outfit Cari's ever worn in her life. A dress of shimmering samite, whiter than fresh-fallen snow. A necklace of glittering gems, rings of gold. She horrifies the handmaidens by insisting that she gets to keep wearing her walking boots – and while they're distracted by that outrage, she slips that sacrificial knife into a fold of the dress and hides it with a belt of gold and emeralds.

She's very, very glad for once that Spar's thousands of miles away and can't see her.

They've taken her stuff, including Ramegos' grimoire and the aethergraph. Twelve Coins Bleeding tells her that she'll get it back, that he'll get her to Khebesh as promised. She doesn't have a choice but to comply. She feels like she's in a den of snakes, where one false step would get her bitten. Typical – the first time in her life she's treated like royalty, and she can't relax and enjoy it.

The handmaidens offer her a plate of grapes and sweetmeats, and she nearly accepts – then she remembers the plate must be empty, that those grapes and sweetmeats are dust and pebbles transformed by the miracles of Rhan-Gis. This city is doing her head in. Food isn't food, walls aren't walls, the thing that talks like Adro certainly isn't Adro, and she's sitting here dressed like a princess, which certainly isn't her. She's got to get out of here.

"You have 'em," she says when the handmaidens offer her the plate again. The girls fall on the plate like hungry ghouls, coughing out prayers of thanks to Rhan-Gis between bites of dust. Cari sits back down on the edge of a bench and tries to stay sane. She has to stay out of the god's influence, to see the world clearly in all its broken horror. It's the only way she'll be able to find her way out of this city.

Long ago, she guesses, Rhan-Gis was just a minor god. The embodiment of the city of Gissa, venerated by a few priests, celebrated in some annual festival or when some new civic building was established. A handful of miracles to His name. Cari's encountered gods like that on her travels, in places yet untouched by the Godswar. Not Kept Gods like in Guerdon, starved of power so they don't become monstrous titans, but slumbering, placid gods, little more than abstractions given a name, a face.

Then there was some wound. Some attack or injury that ruined that tranquil order, damaged the god's perfectly ordered domain. A first cause. The god sought power to heal the wound, to correct the wrong, or the people turned to the god with more fervent prayers, more votive offerings and sacrifices. Maybe Rhan-Gis inspired his people to start moving the city, to bring Gissa out of danger or shift it closer to some font of magic. Maybe the priests thought the best way to aid their god was to offer him sacrifices, or to steal power from another deity. Cari imagines the world as some great invisible machine, the gods as spinning cogs, each in their place, each serene and balanced. Then one wheel flies off its axle, knocks into another, and it all collapses into chaos. Into the Godswar.

"Carillon. It's time." Adro's voice.

Now, to avoid getting crushed by a spinning wheel.

Up close, Rhan-Gis is easily the most beautiful human Cari has ever seen.

The young saint-king of the city, the avatar of the god Rhan-Gis, supreme master of the eternal city of Gissa offers her a glass of wine. "My Crawler tells me that you are Queen of Guerdon. I traded with you, before the barbarians laid siege to my walls! Had you presented yourself to me openly, instead of fleeing and entering my temple by stealth, I would have welcomed you with all proper ceremony. Nonetheless, let our friendship be renewed. We champions of civilisation must stand against the madness of this war. We shall protect the blazing lamp of civility, you and I."

Rhan-Gis' eyes are finely inlaid stained glass, and there's nothing behind them, nothing at all. The mortal man in front of her has been hollowed out. There's nothing left of him except the mad god.

Cari gives him a weak grin and pretends to down the wine. The glass is empty while she holds it.

The rest of the people in this palatial council chamber aren't much better. The Crawling One's slithering around, whispering in Rhan-Gis' ear, in Cari's. "Trust me, Cari, I've got this. We'll be home and dry in no time," he whispers. He talks to her in Adro's voice, but switches to an older, deeper voice when speaking to the saint-king.

On the other side of Rhan-Gis is his court wizard, who looks like he's stepped out of a storybook — sky-blue robes, long white beard, stupid hat and all. Twelve Coins Bleeding introduces him to Cari as Xargor Bane, Master of the Star Tower, and it turns out that the chief advantage of the porcelain mask is that you can keep a straight face when introducing someone as Xargor Bane, Master of the Star Tower. He strokes his chin with a wizened hand as he pages through the grimoire, muttering to himself. The aethergraph and their supplies are next to him, too, tucked under his chair. He holds the heavy book up to the light of a lamp hanging beside the throne to see better. Unlike Myri, whose body bears the marks and scars of her sorcery, the court wizard's body bears the marks of too many pastries and fine wines. "Very interesting, very interesting," he mutters to himself. "Yes, yes, clearly Khebeshi."

Cari decides that Xargor Bane, Master of the Star Tower, is dumb as a gullhead.

Rhan-Gis gestures at an empty spot next to his throne, and a chair rises from the stone floor. A servant darts over with a silken cushion, and Cari sits down, adjusting her ridiculous dress to keep the knife hidden.

Rhan-Gis leans over. "The hateful emissaries of the Sacred Empire are at my gates. My Crawler tells me they hunt you, but you are under my protection. No harm will come to you while I watch over you."

"Uh, thank you, your honour. Your majesty."

"He is the Cornerstone of the World," says Xargor Bane, "and properly referred to as 'his divine radiance'."

"However, I have a duty, too, to my city, and the people who dwell within the holy walls of Gissa. A thousand armies have broken on those walls! And a thousand times a thousand brave souls have given unto me to bolster the city's defences. The forces of the Sacred

Realm are not as great as they once were, and my Crawler tells me
I have you to thank for that—"

He reaches out and strokes Cari's cheek. For a moment, the spell
of the god is all-consuming, and she's filled with ecstatic joy at
being in the presence of Rhan-Gis, here in the heart of the holy city
of Gissa, and she can see the towers and walls rising through the
windows of the temple. She pulls back, fights it off, but she's missed
what he was saying to her. Plus, now she's got a pounding headache,
like the sandpaper's scoured her brain raw and bloody. On the bright
side, her wine glass is now brimming with the genuine article.

" . . . Assures me he can broker an arrangement." Rhan-Gis claps.
"Bring in the prisoner!"

A set of double doors open, and two guards enter, carrying Myri
between them. She's bound hand and feet, gagged – and looks furious, eyes flashing with anger. The guards hastily shuffle her over
to a spot in front of Rhan-Gis' throne, and Twelve Coins Bleeding
kneels down to draw another containment circle on the ground, his
worm-fingers searing sigils and arcane curves into the tiles. Xargor
Bane nods approvingly. "Yes, yes. Excellent work. I would have used
a dampening monad in that quadrant, but what this design lacks
in subtlety it compensates with animal vigour. Good. I deem the
sorceress secure, my lord."

The Crawling One whispers to Myri, too. He's too far away for
Cari to eavesdrop, but she doesn't get the impression it's a threat or
insult. He's careful not to cross the line of the binding circle.

"And the grimoire?" asks Rhan-Gis, with a disinterested wave
of his hand.

"Ah, yes, yes," says Xargor Bane. "It's Khebeshi. Doubtless one of
their akashic records. Of little value, save to scholars, O radiant one."

"Then with his divinity's permission," says Twelve Coins Bleeding
hastily, "I shall take custody of it." He kneels in a fluid motion,
touching the brow of his porcelain face to the ground in front of the
throne. Rhan-Gis, though, raises one finger, and Xargor Bane crosses

his hands atop the book. The Crawling One clearly isn't getting Ramegos' grimoire that easily.

"Gissa shall never fall," announces Rhan-Gis. He's not talking to Caro, or anyone in this room; his words echo from the bricks of this broken city, spring from the lips of the guards at the doors. "Gissa's glory is eternal." Then he frowns, and a little drool escapes his slack lips before he gathers himself and says, "Show in the emissaries of Ishmere."

The guards open another set of doors, and Cari has to fight her instinct to spring up and run. Artolo strides in, those metal-shod riding boots of his clacking on the tiles. He's flanked by Eshdana guards, nervous-looking folk from Ilbarin, and a few Ishmeric soldiers, sigils of Cloud Mother on their armour. Unlikely allies. *Big round of applause for Eladora and her Armistice*, thinks Cari, *bringing together bastards who want to kill me.*

Following Artolo comes an old hag of a priestess. "Damala," mutters Xargor Bane, and Cari assumes that's her name.

On seeing Cari, Artolo's face darkens. He strides forward, fingers clenching — hey, the bastard has fingers now, boneless tentacle-tumours sprouting from his ruined knuckles. Good for him!

The wine of Rhan-Gis, she realises, is really strong.

"She is mine!" snarls Artolo, jabbing a tentacle at Cari. "I've chased her from Ilbarin. Hand her over, or I shall put your joke of a city to the torch!"

"Gissa is eternal," says Rhan-Gis, and Artolo's struck across the face by the words. He staggers back, knocked on his heels. The words hang in the air for a long moment, like there's some improbable solidity to them, a physical barrier. The lamps on either side of the throne blaze with an unearthly light.

"High Umur," says Damala quietly, like she's remarking on distant events, "has decreed the destruction of greater cities than Gissa, and his will cannot be denied."

Xargor Bane leans across and whispers in Rhan-Gis' ear. "My

lord, my scouts tell me that there are considerable Ishmeric forces
to the north of the city, including war-saints. Of course, Gissa is
eternal and our victory is assured – but it would, I fear, be costly."

Cari shivers at the mention of *war-saints*. She saw too much when
Guerdon was invaded, and her city was much better protected than
ragged Gissa. If it's war here, everyone's going to die, or worse. Rhan-
Gis surely can't risk that. Back when Cari was the Saint of Knives,
she could see, could feel, everyone in the New City. She knew when
they were suffering, or scared. She couldn't run away, nor stand aside.
She couldn't abandon Spar to that knowledge.

"My people would bear the cost joyfully. We shall build new
walls from the bones of the dead," says Rhan-Gis, and he sounds
horribly enthusiastic about it. "We cannot deny them the privilege
of martyrdom!"

Bastard, she thinks. Does he not care? Or does he buy his own
claims that Gissa is a city of joy and plenty? Or does being a god
mean believing your own bullshit is an inherent part of the deal?

"Nevertheless, divine one," says Xargor, his voice both soothing
and panicky at the same time, "the city is still rebuilding after the
affray with the Moon-Eater. If more of your people perish, who
will praise your name in the Festival of Clay Words? Will there
be enough maidens to dance the maze at midsummer? Who will
proclaim you Cornerstone of the World?"

Cari revises her assessment of Xargor. He may be a shit sorcerer,
but he seems to be something much more valuable – a voice of
sanity, balancing the mad whims of the god with the needs of the
people. Xargor's trying to keep everyone in the city alive, while
Rhan-Gis would happily see them all perish if they die with his
name on their lips.

The Crawling One slithers to the middle of the room. "Great
Ones, there is no need to make such threats. All of us have other
foes to contend with. This matter can be resolved peaceably." He gestures at Cari, and at Myri's bound form. "Both these women claim

sanctuary in Gissa. Both these women are sought by Artolo of the Ghierdana. The matter before us is to agree on mutually acceptable terms for the surrender of one or both of them."

Artolo starts blustering about how the Crawling Ones have no business here, threatening to do to Twelve Coins Bleeding what he did to the colony on the Street of Blue Glass. Cari ignores him, and tries to work out what game the Crawling Ones are playing. She certainly didn't claim sanctuary here, and she doubts Myri did either, not unless blasting a host of soldiers with sorcery is part of the application process. So, is the Crawling One lying to protect them, bolstering their case like a defence lawyer, or is he after something else?

"This one," says Twelve Coins Bleeding, pointing to Myri, "broke her oath to the Ghierdana. She is a powerful sorceress, and a known criminal. She orchestrated the escape from Ilbarin. While this poor girl," indicating Cari, "was but a prisoner, a hostage to the sorceress. She seeks to withdraw from the world, and searches for the peaceful refuge of Khebesh. If Artolo seeks revenge, let him have Myri, and this other one shall remain here as a guest of Rhan-Gis."

He lets a little of Adro's voice bleed in at the end, and Cari knows he's lying. It's all too neat.

Once, back in the New City, she watched a con man running the old shell game. Through Spar's gifts, she could watch him move the shell hiding the coin and track it no matter how quickly he shuffled. She could tell when he palmed the coin, too. The whole game was laid out in front of her, and she could see every move.

It's like that here. The Crawling One's goal hasn't changed – all it wants is to get one of its worms into Khebesh. They'll feast on the dead there, like they did in Guerdon, and Ilbarin, and here in Gissa. Like they did to Adro. Everything's just a means to an end for those grave-cold bastards. The sorcerers of Khebesh won't let the Crawlers in, though, so it needs a plausible candidate to smuggle the worm through the doors. Cari's more tractable – she's got no defences against its spells – but the Sacred Realm are here for her. Myri may be harder to deal with, but the Crawling One will take her in a pinch. It takes Myri and the grimoire, acts as a broker between Rhan-Gis and the Sacred Realm, and sells Cari to Artolo.

The shell on the left. Twelve Coins Bleeding takes Myri with him to Khebesh, and Cari's murdered by Artolo.

The middle shell . . . no deal. Everything falls apart. The Sacred Empire attacks Gissa, and it's slaughter. The streets, such as they are, run with blood. She can't allow that.

The right shell. By some miracle, Artolo takes Myri and lets Carillon go free. Cari gets to Khebesh, but Myri's dead and the Crawling Ones get even more powerful. She'll be the prisoner of a mad god and his evil vizier all the way to Khebesh. Some instinct tells her that Xargor Bane will get bricked up in some wall within five minutes of a deal being struck, his position fully eclipsed by Twelve Shits Conspiring.

Thing is, that's the one shell she might be able to pick. Rhan-Gis is already infatuated with her, or at least amused by the novelty. Maybe she can push him, get him to protect her. Play to his city-sized ego. The Sacred Realm may want her dead, but how badly?

Anyway, she's mortal and they're immortal gods. If nothing else, they can wait her out and dance on her grave, like she danced on the grave of the goddess Pesh.

Spar, what the fuck should I do?

Artolo and Rhan-Gis bicker, and the argument swirls around Cari. She's only half listening to it anyway, and it's peppered with references to places or gods she doesn't know, and a lot of posturing. Twelve Coins Bleeding's in the middle of it, too, unctuous and all too calm, trying to sell Artolo on taking Myri as a consolation prize. The Crawling One will pretend to give in any moment now, shrug the shoulders he doesn't have and then start haggling on a price for Cari. He's as transparent as any junk dealer in the market.

You've got a knife. Cari doesn't know if it's a memory of something

Spar said, or her own brain playing tricks on her. It's true, though. She has the sacrificial knife, and that concentrates the problem. Knives have a way of cutting through bullshit, making everything bloody simple.

The problem of who to stab, though, is vexing. Most people in the room are too far away, or won't be affected by a mere knife. She guesses Damala's mortal enough to die from a knife wound. Xargor, too, if his heart doesn't get him first. And Myri's so weak that ending her would be easy. But none of those are helpful options.

So. Rhan-Gis is a powerful saint, and she'd lay money that he can pull off the same damage-redirection trick that Spar did for her. Her little knife isn't going to hurt him. And knives definitely don't hurt Crawling Ones.

Artolo. She can get to Artolo. No one's paying attention to her; they're all arguing over her, around her. She's got no power here, no influence, no god backing her up. All her friends – *all my living friends*, she thinks bitterly – are far away. Taking out Artolo would be satisfying if nothing else, but that's not enough. And, anyway, she's not that strong, not that fast. There's little chance, unless she gets very lucky, of inflicting a mortal wound from here. It's a small knife, not a giant flaming sword.

"The sorceress is of no concern to the Sacred Realm. It was Carillon Thay who blasphemed against Pesh," says Damala. Twelve Coins Bleeding shrugs, holds out his hands, gives a resigned sigh, the universal shrug of the con artist. *I'm cutting half my own throats here, but maybe I can do you a deal on one lightly soiled Cari.*

Think, she screams at herself. *Do something.* She digs her fingernails into her palms, almost hard enough to draw blood.

Blood.

Back in Guerdon, years ago, Cari fought a Raveller, a servant of the Black Iron Gods. Those creatures couldn't be injured by mortal weapons, either – but she'd smeared some of her blood on her knife, and that was enough to wound the creature. Of course, that was because Cari was Herald of the Black Iron Gods, birthed by a Raveller, kin to the creature she fought. Alike enough to get past its defences. Rhan-Gis' nameless saint is like her, too, right? People are always going on about *congruency* and *sympathetic resonance* when it comes to saints. Her grandfather *made* her to match the slumbering Black Iron Gods; now, though, she's a better match for Spar.

And things like Spar.

She runs her palm across the edge of the sacrificial blade. It's sharp.

Don't pick any shell. Kick over the table.

Cari jumps up and stabs the Cornerstone of the World in his beautiful throat.

CHAPTER THIRTY-THREE

There is time, in those days before catastrophe, for confessions.

A note from Karla, delivered by a messenger. Baston's careful only to open it when he's outside the New City, away from prying eyes. It directs Baston to a house in Newtown.

A stone's throw from where they grew up, but two or three worlds away. Newtown's quiet, law-abiding, unlike the rookeries of the Wash on the far side of Military Road. Free city territory. No god has ever walked here save the tame deities of the Keepers, and then only lightly; but Baston can smell the incense from the temples in the IOZ from here. Newtown even escaped significant damage during the invasion. A few patches and spots of fresh whitewash are the only scars left on these regimented terraces.

He raps on the door of one house, and it's answered by a veiled woman.

"Mr Hedanson! Come in, come in. I was just making tea."

They follow the woman in. No – the ghoul, as he catches a glimpse of hoofed feet beneath her skirts. A ghoul, dressed in human garb. He might have walked by her on the street and not known. He recalls a ghoul hanging around the Brotherhood clubhouse, years ago, but she was dressed in stolen rags then, an absurd scarecrow figure. Silkpurse, they called her.

The smell of fresh-baked bread mingles with thick perfume.

Incongruous posters on the hallway walls – old theatre posters, rain-streaked, peeled off the walls and kept as treasures. Baston spots his mother's face in one of them. Elshara stares out at him across thirty years. The ghoul leads them down the hallway to a side door, and out into a little garden.

There, seated in wicker armchairs, are Karla and his mother. Baston blinks, momentarily confused. He knew Karla had moved their mother out of Hog Close for protection, but he'd assumed she had hidden Elshara with some old family contacts, or put her on a train to some outlying town like Maredon. This is something else.

He leans down to kiss his mother's cheek. She frowns, examining the bruises on his face. "You've been in the wars. They've sent the Tallows after you."

"Did the smoke show you that?"

"I cleaned up your father's wounds often enough," snaps Elshara. "I don't need the Smoke Painter to recognise Tallowmen's work."

"We'll name no gods here," says Silkpurse hastily. "Karla asked me to take care of your mother, after the recent unpleasantness." Her voice lacks the rough growl common to ghouls.

"Thank you."

"A pleasure, dearie. To be honest, I've been a fan of Elshara for years, so this has been a treat for me! We've become such good friends! I'll fetch you some food. Surface food of course!" Silkpurse scurries off.

"Keep your voice down," whispers Karla. "Silkpurse is safe enough, but she's still a ghoul – and close to Eladora Duttin, too. We can't trust her."

"You look tired, Bas," says Elshara. "I wish you could rest here." He feels tired. He's been running on adrenaline since the alchemists killed Vyr at the Inn of the Green Door. It's so tempting to sit here, in this quiet sun-drenched garden, and listen to the distant murmur of the city. There are no Tallowmen here, pressing on the windows, stalking him from the rooftops. The New City seems like a distant and improbable dream. He could close his eyes and forget that Guerdon's changed.

But he can't.

"Rasce wants me back soon."

Elshara drops a lump of sugar into her tea like a bomb. "Bas, I've got instructions for you. These come from the master of the Brotherhood, understand?"

"From Heinreil? You're in touch with *him*?" Baston snarls.

"Yes, I am." Elshara stares at her son. "I know how you feel about him, I do. But he's Brotherhood. He's on our side."

"He's got a plan, Bas," adds Karla. "A plan to bring the Brotherhood back, as strong as we ever were. Duttin and her lot, they think they're using him, but he's using them. He's the one who made sure you were recruited by Sinter. You're where the master needs you to be. Heinreil still has connections with the alchemists. We protect their yliaster supply, and they'll owe us. But we've got to act fast, before Rasce makes his move and before the dragon comes back. Imagine what we could do in the Wash, Bas. We go home with all the weapons, all the mercenaries that the dragon's gold can buy. We retake our streets." Karla grabs his hand. "We can have it all back. The Eshdana will follow you. You've been running things for weeks – they trust you."

"What about Rasce?"

"He'll have to go, Bas," says his mother. "He's the linchpin. It would have been better if he'd stayed sick, and we could have kept him as a figurehead until it was time to act. But the alchemist, ah—"

"Vorz," supplies Karla.

"He's forced our hand." Elshara frowns. "Your hand, Bas. It has to be you. You can get close to the Ghierdana. Kill him, kill the alchemist."

Of course Heinreil would use him like this. No matter how he tries to escape it, he's still the master's vicious dog, his brute. He can't build, only break things. He shakes his head. "I can't."

"Heinreil's got that figured out, too," says Karla, misunderstanding his reluctance. "He knows how you get a weapon that can overcome Rasce's powers."

"It's not that," says Elshara, studying her son's face. "Go on, Bas."

Baston stares at his hands. Feels the strength in them, the power in them. Hands used to holding a blade, or a gun. Hands drenched in blood. "That night after the first Tallow attack, Karla, after Vyr threw us out – I got an alchemical bomb. I was going to blow up the Ishmeric temple, and me along with it. Rasce saved me. I owe him my life."

Karla opens her mouth to speak, but Elshara shushes her.

"Do you know why you took that bomb, Bas?" asks Elshara, gently.

"It was a mistake. It doesn't matter now."

"It was a choice. I want to know why you made that choice – if you can tell me. Gods know I've made plenty of stupid choices in my time, and I couldn't always explain them to myself afterwards. But other choices ... marrying your father for one – those I could explain. Those, I had my reasons. What about you? What was the reason you wanted that bomb?"

He shakes his head. "I wanted to fight back," he says after a long pause. He can't find the words to describe his thinking on that night. "I wanted to hurt them. I didn't know how else to do it."

"When I didn't know what my next line was on stage," says Elshara, "I'd call for a prompt, instead of trying to end the whole show. It's hard, I know. Everything's changing, with the Godswar so close. It feels like everything's slipping away, and nothing makes sense. Gods, I know it. Nothing's been right since ... since the Tower of Law burned, maybe. But Heinreil can set it all right again."

"You want to hurt them, Bas," echoes Karla. "We can do that. Heinreil can bring the Brotherhood back, too."

"Heinreil. You're talking like Heinreil's going to walk back in the door. He's in prison, and the only way he's fucking leaving is in a box. And even if they did spring him – the bastard ruined the

Brotherhood! No wonder he's with Duttin and her lot – they're all the same. Using us! Lots of talk about what's necessary and all their clever bloody stratagems, but it's still us dying on the streets! To hell with all of them!" He's shouting now, roaring in his family's faces. Elshara recoils from him.

Karla leaps up. Defiant, anger in her eyes.

"Fine!" she spits. "I'll do it, then!"

"Biscuits!" sings out Silkpurse, re-emerging into the little garden carrying a tray laden with more cups of tea and a plate of biscuits and sandwiches. The ghoul blinks at the tableau before her – Baston and Karla glaring at each other, Elshara pale and shaking.

"Give us a moment," snaps Karla.

"Oh, I can't do that, dearie," says Silkpurse. "I'm being called below – we're off to the Fog Yards, tonight, all us ghouls. Lord Rat's orders. I need to get some surface food in my belly before I go into the dark, so I'm going to sit here with your mother and eat my supper, and we'll have no more shouting." Silkpurse drags over another chair with one hoofed foot, then lays the tray on the table. With ghoulish strength, she yanks Baston and Karla down to their seats.

"Thank you," says Elshara.

Silkpurse removes her veil and lays it aside. Karla absently takes it and folds it. "So pretty," says Silkpurse, glancing at Karla's features. The ghoul scoops up a handful of food and stuffs sandwiches into her wolfish mouth, gagging with every bite, but still forcing them down. She speaks around each mouthful. "I couldn't but overhear. It's maybe not my place to speak, but I'll say my piece anyway. Take it from a Guerdon ghoul – there are always monsters and powerful folk in charge, scheming and squabbling with each other. Sometimes they'll help you and sometimes they'll hurt, but they never give a damn about us on the streets."

"Idge wrote—" says Baston.

"I knew Idge," says Silkpurse. "Lovely man, but not very

practical. He'd walk into an open manhole while talking about moments of destiny. Or Mr Kelkin – I'll always support him, after what he did for the ghouls, but I don't pretend he did it out of love for us. It was Mr Kelkin against the priests, and he could use the ghouls against the church, back in the day. Or . . . " Silkpurse swallows another bite of meat, and sighs. "Or Miss Duttin, whose name I heard mentioned in most unpleasant terms earlier." She kicks Baston's shin, sharply. "Miss Duttin bought me this house, and she's been a good friend to me. She's trying to keep the peace in this city – but Baston's right, she doesn't give a damn about any of us. Not really. I don't mean to be unkind, but when times are hard, it's the folk at the bottom who suffer." She looks at Baston, shading her eyes against the sunlight with her clawed hand. "Does Rasce give a damn about you?"

Baston shakes his head slowly. "I don't know. But Spar does. What if we lose him, too?"

"Spar Idgeson's dead, dearie." Silkpurse finishes the last sandwich, then sucks her fingers. "The ghouls know. Everything comes to ruin in the end." The ghoul stands and bows, like she's stepping offstage. "We'll eat together again, some day soon," she says, "one way or another."

And then she's gone.

For a few moment, the sounds of the city fills the silence of the garden. Distant bells up on Holyhill, and ship engines down in the harbour.

It's Karla who speaks first.

"The ghouls can hide. We can't. We've nowhere else to go. It has to be done."

"It's not just Rasce," says Baston quietly. "It's Spar."

"We've seen no sign of him since Vorz came back." Suppressed panic in Karla's voice. "And the dragon follows after Vorz. We've no time. We have to act now."

"We do have a choice," says Elshara. "Let's be honest with

ourselves. Baston – you'll be the one pulling the trigger. What do you want to do?"

He closes his eyes. In a way, it would be a relief to be told what to do again. To give in and just be a weapon again, instead of a man who has to think and to live and to feel.

"It's not enough to go back," he says slowly. "Nothing will ever change for the better while the alchemists and Duttin and their sort are in charge. What's Heinreil's plan?"

Baston listens as Karla outlines what he's supposed to do next, what Heinreil's plotted for him from his prison cell.

The girl in the tailor's shop on Greyhame Street ushers Baston into the back room again and unlocks the cabinet that conceals the aethergraph. It takes a few minutes before the machine goes live, before Baston senses the ugly presence of Sinter on the other end.

NEED TO TALK IN PERSON. IT'S URGENT, he types.

USE AETHERGRAPH, comes the reply.

NO.

He hits the power stud, shuts the machine down. And waits.

The girl comes in, tells him to leave. He doesn't hit her, but he twists her arm in the way the Fever Knight taught him, tells her softly not to scream. Tells her that he's not going until he gets to talk to Sinter.

She runs off. Comes back in a few minutes with two big louts. Baston's last few fights have been with Tallowmen, so it's nice to hit someone who feels pain, to hit someone who can't dodge so quick. To hit someone who goes down when you smash a head into a cabinet, or who roars in pain when you put their face through a dressing-room mirror.

He sits and waits amid the devastation for the priest to show up.

"Fuck me," says Sinter, stepping over the unconscious bodies. "But you're the shittiest spy I've ever run."

"I want to make a deal."

"We had a deal. You tell us what Rasce's up to, and we spare your slut of a sister. Your ma. Your drinking pals down in Pulchar's. Most of them are still alive, despite you being singularly bad at telling us what we needed to know. For example, just a passing thought, why the fuck was there an Ulbishe-made aethergraph in the room where young Vyr got killed?"

"I don't know anything about that."

"No? Clever thing, I'm told. More advanced than even the ones our alchemists can make. Long range, no fecking wires. Why, they'd love to have a poke at it – only someone took a knife to it, smashed it all to pieces first. See any fuckers from Ulbishe running around the New City?"

"Not that I know of."

"What do you know?"

"It's you and Nemon and Duttin running the Tallowmen now – I want you to pull the jacks back. They're killing us."

Sinter scratches his nose. "Seems to me," he says slowly, "that you're falling short on your end. You've given us chickenfeed. Why, in the name of a goddess I shan't name, should I help you scum? Brotherhood or Ghierdana, you're all a gang of fucking thieves."

"I told the Ghierdana that the tunnel into Mandel's refinery was blocked, just like Duttin ordered. But . . . Rasce can work miracles now. Like the Saint of Knives. He's got her gifts. Her sainthood. And there's some alchemist, too, now – he knew it was going to happen."

"How could—" Sinter interrupts himself. "You shits!" He leaps to his feet, admiration mixing with anger in his voice. "That's *my* trick, you bastards. Ha! Damnation, damnation, I should have trailed a vestment myself." Sinter shakes his head. "Who's this alchemist? Is he the dragon's counsellor? Name of Vorz?"

Baston nods. "He knew Rasce could do what Cari did."

"Ach. So, what's Rasce doing with this gift?"

"He looked inside Mandel's fortress. He knows the way in still exists. Then he captured the Rat, and now the ghouls have agreed to bring the Ghierdana through the undercity. He's going to go after the Fog Yards." Baston hesitates for a moment. "I'm telling you this, so you can make ready. Warn Mandel."

"Rasce is a single-minded little shit, isn't he?" Sinter rubs his bald pate. "Aye, we'll make preparations."

"Preparations that'll get my lads killed. So, I want out. And I want the Brotherhood safe."

Sinter raises his three-fingered hand. "Knowing about Vorz is useful." He curls one finger down. "Confirmation about young Rasce's plans is useful." Two fingers. Only one left. "But it's not enough. Won't be enough for the lady." The priest scratches his nose with that one outstretched finger. "Duttin would prefer something quiet. So – can you kill him quietly?"

"He's like the Saint of Knives. Your Tallowman couldn't cut his throat. What makes you think I can?"

"Fair point. Fair point." Sinter nods, slowly. "I had this made, when I was looking for a way to dispose of Carillon Thay safely. It's a bullet carved from a holy relic of Saint Aleena Humber. She killed a lot of Thays in her day, you know. If young Rasce is borrowing Thay's sanctity, the bullet should work on him, too." He hands Rasce a loaded pistol.

The weapon seems unusually weighty in Rasce's hand. He stares at it, then thrusts it hastily into his pocket.

"Well then, there we are. Good lad. Now, do it sharpish, before he causes any more trouble. Rid us of this troublesome saint, and I'll let your pack of thieves get clear of the New City. I'll have Nemon give you a fair head start, too, before we start hunting you." The priest grabs Baston's arm with his maimed hand. "Fair warning, though – last time I tried killing a saint like that, it cost me dear. You'll get one shot. Don't miss."

Baston brushes against the priest, pulling free as he makes for the door. "Got to get back before I'm missed."

"It's fine," complains Sinter. "Leave me here to clean up this mess." Groaning, the priest bends down to tend to the unconscious thugs, little shards of broken mirror cracking under his feet.

He doesn't notice the pebble that Baston slipped into his pocket.

Rasce visits the Lyrixian military enclave in the New City. The walls of this dome are strong and proud, the doors rebuilt and fortified by the occupying military forces. The battlements bristle with cannons and artillery pieces purchased from the forges of Guerdon, and he can tell that there are more such weapons in the bowels of the compound. Ahead of him are the dragon-gates, a wide breach in the dome, blasted open so the dragons can enter the clave; to his left, the wide plaza where the dragons land. He remembers his last flight with Great-Uncle, when he circled over the city. Soon, he'll fly again.

The guards at the doors regard him with a familiar mixture of wary respect, for they know he is Chosen of the Dragon Taras, and scorn, for the Ghierdana are criminals. They bar his path as he approaches.

"I wish to enter," says Rasce.

"Your dragon is still absent," replies the captain of the guard. "You have no business here."

"He's diseased," whispers another guard to one of his comrades. He's out of Rasce's earshot, but close to the living stone of the wall, and so Rasce hears him.

"I shall enter," says Rasce again, and he reaches out his mind and *moves*. The stone wall cracks, splits, rolls back, making a door just for him. He strides forward, his footsteps shaking the ground, knocking the guards away. Even as he glories in his miraculous gifts, Rasce can feel his power ebbing. Each miracle costs him, depleting the strength gleaned from Vorz's experiments on Lanthorn Street.

But soon Great-Uncle will return, and Vorz has promised him all the power he'll need.

He strides into the dome. The dragon Thyrus is there, freshly returned from a combat flight. She's half clad in battle-scarred armour; alchemists are spraying her with exorcising foam to rid her of lingering miracles from the battlefield. Her Chosen rider lies on a stretcher nearby.

Major Estavo emerges from a side office and hurries up to Rasce. Medals jiggling as he runs. "You shouldn't be here, boy! You think I don't know what you're up to? Theft, arson, provoking the alchemists! You're endangering the war effort! The longer Taras stays away, the thinner my patience grows! I cannot—"

"That is why I am here, Major." Rasce smiles. "Doctor Vorz tells me that my Great-Uncle returns tonight."

"To active duty?" The major's relief is palpable. With his inner eye, Rasce can see the maps and reports in Estavo's office; he can see the battle lines in the south, the precarious situation of the Lyrixian expeditionary forces.

"I cannot speak for his plans after he returns, but I would assume so. My Great-Uncle is a patriot, after all. We all look towards securing the future of Lyrix, and the defeat of the mad gods."

Thyrus pulls herself free from the exorcism rig and stomps across the floor of the dome, shedding pieces of broken armour like dead scales.

"Rasce. I thought you were on your death bed." The dragon lowers her massive head, sniffs at him – and recoils, snorting fire in alarm. "What is this? What are you?" She spreads her wings, filling the dracodrome. "What has Vorz done to you?"

"Nothing that need threaten you, O Thyrus," says Rasce. "But to both of you, I say: tonight, do not interfere. I give you my word that neither the military enclave nor the holdings of the other Ghierdana families will be endangered."

If they object or argue, he has many darts to throw, arguments honed in discussion with Vorz. Rasce knows all their secrets now. He knows that Estavo is a habitual user of blackmarket elixirs, knows that two of Estavo's staff are secret spies for Haith. He knows that

Thyrus' Chosen murdered the Chosen of Carancio in a backstreet duel, and that the truth of the incident was concealed from both dragons. Knows, too, that there's a warehouse down near Shriveport that contains the cargo from a Haithi vessel, and that Thyrus took the ship in Guerdon waters, in breach of the Armistice.

But there's no need for all these weapons. He can hold them in reserve, conserve them like his stock of miraculous power. The threat is enough.

"Have your Great-Uncle report to me when he returns. At his convenience, of course," mutters Estavo, smoothing his moustache. Relieved, as if he's navigated some dispute he didn't quite understand, but is now resolved.

Thyrus bows her head. "Hail the new saint of this strange city," she says, "but do not forget what became of the last one."

Rasce laughs. "The Saint of Knives fought alone. I have many friends."

Lanthorn Street has become a military encampment. Thieves and mercenaries fill the street outside, and Baston cannot tell one group from the other. The dragon's gold and a lot more beside has been spent on alchemical weaponry. The host bristles with rifles and hand-cannons. Baston pushes past men he might once have known, now rendered beetle-headed and anonymous by the protective gas masks they wear. Loose tarpaulins on wagons promise other horrors – there are canisters of knife-smoke there, and blasting dust. Maybe some of the weapons were made by Mandel, and now they shall return home.

Baston lingers a moment by a phlogistonic siege charge. He runs his gloved hand over the metal sphere, remembering the heat of the flash.

All these weapons, and none of them could be sure of killing Rasce – yet the little gun in his pocket could manage it. Strange indeed are the ways of divinity.

A beetle-mask hails Baston. It's Gunnar, his voice rendered

strange by the breathing apparatus. It reminds Baston of how the Fever Knight spoke. "Where've you been? It's been a hell of a job, getting all this ready."

"Orders from above," mutters Baston. "Where's Rasce?"

"Inside. I'll let him know you're back."

"He knows."

Baston approaches the house. The sniper on the rooftop tracks him as he walks, and the gunman's eyes aren't the only ones watching Baston. Karla's in the crowd, too, somewhere. She's one of the beetle-masked people, too, and the thought of his sister perishing in the underworld chills him. Their father went down into the darkness, too, and never returned.

He enters the house, the gun heavy in his pocket. The Eshdana guards don't search him as he crosses the threshold, and no one stops him as he heads to Rasce's chambers.

Rasce's half dressed, his torso bare. A half-dozen needles laid out on the table, and one big syringe of alkahest next to a bottle of arax. Vorz leans over the younger man like a vampire, working through the row of syringes. "You left the New City," says Rasce, wincing as another dose of Vorz's tincture shoots through his veins. "Is all well?"

"Boss . . . I need a word."

"Speak."

Baston pulls out the gun, and in one practised motion ejects the phlogiston charge. "Eladora Duttin sent me to kill you. That bullet's magic – it can wound you. They've had me spying on you since the start."

He drops the weapon on to the desk, the holy bullet rolling across the green baize surface to clink against the arax.

"I planted a pebble on Duttin's spymaster. I figured you'd want to return the favour."

CHAPTER THIRTY-FOUR

R han-Gis gurgles blood.

He looks at Cari in confusion. For a moment, she swears there's a look of *relief* on his face, but she can't be sure, because he topples over backwards and then—

Oh god, and then—

Wrath strikes the throne room in the temple of Rhan-Gis.

Without the presence of the saint, the god's wrath is unfocused. Indiscriminate. A skyquake, the heavens shattering and exploding in fury. The temple cracks asunder, one of the great teak runners supporting it falls away, tipping the whole structure over to the side. The sky blackens like a bruise, and the stones cry out in anguish and anger.

This is what Cari knows: everything's fucked. The air full of dust and smoke and thunderous fury. She can barely see, and she's drenched in hot blood. Her right hand's numb and weirdly heavy. All around her, people moan or shout or scream. Or let off guns, which really doesn't help. Half-blind, she crawls across the cracked tiles, feeling her way. Sandpaper no longer describes the sensation of divine proximity – no, now her brain is bathed in some acidic stew that's seeping down her spine.

Clambering over bodies. Something squishes beneath the weight of her numb right hand, and then she feels rubbery, writhing worms against her cheek. Twelve Shits Conspiring has collapsed into his constituent parts, all slithering around on the floor. The worms crawl towards her, tumbling over each other.

One of them – some of them? All of them – is Adro. Everything her friend was, consumed in death and preserved in the worm. Eladora told her about their grandfather, Jermas Thay – he became a Crawling One, but he was still *himself.* Could Adro still be saved? Could she sift the worms, find the one that's him? It's madness, but is it crazier than saving Spar? Or are some forms of survival too awful to contemplate?

The worm brushes against her skin, and she recoils, acts on instinct. One of the lamps is nearby; Cari gives it a shove with her leg so burning lamp oil sluices across the sloping floor, catching the bulk of the worms, never mind that she's now scalded on top of everything else. *I'm sorry. I couldn't save you. I tried.*

Through a gap in the smoke, she glimpses the Ishmeric priestess, Damala, half buried by falling masonry.

You, I don't give a fuck about, whoever you are.

She crawls on, ducking her head as there's another burst of gunfire, heading for Myri, heading for the fucking book, lying next to the stunned body of Xargor Bane.

She nearly makes it.

Artolo grabs her from behind. He roars, an animalistic noise louder than the wrath of god in her ear. His tentacle-fingers grabbing at her hair, lashing around her neck. His face is a mask of blood. She struggles to breathe, her fingers scrabbling against the tiles as he tries to yank her backwards. Her numbed right hand scrapes across the floor, breaking through the binding circle around Myri. There's a flash of sorcery that stuns Cari and sends Artolo flying across the room.

Next thing Cari knows, they're stumbling down a narrow stairway, leaning on each other. Cari's got the grimoire and the aethergraph under her arm, although she can't remember picking them up. Her skull's ringing like a bell. The whole building is heaving and thrashing, as if it's alive and wounded. More skyquakes overhead, artillery bursting in heaven.

"What were you thinking?" screams Myri in her ear.

Good question, but not the time for it. And the honest answer is *"I tried to actually really carefully consider the outcomes of my action, and it turned out pretty much the same as acting on instinct, and everything exploded."*

The light in the smoke-filled stairwell looks weird to Cari, and then she works out that Myri's tattoos are glowing like they're on fire. Shielding them from divine assault, or divination, or some other horrible fate. Cari feels a stab of misplaced jealousy – even in her wounded, exhausted state, the sorceress is vastly more capable than she.

Outside is like inside with more mud. The city of Gissa started out ruined, but now it's falling apart in places. Falling *together* in others, as the divine attention of Rhan-Gis sweeps across the wreckage, and, wherever the god's presence passes, the city reasserts itself, stone crawling on stone to rebuild. Rhan-Gis is looking for another saint, a replacement for the avatar that Cari just shanked. Cari's heard people compare sainthood to getting struck by lightning, and she's just unleashed a great big thunderstorm. Some poor soul is going to find they're the tallest tree in the forest when Rhan-Gis chooses them and fills them with His divinity.

Until then, absolute chaos. The faithful pressing their faces into the mud, screaming prayers to their disrupted god or running riot. Resurrected guards and soldiers stumbling around, holding on to their brickwork patches, mortar running between their fingers like blood. Gunfire, off in the distance. Cari doesn't like the look of the clouds on the northern horizon, either. They remind her of Artolo's new fingers, writhing and grasping. Ishmerian cloud demons, the spawn of Cloud Mother. Fuck.

A trio of kids run past them, burdened with loot. Cari has no idea what one would pillage in this broken place, but somehow the sight cheers her. She hefts Myri, helps her stumble down the street.

Myri mutters a spell. It must be a big one – the backlash staggers her, arcane energies lighting up her bones and twisting her muscles, and Cari has to carry her until the fit passes. Still, Cari guesses the spell works – everyone's ignoring them now. People look at them and don't see them. The same trick Twelve Suns Bleeding did back in Ushket.

"Go south," hisses Myri, "you're going the wrong way."

"East," says Cari, "we're going east. Back to the sea."

To the fishing village. To Yhandis.

Artolo staggers through the ruins of the throne room. Worms shriek with human voices as they burn. He steps over bodies – the dead avatar, some of his own men, some of the city guards – to follow after Carillon Thay. She was within his grasp! How can she escape, again?

A hand reaches from the rubble, clutches at his foot. Damala. He kneels down and clears away the fallen stones. They're sticky with the old woman's blood. He lifts away another brick, revealing her bruised and broken face.

"The gods have foreseen—" She tries to speak, her voice a broken whisper.

"I shall kill her," he says. He prizes her hand away with his Kraken-fingers.

"Give . . . me . . . drown . . . my body," she gasps, her eyes pleading. The Kraken-burial. Her soul can only be claimed by her god if she's given a water burial. Otherwise her residuum will curdle in her corpse until it's taken by some other god or psychopomp, or until it seeps into the earth and dissipates.

The sea's on the other side of those mountains. Carillon has no boat now. Her only route is south, across the wastes. Every second he lingers here gives her more time to escape, delays his revenge.

But he owes Damala's gods. His gods, now. He has to honour the

Kraken and all the gods of Ishmere, make the proper offerings — even if it gives Thay another day of unworthy life. He takes the heat of his anger, quenches it in dark, icy water.

Gunfire, close at hand. He ducks down again, crawls through the dust and smoke to the door. His Eshdana soldiers hold the main entrance to the throne room against the servants of Rhan-Gis. "Boss! Too many of them! We've got to fight our way out!" One of them thrusts a gun into Artolo's hand.

He holds the weapon, feels its weight, then lets it slip. That's not his weapon, not any more.

"Bar the doors," he orders.

"There aren't any other ways out. We're trapped."

"Bring the remains of Damala," he orders.

He walks back into the devastation. He finds the overturned throne, shoves off the body of the saint of Rhan-Gis. There are already a few grave-worms, escapees from the fire, nibbling at the corpse's ears and nose, and he brushes them aside and crushes them underfoot. "Check Damala's remains for worms," he shouts. The Crawlers will not take her soul. The worms desperately crawl away, wriggling down cracks in the tiled floor.

The body of a saint has special potency. So much of the god was channelled through this mortal frame that what remains must be a rich offering. He lifts the body of the saint of Rhan-Gis. It's oddly heavy, like it's a sack of bricks, but he's strong enough to lift it. Strong enough to carry it one-handed as he scales the wall, his tentacle-fingers extending to find cracks and finger-holds, lifting him up to one of the deep-set apertures that let light into this throne room, the uppermost chamber of the pyramidal temple. He climbs out on to the sloped roof, clambers up to the apex.

From here, he can see all the city.

Gissa convulses beneath him. A vast crowd, virtually all the population of this cursed city, surrounds the temple, a sea of mad humanity. They hammer on the doors, claw at the walls. Weep and scream, the anger of the god echoed in the souls of his worshippers. They will kill him, kill all the trespassers. He scans the crowd, looking for two women moving against the mob, but he can see no sign of Carillon and the witch.

His revenge will not come today. But the gods have promised it to him. And the gods of Ishmere keep their promises.

He takes the still warm corpse of the saint of Rhan-Gis and splays it on the roof of the pyramid. He digs his tentacle-fingers into the saint's belly, pulls out hot steaming ropes of entrail and organ, throws them down the roof.

For a moment he's back in his chambers in Ushket, when he murdered that stupid servant. Then, he spilled the boy's entrails out of hatred and frustration and anger. Now, on this rooftop, he moves with a quiet reverence.

This is an offering.

Cloud Mother takes her souls in the air burial, and this is a rich bounty of soul-stuff indeed.

And he is rewarded. Tendrils of solid cloud reach down from the chaos in the sky, lift him off the pyramid. Other tendrils pick up his surviving followers, and the body of Damala, and carry them into the sky.

East, towards *Moonchild* and the sea.

Dark clouds gather over Gissa, like the gods have poured ink across the sky. Saints ride there; hands of fog reach down towards the broken temple. Cari hustles Myri out of the city, following the trail left by the marching hosts. No one pays them any heed. Cari can't tell if Myri's attention-deflection spell is still working, or if everyone's too shell-shocked to notice two women fleeing.

Myri stumbles, her legs giving out. She lets out a snarl of frustration that's somehow also an incantation, her tattoos flaring with defiant light. Cari picks her up. "Come on. Come on. Move, wizard." She's like Spar was, towards the end. Inhumanly strong in his way, but also kitten-weak, fragile, prone to collapsing. Although Myri's a lot lighter, which is a relief.

"Come on," urges Cari. Shit, she's no good at being encouraging. She starts telling Adro's story, about how they stole a cargo load of blue jade from the Eyeless priestesses on Mattaur. She tries to tell it the way Adro did, a farcical yarn involving a lot of running around pitch-dark tunnels – turned out stealing from blind priests wasn't that easy – but she can't remember half of his jokes. It sickens her that the worms have stolen that from her, too. There's a Crawling One out there who could recite Adro's story note-perfect, word for word, laugh for booming laugh, but her friend is gone.

Myri isn't even listening to her anyway, but Cari keeps telling the story. Reciting it like a prayer, like she's staking a claim. So much has been taken from her, and so much of her life has become entangled with gods and sorcery and alchemy and everything else she flings into the bucket marked "magic shit", that she's determined to keep this story unsoiled. It's a funny tale about incompetent thieves, and that's all it is.

In the distance, she hears the thunder of an antique cannon, firing wildly into the air. Mercifully, though, it's not a full-on invasion by the Sacred Realm. The people of the city get to live, at least today. And hell, while Rhan-Gis is disorientated, maybe some of them will find the courage to walk away. There's got to be something better out there, right?

By nightfall, she's not so sure. Hours of travel across the god-blasted wastes, and she's seen nothing but desolation and horror. The landscape's a palimpsest of broken miracles. Other than Myri, she doesn't encounter another living soul – and, to be honest, Myri's right on the borderline. Cari gives her the last of her painkilling drug – fumbling with the little vial, her frozen hand making everything awkward – and the sorceress slips into unconsciousness.

Sighing, Cari picks up the sorceress again, staggers around until she finds a sheltered hole in the mud. It's a big hole – a shell crater, probably, or some sort of blasting miracle. Either way, it tore a chunk out of the ground.

"I mean," says Cari as she drags the sorceress down the slope, "can you imagine a better fucking mud-hole in the middle of the Godswar? This is a great hole. Absolutely top-class."

She lays Myri down to rest in a cleft in the earth, and lies down next to her, trying to ignore the pangs of hunger gnawing at her belly. The Fucking Book between them like a metal child, all hard corners and edges. Cari's hand remains numb. Divine punishment, she guesses. She blasphemed against Rhan-Gis by striking his saint.

Nothing she can do about it now, and her mind's too numb for fear. Maybe in Khebesh they can remove the curse.

It's a horribly warm night, like someone's breathing on Cari's skin all the time, so they're not going to freeze to death. She's still wearing the absurd temple-handmaiden outfit that they gave her in Gissa, although the skirts are no longer white as polished ivory. The belt of gold and emeralds is still gold and emeralds, though, so technically Cari's richer right now than she's ever been in her whole life. She'd trade it all for a sandwich. For Hawse's fried fish. For Eladora's soup, which in Cari's head is still bubbling away on the stove on Desiderata Street, years ago and worlds away ...

She sleeps, thoughts breaking up, fracturing, dissipating into dream.

Dreams are dangerous in the Godswar. Another attack vector, a way for the ghosts of broken gods or other spirits to strike. Before Gissa, Myri would draw protective wards every night so they could sleep safely, but she's too exhausted to act. But no strange god or spirit troubles Cari's dreams this night. Instead, she dreams of Desiderata Street, of the Raveller that chased her, emissary of the Black Iron Gods. In the dream, she flees across rooftops.

Guerdon blurs into Ushket, another rooftop escape, and the Ravellers still pursue. The streets below seethe with writhing, glistening, fluid forms. The Ravellers are thieves of form, stealing shapes and faces from their victims. Flensing their souls away, stealing the bodies.

Ushket into Ilbarin. The Ravellers are a flood, a tide of darkness, washing over the buildings below. The waters are rising. Kraken-tentacles rise. (*Why do all these fucking gods and monsters love their fucking tentacles so much*, she thinks.)

Ilbarin into Gissa. The Ravellers wanted to raise her up, make her their queen. Make her into something like the saint of Rhan-Gis. She dreams of a dark city, a nightmare Guerdon, where writhing towers reach up and tear the stars from the sky, where terrified people flee down constricting streets until the city consumes them. A dragon soars over the city, and the towers burn.

The floodwaters wash over the edge of the roof, leaving her with nowhere else to climb, nowhere else to hide, caught between the flood and the fire.

Darkness consumes her.

Waking in a panic, breathless, screaming. Tentacles become hands, pawing at her. Clawing at her, biting her. Fractured moonlight shows her a half-dozen humanoid figures crowding around her and Myri. Cari leaps up, slipping in the mud. No knife, no sword, no weapon – except the Fucking Book. The book, armoured in its steel-edged case. She grabs the Grimoire of Doctor Ramegos, a tome that holds secrets that wars have been fought over, gods have killed for, and uses it to club at her attackers.

With a desperate, unexpected strength, she catches one of them in the side of the head, driving a corner of the book into the creature's skull. The thing staggers back, falls, tumbling and sliding down into the crater. She turns, brings the book down hard on the forearm of one clawing at Myri's unconscious form.

The attackers shriek, turn and flee. As they crest the rim of the crater, the moonlight catches them and she gets a brief glimpse of what they look like. Small, thin-limbed, greyish flesh drawn tight over limbs and spines. Gods below, she can't tell if they're humans or ghouls or something else, but they're no bigger than children. They scramble away, crawling on all fours, flinching as distant thunder rolls in the sky. Reciting a chanted litany of blasphemy, rote-learned, to fend off the attention of any passing gods.

That's what human survival looks like in the Godswar. Those are your choices – submit to the whims of some insane husk of a deity like in Gissa, or end up like a feral ghoul, an animal.

"Come on!" hisses Cari. "We're going, now!"

"Sleeping," mumbles Myri, curling around the rock she's using as a pillow.

"Come on!" Cari urges her. She transfers the Fucking Book to the crook of one arm, uses her good hand to yank Myri upright. They're not spending a minute longer than necessary here.

They struggle up the slope and march off across the wasteland. Weirdland, wonderland. It's like some god reached across Guerdon and grabbed all the unused backdrops and stage sets from the Metropolitan Theatre, and all the altar paintings and statues from all the temples, and then dropped them all in the mud. Stamped on them a few times, then vomited copiously on the mess. Oh, and then had an artillery battery shell the shit out of it all, for good measure.

Around dawn, they shelter from an unlikely snowstorm in the hollow of a gigantic skull the size of a house, half sunk in the mud. They watch through the eyeholes as a titanic black serpent – beautiful beyond measure, its scales marked with astrological symbols – slithers by outside. The snake fades as the sun rises, dissolving like mist. It's still there – just looking at it gives Cari that god-sense headache – and she guesses it's slipped out of the mortal world, moved back to the aether.

"You never finished the story," says Myri.

"What story?"

"About blue jade. About you and Adro and Hawse, and the *Rose*."

"I did." Cari feels oddly embarrassed. "You passed out."

"Oh. I was enjoying it." A pause. "I can smell the sea."

Myri's right – the wind has changed, and it's fresher, cleaner. They're nearly out. They're nearly through.

"We're far enough south now, maybe, to be clear of the Kraken," says Cari. "We get a boat at the fishing village. Sail as close as we can to Khebesh." *The sea is bigger than gods*, she thinks, and it's an odd thought, and not entirely hers.

"It's not far inland," agrees Myri. She licks her broken lips with a blackened tongue. "In Khebesh, there are golden orchards of apples and figs. Wheat waving in the sun, behind the Ghost Walls." Myri leans back against the inner wall of the skull. "I mean, fuck the masters of Khebesh, but it'll be nice to get some real food. And to rest." She closes her eyes.

Only one of us gets to pass through the Ghost Walls, though. We only have one book.

Cari lifts the Fucking Book. One corner is still stained with blood from when she fought off the ghouls. And Myri's weak. Defenceless. One good swing . . .

"Captain Hawse waited for us," says Cari. "He kept the *Rose* riding at anchor in the bay, until Adro and I found our way out of the tunnels. Nearly drowned carrying the jade, so most of it's at the bottom of the sea off Mattaur. But we made it."

She slings the pack on her back, the ornamented edge of the aethergraph digging into her sore ribs while the book scrapes the same vertebra as always. She's really sick of dragging this stuff across the world.

"Come on," she says again. "We'll rest in Yhandis."

Yhandis is wonderfully dull. It's a few huts, a few leaky little boats, masts outlined against the tortured sky like armless signposts, as if to say "there's nowhere to go from here". Stony fields with a few goats grazing there. It's all in a little enclave, surrounded on two sides by the new mountains and on the other two sides by the sea, with only a narrow pass affording access from the land. A sheltered place. Even the weather is dull and damp.

Cari hides her cursed hand in a fold of her skirt, and bribes the sentries at the pass with emeralds. It's that or have Myri blast them.

The villagers look at them with suspicion. Cari tries to bargain for passage to Khebesh, but it turns out most of them never sail further than a few miles out. There's one fisherman who might be willing to risk a longer voyage, Mad Quint, but he's not due back until tomorrow.

"We'll wait," says Cari. Like they have a choice.

The villagers aren't happy about that. Strangers out of the Godswar could bring anything with them, and it's always more perilous at night. No one's willing to offer them shelter.

Cari points to one building, longer than the rest. A thin wisp of smoke rises from the roof, and the poles outside suggest it's being used to smoke fish. Something about its outline reminds her of . . . of Captain Hawse's books. There were once carvings on the door, too, but they've been hacked away. It was a temple to the Lord of Waters before it was a smokehouse. Declaring allegiance to a god here is probably like wearing a uniform in a regular war, or wearing the Five Knives gang kerchief in the Wash back in Guerdon.

Still, people remember old oaths. Cari dredges up the memory of a prayer to the Lord of Waters, a plea for aid made by shipwrecked sailors. She leans towards one of the villagers, whispers it in the old man's ear.

"One night," he says. "You can stay one night."

CHAPTER THIRTY-FIVE

"You spied on us?" Vorz bares his teeth and lunges for his bag of tricks. Baston grabs the alchemist's hand, pins it to the desk, then punches Vorz in the face, stunning him, breaking his nose again. The pale man goes down in a tangle of limbs.

Rasce doesn't react. He picks up the bullet, holds it up to some light Baston cannot perceive. "I see it," he says, dreamily. "There's holy fire in this." He reaches out his hand, holding the bullet above the stone floor. Then he tips it out. The bullet falls, and it's like the stone is suddenly liquid, a marble pond. The bullet vanishes, ripples spreading out from the point of impact to break on the legs of the wooden desk, to splash against the toe of Baston's boot. "And that's that. What else did they have you do? What else did you tell them?"

Baston shrugs. "Little enough they didn't already know. But, boss – the gods in the street know that you're going after Mandel & Company. They know about the tunnel. They'll be waiting for you."

Rasce pours a glass of arax for himself, passes another to Baston. The Ghierdana prince sips the liquor. "You know, my friend, if you *had* taken the ash, I'd be obligated to kill you for this betrayal. Instead, I can act as I see fit. Tell me, Baston, if you were me, what would you do?"

"Use the stone I planted and find Duttin's Tallow Vats, and end them. Free the Rat, and work with the ghouls, the Brotherhood.

Since the invasion, there are a lot of angry, scared people in this city. Give them weapons. Give them a champion. Give them . . . give them a future." As he says those words, something touches Baston's soul, and for an instant he sees as Rasce sees, as Cari must have seen. The whole shining promise of the New City whirls around him, a city made to be a refuge from the madness of the Godswar and the cruelty of tyrants. For an instant, it's like a bomb going off inside his brain, and he soars.

And then it's gone. Baston staggers, holding on to the desk for support.

Rasce leans back. "And the dragon? My Great-Uncle's commands?"

"He'll have to be patient, won't he? We can retake what we've lost, but not overnight. Take out Duttin's Tallow Vats first. And then . . . gods below, Rasce, look out of the window. We've got a fucking army there. Give me time, and—"

"Idiot!" spits Vorz from the corner. "There is no more time. The dragon returns tonight!"

"You don't know my Great-Uncle, Baston," says Rasce. "Patience is not among the virtues of the dragon. Doctor Vorz, go you to the cellars. I shall have need of more residuum, for the visions I must seek."

The doctor drags himself upright. "I'm not finished your injections," he says sourly.

"Baston will attend to those."

Vorz skulks out.

Baston picks up one of Vorz's tinctures. The vial contains something reddish, like diluted blood. Dark shapes congeal and then unravel, forming and unforming. "Are you sure you want this in your veins?"

"Look at me, friend." Rasce gestures to the stony plates that have spread across his chest. "A little more adds little to my burden." One by one, Baston injects the syringes into Rasce. Finally, he picks up the heavy alkahest syringe. Unlike the tincture, the alkahest must be injected into the flesh beneath the stony plates. The needle is made of steel, to punch through the stone.

"Should I summon Karla?" asks Rasce. "She has the knack of it."

"No," says Baston hastily. "I'll do it." His fingers fumble with the heavy syringe. As the alkahest diffuses, Rasce shudders with release.

"Now. I shall see."

The vision shows Rasce a room he has never seen before, but it's thick with familiarity, a patina of Idgeson's memories on every surface. It's a prison cell of sorts, a large room, mostly flooded with stagnant water, with a small artificial island in the middle. A cell for Stone Men, who might otherwise use their tremendous strength to smash through the bars.

Jere Taphson's lithosarium, although he has no idea who this Taphson is or what he meant to Spar.

His mind drifts in the vision, passing through the walls like a ghost.

Many of the cells are occupied, but not by Stone Men. Other saints, other powers. In one of the flooded rooms, he glimpses a god-touched mermaid swimming through the water, her body partially transformed into a Kraken. A young red-haired woman lying motionless in a bed, eyes glassy and unseeing. A sailor, with bronzed skin and blue-tinged lips, bloodied by a recent beating.

A collection of oddities.

Tallowmen stand watch outside. The flames burning in their heads flicker as Spar passes by.

Voices draw him in. His awareness moves down the corridor, towards an office. Now, he's an invisible presence, his entry permitted by a pebble hidden in the pocket of a priest's robe, hung on one of a pair of a hooks on the wall.

Three people. Rasce recognises two of them – Eladora Duttin and Alic Nemon. The third is an ugly man in a priest's cassock.

"Still nothing?" asks Eladora. She's seated behind a heavy desk. Two aethergraph machines on her desk, and a third – disconnected, looped into itself – on the floor by her feet. A cold cup of coffee, undrunk next to a stack of reports.

"Nothing." Sinter sucks at his broken teeth. "I don't know if Hedan's boy took the shot and failed, or if he lost his nerve."

"What about our other informants?"

"Hard for any of my street-scum to get close. Not with the fucking *streets* watching. And there's no time, anyway. They're hitting the Fog Yards tonight. It's going to be a fucking mess."

"We have our own interests in Mandel & Company to consider, of course," says Nemon. The minister is not a small man, but he has the knack of fading into the background when he wishes to be forgotten. He looks around the room, and Rasce's suddenly worried that Nemon can tell he's being watched. "But Mandel assures me his defences are ready for any assault. Our task will be to contain the damage – and convince Ishmere and Haith that the Armistice holds."

"With the fucking Ghierdana running rampant across half the city? The only fucking reason the war *stopped* is because Haith needs the weapons we supply 'em. If they hear the Ghierdana are going after the alchemists . . . " Sinter groans and buries his face in his hands. "Godshit. I remember smuggling relics out of the monastery on Beckanore ten years ago, before the Haithi torched it. All part of the same fucking deal. Without alchemical weapons, Haith's fucked. They won't stand aside. It'll be a fucking mess, I tell you."

"To my mind," says Nemon, "the situation has run its course. The threat from Rasce's attacks was enough to force the alchemists to put the Tallowmen under our control, and prompt parliament to reverse the ban on making more. We have the Tallows now."

"'We'," echoes Sinter scornfully. "Do we now, minister?"

"Enough," snaps Eladora. "Say you're right, Alic. What do you propose?"

"The other Ghierdana families are already irritated by Rasce. Doubtless nervous, too, if they know what he can do. We send the Tallowmen into the New City – tonight, before Taras returns. We pray that the other dragons do not intervene."

"An attack on the Ghierdana has to be met with retribution. That's their code. 'S'why we needed Hedanson to pull the fucking trigger," adds Sinter. "Little shit. Can't get the staff, these days."

"I won't countenance an attack on the New City," says Eladora. Nemon opens his mouth to object, but Eladora drops one hand beneath the desk and taps on the aethergraph.

"All right," says Nemon, "then set them on each other. We let Rasce know what happened in the inn."

"How will you do that?"

"Walls have ears." He crosses the room and plucks the pebble from its hiding place.

Baston leaves the house on Lanthorn Street. As he closes the door, strange lights blaze from the walls in Rasce's room. The air's thick with magic. Static electricity crawls and leaps; Baston orders some of his lads to move the stocks of phlogiston away from the house, in case of explosion. When he opens his mouth, though, he finds himself reciting lines from the writing of Idge. Baston clenches his jaw and gestures at the crates instead.

Outside, the sun's setting over the harbour, the sullen red light touching the ruins of Queen's Point fortress across the bay. Baston climbs up one of the other towers to get a look at the border. There are a few candle-flames visible on rooftops, but fewer than other nights. He can guess where the Tallowmen have gone – they're waiting at the other end of the tunnel.

Karla joins him. A rifle slung over her shoulder, a breathing mask hanging from her neck. Ready for the attack.

"How did it go?" she asks.

Baston glances back towards the house. Light still blazes from the windows, where Rasce communes with an unseen power.

"I got to punch Vorz."

"That's something." She leans her head on his shoulder. "I don't want to go below, Bas," she says softly. "Not like Dad. I don't want to die in the dark."

He nods towards the distant fires of the Tallowmen. "I was always more scared of those lights."

"I guess we'll have our pick of troubles," says Karla.

"I've told him that it'd be madness to press on. He'll listen. Spar will make him see reason."

Baston glances back. The light has faded from Lanthorn Street. Rasce is done.

The city trembles, almost imperceptibly. Then again, a bigger quake.

"Something's wrong." Baston can feel the magic in the air turn sour.

"Oh gods," breathes Karla, and then she breaks into a run, dragging Baston down the stairs, out onto the street. "He knows! Rasce knows!" Terror in her eyes, like the mad gods are at her heels.

Hand in hand, the two stumble down Lanthorn Street, but it's too late. The ground beneath their feet turns treacherous and clutches at them, slowing their steps. Hot, angry winds blow down the canyons of the narrow streets, buffeting them. Everyone – even Baston's thieves – backs away from them, a circle forming around them.

Like they're the target for an artillery bombardment, and everyone's trying to get clear of the blast zone.

Karla unslings her rifle, but it's too late.

Rasce approaches, like a wrathful god. The stone burns beneath his feet. His jacket hangs open, and his chest is bare. The stone scabs on his side blaze with the same light. He limps towards them, every step causing the city to convulse. His eyes are closed, but his wrathful gaze is every window, every tower.

In his hand, the dragon-tooth knife.

Vorz comes running after him, alchemist's robes like wings, panic on his face.

Rasce gestures, and Karla falls, like a trapdoor's opened up in the ground beneath her. She drops two feet in an instant. The street has swallowed her legs, the stone turned to quicksand, now solid again. She's trapped, half entombed in the New City.

"You killed my cousin!" shouts Rasce.

"It was Mandel!" she shrieks. "Mandel! Vyr was plotting against you, you said it yourself! You're wrong! Baston, tell him he's wrong!"

Baston opens his mouth, but no sound comes. *He's not wrong.*

"How much of the dragon's gold have you stolen? How else have you betrayed me? You broke your oath, *Eshdana*! You all conspire against me." Rasce's voice becomes a wail, almost child-like in its anguish. "I thought you were my *friends*!"

Baston steps forward, putting himself between Rasce and Karla. His hands close into fists, but he knows that Rasce's invulnerable to any weapon he could bring to bear. The only thing that could kill him was Sinter's bullet, and that's gone. Baston cannot protect his sister against Rasce, any more than he could hold back the floodwaters. *The saint trick*, he thinks, desperately. *Name him.*

"I am your friend. Rasce of the line of Taras," he says slowly, carefully, "Boss. Chosen of the Dragon."

Nothing happens. It's not enough.

"My friend," says the saint, "stand aside of your own will."

"I can't, boss. She's my sister."

"She betrayed me. She has broken her oath to the Ghierdana. But, oh!" Rasce grins, and his teeth glow with the same holy light, "she can still serve the dragon. Doctor Vorz tells me we shall need sacrifices." He gestures with the knife, a little flick of the blade, and Baston's flung aside. "Give me your heart, my love! An offering! A bloody sacrifice!"

NO.

The word is unspoken, but it's like thunder, a hammer blow that hits all of them. Karla screams. Baston staggers, half-blind. Rasce brandishes his knife at the city around him.

"You betrayed me, too! Wretch! You stood by as she poisoned me! I shall——"

The city convulses, and so does Rasce. Tremors race through the stone. The stone plates on Rasce's chest blaze, and then begin to grow. Rasce's breathing becomes laboured. He falls to his knees and stabs at the pavement with the dragon-tooth, screams words in a tongue Baston doesn't understand. Baston grabs Karla, tries to pull her out of the ground, but she's stuck fast.

"The dagger! The dagger!" shouts Karla.

The dragon-tooth can cut stone. Baston crawls across the quaking ground, and every inch he gets closer to Rasce, the pressure redoubles, as though the whole of the New City is falling on him. Rasce is screaming, blood bubbling from his mouth. The dagger falls from nerveless fingers.

Suddenly, Vorz steps into the middle of that divine whirlwind. He holds aloft a black amulet. *Carillon's amulet*, Baston thinks distantly. *Cari wore that.* Vorz has to strain to move the amulet – it's caught in the grasp of invisible forces.

"Spar Idgeson!" shouts Vorz. "I compel you! Remember your death! Remember the fall! Remember!"

WHERE'S CARI?

If Spar's first word was like thunder, this is a cannon-blast. It smashes Vorz aside, sending him flying. The amulet tumbles – and Rasce catches it.

"This is my city now. The dragon takes what he desires. If you shall not claim this power, I shall."

He slams it down into the ground.

"Begone!"

And it's over. The sense of divine presence vanishes, snuffed out in an eye blink. There's only Rasce, terrible and glorious. He draws himself back upright. Picks up the dagger with his other hand and takes a lumbering step towards Karla. "Your life is forfeit." She scrapes her fingers bloody trying to claw her way out of the stone trap. She grabs her rifle from where it fell and fires it point-blank into Rasce's chest. The walls of Lanthorn Street echo with the gunshot, but Rasce is undamaged. "Monster!" she spits at him.

"Wait!" Baston pleads desperately.

"Not you, too, Baston." Rasce wipes blood from his mouth. "Not more treachery."

"I'll take the ash. I'll be Eshdana." The words stick in his throat. They're like a noose around his neck.

Vorz sneers as he stumbles to Rasce's side. "An irrelevant technicality."

"A measure of indulgence," says Baston. "Please."

The whole city seems to wheel around them. Everything's unmoored.

"Doctor Vorz," snaps Rasce. The doctor extends his hand. He's wearing black leather gloves, but they're dusted with ash. Rasce dips his finger in the ash, then marks Baston's forehead.

The ash is still warm, as if fresh from a crematorium. Some part of Baston's mind wonders what the doctor was doing with the bodies in the cellar.

"Swear," commands Rasce.

"I'll serve you in all things, you and the dragon. My life for the Ghierdana." Baston swallows. "And if I break my word, my life's forfeit."

Rasce extends his hand, helps Baston stand. "My friend, you have to understand. The ash buys only a measure of indulgence. Not forgiveness."

A pit opens beneath Karla. She vanishes, falling into the darkness. Her scream's cut off by the street closing above her. Baston jumps forward, tries to catch her, but his hand meets only solid stone.

"Karla!" His cry echoes off the walls of the city and the heavens above, and is ignored by both. Karla's gone in an instant, swallowed up as if she never existed. All the strength and courage seem to drain from Baston, leaving him hollow and broken.

"She is alive," says Rasce. "I've sent her away. All the way down to Rat."

Baston turns, slowly, to face his new master. He thought himself bigger than Rasce, taller and stronger, but he now realises he's very, very small in comparison to the creature that stands before him. Everyone else on the street, all the onlookers, all the thieves who've rushed down from the House on Lanthorn Street, even Doctor Vorz – they're immaterial now, living ghosts, no more substance than a candle-flame. Easy to snuff out. Just like him, just like Karla. Rasce's the only solid presence, the only truly real thing.

No longer human. He's stepped through some unseen door, risen to some exalted height no mortal can attain. Once, they were on the same side, allies despite the tangle of oaths and duties and family. Now, that's no longer possible – they are of different orders now. As scythe to the corn, as fire to the forest, so is Rasce to them all now.

He desperately wants to vomit, to scream, to get away from the horror of the living god.

"I'd like to trust you, my friend," says Rasce, "but you must atone first. My Uncle Artolo cut off his fingers with his own knife to prove his loyalty to the dragon. Tiske took the greatest risk at Dredger's yard. I have something in mind for you, now.

"It's time for you to go home."

CHAPTER THIRTY-SIX

Carillon and Myri feast on a banquet of dried fish, with a delicious appetiser of dried fish, two main courses of dried fish (prepared in the traditional Yhandisian method, that is to say, drying), and polished off with a dessert of dried fish. It is unquestionably the best meal Cari has ever had in her life.

And fresh water, too! This little village is better than any of the broken heavens they've travelled through on their way here.

When they're finished, it's Cari who breaks the silence. She takes out the book, props it up like a gravestone against the aethergraph set. Balanced between the two of them.

She takes out a fish-gutting knife, lays it on her lap.

"So—" she begins.

"What's wrong with your hand?" Myri interrupts her, leaning forward with curiosity.

Cari holds up her numbed hands. "It's been like this ever since I stabbed Rhan-Gis." She can still bend her fingers, a little, but only with great effort, and the flesh is greyish-white and mottled.

"You blasphemed."

"I figured."

"Does it hurt?" asks Myri.

"Aches a bit."

"Here." Myri fishes in her robes, digs out a small glass vial, and tosses it across to Cari. "Rub a little along your wrist." It's a vial of Myri's pain medication.

"Hey, I stole all these off you back on Ilbarin!" Cari cracks the vial open, lets the liquid inside drip on her wrist.

"A sorceress always has something up her sleeve," says Myri, then she shrieks, "Don't use it all! Just a few drops!"

Cari throws the vial back, and Myri pours the remainder down her throat. Even a few drops absorbed through her skin makes Cari feel like she's floating, the tugging weight of her maimed hand suddenly gone. She has no idea what drinking a whole vial would do to you, or what internal fires Myri has to quell. She flexes her hand, and it feels somewhat better.

"Fuck it," says Cari, "let's assume we can get a boat to Khebesh from here. Do you want to sort this out now? That was the bargain, wasn't it? We help each other until we get there, and then . . . "

"And then we kill each other?" Myri's scar of a mouth twists into a wry smile. "Here and now?"

"Winner takes the book."

"Winner," echoes Myri, "takes the book."

"Only . . . it's not like it's a ticket, right? It doesn't say 'admit one only to the fabled city of Khebesh', does it?" Cari's seized by a brief moment of doubt; she can't read Khebeshi in the slightest, so it might say exactly that.

"It's not."

"So. Fuck it?"

Myri sounds exhausted and amused at the same time, punch-drunk. "By that, do you mean you don't want to kill me any more?"

Cari considers it. "I'm not going to cry over you when you go. You worked for that fucker Heinreil."

"Doesn't it get tiring," asks Myri, "holding grudges so long?"

"Hate keeps me going. You have to fuck the fuckers before they fuck you."

"Very eloquent."

"What about you? You still want to dissect me?"

"Honestly? Yes. But—" Myri raises a finger. "Only in the spirit of research. Bred from a Raveller, Herald of the Black Iron Gods, Saint of Knives ... they make the most fascinating things in Guerdon. But I'll be patient. I'll wait until you're dead first."

Cari looks at the blasted, withered, spell-wracked woman opposite her and laughs. "Yeah, I think I'm safe there."

Despite her weariness, Cari can't sleep. It might be excitement at the thought of nearly reaching Khebesh, or the stress and terror of the last few days catching up with her, but, honestly, it's mostly the fish. She decides to try the aethergraph again, now that they're clear of the blasted region on the other side of the mountains. Maybe there's some sort of divine interference blocking the messages. It's worth a shot.

She leaves Myri sleeping by the warmth of the brazier, the Fucking Book still propped up like a sentinel, and slips out of the longhouse. Some impulse catches her, and she brushes her hand against a mostly erased carving of the Lord of Waters just inside the door. The rough wood is pleasant to the touch, but it puts her in mind of other half-erased carvings. In the Seamarket back in Guerdon, she remembers carvings of the Black Iron Gods. Worn smooth by centuries, hidden away, but still there. Like the gods they depicted.

Gods cannot die. *Except when I shoot 'em*, she thinks, *then they stay dead.*

She walks through the silent village, the moon bright enough to make out a path. Off to the west, godlights flicker beyond the mountains. If anyone else is still awake, they stay indoors in their huts. She wanders down to the little strand, walks barefoot on the sands, the lamps of the village far behind her. Her gown glimmers in the moonlight, despite the caked mud. *Tomorrow, I'm going to spend another fucking emerald on something sensible to wear.*

The waves brush quietly against the shore. One fishing boat rocks softly against its neighbour. Cari finds a rock to sit upon, looks out at that black expanse of water. *I'm facing east, so – that way, beyond the mountains, is Ilbarin. And that way is Khebesh.* She looks one way, then the other, but the vistas are identical. A voyage across darkness.

Almost identical. A light shines on the horizon. A ship.

And – with the addition of a lot of shit – these waters are the same as Guerdon's harbour. That anonymity of the sea goes both ways. The sea's bigger than the names and charts mortals try to put on it. The sea's bigger than gods. No sea-god, Captain Hawse once told her, can claim the whole ocean.

He'd settled down with one god, though, in the end.

Cari wriggles forward, dips her toes in the water. *Spar*, she thinks, *are you there?*

The same water, after all, washes against the seawall of the New City. She's as close to him now as she was there, right? *Spar, can you hear me?*

Nothing. She sits down with the aethergraph set and opens the case. The moonlight's too dim for her for her to make out the details, but she can feel the letters embossed on the keys, the unnatural chill of the glass tube. She touches the activation stud.

Nothing. The set's dead. She shoves it aside, angrily, embarrassed at her foolishness. She's dragged the stupid thing all the way from Ilbarin, and for nothing! She stands back up, ready to throw it into the water—

And sees the light.

That light out there – it's getting brighter. Getting closer. Moving against the wind, against the tide.

It's the *Moonchild*. Artolo's ship. It's coming right towards her, descending on her like the dragon did. There's nowhere else it could be going – barren mountains to the north, salt flats and more waste-lands south. It's heading for Yhandis. Even if they don't know Cari's here, they'll stop to take on water, supplies. Fucking dried fucking fish is going to get her killed.

Run, screams every instinct.

She dashes through the surf, water splashing underfoot. In her mind's eye, Artolo's already here, grown gigantic and distended in his hatred. Tentacles thrashing, razor-sharp, murdering everyone in Yhandis to get to her. They'll kill Myri, too. Just like she brought Artolo down on Hawse, on Adro and Ren. Just like she brought ruin on Guerdon.

Just like she got Spar killed.

Don't let it happen again, she thinks, and *that* sounds like Spar.

Her hands shove one of the fishing boats out into the water. She follows it out, wading, water cold against her thighs, her midriff. Throws the stupid aethergraph in, and then she hauls herself on board. Not thinking, just acting, a reflex. *Run*.

The breeze blows from the south. She tacks into it, and the sails fill, carrying her north. Aiming for the narrowing gap between *Moonchild* and the mountains. If she can slip past the approaching freighter, if she can make it out into open sea, maybe she can lose them in the darkness. And *Moonchild*'s slow to turn. There's a brief, brief window in which she can make her escape, but she has to go *now*.

Something bumps against the hull. A rock? She doesn't know this shitty harbour at all, she's sailing blind. But her stolen boat isn't impeded – if anything, it picks up speed.

"Carillon? What are you doing?"

Myri's on the shore, dwindling as Cari sails away.

"It's Artolo!" shouts Cari back. "Get away!"

Myri shouts a reply, but it's lost in the wind.

"Take the book! Get to Khebesh!" Cari bites her lip, then shouts, "And then you owe me! Tell the masters to do something!" All that power, locked up behind the Ghost Walls while the Godswar breaks the world. They have to do something.

Like she's doing something. Only in her case, it's something stupid.

Her boat suddenly accelerates, the jolt nearly knocking Cari overboard as the wind redoubles, concentrates, a gale blowing at her back. It's Myri, casting one last spell, giving her the wind.

A searchlight stabs out from *Moonchild*, a ghastly beam like a finger, probing at the darkness. Crawling and jumping across the black sea. Illuminating shore, then breaking wave, then empty water.

For an instant, it catches some living thing, a fish or dolphin, a domed shape breaking through the surface. Then the thing's gone, and the hungry light moves on. If it lights up the shore, it'll find Myri, slowly limping back up towards the village. Artolo will send men ashore to kill her.

Cari hunches, a thief's instincts. Fly-the-light, stay hidden, you're nearly there.

But that's not the point, is it?

"THIS WAY, FISHFACE!" she shouts at the top of her lungs.

The searchlight in her face, like an explosion.

"Mark! A boat! A boat!"

Artolo strides across the iron deck of *Moonchild* to the rail. *There* she is. A savage satisfaction rises in him and becomes an unexpected prayer of thanks. Damala was right – this meeting is ordained by the gods. Fate Spider has woven his destiny. Kraken has blessed him with a mission of divine vengeance.

"After her!" he roars. "Turn! Turn!"

Moonchild wallows, the engines roaring as the heavy ship turns. The wind that buffets her has little effect on the massive freighter, but it still cracks and spits like a whip, forcing the other crewmen to take shelter. Only Artolo stands in the full fury of the wind.

Dol Martaine on the searchlight tracks the movements of the fast little boat as it skims over the water, fleeing north-east, back towards Ilbarin. Aiming for the narrow gap between Ram's Head and *Moonchild*.

"Turn!" roars Artolo, but they're going too slowly. Snarling, he grabs a rope and loops it around himself, then abseils down the side of the hull. His tentacle-fingers possess inhuman strength – one hand twists and grasps the rope so tightly he's held in place even as the ship lurches, even as the gush of spray strikes him with terrible force.

He reaches his other hand down, to touch the churning waters.

At Ilbarin, it was another who did this, a Kraken called up by one of Damala's prayers. Artolo does not know if the thing was a spirit, or a godspawn brought into the world by the Kraken. He suspects it was once human, warped by sainthood. Then, he'd recoiled in horror, suddenly suspecting that the priestess had tricked him, doomed him by healing his maimed hands with Kraken-magic. Now, he sees the truth – there is no distinction between such things. The material world around him is nothing more than the chaos of the water, flowing and formless. Only the gods have meaning. Only the gods impose order on this base matter.

Even he is nothing. The flesh that is Artolo is a passing wave, a momentary arrangement of matter. His revenge is holy. He is a holy purpose, cloaked in flesh – the instrument of Ishmere's revenge on Carillon Thay. His defeat, his maiming, all are part of the will of the gods.

Blessed above all things is the Kraken. All things that cleave to the Kraken are part of the Kraken.

His tentacles dip into the water, work the Kraken-magic. His fingers branch again, and again, and again. He feels them stretch out, unfurl, branch, and he's conscious of them all, all those millions of filaments snaking out into the sea ahead of *Moonchild*.

He can feel Cari's little boat, fragile as an eggshell, scudding over the waves. He extends his tentacle-fingers around it, his hand now a mile long, his soul stretched into something much greater than it was before. Even *Moonchild* is small to him now, a little flake of iron near Cari's speck of wood. The ocean is deeper than these mortals know, colder and darker. Unfathomable leagues below, the Kraken waits.

Now.

He clenches his fist – but as he does so, there's a flare of pain, and one of his tentacles is cut! Carillon's boat slips through the gap in the Kraken-water. Artolo roars in pain, reaches out again, two tentacles sprouting where the one was severed. He's more cautious this time, employing senses previously unknown to him, new forms of perception opening as Kraken moves through his veins. As above, so below – the same pattern, repeated on many scales. Kraken seizes his brain like he seizes the water, and he sees—

—In the water, a shoal of fish swimming alongside Carillon's boat. Dark wings of rays spread out, holy sigils marked on their hides, vestigial human remnants trailing along behind them. *Bythos*, thinks Artolo, *idiot vermin*. At the same time, though, there's another thought in his mind, a thought that isn't his: *Bythos. Servants of the Lord of Waters. Demons. Heretics. Enemies of the one true god of the sea.* He strikes with the Kraken-miracle again, and another of the Bythos hurls itself into the path of his tentacle, countering his magic. The creatures are *protecting* Carillon! He snarls in fury. The Kraken has uncountable tentacles, and they cannot stop them all!

He lashes out – and *Moonchild* lurches. Iron screams and tears. Artolo is flung forward on the rope as the ship grinds to a sudden halt, then he swings back to slam painfully into the hull. Winding him. Kraken withdraws from him, his power vanishing in a heartbeat. He's back in his body, made terribly small again.

"Captain! Captain! Haul him up!" Dol Martaine calls from the deck above. Hands haul on the rope looped around Artolo's chest, pulling him up. He dangles, helpless from the line, a sack of garbage, until they bring him over the railing and dump him on the iron deck.

A knife in someone's hand. Treacherous dogs, he can't show weakness in front of them. He staggers upright, spits blood.

"Why have we stopped?" he snarls in the face of the sailor with the knife, so the rogue steps back.

"Captain – we struck a sandbar," says Martaine, nervously glancing at Artolo's elongated fingers as they twist and coil.

"Reverse the engines, then! Pull us off and—"

"We need to wait for the tide to lift us. The keel's stuck fast."

"She escapes!" Carillon's boat has vanished into the darkness. The searchlight has lost her.

"We need to wait for the tide," insists Martaine. Pitching his voice so the whole crew hears him.

Moonchild's engines are gigantic, furious – and wholly mundane. Whatever lingering power of the Lord of Waters that counters the Kraken can surely have no effect on the engines. Come the rising tide, they can catch Carillon long before she escapes. Where is there to go? There are no landing places on the west coast, not with that line of errant mountains. Does she flee back to Ilbarin? To the Isle of Fire?

There is no escape from Artolo.

Only another delay. An infuriating, knife-twisting delay, but soon . . .

"We wait for the tide," he agrees.

CHAPTER THIRTY-SEVEN

I t is an army of the unseen, a thieves' invasion.

They descend through hidden ways into the tunnels under the New City. Rasce shows them the way, or opens the way where necessary. He can see the fear on the faces of the Brotherhood thieves, many with the ash still fresh upon their faces. These men and women are dockworkers, tanners, factory workers and furnace-stokers, labourers and pedlars first, thieves second. They followed Baston into the New City hoping for relief from the mad gods who occupy the Wash, and now find themselves conscripted into another strange conflict. They clutch their Ghierdana-bought guns as they step gingerly into the shadows.

Others in Rasce's army are made of harder stuff. Eshdana enforcers, who earned the ash in pirate raids or "business" overseas. Mercenaries and veterans of the Godswar. Even these soldiers might quail at setting foot in the tunnels under Guerdon, but they have nothing to fear tonight, for, as they descend, they're joined by the third portion of his army. The ghouls wait there in the darkness, yowling and tittering. They grab the thieves, drag them into the underworld in crazed waltzes, or tug them forward down pitch-dark tunnels.

Vorz accompanies Rasce, looking distinctly uncomfortable, his pale features rendered even more unnatural by the light of his aetheric lamp. One of the ghouls points and laughs at the little light. "Shut it off," says Rasce, "we won't need it. Trust our guides."

Alone of the company, though, Rasce can tell where they are. Even deep underground, he has reference points to navigate by. He knows the location of the New City at his back as surely as he knows his right hand, and he can also dimly perceive five points of light ahead of him, the five pebbles hidden by Baston within the walls of Mandel & Company. As his physical body moves away from the New City and closer to those five stones, he can track his progress through the underworld.

They pass beneath the border of the New City, leaving the Lyrixian Occupation Zone. A breach of the Armistice and act of war if they walked down Mercy Street; instead, they walk a hundred feet beneath Mercy, through tunnels gnawed by the ghouls long before the streets above were named. They approach the Ishmeric Occupation Zone, and, as they do so, the ghouls begin to yowl in unison, a subterranean cacophony that hides them from the eyes of the gods. They pass by without incident.

The Haithi Occupation Zone would be more of a challenge – the dead now patrol the labyrinthine tunnels under Holyhill. To avoid any confrontation, the ghouls lead Rasce and company on a long looping detour that runs under the northern portion of the Wash, under Duttin's lithosarium, under ancient Castle Hill, to emerge briefly from a disused railway tunnel into the night air. Then they plunge back underground, down and down and down, into the ghoul tunnels that catacomb Gravehill.

St Styrus' Shaft is not far away, now.

Rasce shifts his perception to the New City. For an instant, he senses a faint ghost of Spar Idgeson, in the same way one can tell that a room was recently occupied. The shade flees, and it's much too small and weak to be conscious, let alone challenge him. *No doubt lost in memory again*, thinks Rasce. Perhaps that was as much the key to his triumph as any of Vorz's tinctures and transfusions. Spar was consumed by thoughts of the past, but Rasce always looks to the future, to the days when he will soar again as Chosen of the Dragon.

From the heights of the New City, he looks across Guerdon. A few candle-flames burn along the perimeter of the IOZ – and many more in the Fog Yards, guarding Mandel & Company. No doubt there are more Tallowmen waiting below in the darkness, or stationed at other watch posts. The creatures can cross the city with terrifying speed, leaping from rooftop to rooftop almost as fast as a dragon flies. As soon as the attack on Mandel's begins, there will be a wildfire of reinforcements.

Rasce looks to the south.

A distant light. Fire at sea.

It's time.

Karla wakes in utter darkness. She's battered, every inch of her scratched and bruised as though she'd rolled down a mountainside, instead of . . .

Instead of . . .

Stone becoming liquid as it touched her. Sinking, the city passing through her, swallowing her. Devouring her. Entombed alive in a landslide that seemed to last for years.

She screams, and her scream echoes off the vaulted ceiling of hell.

And then she hears a voice, and it's coming from her own mouth.

"HELLO, KARLA."

The stink of ghoul, close at hand. The creaking of massive tendons as Rat squats down next to her.

"Am I dead?"

The sound of a rough tongue scraping over scaly lips. A lick of drool. "NOT YET. SOON MAYBE. BUT THERE IS WATER YOUR KIND CAN DRINK. AND THINGS LIVE HERE THAT I CAN KILL. THEY ARE NOT PLEASANT TO EAT, I THINK."

He throws something down nearby. Karla reaches out, probes it with her fingers. Matted fur, sticky blood . . . some sort of animal. But her blind exploration finds bird-talon feet, too, and a scaly tail, and soft, yielding eyeballs where no sane creature has eyes. A thing bred in the alchemists' vats by mistake.

"What is this place?"

"A PRISON FOR DANGEROUS THINGS. WE KEPT THE LAST OF THE BLACK IRON GODS DOWN HERE. BUT AFTER CARILLON LEFT AND SPAR GREW WEAK, ELADORA DUTTIN CONVINCED ME WE SHOULD MOVE THEM TO ANOTHER HIDING PLACE. I WAS WRONG. I SHOULD NOT HAVE LISTENED."

Rat rises, stalks away from her in the darkness. She hears his hoof steps receding into the unknowable distance, but the voice that comes from her mouth is undiminished.

"BUT I WILL PUT IT RIGHT, AND, OH, THEN I SHALL HAVE REVENGE."

He looks back at her, orange eyes glowing in the darkness. "EAT, CHILD. LIVE, AND SEE THE SURFACE AGAIN."

"This is going to be a mess," mutters Sinter. He ambles across the little office in the lithosarium to the window, unable to sit still. "Come on, damn you. Sooner started, and sooner done."

Eladora Duttin looks up from her book. Sighing, she closes the heavy tome – Mondolin's *Aseria: A History Reconsidered* – and puts down her pen. "We gave Mr Hedanson ample opportunity to take action. It's certainly regrettable that he didn't prove to be a more suitable agent."

"Damn right." Sinter crosses the room again, looks down the corridor of cells. "I used to be good at this, you know. I ran the Keepers' sanctified operations for ten years. I could tell you who makes a good tool. The right strings to pull. Now, I can't even get one little grasping shit to kill another one. Assuming he could have managed it. Killing a saint is fucking hard. I know." He turns back, crosses the room again.

"This mood," says Eladora, "does not become you." She's read this same page a dozen times. Noises from the dark city outside the window distract her. Every shout on the street outside, the rattle of carriages and the rumble of trains, all seem portentous, edged with danger. Tonight, she fears, is indeed going to be a fucking mess.

Sinter stops his nervous pacing long enough to fix Eladora with a quizzical glare, then continues. "Any word from his highness?"

Eladora gestures to one of the aethergraph machines on her desk. "He's still cloistered with Kelkin and the guildmasters. When he last reported in, he said that the alchemists were still being ... difficult."

"Keep a tight grip on that boy of his. Only real leverage we've got over a thing like him." The defrocked priest scowls. "I remember the Patros saying the same about the alchemists to me when I was a noviciate. Faithless bastards. They'll sell us all out if we don't keep a tight leash on them."

"A city of nooses." Eladora steeples her fingers. "That worked so well in the past." *And I have a noose of Black Iron around my own neck. A bargain unfulfilled.*

"We don't know how far Vorz has taken the brat. Is he just god-touched, or has he fully beatified? Maybe we should have gone to the Keepers. Or the Bureau, and got a Haithi saint-hunter. Or—"

"The weapons are available to Mr Hedanson," says Eladora. "Clearly, the will to act was not. So, we must trust in Alic's methods. And, failing that, we contain the problem as best we can."

Sinter opens the window, looks out south across the Wash. The heights of the New City glimmer in the distance. "Should have bloody started by now, shouldn't it? Nemon set the dogs on each other. We should hear something from the watchers soon. A fucking mess."

"His scheme may not have worked. Rasce might not have turned on the Brotherhood, or they might have come to some arrangement. We have to proceed on the assumption that they still intend to attack Mandel & Company, and endanger the Armistice." Eladora reaches for the second aethergraph. "I'll check—"

The first gunshot shatters the window.

Sinter falls.

Shattered, too.

The second blows a hole through *A History Reconsidered*, showering Eladora in splinters and dust.

She ducks under her desk as a hail of gunfire rains down on her lithosarium. The gunmen are on the rooftops opposite.

"S-Sinter?" calls Eladora. The priest's body quivers in the moonlight, then goes still. She stares at his corpse from her hiding place under the heavy desk, frozen in terror. Stares in horrified fascination at the ruin of what used to be his head. Broken teeth, and now a broken skull. Sinter's brains, a lifetime of secrets and intrigue, spill out across her floor.

Another barrage of gunfire. Bullets ricochet around the office. Plaster dust chokes the air. Gods, if one stray shot hits the wrong place . . .

Another shot hits her desk, and she hears the delicate aethergraph machines shatter. She's cut off. The city suddenly shrinks – a moment ago she was worried about all of Guerdon, connected to her agents in Castle Hill and the Fog Yards and the New City and further afield, the whole city occupying her thoughts. Now, all that exists for her is the little square of shelter offered by the heavy desk, while the gunfire rains down all around her.

Eladora reaches over, grabs the third aethergraph, the one hidden under her desk. The soul of Alic Nemon's son Emlin is in there, trapped in a constant loop. She shields it with her body, conscious of the fragility of the precious machine.

Think. The aethergraphs are broken, but the cables are intact. The machines are alchemical reifications of sorcerous incantations, spells cast with wheels and wires and potions in jars. But she's a sorcerer now, of sorts. Perhaps the least qualified Special Thaumaturge in recent history, but talented enough to replicate the aethergraph for long enough to send a message, a call.

Send help.

Baston wipes dust from his eye as he reloads. He knows the old lithosarium well – as a boy, friends had dared him to trespass in its abandoned cells, where people claimed the ghosts of Stone Men lingered. Later, when the thief-taker Jere Taphson and his crew took over, he recalls studying it, reporting back to the Fever Knight. Learning how to besiege the place, just in case the Brotherhood's patience ran out and they wanted Taphson gone.

There's only one entrance on ground level, right in the middle. West wing is all cells, east wing has Taphson's offices, barracks, an armoury. Least, that was what it was back when Taphson was alive. Now, it's something else.

He fires again, targeting the windows. Somewhere in there, Rasce told him, is the pebble Baston planted on Sinter. This is Duttin's headquarters, her secret off-the-books lair. Baston's surprised that she chose somewhere in the Wash. He'd have expected somewhere fancier, with the quality. A mansion in Bryn Avane, maybe, or a government building up on Castle Hill. Somewhere far away from the front lines, from the parts of the city Duttin sacrificed for her Armistice.

Reload. Fire again.

This is for you, Karla, he thinks, as he pumps shot after shot into what was once Taphson's office. Maybe if he does enough damage, he can fix what was broken. Convince Rasce to step back from the brink, somehow reconcile him with Karla, free her from that prison. He curses himself for trying to play the game, trying to take the lead. All he's good for is hurting people.

He knows he hit someone with his opening barrage. Maybe Duttin's already dead.

This is for you, Fae. Another barrage of fire, the barrel hot enough to burn his gloved hand. The stink of phlogiston. Discarded cartridges fall from the rooftop, smouldering as they tumble down to the street below.

Baston swings his rifle around, trains the scope on the gap between Castle Hill and Holyhill. There, leaping over the rooftops like a host of angry fireflies. The Tallowmen are coming, swarming up from the Fog Yards.

Even if she's bleeding out on the floor, Duttin won't let her Tallowmen cross into the Ishmeric Occupation Zone. She has to preserve her precious Armistice to protect her Guerdon.

Not his.

His Guerdon is lost forever.

He turns and flees into what was once the Wash, but is now the domain of mad gods.

The armies of thieves go down the corpse-shaft.

Perhaps it's the only way down, but Rasce suspects the ghouls chose this route to mock their fellow travellers.

The ghouls, inhumanly strong and agile, can scale the walls or swing from the chains that once used to lower corpses down for the ghouls' feast. The humans have to descend in single file, down a stair that spirals along the edges of the shaft, steps unmentionably slick. Some, including Doctor Vorz, lose their nerve and have to be lowered on ropes, like corpses that don't know they're dead yet.

Rasce is the first down. The first to search around the base of the shaft, wading through a mire born from the filth of centuries, gnawed bones protruding from the black slime like tree roots. He finds the entrance to the tunnel that Baston spoke of. It's old, older than the shaft it connects to. He runs his fingers over the walls, and the carvings seem to writhe under his touch.

"A temple of Black Iron," whispers Vorz from behind him. The Dentist raises his lamp, conjuring shapes out of the darkness. "Ravellers, consuming sacrifices for the Black Iron Gods."

The amulet on Rasce's chest squirms against his skin in an

unsettling fashion. He lifts it out, tucks it between his undershirt and his leather cuirass. The motion makes his side hurt, the rocky scabs digging into the tightly laced armour.

"Do you need more alkahest?" whispers the Dentist, opening his black bag.

"No."

"More, ah, tincture?"

"No." Rasce checks his inner eye, looks out from the New City. At this distance, it's an effort – he can dimly feel his mortal body stagger, the Dentist holding him upright – but he's able to look out from the windows of the New City. He can see the lights of the Tallowmen moving, a swarm of fireflies, congregating at the lithosarium. Moving away from the Fog Yards. Good.

"Up the tunnel!" shouts Rasce. "Smash the yliaster vats first, then take anything that isn't nailed down! The dragon takes what he wishes, and, tonight, you are all blood of the dragon!"

Ragged cheers, but the thieves are too cold and nervous to charge. There's a great deal of hesitation over who should be first to navigate the tunnel. Rasce would prefer to lead the way himself, but the time is not right. *Baston could keep them in line*, he thinks to himself.

The ghouls jeer at the idea of being sent to the front lines, so it comes down to the Ghierdana and the Brotherhood, and it's the Brotherhood thieves who are pushed forward. They advance into the darkness.

What will they find there, Rasce wonders. Wards? Traps? Armed guards, the narrow corridor a killing ground for alchemical weapons like heavy gas or knife-smoke. The sort of things Rasce has seen on battlefields from far above.

Vorz makes him sit down. Insists on giving him more injections. "Wait until we have drawn out Mandel's defenders," whispers the Dentist, like he's talking about pulling teeth. The ghouls cluster around, curious, leering at him. Jabbering among themselves, as if betting on when he'll perish and be ready for eating.

There's every chance it might be very, very soon.

The sound of gunfire echoes down the tunnel. Distant explosions. The attack has begun.

It's time.

The dragon returns to Guerdon.

This city is a wounded beast, thinks the dragon. The scars are plainly visible. He flies over the ruins of Queen's Point, over the burned remains of Dredger's yard. Wreckage from the invasion, scattered along the shore. The Haithi and Ishmeric Occupation Zones, like patches of disease.

Even the New City is a mark of injury. A stone scab. *This city is dying*, thinks the dragon, even if it is in denial of its own mortality. Taras has sacked cities before. Feasted on their remains, and this will be little different.

He circles down towards the towers of the New City. He can smell the mortals in those crowded towers, a mingling of scents. Guerdonese, Severasti, Haithi. Folk from Jashan, from Mattaur, from Varinth and a dozen other lands.

And beyond those towers, more towers, empty ones. Burned-out ruins.

Vorz has made a study of those towers. Once, Carillon Thay fought a Keeper saint who wielded a flaming sword. The touch of the sword burned Carillon's soul, and the city took the wound. The soul of the city burned.

Vorz has determined that the reverse is also true.

The dragon opens his jaws, and again the towers burn.

For Rasce, it's standing in the path of a raging hurricane – and the exhilarating joy of reaching up and seizing the wind, of *directing* the hurricane.

He is with them as the people burn, as the dragon-fire consumes the towers and everyone inside them. The fires are so hot, the victims are consumed utterly, skin and muscle burning away in an eyeblink, the skeleton lingering a moment longer, then it too dissolves into the inferno.

And the souls, the souls are captured in an alchemy of atrocity. All gods are carrion gods. The souls become fire, too, fire of a different sort. Raw power, flooding through the New City. Raw and full of pain. The dead don't know they're dead yet, don't know they've been snatched from mortal existence and turned into fuel for miracles. Thousands of fiery meteors, souls crashing across the aether.

Rasce draws on that power, channelling and shaping it. His blood burning, the stone scabs on his chest burning, everything's fire and stone now, no distinction between the two, the aether and the material overlapping, god and man overlapping, and there's nothing except his will, his power. He exhales, and his breath is hurricane fire. At this moment, he is the dragon.

The magic leaps across Guerdon, drawn into the depths of the New City and then spat like an artillery barrage across to five targets in the Fog Yards.

There are five pebbles hidden around Mandel's fortress. Five little pebbles cut from the New City. They'd fit into the palm of your hand.

The whole of the New City sprang from the corpse of a single Stone Man.

The five pebbles erupt, hissing like angry dragons. They sprout like vines, flow like lava. They smash through walls and pierce containment vessels. They rear up, five earthquakes, and shatter the fortress. It's an explosion of solid stone, an ongoing devastation. Guards flee, firing desperately at the onrushing stone before they're entombed or crushed. Tallowmen cackle, dancing through the chaos of living stone, slashing at it in confusion with their knives and axes, unable to comprehend this miracle.

The rushing stone sheds dust, and the dust is also alive. Where the dust touches human flesh, it burrows in like a spore. The Stone

Plague can be a weapon, too. Dust clouds billow though the yliaster processing sheds at Mandel & Company, catching the workers there unawares. They pass through all the stages of the plague in an instant, beyond the help of any alkahest. A single Stone Woman, her lungs calcifying, her eyes gone to marble, stumbles out into the courtyard and fails to scream.

Where the dust cannot find purchase in flesh, it clogs vents, adheres to breathing masks and goggles and the joints of protective suits. Mandel's guards are equipped to fight the Godswar, but even they are taken by surprise, easy prey for the host of ghouls that follows in the wake of the explosions. It clings, too, to the blazing wicks inside the heads of the remaining Tallowmen, snuffing them out.

In the space of ten heartbeats, the unvaniquishable fortress is conquered.

Rasce sinks back to himself. Sharp spikes of pain sear through his body – the stone plates in his side have sprouted five matching spurs, five stag-horned growths driving into his lungs, his bowels, reaching for his heart. The pain is enough to stagger him. His vision blurs.

"I was right," breathes Vorz, his voice full of quiet amazement. "I've done it." Almost absently, the alchemist produces a syringe and injects it into Rasce's neck. More tincture or more painkiller, he can't tell.

"I have to see," says Rasce. He stumbles up the tunnel, coughing despite his breathing mask. He has to see what he has done.

It has to be enough for Great-Uncle. It has to all be worth it.

CHAPTER THIRTY-EIGHT

The mage-wind drives Cari through the darkness. She's no idea how fast she's travelling. For that matter, she's hazy on where she's going – she can navigate by the stars and keep the tiller straight on this heading north-east, but she can't tell if she's on course for Ilbarin or Firesea or if she'll miss them both and break out into the Middle Sea.

She'll run out of food long before then, of course.

And run out of water before that.

Oh, but she'll probably fall unconscious out of sheer exhaustion even before *that*.

On the whole, one of my better plans, right?

All during that long night, the wind in her ears and the spray in her face, Cari has time to think. At first, she berates herself, cursing herself for once again doing something immensely stupid. Acting on instinct, mistaking an escape route for a plan. She can't outrun *Moonchild*. She can't lose Artolo either, not when he's got the Kraken on his side. Even if the Bythos block him from directly striking her with miracles, he can find her by looking for the gaps, for the places they protected her. She remembers looking for Heinreil that way, long ago in Guerdon. The guildmaster stole her amulet, and that amulet blocked her from perceiving him through the visions sent by the Black Iron Gods. In the end, she worked out how to find the amulet by looking for blind spots. Artolo can do the same.

She glances over her shoulder, tries to draw on this knack for sensing godshit she's developed. She strains her inner eye, searching for the knot of Kraken-shit around Artolo, but it's too much for her. All she finds is a headache – and the feeling of a gathering storm. Tension all around her, electricity in the air. Power in the water, the spray tingling when it touches her skin. But there's no hostility in it.

She tries to analyse the sensation, to put words to it. It's not like back in Gissa, where she could sense that she and Rhan-Gis were kindred spirits of some sort, so she was able to slip inside his defences and stab him with her bloody dagger.

At the same time, it's not like it was on the Rock of Ilbarin, before Usharet attacked here. There, it was a sense of opposition, of hostility. Usharet saw her as an enemy and struck at her. She got the same feeling when *Moonchild* approached Yhandis – a god perceiving her as something dangerous or unclean. A servant of a rival deity. That makes sense to her – she's the Herald of the Black Iron Gods, Saint of Knives, Other Portentous Titles Pending. Eladora and Ongent were always going on about gods as patterns, as currents of psychic force. So, if Cari's part of a current that flows one way, and she runs into a god flowing the other way, that causes friction. Hostility. Push far enough, and you get angry manifestations, the wrath of god.

She drums her fingers off the side of the boat. They're so numb, she can't feel the timbers. So, think of it like trespassing into another gang's turf. She had the right idea in Yhandis, she decides, when she compared religious symbols and faith to declaring membership in a street gang. What does that mean for the Lord of Waters? Why doesn't she get the same feeling of hostility from that god?

Almost experimentally, she nudges the tiller to starboard. For a moment, the feeling of friction increases by an almost imperceptible amount, then it fades away again. The Lord of Waters *should* be antithetical to her, but for some reason it's suppressing that hostility. A temporary truce.

Cari tries again, and again, picking at it like a scab, until she's sure.

Hawse said the Lord of Waters had a plan for her. He'd tried to help her escape Ilbarin because of that conviction. Hawse thought the god wanted him to assist her; she thought that it was non-sense, that Hawse was just dressing up his own desire to help her in religious trappings. Now, she's beginning to suspect they were both wrong.

She nudges the tiller again, finds her course.

The mage-wind fails in the afternoon of the second day, but by then the storm's already gathering. Behind Cari, lightning crawls and slithers over the dome of the sky, the bolts branching like the ten-tacles of the Kraken. Soon after that, sections of sea begin to freeze, the Kraken stealing the water and leaving razor-glass ghosts behind. Waves ahead of her bulge, then scab over like blisters, the Kraken sowing obstacles in her path. She weaves through them. Glances over her shoulder to see *Moonchild* on the horizon, the plumes of smoke from her funnels mixing with the gathering darkness of the storm clouds.

Just a little further. They're nearly in Ilbarinese waters.

Ahead, more clouds. More darkness. Two storms at sea, rushing towards one another. An overwhelming sense of pressure weighs down on Cari, crushing her. She has to strain to lift her head. She shifts her grip, putting her heavy stone hand on the tiller, to keep the boat on course as the world howls around her, wind and wave and, horribly, her own voice joining in a wordless scream.

Moonchild's closer now, cutting through the surging waves like an iron blade. She can see a figure on the prow, arms upraised, and she knows it's Artolo. She can imagine him, bloated, skin growing scaly and blue-tinged, as the Kraken claims him. It's not just the Ghierdana crime boss chasing her – he's just the focus, the barrel of the gun. It's the Kraken and the rest of the maimed pantheon of Ishmere that pursues her.

Just a little further.

A rushing wave tears the tiller from her hand. Her fishing boat spins this way and that, buffeted by the wild weather. Spray lashes over the side, nearly blinding her. All Cari can do is cling to the side and pray.

In the distance, Artolo moves his right arm in a sweeping arc, and a huge wave rises up, mountainous, a blasphemy against gravity. The foam atop the wave is a forest of white tentacles. Kraken-shapes move within the wall of water. The wave mounts, and mounts, tall enough to swallow the New City and all its towers.

Then Artolo clenches his left fist, and the wave turns to Kraken-glass, every droplet a lethal knife. The miracle explodes invisible around her, filling sea and sky. So close she can see the gods, see the Kraken in the water. The waves are his writhing, hungry tentacles.

Cari shouts one last obscenity, but her word is lost in the roaring waters as the wave comes crashing down.

Artolo is gigantic, bigger than the sky. Only his steel boots keep him on the ground – without them, he would bestride the world, step from Ilbarin to Ishmere in a single bound. Another step would bring him to Guerdon – he will swallow Thay's soul and carry it with him, make her watch as he washes away her New City like a child's sandcastle in the rising tide. He shall throw Great-Uncle down, too, knock the dragon from the sky and quench his fires in the cold deeps.

Artolo's skull is fit to burst with furious joy. Irritated by the constraints of bone, he dissolves it with a thought, drawing ever closer to the perfection of his new God – for his new god is very close, now. The waves are Artolo's racing pulse; the seas his cold blood.

"We have to turn back!" shouts Dol Martaine over the tempest of wind and wave.

"No! Not until she is dead!" Thunder booms in the clouds, echoing Artolo's words.

"It's like the invasion of Ilbarin! We have to turn!" Martaine tugs at Artolo's arm, disrespecting the living god. With a twitch, he flings Martaine across the deck; with a thought, he turns the seawater sluicing across the forecastle into razor-water, stripping the flesh from Martaine's hands and knees.

Artolo reaches out into the churning waters and searches for his prize. Around him, *Moonchild* groans, pitching wildly from side to side as the storm pummels her. A few crew fall overboard, offerings for the Kraken. The whole ship could shatter, and Artolo would not be dismayed. He's a thing of the sea now, a saint of the Kraken. His desire – the god's desire – for revenge outweighs mortal necessities like shelter from the storm.

A tongue of water lifts the wreckage of Carillon's little boat on to the deck before him. He sifts through broken timbers, finds her battered body.

A memory flows into Artolo's brain, unimpeded now that his skull has become a fluid sac. He remembers when the gods of Ishmere made war upon the gods of Ilbarin, when he and his sisters brought low the Lord of Waters. Glorious was Pesh on that day, Lion Queen, war goddess, blood-crowned! And glorious was the Kraken on that day, diamond-dappled, master of the seas, and a million souls in Ilbarin drowned in celebration of His victory!

But Pesh died. It was another city, another sea, another war – but Pesh is on every battlefield, just as Kraken is in every sea. For the gods, there is neither space nor time, only the infinite iterations of their divine litanies, holy monads drawn in the heart of all things. Gods are beyond time, and cannot die – but Pesh died, her pattern overwritten by the abomination of Black Iron. It was Carillon Thay who struck her down, Thay who maimed both Artolo and Ishmere.

A death for a death. He lifts Cari's limp body out of the wreckage, wraps his fingers around her throat. His touch is careful, almost gentle. This must be savoured. This must be sacred.

She must know it, too. He raises a slimy tentacle-finger, strokes Cari's cheek. Traces the marks on her body – the burns from the shattered Black Iron God, the scars where the dragon bit her, a hundred other cuts and bruises. Her body a map of her failed journey. He can taste her skin through receptors that sprout in the suckers on his Kraken-fingers.

He examines the pale grey skin of her cursed hand, runs his new fingers – so wonderfully soft and adaptable! – between her frozen ones. It's the only part of her that isn't limp and unconscious. That won't do at all.

He nibbles her earlobe, then bites, tasting her blood. "Carillon Thay," whispers Artolo, "the gods say I shall kill you."

" . . . what gods?" she whispers, still stunned, only semi-conscious.

"Pesh, the Lion Queen, shall be avenged. Kraken made me whole again." The litany comes spilling out of him, like he's just a mouthpiece for the unseen gods. As he speaks, the feeling of power grows, divinity pressing against his exposed brain. "Fate Spider set my destiny. High Umur judges your crime. Smoke Painter, Blessed Bol, Cloud Mother—"

"Lord of Waters!" she cries.

And the god rises.

For it is said in all the lands, gods cannot die.

The Lord of Waters, fortified by all the souls salvaged by his loyal Bythos, drawn by the blasphemy of the invaders, surges from the deeps. This reborn incarnation of the god is diminished, changed from the kindly deity who blessed the harbour at Ilbarin and guided the ships home safely. His once-glorious visage is ill-made, his body laden with seaweed and debris. His eyes are bleary, and his voice is no longer the booming of thunder, no longer full of wisdom and foresight, but an animalistic roar of hatred.

But his spear is sharp and true, and for a moment his face is that of Captain Hawse.

*

It wasn't a physical blow.

Cari can't tell what's happening in the physical realm, and what's bleeding through from the realm of the gods. She's seen gods walk in the mortal world, so fuck it, maybe the Lord of Waters *did* just rise from the ocean depths and strike down Artolo. If he did, though, the attack left no physical mark. Artolo's bloated torso doesn't have a giant hole in it.

The effects, though, are undeniable. Artolo topples, bonelessly, collapsing to the deck. All around them the storm rages. *Moonchild* spins wildly, thrown by the churning seas. Dimly, Cari's aware that a blow has been struck in the Godswar, that Kraken has been wounded and thrown into disarray. The storm around them shifts in a way she can recognise but not name, like the wind's howling in a different key. It's still about to sink the *Moonchild*, though.

Cari crawls away from Artolo's unmoving form, finds Dol Martaine lying there, face pressed against the deck, hiding from the gods. She grabs him, shakes him until he looks at her. "Pray!" she shouts, "tell them all to pray!" She shoves him towards the nearest hatch.

The crew are mostly Ilbariners. Some taken as slaves, others wiping away the ash-marks from their foreheads, but all take up the prayer, following Dol Martaine as he recites words Captain Hawse taught him. A prayer for deliverance from the storm.

It's not enough. *Moonchild* begins to capsize as the raging waters crash against her.

Cari bends over Artolo's body. Boneless, it sags and spreads over the deck like a beached jellyfish. He's still alive, staring glassy-eyed into the sky. A bloody stain begins to spread beneath the unbroken skin of his breast. Divine stigmata.

"Hey, fucker." By a stroke of luck so apt it must be divine, she still has her fish-gutting knife.

His slack lips twitch, like he's about to try to speak, but it's too late. She drives the knife in, starting with the old scar, the place where she cut him in Guerdon, but she keeps going. His Kraken-touched flesh yielding to the knife, parting like a wet bag as she carves him up. She dives into Artolo's body, searching for his heart.

A terrible, intoxicating feeling of rightness flows through her. *You were made for this*, it seems to say.

She finds her enemy's soul, seizes it, and flings it into the sea. The Bythos will take it to the Lord of Waters. The soul of a saint is a great prize, easily enough to pay for their passage to safety.

The storm subsides. The clouds clear. *Moonchild* rests on a calm ocean, so tranquil that Carillon can see the flooded ruins of Ilbarin City beneath the keel.

The surviving crew emerge from below. In their terrified eyes, Cari can see how she must appear to them – clad in the tattered remains of a royal gown, knife in hand drenched in blood and gore. Beautiful and terrible at the same time, a saint of terror and dark-ness who has come out of the Godswar to bring ruin upon them all.

Dol Martaine crawls towards her on his bloody knees, babbling about how he tried to stop them killing Adro, how he's protected Ren and Ama, pleading for her mercy. He thinks that she wielded the power of the Lord of Waters. He doesn't know that she's got no miraculous power here, that she's far from Guerdon's New City. That she's human.

Mostly human, anyway.

But there are other forms of power, and other ways to wield it. Cari looks down the length of *Moonchild*, feels the vibrations of the alchemical engines through her legs, notes the deck cannon installed by the Ghierdana. *Moonchild*'s not the *Rose*, but Cari's not the scared girl who ran away to sea any more, either.

"Set a course for the Rock of Ilbarin," she orders, "and ready the guns."

CHAPTER THIRTY-NINE

R asce emerges from the mouth of the tunnel into what must be the heart of the old temple, a great high-ceilinged hall that nevertheless reminds him of a slaughterhouse. The place is thick with ghouls, laughing and hooting. The beasts cluster around two ugly lumps of twisted metal. The ghouls are tying ropes around them, preparing to drag them into the abyss.

Those have to be the two surviving Black Iron Gods, stolen from the vault under the New City, and brought here. More prizes for Great-Uncle. Rasce advances into the temple.

"What are you doing? Onto the surface! Get to the yliaster vats!"

The ghouls ignore him. They haul on the ropes, pulling the two bells towards a shadowy archway. The misshapen lumps of shrapnel catch on the flagstones, like they're trying to keep themselves from being dragged away into the depths.

"Those are mine!' shouts Rasce. "They belong to the dragon!"

A ghoul breaks from the pack, lopes towards him. It's Silkpurse, but it's Rat who speaks through her. "NOT YOURS. NOT FOR YOU. WE WILL KEEP THEM SAFE. AWAY FROM FOOLISH MEDDLERS."

"Leave them be," demands Rasce, "or I shall crush you!" It's bravado – he spent all his power on that catastrophic miracle. He doesn't have the strength for another invocation, not at this range.

"HURRH," laughs Rat-through-Silkpurse. "RUN, LITTLE MAN. WE WILL EAT YOU."

The ghouls close on him, snarling, baring their teeth. Rat's hunger glowing in all their eyes.

He runs.

Baston, too, runs.

It's said that no one, except maybe the eldest of the ghouls, knows every path through the Wash. The old city of Guerdon is layered thick with previous incarnations of the city, wormed through with tunnels and secret passageways, ghoul-runs and back alleyways. The streets are only one way to traverse the Wash; there are other ways, above and below. Guerdon plunges underground, following the buried rivers through old sewers, cellars, measureless labyrinths. Guerdon soars skyward, reaching for the heavens with stairs, ladders, walkways and gutter-paths, buildings that lean so close together a man can step from one window to its opposite neighbour without breaking stride. String all these secrets together, and the freedom of the city is yours.

Can't catch a Guerdon ghoul, they say.

Baston's no ghoul, but tonight he runs like one. Hauling himself up the side of a building, wriggling in through an attic window. Crossing to a drainpipe, shimmying down the pipe to the ground, slipping in through a coal chute on the far side, coal cellar to a passage that runs under the next street to emerge in the toilets of an inn, up the stairs to the common room, shove through the crowd, out the back door, then doubling back, down Shabber's Close, crossing back towards Sumpwater, then up again, racing up the stairs in a tenement block, heart pounding, lungs burning.

If he had Rasce's gift, if he had Spar Idgeson guiding him, then he would know what awaited him behind each door, or around the next corner. He doesn't.

If he was faithful to the gods of Ishmere, then maybe Fate Spider would bless him with luck. He's not.

But these are his streets. He runs through familiar alleyways, climbs walls he climbed as a child, Karla daring him to go higher. The occupation has changed the Wash, warped it almost beyond recognition in places, but there are still patches of the old city, and there always will be.

Baston runs, always one step ahead of his pursuers. The forces chasing him change. The Tallowmen are first, of course, monsters out of his adolescent nightmares, wax horrors that flicker fast on his heels. Faster than he can run, so he has to be clever. He leads them on a dance, using the Tallowmen's hesitation to cross into Ishmeric Occupation Zone to avoid capture. But it's dancing over a pit of snakes – the Wash is now full of Ishmeric sentries and monsters. He exchanges one set of pursuers for another, with umurshixes chasing him down alleyways, spider-sentinels combing the rooftops for him. Where he can, he pits one set against the other, Tallowmen spitting hot wax at the Ishmeric sentries who bar their way.

He's not going to make it. He never really entertained any hope of escaping alive. At best, he hopes he can buy time for the other thieves to escape, buy time for Rasce to complete his assault on the Fog Yards. While the Tallowmen are chasing Baston *here*, they won't be fighting there.

He hopes his death will buy time for Karla, too. He really wants to have one last conversation with her. To shout at her for plotting behind his back, for not trusting him. He wants to hug her, make sure she's all right. He wants to see her, one more time.

Temple bells ring wildly. The priests are closing in. He turns down another alleyway, scrambles over the gate at the end, drops into a stable-yard. He runs, leaping over the murky green-scummed waters of a drinking trough, then vaults up on to another roof. He can maybe get to Lower Queen's Point from here by following the canal, then down to the docks, then loop back towards the New City.

Baston stumbles as the coins in his pocket suddenly become heavy as millstones. A curse of Blessed Bol, the trade-god of Ishmere. He topples from the roof, gold coins pulling him over, like he's got a landslide in his pocket. He rips the lining with a knife, lets the coins smash through a wall and splash into the canal. Off to his left, the roaring of another umurshix.

Go right, then. Away from the harbour, back into the free city. Doubling back towards the lithosarium.

He runs, lights of Tallowmen keeping pace with him, wax bastards following the line of the border.

Left, the line of the Newtown Wall like a dark wave ahead of him. The streets ever more familiar as he climbs up the hill towards Hog Close. Back towards his childhood home. Behind him, the whispering of a spider-sentinel. He can feel it extend feelers into his mind, probing his thoughts. Knowing what he's going to do before he does it.

He tears off his wedding ring, kisses it, then flings it aside. Lets his memory of Fae go with it, the ring holding the best part of his soul. He feels the awful attention of the spider turn aside for a moment to follow the ring's arc, giving Baston a chance to turn again, dodge down an alleyway into Hog Close.

The close is dark as he enters it. Curtains drawn in every window, except for his mother's house which is just lightless and empty. He runs through the little back garden, brambles tearing at his ankles. The place gone to ruin since his mother left. The Newtown Wall at the back of the garden is as tall as he remembers it, unclimbable. He remembers, one summer afternoon, when his father Hedan and a few other worthies of the Brotherhood tried to climb that wall. They were all drunk, laughing, betting on one another, and none of them made it all the way to the top.

Baston starts to climb. Blind, in the dark, his fingers searching for handholds in the stone. Hauling himself up by brute force. The spider-sentinel is close now, long hairy legs carrying its phantasmal body over the roof of the house – but the Ishmeric Occupation Zone ends at the top of the wall, and he seems to have lost the Tallowmen for now. If he can just get to the top of the wall . . .

Climb. Don't think. Don't hesitate. Run, little mortal, before the gods see you. You cannot endure their gaze. You cannot survive their presence.

His hand finds the parapet. He pulls himself over, takes one gasp of air, then rolls and runs again. He's not clear yet. The spider-sentinel's climbing after him, risking a brief trespass into the free city in order to capture him.

Baston races down a steep stairway on the Newtown side, runs into the clean, quiet streets. Newtown's feigning sleep, the whole district hiding under the covers, pretending that if they can't see the plumes of smoke from the Fog Yards or hear the gunfire from the Wash, then everything's still normal in Guerdon. He runs, every muscle in him burning, until he comes to one small house, one anonymous door.

A moment later, the spider moves down the street. Picking its way carefully, legs delicately planting themselves down with sinister intent. Hairs vibrating to the thoughts of those nearby, tasting the dreams of the lucky sleepers, the mounting terror of the wakeful. It stops outside the same door. Eight eyes glitter as it probes the mind it finds inside that house, scanning the thoughts for any trace of the fugitive.

Nothing. The spider withdraws, fading into nothingness. Ishmere dares not risk a breach of the Armistice tonight, not when fate is in flux, and the trail of the fugitive has gone cold. He did not pass this way.

Inside the house, the greatest actress of her generation smiles, beckons her son to emerge from his hiding place.

"And, scene," says Elshara.

Rasce runs. The chamber – the ancient temple of Black Iron – beyond has been shattered, the ceiling torn asunder by a spear of stone. Liquids cascade down from breached tanks on the levels above. He steps over corpses so blasted or encrusted with stone dust that he cannot tell what they once were. Human or Tallow, friend or foe, all anonymous in death. Even the ghouls don't want these bodies.

He moves on. There are knots of survivors, thieves and Eshdana, stumbling around in shock. He shouts at them to find their way upstairs to the yliaster vats. A thief stares at him in confusion. "It's death up there."

Rasce ascends. The spear of stone becomes a staircase for him to climb to the next level. More bodies. More dead thieves, killed by something with claws and teeth, something strong enough to snap necks.

He pushes on through this battlefield, following the sounds of fighting – and, more and more, the sounds of chewing. Broken glass crunches underfoot. Twice, he has to retrace his steps. It becomes harder to see, and his second sight is no use here. The stone he's conjured from Spar's pebbles is wrong, somehow, and it's like looking through melted glass.

He comes upon a body lying on the ground, a figure hunched over it. He raises his knife, assuming the second figure is a foe, but, no, it's one of the thieves, looting the remains.

"Where is—" Rasce begins, but the thief scrambles to her feet and runs without looking back, jumping over the corpse.

He recognises the dead man, although he's never laid eyes on him directly. It's Mandel himself, his throat cut. His beard is matted with blood. His fingers have been cut off to get at the rings he wore. The golden sigil of the alchemists he wore around his throat is gone, too.

"We offered you the chance to take the ash," Rasce says, choking on the dust, trying to find his bravado, but he has the horrible feeling that even though Mandel's lying there dead at his feet, the old alchemist still knows more than he does.

Near Mandel's body, he finds another corpse, burned beyond recognition. The slightest touch causes the remains to crumble and blow away on the hot winds that rush through the tunnels. Stepping out of the path of the swirling dust, Rasce stumbles over a heavy ledger, discarded in the chaos. He's seen it before, too, through other eyes – it's the ledger held by Mandel's scribe. Rasce kicks it over, discovers to his confusion that it's a scrawl of incomprehensible arcane glyphs. Khebeshi, maybe.

It's irrelevant. A distraction. He kicks the ledger into a puddle of some caustic slime that drips from the ceiling. He hurries down the corridor, but the double doors at the end are sealed with fresh spell-wards so strong that his dagger cannot even scratch them. The stone spears that impale the fortress have not penetrated this inner vault either – some tremendous act of sorcery deflected them, preserving the contents of the vault. Rasce steps back, dumbfounded. He tries to imagine what treasure might be worth such defences – but there's no time to linger.

The yliaster vats. He has to get to the yliaster vats. Has to do as Great-Uncle told him. The vats will be on the surface. Turn back. Find a way up.

He finds another staircase, climbs to a saner level. The basement of the alchemical works, a realm of pipes and wires and storage vats. All ruined by his miracle. He hurries on through the devastation. More bodies. Is this what war is like from the ground? It's not right for him to have to see all this. He has to get up, get out to the air. He won't stay trapped in this tomb.

More stairs, more corridors. He tries one way, finds the door hot to the touch, and the glow of flames visible beneath. He backtraces, finds another, trying to remember the route the Tallowman took in his vision, but everything's changed. He's broken this place, rewritten it. Everything's rubble and broken metal now, smoke and stone dust. He's not even sure if he's looking out through the eyes of his body, or if he's watching himself.

He clambers up another set of stairs, passes through an arch, and suddenly he's outside, in the great courtyard of the fortress. Burning metal towers above him, impaled on stone spikes. Everything encrusted with white dust. He glimpses patches of night sky through the pall of smoke.

"My lord! Over here!" A Lyrixian accent. One of the Ghierdana emerges from the smoke, his face hidden behind a breathing mask. "We've found their yliaster warehouse!"

"Who are you?"

"Gallerus."

Gallerus. A distant cousin. Blood of the Dragon.

Rasce clasps him on the shoulder. "Great-Uncle will be pleased!"

Behind the mask, Gallerus beams with joy.

Rasce follows Gallerus through the burning courtyard. Someone thrusts a gun into his hand, and he puts it to good use. There are Tallowmen scaling the outer walls of the compound, hidden by the smoke. Rasce can see them through the stone, triangulate his shots from a dozen angles. He snaps off a few rounds, splattering the waxy heads of the monsters.

The yliaster warehouse. Rows of casks, stacked high. The Eshdana plant explosives, tuck sticks of jellied phlogiston amid the casks. Dangerous work, with all the world on fire. *Someone should put up a red flag*, thinks Rasce, and the thought is so funny he starts laughing. He can't breathe in this smoke. He's getting light-headed, but how can that be, when he's got a whole city in his head?

"Burn it all!" Rasce giggles.

He reloads the rifle, ducks down into the cover of a shattered storage tank. More Tallowmen crawl over the walls. He fires at them, holds them back while the Eshdana work.

Gallerus, brave soul, moves forward with a burning brand to light the fuse. "Once I light it, get clear!" he shouts. "Back down to the shaft!"

Then a Tallowman breaks through. The thing flings itself down from the parapet, landing heavily atop Gallerus. His head smashes into the ground, cracking his breathing helmet and the skull underneath. More Tallowmen converge on the warehouse, scuttling from all angles now. Knives go in and out, spilling more blood on the floor. The blood of the dragon.

No one crosses the dragon.

Rasce levels the gun. He sees through the stone, letting him precisely aim one perfect shot, targeting the phlogiston charges.

The fire consumes him, just as it did the towers in the New City.

INTERLUDE II

By tradition, Keeper priests are burned, not buried or sent down the corpse-shafts. On another day, Eladora might have quibbled at using the university chapel in the Haithi Occupation Zone, but the whole city's choked with black soot after the Fog Yard fires, so one more pyre won't make a difference.

Sinter's funeral is thinly attended. Eladora. Two old aunts, and a girl who worked in a tailoring shop Sinter owned. A man from the Haithi Bureau, bearing a private letter from the Crown of Haith, currently embodied by Lyssada Erevesic, but that's all. It's sadly fitting that a man like Sinter, a spymaster at the centre of so many plots, could vanish with so few traces. The only person who weeps is one of the aunts, and she cries because it's not an official church service. *Well, he was defrocked for proposing a mass slaughter*, thinks Eladora, *he's lucky to get this much recognition.* She wants to feel nothing. Sinter was a tool, at best; a callous, cruel fanatic. She wants to not miss him, to not feel horribly alone.

A door at the back of the chapel opens, and Alic Nemon slips in. He takes his place at Eladora's side, and avoids looking directly at the shrine at the top of the room, where a statue of the Mother of Mercies stands, marble hands open in a gesture of welcome.

The eyes of the statue seem to stare directly at Alic; somehow, even though the stone face has not moved.

"Kelkin couldn't get away?" she whispers to Alic, as the aunts haltingly sing the *Litany of the Keepers*.

"I shouldn't be here," murmurs Alic. "Kelkin's taken ill. The healers are with him, of course. Are you all right? I know you weren't injured in the attack, but . . . " Alic's presence is warm, reassuringly competent, enfolding. Like being swaddled in webs. She has to watch that. The god wearing a human face is not her friend.

"I'm fine. Tell the Haithi and Ishmerians that it was an alchemical accident. Tell them it doesn't threaten the Armistice." The story has already gone out to Guerdon's newspapers.

"The Haithi know the truth already, though, and my, ah, former counterparts will divine what happened."

"The ghouls have recovered the Black Iron G-Gods." The statue of the Mother of Mercies doesn't move, but still, its eyes seem to flicker to stare at Eladora when she mentioned those dread gods. "Not ideal, but it seems acceptable. And the other relics stored in Mandel's remain secure."

"How can you be sure? The place looks like it got hit by dragon-fire. The lower levels are still inaccessible."

"A family friend assured me the wards would hold."

She takes a little pleasure in Alic's look of confusion. She still has secrets even Fate Spider doesn't know. Eladora examines the blackened fingernails on her hand, testament to her own use of sorcery. All things considered – her failure to hold the Ghierdana back behind the truce line considered – they, too, have escaped relatively unscathed. The Armistice remains intact. The city has survived.

"Mandel's place is a ruin, and the whole of the Fog Yards are shut down. Venture Square's in a panic, and the price of yliaster is twenty times what it was last year."

Something of Kelkin is rubbing off on Alic, it seems. Worrying about the speculators and the moneymen.

"Nothing of importance, then," clarifies Eladora.

"You don't understand," whispers Alic, loud enough to get a dirty look from an aunt. "This was sent to Kelkin this morning, straight from Guildmaster Helmont." He slips her a note, and she reads it by the light of Sinter's pyre.

"The alchemists are leaving."

CHAPTER FORTY

The ceiling's familiar to Rasce. He's spent a lot of time, these last few weeks, staring up at that ceiling. Or staring down through it.

Lanthorn Street. He's back at Lanthorn Street.

He's not dead.

Panic seizes him, and his point of view flickers. He's looking down at the bed now from above, and – to his relief – the body in the bed is still alive. His face is blistered in places, but no worse than it would be after a burning raid with Great-Uncle. The smell of the alkahest poultices on his bandaged skin is overpowering. His throat is very dry, and tastes of metal.

"Boss."

Baston's slumped in the chair by the bed.

"My friend," croaks Rasce.

Baston frowns at that. "You survived." Baston's matter-of-fact delivery can't quite conceal the awe in his voice. "The whole of Mandel's burned, and you survived."

"So . . . so it would seem. I can't remember . . . Gallerus set explosives to blow up the yliaster."

"A lot of things burned that night. The stone you conjured took the fire for you. Hell of a miracle." Baston walks across the room, opens a window. From outside, the sound of angry shouts. "Course, everyone knows how you managed that."

The burning of the tower. Great-Uncle's offering. They know.

Rasce leans back, lets his mind slip into the New City. The mob presses on Lanthorn Street, surrounds the Ghierdana enclave, the Lyrixian military compound. He feels them all, all those feet stamping on the stone, all those upraised fists and shouts of protest. Karla's name is on the lips of many of them – she's become a martyr for them, a heroine. He feels individual tears fall and splash on the ground as they weep for her; feels their cries echo off his walls.

There are more bodies on the ground – fresh-killed corpses, shot by Lyrixian soldiers when they tried to breach the compound walls.

And thanks to Vorz's experiments, Rasce feels a horrible ghoul-hunger when he perceives those dead men. There are still souls within the corpses, fresh and untapped residuum that he can access if only they're buried in the basement at Lanthorn Street.

He moves on, his mind sweeping through the city. *Spar*, he calls, *show yourself*. He can feel traces of the ghost, comes upon calcifying memory-shells cast off by Spar as he fled, but whatever remains of Spar's mind hides from him.

"Great-Uncle," he mutters to himself. "Great-Uncle has returned."

His questing mind finds the dragon down by the docks, in council with Thyrus and Carancio. His heart soars at the sight. Everything's gone to hell, but Great-Uncle will know what to do.

"He carried you out of the fire," says Baston. "The dragon did. Flew across Guerdon like a fucking thunderbolt, swooped down and scooped you out of Mandel's. Everyone else had given you up for dead."

"I must go and see him," he tells Baston.

Baston nods. He doesn't move.

"Are you still with me?" asks Rasce, hesitantly. "Now – now that my task is done here in Guerdon, I am sure I can be more forgiving. Even of . . . " His breath catches as his lungs press against the stone scabs on his ribs. "Maybe . . . maybe even of your sister. And you, you did well. Together, surely we can make things right."

Baston's face is unreadable. "Aye. I'm still here, aren't I? I swore an oath."

Baston walks two paces behind Rasce as they go through the New City. At the boss's right hand, watching for trouble, just like the Fever Knight trained him. Today, of course, there's no need to look for trouble – just step out on to the street, let the mob find them, and there it is.

The burned towers are visible everywhere in the New City. An accusation, black against the sky.

"Did you know?" asks Baston.

"I knew Vorz had a plan to deliver me the strength I needed to bring down Mandel. I did not know the details."

The details. The details were named Enry Sarrason. The details were named Muira Longwater. Thamas the Carpenter. Stonewoman Jal. Two families from Mattaur, three from Severast, three from Jashan. Eighteen children among the details. Rescuers choking on the ash from the details' scorched flesh.

"I shall make this right," says Rasce. "It's war, my friend, and there is always suffering in war. But we have won a great victory, and there shall be a share of the spoils for the deserving." He glances back at Baston. "They don't know which dragon it was. You must not tell them."

"I'll keep my mouth shut."

They emerge from a warren of alleyways and descend down steep slopes towards the harbour. The seawall rises high above them, a frozen wave of stone. The New City docks are under Ghierdana control, Eshdana muscle keeping the mob at bay, and the sound of shouting and weeping fades as they descend.

Only the waves on the shore, now, the crying of the gulls – and the rumbling colloquy of dragons.

The pain in Rasce's leg vanishes when he sees Great-Uncle. His breath comes more easily when he sees Great-Uncle. His worries dissipate like ice, melting in the heat of the dragon's presence. Seeing him approach, the dragon turns from Thyrus and Carancio, and mantles one wing, offering Rasce a private conference. The dragon's head, eyes glowing with wisdom, fills the world as Taras enfolds Rasce.

"You have done well, my nephew," says the dragon. The rumbling of his voice can be heard through the stone.

"It has been hard," admits Rasce. Gods, he's missed Great-Uncle. He's missed that guidance, that certainty. "Very hard. We lost . . ." His voice breaks, and he gestures helplessly with his hands. His own injuries to body and soul. Vyr's death. So many betrayals. So much death and suffering. "But I did what you ordered."

"Forget what has been lost. Consider what has been gained. The only question, nephew, is whether we are in profit or not, and what coin to measure that profit in. We have spent blood and gold, yes. You have suffered, yes, I see that. But from all this, we have won *power*, and from power all else flows. We have won a greater victory than you understand."

"Then tell me. *Show* me. Take me aloft."

"In time," rumbles the dragon. "Patience, O Chosen of the Dragon. Patience. You are still needed here," says the dragon, uncoiling. "Major Estavo has work for you." Great-Uncle folds his wings back, leaving Rasce blinking in the harsh light. The dragon slithers away, returning to his conversation with the other two wyrms.

A flurry of activity. Doctor Vorz, first, with his black bag and his vials. Muttering to himself, talking about absorption rates, conversion efficiencies, projection quotients. Injecting more of his tinctures into Rasce's battered flesh. Small stone scabs have formed over the injection sites, and Vorz curses as one of his needles snaps. Rasce feels like some alchemical apparatus, being checked and calibrated.

As Vorz works, Rasce watches a graceful young woman cross

the dockside. She has a breathing mask tucked under one arm, her other hand resting casually on the hilt of a blade at her side. She moves like a lioness, proud and cruel. Her features remind Rasce of one of his younger cousins, Vyr's sister. The woman glances over at him, a look of pity on her face – and then Vorz injects something into Rasce's face that makes his eyes water, and he loses sight of her with his human eyes. His inner eye, though, tracks her as she saunters up a gangway and vanishes aboard Vorz's ship moored at the dockside.

Then Estavo, the major mopping his brow, looking back towards the dragons for support. He has a bundle of papers in his hand. Architectural drawings, hastily prepared, the ink damp in places. A plan for fortifying the Lyrixian military compound, for sectioning off the Ghierdana compound from the rest of the New City. Wide, wide streets, deep trenches. New walls and barriers, all to be conjured from the mutable stone.

"The dragon Taras assured me you could do this," says the major, wiping his moustache. His voice low, like they're engaged in something shameful.

"I don't know if I have the strength," says Rasce.

"Oh, don't worry," says the major. He pats Rasce on the shoulder, careful to avoid any contact with his skin. "Doctor Vorz explained that he has some sort of, ah, alchemical engine down on Lanthorn Street. We shall supply you with, ah, the necessary fuel."

Baston's waiting for him at the foot of the stairs.

"What's the word, boss?"

"They will bring more ... offerings to Lanthorn Street. We should return there."

"And then what, boss? You destroyed Mandel. What's next?"

"Yliaster," croaks Rasce. He can't even remember what the stuff does. "There's a shipment of yliaster coming up from Ilbarin. We control the city's yliaster trade." Baston starts to shake his head, but

Rasce presses on. He clutches his dragon-tooth knife, and his plague-granted strength is enough to crack the hilt. "When the shipment comes in, there'll be coin enough to solve everything. It's ... it is business, my friend. It will all be worth it."

But there will be no shipment of yliaster from Ilbarin.

Across the sea, the yliaster refinery on the edge of the drowned city lies in ruins. *Moonchild*'s guns bombarded it while Carillon, Dol Martaine and the rest of the crew broke open the work camps. Then on to Ushket where they looted the contents of the Ghierdana warehouses, taking on food and supplies for the long voyage home. Some of the survivors of Ilbarin joined her crew there, abandoned the dying land for the promise of distant Guerdon. Others stayed behind, prisoners of their own pasts, or chained by fears of passing through the Godswar again. All were free to choose.

The Saint of Knives has little patience. After three days, *Moonchild* cast off from Ilbarin, never to return. Now she sails for Guerdon. Her decks are crowded, every hold occupied. The freighter becomes a floating city.

No Bythos ride the bow wave of *Moonchild* as she steams out of Firesea. The wounded Kraken does not reach for her, and she sails into open ocean where no gods hold sway. Her engines groan and roar as they are pressed to the limit of the capacities built into them by the alchemical engineers of Guerdon. The Saint of Knives does not tarry. She's going home, as quickly as *Moonchild* will carry her.

A city needs order. Ren proves to be an able administrator, Cari's right hand. He oversees the distribution of rations, ensures that everyone gets a fair share. Oversees the engines, ensures they have enough fuel to make it all the way to Guerdon. There are refuelling stations en route, but they're all controlled by warring parties in the Godswar, by Old Haith or Ulbishe or Lyrix, and none of them would trade with *Moonchild*. Ren watches the gauges tick down, and knows that Adro would tell him not to worry. They'll get lucky, Adro would say. It'll be tight getting to Guerdon, but with a fair wind and calm seas they'll make it.

A city needs hope and purpose. Ama, Ren and Adro's daughter, plays in the sun, and laughs for the first time in months when they cross west of the cape of Eskalind.

A ship, though, needs a captain. Cari's spent half her life at sea, but *Moonchild* has no rigging to climb, no sails to trim. Alchemical engines are a mystery to her. Still, she does her best impression of Captain Hawse, rallying and training her amateur crew, making them ready for the trials to come. They sail through disputed waters now, seas prowled by saints and monsters.

A ship needs a navigator, too, and again Cari fulfils that role. Hawse taught her to read charts, but she doesn't need any map to tell her the bearing to Guerdon. She can sense the New City when she closes her eyes – but she can't sense Spar. Her prayers go unanswered, and every day her worries grow as the silence remains. *I'm too late*, she thinks. She's returning empty-handed from her quest, and she's coming back too late even to say goodbye.

She hides her fears from her crew. She's become their champion, their saint, and she has to show courage for them. She's promised them a better home in the New City.

The crossing takes three weeks, even with *Moonchild* at full throttle. Supplies run low; disease stalks the lower decks. The voyage is not without sacrifice.

But, as Adro would have said if he was there, they get lucky.

The waters near Guerdon are empty. Far fewer now seek sanctuary than before. The war has moved, and the city is no longer as safe as it was. Still, the people of *Moonchild* cluster at the railing, searching the horizon for the first glimpse of their new home.

At last, ahead lies Guerdon's wide harbour. Cari can feel the weight of the distant city. Past the Isle of Statues, where the old

Stone Men go. Past the skeleton of the new lighthouse on the Bell Rock, past the quarantined Hark Island, the low sandbar of Shrike. She can almost see it now, see the towers of the New City reaching for the sky ...

"Turn the fucking ship," orders the Saint of Knives.

CHAPTER FORTY-ONE

Glass crunches under Baston's boots. The tavern's windows were blown out by the fires inside. He steps through the scorched doorway, steps gingerly through the still-smouldering embers. It's professional work, he has to admit. There were times when Heinreil would send the Fever Knight to torch some business that hadn't paid its dues to the Brotherhood. *If you won't support us in the struggle, Brother, we have to assume you're on the side of the Guilds.* Heinreil's words, making a mockery of Idge's ideals.

For a tavern like this, you want to get the fire burning near the bar, near all those casks and bottles of flammable alcohol. An amateur, or someone who just wanted to send a warning, would toss a firebomb in the door. Sow terror and cause a bit of damage, but if you want the place destroyed efficiently, you set your phlogiston charge behind the bar.

The bar was popular with Lyrixian soldiers. When the fire started, the place was full of them, some just arrived from overseas, others just back from the Godswar down in Khenth. Major Estavo's furious, according to Rasce, threatening retaliation.

Scuffed patches where the bodies were removed. Already, they've taken the corpses down to Lanthorn Street, so Vorz can drain them of what residuum might remain. The arsonists barred the doors to ensure no one could escape the blaze. Baston spots a little half-melted metal amulet behind the bar and bends down to examine it. A sigil of the Kept Gods of Guerdon.

He picks up the talisman, weighs it in his hand. Keepers burn the dead – the flames of Safid carry the soul to heaven, that's the litany. He wonders if there'll be any residuum at all left in that body, and if whoever died here knew what they were doing.

Like the rest of the New City, the tavern sprang from the stone, and Rasce has eyes in the stone. The attackers will be found and judged by the living saint.

Glancing out through the shattered windows of the tavern, there's two dozen or so people on the far side of the street, staring at him. Faces soot-streaked. All silent, all unmoving like statues, except when a mother wraps her arms around her son to keep him safe. All judging Baston with their eyes. It reminds Baston of the days after the invasion last year, when people emerged from their hiding places in cellars and shelters and found themselves in the shadow of strange powers.

He recognises some of them. A cousin of Fae's there – Baston met him at the wedding. That woman taught in an alley-school. Another woman in a black shawl – her husband was Brotherhood, back in Heinreil's day, before they sent him to the Tallow Vats. All of them left the occupied Wash behind, came here drawn by promises of safety from mad gods and occupying armies. Now look at them.

"Karla's brother," one of them says to another, "he betrayed her."

Baston wants to cross the street and greet them. Tell them that he's still on their side. Tell them that he'll look out for them, make things right. He can't make them understand. If he says a word, Rasce will hear it.

There's a barrier between him and the other side of the street so wide and deep he cannot imagine how to bridge it.

A shadow darkens the street outside, like a cloud moving across the face of the sun. The crowd breaks up, dissolving, people hurrying away without a word.

A dragon passed, he realises.

He returns to Lanthorn Street. The buildings around the house have been transformed by Rasce's miracles, reshaped into a guarded compound. Baston passes through the outer gatehouse, marches across the courtyard towards the fortified house. He can't even see the spot where he last saw Karla, the place where Rasce banished her to the underworld. It's all been erased.

She's still alive, Rasce told him. He has no idea if that's true or not.

Eshdana guards stand at the door, but they don't stop him entering. Inside, the house is quiet. The ground-floor room where the Brotherhood thieves used to gather is empty. Like an abandoned ship, half-played games of cards, undrunk bottles of arax and whisky, all preserved in the moment before they left for the raid on Mandel & Company.

He ascends the stairs, one step at a time, as if carrying a heavy weight.

Rasce is asleep, or in a trance. Doctor Vorz sits on the edge of the bed, like some vampire out of the Haithi uplands – but this leech injects blood, instead of sucking it.

"I'll come back," mutters Baston.

"No. Stay," orders Vorz. A forced smile, as if to say *we're all Eshdana now.* "I have to leave the city soon, and it would be best to have someone reliable to handle further injections."

"I don't know anything about alchemy."

"Don't boast about ignorance. Take every opportunity to improve yourself." Cold white fingers grab Baston's rough hand, guide it into place over the syringe. Rasce shudders as Baston pushes down on the plunger, but doesn't wake. "See, the tincture is injected into the vein. It's dilute – mostly water. A little yliaster – note how there's a residue left in this vial, so be sure to shake it before injection. And the active ingredient, of course." Vorz holds up another vial, reddish-black liquid clinging to the inside of the glass.

"Blood."

"More or less." Vorz carefully returns that vial to his bag. "I shall prepare a number of tinctures for you to have on hand." The Dentist peels back the blankets and examines the stone plates on Rasce's ribs.

"What does it do, exactly? The tincture." It's not idle curiosity. More like pushing on a scab. Baston wanted Rasce's miracles to be a genuine blessing, a sign that the Brotherhood could be reborn, that Spar Idgeson and Idge's ideals were still alive. Better to be thoroughly disabled of such fancies, to drain the pus of illusion from the world. Deal in certainties.

"It increases Rasce's congruency with the Guerdon entity."

"With Spar Idgeson, you mean."

Vorz frowns. He lowers his voice and makes a curious gesture with his hand before continuing. "I do not misspeak. The entity was conjured *through* Idgeson, and they are entangled, but still distinct. The entity is a sort of formless deity without ethos or purpose or intent. Little more than a holding vessel for the power of the Black Iron Gods that was stolen by Carillon Thay. A null god, which retained a fleeting impression of Spar Idgeson." Vorz scratches the bridge of his nose. "It would be fascinating to study thoroughly, but other projects take precedence."

"What if I run out of tincture while you're away?"

"You will be left with an adequate supply."

Baston watches the Dentist work in silence for a few minutes.

"I need some scrying done."

"He must rest. Just say what you need done. He will hear you."

Self-consciously, Baston recites what he found at the tavern, asks Rasce to find those responsible. Like he's visiting a Keeper church and whispering prayers to the Holy Beggar, or staring into the vapours in the temple of the Smoke Painter with his mother. Rasce moans, tosses and turns on the bed, reddish sweat staining the pillow. Lights flicker in the depths of the stone.

"He will know." Vorz fastens his bag shut and rises. "He will sleep for some hours now, though. Come along. Great-Uncle calls for me."

"I'll stay a bit."

"As you wish." Vorz makes that gesture again, leans in close to Baston. "You know, I will soon have need of a reliable bodyguard. I could speak to the dragon, have you given into my service instead of Rasce's. We both know the true value of an oath."

He doesn't know if it's meant as a peace offering or a threat.

"I'm not sure that we do."

Vorz departs. Baston settles into the heavy armchair opposite the bed, and waits.

The town of Maredon is Guerdon's younger sister. More sensible, one might say – here, there are only the Kept Gods, no dalliances with alien gods, no wild speculation. Old church spires dot the skyline, mixed with the chimneys of the alchemy works and the cranes of the town docks. Maredon's the home port for Guerdon's navy, and the little harbour's ringed with forts and gun emplacements.

Moonchild's met by naval escorts, who race around the armed freighter, their white wakes like a sigil of containment around the strange ship. It's Ren who makes contact, Ren who goes ashore to negotiate. Refugee vessels were a common sight in these waters before the Armistice, but those days are gone.

So, they wait. *Moonchild* sits at anchor in the middle of the harbour, a dozen cannons trained on her. The people on board huddle on the deck, staring at the brilliant green fields around the town, so close yet still out of reach. They've crossed ocean and Godswar, crossed hundreds of miles, only to be stopped short at the last few hundred yards.

Dol Martaine waits. His rifle's nearby, and its presence is like a sore tooth. Ren told them to take no hostile action, so they've spiked the cannons on *Moonchild*, surrendered their swords and guns to the city watch, but Martaine's still got a smuggler's instincts. The rifle and a few other necessities wait concealed in an air vent.

Right now, he's in charge, in the absence of Ren and Cari.

Carillon Thay was never good at waiting. She's already gone.

Ama can't wait. She squirms, unable to understand why they're not *there* already, why they're not landing at the magical city that Cari told her about, the earthly paradise where they'll be safe. Martaine tells her to stay below, out of the wind and rain.

He's slow to see it. It's only when he spots the Maredon guns hastily turn to track an approaching target that he realises the peril.

The dragon swoops low, flapping lazily over the harbour. It's not an attack – if the dragon meant to attack, Great-Uncle would come in faster than the wind, a hurricane of fire and scales, striking like a thunderbolt. This is something else – the dragon descends, the beating of its wings whipping up the waves, sending white spray crashing over the deck. Closer and closer the dragon descends, hovering above *Moonchild*.

The naval escorts that circle *Moonchild* turn and race away. The harbour guns crank around to aim at the dragon. *Fire, you bastards*, prays Martaine. *Fire before he breathes.*

But the guns remain silent. The dragon's not attacking Maredon, not breaching the terms of the Armistice. They're alone, without help.

The dragon's gaze sweeps over the ship. Ama screams in terror and runs to hide; people on deck cower before the dragon, or stare back at Great-Uncle, too tired to flee. The dragon's gaze falls on Dol Martaine, and the monster's mouth curls into a smile.

"Where is my yliaster, Dol Martaine?" asks the dragon. The heat from the monster's maw is so intense it's like standing in the noon-day sun in Ilbarin. Martaine feels the skin on his forehead blister.

"In . . . " Martaine's voice comes out a whisper. He swallows. "In the fucking sea."

"Eshdana . . . " says the dragon, drawing out the word. "You know your life is forfeit."

"Aye." Martaine steps forward, and looks up at those massive jaws. "To hell with it."

Flames dance in the dragon's smile. "Not here, Dol Martaine. Not yet."

And then he's gone. Great-Uncle twists in the air, his tail cracking like whip, and then he flaps his mighty wings and climbs, rising out of the harbour.

Ama runs up to Martaine, slipping on the wet deck. "Are we safe? Is the dragon gone?"

Martaine looks down at the girl. "No."

Scratch.

Scratch.

There are ghouls in the cellar, and they trouble Rasce's sleep.

Not the cellar of Lanthorn Street, of course – though the corpse-stealers would love to break in *there*, wouldn't they, a rich bounty of rotten flesh and residuum. No, he can sense the ghouls far, far below, in the tunnels beneath the New City. His attention flickers through the stone, leaving his body far behind, and observes the ghouls in the darkness below. Lots of them, skulking and scraping, like an itch at the base of his skull. Tormenting him. A chorus of yelping and yowling, mocking him.

It's within his power to crush them. He could bring the tunnel walls smashing down on them, squeezing them like he'd squeeze a fist, but it would cost him. The magic comes dripping slow, miracles distilling from the rot in the cellar as the city slowly digests the souls of the dead. It would be satisfying to crush them, but foolish.

He could tell Baston. Have him send a squad of armed Eshdana down into these tunnels, but the ghouls would be long gone by the time they arrived. No, the sensible thing to do is to ignore them. The wise thing. They haven't attacked him since they stole the Black

Iron Gods, and he still has their Lord Rat trapped. So, ignore them as they scratch.

Scratch. Scratch.

Other voices trickle into his consciousness, unwanted revelations. Plotting against the Ghierdana. Major Estavo broke the initial protests – Rasce heard the crack of the rifles echo off every wall, felt the blood spray splatter over the stones. Watched as a dozen died, and the rest fell. Watched as Vorz's Eshdana dragged the bodies away to Lanthorn Street.

Wearily, Rasce rolls over in bed – wincing as his stone plates catch – and finds Baston sitting in the chair opposite, looking at him. His expression unreadable.

"What?"

"Someone hit the Gull's Perch tavern." Baston hands Rasce a little piece of half-melted metal. Visions flicker into Rasce's brain, embedding themselves there like hot stones.

"It was Gunnar Tarson. He planted the bomb." The vision burns in Rasce's mind, an echo of the flames. "He's on Horsehead Street."

Baston nods. "I'll deal with him. Be ready in an hour."

"He was your friend—" begins Rasce, and Baston shrugs.

"No one crosses the dragon. That's how it is, right?"

Rasce watches him walk down the hallway, down the stairs, march across the courtyard outside Lanthorn Street. All the visions tangled now. He can see Gunnar Tarson, too, like he's watching him through a spyglass from some tall tower. Tarson's meeting with enemies of the Ghierdana. Plotting revenge for the burning of the towers, whispering about the attack on the tavern.

He redirects his spyglass. There's Major Estavo, secure in his newly reinforced dracodrome. A thicket of flags, indicating targets for the dragons, planted across the lands south of Guerdon. Khenth is on the defensive, the Silent Conclave driven back across the wastes by forces from the south. Jashan, it seems, is newly allied with Ulbishe, an alliance bought with alchemical weapons from Ulbishe's foundries. That alliance secures Ulbishe's southern and western approaches, leaving Lyrix as its only potential rival to the east.

When he flies with Great-Uncle, they'll set that thicket afire, won't they? They'll soar, dive, deal out life and death as they choose. He wants to be free of Guerdon, free of the New City. Free of the visions and the voices in his head.

Now, though, he scours the New City again, his mind a droplet of quicksilver through the streets. Enemies within and without; Tallowmen on the border, oath breakers and traitors within.

He has to prove himself to Great-Uncle. Only Great-Uncle can take him away from here.

CHAPTER FORTY-TWO

C arillon Thay returns to Guerdon.

Last time she came by ship, a stowaway. She crept ashore in the middle of the night and vanished into the tangle of warehouses and taverns along the docks. That was before the New City, before the Armistice divided Guerdon into four zones. That was before she knew what she was, or what the name *Thay* really meant. When she owed nothing, owned nothing, loved nothing.

This time, she arrives by train from the outlying town of Maredon. She gets off at a station on the edge of Meredyke Park and walks across the green, under the shades of trees, a heavy satchel at her side. Unremarkable, forgettable, a world away from the deck of the *Moonchild*, when her hands ran red with Artolo's blood. Carillon Thay walks through the park, her eyes fixed on the distant spires of the New City, visible around the shoulder of Castle Hill.

The skies over Guerdon are unusually clear today. The alchemists' factories in the Fog Yards and on the far side of Holyhill have stopped for want of yliaster. The train was abuzz with rumours of some great change in the alchemists' guild, a shift in power. Merchants and naval officers, scanning the newspapers like soothsayers trying to read omens from the gods.

Cari walks, looks for her own omens. Finds none.

Leaving the park, she passes through Newtown. The border of

the Ishmerian Occupation Zone lies just ahead. She hunches her shoulders, fixes her gaze on the cobbled streets that follow the curve of Castle Hill, down past the King's Nose tavern and into the upper Wash. She must look like a madwoman, she thinks, as she walks in two worlds. Choosing her route to avoid even the smallest prickle of divine friction, twitching in reaction to the unseen presence of a spider-sentinel or other spirit. Keeping her soul down. If she's caught here by the gods of Ishmere, without Spar or any other defences, she's doomed. And it'd be just fucking typical for her to escape the Kraken's wrath down in Ilbarin, to cross half the world back again, and then to get picked up around the corner from Spar's old place on Crane Street.

Ahead, the lithosarium.

The wax sentries on the roof catch her off guard. Old fears rise in her, but she batters them down. If the Tallowmen are here, she's in the right fucking place.

There are back ways into the building. Cari slips through the archway of a tenement that adjoins the main body of the lithosarium and clambers out of a window on to the slick roof, just out of sight of the Tallowmen. The cells in the lithosarium are partially flooded. The Stone Men were once confined to little islands in the middle of these large open spaces, the threat of drowning restraining them where iron bars or walls could not contain their plague-granted strength. Cari dives into that foul, greenish water, and two strokes carry her to the cell door.

It's not locked.

At the end of the corridor, another door. The sound of someone leafing through a book. And that door, too, is ajar.

"I'm back," says Carillon.

"I know," replies Eladora, marking her place in her book and closing the heavy tome. "Admiral Vermeil told me two days ago that a ship from Ilbarin had been sighted. Why did you land at Maredon instead?" Eladora sniffs. "And you could have come in the front door, instead of dripping mud everywhere. I think there's a change of clothes in that locker behind you."

"There are fucking Tallowmen at the door, El."

"They will not harm you. I gave them strict instructions."

Cari tips the liquid out of her satchel on to the floor, then grabs a towel. It's awkward with one hand still sore, but she wrings most of the slimy water out of her short hair. "There's something wrong in the New City. I couldn't feel Spar at all. It's like he's hiding – and not from me."

Eladora lays one hand on the leather-bound book. "The Ghierdana have a rival saint. A troublesome young man named Rasce."

"How did they do that?"

"The same way you became a saint of the Black Iron Gods, or Sinter used me to disrupt my mother's link with the Kept. Congruence via sympathetic magic. Enough to fool the gods."

"Spar's not a god."

Eladora shrugs. "I don't know what to tell you, then, Carillon. Whatever term you wish to apply, it worked."

"Shit."

"I take it your expedition to Khebesh was unfruitful."

"I didn't make it to Khebesh." Cari buries her face in the towel. She doesn't know if she wants to scream into the towel or hide her face while she weeps. Or twist the towel into a garrotte and strangle Eladora.

"I'm sorry." Eladora moves some documents on her desk, nervously. Her fingers shake, blackened nails leaving half-moons of soot on the white paper. "If it's any consolation, Rasce's actions may have, ah, restored some of Spar's strength."

"They burned people alive. I dreamed of it." Cari shudders.

Eladora nods, like Cari's just given her a clue in a crossword. "I assumed that the dragon's attack on the New City was connected, but it's good to have confirmation. One can never be sure with the Ghierdana – feuds between families are not unknown. That raises the stakes."

"The stakes," echoes Cari.

"Right now," continues Eladora, "the various factions appear to be holding back and letting things settle. The Ghierdana have stopped trying to push beyond the boundaries of the Lyrixian Occupation Zone. It's exceedingly hard for me to get information out of the New City, as Rasce has the same, ah, supernatural awareness you possessed. However, there are reports only of comparative minor miracles, and no further sacrifices." She coughs, a horrible hacking cough, then continues. "Of course, your return may precipitate further trouble."

"Fuck you."

A thin smile. "The alchemical works need yliaster. The Ghierdana have disrupted the supply lines. And you just showed up in a freighter that was supposed to be loaded with the substance, but instead arrived bearing a very different cargo. That will agitate events." She sniffs. "The dragon Taras overflew the naval base at Maredon. They know you returned – or at least, they know that the *Moonchild* is here, and I assume—"

"I don't give a shit about any of that."

"You should. The freighter *Moonchild* is owned by Lyrix, and they have requested that it be returned to them – with all its current passengers aboard. Parliament has agreed to do so."

"The Ghierdana are fucking pirates! To hell with them! You can't do it! I got those people out of Ilbarin. They're supposed to be safe here!"

"'Safe' is not a natural condition of the world, Carillon. A place must be made safe – and here, that is achieved by maintaining the Armistice. If it means anything, the Lyrixians have offered assurances that the passengers on *Moonchild* will be treated hospitably."

"It doesn't. You can't trust the dragons."

"I am aware of that. But preserving the peace is—"

"Worth their lives?"

"Yes. I shall do everything I can to avert such a tragedy, but, yes – if one must choose between a handful of lives and thousands – not to mention the accumulated learning and cultural wealth of this city – then the choice is obvious. In any event, it's parliament's decision." Eladora shuffles the papers on her desk, holding them up like a shield.

"What's the book?" asks Cari suddenly.

"What book?"

"That book. The one you've been trying to hide from me."

Reluctantly, Eladora moves the documents, revealing the leather-bound tome once more. "It's one of our grandfather's diaries. Jermas sent them to my m-mother long ago, when he sent you to live with us. I only obtained them after Silva's funeral."

Cari draws a knife. "Tallowmen at your door. Jermas' diaries. Talking like a fucking politician. Who knows what else you've got here. Gods below, El, what are hell are you doing?" It's not like Guerdon was ever a shining beacon of moral clarity, but Eladora was always the good girl, the polite one, and Cari was the troublemaker, the one who didn't give a damn.

"Saving Guerdon. Preserving the Armistice." Sorcery flickers around Eladora's hand, a corona of incipient lightning. "I do have influence in parliament. Maybe I can help – but I'll need your assistance. The balance of power has to be restored, and quickly. The alchemists' guild is threatening to flee the danger by decamping to Ulbishe, and without the alchemists the city will be considerably weakened. I'm trying to bargain with the guildmaster – I still have certain things they desire – but it would help immensely if the threat was, ah, diminished. I need you to counter Rasce."

"You mean kill?"

"If it comes to that. If it can be done. We tried, and that was before he came into the fullness of his power. The key, though, is returning the three occupied zones to balance. If Haith or Ishmere believe that the Lyrixians can strike outside the borders of the LOZ without impediment, the peace will collapse. I think I have General Bryal of Haith convinced, but Ishmere is . . . well."

"Yeah, I think I have some idea." Mad gods all around. Cari shakes her head. "I want to talk to Rat, first."

"The Ghierdana have imprisoned Lord Rat in the vault under the New City. He is alive, the ghouls tell me."

There's a chair nearby, and Cari sinks into it. "Fuckers." A thought strikes her. "So where are the Black Iron Gods, El? Do they have the other bells, too?"

"No. While you were away, I removed the contents of the vault for safe-keeping."

"What do you mean? What are you doing with the bells? No one should ever touch those things, ever. Fucking ever." Her grip on the knife tightens, to fight her rising panic. She judges the distance between them. "You never told me what really happened, last year, when you went into the vault. The Black Iron Gods teleported you to the isles of the Ghierdana. What was the price, Eladora? What did you promise them?"

"*Owe* them," whispers Eladora. She stands. "Come here. I want to show you something." Eladora beckons Cari across the room, brings her over to a trapdoor set in the floor. "It's warded against me. I can't touch it. You have to open it."

Cari hooks her hand around the iron ring, pulls the hatch open. Wards glimmer on the trapdoor for a moment. There's a small storage space beneath – Jere Taphson kept vials of alkahest down there, once.

Now, something else.

"Why," asks Cari, "do you have a phlogiston siege charge under your chair?"

"Because I don't know when the Black Iron Gods will call in their debt. I don't know how much time I have, Cari. I've gathered all the power I can, as fast as I can, to use for the betterment of Guerdon. But when the bells call for me, I shall deny them as b-best I can." Eladora's clearly rehearsed this speech before, over and over, but her voice still quavers at the end. "I need your help. Please. I can't do this alone."

Cari crosses to the window. The pane of glass is new, and she absently notes the afternoon light glinting off little shards of glass in the cracks of the sill. She stares across the Wash at the towers of the New City. Closes her eyes, and there's an after-image, like she's been looking straight at the sun. A dragon coils around Spar, trapping him.

She wants to run to him. To sneak across the border, to trust that she'll get her power back. The Saint of Knives, reborn. To do what she did to Artolo, only this time she won't leave an enemy behind.

Breathe. Swim up. Turn away.

"I need to know what I'm walking into," says Cari.

"Our sources in the New City are gone," admits Eladora.

"Forgive me," says a voice from the door. "I don't mean to eavesdrop."

Eladora hurries over to the newcomer. "Ah, Cari, permit me to introduce Minister Nemon."

"We've met," snaps Cari. "Sort of. Back during the invasion, just before I killed Pesh, I saw him on Hark Island. And I saw him die in the New City before that. What the hell?"

"An unlikely series of events," says Alic, smoothly, "none of which are germane now. Welcome back to Guerdon, Carillon Thay." He smiles, and it's not reassuring. Then he points at Cari's satchel. "You have something for me."

Cari frowns. "What do you mean?"

"As I was saying, Cari, permit me to introduce Minister Nemon," says Eladora. "Minister for security." She makes a magical gesture with her hand, as if warding off unwanted attention, and plunges on. "Also, godshade of the Fate Spider, incarnate deity of spies and thieves."

"The fuck?"

"We didn't discuss this amount of disclosure," mutters the spy to Eladora, then he smiles again at Cari. His expression is in a different register now, and it's like she's seeing him for the first time.

The muscles beneath his skin are oddly taut, an articulated mask thick with strings he can pull. His smile is as artificial as something grown in an alchemist's vat.

"He's a god? Not a saint or something like that, but an actual god?" *If he can do it, why not Spar?*

"Only in the most diminished sense," says the spy.

"Everyone's always telling me that gods are repeating patterns," says Cari. "Whirlpools in the aether, spells that cast themselves. They don't think like we do, you said. So – how?"

The spy takes Eladora's chair. "By means of a great sacrifice. You are correct, Carillon, that gods exist – and I once existed – outside the constraints of mortal time. Saints are our masks, allowing us to interact and understand the material realm. When Ishmere attacked Severast and threw down my temples, some of my priests escaped through secret ways. Their prayers preserve the thread of my existence. As long as they live, so do I."

"So if I stab you," asks Cari, "what happens?"

"Why," says Eladora, a note of despair in her voice, "does your mind go *there* instantly?"

"Considering what we're asking her to do," replies the spy, "it's a good question. Kill me, and I return. I am a god, and gods cannot die easily. Rasce, though, is still a mortal. Kill him, and he dies."

"El said you already tried that, and it didn't work."

"Ah," says the spy. "But now we have you, and you can bypass his defences."

Like Rhan-Gis, she thinks. Hesitantly, Cari reaches into her satchel, pulls out a cloth-wrapped bundle.

"Doctor Ramegos' grimoire," says Eladora with genuine joy, the eagerness of a librarian when a long-lost book is returned, "you brought it back!"

"No." Cari unwraps the oilskin. Inside is the aethergraph taken from Vorz's laboratory in Ilbarin. She's carted the damn thing all the way home. "I could never get it working. Stole it off an Eshdana sorcerer called Vorz who works for the dragons."

"I have heard of this Vorz. A backstreet alchemist, by all accounts," Eladora says, "but this aethergraph wasn't made in any back alley."

Nemon examines the machine. "It's intact, unlike the one from the Inn of the Green Door. We can pull psychic echoes off it, find out what they were talking about. A valuable prize.

Cari shrugs. "How long will that take?"

Eladora gives a sad little smile. "I have a singularly talented alchemist on staff. It won't take long."

"And I have something for you in return," says the spy. He reaches into his pocket, takes out what looks like a grey silken handkerchief, as delicate as a cobweb. He shakes it out, and a little pebble of pearly stone falls.

Hanging in the air for a moment, plummeting end over end.

To crash on to the surface of Jermas' diary, coming to rest on the dark leather of the binding.

Cari exhales. Wipes her eyes, her face suddenly wet with tears.

She lays her hand on the table, fingertips brushing the stone.

Spar, are you there?

Yes.

Cari and Spar begin with words. Fumbling, awkward, misplaced.

I'm sorry I was gone so long

I couldn't hold out

I've made mistakes

I missed you

The words give way to a flood of emotions and memories. In the technical argot of sorcerers and theologians, their souls are congruent.

For Cari, Spar's presence is shelter against the storm. He's home, the one place where she never feels that nervous restlessness, never feels that she has to move and fight to survive. The place where she doesn't need to lose herself. She returns to him now with new eyes. She's seen the Godswar. The horrors that lie ahead for Guerdon if the fragile Armistice breaks and the war returns to the city – internment camps watched by armed guards, prisoners dredging the last scraps out of a dying world for cruel men. Mad gods for mad worshippers, denying the world around them, stumbling towards oblivion.

At the end, nothing but worms.

And for Spar, Cari is life and fire, a light that guides him. Behind him, the stony pit of despair. Above him, always unreachable, is the duty passed down to him from his father. Idge is always there in memory, dangling from the noose, at once sacrificed to and liberated from the dream of a better city. Like alkahest, Cari frees him to move, to think, to find another way.

Welcome home.

"I didn't think I'd make it."

I knew you would.

"Liar. You told me not to go."

It was hard. His thoughts carry that darkness with him, the memory of his broken time. Cari shudders – even experiencing that dissolution, that unravelling, second-hand is terrifying.

"What are you, now? I saw the New City as we approached, and . . . it wasn't you."

I was driven out. Spar's voice is thoughtful. *Although I'm not sure what "I" really means, any more. What are you, Cari? Your soul? Your thoughts? Your memories? The body that houses them? We are all more fluid than we imagine, I think. We seek meaning to give ourselves form.*

She clenches her fist around the stone so tightly it digs into the skin. "I'm here. I came back for you. I don't give a shit about philosophy. How's that for an answer?"

A distant flicker of amusement. She'll take it.

"I hear," she jokes, "you've been cheating on me with another saint."

Rasce. He's . . . I thought he had it in him to be a good man. I still do. But his loyalty to the dragon poisons him. Spar's voice fades in and out in Cari's mind. The psychic equivalent of a furtive whisper.

"You're hiding from him."

He drove me out.

"How did he force you out? I mean, it's your . . . " She searches for the right word. Body? Domain? Miraculous gift?

My consciousness is fragile, says Spar. *I can't fight him without . . . losing the thread of myself.* Cari can sense his fragility, Spar's mind is like a soap bubble on the surface of the stone. Something beautiful and precious and fleeting. She crossed the world to find a way to save Spar, and now he's in more peril than ever. She glances across the room, to where Eladora and Alic Nemon whisper to each other. Eladora and a renegade god, wearing a human mask. *Their prayers preserve the thread of my existence,* Alic had said, like it was something to be proud of. Using people like stepping stones across the mire.

Could Spar do the same? Cari would gladly bear that burden. But he was fading even when she was right there with him as the Saint of Knives – that's why she left in the first place! There's something different about Spar, so the trick that Nemon's using won't work for him. All these sorcerers and alchemists and priests running around conspiring against each other, and none of them willing to tell her how to put things right.

Cari, it's all right. It's not your job to save me.

His thought comes as a shock. She's been travelling alone for so long, she'd forgotten what it was like to have him reply to her thoughts.

"Of course it is," Cari replies.

No, it's not. Some things cannot be fixed.

"Fuck that. The Ghierdana stole my blood, Spar. They stole my amulet. The only reason Rasce was able to do what he's done is because of magic shit and alchemy."

I don't think it was just that. My first connection with him was before that. I think I recognised something in him. Some . . . potential, maybe?

Cari runs her fingers through her hair in frustration. "Eladora wants me to kill him. So, we kill him. He deserves it for all he's done. Burning the towers and—"

We burned the towers, too.

"Not the same. That was an accident—"

We didn't know what would happen, and we tried to put it right afterwards. We made amends as best we could. We should give Rasce the chance to make amends, and resolve this peacefully. The city's seen enough death.

"Godshit, no. This all fucking *began* because I didn't kill Artolo when I had the chance. No more leaving enemies behind us. Spar, I've spent months running from the Ghierdana. The bastards don't give up. They're all, I dunno, inbred or something."

Brought up from birth to serve the dragon. But you of all people, Carillon Thay, should know something about breaking free of one's monstrous family and their intentions for you.

"Oh, fuck you."

Sorry, but . . . we can do this. Remember in the Crisis – before I died – when we thought we could gain control of the Ravellers through you? It's a moment like that one. Idge wrote that there are moments when individuals can break free of the historical forces that constrain them and make a change.

Carillon groans. "You're so bloody stubborn. All right. We'll try – but we get Rat first."

Because Rat is always so eager to forgive those who have wronged him, says Spar with a wry note of relief in his voice.

"Yeah. I'm hoping he brings you down to the gutter with the rest of us mere mortals." Cari rifles through Eladora's desk – ignoring Eladora's horrified glare – and finds a small silver necklace with an amber pendant. She draws her knife, pops the amber out of its housing, and slots the Spar-pebble in its place. "Saving you bought Rasce one chance. If he doesn't take it, I'm going to kill him."

Rasce is watching the tunnels. He sees like you saw. If you enter the New City, he'll know.

"He has to catch me first."

Tallowmen hiss and leer as Carillon leaves the lithosarium. She pauses at the threshold, looking back at her cousin. Eladora stays in the shadows of the doorway, careful to stay out of sight. Flinching at every movement on the rooftops, cautious of both gods and men with guns.

"Be careful, Carillon," says Eladora. "Please, return here once you've dealt with Rasce. Finding a way out of this present peril will require delicate diplomacy. Once balance is restored between the occupying forces, we shall need above all a period of stability. We'll need time to, ah, reassure the alchemists that Guerdon is still safe for business and convince them to reverse their decision to leave."

Cari stares up at the towers of the New City. "I'm not coming back, El."

"You're leaving Guerdon?"

"No." Cari closes her hand around her necklace. "But I'm not going to be one of your tools. I'm not going to hold back. That's my city up there."

"I need the Ghierdana, Carillon. Without the dragons, the Armistice won't hold. The whole damn point is that the three powers counter each other – if one breaks the truce, the other two are bound by treaty to attack." Eladora steps forward to grab Cari's arm. "If you weaken the Ghierdana too much, you'll ruin everything. Or g-get yourself killed."

"I'm not going to weaken them. I'm going to drive them out. I'm not going to let them suck us all dry in the name of *stability*. Fuck that. El, I've seen where that goes, how everything rots and goes bad. I'm going to save Guerdon from that. I don't know how, but it starts with saving Spar."

CHAPTER FORTY-THREE

"**O** n three," whispers Baston.

One, and his hand brushes against his pistol. He shouldn't need it, but in the aftermath of the raid on Mandel's, there are a lot of guns slopping around the New City.

Two, and breathe. Steady head, steady hands. Like the Fever Knight taught him. Push all thoughts of Karla away. Remember your oath. He glances down the street, checking to ensure his men are in place. Eshdana from Lyrix, all of them.

Three, and he's kicking in the door. The place on Horsehead Street is typical of the New City – a stone mansion, conjured from Spar's dying dreams, now turned into a slum. In fact, Baston recognises it – there was a kid's book of fairy stories that Spar had when he was a boy, and Karla inherited it when Spar outgrew it. Baston remembers the faded illustration of some brave knight's manor, and now he walks through Spar's memory of it. He steps over ragged bedrolls, scavenged from some wrecked ship. Pushes aside a tattered curtain. Dirt smeared on the walls.

One guy by the entrance, scrambling to his feet. Reaching for a blade. Baston punches him in the face, kicks him to make sure he stays down. Scoops up the blade without breaking stride.

There are shouts of alarm from other rooms. Groggy confusion – it's early in the morning, pre-dawn.

"Hold 'em," he orders. His men sweep forward, securing the lower floors. "Don't hurt anyone," orders Baston, "unless they move."

He marches upstairs. Third door on the left, Rasce told him. The walls of the corridor are covered in a scrawl of black paint, a litany in some tongue he doesn't speak. Folk of Mattaur do that, he's heard. The stone beneath the paint glimmers with its own internal light for a moment. He's not alone.

Third door on the left. Baston pauses, sniffs the air. There's a faint smell of phlogiston.

"Gunnar," he calls out. "It's me. Don't make this messy."

"Baston," shouts Gunnar. "I've no quarrel with you. Send in the dragon boy."

"He isn't here."

"Join us, Baston! You owe that bastard nothing, not after what he did to Karla."

"I gave my word."

The tombstone click of a breech snapping shut. "Come in then. Let's talk."

"Door," whispers Baston.

The corridor wall to the left of the door ripples, the stone softening. Baston puts his head down and charges through the gap – it's like pushing through mud – into the room beyond. Gunnar's there, facing the door with a gun in hand. His eyes widen in surprise, but he's too slow. Baston's strong hands close on the barrel, force it to one side. Baston's forehead crashes into Gunnar's face, and the boy falls to the ground.

Baston wrenches the weapon free, flips it around, aims it at the woman in the bed.

"Don't," says Baston.

"Her family died in the dragon's fires." Gunnar spits blood across Baston's boots. "How many of our friends did the Tallows get? And you don't give a damn. You spent their gold and you spent our lives, and you don't give a damn. The dragons and their fucking cult, and you're one of them."

"You took the ash first."

Gunnar wipes his bloody hand across his forehead. "Aye, and you told me to take it. Karla said it meant nothing, that we'd get back what they took from us. But now . . . " He looks up at Baston. His voice shakes with fear. "Are you going to kill me?"

Baston reaches down, pulls Gunnar upright. Presses the gun into his side. "You broke your oath. It's up to the boss."

Baston finds Rasce waiting in a café nearby. Four Eshdana at the door, two more inside, and either end of the street under guard, too. Baston catches a few people glancing fearfully at him as he marches Gunnar down towards the little eatery. The owner – a Mattaurese woman, eyes marked with dark kohl, her wooden shoes clattering as she clears plates – frowns when he enters with Gunnar, but quickly conceals her distaste. The place has been cleared of other customers – it's just Rasce and his guards.

Rasce is looking stronger. Only a little stiffness in the way he turns reveals his injuries. His high-collared jacket and gloved hands conceal any trace of the Stone Plague.

"Gunnar," says Rasce. He puts down his butter knife. Picks up his dragon-tooth. "You plotted against the Ghierdana. You attacked the tavern."

Gunnar swallows. "No, sir."

"I heard it from your own lips, friend."

Gunnar hawks up a gobbet of phlegm and spits. Rasce doesn't dodge. The spittle drips down his cheek. He takes a napkin and wipes it carefully away. Drops the napkin back on the table. Then, with the same hand, he grips Gunnar by the throat, and lifts the bigger man up. Rasce's arm quivers with the effort, but the added strength granted him by the Stone Plague is obvious.

"This man swore an oath to the Ghierdana, did he not, Baston?"

"He did."

"And what is the punishment for oath-breakers?"

"Death."

"But perhaps," says Rasce, "I could be merciful." He drops Gunnar. "What do you think, Baston? Maybe we could use an informant?"

Gunnar gasps for air, unable to speak, but his eyes stare pleadingly at Baston.

"The punishment for breaking the oath," says Baston slowly, "is death. He knew it when he took the ash. And you see everything. You don't need any spies in the New City."

"I suppose not." Rasce sighs. "Very well."

Heinreil would have had the Fever Knight kill Gunnar, thinks Baston. *Or he'd have had me do it.* On the streets of the old Wash, Heinreil was the generous boss whose hands flowed with silver. He was the man you went to for favours, the court of last resort. It was lieutenants like the Fever Knight or Baston who did the killing, who bore the sin. Baston's already carrying his damn oath to the dragon, and that's burden enough. Rasce will carry this killing. The people of the city will see him do it.

"You should do it yourself. Do it outside," says Baston. "Show people what happens when they cross the dragon."

"Are you sure?"

Baston clenches his teeth, and nods.

They drag Gunnar outside. Baston watches through the window as they force the boy to kneel. One of the Eshdana pulls back his head, exposing his throat.

Heinreil knew how to lie and keep his own hands clean.

Rasce brandishes the dragon-tooth, then draws it across Gunnar's throat in a red rush. Blood gushes out across the pearly stone of the street, running into the hungry throats of gutters. Once Gunnar stops twitching, they pick up the body, throw it in a cart. Down to Lanthorn Street, down to the cellar. Cellars, by now – Vorz's crew have expanded their makeshift catacomb, to cope with increased demand.

A hundred eyes watch Rasce murder Gunnar. Baston doesn't have Rasce's supernatural awareness, but he knows Guerdon. Whispers on the streets, like poison poured into every ear. The city turning sour. Baston's bound by his oath, but he can undo his mistakes. He can drive a wedge between the Brotherhood and the Ghierdana, push people to rally against the tyrant god that's growing in their midst.

Heinreil taught him to be a monster. Very well – he'll be a monster. He'll force some Brotherhood to stand up. The guilds' oppression made Idge. He'll force some other hero to rise up.

Rasce comes back in. He throws a handful of coins down on the table, but the café owner doesn't touch the money. She vanishes into a back room to fetch a bucket of water for the stained pavement outside. No doubt she fears that her coffee shop will be hit next, targeted for collaborating with the occupying forces.

"You know," Rasce says, "Great-Uncle shall move on soon. Back to Lyrix, or back down to Ilbarin to clean up the mess my Uncle Artolo left there. I shall fly with him, of course, but there's a place for you, too. A high rank in the Eshdana, wealth and power beyond measure."

"Whatever you say, boss."

Rasce takes a step towards Baston, and Baston steps back. "The plague, boss. Better I don't get too close."

"Of course." There's a weight to Rasce's voice, a leaden resignation. He turns away, eyes half-closing as his mind flickers through the stone.

"Boss . . . " says Baston.

"Yes?"

"Did you really speak to Spar Idgeson?"

"For a while. But he's gone now. The New City belongs to the dragon." Rasce turns. "Keep going through the list of names I gave you. Send them all down to Lanthorn Street." He wipes the dragon-tooth on a napkin, throws it on the floor. "Great-Uncle calls for me."

*

Great-Uncle suns himself on the plaza. Rasce approaches and bows, wincing as the stone plates dig into his ribs.

"My boy," rumbles the dragon. "How fares your city?"

"It is unsettled," Rasce admits, "but the trouble will subside."

"It is good for them to know fear." Great-Uncle stretches his wings. "Walk with me, Rasce."

Great-Uncle leads him across the plaza. For a moment, Rasce is comforted by the presence of the dragon; he can feel Great-Uncle's thunderous footsteps as he ambles across the courtyard, feel the scales of the dragon's tail slither across the flagstones. He beholds Great-Uncle's radiant glory from every angle. It reassures him – *Great-Uncle will help him with this cursed sainthood* – but he cannot rid himself of the troublesome impression of how *small* the dragon is, compared to the New City.

"Look," rumbles the dragon. Rasce looks out up at the serried ranks of grey clouds marching in from the sea, the dazzling patches of blue sky in the gaps between. He imagines flying with Great-Uncle, soaring up above that dull canopy to the bright realm beyond, liberated from the sullen earth.

"Not there, Rasce," chuckles Great-Uncle. "The harbour."

"Oh." Rasce looks across the island-spangled harbour. "What of it?" With a pirate's eye, he distinguishes traders and freighters from fishing boats and warships.

"During the invasion, Carillon Thay used her miracles to raise the wreck of the *Grand Retort*. She conjured a new island." Great-Uncle pauses and digs his claws into the plaza, ripping up the flagstones and cracking them into smaller pieces. Rasce winces as the claws scratch his borrowed flesh. "Doctor Vorz proposes that I scatter stones like seeds, and you make them sprout. Imagine it – a barrier we can command, nephew. Every ship passing through the harbour shall pay us tribute – and should we desire, we can close it. Doctor Vorz is a man of vision."

Rasce closes his eyes and imagines it. The same miracle he

conjured in the Fog Yards, over and over again. The last time he did that, the stone tore through his innards even as he shattered the world.

"Such a miracle," he whispers, "would be costly."

"Have no fear," says the dragon. "All is arranged."

On the horizon, a great freighter steams into the harbour under armed escort.

Moonchild has returned to Guerdon.

It's twilight by the time Rasce returns to the House on Lanthorn Street. There are thirty-seven guards stationed there, in the house and in the surrounding buildings, watching the courtyard and the alleyways.

Two hundred and four people in the buildings immediately nearby, and at least one hundred and fifty of them hate him. He can feel their anger through the stone.

Under cover of darkness, two young boys daub Karla's name on to a wall in an alleyway. In a nearby tower, one of the few thieves to make it back from the Fog Yards lies slumped in a corner. She's taken lotus-dust to numb her mind, but she still has nightmares of the stone walls around her coming to life, erupting into spikes and knives. Rasce hears his name over and over, whispered over dinner tables and in clandestine meetings in taverns and temples.

I didn't ask for this, he wants to shout. Even contained, his anger sets the stone around him burning, ripples of ghostlight blazing beneath the courtyard as he walks towards the house.

Twelve guards there, including the sniper in the attic. Four working down in the basement, their pickaxes hewing at his body, tearing new holes in him to match those made by the needles. They've already interred Gunnar Tarson. Rasce can feel the boy's corpse like he's a lump beneath the skin, feel microscopic particles of dust invade the body, sprouting within the dead man like marble fungi. A New City in miniature, growing within Tarson, those tiny

towers like cilia through the gaping wound in Tarson's neck, pushing through the dead flesh in search of the man's soul. Tarson's hate
comes flooding out with the residuum, the last vestiges of the soul
flowing into the hungry stone.

Rasce can't stay here. He'll go mad. He doesn't want this sainthood any more. Has he not been faithful? Has he not shown his
devotion? He did everything that was asked of him and more. He
didn't fail like Uncle Artolo. He didn't skulk and conspire, like Vyr.
He did what was asked of him.

In Lyrix, they lock saints up in madhouses and call them
monasteries.

Rasce turns and runs, fleeing the courtyard. Fleeing that awful
house, this awful city. He has to go back to the plaza, back to Great-
Uncle. The dragon will fly him away from this. Lift him away from
the stone and the slime, carry him to the cool airs above. Great-
Uncle will save him. The dragon is ancient and wise. The dragon
chose him; he must be more precious to Great-Uncle than any jewel.
Great-Uncle will save him.

Guards shout at him in alarm, call for him to return. Running
feet behind him, like a drumbeat on his spine. He twists the street
behind him so they cannot pursue. The paths bend ahead of him, a
convenient earthquake. Across the city, he knows that the dragons
Carancio and Thyrus take to the air in fright, knows that Major
Estavo hunkers down in the dracodome, mistaking Rasce's headlong
flight for the opening thunder of an artillery bombardment.

He closes his eyes and runs blind, but he can still see. The city
parts for him. The stone will not impede him. Right now, right
this instant, he can see Doctor Vorz down at the docks, standing
on the deck of a ship as his servants quarry lumps of stone from
the seawall. He feels every blow of the pickaxe, and every block is
a torment in waiting.

It's almost a relief to run into the mob. A dozen ruffians – he
could summon up their names with a thought, retrace the paths

they took through the streets if he wished. They know him, too – who does not know Rasce, Chosen of the Dragon, prince of the city?

A fist cracks across his jaw. A boot slams into his stomach. One of them kicks Rasce in the back of the knee, sending him sprawling, then draws a knife across his throat – but none of them can hurt him. The impacts of all their blows are swallowed by the streets around him. He is cursed with invulnerability. Even the knife cannot bite him.

Baston comes charging down the streeet, but only Great-Uncle can save him. Rasce lies in the street and watches with detachment as Baston scatters the attackers with efficient brutality. Sends them fleeing down the streets.

"Go after them!"

"I'll put their names in the book," says Baston, and Rasce has to laugh. The list is already too long. He can't stay here until it's done. Let some other servant of the dragon take over here. He cannot endure.

Baston helps him walk back to Lanthorn Street, brings him upstairs to the bedroom. A series of sharp pains. Tincture injections? Alkahest? Sedatives? He can't tell, but it melts his soul.

"Baston," croaks Rasce. "I can't go on."

"The gods send dragons to scourge the sinner and honest man alike," quotes Baston, and he's gone.

That night, he dreams of one name that isn't on the list.

Carillon Thay.

CHAPTER FORTY-FOUR

Dol Martaine spits over the side of their little boat. "This is the sort of nonsense scheme you and Adro tormented me with for years, so now I will show you how to do it properly."

Cari heaves on the oars, rowing towards Shriveport, the New City rising above them like a mountain, dark against the clouds. Only the lights of Guerdon can be seen on this foul night – the lamps up on Holyhill, the distant glow against the clouds of the alchemists' furnaces, and the glimmer of the luminescent stone. A few candles burning on rooftops, making Cari shudder.

"Stay down," mutters Dol Martaine. Cari ducks under the pile of burlap sacks, hiding while they sail past a Ghierdana patrol. Martaine calls a greeting, some Lyrixian joke, and the Eshdana on the patrol boat laugh and let them pass.

"Just get me close enough that I can swim to shore," whispers Cari, "then you go back. You don't have to come with me."

"Ach, and what would I tell them if I let you die?" He brings the boat alongside a larger freighter, finds a line trailing in the water. They creep aboard like ghosts, and from there make their way on to the docks, disappearing in the maze of alleyways. Cari takes the lead here, leading him through the labyrinth. Brick warehouse walls give way to pearly stone, a frozen wave of creation.

"One moment." Cari takes a deep breath, reaches out and touches the stone of the New City. The stone feels empty at first, hollow – but then it seems like the whole New City is slithering down towards her, unwinding, something scaly and titanic. There's another presence there, where once there was only Spar.

Looking for her. Hunting for her.

"Shit."

"What is it?" Martaine looks around, as if expecting enemies to leap out of the shadows.

"Nothing you can fight. Come on."

They backtrack, skirting around the fringes of the New City. Rain sweeps in from the harbour, drenching them both, turning the alleyways into tributaries. More rain falling in a minute than Cari saw in all her time in Ilbarin, water gushing through drainpipes, gurgling in gutters—

Hissing in the candle-flame. A Tallowman drops down in front of them, blocking their path, flooding the alleyway with harsh light. The thing's taller than Dol Martaine by a foot or more, hideously distended. Wax flesh contorted into an expression half-quizzical, half-feral, as if it's trying to remember why it's not dismembering them right this instant.

Cari's got her knife, but she knows the creatures heal minor wounds instantly. Martaine's loaded down with alchemy, but most of the weapons either have no effect on Tallowmen, or would kill Cari and Dol Martaine if they tried setting them off at close quarters.

The Tallowman's lips part, stringy gobbets of hot wax dribbling from its candle-lit mouth. "Paperrrsss."

"In here," says Martaine confidently. "In this bag." He holds out a yliaster sack, shakes it. "Take a look."

The Tallowman leans forward – and Martaine whips the bag over the monster's head, pulls the drawstring tight. Cari darts forward and grabs the other end of the cord, the two of them struggling to hold the bag in place. The Tallowman screeches, but its cry is partially muffled. It thrashes around, one flailing limb catching

Martaine and sending him sprawling, but the Tallowman's more focused on trying to get its head out of the bag than fighting. Its fingers claw at the sack, but the fibres of the sack are tough, and the bag's airtight. The lack of oxygen snuffs out the flame in the Tallowman's skull, and it freezes in place, caught in the middle of its writhing.

"Bastard thing," mutters Martaine as he pulls himself up.

"There'll be more. And worse."

Worse is the way down.

Worse is ghoul tunnels under the city. Martaine's bravado ebbs the deeper they go, as Cari leads him down into Guerdon's depths. In the unknowable distance, echoing up the tunnels, the hyena-calls of ghouls.

"You trust the ghouls?"

"Some of them."

"The one we're here to find?"

"Rat." Cari toys with her new necklace. "Rat's complicated."

They slip and slide on muck, clamber over rubble. The dark places under Guerdon are comfortable to Cari now. The cool, moist air delights her skin. Her eyes have adjusted to the blackness, and she barely needs the little lamp she brought with her. She's at home here in a way she never expected to be.

Martaine's litany of muffled curses and oaths suggests he's having a different experience.

"We're here," she tells him. "Turn up the light."

His breath catches at the sheer size of the outer vault.

I did this, Cari thinks. *We did this*. She gave Spar the power to rewrite the city, to cast down the alchemists and bury them in this vault. In an instant, they wrought a transformation that remade Guerdon, the work of centuries upended in a moment.

You get it wrong, and then the whole world is your fault.

It's strange, to stand in this titanic cathedral littered with the shattered remains of the alchemists' machinery, this monument to her own moment of desperate power, and recognise her own arrogance. Back then, she thought that everything in the whole world turned on the decision she made. Now, she sees the truth – the Godswar is much, much bigger than Guerdon. Even if she'd taken command of the Ravellers, become the queen they wanted her to be, and seized control of the city, the world beyond Guerdon would have continued to grind on remorselessly. The poor bastards in the camps in Ilbarin don't care who's in charge in Guerdon's parliament; the mad gods continue their blind struggle for supremacy.

A burden lifts from her as she crosses the vault. It's not *all* her fault, no matter how much power she has. There's a path between vanishing into the anonymity of the open seas, and the throne of Black Iron they showed her in visions.

She leads Dol Martaine across the chamber, looking for the weak spot. There's a scorched section of wall, somewhere in the darkness, that marks where Haithi agents tried to break into the vault and steal the Black Iron bombs. Cari and Rat and Spar kept them safe.

Maybe they should have destroyed the Black Iron bells. Found a way, somehow – although Cari's unsure what effect that would have on her. She's still connected to those gods. So's El. So is Miren, although that's a tick in the pro-destruction column.

Scratch. Scratch.

And then a voice, out of her own mouth. The taste of mud and bad meat.

"CARI. WELCOME HOME."

"Hey, Rat. Stand back."

Dol Martaine plants a small explosive charge. It's terribly small compared to the siege charge the Haithi sappers used, and Cari knows how thick she made that wall. They scurry for cover. The bomb explodes with a sharp crack, punching a small hole in the wall of Rat's prison. It lacks the grace of a miracle, but it's all they have.

When the soldiers from Haith blasted open the wall, Cari felt it.

She has to assume Rasce can do the same, that he's already moving. The gap is nowhere near wide enough for Rat to crawl, but he tears at the stone, his big ghoul claws tearing at the broken wall.

Cari grabs a bar of twisted metal from the debris and rushes over, works from her side, trying to pry chunks of rock away to widen the gap. It's slow going, and every instant they wait here the danger increases.

The sandpaper sensation, in the back of her head. Rasce is coming.

Rat stops clawing at the wall, and instead shoves a limp human form through the gap. A woman, her face vaguely familiar to Cari from the old days. Karla Hedansdir, filthy and bedraggled, but still alive. Cari pulls the woman out, pushes her into Martaine's arms.

"RASCE IS CLOSE. TAKE HER," says Rat, through Martaine. "GO. I'LL GUIDE YOU THROUGH HER."

"The hell with that," snaps Cari. She fishes out her new-made talisman, presses it to the wall. *Spar. Miracle. Take what you need from me.*

The wall tears. Cari shudders, but she's gone through far worse on her journeys, and barely notices the pain. Rat steps out of his prison, the rank stench of his presence bizarrely reassuring as he sweeps her up, his hug nearly crushing the life from her.

"Yours is marrow I shall be sorry to eat," he whispers in her ear. Then, through Karla. "THERE IS SAFETY IN THE DEEP PLACES. COME DOWN TO THE REALM OF THE GHOULS."

"I'm not running. I want to take Rasce down. Get back my sainthood."

"AND THEN?"

"Take down the rest of them."

"HURRH. UNWISE. FOOLISH TO GO LOOKING FOR FIGHTS. BETTER TO LET YOUR ENEMIES WITHER OVER THE YEARS. YOU HAVE NO PATIENCE, CARILLON THAY."

"Spar doesn't have time to wait. Neither do my friends on the *Moonchild*. We sit around waiting for the right moment, maybe it never comes. Are you with me?" It's a gamble. There are two sides to Rat – there's the street ghoul who was her friend, and the Elder Ghoul he's become. The Elder Ghoul who was willing to kill her, once.

"THE GHOULS ARE SAFE. THE BLACK IRON GODS ARE SECURE," says the ghoul. He stretches and grins. "I AM AT LIBERTY TO ACT."

"You're going to help save your friend because you've got nothing better to do?"

"HURRH. AND I AM HUNGRY. HUNGRIER THAN I HAVE BEEN IN A LONG TIME."

"Spar doesn't want to kill him unless we have to."

Rat presses his claw to his forehead. "OF COURSE HE'D SAY THAT. DO YOU HAVE A PLAN?"

"I talk to Rasce. Failing that . . . " She holds up her knife.

"FORTUNATELY FOR US ALL, I HAVE HAD LITTLE TO DO BUT THINK FOR SOME TIME. IS THAT NOT RIGHT, KARLA?"

Karla struggles to lift her head from Dol Martaine's shoulder. "Lanthorn Street," she whispers with difficulty.

In the distance, rumbling down the tunnels, a sound like thunder.

"TEMPLE DENIAL," says Rat. "AS IN THE GODSWAR. YOUNG RASCE USES LANTHORN STREET TO CONSUME THE SOULS OF THE DEAD. WE NEED NOT RECLAIM THE WHOLE OF THE NEW CITY. WE TAKE THAT PLACE OF POWER, AND THE REST WILL FOLLOW."

"You sure?" asks Cari.

"TRUST A GHOUL TO KNOW THIS."

"I have no fucking idea what's going on," says Dol Martaine. "Not one single clue. But that—" he jerks his thumb towards the rumbling noise, "sounds like trouble."

The underworld reshapes itself to make a path for Rasce.

He descends like a swooping dragon, every step carrying him

closer to Carillon Thay. The memory of her runs through the stone, like her tainted blood runs through his veins.

He can see her in the visions, although it hurts to look at her, psychic feedback stabbing his mind's eye. She's in the depths of the New City. She's not alone – he's aware of the Rat, of Karla, of another mortal man, but Rat only barely exists to him, and even Karla is just a smear of greasepaint, a fleeting wisp of flesh and bone. Carillon, though – she's like him.

The dragon-tooth blade in his hand. He's barely conscious of having a mortal body – so much of him is in the city around him, now.

She senses him coming. She and her companions scatter, like ground troops before the flaming breath catches them. Rat and the mortals hastening down one tunnel, Cari fleeing a different way. Experimentally, he reaches out with his mind and tries to squash her, to close a fist of stone around her, but the miracle's countered. Does she still have some claim on his city, or is this some lingering reflex of Spar?

It's better this way, though. More personal.

He slams the tunnel ahead of her closed, the stone melting and re-forming in an eye blink. Cari spins around, a cornered alley cat, a knife in her hand. She draws her blade across her palm, bloodying it.

He conjures a doorway for himself and steps into the passageway. The floor's littered with pipes and broken machinery, more debris from the old Alchemists' Quarter swallowed by Spar's rebirth. He's a creation of that alchemy, too, in a way – Doctor Vorz's tinctures burn within him as he works the miracle, sending a pulse of light through the stone.

Rasce sees her at last with his own eyes.

"You look like him," says Cari. "Artolo." She steps lightly over the treacherous debris, a sure-footed thief. Circling around, knife in hand.

"My uncle. You maimed him." The memory of the brief, one-sided duel between Artolo and the Saint of Knives runs through him, something else he's taken from Spar. "And I'm told you stole his ship. Is he still alive?"

"People – and gods – who come after me and mine end up dead. Ask the fucking Lion Queen."

Rasce laughs. "Behold! The dread Saint of Knives! And your Cousin Eladora, the grey eminence behind the scenes. Sending spies and assassins to torment me."

"Something like that." Cari adjusts her grip on her knife. "Listen, we don't have to fight. Spar says—"

"The ghost still speaks to you? Where is he hiding?"

Cari scowls. "Never mind that. Spar says that you're not a complete shit. There don't have to be more killings. The city's big enough for both of us, right?"

"To hell with this city. I shall be gone, soon. I shall fly with Great-Uncle."

"Fuck it, I'm fine with that. You go. I'll stay with Spar. I'll . . . " The Saint of Knives spits on the floor. "I'll even come to some arrangement with the dragon. Keep Eladora's bloody peace, right? Look, I've seen how bad things can get. The world's fucked enough without us adding to it."

Rasce steps closer. "Then take the ash. Swear to serve the dragon. You take my place here." He makes the proposal lightly, but as soon as the words pass his lips he realises how perfect it is. She'll take on the burden of the city, the role she was made for. He can fly with Great-Uncle again – and he'll return to Guerdon between flights.

Return to her.

It's a solution as perfect as the architecture of the New City, as elegant and soaring as the towers. His heart leaps. "Cari. Gods – I've shared Spar's memories. I've been him. There are things he never told you. I know how he loves you. He is dead, but I – I am alive. I can love you. We are alike – who else knows you as I can? With your gifts added to mine, my place as Great-Uncle's favourite is assured!"

"Fuck that." Cari stares at him with disgust.

"Join me! You want your sainthood back? Have it! I shall give up that power gladly. The gods of Ishmere want you dead? To hell with them! Become Eshdana, and we shall protect you! Only take the ash, beg Great-Uncle's forgiveness, and all shall be well, yes?"

"What about *Moonchild*? What about the people I brought from Ilbarin?"

"They crossed the Ghierdana. Their lives are forfeit to the dragon – but I am Chosen! Great-Uncle will spare their lives, I promise." He spreads his arms and proclaims his words with pride. "I say to you, you have the word of the dragon!"

Cari's eyes widen. A shiver runs through her.

"Adro," she whispers. The name means nothing to him.

Then, in a swift motion, she drives her knife into Rasce's ribs.

Baston's woken from an uneasy sleep by rumours of fire up near the dracodrome. Someone's set a storehouse full of Lyrixian military supplies alight. Explosions and the flash of burning phlogiston light up the night sky, like Dredger's yard all over again. A thrill of pride runs through him, and he wants to run out there and join them, but they'll never trust him again – and his oath still binds him, anyway. If he betrayed the Ghierdana, he'd only bring more trouble with him. Better to stay here, in this lonely house, and do what he can from within.

There's no sign of Rasce. Baston put guards on the door of the bedroom, but now there's a second door in the room, leading outside. Rooms can't hold someone who can reshape the city. Without Rasce's miracles, they're blind – no idea what's going on beyond the walls of the compound. All they can do is hunker down. Hold the Lanthorn Street compound and wait out this storm.

Baston walks the walls, a loyal sentry. A few troublemakers throw stones at the compound. There's a moment of excitement when one lad flings an empty tin can over the wall, and everyone fumbles for gas masks thinking its withering dust. But aside from that, the first few hours are quiet.

Then, outside, a gunshot.

Baston moves to the window, carefully standing to one side so he's got cover. The courtyard outside is dark and empty, but the gunshot was close at hand. By the main gate, maybe.

There should be more guards out there. He left half a dozen watching the walls.

Baston moves to the hallway. He checks the locks on the main door — it's heavily barricaded, just like it should be. He shouts up the stairs to the sniper. It's young Nic tonight. A Brotherhood boy.

"Nic? See anything?"

Gurgling, like the boy's swallowed his tongue. The sound of a body falling in the attic. Then a voice, oily and thick, from his own mouth. "BASTON. OPEN UP."

Scratch. Scratch from the far side.

"OPEN THE DOOR, BASTON."

"I can't do that, Rat."

"HURRH. QUICK NOW. DON'T BE A FOOL."

"Is Karla there?"

"SHE IS ALIVE. OPEN THE DOOR AND YOU CAN SEE HER."

"I can't. I swore an oath." He backs away from the door. "Go away, Rat. Go back to your tunnels. Leave here in peace, and the Ghierdana won't come after you."

"NO."

The door shudders as a huge weight slams into it.

As soon as the knife goes in, Cari knows she's fucked up. She feels the blade skitter off some barrier — an armoured vest beneath Rasce's jacket, maybe — and slash Rasce's side, a shallow cut. Not the lethal blow she needed, and she knows that was her only shot.

So now she runs, pushing past him to flee the way he came.

The tunnels become a nightmare. Rasce can't attack her directly with a miracle, but he can throw up obstacles, conjure chasms beneath her feet. She finds a stairway leading up, but it melts away when she sets foot on it. Another tunnel she tries suddenly floods, a spasm in the stone breaking open a water pipe.

All the while, Rasce pursues her. He's slow, limping, clutching his side with one hand, but he won't stop. The Ghierdana never stop.

Then — she's out. She races up a staircase, each step vanishing behind her, but she's too fast. Night air on her face, honest Guerdon drizzle, and she's out. The towers of her home rising above her. Rasce lashes out with a miracle, and the tower above her convulses and calves a huge chunk of masonry. Spar used that trick before, to squish invaders, and Cari's ready for it. She steps to the side, knowing exactly where it will land. She springs atop it, and from there to a windowsill. From there, up to the fresh scar in the building's flank, climbing for the rooftops and the gutters that have always been her domain.

Rasce follows, but he's slow and she's got the edge. She can't draw on the stone the same way he can, but she can twist his miracles, blunt them and steal them. He conjures a spear of stone, and she uses it as a stepping stone to reach higher ground. He conjures a wall, and she hides behind it, uses it to get close enough to cut him again.

"Hey, I killed your uncle," she taunts him.

"My uncle failed the dragon. I will not!" shouts Rasce. He picks up a lump of rubble from a rooftop and flings it at her with inhuman strength, but she dodges. Someone cheers from one of the nearby towers, and the call's taken up by other voices. The city's turning on Rasce.

"Going to kill the dragon, too!" shouts Cari, and a shout of approval goes up. "I killed Pesh, remember? You think one lousy dragon is going to—"

A shadow falls across the rooftop, blocking the light from the glimmering towers. Snuffing out the shouts and cheering.

"Yes," whispers Rasce. Cari's distracted for an instant, terror clutching her heart. For all her bravado, she's still powerless here. And an instant is all it takes – the stone beneath her liquifies, catching her and trapping her in place.

Rasce approaches, slowly, painfully. Limping like Spar. For him, the stone is solid, and he walks unhindered.

"You still lose," Cari gasps. "Rat knows about Lanthorn Street. And he's got Spar. Temple denial, fucker."

The dragon's shadow passes. Taras does not land here.

"I always win," Rasce whispers, and there's no joy in his voice.

The door shudders again as the Elder Ghoul smashes into it.

When Baston knew him, Rat was a scrawny little wretch, wiry with ghoul-strength, but small. He's grown since then. The beast on the far side of the door is as heavy as an elephant – but the door holds.

Another crash. The whole of Lanthorn Street shakes, but the door's reinforced, stone bound with Rasce's divine will, and the ghoul can't break through.

A scuttle of claws. Rat's moving, climbing the outer wall of the house. Think. Where would he go? What's the easiest way in?

The attic window. The sniper's nest. Baston grabs a weapon and runs, pounding up the stairs. Once the ghoul gets inside, there'll be no way to stop him.

He rounds the top of the stairs and fires blind. The heavy blunderbore, Dredger's cannon, roars as it fills the attic room with shrapnel. Rat yowls in shock as the blast catches him in the face. The ghoul topples backwards, falling from his perch to crash into the courtyard below. Black blood stains the white stone of the attic windowsill.

Baston darts over to the edge and looks down. Rat pulls himself upright, paws at his head. One of his horns cracks and comes away when he touches it. The whole side of his face is a bloody mess, one eye dark and ruined.

"Give it up, Rat! We belong to them now, the dragons and the gods. You can't beat them. We can't beat them." He reloads the blunderbore, aims it at the Elder Ghoul. Dares Rat to try climbing again.

Instead, the ghoul glares up at him, and Baston feels tendrils of Rat's thought creeping into his mind. Penetrating him like tree roots, pushing blindly at the foundations of his mind. A slurry of rot and fetid grave-earth slithering into his throat. "HURRH. MY KIND EAT THE BONES OF GODS. YOU CANNOT STOP ME, MORTAL CHILD." The Elder Ghoul is a demigod of sorts, with powers far beyond those of its lesser kin. The tendrils press on, a chill creeping through Baston's spine, his stomach. His fingers become utterly numb, and the blunderbore falls from his frozen hands.

Rat chuckles, wipes away the blood, and begins to climb again.

But Baston's done his duty. He's held the line for long enough.

Taras swoops down like a thunderbolt.

One swipe from the dragon's mighty claws knocks Rat from the side of the building, smashing him back down to the courtyard below. The dragon lands, its massive wings filling Lanthorn Street. Rat, who was so large and potent a moment ago, is a tiny, fragile thing compared to the dragon.

And tiny, fragile things can easily be broken. Great-Uncle's jaws close on the ghoul's torso, and he lifts and shakes, snapping him like a hunting dog kills a rat.

CHAPTER FORTY-FIVE

Victory is heralded by a greyish morn, the low clouds laden with sleet. Rasce shivers at the table, and the delicate Lyrixian pastries on his plate are as unappetising as ash. Arax does little to settle his stomach, but he still pours himself a second glass, then a third, before he closes his eyes, looks inward.

Three prisoners. The largest, Lord Rat, is still unconscious out in the courtyard. They've manacled the ghoul while Great-Uncle decides what to do with the creature. If the ghouls want their chieftain back, then the Ghierdana shall demand a high price. The stolen weapons of Black Iron, perhaps. It would be good, Rasce thinks, to correct Uncle Artolo's failure at the last.

The second prisoner is downstairs in the cellar. Rasce stumbles downstairs, the steps warping themselves to conform to his unsteady gait. He will not fall here.

The cellar's almost empty. Doctor Vorz's acolytes are down in the harbour, weaving the noose they shall throw around Guerdon's sea trade. Rasce is alone in the cellar apart from one other living soul.

With a wave of his hand, he causes one of the graves to yawn wide and vomit up its contents.

Carillon Thay.

There's an ugly purple wound on her forehead, where he struck her last night. She appears unconscious at first, but she's watching him through half-closed eyelids.

Rasce's finger probes the spot where she stabbed him. A new stony plate is growing there, a scab like wet concrete. "I did not ask for this," he says quietly. "Any of this. I did not ask for this gift of sainthood. I did not want to fight you."

"Fuck you."

Rasce smiles, thinly. "I knew you would say that. I have learned much from Spar." He toys with his dragon-tooth. "I thought you would understand, you of all people. You, too, knew the burden of this sainthood. To be a saint without a god. To command such power, and to feel the weight of the New City on your brow. I hoped you would understand."

"Fuck you," she says again. "You stole that power, and you crawled up the dragon's arsehole. Spar's worth a hundred of you – you should have listened to him, not Vorz. I fucking understand you, all right. You're weak."

"You have no idea of the sacrifices I made. Spar Idgeson had not the strength, so I carried him. I broke Mandel! I broke the alchemists! I beat this city."

"And all for the dragon." Cari gingerly touches the bruise on her forehead. "Second fucking time I've been hit there," she mutters to herself. Then, to Rasce: "What do you get out of it? What's the point?"

"Love."

"Oh, gods below."

"Great-Uncle loves me." He takes a deep breath, drawing on the well of that knowledge. It's warmer than alkahest. "You think he is like the Black Iron Gods, and that I am a fool for serving him. But what would you know of such things? You were born in a vat, Vorz tells me, bred by cultists for a singular purpose. I am Ghierdana, blood of the dragon. For a hundred generations, the dragon and my family have been one."

He stands. "Great-Uncle has decreed your fate. First, Doctor Vorz shall bleed you dry, to make more of his potions for me. Then, you shall be traded to the Sacred Realm of Ishmere. The blood of Pesh is on your hands, and the Sacred Realm will pursue you to the ends of the world for that crime."

"What about Spar?" Cari's voice is very small and scared. "Send me to Ishmere, but . . . please. It's not fucking fair."

"The gods sent dragons to scourge the living and the dead alike." He pauses before entombing her once more. "I wish things were otherwise."

Rasce allows himself a moment of indulgence before visiting the third prisoner. His mind ranges over the New City once more. He sees Great-Uncle up on the plaza, curled up. Rain drums on the stretched membrane of the dragon's wing – Great-Uncle is in private conference with Doctor Vorz. For a moment, Rasce feels like he's a child back home on the isles of the Ghierdana, watching older members of the family in similar confessionals. The man-tled wing is an ancient symbol of trust and secrecy among the dragon families. Nothing discussed in the shadow of the wing can be discussed without Great-Uncle's permission, not even with other members of the family. When he was a child, he craved to be admitted into that innermost sanctum, to be initiated into that secret.

Now, he pauses at the threshold. He can see all things, hear all things in the New City – even under the shadow of the wing. Neither Great-Uncle nor Vorz would ever know if he eavesdropped through the stone.

It would be wrong to listen, would it not? But the dragon takes what he desires.

Rasce's consciousness flickers forward, enters the sanctum.

" . . . Aethergraphed me this morning," says Vorz. "The target is the rail junction at Limerock."

"What about the junction's air defences?" rumbles Great-Uncle. "I am too old, Vorz, to fly blind into their guns."

"Master Helmont has supplied a list of the weapons stationed there, and he shall ensure the guns run low on phlogiston before you attack."

"Very well." Great-Uncle chuckles. "When this is done, I shall sleep for a century."

Rasce recalls the rail junction at Limerock. His mind flickers to Major Estavo's office in the dracodrome, to the map that hangs there. Limerock junction lies to the south-west of Guerdon, a lonely outpost on the edge of the Godswar, where rail lines from Ulbishe and the other cities of the south meet. A return to action, at last! A return to the sky!

He withdraws. His mind moves on, searching and probing, until he finds her. Karla's sleeping in a shelter in the New City, an almshouse run by an old Brotherhood man called Cafstan. A den of traitors, Great-Uncle would call it. All those names should go on the list. Rasce lingers a moment, looking at Karla's sleeping features. He could reach out and destroy her now with a thought – Cafstan's shelter is not so far from Lanthorn Street. He could squeeze with his mind and crush them all. He could open the ground beneath them and swallow them.

Rasce opens his eyes. Returns to his body.

"Baston," he says softly, and Baston appears. A loyal dog, coming when called.

"I've found your sister. She's at Cafstan's."

Baston nods. "What do you want me to do?"

"I spared her at your request. But there has to be a limit to my indulgence. She is well loved, I know, by the people of the New City." A twisted grin crosses Rasce's face. "Love bought with the dragon's gold. My Great-Uncle will wish to make an example of her. She will be permitted to live, Baston, but more than that I cannot promise."

Baston nods again. He turns and walks out of the door of Lanthorn Street, shoulders hunched against the rain.

The pebble lies on Rasce's desk.

One last conversation. One last prisoner. One last hiding place.

"Spar, are you there?"

Yes.

"Ha! You have become very, very small, my friend. When I met you, you were a great city, home to many thousands. Now, an ant would find you a cramped house."

Where's Cari?

The question irritates Rasce. It's not merely that so many foes conspire against him, it's that they are so damnably loyal to one another, even the rogues. Karla, choosing Baston and the Brotherhood over all Rasce could have given her. Spar, still asking after the fate of the street thief when Rasce has defeated her completely.

Even his *allies* cannot be trusted – Vyr schemed against him. Doctor Vorz *uses* him. The other dragons mistrust him. He is everywhere and everything in this cursed city, and he is terribly, completely alone.

He's broken Guerdon, survived every attempt to bring him down, and still he's alone.

Only Great-Uncle can be trusted. Only the dragon knows the lonely burden of power.

"Still alive," says Rasce, grudgingly. "But you have failed, all of you. The dragon is invincible. All that is left now is to dole out punishments."

Kill me. If I'm gone, Cari has no reason to stay in Guerdon. I'm all that keeps her here. You can let her go.

Rasce rolls the pebble around the desk. He knows that Spar is a spirit or ghost or some other thing of aether – no doubt Doctor Vorz has some cryptic definition – but he cannot shake the mental image of a tiny man, no taller than his fingernail, living inside the stone, hurled this way and that as Rasce toys with the pebble. "When I first encountered you, my friend, you were nearly gone. I do not know anyone who has gone so close to the borderlands of death as you. Do you not fear death?"

Of course I do. But . . . I lived with the plague for so long, I had time to consider it. The world is full of injustices and imbalances, and death is but one of them. You can rail against it, fight against it, but it comes for all of us.

"Save the gods."

I don't believe that any more. We've seen gods die, like Pesh. And even the ones who don't perish are so diminished they hardly count. I've seen Stone Men who are so far gone they're just shells – rocks with a few vestigial human organs, incapable of thought or speech. Death takes many forms.

"I think there is a natural order to all things, and it is this: the lesser kneel down to the great, and the great give reward and punishment as they see fit. There are but two truths in the world, luck and strength, and to have both is to be great. If I were to spare your friend Carillon, I would be sowing bad luck for myself. No, she must die, so the Ghierdana may prosper."

My father believed that all tyrannies must eventually fall – that they shall be overthrown, or else grind themselves into the dust.

"Mortal tyrants and mad gods, maybe. But Igde never knew the dragon." The dragon's victory is inevitable. He's seen that here in Guerdon. All other powers – Eladora Thay and her Armistice, the alchemists, even the gods – they're bound by rules and laws, beholden to debts and obligations, caught in complex webs of intrigue. The Ghierdana, though, we soar above such restrictions. Everything is simplified, uncertainties flensed away. You're either with the dragon, part of the family, or you're an outsider to be used or robbed or slain as the dragon desires. Rasce picks up the pebble. "What about you? Could you take the oath, I wonder, as Baston did, and serve me in all things? Or should I do as Doctor Vorz said, and destroy the last of you? What shall I do with you, little ghost?"

I can't fight you, Rasce, and I won't serve you. You've nothing left to take from me, so you cannot threaten me.

"Always the martyr! I have suffered, too! I have endured!" He's sick of Spar's moralising, sick of his detachment. Spar's no longer the moral high ground, damn it. The city belongs to Rasce.

Enduring suffering in itself means nothing. It's only if you draw perspective from it that it becomes worthy. The Stone Plague taught me patience. It taught me that things happen in degrees, a fraction at a time, until suddenly the world changes. That what is within counts more than what is without. But you – you still see everything as kindling. Offerings to please the dragon.

Of course they are, thinks Rasce. *That's how it works.* The Ghierdana speak for the dragon, the Eshdana serve, and everyone else burns in the end. "Do not speak!" he snaps. "The decision is mine alone. Your life, in my hands." He throws the pebble into the air, catches it. "I am leaving Guerdon with my Great-Uncle. My work is done; the war is won. My place is in the skies, at Great-Uncle's side. I will leave, and never look back!"

Rasce flings the pebble across the room. The door opens. Baston catches the stone in midair, stares at it in confusion, then tosses it back to Rasce. "Boss."

"I sent you to secure your sister."

Baston ushers another woman into the room. "You're going to want to hear this."

Eladora Thay draws back her hood.

"Miss Duttin. You are very daring, to enter into the Lyrixian Zone alone and unarmed."

"It seems I am not safe from the Ghierdana even in my own office," sniffs Eladora.

Rasce spreads his hands. "Who knows what rogue attacked you there? Some turncoat spy, perhaps, bitter at being used? What do you think, Baston?"

Baston shrugs. "We'll never know, boss."

"Are you here to offer a ransom for those who trespassed against the Ghierdana? The price shall be high indeed, I warn you."

"No ransom." Eladora reaches into her bag. "Your attack on

Mandel & Company may not have ended the ceasefire, but it has wounded Guerdon, perhaps mortally. The alchemists' guild—"

"What of them?" snaps Rasce.

"They are leaving. The guildmaster has already departed, taking with him the contents of the alchemists' treasury. They have signed a memorandum of understanding with their counterparts in Ulbishe. They won't immediately abandon Guerdon, but everything of worth and all future research shall go to Ulbishe. They fear that Guerdon is no longer safe, and they have little loyalty to the city."

Rasce shrugs. "What has this to do with me? Should I fall down and weep at your misfortune?"

"At your triumph. Doctor Vorz – what do you know about him?"

Vorz looming over him, injecting him with the tincture. Vorz, in endless private conferences with Great-Uncle. The brief stab of jealousy, all those weeks ago, when Great-Uncle declared Vorz would fly with him in Rasce's place. "He . . . he's an alchemist. A renegade from Guerdon, he told me. Thrown out by your guild."

"He's from Ulbishe. An agent of the Glass Court. I have proof if you want it. Carillon brought me Vorz's aethergraph, and we were able to read traces of his correspondence." She places a glass vial on the table, a component of an aethergraph. "All along, your true mission was not to profit from the trade in yliaster. It was to choke it off, and force the alchemists' guild into the arms of Ulbishe. To convince them that Guerdon could not protect them."

"Why would Great-Uncle keep this from me? I'm Chosen of the Dragon."

"Because he has no intention of taking you with him," says Eladora. "He intends to leave you behind."

CHAPTER FORTY-SIX

The last day in the life of Carillon Thay dawns bright and almost cloudless. The city's factories have ground to a halt, and sea winds drive away the smog.

Rasce comes to exhume her from her cell. Baston Hedanson reaches in, pulls her roughly from the grave. Marches her through the too-familiar streets of the New City.

They walk in silence. Faces look down from every window, eyes full of pity for Cari, full of hatred and resentment for the Ghierdana. It's Ilbarin again, almost. There's still resistance here, in places – even with Rasce's divine presence guarding them, the Eshdana guards are nervous as they make their way through the twisted streets. Dragons circle overhead, sunlight flashing off the lenses of the goggles worn by their chosen riders. Rasce signals to them with a wave.

They come to the seawall, a cliff of stone that guards the portion of the city that juts out over the harbour. Cari remembers the feeling of the waves against the stone, the way the water rushed and drained through channels and cracks, the unseen entrails of pipes and sewer left over from when all this was the Alchemists' Quarter. But this morning she's just herself, cut off from Spar and the city. No voices in her head.

Moonchild waits below. Waves push her against the shore, bumping her steel hull against the stone. There's a narrow ledge down there, at sea level, a walkway running along the foot of the wall. Even at this distance, Cari can make out individual figures on the deck – Ama near the prow, Ren standing behind her protectively. Dol Martaine's lanky frame, and, gods below, she's *happy* to see the bastard, even from afar. All the others she brought out of Ilbarin. She promised them a better future, and instead they get this. She snarls, tries to break free, tries to do *something*, but Baston grabs her, locking his arms around her, and he's too strong. He forces her to submit, kicking the back of her knee in a way that sends pain shooting through her spine.

But as he releases her, his fingers brush against her shoulder, and he makes the Brotherhood sign for *trust me*.

Rasce watches the passengers disembark from *Moonchild*, far below. The Eshdana guards make the refugees from Ilbarin line up along the narrow ledge of the shore, pressing their backs against the walls of the New City, prisoners waiting for the firing squad. Sacrificial goats, helpless and penned against the stone.

Further off, Vorz's ship. It's beyond the reach of Rasce's preternatural senses, so he cannot feel it the same way he senses *Moonchild*. He doesn't know if Vorz is aboard that ship, cannot eavesdrop on the Dentist while he's at sea. He wonders if Vorz has already extracted another tooth from Great-Uncle's mouth, carved it into a new dagger.

The sheath at Rasce's side is empty.

He pulls the long coat he borrowed off Baston close around him. The coat smells of soot and sweat, leather and alchemical run-off. It smells of Guerdon.

Vorz's ship is still within the waters of the Lyrixian Occupation Zone. Beyond, city watch gunboats prowl, aetheric searchlights instead of Tallow-flames, but bound by the same Armistice. They cannot cross the treaty line, cannot interfere. They are powerless to stop this offering.

The ragged peace births its own sorrows. Guerdon is a trading city – in the books of the accountants down on Venture Square, to exchange the threat of invasion by Ishmere for the slow rot of corruption and compromise was a trade worth making. Rasce came to this city thinking himself a pirate prince, Chosen of the Dragon. Now he's sickened by divinity. Unfriendly eyes stare at him from every window. The stone speaks to him of hateful whispers; his name is a curse here now.

He thought he came here to fight a war. To strike like the dragon – the swift blast of fire, the hurricane wings, the directed catastrophe. But it was something else. He was heat applied to an alchemical reaction, nothing more than a tool.

He glances at Baston, who walks a few steps behind him, a grim shadow. Baston's face is unreadable. Fresh vials of tincture in his pocket, to prepare Rasce for the next – the final – miracle. Baston drags Carillon Thay along. The girl is pale, woozy from injury and loss of blood.

Great-Uncle awaits them at the end of Sevenshell Street. The sun gleams on his red scales, his golden underbelly. The scars of the war have healed, and the dragon is glorious. Great-Uncle's claws and teeth are wrath made manifest, and to see the dragon – to know that he is kin to *that* – still sets Rasce's heart afire with pride.

Even Baston is cowed by the dragon's presence. Carillon struggles as they draw close, but Baston holds her tight.

"Rasce," purrs the dragon. Then his reptilian gaze flickers to Cari. "Thief."

"Fucker."

The dragon extends his neck, bringing himself face-to-face with Carillon. The heat of his breath is enough to scorch her skin. "Vorz tells me you were made for a purpose. The waking and scourging of the Black Iron Gods. I, too, was made for a purpose. Long ago, the gods of Lyrix made me and my siblings to torment the sinful. I am divine, and you have sinned against me. No god will absolve you. You have come a long way to perish, Carillon Thay."

Another procession approaches, heralded by horns and defensive chants. The priests of Ishmere, given special dispensation by Major Estavo to cross the border of the occupation zone. Although they've been ceremonially gentled, spiritually disarmed, they still come in pomp and grandeur. Saints of the Smoke Painter conjure vaporous banners of purple and red. A grinning priest of Blessed Bol, the golden god, squatting on a sphere of solid gold that rolls along under its own power. Priests of Kraken and Cloud Mother, in their regalia. On a palanquin rides a saint of High Umur, Lord of Judgement. Beside him, clad in grey, a priestess of the Fate Spider.

Following them, tended by acolytes, is a man wearing a jewelled headdress in the form of a lion. A sword has been strapped to his limp hand, and his head lolls about. His once-mighty torso bears a hundred scars, marked by a hundred triumphs in war, now run to seed. A sickly grey pallor to the mangy fur that sprouts on his neck and shoulders. Once, he was a saint of Pesh, Lion Queen, goddess of war. A saint shackled to a dead god, and the cost is plain for all to see.

The Smoke Painter saint steps forward and bows. Its face is hidden behind a mask of tattooed flesh, its body twisted and elongated grotesquely, but its fingers are beautiful in their elegance as it conjures a harp of golden smoke from thin air and plucks the strings. It plays haunting music that's also somehow a voice.

"Hail, Taras, eldest of scourges, father of the Ghierdana. The bargain is struck. The Sacred Realm shall not speak against your works here" – the long fingers, trailing tendrils of smoke, gesture over the glittering harbour – "in exchange for the murderess." The Ishmerian's satisfaction at the bargain is palpable. Of all the belligerents in the Godswar, Ishmere makes the least use of alchemical weapons. The collapse of Guerdon's alchemical industry is a boon to the Sacred Realm.

Great-Uncle nods his head in acknowledgement. "May her death renew the fortunes of Ishmere."

With brutal efficiency, Baston drives his fist into Cari's spine, twists her arm painfully, sending her to her knees.

The dragon spreads his wings, so wide they stretch across the world, casting all of Guerdon into deep shadow. He shuffles to the edge of the seawall, feeling for the rising winds.

Rasce steps forward.

"My beloved Great-Uncle. A word, please, in private."

Cari watches as the dragon mantles one wing, creating a hollow for Rasce to enter into. The dragon coils around his great-nephew, the massive bulk of his scaly body and long tail becoming a wall, building a sanctum only for the Ghierdana.

No one can hear their conversation. No one else is privy to their words.

The Ishmeric priests glance at each other. Fate Spider whispers urgently in High Umur's ear. Smoke Painter casts divinations, but the wind catches them and blows them away.

Far below, the prisoners from *Moonchild* shuffle nervously. Cari wishes she could protect them, be the Saint of Knives one last time, but she's got no power here. She can't even say goodbye.

Baston keeps hold of Carillon's upper arm with one hand, restraining her from running. His other hand on his gun. She can feel the tension through his skin, the barely suppressed violence.

Wait. Hold for the moment.

A muffled shout, from within the belly of the beast, and a roar of anger.

Then an explosion of movement. The dragon unfurls, wings spreading, rearing back, eyes burning with fury. It looms above them, blotting out the sun, darkening the sky.

But Rasce's faster. He's moving, dodging to the side, opening the long coat. It billows behind him, his own leather wings, and he brings up a weapon. It's a fucking blunderbore. He fires at point-blank range, vanishing for a moment in the billowing smoke. Great-Uncle bellows in shock and pain. The dragon's hide is tough enough to shrug off artillery shells or divine wrath, but the blunderbore's loaded with a dragon-tooth dagger. The discharge shatters the knife, turning it into a hail of bone shards, razor-sharp, driven deep into the dragon's flank. The shards tear gaping wounds in Great-Uncle's side, cutting through its scales to the flesh beneath.

The dragon topples backwards, thrashing. It slips over the edge of the seawall, and gravity tugs at it, pulling the beast down towards the crashing waves below. The dragon's claws dig into the stone, arresting its fall. Great-Uncle inhales—

And Carillon breaks from Baston's grip, runs towards the dragon-fire. Acting on Spar's instinct, that redemption's possible even for Rasce. Her fingers intertwine with his, and in that moment she's aware of the New City again, aware of the miraculous realm all around her.

The dragon roars, and lets loose the fire, but Cari's ready with a defensive miracle. With a twist of divinity, she shunts the fire into the New City, transferring the injury away from herself and away from Rasce, two saints shielded by the same miracle. This time, she's able to redirect the devastation away from the surface, away from the parts of the New City where people live. She takes that fire and buries it. The ground shakes as the vaults below explode in stolen flame.

Baston ducks behind a wall. Down the street, the Ishmeric priests scream and fall back. They incant desperately, calling the attention of their gods, but they're gentled and out of position, and their prayers go unheard in the moment.

Through the fires, Carillon screams as the miracle takes its toll. The city's store of magic is depleted. Through Rasce, she can draw only on the scant residuum of the few bodies in Lanthorn Street. Like a sorcerer, she must pay the debt in the coin of her own body and soul.

And in the same moment, Rasce reaches out, and Great-Uncle's wounded flank explodes.

The dragon-tooth was not the only material loaded into the blunderbore. A handful of pebbles, too, cut from the living stone of the New City, from Spar's transmuted flesh. The miracle causes the pebbles to erupt with conjured stone, spears and buttresses metastasising beneath the dragon's hide. The same miracle that shattered Mandel's fortress now impales the dragon.

Dragons are not gods.

Dragons can be killed, and never return.

Great-Uncle's wings beat in agony, once, twice, fighting against the sudden weight of the stone. Then he falls, breaking as he plummets, rending and shattering at once. Dragon's blood falls like rain across the harbour, hissing on the waves, as the magnificent wreck of Great-Uncle crashes into the water. City watch boats nervously circle the gigantic carcass. Waves from the impact grind *Moonchild* against the shore. Thick clouds of smoke and steam cloak the seawall.

Rasce leaps to the edge of the fire-blackened wall and howls, a feral cry. "I did everything you asked of me!" he screams at the titanic corpse below. "I sacrificed so much for you – and all the while, I was *nothing* to you! But I win, Great-Uncle! You are dead, and I am a living god!"

He turns to Cari. Extends his hand to help her up, a crazed grin of triumph on his face. "Listen to me," he hisses in her ear. "I bargained with your cousin last night! She gave me proof, yes, that Vorz is an agent of Ulbishe! He conspired with my Great-Uncle, betrayed me. Betrayed the Ghierdana, betrayed Lyrix. Everyone. I shall take over the yliaster trade and endure the guild's supply. But you—" He wipes ash from his face. "You must run! There's a boat waiting in Shriveport. That is the bargain – everyone will be told that it was you, the Saint of Knives, who killed the dragon! You slew Pesh – they will believe it!"

"I just got home, I can't—"

"Go!" insists Rasce. "Or you shall bring both the wrath of the Ghierdana and the Sacred Realm down on your precious fucking city!"

Cari wants to scream. Through gaps in the smoke, she sees the glittering waters of the harbour, and beyond, the open ocean. Not an escape, not blessed anonymity and a new life – just eternal exile.

But everyone gets to live if you go. Everyone down there on the Moonchild, *everyone up here. Rat and . . .*

"Take care of Spar for me. If you don't, I'll come back and I'll kill you."

He clasps her hand. "I shall."

Then, out of the smoke and ash, comes Baston Hedanson. The dragon-fire caught him badly – his right side is badly burned, arm and face seared almost to the bone. But in his left hand is a gun, and he holds it perfectly steady.

His boots crunch as he steps on discarded glass vials.

"You crossed the dragon," says Baston. "By the laws of the Ghierdana, your life is forfeit."

He fires. The bullet, washed in Vorz's tincture. In her blood.

And Rasce, too, falls.

Cari sees the gun, the flash of discharge, out of the corner of her eye. She turns, but Rasce is already stumbling back, dragging her with him. In that split second, she reaches for one of her old saint-tricks – tries to anchor herself to the stone of the New City – but it doesn't work. Spar doesn't have the strength to work the miracle, or the dragon-fire has burned away the magic.

Rasce still holding on to her hand, and he carries them both off the edge of the seawall.

The sickening moment when she goes over the edge.

Falling now.

Tumbling towards the rocks and the waves.

Everything wheeling around them, sea and sky and city. Spar described his fall from the Seamarket to her, and for a moment she's back there again, back in the Crisis, back next to the Black Iron Gods. She feels like she's watching herself fall, her and Rasce.

And then . . . then Rasce's not falling. A ring on his finger blazes with magical light, and suddenly he's drifting down gently, like a leaf on the wind.

Cari, though, falls like a stone until she hits the bottom.

Instinct takes over. Training takes over. Rasce tears his hand free from Cari and activates the Ring of Samara. His fall's arrested, going from headlong plummet to gentle descent in an instant. But Carillon keeps falling.

Tumbling, head over heels, until there's no more cliff, no more air. He lands gently, knee-deep in the surf, by that little ledge at the base of the seawall. The white stone, now stained red.

The sea surges, pulling at Cari's broken body.

Blood in the water, so much blood, but he doesn't know if it's his or Carillon's or the dragons. Ash, too, falling around him. The New City above him, a mountain about to topple, but the way the sun reflects off the stone is heartbreakingly beautiful. Guerdon's beautiful from the ground.

Shouts from the direction of *Moonchild*, people wading towards him. A boat's coming, out there beyond Great-Uncle's corpse. The blood loss from the gunshot wound begins to slow, blood speckled with grit bubbling from between his fingers. The plague has saved him, he realises. The stone plates took the bullet, too. He's going to live.

He laughs, bubbles of blood bursting at his lips. He always wins. Great-Uncle may be dead, but he's still Chosen. Some god has blessed him with strength and luck, and he can never fail! Look on his works! He has brought this great city to its knees! He has slain the dragon! He has brought ruin to all who stood against him — even the dragon!

He falls to his knees. What is left to him?

The amulet at his neck – Cari's stolen amulet – spasms like a living thing. Nearby, the blood on the water turns black, a liquid shadow dancing on the waves. Rasce recognises, in that moment, exactly which god blessed him and preserved him.

Behind him, he can hear the approaching engine of Vorz's motor launch, but the alchemist will arrive too late.

He opens his arms as the darkness enfolds him, rising up like black wings.

CHILD/SISTER/HERALD call the broken bells from far away across the city. Broken bells calling to a broken body. Cari hears them, as she always did. The calling of the Black Iron Gods drove her away to sea, where she found shelter on the *Rose*. Later, after the Crisis, Spar's presence in her mind shielded her from the last of the bells. The calling of the gods silenced at the last.

She wants very much to live. She's fought for so long to find this home again.

Spar. Forgive me.

Now, as she lies dying, Cari listens again. She strains to hear the sound of the bells. She names the Black Iron Gods, speaking their secret names with her last breath, squeezing the air out of punctured lungs, past shattered ribs, through broken lips. A reluctant, desperate claim on the legacy of the Thay family.

Saint of Knives. Saint of Thieves.

Saint of Black Iron.

Carillon Thay unravels her broken shape and steals another.

EPILOGUE

Months pass. Alchemists, gulls and other scavengers pick the carcass of the dragon clean, leaving only a few bones visible at low tide.

There's less traffic, now, at Guerdon's docks. Fewer ships sail past the dragon's bones. Trains and carts roll south, carrying the wealth and knowledge of the alchemists, and do not return. The city falls into a sullen, weary mood. Turns inwards, against itself. District against district, zone against zone. Not outright war, but suspicion, jealousy. It goes unspoken for the most part, but everyone knows the city's in decline. The Fog Yards and the new Alchemists' Quarter are twin urban wildernesses, full of half-finished or half-destroyed factories. The alchemists' guild has ruled Guerdon – openly or not – for nearly fifty years, but now it's gone. The city has lost its animating spirit.

For a time, suicides on Venture Square are commonplace, ruined speculators falling from towers like overripe apples at the end of autumn.

But if there's one thing Guerdon understands, it's commerce. Someone's always buying. Someone's always profiting. Haith, for instance – with Guerdon diminished, the influence of the Crown of Haith over the northlands grows. Haith's allies in the HOZ, too, feel the benefit of Guerdon's slump. The churches of the Keepers are thronged, and the king's influence waxes as parliament's wanes. A new crop of alchemical salvage workers, in imitation of Dredger, searches through the ruins of Mandel's yards and the other wreckage for scrap and wonders.

The Brotherhood, too, benefits from this diminishment. The New City is a thief's city, in the end. Oh, it's still *technically* the Lyrixian Occupation Zone, still *technically* under the control of the Lyrixian military and their Ghierdana allies, but it's the Brotherhood's city now. The war's shifted south again, to Ulbishe and Khenth, and the dragons fly south, too, to new dracodromes closer to the front lines – and closer to the shipping lanes, for a little piracy on the side. As for the Lyrixian military – a knife at Major Estavo's throat, and an explanation of the new order, and that's that.

There are still Tallowmen, but fewer than before. Rebuilding the Tallow Vats is expensive, and parliament no longer has the coin to spare. The closure of the factories, too, puts a host of newly unemployed workers on the streets of the Wash. Baston's men move among them, speaking of Idge and Karla, of other martyrs to the cause. Discontent rumbles in Guerdon that winter, but no one knows how to put things right. The city is no longer safe, no longer prosperous. What is Guerdon, if the streets don't run with silver and the factories don't run at all?

The future becomes shapeless and uncertain. The threads of the city's destiny unravel.

Months pass, and a ship from Ilbarin docks at the quayside of Shriveport.

The sorceress walks the streets of the city warily. Familiar routes are closed to her. The old Brotherhood clubhouse in the Wash, for example, is locked away within the IOZ, and the streets there are all changed. On Valder Street, where she once lived, she discovers houses reduced to rubble in the invasion. Some have been partially rebuilt; one is surrounded by yellow tape flapping in the breeze. It marks places tainted by alchemical weapons. The tape is old and faded, and flakes away when she touches it. No matter.

A poster on one wall advertises sorcery-for-hire. A Crawling One. She's heard they've returned to Guerdon, filling gaps left by the departure of the best of the alchemists. Hired by rich families up in Bryn Avane – and, she's willing to wager, criminal bosses over in Five Knives. It's how she first came here, after all.

She turns, heads south, parallel to Mercy Street. A carriage passes her, drawn by a pair of raptequines. Troubled by the sight, she ducks into a tavern. There are some half-familiar faces there, in the shadows, but they don't recognise her spell-blasted features. Still, a few coins gets her what she needs to know.

South, towards the shining mountain of the New City.

There's a checkpoint at the border. The slovenly guards are in civilian clothes, the only mark of their authority a tattered notice tacked to the wall, signed by a Major Estavo. Not one of the guards at the LOZ border is Lyrixian by their accents. Initially, they refuse to let her pass without a hefty bribe – her licence to practise sorcery is out of date, they tell her – but she makes the old Brotherhood recognition sign, and that opens the gates of this city. A hell of a lot easier, she reflects, than the Grimoire of Doctor Ramegos.

On Lanthorn Street she meets her first familiar face. Dol Martaine approaches her cautiously, mindful of her power.

"Guessed it was you from the border guards. Are you here to make trouble, witch?"

"Here to pay back a debt. And I actually mean a debt. If I meant 'take revenge on someone', I'd say that, all right. Books have to be balanced."

"Right." Martaine relaxes a little. "Is this about Ilbarin?"

"No. Not really." She glances up at the twisted spires. The light catches her face, and Dol Martaine flinches at the sight. "Is it safe here?"

"Nowhere's safe. But it's all right for now." Some passers-by stare curiously at Myri's strange garb, and Martaine hurries them along with a growled threat. "Carillon told me you pulled her out of the work camp."

"Is she here?"

Martaine shakes his head. "She died. Just after we arrived. She fell from the seawall. I saw it, we all did. All those who made it here on *Moonchild*. Saved us from the dragon, then died on the rocks." He sighs, rubs his hands on his stained trousers. "I always knew she'd fall to her death. Told the captain so. You couldn't keep her out of the rigging, or off the rooftops. Always climbing, always running."

"And Vorz?" Unable to keep the note of loathing out of her voice.

"He's gone. His men fished the dragon boy, Rasce, out of the sea and fled. Went down to Ulbishe, I hear."

"Ulbishe," she repeats.

"Were you looking for Vorz?"

"Books have to be balanced, but that's my business." She removes her glove, carefully tugging at the fingers, one by one, to avoid tearing the skin. She touches the wall with her spell-scorched palm. "I'll see the boss, now."

The new master is younger than Myri expected. Her face, too, is familiar. She sits behind a heavy desk in the house on Lanthorn Street. She's richly dressed, a jewelled pin at her throat like a respectable guildmaster.

"You're Hedan's daughter, right?"

The master's face is impassive. "I remember you, too. You were Heinreil's sorceress."

"Is he—"

"I am master of the Brotherhood now." She toys with a little golden casket, the only ornament on her desk.

"Didn't you take the ash?"

"I did. But the dragon I swore to serve is dead, and my brother negotiated a bargain with Thyrus and Carancio. They had little choice but to accept. Now, the Brotherhood has an understanding with the Ghierdana. This is our city once again."

"And your brother?"

"He crossed the Ghierdana. He had to go."

"All right. I'm not getting involved. I'm not staying. I was done with Guerdon years ago."

"So why are you here?"

"I owe a debt to Carillon Thay."

"She's dead," says Karla. "She fell from the seawall, and the sea took her. Her body was washed away."

"She had a friend. Spar."

Karla rises. "I can show you his grave."

The dark cellar would smell foul, if she could smell anything.

"Watch your step," warns Karla, and Myri conjures a werelight in response. The floor of the cellar is pockmarked with old graves, hastily dug out of the solid floor with pickaxes and then refilled, urban cairns. Karla leads her to one open grave. A single pebble rests there.

"I didn't know what else to do with it," says Karla, suddenly nervous. "He was . . . in there, I think. I don't know. He never spoke to us. Only Rasce."

Myri kneels down in the dirt of the cellar and begins to inscribe a complex glyph on the floor. Her fingers trace silver lines of sorcery over the empty graves.

"He doesn't need to speak to me. Just listen."

A distant flare of light.

Not light.

Sorcery. A light in the aether, an invisible sun. It draws Spar back together, gathers him. Fragments of awareness gone feral, rats creeping through the walls of what was once his mind.

A stranger's voice, but the light's enough to keep his attention.

He can string his consciousness along the trail of light, for a little while. Remember what it was like to *be*.

"I went to the masters of Khebesh. I told them everything I knew about the Gutter Miracle. About the New City, the Saint of Knives. Everything I knew about Jermas Thay's work, about Carillon's creation. Everything.

How do I put this?

Gods are patterns. Patterns in timeless motion in the aether. Living spells, if you want to think about it that way. Mortal thought agitates the aether. Individual mortals don't count for much, but the right thought makes a spell. And a lot of mortals ... Gods are born out of our collective thoughts. Into the pattern of their divinity, they channel prayers, channel the residuum of the dead. That's what keeps the god moving through the aether. The pattern retraces itself, over and over.

And then there's you. A mortal soul, given the accumulated power of a pantheon. The masters didn't believe me when I told them you'd survived in any form. You're an anomaly, Spar Idgeson. Caught halfway between god and mortal.

So, if you're not a god, how was Vorz's pawn able to make sacrifices to you? Not to the Black Iron Gods. To you.

My theory – and the masters agree – is that you're holding yourself back. You're caught between the mortal world and the divine – between being a timeless pattern of magic, endlessly renewing itself, and being a mortal mind anchored to the material world, to mortal time.

There's the choice before you. You can let go of your linear consciousness, stop clinging to anchors like Carillon, like your memories. You won't *think* any more, not like you do now, but you'll still exist. You'll be ... a pattern. A living spell. If people worship you, you'll gather power, influence fate. Maybe even accrue saints, think through them. Like Pesh was all war, like the Mother is all mercies, like the Lord of Waters is the seas of Ilbarin, you'll be ...

well, I never knew you, Spar Idgeson. I don't know what sort of god you might be. A tyrant, or something else. Maybe something good. I don't know.

Or, you stay as you are. This beacon I've conjured to draw you out – I can inscribe it, make it a lasting enchantment. It'll keep you together, for a while. It will be an anchor for you, a sort of artificial saint to give your consciousness a reference point. The spell will run out eventually . . . but not before you. Your mortal body is long dead; your thoughts are fuelled by the stolen power of the Black Iron Gods, and by whatever's left of the sacrifices the Ghierdana gave you. Maybe more residuum from corpses would prolong you for a little while, but you can't process it cleanly. Human thoughts are too messy.

So. That's it. I don't even know if you can hear me, or if you're too far gone already. If you can answer, give me a sign."

The city sorely needs inspiration. The dream of the New City is rotting around him. It's a thief's city, but thieves in the manner of Heinreil, in the manner of the dragons. Taking from the poor and the desperate, instead of the guilds and rich merchants. Idge wrote of a better way. Spar allows himself to imagine rebellious saints, holy thieves. Champions of the gutters and the alleyways, casting down the corrupt guilds, demanding a fairer city. The Tallowmen and the other obscenities and cruelties of the alchemists destroyed, the mad gods driven from the city.

A holy revolution.

But Spar Idgeson is not his father. He's been the custodian of Idge's dream all his life, all his temporary after-life too. He's served Idge's memory as Rasce served the dragon, thought himself chosen to carry on the dream of a fairer Guerdon.

But in his own way. Not Idge's.

Spar draws all his remaining strength together. With an unseen finger, he writes on the cellar wall, burning his message into the stone.

I'LL WAIT FOR HER.

ACKNOWLEDGEMENTS

It's 13 July 2020 as I write this, and honestly some days the future feels so unpredictable it's an act of absurd optimism to write. I hope, gentle reader, that you're well as can be expected under the circumstances, whatever those happen to be when you read this.

Thank you, by the by, for reading this; special thanks to all those who read and reviewed *The Gutter Prayer* and *The Shadow Saint*. Special and heavily armed thanks to BookNest.eu.

Endless gratitude to the editorial team of Emily Byron, Bradley Englert, Jenni Hill and Joanna Kramer, cover artist Richard Anderson and the rest of the Orbit team.

Even Nazia. She knows what she did.

Portions of this book were written during lockdown. My condolences to Edel and the kids, who were trapped in a house with a writer on deadline and no access to coffee shops.

I remain indebted to stalwart agent John Jarrold, beta readers John Nephew and Neil Kelly; also to the Pelgrane crew, the Twitterati, and the circle of friends that became a set of squares on Zoom in recent months. Here's to better times ahead.

extras

orbit

orbitbooks.net

about the author

Gareth Hanrahan's three-month break from computer programming to concentrate on writing has now lasted fifteen years and counting. He's written more gaming books than he can readily recall, by virtue of the alchemical transmutation of tea and guilt into words. He lives in Ireland with his wife and children. Follow him on Twitter @mytholder.

Find out more about Gareth Hanrahan and other Orbit authors by registering for the free monthly newsletter at www.orbitbooks.net.

if you enjoyed

THE BROKEN GOD

look out for

THE BONE SHARD DAUGHTER

by

Andrea Stewart

The Emperor's reign has lasted for decades, his mastery of bone shard magic powering the animal-like constructs that maintain law and order. But now his rule is failing, and revolution is sweeping across the Empire's many islands.

Lin is the Emperor's daughter and she spends her days trapped in a palace of locked doors and dark secrets. When her father refuses to recognise her as heir to the throne, she vows to prove her worth by mastering the forbidden art of bone shard magic.

Yet such power carries a great cost, and when the revolution reaches the gates of the palace, Lin must decide how far she is willing to go to claim her birthright — and save her people.

1

Lin

Imperial Island

Father told me I'm broken.

He didn't speak this disappointment when I answered his question. But he said it with narrowed eyes, the way he sucked on his already hollow cheeks, the way the left side of his lips twitched a little bit down, the movement almost hidden by his beard.

He taught me how to read a person's thoughts on their face. And he knew that I knew how to read these signs. So between us, it was as though he had spoken out loud.

The question: "Who was your closest childhood friend?"

My answer: "I don't know."

I could run as quickly as the sparrow flies, I was as skilled with an abacus as the Empire's best accountants, and I could name all the known islands in the time it took for tea to finish steeping. But I could not remember my past before the sickness. Sometimes I thought I never would – that the girl from before was lost to me.

Father's chair creaked as he shifted, and he let out a long breath. In his fingers he held a brass key, which he tapped on the table's surface. "How can I trust you with my secrets? How can I trust you as my heir if you do not know who you are?"

I knew who I was. I was Lin. I was the Emperor's daughter. I shouted the words in my head, but I didn't say them. Unlike my father, I kept my face neutral, my thoughts hidden. Sometimes he liked it when I stood up for myself, but this was not one of those times. It never was, when it came to my past.

I did my best not to stare at the key.

"Ask me another question," I said. The wind lashed at the shutters, bringing with it the salt-seaweed smell of the ocean. The breeze licked at my neck, and I suppressed a shiver. I kept his gaze, hoping he saw the steel in my soul and not the fear. I could taste the scent of rebellion on the winds as clearly as I could the fish fermentation vats. It was that obvious, that thick. I could set things right, if only I had the means. If only he'd let me prove it.

Tap.

"Very well," Father said. The teak pillars behind him framed his withered countenance, making him look more like a foreboding portrait than a man. "You're afraid of sea serpents. Why?"

"I was bit by one when I was a child," I said.

He studied my face. I held my breath. I stopped holding my breath. I twined my fingers together and then forced them to relax. If I were a mountain, he would be following the taproots of cloud junipers, chipping away the stone, searching for the white, chalky core.

And finding it.

"Don't lie to me, girl," he snarled. "Don't make guesses. You may be my flesh and blood, but I can name my foster son to the crown. It doesn't have to be you."

I wished I did remember. Was there a time when this man stroked my hair and kissed my forehead? Had he loved me before I'd forgotten, when I'd been whole and unbroken? I wished there was someone I could ask. Or at least, someone who could give me answers. "Forgive me." I bowed my head. My black hair formed a curtain over my eyes, and I stole a glance at the key.

Most of the doors in the palace were locked. He hobbled from room to room, using his bone shard magic to create miracles. A magic I needed if I was to rule. I'd earned six keys. My father's foster, Bayan, had seven. Sometimes it felt as if my entire life was a test.

"Fine," Father said. He eased back into his chair. "You may go."

I rose to leave, but hesitated. "When will you teach me your bone shard magic?" I didn't wait for his response. "You say you can name Bayan as your heir, but you haven't. I am still your heir, and I need to know how to control the constructs. I'm twenty-three, and you—" I stopped, because I didn't know how old he was. There were liver spots on the backs of his hands, and his hair was steely gray. I didn't know how much longer he would live. All I could imagine was a future where he died and left me with no knowledge. No way to protect the Empire from the Alanga. No memories of a father who cared.

He coughed, muffling the sound with his sleeve. His gaze flicked to the key, and his voice went soft. "When you are a whole person," he said.

I didn't understand him. But I recognized the vulnerability. "Please," I said, "what if I am never a whole person?"

He looked at me, and the sadness in his gaze scraped at my heart like teeth. I had five years of memories; before that was a fog. I'd lost something precious; if only I knew what it was. "Father, I—"

A knock sounded at the door, and he was cold as stone once more.

Bayan slipped inside without waiting for a response, and I wanted to curse him. He hunched his shoulders as he walked, his footfalls silent. If he were anyone else, I'd think his step hesitant. But Bayan had the look of a cat about him – deliberate, predatory. He wore a leather apron over his tunic, and blood stained his hands.

"I've completed the modification," Bayan said. "You asked me to see you right away when I'd finished."

A construct hobbled behind him, tiny hooves clicking against the floor. It looked like a deer, except for the fangs protruding from its mouth and the curling monkey's tail. Two small wings sprouted from its shoulders, blood staining the fur around them.

Father turned in his chair and placed a hand on the creature's back. It looked up at him with wide, wet eyes. "Sloppy," he says. "How many shards did you use to embed the follow command?"

"Two," Bayan said. "One to get the construct to follow me, and another to get it to stop."

"It should be one," Father said. "It goes where you do unless you tell it not to. The language is in the first book I gave you." He seized one of the wings and pulled it. When he let it go, it settled slowly back at the construct's side. "Your construction, however, is excellent."

Bayan's eyes slid to the side, and I held his gaze. Neither of us looked away. Always a competition. Bayan's irises were blacker even than mine, and when his lip curled, it only accentuated the full curve of his mouth. I supposed he was prettier than I would ever be, but I was convinced I was smarter, and that's what really mattered. Bayan never cared to hide his feelings. He carried his contempt for me like a child's favorite seashell.

"Try again with a new construct," Father said, and Bayan broke his gaze from mine. Ah, I'd won this small contest.

Father reached his fingers into the beast. I held my breath. I'd only seen him do this twice. Twice I could remember, at least. The creature only blinked placidly as Father's hand disappeared to the wrist. And then he pulled away and the construct froze, still as a statue. In his hand were two small shards of bone.

No blood stained his fingers. He dropped the bones into Bayan's hand. "Now go. Both of you."

I was quicker to the door than Bayan, whom I suspected was hoping for more than just harsh words. But I was used to harsh words, and I'd things to do. I slipped out the door and held it for Bayan to pass so he needn't bloody the door with his hands. Father prized cleanliness.

Bayan glared at me as he passed, the breeze in his wake smelling of copper and incense. Bayan was just the son of a small isle's governor, lucky enough to have caught Father's eye and to be taken in as a foster. He'd brought the sickness with him, some exotic disease Imperial didn't know. I was told I got sick with it soon after he arrived, and recovered a little while after Bayan did. But he hadn't lost as much of his memory as I had, and he'd gotten some of it back.

As soon as he disappeared around the corner, I whirled and ran for the end of the hallway. The shutters threatened to blow against the walls when I unlatched them. The tile roofs looked like the slopes of mountains. I stepped outside and shut the window.

The world opened up before me. From atop the roof, I could see the city and the harbor. I could even see the boats in the ocean fishing for squid, their lanterns shining in the distance like earth-bound stars. The wind tugged at my tunic, finding its way beneath the cloth, biting at my skin.

I had to be quick. By now, the construct servant would have removed the body of the deer. I half-ran, half-skidded down the slope of the roof toward the side of the palace where my father's bedroom was. He never brought his chain of keys into the questioning room. He didn't bring his construct guards with him. I'd read the small signs on his face. He might bark at me and scold me, but when we were alone – he feared me.

The tiles clicked below my feet. On the ramparts of the palace walls, shadows lurked – more constructs. Their instructions were simple. Watch for intruders. Sound an alarm. None of them paid me any mind, no matter that I wasn't where I was supposed to be. I wasn't an intruder.

The Construct of Bureaucracy would now be handing over the reports. I'd watched him sorting them earlier in the day, hairy lips fumbling over his teeth as he read them silently. There would be quite a lot. Shipments delayed due to skirmishes, the Ioph Carn stealing and smuggling witstone, citizens shirking their duty to the Empire.

I swung onto my father's balcony. The door to his room was cracked open. The room was usually empty, but this time it was not. A growl emanated from within. I froze. A black nose nudged into the space between door and wall, widening the gap. Yellow eyes peered at me and tufted ears flicked back. Claws scraped against wood as the creature strode toward me. Bing Tai, one of my father's oldest constructs. Gray speckled his jowls, but he had all his teeth. Each incisor was as long as my thumb.

His lip curled, the hackles on his back standing on end. He was a creature of nightmares, an amalgamation of large predators, with black, shaggy fur that faded into the darkness. He took another step closer.

Maybe it wasn't Bayan that was stupid; maybe I was the stupid one. Maybe this was how Father would find me after his tea – torn to bloody pieces on his balcony. It was too far to the ground, and I was too short to reach the roof gutters. The only way out from these rooms was into the hallway. "Bing Tai," I said, and my voice was steadier than I felt. "It is me, Lin."

I could almost feel my father's two commands battling in the construct's head. One: protect my rooms. Two: protect my family. Which command was stronger? I'd bet on the second one, but now I wasn't so sure.

I held my ground and tried not to let my fear show. I shoved my hand toward Bing Tai's nose. He could see me, he could hear me, perhaps he needed to smell me.

He *could* choose to taste me, though I did my best not to think about that.

His wet, cold nose touched my fingers, a growl still deep in his throat. I was not Bayan, who wrestled with the constructs like they were his brothers. I could not forget what they were. My throat constricted until I could barely breathe, my chest tight and painful.

And then Bing Tai settled on his haunches, his ears pricking, his lips covering his teeth. "Good Bing Tai," I said. My voice trembled. I had to hurry.

Grief lay heavy in the room, thick as the dust on what used to be my mother's wardrobe. Her jewelry on the dresser lay untouched; her slippers still awaited her next to the bed. What bothered me more than the questions my father asked me, than not knowing if he loved and cared for me as a child, was not remembering my mother.

I'd heard the remaining servants whispering. He burned all her portraits on the day she died. He forbade mention of her name. He put all her handmaidens to the sword. He guarded the memories of her jealously, as if he was the only one allowed to have them.

Focus.

I didn't know where he kept the copies he distributed to Bayan and me. He always pulled these from his sash pocket, and I didn't dare try to filch them from there. But the original chain of keys lay on the bed. So many doors. So many keys. I didn't know which was which, so I selected one at random – a golden key with a jade piece in the bow – and pocketed it.

I escaped into the hallway and wedged a thin piece of wood between door and frame so the door didn't latch. Now the tea would be steeping. Father would be reading through the reports, asking questions. I hoped they would keep him occupied.

My feet scuffed against the floorboards as I ran. The grand hallways of the palace were empty, lamplight glinting off the red-painted beams above. In the entryway, teak pillars rose from floor to ceiling, framing the faded mural on the second-floor wall. I took the steps down to the palace doors two at a time. Each step felt like a miniature betrayal.

I could have waited, one part of my mind told me. I could have been obedient; I could have done my best to answer my father's questions, to heal my memories. But the other part of my mind was cold and sharp. It cut through the guilt to find a hard truth. I could never be what he wanted if I did not take what I wanted. I hadn't been able to remember, no matter how hard I'd tried. He'd not left me with any other choice than to show him I was worthy in a different way.

I slipped through the palace doors and into the silent yard. The front gates were closed, but I was small and strong, and if Father wouldn't teach me his magic, well, there were other things I'd taught myself in the times he was locked in a secret room with Bayan. Like climbing.

The walls were clean but in disrepair. The plaster had broken away in places, leaving the stone beneath exposed. It was easy enough to climb. The monkey-shaped construct atop the wall just glanced at me before turning its limpid gaze back to the city. A thrill rushed through me when I touched down on the other side. I'd been into the city on foot before – *I must have* – but for me, it was like the first time. The streets stank of fish and hot oil, and the remnants of dinners cooked and eaten. The stones beneath my slippers were dark and slippery with washwater. Pots clanged and a breeze carried the sound of lilting, subdued voices. The first two storefronts I saw were closed, wooden shutters locked shut.

Too late? I'd seen the blacksmith's storefront from the palace walls, and this was what first gave me the idea. I held my breath as I dashed down a narrow alley.

He was there. He was pulling the door closed, a pack slung over one shoulder.

"Wait," I said. "Please, just one more order."

"We're closed," he huffed out. "Come back tomorrow."

I stifled the desperation clawing up my throat. "I'll pay you twice your regular price if you can start it tonight. Just one key copy."

He looked at me then, and his gaze trailed over my embroidered silk tunic. His lips pressed together. He was thinking about lying about how much he charged. But then he just sighed. "Two silver. One is my regular price." He was a good man, fair.

Relief flooded me as I dug the coins from my sash pocket and pressed them into his calloused palm. "Here. I need it quickly."

Wrong thing to say. Annoyance flashed across his face. But he still opened the door again and let me into his shop. The man was built like an iron – broad and squat. His shoulders seemed to take up half the space. Metal tools hung from the walls and ceiling. He picked up his tinderbox and re-lit the lamps. And then he turned back to face me. "It won't be ready until tomorrow morning at the earliest."

"But do you need to keep the key?"

He shook his head. "I can make a mold of it tonight. The key will be ready tomorrow."

I wished there weren't so many chances to turn back, so many chances for my courage to falter. I forced myself to drop my father's key into the blacksmith's hand. The man took it and turned, fishing a block of clay from a stone trough. He pressed the key into it. And then he froze, his breath stopping in his throat.

I moved for the key before I could think. I saw what he did as soon as I took one step closer. At the base of the bow, just before the stem, was the tiny figure of a phoenix embossed into the metal.

When the blacksmith looked at me, his face was as round and pale as the moon. "Who are you? What are you doing with one of the Emperor's keys?"

I should have grabbed the key and run. I was swifter than he was. I could snatch it away and be gone before he took his next breath. All he'd have left was a story – one that no one would believe.

But if I did, I wouldn't have my key copy. I wouldn't have any more answers. I'd be stuck where I was at the start of the day, my memory a haze, the answers I gave Father always inadequate. Always just out of reach. Always broken. And this man – he was a good man. Father taught me the kind of thing to say to good men.

I chose my words carefully. "Do you have any children?"

A measure of color came back into his face. "Two." He answered. His brows knit together as he wondered if he should have responded.

"I am Lin," I said, laying myself bare. "I am the Emperor's heir. He hasn't been the same since my mother's death. He isolates himself, he keeps few servants, he does not meet with the island governors. Rebellion is brewing. Already the Shardless Few have taken Khalute. They'll seek to expand their hold. And there are the Alanga. Some may not believe they're coming back, but my family has kept them from returning.

"Do you want soldiers marching in the streets? Do you want war on your doorstep?" I touched his shoulder gently, and he did not flinch. "On your children's doorstep?"

He reached reflexively behind his right ear for the scar each citizen had. The place where a shard of bone was removed and taken for the Emperor's vault.

"Is my shard powering a construct?" he asked.

"I don't know," I said. I don't know, I don't know — there was so *little* that I did know. "But if I get into my father's vault, I will look for yours and I will bring it back to you. I can't promise you anything. I wish I could. But I will try."

He licked his lips. "My children?"

"I can see what I can do." It was all I could say. No one was exempt from the islands' Tithing Festivals.

Sweat shone on his forehead. "I'll do it."

Father would be setting the reports aside now. He would take up his cup of tea and sip from it, looking out the window at the lights of the city below. Sweat prickled between my shoulder-blades. I needed to get the key back before he discovered me.

I watched through a haze as the blacksmith finished making the mold. When he handed the key back, I turned to run.

"Lin," he said.

I stopped.

"My name is Numeen. The year of my ritual was 1508. We need an Emperor who cares about us."

What could I say to that? So I just ran. Out the door, down the alleyway, back to climbing the wall. Now Father would be finishing up his tea, his fingers wrapped around the still-warm cup. A stone came loose beneath my fingertips. I let it fall to the ground. The *crack* made me cringe.

He'd be putting his cup down, he'd be looking at the city. How long did he look at the city? The climb down was faster than the climb up. I couldn't smell the city anymore. All I could smell was my own breath. The walls of the outer buildings passed in a blur as I ran to the palace — the servants' quarters, the Hall of Everlasting Peace, the Hall of Earthly Wisdom, the wall surrounding the palace garden. Everything was cold and dark, empty.

I took the servants' entrance into the palace, bounding up the stairs two at a time. The narrow passageway opened into the main hallway. The main hallway wrapped around the palace's second floor, and my father's bedroom was nearly on the other side from the servants' entrance. I wished my legs were longer. I wished my mind were stronger.

Floorboards squeaked beneath my feet as I ran, the noise making me wince. At last, I made it back and slipped into my father's room. Bing Tai lay on the rug at the foot of the bed, stretched out like an old cat. I had to reach over him to get to the chain of keys. He smelled musty, like a mix between a bear construct and a closet full of moth-ridden clothes.

It took three tries for me to hook the key back onto the chain. My fingers felt like eels – flailing and slippery.

I knelt to retrieve the door wedge on my way out, my breath ragged in my throat. The brightness of the light in the hallway made me blink. I'd have to find my way into the city tomorrow to retrieve the new key. But it was done, the wedge for the door safely in my sash pocket. I let out the breath I hadn't known I'd been holding.

"Lin."

Bayan. My limbs felt made of stone. What had he seen? I turned to face him – his brow was furrowed, his hands clasped behind his back. I willed my heart to calm, my face to blankness.

"What are you doing outside the Emperor's room?"